ALOHA

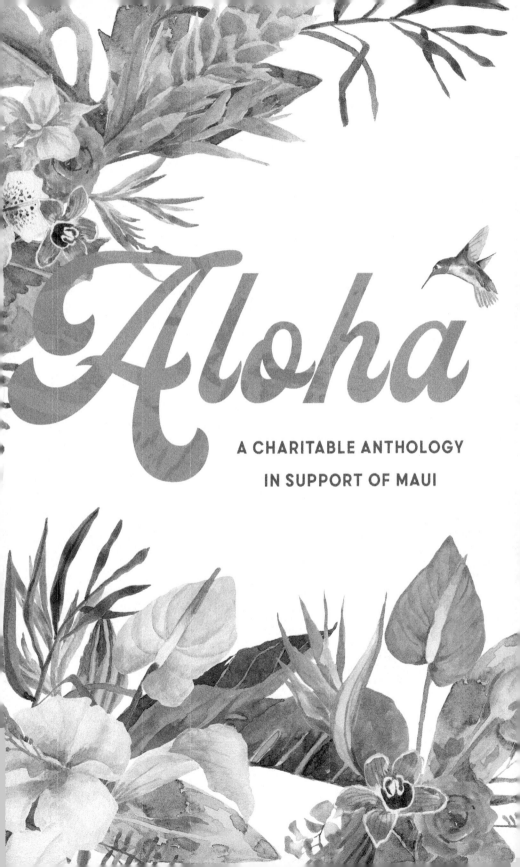

Aloha

A CHARITABLE ANTHOLOGY
IN SUPPORT OF MAUI

CONTENTS

FOREWARD

Dear Reader,

My parents first official move when my dad joined the Air Force was to Hawaii. They were in their early twenties, got to spent six weeks on Waikiki Beach, and three years in an apartment on the beach in Oahu. My oldest sister was born in Honolulu. When we were sent to Australia, more military orders, of course, we spent a day in Hawaii there and coming back. I have pictures of myself in a grass skirt at a Luau as a baby.

Last summer, my parents took us all back to make more memories where our little family had started. We went to the Big Island and spent a day driving around Oahu, my parents reminiscing what the island looked like nearly forty years early.

It was magical. Hawaii is magical.

So it was with a heavy heart that I watched this beautiful island full of rich culture, stunning vistas, and incredible people burn to the ground.

As you saw on the news, the island of Maui, specifically the town of Lahaina had devastating fires that caused widespread damage, obliterating the village, killing more than a hundred people and leaving hundreds more missing.

I couldn't sit back and do nothing. So, I reached out to as many of my author friends as possible to see if they would be interested in putting something together to raise money for those impacted by the fires. I hoped a few would say yes. I'm pleased to bring you more then fifty original stories from some of the best in the industry.

Thanks to you purchasing this anthology we will be able to help ease the suffering of those impacted.

Sit back. Turn the page. Dive in deep.

Enjoy ALOHA!

K.A. Linde

ONE CRUEL GAME

K.A. LINDE

CHAPTER 1

"Sorry, folks, this weather system means we're going to be here for a while," the pilot announced over the speaker. "Hope you don't mind an overnight in Hawaii."

The rest of the plane groaned.

In consternation, I looked up from the sketches on my iPad. I'd been reviewing the sketches of the runway outfits Harmony had designed and sent over. "What did he just say?"

The man across from me in business class winked at me. "He said we're spending a night in Hawaii."

I pursed my lips. This couldn't be happening. This didn't happen to *me*.

Normally, I would be flying private. However, that plane had been occupied, and so I was stuck on a commercial flight, coming back from a modeling gig in Australia. I'd popped a Xanax on the way over and only woken up a half hour ago. I was supposed to be back in New York City by the morning to relieve the nanny and see the kids. Instead … this.

"Great," I grumbled.

While we taxied into the terminal, I made arrangements with the nanny for her to stay an extra night with the kids. My mother obviously couldn't be trusted to watch them. She shouldn't have been trusted to watch *me*.

Then I slung my Birkin onto my arm and strode off the plane. The thunderstorm that had grounded us raged as I stepped into the airport. Arrangements would need to be made for the night. A car service, hotel, dinner. I'd texted my travel agent on the way, but I hadn't heard from her yet.

Usually, she was on top of things, but it would be the middle of the night back home.

"God, I need a drink."

My heels clicked against the tiled floor as I navigated the airport past hundreds of other disgruntled travelers. An extra night in Hawaii would be a dream ... had it been planned. Instead, all of us were stuck in a torrential downpour without hotel accommodations or any information about when exactly we'd be able to get out of here.

I found the first-class airport lounge. Glass doors slid open to reveal a crisp modern interior, a business center, and best of all ... a fully stocked bar. Already, several dozen businessmen in stark black suits were seated around the room. Only a handful of other women were present, dressed in their own dark suits, on calls or buried in their computers.

Men and women alike looked up as I strode into the room in my sleek red dress and Louboutin heels. My dark hair was down in loose curls. Ever-present cherry-red lipstick perfectly applied on my lips. Despite the circumstances, not a single strand was out of place.

"Can I help you?" the bartender asked when I took the only unoccupied seat.

"Vodka martini, extra olives."

"Coming right up."

"Going to be a long night," the man next to me said.

"Mmm," I said noncommittally.

I pulled out my cell phone and jotted out texts to friends. My martini came, and I ordered a second after the first was finished. I still hadn't heard from my travel agent. Just how I wanted to spend my evening.

A hush fell over the lounge as the doors opened again. I lifted my gaze, and my heart stuttered. The man at the front might as well have been a god descended from Olympus to grace us with his presence. He was as terrifying with his intensity as he was gorgeous. A strong jawline, cold eyes, and perfect lips on a solid frame encased in a several-thousand-dollar suit tailored to his incredible build.

Those dark eyes moved across the room, command in every gesture. Until they found me. A shiver ran down my spine. I lifted my martini to him. He arched an eyebrow and then turned his attention to the concierge who had approached him. After a few moments in deep conversation, he took a phone call and left the suite.

I sighed. Fine then.

I pulled my iPad back out, connected to the Wi-Fi, and navigated the list of airport hotels. I usually stayed in Percy Tower when I was in town, but did I want to brave the storm without car service? Probably not.

A dwindling number of hotels still had a few rooms available, but none seemed like much of an option. My daddy used to have property here before he lost everything. Luckily, he'd given me my apartment overlooking Central Park before the IRS could take it, too. My life would have been much easier if he wasn't such a scumbag.

When I finished off the second martini, I felt a presence at my back.

"She'll take another," the man said behind me.

I shifted to make out the features of the gorgeous gentleman from earlier.

"And I'll have a scotch. Do you have Blue Label?"

The bartender shook his head. "Sorry, sir. We have Black Label though."

"Fine." He slid a black credit card across the bar. "Put hers on mine, too."

"Presumptuous," I teased.

His dark eyes met mine. I saw unbridled power and control.

"We're both stranded here until morning. We might as well have a good drink."

I set the iPad down, ignoring the hotel information. I'd already found a better option. "Surely, you're not staying in the lounge overnight."

He scoffed. "Of course not." His eyes caught the open website on my screen. "And you aren't either."

"No, I'm not. I'll get a hotel room."

He shifted closer to me. "Or you could take mine."

I fluttered my eyelashes. "Then, where would you stay?"

He smirked, a small guffaw escaping him. "You're cheeky."

"I've been told that before."

"I bet you have."

"You'll be staying with me," he said.

There was no second-guessing the bold statement. I would be lying if I said I didn't like his daring authority. He went after what he wanted, and tonight, that was me.

"Perhaps presumptuous is your middle name."

He fingered a strand of my dark hair. "You don't seem to mind."

A shiver went up my spine. "I don't."

Another martini was placed before me. His scotch was set down in a crystal glass.

"Closed or open?" the bartender asked.

"Closed. I don't think we'll be here much longer."

I swallowed. The tension bristling between us. He was only a hairbreadth away from me, and my insides felt like they were made of jelly. Perhaps it was foolish to feel anything for a man like this, stranded in the same place. When I went home, I'd return to a million responsibilities—work, my charity, the children. Right at this moment, I was just a woman, and all I wanted was this man. In fact, it felt like the thunderstorm had engineered this fortuitous meeting.

I stuffed my tablet back into the bag. "Where to?"

He tossed back his scotch, and with one wicked grin, I was lost. "Follow me."

CHAPTER 2

I caught my first sight of the torrential downpour as we stalked toward the airport exit. The glass sliding doors opened, and a whoosh as loud as a hurricane catapulted into the lobby. For a moment, I second-guessed whether or not we should even leave the airport. There were reasons people were sleeping inside and not braving the treacherous conditions. Not all of them had to do with the fact that nearly every hotel in a five-mile radius was completely booked.

But he had my hand in his and was walking with all the purpose in the world toward two men holding large black umbrellas.

"This way," the first man said.

He held an umbrella up, and we continued our stride as if nothing could stop us.

A black Escalade waited at the curb, and I was quickly helped into the backseat. My beau carefully unbuttoned the top of his suit coat before taking the seat beside me. The door slammed. A moment later, the two men got into the front, and the car pulled away.

Silence stretched between us, filled with momentous wonder. Who was going to break the quiet? He wasn't the type of man to break for anyone or anything.

I let my gaze skip over his strong features a moment before pulling my phone out. A message was there from my travel agent.

"Finally," I muttered.

She listed hotel accommodations, along with a rebooked flight for tomorrow afternoon at three, as long as planes were taking off.

"What's that?" he asked, looking over my shoulder.

"New flight. Did yours get rebooked?"

He smirked. "The plane leaves when I'm on it."

Of course it did. And normally, I'd be on that private plane. It was really a travesty that I was flying commercial. I'd forgotten how much I disliked it.

"Perhaps you can just fly me back to the city then," I teased.

He arched an eyebrow. "We'll see."

Then he returned to his own phone. I responded to my travel agent that I had a place to stay for the night, but to be on top of things in case more flights were canceled in the morning. I did not want to be stuck in this storm forever.

The traffic into Waikiki was a disaster, taking twice as long as it had any other time I'd been on the island of Oahu. Finally, the Escalade pulled into a covered interior, the deafening storm deadened by the building. He got out first and offered me his hand to help me out. Then he pulled my hand into the crook of his arm and directed me into the hotel with the name Percy in big gold letters on the exterior.

Inside, the lobby was immaculate with white marble everything and black and gold accents. It was sleek and modern and expensive, all rolled into one perfect package. We entered the elevator and he used a key card to get to the penthouse, and we shot straight upward. Instead of opening to a hallway, the elevator revealed a white marble foyer. Orchids were on display in vases, and beautiful artwork hung from the walls. He slid the card on the door, and we entered paradise.

The penthouse must have taken up the entire floor. It was enormous with multiple suites, a dining area, living room, and full kitchen. The far wall exposed an impressive display of the thunderstorm cascading into an infinity pool. The water slashed across the windows like an intruder attempting to infiltrate the place. Lightning broke the skyline, momentarily revealing the sandy beach below and the Pacific Ocean beyond.

"Drink?" he asked.

"Absolutely."

He strode to a fully stocked bar and poured himself the Blue Label scotch he'd requested at the airport lounge. Then he grabbed a bottle of champagne and held it up for my inspection. "Yes?"

"Well, it's not a dirty martini."

He ripped the foil off the cork. "You've had enough of those."

I scoffed. "That so?"

"Yes. Now, we're celebrating."

He poured the champagne into a flute and passed it to me. The bubbles tickled my nose when I inhaled the dry scent of the alcohol.

"What exactly are we celebrating?"

"The storm, of course."

"You want to celebrate getting stranded in Hawaii for a night?"

His dark eyes gleamed. "With you."

I bit my lip and then lifted my glass. "To fate then."

"A little on the nose," he said, moving his head side to side, as if debating whether to agree. "But I accept it."

Our glasses came together, and he took a long swallow. He set his glass aside and watched me sip on my champagne. It was my favorite vintage. I'd visited the winery years ago, and I kept bottles of it chilled at home for every occasion.

Yet I could barely concentrate on the stuff with his intense gaze on me. I wanted to ask him what he was thinking, but there was no point. He'd never tell me. He was an enigma. It was written across his broad shoulders and strong jaw and mysterious eyes. Scrawled over every inch of that toned body, hidden in that fancy suit.

"What?" I finally asked, twirling the flute in my hand.

"Come here."

My body heated at the command in those two words. The desire laced in every syllable.

I set my glass down and stepped into his orbit. The rest of the world was spinning, but here he was, the center of the universe.

"Yes?" I asked breathily.

His hand came to my chin, tipping it up so he could look directly into my eyes instead of the hooded look I'd given him through my lashes. He roved my face, memorizing every inch of it. I swallowed at the assessment, unable to keep myself from squirming just a little at his attention.

He rubbed his thumb across the red of my bottom lip. My lips parted slightly as my body thrummed to life. I darted my tongue out, catching the tip of his thumb. He didn't flinch or move an inch, but I watched the desire ratchet up in his gaze.

"Tonight, you're mine."

He tugged me forward until our lips were a breath away. My eyes still lingered on his. A puff of need escaped me at those words.

I was his. I was all his tonight.

"Yes," I breathed.

That was all the permission he required before his mouth descended, fitting to mine like the piece I'd always been missing.

CHAPTER 3

He tasted like pure sin.

His lips were sweet torture.

His hands fisted in my hair, a brutal tenderness.

None of it made sense. How much it hurt and how perfect it was, all at the same time. The complete control in his every movement. The precision of his mouth moving against mine. The dominance as his tongue swept inward.

It was like my first kiss all over again. It sundered me. I was in the midst of it and already knew it was the end of everything else. The kiss that told me I'd never want anything else but this. His hands in my hair, his body pressed against mine, and his lips devouring me whole.

My heart was in my throat as I tried to drag him closer, but I was held in place. There was no escape from his embrace. And I didn't want to escape either. I wanted to drown in this kiss. Drown and drown and drown.

I was so far underwater that I could barely breathe as he broke away from my mouth and stared down at me with his mercurial eyes. The fascination in them evident. My red lipstick a slight smudge against his mouth.

I reached forward to brush it off, and he caught my wrist tightly in his grip.

"Don't."

"My lipstick," I said by way of explanation.

He rubbed his knuckles across his lips. The movement harsh and deliberate. My pulse quickened at the smear of red that came back across his hand. And then the slow, wicked smirk that crossed those pouty lips at the sight of the red.

"It's supposed to be kiss-proof."

"You smeared it all over my lips. Where else will you smear it?"

I opened my mouth to object, but that was the wrong thing to do. His thumb pressed inward, invading my mouth in the best way. I closed around the digit. My eyes were intent on his heated expression as I flicked my tongue against him and then dragged it out of my mouth.

But he wasn't looking at me when I was through. His eyes were on his own hand. A red rim was around the end of his thumb. An example of what my lips had done to him.

"Perfect." His eyes finally lifted to me. "Now, on your knees."

"I—" I began.

But he interrupted me, "Now."

I swallowed, clenching my hands into fists. I hated him for the words as much as they heated me through. If I'd thought he was being condescending or degrading rather than turned the fuck on, I might have left. But I saw the way his pupils dilated and the thump of his heartbeat in his throat at the sight of my lipstick.

So, despite everything in my blood telling me not to, I slowly sank down on the hard tiled floor. The cold ground already biting into my knees.

He stared down at me with mischievous delight. As if he knew exactly what kind of torture it had taken for me to obey like that. Then he just left me to kneel next to the wet bar. A submissive stance that he clearly enjoyed as he removed a handkerchief from his pocket. An honest-to-god handkerchief with the letter *P* in tiny golden font across the silken material. He cleaned the lipstick off of his thumb and knuckles, then he tossed it carelessly onto the counter.

I knew what was coming next, and yet I couldn't make the move. I just knelt and waited.

He cupped my chin in his large hand. "And here I thought, you'd fight me."

"Would you like me to?"

"Always," he teased.

"I don't believe you," I told him. My gaze slipped to the front of his pants, where his cock strained against the expensive wool trousers. "Your cock is hard from me following orders."

"Ah, there's my little brat."

I shivered at the words. So humiliating, and somehow, they made everything in my body shudder with need. "I'm not—"

"Shh," he commanded.

He slipped his suit jacket off of his broad shoulders and tossed it on top of the handkerchief. He undid the buckle on his belt, and the snick of it leaving the loops made me tremble with desire. He pulled the two ends together and gave an experimental snap with it. I jolted at the sound, and he grinned wider. The belt followed his jacket, and then he was undoing his pants, letting them hang low on his narrow waist. His cock jutted forward against the black of his boxer briefs. Then he reached within and removed the thick length of him.

My mouth watered at the sight of him, long and veiny. He pumped it in his hand a few times as he watched me watch him. My body clenched all over as I imagined him pumping that inside of me. The feel of his cock taking everything that I would give.

"Open your mouth and take this like a good little brat," he said, gripping the back of my head and pulling me onto his cock.

I opened wide, wide, wider, coughing around the immense length of him. I swallowed him down to try to make more room, and he grunted in appreciation. The sound alone warmed something deep in my core.

"So good," he praised. "So very good."

He pulled back, giving me room to breathe. I took the opportunity to seize some control of the situation. My hand found the shaft, and I worked him while I bobbed on his cock.

"No," he said, taking my hand away. "I want that red lipstick like a rim around my cock."

I had no words. I couldn't speak even if I wanted to. His hands were back in my hair as he thrust into my mouth. The red lipstick leaving an imprint all over him. And I couldn't even complain. Everything was on fire as he used my mouth.

I felt him swell inside of me.

I prepared myself, knowing what was coming as he pushed to the back of my throat and grunted out, "Swallow."

There was no other option as hot spurts splashed into my mouth. I swallowed hard as he jerked a few more times and then finished. He pulled out of my mouth, and I rocked back on my heels, delirious. He gripped the counter with one hand as his eyes raked over the red ring on his cock.

His look was one of triumph. "Perfection."

CHAPTER 4

He didn't wait for me to come back to coherence. He just tucked his still-wet cock back into his pants, bent forward, and lifted me over his shoulder. I gasped in shock as my head dipped toward his muscular ass. My Louboutin heels dangling precariously on my feet.

"What are you doing?" I gasped.

But he tightened his grip around my thighs and carried me out of the living space and into a bedroom. From the glimpse I got of the room while upside down, it looked massive with a king bed, dressers, and elegant artwork. An open door led into an all-white bathroom while the opposite wall sported more floor-to-ceiling windows, revealing a covered hot tub that still couldn't escape the tropical storm thundering outside.

He tossed me unceremoniously onto the bed. The layers of bedding and the thick mattress pad cushioned my fall.

All I got was a look at the back of his head as he headed toward the bathroom, yelling, "Don't move," over his shoulder.

And so, I didn't. Not a muscle.

Even though every inch of my body was warring with me to do anything but what he'd said. I wanted to *want* to take orders. The commands themselves made me hot all over, yet I chafed at every single inflection out of his mouth.

The look on his face when he returned to find me still lying on my back in the bed made it worth it. He'd stripped out of his button-up shirt, revealing the muscled torso beneath. His trousers had disappeared as well, and his powerful thighs were on display as he strode back across the room to where I lay.

"What were you doing?"

He smirked, but said nothing. Just grabbed my ankles and tugged me further down the bed. My ass was nearly hanging off the end. He gripped my hips and flipped me over, burying my face into the soft white comforter.

His fingers snaked up my bare calves, then brushed aside my red skirt to skate up my inner thighs. I shivered at the touch. He stopped just before reaching my pussy. Instead, he pushed my dress up over my hips, slipped his hands under the material of my black thong, and dragged it down my legs.

I whimpered as he brushed lazily against my sex. A chuckle sounded behind me. Soft and unmistakably cruel. He knew exactly what he was doing.

He discarded my panties, and his fingers ran back up my legs. I clenched my red-lacquered fingernails into the comforter. When he approached my pussy this time, I pushed backward. My body was still pulsing with need from the blow job. I wanted what was mine. And the more I wanted it, the more he'd deny it. Still, I couldn't stop myself.

"Ah-ah," he said.

His hand came down on the sensitive flesh. A tap more than a slap but enough for my entire body to jerk forward, like he'd just caressed my clit into submission.

"Fuck," I ground out.

"If I slide my fingers into this wet pussy, are you going to let me fuck you with them?"

He circled my clit before dragging two fingers through the slick wetness of my pussy.

"Yes," I moaned. I would have done anything at that moment.

"Are you going to ride my fingers?"

He pushed one finger in, and I had to bite down to keep from moaning.

"Yes."

"Be my little slut?"

"I'll do whatever you want," I offered.

"Whatever I want?" he asked with a harsh laugh. "Why do I have doubts about that?"

"Because I'm a brat."

He laughed again. "That you are."

His bare palm came down on my ass. It stung, and I hissed at the contact. Yet craved it again. I pushed backward, hoping for more. He tsked me but delivered. Another smack came, followed in quick succession by two more. I shivered all over at the pain of it blossoming on my now-rosy ass.

"Fuck," he said with a sigh, as if he was disappointed. "I was going to take my time with you, but now that I can see your wet cunt, I want to bury my cock in it."

I moaned an incoherent, "Yes."

He slid his fingers out of me, lifted my ass higher in the air, and rained a few more precise smacks. I ached with need by the end of it. My mind beautifully empty and my body begging for release. I could come just from the spanking and his fingers. If I could get to my clit, I would come undone instantly.

But he never let me.

His boxers fell to the wayside, and then his hands were on my ass, spreading my cheeks. The grip stung my aching backside. A sweet yet terrible tenderness that made me want him all the more.

He wasn't gentle. He didn't have a gentle bone in his body. Not when it came to this.

He angled himself to fit into me and then slammed inside. I jolted forward against the bed. If it wasn't for the arm he'd placed under my stomach to hold me up, I would have fallen flat. Instead, he kept my ass high and his thrusts deep.

I rocked back into him even though it already felt like I was being split in half. Yet I couldn't want anything else. Not as he took me just as I always wanted to be used.

His other hand held tight to my ass, setting the bruising pace. Our bodies collided over and over again. A wet slapping sound that hit a perfect rhythm.

"Anything I want?" he asked between grunts.

"Yes," I gasped.

Then his thumb moved to the crease of my ass. He pressed down on the pucker of my hole. Everything went black at the edges. The pleasure I'd barely been holding back swarmed up my throat, as if it were trying to claw its way out of me. Warmth suffused my body, and then I let go.

I screamed into the empty penthouse suite. My climax hitting the top of a roller coaster and then cascading over the cliff. He kept pumping into me, wringing out my orgasm, before he finally bottomed out inside of me and roared his own approval. He jerked a few times, releasing every last drop before withdrawing.

I collapsed onto the bed and turned over to gaze up at him with a delirious look on my face. The jet lag from Australia was already terrible, but add in the best sex of my life, and I could barely keep my eyes open.

He headed to the bathroom and came back with a towel. He carefully cleaned up our mess before helping me out of my dress, yanking back the covers, and carrying me into the oversize bed.

Our eyes met briefly as he tucked the covers around my shoulders.

"Wait … are you …" I trailed off.

He seemed to know what I was asking. "Where else would I go?"

He stepped away, and a second later, I heard the shower running. I must have drifted off because what could have only been a minute later, he was under the covers. His warm body cocooning mine. His hair still wet from the shower. His breath hot on my shoulder as he held me against his chest.

I snuggled deeper against him. He pressed a kiss into my hair.

"Sleep now," he ordered.

And with a sigh, I fell into a perfectly dreamless sleep.

CHAPTER 5

He was gone in the morning.

The bed was cool to the touch. His clothes from the night before were missing. Mine were carefully folded on a nearby chair. The rain had stopped sometime in the middle of the night. Only dark, ominous clouds still hung heavy in the sky.

I stepped out of the bed with a sigh. I shouldn't have even been surprised. Of course he was gone. Typical.

I had time before I needed to be back at the airport, so I used the amenities. After my shower, blow-dry, and makeup reapplication, I felt more like myself. I checked my phone, answering texts from my travel agent and a few from friends that I'd missed the day before. I admired the penthouse suite and left.

A black car waited for me at the front. My last hurrah from my late night rendezvous. I was at the airport and before my gate at precisely the right time. My business-class flight took off at three p.m., and I was taking the elevator up to my home in New York City by seven the next morning.

I dropped my Louis Vuitton luggage at the entrance of my penthouse and heard familiar footsteps.

"Mommy!" a little girl said as she rounded the corner.

Helena dashed the rest of the way, tackling me at the ankles. I laughed and bent down to pick up my two-year-old daughter. I swung her in a tight circle.

"How's my best girl?"

"Best!" Helena cheered.

The nanny, Kimberly, strode into the living room. Beckett was in her arms. His eyes lit up at the sight of me. He reached his arms out and kicked his little feet.

"Ma! Ma!"

"Welcome home, Katherine," Kimberly said. "They've missed you."

I set Helena down and took Beckett from her.

"I've missed them like crazy." I kissed his giant chipmunk cheeks. "Mommy missed you so much, dumpling. How'd they do?"

"Excellent. Everyone woke up about a half hour ago. Slept like a dream."

"Good," I said with a smile. "Next time, you'll come to Australia with me and the children."

Kimberly laughed. "You've convinced me."

I waved her off as she headed home. Having the kids alone for all this time must have been draining. I knew what those days were like. Even with all the help I'd hired over the two years since becoming a mother, nothing could replace what a mother did. Not even their father.

"Oh, Mr. Percy," Kimberly said, stepping to the side as the elevator dinged. "Welcome home."

"Thank you, Kimberly."

Kimberly waved at me once more and then stepped into the elevator.

"Daddy!" Helena said before rushing to her father.

Camden's eyes were all for his little girl as he swung her into his arms. He pressed a kiss to her temple as she began a long-winded babble about everything that had happened in his absence. Beckett held his hands out, too. He took him as well, carrying them into the playroom.

All the while, my eyes followed him.

"You're late," I told him with an arched eyebrow.

He smirked up at me. "I had business in LA before I came home."

I tsked. "You could have told me."

The gleam in his eyes was all desire and danger and detonation.

"Was that part of the game?"

I shook my head at him. "You're the devil."

He set Beckett down and extracted himself from Helena. "You married the devil, love." He slid a hand around my waist and drew me in close. "You knew what you were getting into."

"You could have at least flown me private."

He laughed then. "So, that's what this pouting is about."

I rolled my eyes at him. "You like when I pout."

"That I do."

"And I thought you didn't like playing games."

He lifted my chin the way he had the night before, taking complete control of my body in that one gesture. "I like ones that I win."

Then he kissed me. Our tryst in Hawaii ignited between us. The man I'd married, the man I loved, the man I came home to. And no one else. Even when we played one cruel game.

Thank you for reading Katherine & Camden's short story! I hope you loved them as much as I do. They're my forever favorite villains. If you want to know more about them, you can read their story in Cruel Marriage.

BEGINNINGS...

A HAPPY EVER AFTER SHORT STORY SET IN THE AARTI-VERSE

AARTI V RAMAN

CHAPTER ONE - NIHAAL

Somewhere over Indian airspace

"I didn't know you read books, at all." I peeked over Mili's shoulder, to check out said book. Ignoring the twinge of my own from where the GSW (gunshot wound, for those who don't know) throbbed dully. It was healing nicely, *thank* fuck or I'd be even more pissed at the piece of shit who almost got away with murder before biting his own bullet, in a manner of speaking.

I looked in distaste at the sling my wife – God, I loved saying that in my head – insisted I wear on our journey. Apparently, airports were full of jostlers, and she wanted me protected.

My wife was efficient, practical, and hot AF while managing our life.

Mili gave me a look, one I'd never seen on her lovely face before.

She was slightly sheepish. "I picked it up at the airport. Usually, I work or nap on flights but this was a ninety-minute journey so I figured I might as well read."

I continued peeking into her reading material. My eyes widened and then narrowed as a word caught my eye.

"Is that…" I looked around the crowded airplane. "A Jacob's ladder?" I murmured the words in a sub-vocal tone.

I was ever mindful of our audience, even if we were in first class, which only meant more leg room and free water refills on this airline. And I did not look the part of the suave and sophisticated Formula One driver I was, because I was on honeymoon with the love of my life.

Mili shrugged, her shoulder bumping into mine. "Yeah."

"A Jacob's ladder is a…"

"I know what it is," she hissed. Red crept up her neck and icepick cheeks dusting her skin with adorable color. "Do you have to be so loud, Nihaal?"

She was obviously embarrassed now.

I didn't immediately get it. Mili was the most confident, brilliant, stunningly smart person I knew. She had nothing to hide or be ashamed of, including her reading choices.

I grinned, irrepressibly. "I wasn't being loud at all, love." I nodded at the page, curious to know more about the Jacob's ladder and its...use. "It's reading time now. Back at it."

She snapped the book shut, drumming her fingers on the book with an innocent cartoon couple cover. The ring I'd given her just a few months ago in a hasty civil ceremony that was over before it began, glinted in the harsh airplane lights.

In a flash of memory, I remembered how she looked on our wedding day. She'd worn a blood-red sari and flowers in her long hair.

Mili had a quiet unstoppable beauty that she'd honed through the use of makeup and wearing really good outfits but on our wedding day, she'd been... sexy and unattainable.

I almost swallowed my tongue when I saw her that day, which explained why I was a dick to her later that night. At least, that was the story I told myself when I thought of the dark, destructive first week of our marriage.

I knew Mili would have a different version of the events...

...And she just might be right.

"I'm not going to read it if you're..." Mili pushed gently at my uninjured side. "Going to hover."

"Why not? It looks like so much fun." I murmured throatily.

I fingered the spine of the book suggestively. Running one long finger down it, while making fiery eye contact with Mili. But I couldn't hold it for more than five seconds.

My lips twitched as I tried to flirt, unsuccessfully, with my wife.

She smiled too when she leaned into me, no longer sheepish. "It *is* fun. So, I read it, idiot."

"You read about men with pierced peens when you're not napping or working, woman." I mock-frowned. "Is this something we should talk about?"

I was extremely curious about her preferences in this area. So far, we were doing bangingly well for being newlyweds in the most untraditional sense of the word. But, as my Tio Paul was fond of reminding me, 'Practice makes a man win races, Nihaal. So fucking practice'.

I was inclined to agree with my mentor and racing team Menzo Monadnock's Team Principal on this point. 'Practicing' with Mili was infinitely better than alone, in the cockpit of a tin can hurtling through concrete beyond the force of gravity.

"Nihaal." Mili chuckled, a rich, feminine sound that went straight to *my* unpierced peen.

I sat up a little straighter.

"Mili." I grabbed her hand in one of mine, the hand that wore her ring. A simple golden band, nothing fancy or unique.

Maybe we needed something a little more…us, I mused.

"Nihaal." Mili took her hand back. "It's just a book," she assured me. "It's fun. And escapist. And I learn something new every time I read one."

"Like the proper way to service a Jacob's ladder?" I couldn't resist teasing her.

She burst out laughing. A sound that turned a few heads in her direction, mostly from disapproving older women and men who had a distinct gleam in their eyes when they saw her.

I outstared them all with a hard glint I'd honed over battling it out on the toughest racetracks for years.

That's right, people. She's gloriously mine.

"You're never going to let that go, are you?"

I shrugged. "I could be…persuaded. If you…" I recalled the exact phrase the author had used in the book. "STFUATTDLAGG."

My jaw dropped a second later. As I suddenly understood what the phrase meant, especially when paired in context of servicing a Jacob's ladder.

"Good fucking God, Mili." My face heated up at the graphic image forming in my head of two faceless people doing that in a men's club. "What *are* you reading?"

Mili grinned again, secretively. Seductively. "Fun. Escapist." Tapped on the book with a nude-painted nail. "Educational."

I shook my head. "I would never, in a million years, imagine that the brightest mind from Yale and Cambridge, Drake Fallahil's right-hand, Mili Iyer-Bhatnagar, would read—"

"Spice," she said primly. "It's called spicy romance. And I love it. Any problems?"

I shook my head again. Because she had another glint in her eye. This one was more battle-like and less fuck-me. I'd never won against that look.

"Of course not. I'm just…" I searched for a word that would accurately describe my feelings *and* not get me killed on this flight, "Surprised."

Mili subsided at my honest answer. "We've been together for such a short time, Nihaal. Obviously, we don't know everything about each other."

"Eighty-one days of knowing each other." Her face melted in pleasure because I knew the date of us meeting. "And fifty-nine days being married, Mils." I toyed with her ring again. And she let me, so I was in the safe zone.

"You kept count."

I grinned now. "It was a memorable meeting, sweetheart. Of course, I'd remember the day I met you."

And it had been. I'd just won the Emilia-Romagna Grand Prix and was taking a much-needed shower in my hotel suite assuming I was alone, when she barged straight in and I…

"It doesn't feel like it, though. Does it?" Mili cut into my *spicy* thoughts. "It feels like…"

"I'm not going to say the clichéd thing like forever," I teased her.

Although, if I was being honest with myself, so many events – important, life-altering, and tectonic – had happened in the last three months that it did feel like a lifetime.

"You'd never be clichéd," she murmured.

"You'd never let me," I reminded her.

"You do know the important things about me." She sighed out, laying her head on my good shoulder. It made me feel ten feet tall to see my Mili, my Firecracker, be soft and vulnerable with me.

Because she was so capable – like trying to solve the mystery of the strange and deathly happenings in my home, Bhatnagar Stud and Race Farm by herself and being the best lawyer-fixer ever – it was easy to forget Mili was also fragile.

Especially with me.

Especially now.

"So, is there a reason why we are not headed to Hawaii for our honeymoon, where I get to see you in a coconut bikini and…" I leaned in and whispered something decadent in her ear – like the author in her book would write - that caused Mili to blush something fierce. Watching her do that was fucking amazing.

I couldn't wait to try it when she had far less clothes on, and I could do something about it.

"Behave!" Mili sighed and batted my face away. "Is there a way to block you in real life like I can on the text app?"

I was affronted. "Why would you want to block me anywhere?"

"Because you're too much sometimes," Mili grumbled. But she twined our fingers together again and continued softly, "This last week…I realized I was being unfair to mom. Holding her responsible for a decision she thought was best at the time. Holding her responsible for Appa dying so suddenly." Her husky voice cracked; her golden eyes shone with tears.

She took a deep breath, squeezing my hand tight.

I held on and held my tongue. I knew enough about Mili to know when she needed to collect herself.

"I want to make up with her, Nihaal. And with Krivi and Ziya. My family." She mentioned the seriously scary dude with the blackest eyes she was related to and his svelte and sweet wife. "I want…" Mili hesitated. "I want you to love them like I do." Hope was bright and beautiful in her night-black eyes, giving it the same luminescence as the tears.

But I couldn't believe what she was asking of me.

"I cannot possibly love your government-sanctioned murderer cousin, Mili." I stared at her incredulously.

"Allegedly," she whispered fiercely. "He's a hotel owner now."

"And I'm a GoKart champion," I shot back. "Krivi threatened me with dismemberment if I ever hurt you, right before the wedding. Did he tell you that?" I stopped short of shuddering at the memory of the man telling me casually what he'd do to me if I broke Mili's trust.

And I had, for a little bit. Before I fixed it. And she loved me forever.

It was a different thing that maybe Krivi Karthik Iyer, alleged MI5 spy, would not see it like that.

Mili shrugged casually. "He's insanely protective of me. I am an only child, you see. So Krivi took over big brother duties." She looked like she wanted to laugh.

"Now I feel like blocking you IRL," I grumbled.

"No, you don't. You love me far too much. You even took a bullet for me." She was smug in her declaration.

I shook my head. "I should never have done that."

"Really?"

I kissed the tips of her fingers. "It's given you ideas that you can make me do impossible things. Things I don't want to do."

She opened her mouth, as if to say something. Guilt and chagrin flitted across her normally cool face.

I caught the expression because I spent most of my time learning the ways of my Firecracker. It was endlessly entertaining and made the time spent in rehab instead of prepping for next year's F1 season bearable.

"What?" I asked slowly. "What did you do?"

Mili slid her gaze away. "Why would you say that?"

"Because I do know you. What did you do, Mili?" I spaced the words out evenly.

She muttered something under her breath and said, "I engineered it so your sister could have some time alone to sort out her situation with her...Ben and..." Mili bit her lip. "I think, Nashit."

I looked at her, disbelieving. "What are you *talking* about?"

My younger sister, okay, she was a competent surgeon in Edinburgh and young was just a number, would not have complications in her love life. She was far too level-headed for that. Especially considering the shitshow her life was about to become because of our dearly departed father.

And especially not with Nashit, who was like a son to my father and Pehel's fiercest champion since we were kids.

"I knew you'd go all protective big brother on her, if you knew about Ben and Nashit," Mili said quickly. "And she is in a terrible situation with Krishna Uncle's will conditions and I just...wanted to give her some space to figure things out. For herself."

"Is she into Ben and Nashit?" I gritted out. "Is my younger sister interested in two men?" My gut burned at the idea of her being interested in even one man. At the very idea of any man putting a hand on her, even a filthy rich and smart bastard like Ben Everton but...

"She has been ordered to *marry a man* and save a billion-dollar inheritance, Nihaal. Do not judge her for what she's thinking or feeling, okay?" Mili said quietly, with dignity.

I huffed out an injured breath. "I wasn't…

"Look, we began the same way, didn't we?" she said placatingly. "I.."

"We were different," I growled. "I wanted you from the second I saw you. And you…"

"Really?" Her eyes brightened with soft pleasure at my gruff admission. Then she straightened and continued, "It can't be different for us and for her, Nihaal. That's not fair. Plus, Pehel's a functional adult. Way more than you or I have been the last year, and don't you deny it."

I couldn't, even if it bugged the fuck out of me. "Still…"

"She gets to choose whoever or whatever she wants," Mili emphasized. With the steely look I was intimately familiar with.

It was the look that began our…relationship. Was the bane of my existence till I decided to say fuck it, and just loved her with all my heart.

"You could have told me, you know. You didn't have to keep it a secret from me," I said slowly.

A pinprick of hurt entered the bubble of adrenalin, sheer happiness, and lusty love I was enclosed in. Not enough to fully burst it but the shield sure was penetrated.

"I was going to. As soon as we landed," Mili murmured.

Just then, the pilot announced, "Ladies and gentlemen, this is your pilot speaking. We're beginning our descent into Chandigarh now. The temperature's a balmy twenty-five degrees and we are very much on time today. We hope you have a pleasant stay…"

He droned on about flight instructions.

I gave a stricken Mili a muted look. "You should have told me before we left. We can talk about it after we land. In private."

CHAPTER 2 - MILI

Being in love was a pain in the ass.

No one ever told me that. Not one of the books I read on the sly (about three times a year) told me what came after 'happy ever after'. How difficult it was to consider another person's feelings and navigate day to day life with a man, especially a man like Nihaal Keziah Bhatnagar. My husband, who I was insanely in love with but who still surprised me with his reactions to things.

Like, the way his eyes heated up and gleamed when he talked dirty to me, without knowing what it was he was telling me. I was instantly slick in my core at his clipped British accent asking me to shut the fuck up and take…

Or the offended and *hurt* look he'd given me before the pilot's announcement severed our conversation.

I knew Nihaal cared about Pehel. That, in his own rebellious son way, he'd exiled himself so he could show his sibling they were more than Bhatnagars – heirs to a vast, horse-racing legacy and fortune. Of course, he'd also been criminally selfish when he'd left her at his father's mercy, but I knew what had driven him then, and what drove him now.

Ambition.

The need to be the best, the only in a world full of mediocrity. A champion.

Only the criminally selfish could achieve this kind of brightness. And while I admired him for what he'd done, I could also understand why Pehel blamed him and didn't want him around as she chose a man to marry over the next few days. If Nihaal hadn't left, Krishna Bhatnagar would not have created the iron-clad monstrosity of a will that drew me into Nihaal's orbit and changed the course of my whole life.

It was a pain, being in love and having to *explain* all of this to him. When I knew I was right.

But, because I loved him, I didn't want to hurt him, even unintentionally. And I had promised him I'd not try to fix things alone anymore.

And yet...

"I'm sorry, Nihaal," I said mournfully, quietly, as we disembarked. "I should have told you this before we left Alipur. I'm sorry," I repeated.

He held on to the bag he carried on his good side, his other shoulder was still healing, and waited for the doors to be opened.

We were the first to get off, considering Nihaal was a celebrity even if he wasn't recognized today. Because he had on gray sweatpants, a slouchy hoodie, had grown a beard with sunglasses that covered his face, and his arm was in a sling.

The outside world did not know the real reason why Nihaal did not race at the Abu Dhabi Grand Prix, almost two weeks ago. Ending his career-best season without a Driver's Championship. And we'd made sure he kept out of the public eye as we both recuperated.

"Thank you for flying with us, sir, ma'am." The flight attendant smiled graciously. "Have a pleasant stay."

When we were almost out the door, the flight attendant gasped. Fuck. She'd recognized him.

"We will. Thanks." Nihaal grinned at her, his full-wattage, champion-out-of- bed-and-in-it smile.

A flash of unwanted jealousy writhed in my chest, green and poisonous. This woman needed to be put in her place.

I smiled sweetly at her and grabbed his hand with more force than necessary. "Yes, *we* will."

I made sure to flash my engagement and wedding rings as I waved at her like a princess would and practically dragged Nihaal out. My arm throbbed from the flesh wound I'd sustained when a deranged man had tried to fucking--

I practically thundered down the flight stairs.

"Hey. Hey. Slow down, Firecracker," Nihaal muttered, trying to keep up with me, even though we were evenly matched in height and gait. "You'll open the stitches on your arm. Mili!"

I gave him a forbidding look. "Were you flirting with her as payback for me not telling you about Pehel?"

"Was I flirt…"

Nihaal took a deep breath and gave me an inscrutable look. Then, he strode ahead of me to the waiting Range Rover parked on the tarmac itself. One of the perks of being a world-famous athlete was the tarmac to road service. We figured the pint-sized Chandigarh International Airport would not be able to handle the frenzy of a mob hounding Nihaal if they knew he was here.

We usually chartered a flight or opted for odd times – when the flights would be almost empty – to travel. But in my haste of hustling Nihaal away from his sister, I had booked us on a full flight. In daylight.

My fixing abilities needed a tune up, clearly.

A special attendant was already loading our bags into the car as we swiftly made our way to it.

I took a moment to covertly admire Nihaal's lithe butt in the gray sweatpants. Familiar heat filled me when I saw his long strides eating up the tarmac, confident and just the right kind of arrogant.

Eighty-one days ago, I saw this man's naked ass in a shower while he whistled tunelessly and began my descent into the most delicious madness. *Love*.

Nihaal held the door open for me. My courteous husband, with the Grim Reaper cast to his handsome face. I climbed in and took the bag from him.

He helped to buckle me into the seat belt because my arm was slightly non-functional, and I did the same for him.

He still didn't say a word.

"Nihaal…" I began hesitantly, dread forming in the pit of my stomach.

Were we having a fight or was it something more? It was so hard to tell, sometimes. Before, our issues were black and white – he was black, and I was white – so I could righteously fight with him knowing I was right. I could win.

Now, I *loved* him, I didn't want to win with him, and everything was so gray and murky…

"I smiled at the woman and said thanks, Mils," he said calmly. "I wasn't flirting with her. As payback or otherwise."

I flinched internally with every word he spoke.

He looked out the window, clearly rejecting me as the driver gunned the car out of the tarmac through a private route.

And, for once, I didn't say anything either. I was in the wrong. I had no righteous defense here.

As I looked at Nihaal's marble-hard profile – the straight line of his nose running to the fluffy beard covering his dimpled chin and sculpted jaw - I wondered how to fix this.

There was the word again. Fix. I was genetically incapable of not solving a problem. Whether it was through words or actions. And I knew this was a huge sore point for Nihaal because it fell to him to worry about me when I did something I figured I could handle but that was, sometimes, a bit too dangerous.

To his credit, my husband was actually doing much better in the communication department than me – the fixer whose job it was to talk people into doing whatever it was I wanted.

I did something then that felt unfamiliar to me.

I texted my first, maybe my only, girlfriend Anya Fallahil. The wife of my first and only boss, Caleb Drake Fallahil, the apex predator of the venture capital world.

I checked the time. It was four-thirty pm in India. So, it was about nine pm in Singapore where Drake and Anya were staying for the time being, since Anya was extremely pregnant and preferred to be near her mother, Swati, maker of delicious butter naans and chicken Chettinaad stew.

You there?

Her reply was instantaneous. *For you. Always. Or at least till I have to go pee. Again. For the hundredth time today.*

I smiled a little. Anya was a few years younger than me, but she was an old soul. It wasn't justification for the way Drake basically blackmailed her into marrying him for reasons that still escaped my rational brain, but she reminded me of my sister-in-law, Pehel. They were both calm, seemingly happy people. But with storms swirling underneath.

Certainly, Anya had to be a little bit insane to fall in love with Drake. And *breed*.

Before I lost my nerve, I asked the question.

How do you make it up to Drake when you screw up?

She replied cheekily with a series of emojis - the peach, eggplant, and rain drops ones. AKA code for sex.

I snuck a glance at Nihaal. He was now occupied with his phone. Jumping his bones and fucking his brains out without communicating seemed a bit excessive. And set a bad precedent. For the health of our relationship.

And what if you have to talk about things?

Her answer was impossible to execute and completely simple.

Then you talk.

Three dots appeared under the text chain.

And she sent a video of Drake in his silk monogrammed pajamas now that he was on paternity leave for the baby's birth, sitting hunched on his laptop, glasses on his nose, completely lost to the world. He was stunningly, clinically handsome. In the way the David was – a living, breathing statue come to life.

"Drake, honey?" Anya called out from behind the camera.

I lowered the volume on my phone, mindful of Nihaal.

Drake grunted. But didn't look up from the screen.

"Husband mine, can you answer me, please?" she asked sweetly.

Drake looked up, eyes blinking like an owl. He looked at the camera. "Anya. Who's that?"

"Say hi to Mili. She misses you."

Drake smiled, immediately and affectionately, like the big brother he was to only two women in the whole world. "Hi, Mili. I miss you too."

The video ended.

Anya sent another text after that.

You talk until he listens.

I was afraid this would be the answer. And it required something from me, complete and total vulnerability with Nihaal.

Something I'd avoided till now.

"I wanted you," I said almost soundlessly.

I spoke looking out the window, watching the tarmacked national highway give way to the planned roads of Chandigarh city. After which we'd be on our way to the Himalayas and the mountain town of Manali, where Ziya was currently overseeing the creation of yet another homestay in the Goonj Homestay chain.

"I wanted you so badly I was willing to marry you for it," I confessed. "When I swore to myself, I'd never marry anyone. I'd never even fall in love."

Nihaal stilled but didn't look up from his phone.

I knew I had his attention. A thick ball rose up in my throat and lodged there. But I swallowed past the shame and the secret desire to stay alone so I didn't have to do this – be this naked with anyone – and told him everything.

"I thought I was doing it to satisfy the conditions of your father's will, Nihaal. That I was solving your problem for you. And I was. But that wasn't why I did it. Not in here." I fisted a hand to my chest. Where my heart beat uncommonly fast.

I finally looked at him.

He was grave faced, thin-lipped. But he was looking at me. Progress.

"I...It's difficult for me to not make life easy for you. For your family. I am not built like that."

"I wasn't asking you to stop, Mils," Nihaal offered coolly. "I'd never ask you to change who you are."

My heart twisted at his words. "I know but..." I whispered my secret out loud. "I'm changed by you, Nihaal. You don't know how much I'm changed by you. I'm..." I searched for the right words to make him understand how important he was to me.

"Altered. Forever. By you," I said softly. "But it doesn't mean I'm not still me."

Our marriage, our relationship was fast becoming the lodestone of my existence. It wasn't the only important thing, of course. I was still highly ambitious too but...I wanted to see what we'd build together more than anything.

Nihaal removed his glasses.

I sucked a breath in at the force of feeling in his golden ichor eyes. I was blasted by the heat in them, the sheer depth of what shone from him.

"You blew into my life like inverted G-forces, Mili. I stood no chance against you. Not one. And I wasn't..." Now he searched for the right words so we could communicate and not sulk separately. "Trying to make you feel bad, much." He smiled wryly. "For trying to help Pehel."

Nihaal sighed. His chest moving in tandem with the big gust of breath.

"I messed up my relationship with her when I left home all those years ago, I thought...now's my chance to make it up to her. To rebuild our foundations." He was melancholic. "And it feels like you made a unilateral decision to pause that."

I crawled over to him. And put my arms around his waist, mindful of the sling.

The driver gave us a surprised glance in the rearview mirror. As if he wasn't used to PDAs in the backseat of the car.

I couldn't give a fuck about propriety right now. I was having an important *conversation* with the love of my life.

"I was hoping you'd say that." I kissed his unshaven jaw. "You have the best heart, Nihaal. And I'm sorry, truly, that I didn't tell you my plan. I wasn't sure you'd leave if you knew why I wanted us to go."

His arms came around my waist, traveled down my pants leg so I lay half-draped over him. "I am not sure either." Nihaal ran a hand over my leg. "That's what sucks. That you are fucking right about this. But...next time, just tell me. Okay? I don't want to ever feel like you're trying to control me."

Like his father had tried to, constantly. In life and after he died.

"I won't. I'll try my hardest not to," I vowed.

"That's enough for me, love." He ran a thumb over the inside of my wrist.

"Anya says I should use sex to get you to listen to me."

Nihaal grinned. Cheekily. Sexily. Devilishly. Sparks of lust and heat driving the flames hotter between us. "Anya might be smarter than you."

I looked at the driver's stiff, disapproving form and kissed Nihaal's jaw discreetly.

"Later," I promised. "I'll prove to you just how smart I am."

CHAPTER 3 - NIHAAL

I was going to die today.

The car climbed up the mountain valley town of Manali several hours later, on the way to Goonj Manali. It was soon to be a world-famous hospitality location known for its classy décor, excellent South Asian cooking, and breathtaking views of the snow-capped Himalayas. Krivi and

Ziya were as good at the hospitality business as one of my other friends, Ansh Thackery.

Yet, I was certain today would be my last.

Because, after making up with Mili, which was second to making love with Mili, I remembered the ruthless cool on her cousin's face and the promise he'd made me minutes before I said 'I do' to Mili and tethered our fates together.

I'm watching you. I don't care how rich or famous or talented you are... The minute I see something I know will hurt my sister will be the last thing you ever do...That is a promise. And I always keep my promises.

I was not fully aware of his career prior to helping Ziya manage the Goonj hospitality business, but I had my suspicions. I could have asked *my* cousin, Mason Jones-Tarrant, of the billionaire Manhattan Jones-Tarrants, to look into Krivi and confirm my suspicions but I was not eager to know the ugly truth.

Ignorance was bliss in this instance.

———

"You're worried," Mili observed. "What's gotten you worried?"

I gave her a droll look. "Don't pretend like you don't know, Mils. Your cousin is a terrifying man."

"He's like a cute teddy bear," Mili protested. "You just don't know him very well."

I shook my head at her blind ignorance. "A lethal teddy bear," I corrected her. "And I'm fairly certain he's going to have things to say to me after what happened."

"What happened?" She was so clueless, my smart Firecracker.

"You got hurt. There." I pointed at her midriff, and her arm, which was not in a sling like mine was, but it rankled all the same. "There."

Mili stared at me, nonplussed. "And?"

"I let you get hurt, Mili. This happened on my watch," I said simply.

And that was it. Mili got hurt not once but twice with me. Because of me. And all the love in the world wasn't enough to make me feel better about it. God knew, I deserved whatever hurt Krivi would inevitably dish out.

She opened her mouth as if to argue the point. Instead, she smiled softly. Delicately, with her whole heart.

"What?" I demanded, restlessly. "What are you smiling about?"

Mili shrugged. "You didn't protest, not even once, when I asked you to come here with me. Knowing Krivi might not be exactly welcoming, you still came."

I shrugged. "You missed your mom. You wanted to be with her."

And, in my head, that was the end of the argument. Whatever Mili wanted, she got. Especially if it was time with her family. I knew full well what happened when families spent too much time apart and never really healed, I wouldn't let that happen to Mili if I could help it.

"Getting killed is a small price to pay for you to make up with your mom." And I half-meant it. I liked living but I loved Mili.

Mili sighed and kissed the tips of my uninjured fingers. "You undo me when you say things like that, you know."

"Well…" I narrowed my eyes. "It's certainly more romantic than the things your book characters say."

I kept my chuckle in because she pouted and was about to argue with me. Her eyes fired up and she had that militant tilt to her chin.

But then she sucked in a breath. Mili jerked her head and said, "Look. It's beautiful."

I turned around to check it out. A towering stone castle chiseled from the mountain side came into view. It was stately, imposing, born from the mountain. A terrifyingly beautiful thing come to life.

"God," I breathed. "He can throw me from up there and they won't even find my body."

"You're paranoid, Bhatnagar. Krivi isn't going to hurt you. I promise," she assured me.

"I'm going to stay three feet behind you and your mom to make sure he doesn't," I told her grimly. "You can protect me."

She leaned over and squeezed my knee. Only slightly lasciviously. "Happy to, champ. Happy to."

"Bhatnagar," Krivi said as he opened the car door, ten minutes later. All six-three of him hulked and bulked up in the muscle tee he wore under the cotton shirt and jeans and workman boots.

"Krivi," I said grimly, holding tight to Mili's hand, just in case the slaughter began at the gate itself.

"Krivi!" Mili reached over me and hugged him around the neck, ignoring her injured arm. "Oh my god, Krivi. Let me hug you."

His eyes almost bugged out from the force of her hug. But the light of destruction left them, and he gave me a tentative smile.

I smiled back. I also let go of Mili's hand.

Krivi could do his worst if he wanted. I was still going to be okay. I'd lived through far worse in the last month. And I wasn't going to allow some ex-spy to ruin my happy ever after.

"Good to see you, cousin," I said cheekily, exiting the car.

Krivi looked at my sling, then at me. And, finally at Mili who tightly gripped my hand. She was beaming, happy. I knew it radiated from her – the warmth of her love. And I basked in it, a little of it was because of me.

I squared my shoulders even more, like a boxer getting into the ring.

"Good to see you too, Nihaal," Krivi said quietly.

"This place is heavenly," Mili gushed. "Ziya chooses the best places to do business in."

"She does." Pride and love shimmered on Krivi's expressionless face. "She is the best."

"Milika!" Mili's mom wailed as she came out of the half-finished portico, flat-out running toward us.

She was closely followed by Ziya and Krivi's two-year-old daughter – Noori. Noori waddled on chubby legs clad in light up sneakers with her mother trailing close behind.

I watched, my newly awakened heart a little full as Mili ran from my side to her mom and the two women hugged each other. Laugh-crying as they spoke over each other. In half-phrases and endearments and apologies that only made sense to them.

"Shalini will be happy now," Krivi murmured, to me. "Her daughter's here."

"Her daughter is happy too," I said quietly.

Krivi looked at his wife and called out, "I'll take her." He indicated his daughter, still waddling over to us as fast as her little feet would carry her. She touched Mili's knees when she went past her.

Mili chuckled and wept a little more, clutching her mom closer. "She's grown so *much*," she marveled.

I thought so too but I wasn't going to say anything to provoke the cousin. So, I just smiled.

I even took a step forward to go to my mother-in-law when the little girl barreled straight past her father's waiting arms and collided against my pant legs.

Immediately I scooped her up with my good hand, so she wouldn't bounce down from the impact and fall.

To my surprise, she let me.

"Can I hold you?" I asked the little girl, not sure she'd understand me. But it was always polite and important to ask consent as I'd learned around the new mamas of my racing team.

Noori stuck her thumb in her mouth, her eyes big and black in a face too small for it. She had the cutest nose, rosebud lips, and fluffy, pillow-soft cheeks. And she actually cocked her head, as if considering my question.

"Let me—" Krivi began.

"Okay," Noori said. And lay her head on my shoulder, sucking on her thumb in that endearing way I remembered from the wedding.

I felt a hit in my gut. One made of elastic love for this little girl who just trusted me instantly. It was a massive feeling and I didn't know how to deal with it, except…breathe.

Krivi's eyes widened. And then a light entered his eyes. *Was it approval?*

"Sorry about that. She just got away from me." Ziya skidded to a stop next to her husband. She was shocked when she saw her daughter lying quietly on me.

"She doesn't go to anyone," she breathed out. "She's very particular about who holds her. You are magic, Nihaal."

Mili and her mom came to stand beside me, arms around each other's waists. She snaked one arm around me and gave me a warm, side hug, and I nodded softly at her.

We didn't know each other very well, if at all, but that was going to change over the next few days.

I was going to make sure of it.

"Hello, Shalini Ma," I said pleasantly. The words slipped out. Natural and *right*. Mili's eyes widened and softened at hearing me say them. That sealed it for me. "I brought your daughter to you in one piece."

Shalini wiped streaming eyes with shaking hands. "I'm glad both of you are okay, Nihaal."

I looked at Krivi quickly. He was looking at the four of us, consideringly. As if weighing the odds of keeping me alive versus disposing of me while his daughter was tucked against my chest.

"Yeah," he said finally. "I'm glad both of you are okay."

I heaved a sigh of relief, internally.

I wasn't going to die today.

CHAPTER 4 - MILI

Three days later

Goonj Manali

"Where are we going? Nihaal…Nihaal…" I grumbled as I held onto him awkwardly, his strong fingers wrapped around my palms. I was blindfolded so I had to rely on him to lead me safely.

It was a strange thing. Trusting someone like this. For me, it was anathema to do so. But…love was strange and wonderful so when Nihaal tied one of my scarves around my eyes as we were preparing for bed after another raucous family dinner to lead me here, I submitted. The submission was new too. And, if I was being honest, exciting and hot.

So. Fucking. Hot.

My nipples peaked against my bra, in agreement.

"Is this a sex thing?" I asked as he paused.

"There's a step here. Watch for it, okay?" Nihaal instructed.

I drew the sash of my dressing gown closer around my waist and felt the edge of the step with my toe. I did not want a stubbed toe to begin whatever this was. I climbed the step, holding tighter to him.

We walked a little farther, the air becoming colder, purer with each step I took. I knew we hadn't left the property because it was bitching cold in the homestay than outside it. But we had taken a series of turns leading us farther away from the construction and our rooms, almost like a maze, so I was disoriented.

"Where *are* we?" I wondered. The stone was cold to the touch on my fur-slipper clad feet, so I deduced we were somewhere inside the mountain and not out of it.

And I wasn't exactly dressed for an excursion, especially with what I had on under my dressing gown. Besides, Nihaal still wore the clothes he'd worn for dinner - gray sweatpants and a worn silver and black Menzo tee.

I didn't know what he was doing, where he was taking me. I was completely under his control...the notion was new. Exciting. Hot AF.

Dammit. I was such a goner for this man.

"We're here. You ready for it?"

"Can I open my blindfold?" I asked.

His fingers trailed up my neck to my collarbone.

I felt him settle at my back, an insistent male presence. My favorite position in foreplay. Because being held by Nihaal like this was...delicious helplessness and heat combined.

"If you want to." His voice, so beloved and so familiar, was foreign too. Maybe because I couldn't see him. Only feel him.

I swallowed. Suddenly a little too hot for my comfort. I tried to capture his hand with mine. But he slipped from my hold. "I..."

Nihaal kissed my neck. "Say yes and I'll open it."

I moaned and lay my suddenly weak neck on his shoulder. I tried to suppress the shudder that wanted to run through me.

He made me feel so vulnerable, so *powerless* when he held me like this. Because I didn't want to move away and face him. I wanted him to do whatever he wanted to me. While I could only experience it.

My pussy slicked with wet heat. Immediate and clamorous.

"Say it, Mili." He kissed the corner of my lips, bending his head to do so.

I took his healing hand and pressed it against the tips of my breasts, already beading to tight, painful points against his palm. "Nihaal..." I whined.

He squeezed against the silk. Just a little rough. A little painful. "You like being at my mercy," he observed, coolly.

I reached blindly up his thigh and cupped the rough material of his sweatpants. Where his cock was already at attention. "You're at mine too," I spoke through my teeth.

"I like being at your mercy, Mils." Nihaal feathered his lips over my ears. His breath fluttered over me. Showering me with heat and chills at the same time.

"Well." I tried to keep whatever sanity I still could. And untied the sash of my gown with nerveless fingers. "Prepare to fall at my feet, Bhatnagar."

I shrugged out of the gown. But, because I was trapped against his back, it didn't slide down my body, sticking instead to our middle.

He sucked in a sharp breath as his hand collided against my silk-clad breasts.

"What the fuck is this?" Nihaal's growl was sin incarnate.

I smiled. Trailed a hand down his thigh, which was more rigid than it had been a moment ago.

"You said you wanted to go to Hawaii so you could see me in a coconut bikini..." I reminded him. Breathless and out of words.

Because his hand was moving over my belly, my abdomen, touching the waistband of the G-string bikini I wore. His other hand was squeezing and releasing my tits like he wasn't aware of what he was doing. Arousing me endlessly with each rough caress.

"So, what?" He sucked on my throat, his teeth scraping against the tender pulse fluttering there.

I turned molten, fire licking along my nerves, my limbs. Making it hard to concentrate on anything but his lips, his fucking talented hands and the way every time he touched me, I combusted.

"So..." I swallowed. "I...ahh."

Nihaal dipped a finger into my belly button and swirled. Electricity shot from the dip of my spine straight through every part of me.

"I figured, I could give you what you wanted."

"Why?" He toyed with the back of my robe, sliding his knuckles up and down my spine, while the other hand moved down, down, whispering over my neon green bikini panties, hot and insistent. *Possessive.*

I arched into his touch, a wave crashing on the shore. I wasn't sure how much longer I could stay upright with him touching me, teasing me...

"Because I..." I gripped his thigh. Hard. Nails digging into the material. Feeling his bones and muscles contract against my fingers. "I love you."

Nihaal plunged one finger into my waiting heat at the 'you.'

I closed my eyes and nearly gasped at the force of it all. Colors and shapes, the whole galaxy, danced in front of my eyes as I absorbed the feel of him inside me. Thick and invading and so necessary I felt tears prick the corners of my blindfolded eyes, the fabric adding to the sensations I was forced to experience.

He untied the blindfold, the silk sliding from me in a whisper.

"So did I." He kissed my cheek, my jaw.

I opened heavy-lidded eyes. And what I saw struck me mute.

We were in a small cavern, with untouched stone walls. Lit with tiki torches at the moment. A straw umbrella had been set up on one side of the space with two colorful, fruity drinks on a wicker table. The table only boasted one chair though.

At the very back of the cavern was a huge white four-poster bed with sheer white curtains that fluttered in the cool breeze. Fluffy pillows and sheets were piled high on it. And, on the stone wall behind the bed was a huge poster.

It was a beach scene, full of the bluest of waves, the sun dipping in the horizon and palm trees swaying in the breeze. Colorful and cheery and super sunny.

Across the poster were the words, "Aloha! Welcome to Hawaii."

I felt a tear slide down my cheek at his sheer thoughtfulness and romanticism.

"If we couldn't go to Hawaii." Nihaal worked the finger in and out with each word.

I rose on my toes. Trying to catch his rhythm. Unable to stop my body from wanting it so bad. Moving against his cock. The friction making me lose my mind, my inhibitions.

His voice was clipped, cool, at odds with his furnace-hot body, his racing breaths. "Hawaii." *Thrust. Exit.* "Comes." *Thrust.* "To." *Exit.* "Us." *Thrust.*

I cried out as his thumb brushed against my already stimulated clit, rubbing against it in that way I liked and couldn't stand at the same time. Aching and pulling me into orbit.

My orgasm began and took me under in seconds, making a mess of my panties, moisture building, and dripping down my thighs.

Tears blinded me even as I came apart in his arms, shaking and dropping my feet back to the ground.

I searched for his mouth.

Nihaal kissed me roughly. Hard. His teeth bit my lips as he took and took me. I loved every second of it. Feeling cherished and so very loved, more tears fell down.

I tried to wipe them away, but he batted my hand away.

"I like seeing these happy tears," Nihaal spoke against my lips. "It's better than the others you've cried this week."

"I love you," I said brokenly. The words too fucking small, not enough to contain everything I felt, I *was* for him. Treasured and fucked and bold and happy and fantastic. "No one has ever done this for me. No one thinks I need...I need..."

I turned in his arms and threw my hands around my husband's neck in gratitude and utter abandonment. He was forced to withdraw his hand from my core because of my action. And I felt his loss deep in the pit of my stomach.

The gown slithered down between our feet.

I was messy, and half-naked. He was still fully dressed. But I didn't care.

"*I* need," Nihaal said softly, cupping my cheeks with fingers drenched in my pleasure. Sticky and aroused and all his. "I need to take care of you too, love. It's not been an easy time for you with Krivi and Shalini Ma."

I knew what he meant. Having the conversations I'd had to have with my family was soul-wrecking but also healing. And knowing Nihaal was there with me, by my side or giving me space, meant I could face it all without losing myself.

Now, his ichor-gold eyes glowed with uncertainty and love. The need to care for me. His admission was heartfelt. "And I wanted to do something to make you feel...happy again."

"I'm happy." I sniffled, inelegantly. And kissed him. Soft and lingering, the tears drying up. "If I were anymore happy, I'd fly straight into space."

"That's my plan." Nihaal grinned wickedly. Gave the bed a sidelong glance. "On that bed, to be more precise. I fucking deserve it after muscling the thing in with Krivi's construction pals."

"You didn't hurt yourself, did you?" I anxiously checked his shoulder, precisely where the bullet had entered and exited from his flesh. "The doctor said…"

"I didn't hurt myself." He grumbled. "This is a sexy moment. Don't ruin it, will you?"

"I am ruined. I am a blubbering mess," I wailed, leaning back against his arms.

"You're my blubbering mess," Nihaal corrected me and kissed my forehead. "And I plan on ruining you for the rest of my life, Mrs. Bhatnagar. Will you let me?"

I did what Noori said to Nihaal every time he asked her for permission to pick her up, or play with her, or read her favorite storybooks with her. What Amma told him when he announced he'd make scrambled eggs for breakfast for everyone and Krivi actually allowed him near the knives.

I lay my head on his good shoulder and whispered, "Okay."

And it was more than okay.

It was my own personal happy ever after. Every single day.

———

Thank you for choosing to read my short story for such an important cause. You're awesome. If you have burning questions about Nihaal and Mili, all will be answered if you dive into Burn and Blaze by Aarti V Raman.

THE PRE-PROPOSAL

ADRIANA LOCKE

BLAKELY

"Aloha," Ella says, straightening the flower halo on her head. "Welcome to Hawaii."

She offers me a pale-yellow beverage with a tiny red umbrella. I take it from her and then take in my brother Brock's backyard. It's not exactly an island in the Pacific, but it's as close as you'll get in Nashville.

Birthdays are nothing short of national holidays for Ella St. James. There is no such thing as a small celebration with her. When Brock showed the tiniest crack in his veneer, hinting at the most negligible possibility of being open to a party, Ella ran with it … straight to the pin app for ideas. One month later, she's transformed his backyard into a tropical oasis to cheer her boyfriend on into the next year of life.

"Wow," I say before sipping the pineapple concoction. "You really went all out for this one."

"I've been hinting at wanting to go to Maui for months. I thought maybe I could wet his whistle a little bit. Give him a taste of what his life could be like —how happy I would be and how over-the-top I could go in returning the happiness—if he obliged my request."

I smirk at the twinkle in her eye. "Meaning …"

"You should see what I have planned when all of you go home. I know exactly what wish will be granted tonight and involves me, grapes—"

"No, Ella. Stop! That's my brother."

She giggles. "Sorry. I forget there are boundaries. It's the one shitty thing about dating your best friend's brother."

"Work on remembering that."

My gaze sweeps across the event in front of me. Music plays from a DJ booth in the far corner of the backyard. A bar is set up next to the outside kitchen area with two bartenders serving Brock's friends colorful drinks. A Hawaiian backdrop leans against the fence for photo opportunities, and hibiscus flowers, pineapples, and surfboard inflatables float in the pool.

It's fun and special without being stuffy. It's perfect for Brock.

"You did an amazing job, El," I say, nodding in appreciation of her efforts.

"Thanks. It came together pretty well, and Brock said he loved it. So, I'm happy. I mean, I would've loved another bump in the budget so I could've afforded ..."

I don't hear the rest.

It's impossible to focus on anything else when he looks your way.

My breath catches in my lungs. If I was walking, I'd stumble. Every cell in my body overheats as I take in the real focal point of the party.

Renn. Freaking. Brewer.

My brother's best friend owns the space around him without putting in actual effort. He's traditionally good-looking with bottomless brown eyes, a jawline cut from granite, and shoulders that assure you he's capable of tossing you over them and carrying you off to bed. Something I've dreamed about more times than I care to admit. But he's somehow even more than that.

He carries himself with an air of intrigue as if he's on the verge of saying or doing something fun. His confidence is as attractive as his broad shoulders and thick forearms. And the way Renn looks at me like I'm the only person in the room? It's heady. Intoxicating.

And dangerous.

"I have to admit," Ella says, the words laced with a laugh, "it took you about five seconds longer than I guessed to find Renn."

My cheeks flush as Renn smirks. He watches me with the heat of a lover and the mischief of a conspirator. He's neither thing to me. He can't be. For so many reasons.

He lifts his glass my way before slowly returning to his conversation with a couple of guys I know are also on his and Brock's rugby team.

I clear my throat and turn to Ella. "I'm sorry. What did you say?"

She laughs again in reply.

"No, really," I say, feeling Renn's eyes on my back and trying my best not to turn around. "What did you say?"

"I said it took you about five seconds longer than I anticipated to find Renn in this chaos."

"What's that supposed to mean?"

She puts a hand on her narrow hip. "Don't play coy with me. You know damn good and well what I mean."

And I do. I know exactly what she means.

The chemistry between the bad boy of rugby and me is wild. I've been awake countless nights, wondering how to describe what it's like to be with him. How to name the feeling. The electricity. The connection. How to wrap my brain around the intoxication of breathing in the same air, the giddiness of knowing every woman in the room is dying for his attention, and I get it without asking—the heat in his eyes and the fire in his touch.

I should feel nervous around him. He's that beautiful. But, instead, it's as if we've spent more time together than a few parties and a handful of holidays. There's nothing awkward or off-putting, nothing unsettling about Renn Brewer ... except that there's nothing unsettling about Renn Brewer.

"It doesn't matter," I say before taking another sip. "He's Renn, and I'm me, and, in this mathematical equation, one plus one does not equal two."

She grins. "You're right. I'm sure he's good for way more than two."

I smack her shoulder lightly, making her laugh. The levity fades quickly from her pretty face.

"What?" I ask.

Ella groans. "I just saw Kevin—a guy your brother went to college with. He's flying to San Diego in the morning and staying here tonight. And I have a ton of bags and boxes in the guest room that I was hiding for the party, and it's a mess and—"

"Excuse me." A bartender approaches, interrupting her mini-meltdown. "Ella, I'm sorry to interrupt, but I need you for a second."

She turns to me.

"Go," I say, smiling. "Take care of that, and then try to enjoy your work. I'll go upstairs and get the guest room ready for Kevin."

Her shoulders fall. "Are you sure?"

"Of course, I'm sure. Big groups of people make me nervous anyway. I'm kind of happy about going in the air conditioning and avoiding the masses."

"I owe you. Big time."

I smile at her as the song playing overhead changes to a quicker beat. Renn moves to the edge of my periphery. His laughter pierces through the music, floating on the warm breeze straight to me. The sound draws up the corners of my lips. But before I can toy with him back, my brother comes barreling toward me.

"There you are," Brock says, giving me a one-arm hug. "I was wondering when you were going to get here."

"Traffic was a nightmare."

He releases me, taking a step back.

My brother is nearly a foot taller than me and outweighs me by almost a hundred pounds. We may not look alike, but we've always been close; not having a father will do that to you. But our bond grew tighter when our mother died, leaving us on our own—a high school kid and a collegiate athlete with no one to turn to.

"What do you think of your party?" I ask, casually glancing over my shoulder. I intend to leisurely drag over the partiers. Instead, it flips right to Renn.

He's bringing a glass to his lips, his eyes trained on me. The corners wrinkle as if he's amused. He winks.

I lift a brow. And even though I can't hear it, his chest shakes with a chuckle.

"What do I think of this party?" Brock asks, drawing my attention back to him. "I think it's completely unnecessary and over-the-top." He leans forward, lowering his voice. "And I kind of love it, but don't tell Ella."

I laugh.

"I'm kidding," he says. "She knows she killed it. But I know this whole idea did double duty because she wants me to take her to Hawaii. She's trying to lure me in."

"Really?" I gasp. "I had no idea."

He smirks. "Sure, you didn't. Ella has a lot of strengths, but subtly isn't one of them." He waves to someone across the yard. "Do you mind if I go—"

"No, go. Please. Hang out with your buddies. I'm going inside to make sure the guest room is ready for Kevin."

"What? You don't have to do that. He'll be fine on the couch."

"I know I don't have to, but I want to. I need a calm transition from borderline road rage to partying rugby boys. Things will get wild here soon, and I need a few moments of peace."

Brock rolls his eyes but grins. "Whatever. But I don't know what's in there. If you need help moving big boxes or anything, just shout."

"Whatever," I say, giving his sarcasm back to him. "Now go have fun."

He makes a face, but his appreciation and happiness are evident. That makes me happy.

When I turn around, Renn is nowhere to be seen.

"Hi, Mark," I say, passing a light-haired man with a neck as thick as a tree trunk.

"It's good to see you, Blakely," he says.

Good to see you, too, but get out of my way so I can find Renn.

My stomach twists because it's the last thing I should be thinking. Renn Brewer is the epitome of off-limits. But, unfortunately for me, that fact might only add to his lure.

I wind my way through partygoers and head for the house. The late evening sun is low on the horizon, casting a glow around us. It's my favorite time of day. The world is a touch more magical in the golden hour.

Brock's home is warm and inviting as I enter the French door into the kitchen. Even though I've never lived here, it feels like coming home. There are many reminders of our mother—her apron hanging in the butler's pantry and one of her handwritten recipes framed on the island. It's the closest thing to home that I'll ever have.

"Hey, cutie."

I jump at the sound of Renn's voice. The surprise is fleeting and quickly replaced by a heat snaking up my spine.

"You scared the shit out of me," I say, laughing, as I turn to him.

His black polo shirt makes his deep brown eyes even darker—more sinful. They leave a fire trail behind as they drag down my body before returning to my face.

He licks his lips. "Has anyone told you that you look hot as hell tonight?"

"No."

"Then let me be the first." He takes a few steps toward me. "Blakely, you look hot as hell tonight."

I laugh. "You're a charmer."

"My mother says it'll either save my life or destroy it."

My cheeks ache. "I guess it'll depend on who you're trying to charm."

"How's it working on you?"

I smile.

He stops a couple of feet away from me. The smooth, warm notes of his cologne—the same scent that he's paid a hefty chunk of cash to be the face of —caresses me, teasing me with its promise of sexual satisfaction.

"What are you doing in here, anyway?" he asks. "The party is out there."

"I told Ella I'd go upstairs and get the guest room sorted for Kevin. He's staying here tonight, and she left the room a mess."

Renn nods. "Want some help?"

"Sure."

His eyes light up as if he's pleased. "How have you been? I haven't seen you in a while."

"I've been good. Working a lot," I say, following him to the stairs. He stops off to the side to allow me to go first. "I'm being considered for a promotion, so I've been working extra hard to seal the deal."

"I'm sure you've already got it in the bag."

"Thanks. I hope so."

The guest room door is open when we reach the top of the stairs. Ella was right—it's a mess.

Boxes are stacked at the foot of the bed. Some appear empty, while others have papers and packing material spilling out onto the floor. The bed is littered with scissors, tape, ribbon, and magazines. Several empty water bottles and a half-bottle of wine are lined up on the nightstand.

"I bet you regret offering to help now, don't you?" Renn asks, chuckling.

"Actually, no. It's not even as bad as I pictured."

"Really?"

"You obviously don't know Ella," I say, grinning. "She's gorgeous, talented, kind, helpful … and a walking disaster."

He peruses the room. "I've read studies that say that the most successful people in the world are a disaster."

"Let me guess—you're a disaster?"

He smiles. "I mean, I was the Most Valuable Player in rugby the last two years. Just saying."

My laughter fills the room. "You were also suspended for three games, and didn't I see something online about a picture you posted on your Social Stories?"

"Are you following me, Miss Evans?"

"You are kind of hard to miss, Mr. Brewer," I say, stuffing packing material back in the boxes. "You're on every tabloid. I can't turn on a sports station without hearing your name. My co-workers were even talking about you the other day, and I can assure you, none of them know the first thing about rugby."

Renn gathers the bottles and puts them in the trash. "It was about how big my cock is, wasn't it?"

My cheeks turn a deep shade of pink.

"I knew it," he says, smirking.

"I'm not sure that's something to be proud of."

He snorts. "If I'm not supposed to be proud of the size of my cock, then what do you want me to be proud of?"

I flash him a look. "I meant that you shouldn't be proud of the fact that you posted on Social. What if little kids saw that?"

"First of all, it was up for two minutes at three in the morning. Second, I'm a human, and although I'm quite a specimen, I make mistakes. And third, it's not my fault that society has deemed anatomy a taboo subject. Before modern times and everyone's sudden sensitivity to ... well, everything ... they had naked sculptures of men and women sitting around town." He inspects the wine label. "You'd be kidding yourself if you think I wouldn't be the one posing for artists if that was still a thing."

I roll my eyes—but he's not wrong. If Michelangelo were here and looking for a muse, he'd undoubtedly choose Renn.

"You're so humble," I say, breaking down the smallest box and shoving it inside the largest one.

"I'm honest."

I shrug, mostly because I can't deny that he's right. I look up when something rattles.

Renn holds a box of cookies. "Think these are still good?"

I smile. "I have no idea. Take a bite of one and see."

"That feels risky."

"Don't act like you're afraid of risky behavior."

He smirks. "What about you? Are you afraid of a little risky behavior?"

My insides melt at how he looks at me—like he wants to test my cookie and see if it's good.

"Because you're right," he says. "I like a little risk. It makes me feel alive."

A surge of heat ripples through my veins. "I like to feel alive, too."

His eyes darken.

"Which is why I shy away from specific risky behavior," I say, biting my lip to hide a smile.

"What kind of specific things are you talking about?"

I laugh, ignoring the bead of sweat dotting my skin.

Renn knows precisely what I mean. It's the foundation of this little back-and-forth we engage in every time we're together.

Brock would slaughter us both if Renn and I did anything more than this. My brother is a good sport when Renn and I flirt, and he ignores us when we routinely toe the line between friends and friends-with-an-impending-one-night stand. Because that's all it would be—a one-night stand.

I've been tempted many, many times over the years. Renn is the embodiment of what I love in a man. He's gorgeous and fierce, fun and carefree. He makes me feel beautiful and memorable, and I eat that shit up. But as much as he's exactly what I love, he's absolutely what I don't need. And, at the end of the day, he's not what I really want.

My thirtieth birthday is approaching, and the date on the calendar has made me face my future in a way that makes me uneasy. I've lived the last ten years with little regard for the moment when going out on the weekends, hooking up with random bad boys, and doing the walk of shame in the mornings wouldn't feel as fun.

That moment is now.

It's time I begin to make constructive choices, not just those that feel good in the short term. It's time to investigate life insurance and understand how mortgages work. And every day that passes ushers in a deeper desire to have a baby. To start a family of my very own. That won't happen if I continue to humor delicious bad boys ... like Renn Brewer.

He takes a bite of a cookie. I watch his jaw flex with every movement.

Why do I have to be responsible?

"We need to get out of here," I say, gathering the ribbon off the bed.

"Why is that?"

I look up. Our gazes collide, causing sparks to fly across the room.

The temperature rises ten degrees, and sweat drips down my breasts. Renn tosses the cookies on the bed—his eyes never leaving mine.

He holds his breath, and I'm not sure what he will say. Will he crack a joke? Will he change the subject? Will he say something ridiculous?

"Blakely! Where are you?" Brock shouts from downstairs. "I want you to meet someone."

Renn blows out his breath, making me chuckle.

"Coming," I shout back.

"You could've been, but no," Renn says, rolling his eyes.

"Stop it."

"Things women never say to me for two hundred dollars, Alex."

I laugh as we head for the door.

Thanks for reading! For more Renn and Blakely, read The Proposal by Adriana Locke.

TWISTED TIGHTER
A SPARROW NOVELLA
ALEATHA ROMIG

CHAPTER 1 - LAUREL

The dip of the mattress brought me to the present. Inhaling, I blinked my eyes, seeing the handsome green stare of my husband and inhaling his fresh scent. He tilted his forehead toward mine seconds before his strong lips brushed my nose and lips.

The scent of bodywash mixed with the mint of his toothpaste filled my senses. Droplets of water fell from his long hair, dripping onto his wide colorful shoulders. I was immediately drawn to his warmth, the heat within him raging. I reached out, roaming my hands over his back and lower to his firm butt. My exploration confirmed what I suspected. The man above me was completely nude.

"I didn't mean to wake you, Doc." His deep voice reverberated within me.

"I don't mind," I said with a tired grin. "I was trying to wait up for you."

He looked at the notebook now lying to my side. The notes within were chemical formulas of a recently released medication, one that accomplished what I'd set out to do. Their research was solid—the research of Sinclair Pharmaceuticals. Yet it wasn't exactly the same as what I'd been working on. I was curious about the differences.

Mason scoffed, turning the pages. "I'm surprised you fell asleep. This looks like riveting reading."

"Would you believe me if I told you it was?"

"I always believe you, Doc." He tossed the notebook to the floor beside the bed. "I'd believe you if you told me you wanted to go back to sleep."

Running my palms up his back and over his wide shoulders, I read the story of Mason's past written in Braille. It was a tragic story of death and destruction, the obliteration of a life—no, of many—yet the story wasn't complete. Seven years ago, the ultimate twist occurred. No fiction writer could do it justice.

A boy from my past.

I was no longer the girl he remembered, nor was he the boy I knew.

What was meant to be was unstoppable even by death. No, we're not immortal, just damn fortunate that life played out as it had. Today we're together, living and enjoying the fruits of our labors and the bond of our extended families.

Colorful tats covered my husband's body from the nape of his neck to the tops of his feet. And at this moment, they were all visible, every single one of them. A grin curled my lips. "Based on your lack of clothing, I'm not sure you're to be believed."

Mason reached for my waist, and in one quick move—one that only a man with his strength could do, we twisted and spun until his head was on the pillow and I was left straddling his muscular torso. With only my silk pajama shorts and camisole separating us, his smile broadened and the golden flecks in his green eyes shimmered. "I'm very believable."

With my hands on his shoulders, I enjoyed the friction of his skin at my core as well as the probe of his erection at my back. "I think you meant to wake me." I moved my knees, swaying forward and backward. With each pass, my nipples hardened and my core dampened. "I'm glad you woke me. I miss you when things are busy."

Mason's large hands moved beneath my camisole. His fingers splayed on my lower back and stomach as he directed my movement. "I fucking love how soft your skin is." His gaze met mine. "But you're overdressed, and I want a striptease."

The rumble of his request sent a jolt of electricity through me.

Slowing my motions, I reached for the hem of my top and slowly pulled it over my head. My breasts bounced and my nipples grew even tauter at the cool air. Next, I lifted myself on my knees and tugged at the waist of my shorts.

Mason's intense stare was on me. Much like a hot laser, it added heat to my exposed flesh and bare core.

"No panties," he observed as he shook his head. "What happened to my good girl?"

My lips curled. "I'm good, and I can be bad."

I tossed my shorts to the floor as I scooted back and fisted Mason's large erection. The skin stretched beneath my touch, a velvety softness covering a hard-as-steel rod. The first time we'd made love had been in a dark room. That was probably a good thing. If I'd seen how large he was, I might have run for my life. Bending at the waist, I kissed and licked the salty tip.

The muscles in his biceps bulged as he placed his hands behind his head. "Keep being bad, Mrs. Pierce, and you will be sleeping with a reddened ass."

"If that's supposed to be a deterrent, you need to up your game."

I lifted myself until I had his erection positioned. Biting my lower lip and feeling the invasion, I eased myself down, sheaving him with me. Yes, he was large, but I was used to large. I was also wet and ready. Mason was right—I had wanted to be awake or for him to wake me.

Arching my back, I took in the stretch and fullness.

My long brown hair flowed over my shoulders.

Mason's hands came back to my torso, lifting and lowering me. Even if I was the one on top, he was the lead in this dance. I didn't mind. When it came to making love or fucking—because we did both—I was happy to take his direction.

Such as fireflies lighting a Chicago night, my nerves began to crackle, sizzle, and ignite. The buildup was slow at first, but as the night progressed, the flashes of synapses were more numerous, coming quicker in rapid secession. Light after light, explosion after explosion. Our flesh dampened with perspiration, and our bedroom filled with the primal sounds of every couple before us.

As I was about ready to reach my climax, my world shifted.

I was the one with my head on the pillow, and Mason's incredibly handsome face was above mine. My knees spread farther to accommodate this mountain of a man. The muscles and tendons of his neck protruded as his thrusts came faster and faster. The sky was now ablaze with flashes of light.

Fireworks exploded in a finale worthy of the Fourth of July.

A symphony of sounds came from my lips as I held tightly to his shoulders and rode wave after wave of my orgasm. Soon our bedroom filled with a guttural roar as Mason's body shuddered and he joined me on the other side of bliss.

Our hearts beat one against the other as Mason collapsed over me. Again, I ran my hands up and down his back. When he looked up, our eyes met.

"I love you, Doc."

Even after seven years of marriage, those words melted my heart. "I love you, too." I lifted my eyebrows. "Are you going back downstairs?"

Downstairs, a floor labeled 2, was the command center from where Mason and the other top Sparrows ran Chicago. It was also where I had a makeshift lab and office. A few years ago, the Sparrow men broke their own rule and allowed me entry. It was a gesture I appreciated and would never abuse. I knew how sacred that space was to them.

Mason rolled onto his back, severing our connection. "Not until morning."

A smile lifted my cheeks as I snuggled at his side.

Morning was not a specific indication of time.

It could be a minute after the clock struck midnight or maybe not until after all the cohabitants of the tower met in the penthouse for breakfast. As I drifted to sleep, I was aware that I may wake alone, or I may wake to early morning sex.

As long as I had this time with my husband, I was satisfied.

CHAPTER 2 - LAUREL

The sun rose over the city of Chicago as Garrett, a trusted capo in the Sparrow regime, drove Araneae and me to the Sparrow Institute. The institute was Araneae's idea. As the queen of Chicago's underworld, she chose to use her wealth for good. The institute's goal was to bring human trafficking out of the shadows. The institute counseled, housed, and educated victims of human trafficking, helping the women and men to build a foundation that would carry them into the future.

Working with law enforcement and of course, the Sparrows themselves, this endeavor was meant to bring an end to the inhumane and unjust world hidden not only in Chicago but around the world. While the arrangement seemed odd to me at first, now years after entering the glass tower high in the sky of Chicago's skyline, I saw the good that Araneae had done and the possibilities for future efforts.

While I oversaw the counselors and psychologists at the institute, my main objective was refining a pharmaceutical formula designed to camouflage traumatic memories. As it could be assumed, victims of human trafficking had more than their share of disturbing memories. The formula I hoped to perfect wouldn't be limited to use with the people who found their way to the institute. The premise could aid others who suffered from PTSD, no matter the cause. My formula had a different mechanism of action than the one developed at Sinclair Pharmaceuticals and recently approved for sale.

Looking up from my tablet, I turned to my friend, seeing the way her head was tipped back against the headrest. "Are you feeling all right?"

Araneae's lips pressed into a straight line, and her complexion paled as she turned my way. "I'm good," she said with a nod.

"You're pale." I thought back to breakfast in the penthouse kitchen. "I didn't see you eat this morning. Maybe you need coffee."

She smirked. "I do, but I won't be having any."

"Is it your stomach?" I held multiple PhD degrees but was not a medical doctor; however, that didn't stop me from an innate need to help whomever I could.

"I guess you could say that."

The metaphoric puzzle pieces began to slide into place in my head.

"Oh, Araneae," I said in an excited, hushed tone. "Are you pregnant?"

She sighed. "I didn't want to tell anyone, not yet."

Our eyes went toward the rearview mirror, seeing Garrett's attention was on the road. Even if he overheard, he wouldn't say anything. That was an unspoken law in the world where we lived.

I reached over and laid my hand on her knee. "How long have you known? Does Sterling know?"

"Only a few days." Her lips curled upward. "He does. Even though we planned on Goldie being an only child, he's excited." She tilted her head back and forth. "He's concerned and overprotective."

"That's a shocking new development."

She laughed. "It's not, but if I remember back to when I was carrying Goldie, those qualities kick into overtime when I'm expecting."

There was an incident that occurred while Araneae was carrying Goldie that had our entire world on edge; that's a story for another day.

I grinned. "You're on your way to the institute, so he hasn't gone full 'lockdown' yet."

"I'm not spending the next eight months locked in the tower. Sterling knows that hormones can make me...different. He'll send a thousand Sparrows to watch over me before he does an eight-month lockdown—for his own good."

"Different?" I asked.

"You know...there's the morning sickness and in the second trimester, he has to deal with an overactive libido."

"I'm sure he doesn't mind."

"You're right," she said, pink returning to her cheeks. "And third trimester is all sleep. Remember, pregnancy even zapped Lorna, and that woman is a spitfire."

Lorna was my sister-in-law, Mason's sister.

"I know the science behind it." I sighed. "I also knew marrying Mason that pregnancy was something I'd never experience." I sat taller. "Besides, I'm too old."

Araneae tilted her head. "I thought your child status was by choice. I mean, you're great with all the children. And then there's your career. You're amazing at what you do. Children are a lot of work, even with help." She patted my knee. "You are not too old, not if you want a child."

Araneae was the youngest adult in our tower. While all the men were basically the same age, Lorna, Madeline, and I were close to our husbands' ages. The queen of Chicago was six years younger. That didn't in any way mean she was incapable of fulfilling the duties of her position. If you asked... well, any of us, Araneae was the only woman in the world who could handle Sterling Sparrow. Whether the occasion took an equal sparring partner or the gentleness to calm the beast, Araneae was the woman for the job.

"It was by choice," I said, nodding. "I chose to marry Mason and spend my life with him. I also knew that after what he'd been through— physically...basically, the burns, the explosion...well, he can't...we have a wonderful sex life." My muscles were still keenly aware of the workout we'd had last night. "It's that he shoots blanks."

Araneae's eyes opened wide. "I never knew or suspected. Have you talked to Dr. Dixon about it—or any physician?"

I shook my head. "It's not a subject we discuss. It just is what it is."

"You could adopt."

It was my turn to scoff. "Our world is perfect and also dangerous. I don't think I could bring a child into it, knowing what I know." I quickly turned to Araneae. "I don't mean I wouldn't have a child, only that I don't see the Cook County Court being quick to approve an adoption, no matter how much love we have to offer."

"You know that Sterling could—"

Pull strings.

Yes, Sterling Sparrow had power that was basically second only to God.

"I'm happy with the way things are," I said. "I am. I love my husband, and he loves me. We support one another, and we have all of you." I patted her knee. "And more of you on the way. Having our men home safe and all of us secure in the tower each night is all I want."

"What you said, about the danger," she mused. "It's why we planned on only one child. Goldie is now almost four." Araneae sighed. "I'm just thankful she's had Eddie and Jack and she's used to other children. Otherwise, I think springing a sibling on her would rock her world."

"Oh, I would bet it still will, but she'll survive. She's a Sparrow, after all."

Garrett turned the car toward the underground garage at the institute.

CHAPTER 3 - MASON

The sights of Chicago grew grayer as Christian, one of the Sparrows' top capos, and I made our way toward the shipyard. On the shores of Lake Michigan, this area was large enough to be a city within itself. Hell, it was bigger than the entire country of Monaco. If it were a city or country, few people would choose to live here. Rows and rows of containers lined what could be described as roads. In reality, it wasn't a city but a vast enterprise fenced off from the rest of the world.

"Can you imagine patrolling this chaos before GPS?" I asked, speaking my thoughts aloud as I directed Christian toward our destination, watching the blinking beacon on the screen of my phone.

Christian shook his head as his gaze narrowed.

The limited sunlight on this cloudy day was obscured by the rows and stacks of shipping containers. Most people were unaware that one cargo ship could carry about 24,000 TEUs—twenty-foot equivalent units. That was the equivalent to a forty-four-mile-long train. It was why, even in today's world, transporting goods over the waterways was still the most economical and efficient means of logistics. That fact was what made port cities grow.

While Chicago wasn't on the eastern or western coast, the Great Lakes and St. Lawrence Seaway provided the ability to transport cargo from the Atlantic Ocean to Chicago and other major cities through an elaborate locks system. There was a six-hundred-foot difference in water level from Lake Superior to the Atlantic Ocean with sixteen separate locks from A to B.

The reason Christian and I were navigating the maze of giant cargo containers was because one of our Sparrows on the street got wind of a shipment Sterling Sparrow had proclaimed illegal in his city. No one was under the illusion that the underworld side of Sparrow was hearts and flowers. It was a business, similar to many.

Sparrow allowed certain transactions, those that brought wealth and power to groups or gangs throughout the city. He allowed those activities as long as the benefactors paid in kind. In other words, Sparrow got his share.

There were guns.

There were drugs.

There was stolen merchandise.

There were also rules.

Sparrow's number-one rule, the real reason he took over his father's empire, was the abolishment of human trafficking within his borders. The night my life was irrevocably changed was in this same shipyard.

That was fourteen years ago.

We'd upped our game since that time.

There would be no running blind into a building.

Now we had technology that helped us.

Infrared cameras alerted us to heat signatures.

Of course, those only worked when the bodies within the containers were still alive.

The rumors of possible human cargo made it to our command center early this morning. Reid, my brother-in-law and the technological wizard of our foursome, went to work with satellite thermal imaging. By the time we'd finished breakfast and I'd kissed Laurel goodbye for the workday, Reid had a bead on two possible containers.

"These things are fucking massive," Christian said, looking up through the windshield. "I mean, I knew that. But each time we're here, I feel dwarfed."

"We're getting close," I said as the red pin on my screen began to blink.

There was a millisecond of thought on missions such as this—thoughts of a setup. The man who ran into a trap fourteen years ago had a lot fucking less to lose than the man I am today. I didn't need any of the other men to tell me they never leave the tower without telling their wives they love them. I felt it in my bones. Even this morning, as Laurel and Araneae gathered their things to leave for the Sparrow Institute, I tugged my wife to the side, finding a secluded spot in the massive penthouse. We kissed and promised one another we'd see each other tonight.

It was what we did every day.

Christian stopped the SUV.

We both had the same physical reaction.

Christian's hand went to his nose. "Fucking shit. Do you smell that?"

Instinctively, I held my breath and nodded. "It smells like shit—literal shit."

I'd had the misfortune of finding deceased humans. That was an odor unto itself. This wasn't the same. I sent a text message to Reid back at our command center.

"SMELLS LIKE SHIT."

"WATCHING THE SATELLITE CAMERAS. THERE IS MOVEMENT IN THERE."

I looked over at Christian. "What are you hearing?"

We both stilled.

"Shouts?"

"Too high-pitched," I said as I walked around the end of the container. As I listened, I realized the sounds were coming from the second higher-up container, not the one on the ground. "I'm climbing up."

"No, sir," Christian said. "I'll climb up."

Fourteen years ago, I would never have allowed someone to sacrifice themselves for me. In today's world, not only did I have a beautiful wife to return to, but I was one of the top Sparrow men. Just as I'd still lay down my life for Sparrow, any true Sparrow capo would do the same for me.

Unholstering my gun, I stood back as Christian climbed the metal ladder to the second container. He was about ten feet high when he cut the lock and maneuvered the door.

"Oh fuck," he said as the door opened.

An overpowering odor of manure hit me a second after Christian leaned away and dropped to the ground, landing on his feet.

"Goats."

"Goats?" I questioned. "That's not a livestock container."

Christian scoffed. "I'll call the supervisor and let them know what's going on." He shook his head. "They'll want to get this container unloaded as soon as possible. There was probably some mix-up."

"Goats," I said again with a smirk. "Fucking goats. I'll take that over women or children."

As the two of us got back into the SUV, I sent Reid a text telling him about our discovery, and Christian called the construction supervisor in charge of the yard. An hour later, we were finally out of the shipyard and making a few stops around the city.

When you were in charge, it was important to be visible.

Sterling Sparrow would never be seen walking the streets of South Chicago. When it came to public appearances, Patrick and I were the two who canvassed the city. We were as close as many would ever get to the king himself.

By the time we made it back to the tower, Christian took the elevator to 1, and I went to 2. Using the eye sensor, the metal door slid open to our command center.

"Goats," Reid called from his place behind many computer screens. His smile displayed his amusement.

"They fucking stank." I sniffed my shirt. "I think I still stink."

"You do," he said with a grin. "Shower and change clothes. I'll fill you in on what Patrick learned today."

"Something important?"

"Isn't it all important?"

It was.

Even the mundane could be life-altering.

I walked closer to my brother-in-law. "I wish things would slow down."

Reid shook his head. "Man, you really do stink. Did you go around town smelling like that?"

"I guess I did. It was hard to notice when we both stank."

"Why do you want things to slow?" he asked.

"Laurel's and my seven-year anniversary is coming up, and I'd like to take her to the ranch."

"You can still work from the ranch. It's your anniversary—how about someplace new? Hawaii?"

"You think Hawaii is nicer than my ranch?"

"Beaches over horse shit." Reid shrugged. "Just a thought."

CHAPTER 4 - LAUREL

"Thank you for your help with Addison," Araneae said as we rode the elevator up our tower toward our respective floors.

Stifling a yawn, I shook my head. "It doesn't get easier, hearing their stories."

Araneae also shook her head.

"I think she'll be all right." My voice lightened. "She shared with me that before she ran away, she wanted to be a veterinarian."

"Really. I get so excited when they have a goal. Now, we just need to help her see that she can achieve it."

"We talked about taking classes." The elevator stopped on A, the floor that held Mason's and my apartment. I reached out and held the doors open. "I don't say it enough, but you truly make a difference, Mrs. Sparrow. I'm proud to work with you."

Araneae came close and wrapped me in a hug. "First, never call me that again." She scoffed as her countenance lightened. "I feel the same about you. Will you be up for dinner?"

While all of us met each morning for breakfast in the penthouse, dinnertimes were often hit or miss. Mostly, if things weren't chaotic with the men, it was the time for each respective couple or family to have their own time.

"Not tonight," I said. "I'll see you in the morning. I ordered groceries for a favorite recipe that Mason likes." I shrugged. "I can't cook like Lorna, but I can give it a shot."

"Oh, I hope Lorna made our dinner even if she wants to eat with Reid and Jack."

"Has she ever let you down?" I asked.

"No, thank goodness. Reheating is my specialty."

"I won't say a word about your secret."

Araneae grinned. "You're all family. I'll announce at tomorrow's breakfast. I'm sure Lorna has caught on with my coffee and wine consumption."

My eyes grew wide. "That's right, you didn't have wine the other night. How could I miss that?"

Araneae shrugged.

Releasing the doors, I watched as they closed, the elevator taking Araneae up to the penthouse.

As I made my way toward our apartment on the far left, I heard a racket coming from the middle door. Simultaneously, the door opened, and Eddie—Patrick and Madeline's son—came running out.

"Whoa," I said, catching his little shoulders as he almost plowed me over. "Where are you going?"

Truthfully, the tower was childproof. They all needed an adult to access the elevator.

Eddie looked up, his blue eyes—just like his dad's—sparkling, and his dark mop tousled. "Hi, Aunt Laurel. Mom said I could play with Jack until dinner is ready."

I looked up to see Madeline standing in her doorway. "Sorry, the Kelly tornado is loose."

Kelly was their last name.

I shook my head, feeling more tired than usual. "I wish I had his energy."

"Me too."

Madeline was a strikingly beautiful woman who joined our family after I did. However, she and Patrick have a long history. It's a story for another day.

"Have a good night," I said.

"You too." Maddie called to her son, "Edward, knock first."

Instead of listening, he turned the doorknob on the apartment to the right, the home of his friend Jack and Jack's parents, Reid and Lorna.

Once inside our apartment, I sighed, taking in the quiet and tranquility. Beyond the floor-to-ceiling windows, Lake Michigan churned, white caps dotting the surface. The sun from earlier this morning had been overtaken by clouds. A late-summer thunderstorm was in our future. From our lofty height in the building, there were times when the view of the lake would disappear, our building surrounded in the hanging condensation.

I went to the refrigerator and looked inside. In a reusable shopping bag were the groceries I'd ordered. Seeing the fresh vegetables made me smile. A quick look into the freezer and I found my pound of shrimp.

Before changing out of my work clothes, I took the shrimp to the kitchen sink to defrost. I didn't often cook because when given the option, I would usually rather do something else. However, occasionally it was fun to remind myself that I was capable. I also wanted to remind Mason that his wife could do more than mathematical equations all day.

It was my talk with Addison that spurred the thoughts. I'd ordered the groceries after she'd left my office. Of course, they were delivered to the first floor and then brought to 1. Most likely, it was Reid who delivered them to our kitchen. Locking each apartment was unnecessary when the top four floors were as protected as Fort Knox.

With Addison, we'd talked about hopes and dreams. It was rewarding watching the expression of a person who had given up on life's potential realize that a future was possible. There was a spark that ignited in their gaze. Their speech quickened. It was truly a wonder.

I'd asked her what she wanted in life.

Her answer was like a lot of the women and men we counseled. She wanted basic needs: shelter, food, and above all, safety. *Maslow's Hierarchy of Needs* came to mind. His psychological hypothesis was that people are motivated to fulfill basic needs before they move on to higher-level ones. Basically, prior to being found and rescued from her horrific world, Addison's only concern was with the essential—staying alive.

I tried to direct her beyond that, to help her see that she could have higher aspirations.

She shared some fond memories of her childhood, things she enjoyed. One was cooking with her mother before she lost her to a premature death. Addison's expression would radiate pleasure as she discussed special times they shared. Listening to her reminded me of my own childhood memories.

When I was a young girl, I knew I wanted to help people. I'd often go with my dad to a Boys and Girls Club in South Chicago. It was where Mason and I first met. I also imagined a life like my mother's—professional and family.

Mason was my family.

I wanted to do something domestic for him, to let him know he hadn't only married a professional woman. I could be both.

Shedding my work clothes, I donned a pair of soft slacks, warm socks, and a light blue sweater that hung to my thighs. I splashed my face with water and washed away the day's makeup. Next, I released my hair from its ponytail and combed out the long locks. Lastly, I reapplied a little mascara and lip color.

On my way back to the kitchen, the door to our apartment opened.

It was funny that even after seven years, the sight of my husband could still make my stomach do a flip-flop. His strikingly handsome face, high cheekbones, and chiseled jaw were but the cherry on the Mason sundae. A thermal shirt stretched over his muscular shoulders and chest, and blue jeans covered his long legs.

It was then I noticed his wet hair. Tilting my head, I asked, "Did you shower?"

A twinkle came to his green gaze as he moved closer, wrapping his arm around my waist and pulling me close. "You're beautiful." His lips met mine.

Warm, possessive, and welcoming.

My breasts pushed against his chest as I sighed. Once our kiss was done, I took a deep breath—because that was what Mason did to me: he took my breath away. "Shower?"

"Yes, on 2. It's a long story involving goats."

"Goats?" I asked.

"Yeah, you know, short animals about yea high" —he extended his hand near his thigh— "and their shit. A lot of shit."

I couldn't stop my giggle. "That doesn't sound like a normal day in Sparrow world."

"Is there such a thing?"

"I don't know. You don't tell me a lot."

"Oh, Doc, I tell you what I can. For instance, after the goats, Christian and I went around town for a few meetings. I didn't realize how much we stank until we got back to the tower. I'm sure half the underground is talking about how bad Sparrow's men smell."

"Did Sterling say anything?"

"I'm hoping he never finds out." Mason took a step back. "You really are radiant. What are you up to?"

"I'm about to cook dinner."

Mason's eyebrows rose. "Cook? You?"

I playfully slapped his shoulder. "I can cook."

His same eyebrows danced. "I know what I like to eat."

"Later. Shrimp scampi with vegetables first."

CHAPTER 5 - MASON

The delicious aroma of garlic permeated the air throughout the entire apartment. Coming from our bedroom, I paused in the hallway, struck by the vision of my wife. Sometimes when I'd catch a glance of my colorful but marred skin, I'd wonder why a woman like Laurel Carlson Pierce would agree to spend her life with me.

Watching her usual work—that of a scientist—was truly a feat in patience for a man like me who wanted swift results. As with the notebook she was studying last night before falling asleep, Laurel continually demonstrated her tenacity in her ability to stay on task. There was something different about seeing her now. With her casual attire, and super-sexy tight pants, she appeared calmer. Along with the scent of garlic, jazz played from the sound system. She swayed to the tune, while cutting vegetables. Near the cutting board was a glass of red wine.

Relaxed.

That was how she looked.

She turned my way and smiled. "What are you doing?"

"I'm watching the most beautiful woman I know cook me dinner. I'm getting a caveman-type feel."

Her cheeks rose. "Caveman. Did they have state-of-the-art kitchens during caveman days?"

Her presence drew me closer until I once again had my arm snaked around her waist and her hips pulled toward mine. "We can go with this. We can put bones in our hair, and I can beat my bare chest."

"Where would we get bones?" She shook her head. "Never mind, don't tell me if you have a spare body or two on 2." She laid her hand on my chest. "And I don't think being dragged around by my hair sounds fun."

My eyebrows danced. "My woman. Cooking dinner."

"If you don't stop, I'll never do it again."

I reached for her glass of wine and with my pinky extended, I lifted it to my lips. "See, Mrs. Pierce, I can be refined."

Laurel leaned closer and opening her lips, sucked my pinky, sending shock waves throughout my entire body. "What the hell?"

Her blue gaze simmered. "I think I might like you less refined. Not a caveman exactly but maybe a dominant assassin?"

That was who I was when we reunited.

"I can do that."

Pulling another wine glass from the rack, I filled it with wine. "Is there anything I can do to help?"

Soon, I was putting together a salad to go with the shrimp, garlic, and veggie creation she placed in the oven. On the stove was a pot of water, and soon she'd add pasta.

As she did, I asked, "Do you want to go to Hawaii?"

Laurel turned my direction. "If cooking you dinner gets me a vacation, I'll do it more often."

"I was thinking of our anniversary."

"What about the ranch?" she asked.

"I thought...okay, Reid mentioned...maybe instead of riding horses and shoveling shit, you might enjoy a tropical beach, a hike to Diamond Head...I don't know, maybe a helicopter tour of the islands."

Laurel dropped the pasta in the boiling pot and wiped her hands on a kitchen towel. Without taking her eyes off me, she came close and wrapped her arms around my torso. Looking up, she met my gaze. "I love the ranch. I love you. When you're there, you're more...at ease. I don't need a helicopter tour. If I want to be in the air, you can fly me in your plane in Montana."

"I fucking love you."

"That's good because you're stuck with me for at least another fifty years."

The dinner tasted as wonderful as it smelled. As we ate, we talked about everything we could do at the ranch. It made my heart swell that Laurel loved the ranch as much as I did. Whether she was talking about the horses or the mountains, her blue eyes sparkled with anticipation. It had been a few months since we'd been to our property in Montana.

Even without us present, we knew that it was in great hands with Seth, our property manager and overseer. He and his wife loved the land as much as Laurel and I. To take on a job like theirs, there had to be desire to work. It was a 24/7 endeavor.

"So, it's settled," I said. "We're headed to Montana for our anniversary, barring any cataclysmic events here in Sparrow world."

"Don't say that. You'll jinx us."

"Do you want to invite the others?" I asked, hoping she'd say no. It wasn't that I didn't love all the members of our enlarged and eclectic family. It was that I also loved having time alone with my wife.

Laurel inhaled. "The kids have so much fun there. But with Eddie starting school this fall, I'm not sure Patrick and Madeline would be able to come. And then with Araneae pregnant—"

"What? Araneae is pregnant again?"

"It's been four years."

I stood from my seat. "Sparrow hasn't said a word."

"Don't say anything," Laurel said, meeting me standing. "I found out today, and she wants to announce tomorrow at breakfast. Practice acting surprised."

I chuckled and made a face with my lips agape.

"Keep practicing."

Reaching for her hands, I tugged her close. "What if we take off, just the two of us? It's a shit-ton of work to move all of us across the country. You know Sparrow can't travel without a full security detail."

"Just the two of us sounds great."

"I was thinking about something else the two of us could do that sounds great."

Her smile turned sultry. "Who's asking?"

Lowering my tone, I recalled the role-play she'd mentioned. "Me and I'm not asking."

Laurel shook her head. "How do you do that?" When I didn't respond, she added, "Make my nipples hard with only a change in your tone."

"On your knees."

Her breathing deepened and her complexion pinkened. Tugging her lower lip between her teeth, Laurel obeyed.

"No." I released her lip. "I'm going to need you to free my cock and open wide."

My cock grew ten sizes as she reached for the button of my blue jeans.

CHAPTER 6 - LAUREL

Two Weeks Later

As sunshine streamed down, sparse white clouds floated in the vast blue sky for as far as we could see. Dry tall grass swayed in the breeze as strands of my hair floated around my face. With my boots in the stirrups and my ass on a thick leather saddle, I rode horses with Mason over the pasture. While everything was beautiful, I made a mental note to wear a sports bra the next time we rode. My breasts were sensitive, no doubt from the attention my husband enjoys giving them.

Our destination was a stream running through our property.

Watching my husband, I marveled at his skill set.

The gentleness in his touch and the way he cared for the horses on the ranch was tender and loving, not often attributes of a trained killer. The multitude of tattoos covering his body were but an outward sign of the many facets of this man.

His biceps bulged as he pulled the reins, slowing his horse to a trot. I followed suit.

Mason's face turned my way as he brought his finger to his firm lips and pointed. About two hundred yards up ahead was a black bear with two growing cubs. Instead of having fear, we both stopped our horses and watched in amazement as the mother bear led the two cubs into a line of trees.

"She's protecting them from us," I said softly.

"Teaching them about dangers." Mason sighed. "Man is the most dangerous of all animals."

"I've never seen you harm an animal. You wouldn't do that. Instead, I've helped you corral horses to get them out of a lightning storm."

He laid his hand over his holster. "I couldn't blame a mother bear for fighting for her cubs, but if you were in danger, it would be her last fight."

I reached across to his arm. "I know I'm safe with you, no matter what attacks."

He flashed his panty-melting smile. "Come on, we're almost there."

A few minutes later from the crest of a ridge, the stream came into view — an oasis in the valley. Around us were brown and dried grasses. Down near the water, the grass was green and there were even a few trees.

Soon, we had the horses tied to a tree branch and a blanket lying upon the green grass. With a picnic lunch, we both settled onto the blanket.

"Are you feeling better?" Mason asked.

"I am." I unwrapped one of the sandwiches. Turkey and cheese. "I'm also hungry."

Mason pushed his sandwich my direction. "You didn't eat much breakfast. You can have my lunch too." He pulled out a container of blueberries and strawberries. "I can eat the fruit."

"No." I laughed, pushing his sandwich away. "I'm not hungry enough to eat for two." I took a bite. "I'm sorry I didn't do more to help you get the horses ready. I'm guessing it was traveling that has me off-kilter."

He leaned close, kissing my nose. "As long as you're better now. And Seth was up at the barn. He helped me saddle the horses."

We both turned, looking at the two proud, majestic beasts standing near the stream. Earlier in the spring, the stream was more of a river. This late in the early autumn, the flow was much gentler.

After finishing our lunch, Mason tugged off his cowboy boots and socks. Next, he rolled up the legs of his blue jeans. His green orbs glittered with golden flakes as he offered me his hand. "Let's wade in the water."

I nodded, quickly removing my boots and rolling my blue jeans. I shrieked as my foot submerged. "This is a lot colder than I expected." Despite the sunshine, goose bumps coated my flesh.

Mason laughed. "Even now, this is the runoff of melting snow from the high elevations. It's not exactly the Pacific Ocean." He held my hand. "I did offer you Hawaii."

I shook my head. "This is where I want to be." Leaning closer, I brushed his lips with mine. "And who I want to be with."

The scene around us was almost magical — a bubble away from the dangers of the Sparrow world, away from the horrible tales told by the beneficiaries at the institute, and away from the happy chaos that was our family back in the tower.

By the way, Eddie wasn't attending public school. Of course, that wouldn't do for the nephew of the king. Madeline kept us informed as school after school was interviewed and vetted. After all they'd done, I suspected that next year when Goldie entered school, she'd be exactly where her cousin was. No doubt, Jack would follow.

While the children's every need was met, there was a price to be paid being the children of the men and women in our world. Ruby survived. The new little ones will too.

Once we were back on the blanket, I laid my head in Mason's lap and stared up at the beauty of the sky. "Oh," I said, looking up to his eyes. "Did Seth tell you that Lindsey's expecting their fourth?"

Mason shook his head. "You'd think they would know what causes that. If not, they can watch the horses."

I hummed. "Lindsey told me. She's very excited. And I think she likes what causes them."

"How about you?"

"I like what causes them."

"Maybe we should practice."

"They say practice makes perfect."

———

The next morning as Mason and Seth worked with the ranch hands to ride the fence lines, I went for a walk. At first, I wasn't certain if there was a destination in mind, but as I got closer to Seth and Lindsey's house, I felt drawn to it. The structure was much larger than it had been when Jackson lived there. They may need another wing with the upcoming addition to their family.

I found Lindsey outside working in her flower beds as the three children played in the yard. Seth's wife was a tall woman, more like Araneae and myself, with a slender form and bouncing blond curls.

"Good morning," I called.

Lindsey stood and wiped her forehead with her hand covered in gardening gloves. "Dr. Pierce. It's good to see you."

"Laurel, please."

She grinned. "Laurel. Are you lonely up at the big house. We were surprised it was only you and Mr. Pierce."

"I think we wanted a break." I looked around. "And this place is it."

"It's definitely God's country out here." She looked at the children a few yards away. "And a great place to raise children."

The truth was that other than my sister, having true female friends was new to me. I had friends, but not women who I would share my secrets with, not until Lorna, Araneae, and Maddie. Lindsey and I weren't close, but I was about to tell her something I hadn't told my friends back home or even my husband.

"Lindsey, may I ask you something?"

Her expression sobered. "Is everything all right?"

"I don't know."

She shook her head. "Of course." She motioned toward a pair of rocking chairs on the porch. "Let's have a seat. May I get you anything?"

"Water would be nice. It's a long walk."

"Sure thing. I'll be right back."

As I took a seat on her porch, I gave more thought to what had been simmering in my mind for the last two weeks. I was afraid to say the words, fearful that in doing so, I'd learn I was wrong.

"Here you go," she said, handing me a glass of water with ice and sitting with her own glass. "Is this about the ranch or Mr. Pierce?"

"Not really." I inhaled, looking out at the children. "This will sound odd—after all, I'm aware of female biology. It's just that..." I took a drink of the water. "How far along are you?"

"Oh." She grinned and laid her hand over her midsection. "Just passed three months."

"Did you know you were expecting—now or any other time—before taking a test?"

Lindsey nodded. "There are signs. I mean the obvious one is the missed period." She scoffed. "Laurel, you know all of this. Are you saying...do you think you're pregnant?"

I inhaled. "I can't be, but all the signs are there. My breasts are painfully sore. My period is late. Then again, I'm almost forty. Maybe it's early-onset menopause."

"Why *can't* you be?" Pink filled her cheeks. "I mean, surely you and Mr. Pierce..."

"Yes, we do. It's that a long time ago, Mason was in an explosion. He was badly burned. Everything works, but the intense heat" —it was as I'd told Araneae— "he shoots blanks."

"Well, you're the one with all the letters after your name. Surely you realize it only takes one."

Tears came to my eyes. "He doesn't have one."

Lindsey stood. "I'm assuming there hasn't been anyone else?"

"What? Oh, no. I wouldn't even think of that. Only Mason."

"Come with me. I have a test. I keep some on hand because, well..." She laid her hand over her midsection. "Seth and I kind of fuck like rabbits." She laughed.

"I'm scared to take it."

"Because...?" she prompted.

"I'm a scientist. I don't believe in miracles. I'm convinced my symptoms are psychosomatic brought on by an impossible hope."

Lindsey's smile grew. "You want to be pregnant?"

"I do, but it's impossible, and when I see the negative test, I'll be disappointed."

"Let me get you the test, and you can take it up to the house. The rest is up to you."

CHAPTER 7 — MASON

"Doc?" I called for Laurel as I entered the house and made my way toward the kitchen. I was hungry, worn out, and dirty, and I couldn't be happier. Even when I had no idea who I really was, I knew I loved this open country. "Doc," I tried again.

Opening the refrigerator, I drained a bottle of water and pulled out a dish of pulled pork from last night. Grabbing a fork, I set the serving dish on the table and took a seat. It was as if I hadn't eaten in days. With most of the meat consumed, I looked around the kitchen.

Everything was in its place. There was a small bouquet of wildflowers in a glass on the counter. My hunger was satisfied, yet I still hadn't seen Laurel.

Did she go to town?

I hadn't noticed any vehicles missing. Then again, I didn't really look.

Calling her name, I went to the back of the house, first checking the office. It was empty. Next, I went to the deck. The chairs were in place, and there was even the book my wife was reading on the table. I scanned the grounds, looking out to the lawn and beyond. In the distance, snowcapped mountains lay like purple and white giants along the horizon.

"Laurel." My voice was louder and filled with new urgency.

A memory came back of a kidnapping.

The pork twisted in my stomach.

No.

We'd taken care of the kidnappers. They would never hurt anyone again.

I headed toward the big staircase in the front of the house. "Laurel."

My heartbeat accelerated as I took the steps two or three at a time. The thumping of my heart in my ears was all I heard as I ran toward our bedroom. Opening the door, I bolted inside, scanning the room. The bed was made. Everything was in its place.

And then my world righted.

"Oh, Mason," Laurel said, stepping from the bathroom.

"Why didn't you answer?"

"Answer what? Did you call me?" She reached for her phone in her back pocket.

Before she could remove it, I wrapped her in an embrace. As our bodies collided, my heart resumed its normal cadence. "Fucking Christ," I muttered. "I'm going to put a GPS tracker on you."

Laurel scoffed. "I have them. In my shoes."

"Shit, you do." I could have pulled that up on my phone. "I wasn't thinking."

It was then that I took a step back and peered down at her beautiful face. "Are you all right?"

Tears filled her eyes as she nodded.

"What is it, Doc? Are you sick?"

Laurel reached for my hand.

Seeing our fingers intertwined, I realized how dirty I still was. "I should shower."

She looked up at me. "You're perfect the way you are. I need to talk to you about something."

"Can it wait until I don't stink?"

She shook her head. "I mean, it could, but I don't want to wait."

I led her to the stool at the end of our large bed. We both sat. "Okay." My mind was filled with horrible scenarios. A man didn't do what I did or live through the things I had without the ability to conjure grotesque possibilities. "Is it someone in Chicago? Lorna? Sparrow?" My questions came faster. "Reid?"

"They're fine...I think they are. I went for a walk today and visited Lindsey."

I had no idea where this discussion was going, but based on the way Doc's hands were trembling, it was important. "Is Lindsey all right?"

She nodded. "She let me borrow—I guess it was more like she gave it to me..."

"What did she give you?"

Laurel swallowed and stood. "Come with me."

"You're starting to freak me out."

Her lips curled in the first smile I'd seen since finding her.

"Good," she said. "I'm freaked out too."

With my hand in hers, she led us to the bathroom and tilted her head toward the vanity. On the counter was a blue-and-white stick.

It was a test.

"Are you sick?"

"It's not that kind of test—about being sick. It's a pregnancy test."

"A pregnancy..." I took a step closer and lifted the stick.

The voices in my head told me this wasn't possible. The inability to procreate was an added bonus for my time in the Order, a covert government agency. Laurel and I had discussed the inability to have children before we wed. We both said we were satisfied with one another.

I lifted the test and saw the two lines.

"How?" It was the first word that popped into my head.

Tears slid down Laurel's cheeks as her answer came out in a sob. "A miracle."

A miracle.

Do I believe in miracles?

I reached for her shoulders. "We...you and I..." I laid my hand over her midsection. "A baby."

Laurel nodded. "I never thought we would." Her eyes opened wide. "Are you upset? Do you not want it?"

Wrapping my arms around her, I pulled Laurel to my chest so fast that her last question came out muffled against my shirt. "I'm shocked. And I'm as far from upset as any man could ever be." I pushed her far enough away so I could see her sparkling blue eyes. "We're going to have a family."

She nodded.

"Fuck," I said, realizing I was actually crying, perhaps another miracle. I cleared my throat and spoke. "That boy and girl who sat on the rooftop in South Chicago..."

"I remember them."

"This life with you is more than he ever dared to dream."

"Her either." She palmed my cheeks. "You've made her every dream come true. I love you."

"I love you."

Thank you for reading! Mason and Laurel have more stories from the past and into the future. Start at the beginning with the first trilogy, Web of Sin, book one, *Secrets* by Aleatha Romig.

RIPTIDE

ALESSANDRA TORRE

CHAPTER 1

"Hawaii. September 12th. Come with me."

The note was tucked in three dozen red roses that were delivered to the bookstore by one of the Venice Beach potheads who couriered from the bougie Marina Del Rey florist. "Lucky girl," he drawled, setting it on the bookstore's counter with a loud crack. "This thing was crazy expensive."

I plucked the card from the bouquet and reread the message, then flipped it over to see if there was anything more. Tucking the card into my back pocket, I smiled at him. "Thanks. They're beautiful."

They were. The roses were red long-stems with bright pink orchids spilling from the dark green foliage. I lowered my face to the blooms and inhaled their delicate scent.

There wasn't a signature on the card but I knew exactly who they were from. Stewart Brant had a distinct style in everything he did. Always the best, the most expensive, the highest quality. Delivered by a service, not by hand. Even the card was handled by someone other than him. I wasn't even sure what his handwriting looked like, but that perfect calligraphy wasn't it.

A trip to Hawaii. Smiling, I moved the vase to the side of the counter, out of the way, and then picked up the plastic yellow handle of our store phone. I pressed in the number, then waited, curling the long cord around my finger as I watched a girl in a polka-dotted bikini examine our table of dark romances.

The bookstore was smack in the middle of Venice Beach and was half store, half bar, which meant that the place was busiest at happy hour. So far, I hadn't sold a single book, and it had been... I glanced at my watch. Three hours. Other than reading twelve chapters in a Dean Koontz novel, this delivery was the only noteworthy thing that had happened during this shift.

"Hey, Madison." Stewart's assistant answered the phone in her efficient New York accent. "Let me guess, you just got a delivery."

"I did, and they're beautiful. " I paused. "I'm sure you're the one to thank for that."

"Oh, they were his idea. I just implemented it." She laughed. "And I might have reminded him that it's your anniversary. He's taken off for the evening. After 5:45, he's all yours."

"Awesome. Well, thank you for your help with that. There was a note..." I pulled it out of my pocket and studied it.

"Yeah, he wants to take you to O'ahu in two weeks. He has a few meetings with the investors on the hotel deal and will be staying two nights. I booked the jet and hotel, so you just need your suitcase."

I looked out the front doors of the store, to the water, where a group of surfers stood by the surf, their brightly-colored boards shining in the sun. "Two nights?" I asked, thinking over who could cover my shifts.

"Yep." She laughed. "Hey, if you don't want to go, I can. Or maybe--"

"No, I can go," I said, but inside, I was thinking of the reasons I shouldn't.

And then, as if on cue, the number one reason walked through the open doors.

Paul.

He took me in the storeroom, my jean shorts and underwear down around my ankles, my tank top pulled over the tops of my breasts. I bent forward, and the line of book spines scraped against my nipples as I gripped the shelf. His fingers dug into my waist as he pressed his mouth against my neck, his breath hot in my hair, his cock hard between my legs.

When I came, I moaned, and he covered my mouth with his hand, his skin salty. I bit it, holding it gently with my teeth, and thought briefly of the locked storeroom door, the sound of the bar's band easily passing through the thin divider.

It was hot and hard and quick, and he grunted softly when he finished inside of me, his strokes slowing, then shuddering to a stop. I released his hand and sagged against the shelves, my limbs limp.

He turned me to face him, holding me up as he pressed his mouth to mine, then kissed my neck, my collar, then my lips again. "I love you," he said gruffly.

"I love you too." I smiled, meeting his eyes. Damn, the boy was pretty. Vivid blue eyes, tan skin, nose slightly burnt, his blonde hair rough from the water and the wind. He looked like a model, a perfect specimen of masculinity and beauty, and all one hundred percent mine.

I broke our eye contact and looked down at my feet, then went to pull up my shorts.

"Stop." He did the job for me, his fingers tender as he drew the bright orange thong and my baggy jean shorts up my legs, then over my hips.

I heard the ding of the register bell and swore. "I got to go."

He grabbed my hand just as I unlocked the door and pulled me back to him. "Wait."

I resisted. "I can't... I gotta go."

"The roses, those from him?"

"Yep." I twisted the knob and pulled the door open. "It's our anniversary." Another man would be jealous, but it's Paul, and he's always been impossibly understanding about how our relationship works.

"Ah, that's right. Which is why I'm doing tacos and Forensic Files by myself tonight." He grinned. "I'll save some of my queso dip for you."

"You better." My stomach complained at the thought of missing Paul's seven-layer cheese dip. I rose on my toes and gave him another kiss. From the register, another insistent ding of the bell sounded, and I looked around him to see the bikini girl standing there, two books in hand. "I have to go."

He snuck around the Science Fiction section and out the front, and I realized I should have mentioned Hawaii to him before my date with Stewart.

The thought nagged at me, and I texted him as I was getting ready for dinner.

Forgot to tell you... I'm going to go to Hawaii with him in mid-September for two days. Just wanted to give you a heads up.

I sent the text and then opened my closet in Stewart's condo. As a woman in two relationships, I also had two closets. They were laughably different. In my house with Paul, I had an overflowing coat closet filled with colorful tank tops, sundresses, wet suits, bikinis, and cutoff shorts.

Here, I had my own walk-in, with Lululemon matching workout sets, conservative suits, expensive cocktail dresses, loungewear, blouses, cashmere sweaters, and slacks. I picked out a black sweater dress and sparkly stilettos. Laying them out on the fluffy white bed, I stripped out of the outfit I'd worn to work and dropped them into the hamper. By the time I got up in the morning, Stewart's maid would have already washed and folded them, the clothes ready for me to wear home.

I didn't have to keep my outfits separate. I could wear any of these things back home, but it never felt right, walking into my home with Paul, wearing a pair of pressed capris and a cardigan.

His response came while I was in Stewart's giant steam shower. I didn't see it until I was wrapped in a big fluffy robe and adding conditioning oil to the ends of my long hair.

Which island? The O'ahu competition is the week of the 11th. It's not too late for me to get into the tourney, if you want me to. We could get dinner one of the nights... I could take you to Sans Souci beach to see the turtles.

I read it once, then set down my brush and read it again. My heart skipped, then tripped, and I couldn't decide if I was elated or horrified at the suggestion.

My world, our dual relationships... they worked because I was diligent about keeping a clean line of division. Stewart knew nothing about Paul, not even his name, and vice versa. I didn't lie to them, but I respected that there were certain things they didn't need to or want to hear. Both men knew that I had another partner. Both were okay with it. It was Stewart, originally, who suggested it. When I met Paul, I told him about Stewart and gave him the option of accepting the arrangement or walking away. He accepted it, and a year and a half later, here we were.

I loved both of them. I was committed to both of them. I couldn't choose between them, and they would never ask me to. The choice would rip me in two.

Going to Hawaii and having both of them there... it felt like playing too close to the fire.

Then again, how was it any different than dating them both here in L.A.?

I sent him a text before I second-guessed myself.

Sure. I'm not sure how much I'll be able to see you, but would love to try to go to Sans Souci.

Halfway through our anniversary dinner, I decided not to tell Stewart about Paul's offer to come to Hawaii.

In our years together, it was the first time I lied to him by omission. I don't know why I didn't tell him except that I realized, right around the time he cut into his steak, that it was a shitty thing to do - me sharing that vacation with another man.

It didn't matter that Stewart encouraged and allowed my relationship with Paul. It didn't matter that he would be in meetings most of the time.

This was a trip he had invited me on.

A chance for the two of us to go away together... and it was horrible of me to share that experience with Paul.

Right then, I should have excused myself from the table and texted Paul to tell him he shouldn't go. But I didn't. I enjoyed our dinner. I focused on Stewart. I savored the rare opportunity to enjoy his company, and by the time I looked at my phone, late that night, the text from Paul was already four hours old.

Flights booked and I'm confirmed in the tournament. Oneill is paying my way.

Shit. I looked over at Stewart, who was beside me in bed, his glasses on, his computer on his lap, his fingers nonstop on the keys.

I should have told him then, but I didn't. I didn't, and my lie of omission grew bigger.

CHAPTER 2

I stepped off Stewart's jet and into the balmy Hawaiian air. Squinting against the sun, I pulled my sunglasses off the top of my head and pushed them onto my face, laughing a little when my hair blew into my mouth.

"Here." Stewart offered his hand, helping me down the steps and onto the pavement. Moving to my left, he blocked the wind with his body. "Better?"

"Much." I grinned at him. "I need to cut my hair short like yours."

"Don't even think about it," he warned, grabbing the back of my neck and squeezing it gently.

Stewart had rented a Mercedes convertible, and he pressed the button to lower the top, then looped his fingers through mine. I played with the radio until I found a reggae station, then relaxed against the seat and closed my eyes. He accelerated out of the airport lot, and I stretched out my legs, appreciating the sun's warm kiss on my face.

"The air smells different here," I called out to Stewart. "Sweeter."

He laughed. "Oh really, sweeter than Venice Beach?" He shook his head, and I smacked his arm, warning him to keep his thoughts to himself. Stewart hated where I lived with Paul. That was one thing I didn't have to worry about - us bumping into him in that part of town. Stewart stayed downtown, and rarely left the confines of the two-mile loop between his high-rise condo and his office.

Stewart had tried multiple times to buy me a place near him, but I had staunchly refused. Venice Beach may have its seedy elements, but I loved the community and atmosphere there. It was all artists, hippies, and surfers - a creative melting pot that took care of its own and shunned the corporate robots and Beverly Hills brats. Stewart was the epitome of the corporate robot, but maybe that's why I loved him so much. Maybe I needed the stark differences - the additional textures that brought to my life.

And I had to admit, they were *nice* textures. As we checked into the Ritz Carlton, I inhaled the rich scent of coconut and hibiscus and took the steaming towel the attendant offered, cleaning my hands before accepting a chilled glass of champagne.

We rode up the elevator with a tuxedoed butler. I smiled at the man, then poked Stewart in the side. "Did you know that Hawaii has an ordinance against loud laughter?"

He looked up from his phone long enough to frown down at me. "What?"

"I'm serious. You aren't allowed to laugh loudly."

He was shaking his head, about to argue, and I spoke quickly before he did. "They only allow a low ha."

"I don't--"

"A-low-ha." I grinned at him. "Get it? Aloha."

He shook his head in exasperation, but I could see the twitch of his lips.

"You should tell that joke in your meeting with the investor," I suggested.

"I will most certainly not tell that joke to anyone," he responded, wrapping his hand around my waist and pulling it tightly against him.

The elevator car settled, and the doors opened with a quiet chime.

The massive suite had a living room, a giant tub, and a wall of windows that showcased the million-dollar view. I slid open the doors to the balcony as stewards hung up our clothes and turned down the bed.

I'd be lying if I didn't admit I loved the lifestyle Stewart's wealth afforded. I loved it, and I loved him - the brilliant and thoughtful man in the suit with an OCD-level attention to detail and a rigid work ethic.

Love had never been the issue... I just needed more than Stewart was able to give. I needed lazy Saturday mornings in bed. I needed birthday presents that weren't picked, purchased, and delivered by assistants. I needed takeout, trashy television, and dates that didn't have to be booked three weeks in advance.

Everything I needed, Paul provided, and Stewart understood that.

The door closed behind the valets, and Stewart undid the top button of his shirt and looked at me with a dominant hunger. "Come here."

I came. In more ways than one.

First to him... dropping to my knees on the soft carpet. Undoing his zipper. Pulling out his cock. It was long and soft, and when I gripped it, it immediately responded. When I took it in my mouth, it stiffened to full attention.

Then, on my back where he focused his attention in between my open thighs, his firm mouth worshipping the delicate area before zeroing in on the one delicious rhythm that would take me exactly where I needed to go.

Then, on my knees, his pace furious, his fingers biting into my ass as he pumped in perfect staccato, everything in my body binding, exploding.

I was loud and he was loud, and we didn't care. Afterward, I spooned into his side with the doors open, my clothes somewhere on the floor, the salty breeze drifting over my naked skin.

"I have to go soon," he said, kissing the top of my head.

I closed my eyes, not ready for the moment to end. The waves were loud, seagulls crying, and the sounds were so familiar, so much like my Venice Beach apartment, that I got up abruptly, needing to close the doors and block it all out. It didn't feel right, especially given that Paul was somewhere out there, on this beach, on this island.

As soon as Stewart was dressed and on the way to his meetings, I showered and dressed, then went downstairs and out to the beach to find Paul.

CHAPTER 3 - STEWART

Damn, I should do this more often. It's gorgeous here. The cliffs, the sand, the waves, the sun... It's everything Los Angeles wished it could be, minus the rat race of attention and wealth. I stood on the room's balcony and inhaled the breeze.

The memories came with it, and I stopped, compartmentalizing the memories and locking them away. Ah, that's right. This was why I didn't go to places with turquoise water and long stretches of sand. The serenity always brought with it the memories.

The night.

The blood.

The police.

The funeral.

Down at the beach, a crowd was on the far end where the waves were the biggest. Surfers dotted the waves, their bright boards like confetti on the dark blue water. There was a line of tents down there and some sort of a stage.

I hadn't ridden a board in almost twenty years. Maybe it was like riding a bike or maybe I'd fall flat on my face. It didn't matter. I didn't have time to try. Right now, I should be checking my email. Looking over the discussion points for this afternoon's meeting. Double-checking the figures and reevaluating the risks based on this morning's market updates.

"Wow, it's gorgeous." Madison joined me at the railing and turned her face into the sun. She closed her eyes, and a slight smile lifted her lips. With her long blond hair in messy waves across her shoulders, a sheer cover-up over her white bathing suit, she looked like an advertisement for effortless beauty. She looked like what I yearned for... peace. I should call China. Now, before their market closed for the day. If I could put pressure on Huang, there was at least a percentage point still built into the negotiations. That should be used for leverage.

"I'm starving." Madison squinted at me, shielding her face from the sun with her hand. "Do you have time to eat?"

I pulled back the sleeve of my linen button-up and checked the time. I had fifty minutes. Maybe an hour, if I could get ahold of China quickly, before we left.

"Yes, as long as it's someplace close." I nodded down to the beach toward the event. "Something's going down on the beach. Want to walk down there and see what's going on? Looks like they have some food trucks."

It was an unorthodox suggestion, at least for us. Madison and I eat at Michelin-star restaurants with a bevy of waiters standing by to assist, the atmospheres always a quiet hush of respectability and honor. I was confident she would jump on it with zeal. This was, after all, something in line with her other life - the one that seemed to be ruled by chaos and poor planning, her hand in his. She once called me from a rest stop in Kansas, where she was road-tripping to Florida to drop off a van. She went to Burning Man and came back hoarse and sunburnt. She lived a reckless and wild life with him, then came to me, where she recuperated with the help of my chef, the condo's spa, and my giant bed.

"Oh, I don't know." She made a face. "I thought we'd just grab something at the hotel restaurant."

So much for my attempt to walk on the wild side. I turned away from the view. "Sure. I've got to make a call, but I can do that on the way."

The hotel restaurant was closed, and I checked my watch, then looked at Madison. "Want to hit the beach?"

Her gaze darted to the beach, then toward the lobby. "Um... yeah. I guess."

Something was off. I studied her, trying to understand why she looked so nervous. "What--"

My phone rang, an international code on the screen. I gestured for her to go ahead of me and answered the call.

My Chinese contact spoke quickly, and I responded in his language, watching as Madison walked ahead of me, into the sunshine. She was moving slowly, practically dragging her gold sandals along the path. I frowned, reaching for her hand and holding it. She looked over and smiled at me, but the gesture didn't make it to her eyes.

I finished my call, and we were almost to the event when Madison stopped, her hand going to her head. "Shit." She stumbled a little to the side.

"What's wrong?" I tucked my phone in my pocket and moved in front of her.

"I feel dizzy." She closed her eyes. "I think I'm going to faint."

"What?" I looked around. "Here, let me carry you. They've got to have a medical tent at this thing."

"No." She shook her head violently. "Just let me sit down." She pointed to the closest giant palm. "There, I'll sit there, in the shade."

I helped her to the tree, and she dropped onto her butt in the soft sand. "If you won't let me take you somewhere, let me go and get help."

"No." She gathered her thick mane of hair and lifted it off her neck, fanning herself with her other hand. "I just... just give me a minute."

I didn't have a minute. I needed to get her something to eat and make sure she got back to the hotel safely, then I needed to get in the car and head to my meeting. Did that make me a dick? Yes. 100% so. But also, Madison was acting odd. All of this was suspicious.

I scanned the crowd and structures ahead of us. I could see an O'Neill trailer and a giant PacSun sign. Probably a surf competition. The faint scent of hamburgers was in the air, and I scratched the back of my head, looking at her. "What if I go get you some water and food? We can take it back to the room, or you can eat it here, if--"

"Yeah, that sounds good," she interrupted. "I think I just need to sit here for a bit." She angled her body away from the crowd, sitting on the opposite side of the palm and leaning against its trunk.

"Okay." I studied her. "Are you sure you'll be okay? I don't like the idea of leaving you here."

"I'll be fine," she said, and already, she sounded better.

I left her in the shade and walked quickly toward the action. Entering the crowd, I walked quickly, scanning the signage and booths in search of food.

I found a stand and ordered a few grilled shrimp skewers and side salads. I took my number and moved out of the way, to the side, as they prepped the order.

I checked my email and then my workspace app. I was responding to a question from our controller when I heard my name. Looking up, I froze at the man standing before me.

Paul was next to a sunglass stand in board shorts and a Bob Marley t-shirt. His hair was shaggy, his jaw stronger than I remembered, and his expression grim. It was an unsettling look for a guy who had always smiled at everything. "Hey," I said, lifting my chin and meeting his gaze.

"Hey." He glanced around the crowd, then back at me. "What the fuck are you doing here?"

"Here at this event or here in Hawaii?"

He used one hand to rub at the back of his head. "I don't know. Both?"

"I have a business meeting. A few meetings with a hotel chain that's here. I saw the event and wandered down to get something to eat." I noticed the leash band around his calf. "You still surf?"

"Yeah," he said tightly. "I still surf."

It had been years, and the hostility between us hadn't faded. It sucked, but I was as guilty of it as he was.

Paul stepped back. "Well, I gotta go. I'm riding in the next class if you're around to watch."

"I can't, I have--"

"A meeting?" He let out a hard laugh. "Yeah, figured."

I nodded, and he turned, then paused and looked back at me. I held my breath, tensed for what he might say. *Don't say it. Don't say...* I couldn't handle him saying anything about her. Fuck, just her name on his lips - I couldn't hear it. I couldn't take it.

Maybe he could read it on my face, or he could hear my inner thoughts. Whatever the reason, he didn't bring her up. He didn't say a damn thing. He gave me a long look, then he walked away.

Hell, maybe I'm the one who should have said something. Maybe I should have brought her up. Maybe it wouldn't have ended like it did the last time.

But I didn't. I didn't, and he didn't, and when I got our food and carried it back to Madison, I didn't say anything about it.

CHAPTER 4 - MADISON

I knew Paul was there, in the crowd, if he wasn't on the water. When Stewart suggested we go down to the beach, I didn't know how to handle it. Thank God that my faux faintness had worked. If we had gone into the competition, if we had seen Paul...

I'm not sure what would have happened if the two men in my life had finally met.

Maybe nothing. Maybe they would have shaken hands, grabbed a beer, and become best friends.

Or maybe they would have squared off and beat the shit out of each other.

Either outcome was likely, and I didn't plan on ever finding out. I would keep my lives separate as long as I could, or die trying.

Which was ironic, because that's exactly what ended up happening.

———

Want to know more about this cast of characters? Undertow by Alessandra Torre is a standalone love triangle romance featuring Madison, Stewart, and Paul.

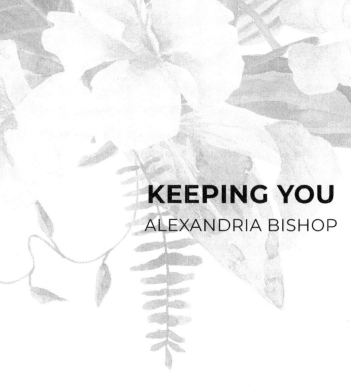

KEEPING YOU

ALEXANDRIA BISHOP

CHAPTER 1

The acrylic toothpick clanks against the side of my glass as I swirl my olives in the drink. I can't remember the last time I had a good martini… just the way I like it. Three olives and just enough brine that I can barely taste the burn of the alcohol.

And this one?

It's perfect. Which means I have to go slow or I'll be passed out on the floor if I try to drink too many of these. But it is just what I need.

The sound of violins play in the background and fills me with contentment and longing. My favorite restaurant is one of those tucked-away places with a few tables that you would only find if someone told you about it. A long bar runs down one side, with patrons crowded at stools.

The bartender is a tall man who goes by the name of Scarface…not that anyone actually knows what his real name is and no one would dare to ask. His eyes are so dark they're almost black and you can just see all the terrifying stories lurking beneath the surface. He wears a white shirt under his black vest and a dyed black bow tie with a skull on it.

Behind him, shelves upon shelves are packed with bottles of every liquor you could imagine. Below that are rows and rows of glasses ready to be filled with every type of drink imaginable, some served cold and others hot, some containing water and others containing alcohol.

There is a constant buzz in the room as people talk about their lives, loves, conspiracies, movies – anything people can think of to talk about. The room smells like cigarettes and alcohol and breath mints and perfume, with an underlying layer of olive brine.

Friday night couldn't come soon enough. The acquisition I've been working on with my partner for weeks, finally went through today. I have an early morning meeting tomorrow but for now I'm going to enjoy my cocktail and see where the evening takes me.

I am in much need of a celebration and a night away from reality.

Out of the corner of my eye, I watch as a man slowly but confidently makes his way toward my place at the bar. His sandy blond hair is cut short on the sides but left longer on the top and styled in a messy just ran my fingers through it look. A thin layer of scruff covers the lower half of his face. His eyes are dark blue and clear, and they light up as they lock on me, as if they are two stars in the night sky.

His feet shuffle now and then, and he draws attention to himself. Not because he's being loud or rude, but because he wants someone to notice him, to notice that he's there. He stands one foot away from me and rests one hand on the bar. His fingers tap lightly against the polished surface. He folds his other arm across his chest, and his muscles tense a little under his shirt, making it pull against his broad shoulders. He cocks his head to one side and grins at me, flashing a wide smile that reveals dimples in each of his cheeks.

"My name is Rick," he tells me with an air of assuredness as he holds his hand out toward me. Rick's smile is sincere, his handshake firm. He towers over me even though I'm wearing four inch heels.

I'm intrigued by the little bit of ink peeking out from the end of his sleeve as it slides slightly up his arm. If I were a judging woman I would see this clean cut guy and assume lawyer or accountant. But if he's hiding a tattoo or more maybe appearance's can be deceiving.

"I'm Ilsa."

"Nice to meet you, Ilsa," he says as the bartender hands him the beer he ordered and he takes a long pull from the bottle. Motioning to the empty table behind us he asks, "would you like to join me?"

A smile spreads on my face, and I say, "I'm waiting for someone."

Rick's face falls just slightly, and he wipes against his forehead with the back of his hand. He asks, "Is he coming?"

I sip my martini and think about it for a moment. "Maybe," I say, "or maybe not." I look back at the restaurant's door for a long moment, then back to Rick.

Leaving it at that, I turn toward the table and let him lead me away from the bar. He pulls one of the chairs out for me, like a gentleman, and pushes it in as I take a seat. Rick starts to take his own seat and motions to my nearly empty glass and asks, "Can I get you another drink?"

That's probably not a good idea. I had already planned on having one drink and then stopping there. We made eye contact and I felt a sudden jolt of electricity. I knew I was going to sleep with him tonight.

I take a sip of my drink, letting the alcohol wash away my inhibitions. I'm starting to feel a little bolder, so I smile and tell him, "I would love another drink, Rick."

His ocean blue eyes light up when I say his name and he gets the bartender's attention.

"What can I get for you?" he asks me.

"I'll have a dirty martini please… extra olives," I reply.

Rick nods and orders another round of drinks. We both sip at our drinks and then he looks back at me, "So, tell me something about yourself, Ilsa."

The stir stick finds its way back in my hands as I fiddle with it. Something about that question always has me freezing up and my mind going blank.

I gaze at him across the table, taking in his handsome features. His full lips and sun kissed skin. But I can't stop going back to those piercing cobalt blue eyes. They're warm, mesmerizing, and I want to be swallowed whole by them.

Who even thinks something like that?

I giggle… jeez, the alcohol must be going to my head already. I should probably slow down. Sliding the glass away, I take a small deep breath and give him my warmest smile. "I assure you that my life is not very interesting. I'd love to know more about you."

"A gorgeous woman like you? There's no way your life could be described as anything less than interesting. I'll get you to tell me something later."

"What makes you think there is going to be a later?" I ask.

Rick shrugs, "Maybe I'm hoping that I play my cards right."

I bet he is. If there's one thing I can say about this man is he hasn't looked at anyone else since he gave me his attention. It's like we're in our own little bubble in the middle of this noisy bar.

"Hmm a gambler...do you work in finance?"

Based on his suit and tie that he's wearing, I could see it. Just a quick stop for a drink on his way home from the office. A nice distraction from the stressors of the day.

"I'm a commercial pilot," he says with a grin.

Definitely not what I was expecting, but I'm also not mad about it. I wonder how many different exotic places he's traveled to around the world? I've been bitten many times with the escape of wanderlust, but responsibilities and life have always gotten in the way.

"That's exciting. Are you just in town for the night? Or do you live around here?" I ask.

Rick smiles, "Just for the night."

Well things definitely just got a little more interesting.

CHAPTER 2

"Where are you traveling to next?" I ask as I lean forward across the table. The noise level isn't deafening but I feel a pull toward this man. Like I need to be closer to him.

"Hawaii," he says nonchalantly with a grin that lights up his entire face.

"I was supposed to go there once…" I leave off as I think about another time in my life when I had less responsibilities and could do whatever I wanted without a care in the world. That girl did not know how easy she had it.

"What kept you from the trip?"

This whole time, I've continued fiddling with the toothpick, but I drop it back in my glass and place my hands on the table. Something about this man brings nervous giddy energy out of me. And I definitely don't hate it.

Smiling, I tell him, "I dated this guy in college. We were madly in love and planning a romantic getaway to Hawaii for spring break. I was so naïve back then."

"What did he do?"

That is such a loaded question. What didn't that guy do? It was my first heartbreak I ever really experienced and even though I know I am better off, that's not something you get over. Sure you grow up, get wiser, but it still doesn't erase the memories of that sting and hit to your ego.

Picking up my martini glass, I sigh and let the salty cool liquid burn my throat in a deliciously refreshing way. "Turns out our definitions of the word love were very different. He loved my body and about five other girls. There was never a trip. He made the whole thing up to keep me around."

"He sounds like a tool. You probably wouldn't have had a good time anyway," Rick says with a confident shrug as he follows my lead and takes another sip from his own beverage.

I laugh at his easy opinion of a man he's never met before. But he hit the nail on the head. "You're right, but I'd still love to go there someday."

And many other places, but I don't add that tidbit of information.

"So do it."

If only it were that easy. But rather than face reality I say, "You know I just might do that. Maybe I'll stow away on your flight tomorrow." I tell him with a wink.

Keeping his hands in his lap, Rick closes the distance between us. Following my lead, he doesn't crowd me. At our small intimate table, he is close enough to reach out and touch me. But he doesn't. I am warmed by his presence.

I can smell his breath on his lips. An intoxicating blend of mint, the citrus from his beer, and a warm smokey scent that must be coming from his cologne. It's wrapping me up like a blanket and doing dirty delicious things to my body.

Our drinks are long forgotten as we get lost in conversation, talking about everything from our favorite movies to our wildest dreams. The tension between us grows stronger with each passing minute, until neither of us can resist any longer.

Feeling bold, I reach across the table and take Rick's hand. His skin is warm under my touch, and my heart pounds in my chest as I lean in closer to him.

"I'm not usually this forward," I admit, "but there's something about you that I just can't resist."

Rick's eyes grow dark with desire, and he leans in closer to me. "I feel the same way," he whispers, his breath hot against my skin. "I've been wanting to do this all night."

As if on cue, he reaches out and cups my face in his hands, pulling me in for a deep, passionate kiss. I moan softly as his tongue explores my mouth, his hands roaming over my body as we lose ourselves in the moment.

The loud noises of the bar patrons, the clinking glasses of drinks being made, and the overhead music all fall away to nothingness as we get absorbed into each other and only each other.

Pulling away, he shakes his head slightly and whispers, "No more talking." I can't help thinking of the word as a growl. In the same deep, husky voice he says, "Let's get out of here." I glance at him again and see that he is staring at me now with a longing so strong I can feel it on my skin.

The way this man has control over my entire body with that one word is exhilarating. A chill runs down my spine. Goosebumps begin to form, and my heart races. Heat pools deep in my core and I lick my lips in anticipation. This man makes me feel excited, anxious, and even afraid all at once.

And I like it.

Two can play that game. I place my hand on his leg and lean in close, brushing my lips against his ear. "Indeed, no more talking," I whisper as I nibble on the lobe. I feel his body shiver and tingle. Grabbing my drink, I hand it to him and whisper, "Finish your drink."

Standing up, I reach down for my purse and smile at the bartender. I turn back to Rick and ask, "You ready to go?"

He nods and hands me back the drink before standing up. Leaning in, he places a quick peck on my lips before pulling away. I feel the warmth of his body as he stands behind me. With his arm draped over my shoulder, I feel like the luckiest woman in the world.

I walk up to the bartender and give him my card. I know I'm already a little too drunk to drive home so I might as well enjoy the perks of having Rick's company.

The bartender hands me my card. "Your tab is paid by an anonymous source."

"Who?" I ask even though I know the answer.

"You'll have to figure that one out."

I turn back to Rick and give him a you-have-got-to-be-kidding-me look. He just shrugs and gives me a grin.

CHAPTER 3

The door doesn't even click close behind us before Rick attacks. His mouth instantly finds mine and with the first touch of our lips, that's all it takes. He's like a man starved and I'm the only meal he wants to eat. The way our tongues collide in a delicious tangle of exploration has me on fire like I'm going to explode.

His hands travel down my body until they stop on either side of my barely covered ass as he hoists me up. My legs wrap around his waist and my dress slides up leaving me completely bare from the waist down.

"Naughty girl," he mumbles into my lips as he caresses the smooth round skin underneath his calloused fingertips.

I don't always opt out of lingerie underneath my clothing but I am so very glad I did tonight.

I want this all so much it's hard to breathe.

Rick hoists me up further and presses me against the wall. I moan as his rough hands find my soft skin. I groan as I feel his hardened cock pressed against me.

His lips break from mine and travel along the column of my neck until they find my earlobe. "You're so fucking sexy," he whispers.

I moan and run my hands through his hair as he kisses my neck. The light scrape of his stubble against my smooth skin sends shivers down my spine.

"I want you to do something for me." His voice is laced with lust.

"Anything," I breathe out.

He slides me down his body releasing his grip on my body and gently places me down on the floor. Our breathing is coming out labored as we stand mere inches from each other. "Take the fucking dress off."

My mouth drops open and I look up at him with a grin. "I'm not that easy," I tease.

Rick tilts his head as if he is thinking it over. "You're right, we should blow off some steam first."

Before I can ask what he means, he drops down to his knees in front of me. His hands tightly grip my legs as they slowly glide upward in an achingly slow pace. My breathing quickens as my heart begins to race in my chest. He is so close I can feel his hot breath between my legs.

"You're already wet for me. It's all for me, isn't it?" he growls against the point where my legs meet my body.

I nod in response.

Rick's hands stop before they reach my aching center and look up at me. "I want to hear you say it."

I breathe out a sigh of frustration. "Yes, it's all for you."

His lips form a lopsided grin as his eyes darken with desire. "Good girl," he whispers just before his mouth finds my aching sex.

My head along with the rest of my body falls back as I let the sensation of Rick's tongue glide up and down the length of my pussy. My hair hangs behind me in waves, making a curtain to hide my blushing face.

"Oh God!" I shout out as the pleasure nearly sends me to my knees.

Rick pulls away and stands up in front of me before I can catch my breath. "Not so fast," he says as he stands me back up.

One of his hands grabs a fistful of my hair while the other cups my ass. I moan as he pushes my back against the wall. His lips find mine again, and the kiss is almost as desperate as the one I was just treated to.

He pulls away from me and nuzzles the nape of my neck before he whispers, "You want this. You want me to fuck this pussy."

I moan and nod in response.

"Say it," he demands.

"Fuck me. I want you to fuck me."

He growls before his lips find mine again. The kiss is intense, filled with need. His teeth nip at my bottom lip as his grip on my ass tightens.

"You want me to fuck you, don't you?" he asks before his mouth trails kisses down my neck.

"Yes," I breathe out.

"Tell me. Tell me what you want."

"I want you to fuck me. Please fuck me."

His lips are back on mine in an instant. "I'm going to fuck that pretty pussy until you scream."

He lets go of my hair and begins to grip his belt. I watch in anticipation as he opens it and slowly unzips his pants. A groan escapes me as his cock springs free. "You like that, don't you?" he asks as he steps closer to me.

"Yes," I moan.

"You want that?"

"Yes!"

With his free hand, he grabs my chin and forces my head up to see him. "Look at me."

I do as he says and I see the passion in his eyes. I see the desire. I see the fire.

"I'm going to fuck you so good you won't be able to walk for a week."

His words have me so hot I can feel the moisture running down my leg. His eyes travel from mine to my bare pussy and back again. He bends his knees slightly and grabs his cock before he pushes it against my entrance.

I suck in a deep breath as I feel his head slide into me. My body tenses as I wait for him to enter me completely.

"You want it slow?" he asks as he looks up at me.

"No," I breathe out. "I want you to fuck me. Fast. Hard. No slow tonight."

"That's what I like to hear," he mumbles before he slams into me.

My head falls back against the wall and I let out a scream of ecstasy. This man knows how to fuck. His cock fills me perfectly.

His hands grip my waist as he slides in and out of me. I can feel myself getting closer to the edge with each thrust he makes. His mouth finds my neck again and I can feel his stubble against my shoulder. His lips latch on to the sensitive skin and he begins to suck.

He bites down into my skin and a shockwave runs through my body. My muscles tighten around his cock as I feel his teeth drag along my soft skin. "Fuck, you're so tight."

My entire body begins to shake. My legs start to tremble and my fingers dig into the flesh of his shoulders. I am so close to coming. I can feel the climax in my fingertips.

Rick continues to fuck me harder and harder until I can no longer stand. My back hits the wall as his final thrust brings me to the edge. My mouth opens in disbelief as I feel the orgasm rip through me.

My breath catches in my throat and I let out a scream as my body falls limp against the wall. It feels like my whole body is shaking.

"That's it, baby," Rick whispers in my ear. "I want to feel you come with my cock inside you."

My body is still twitching as Rick begins to pick up the pace again. His thrusts grow more frantic as he pours his seed deep inside me. "Oh fuck!" he shouts as he spills himself inside me.

He pulls out of me and pulls his shirt off before he turns me around and presses my back against the wall.

"We're just getting started, I'm not done with you yet."

CHAPTER 4

I roll over in bed and grab my cell phone off the charger. Time to turn it back on and re-enter reality.

"What time is your sister bringing the kids by again?" Clarke asks me as he tugs my body back to him and snuggles up against me.

I didn't know when I was in college that I would be spending the rest of my life with this man, but I am so glad that I agreed to go on that first date with him. After my horrific heartbreak, which in retrospect was a blessing in disguise, my best friend Natalie convinced me to go to a frat party with her. I was never into the whole Greek life thing, but she was pledging a sorority and wanted my support.

In five inch heels, we walked ten blocks to the frat house because she had no idea where we were going and got lost multiple times. Those were the days back before everyone had GPS on their cell phones. After nearly breaking my ankle multiple times, we stumbled up the steps to the very loud party and I found the man laying next to me nursing a beer on the front steps.

Clarke was dragged to the party by his best friend. We bonded over our mother's similar love for Gone With the Wind and laughed at our equally silly names. Only mom's like ours would name their children Tara Savannah Scott and Clarke Gable Taylor.

"They should be back soonish. Tinley told me she has a whole day of baking ahead of her. She has a retirement party, sweet sixteen, and bridal shower this next week to bake for."

"That's awesome that her business is booming so much. I'm really happy for her."

"Yeah, me too. She seems really happy these days. I'm proud of her."

"How did the acquisition go yesterday?" he asks as he feathers kisses along my neck and shoulders.

I laugh thinking about the hours I spent on my presentation and then finally presenting it yesterday. "The church finally relented and gave us the okay to rent out their auditorium for Liv and Luna's dance recital. All the negotiations were starting to get heated and I was worried we were going to have to find a new location."

"I was never worried."

"That's because you didn't have to talk to those people."

Clarke pulls my face toward him and in the most earnest way he says, "No, because I know my baby is a master negotiator. Nobody can ever shut you down. Always pulling out the big guns."

He kisses me and I get lost in his mouth as I wonder if we have time for another round this morning. As we break our kiss, reality comes slamming right back to us.

"Mommy," I hear as little feet pad stampede down the hallway toward the bedroom. It's only a few moments before our door is ripped open and our little boy jumps into bed with us and cuddles up in the middle.

I know Olivia won't follow her little brother into here, but I am so grateful Landon is still small and loves his mommy snuggles. And of course the minute I think the thought, he rolls over and latches onto his dad in a giant bearhug.

"I told him to wait until you were both up," Tinley says from the doorway.

I laugh as my sister watches the three of us in bed and ask her, "Did you really think that would work?"

"Of course not, but I at least had to say it, right?"

I roll over and slide out of bed as Landon and Clarke get absorbed into a conversation about the latest superhero movie that our little boy wants to see.

"How about some coffee?" I ask my sister as I reach for my robe draped over the end of my bed.

"Sure," she says, "but I can't stay too long. Marek has the kids and when I left them, they were making a mess of my kitchen."

As we head down the hallway, I can hear Olivia in her room working on her dance routine. My not so little girl has always been a perfectionist when it comes to everything she does, so I'm not surprised that she's right back to it as soon as coming back home.

"So what did you end up doing last night?" Tinley asks from the other side of the island as I work on making coffee.

"Oh you know us. Went to our favorite restaurant for dinner and then watched some Netflix. Nothing too crazy," I tell her as I think about our actual date night.

I can't remember the first time Clarke and I decided to try roleplaying. Pretending to be strangers meeting in the most random of places and letting ourselves get sucked into the fantasy of being someone else for a night but always ending up right back at the same place. Back at home with crazy hot sex.

It might not be for everyone, but I love every second of it. In some ways, we have fallen even more in love with each other over the years. Life can get stagnant and boring but our lives are anything but that.

As if reading my mind, my sister asks, "And that never gets boring? I don't know how you don't get sick of each other."

If she only knew the truth. But if there's one thing I've learned over the decade of marriage, some things you just have to keep to yourself. And as far as I'm concerned, the spark between Clarke and me only burns brighter the longer we're together.

You've met Tara's sister Tinley. Grab the first book in her story, Dating in the Dark by Alexandria Bishop.

LOVE AND FREEDOM

A RELEASE SHORT STORY

ALY MARTINEZ

"Ramsey, wake up," she whispered.

My mind came awake on the first syllable, but it took a second for my brain to process where I was.

It had been three years since I'd come home. Yet, every morning as I roused to consciousness, it never felt real. I'd spent too many years locked behind bars to ever get used to that kind of freedom.

My subconscious defaulted to the cold chill of a prison cell. The walls closing in around me. The stale air filled with sweat and defeat.

But that wasn't where I was anymore.

I was at home—*our home*. In a cushy bed with the subtle fragrance of flowers and honey surrounding me while her soft curves warmed my side.

Thea.

My sparrow.

The woman who had owned me for the better part of my life, including every minute of the twelve years when I'd been in lockup, hell-bent on pushing her away.

She'd never listened though. I'd once cursed that she was so damn stubborn. Now, each night as she crawled into bed, my ring on her finger, the promise of our future bright on the horizon, I had to fight the urge to drop to my knees and thank any and every god in the universe who had brought her into my life.

"Ramsey," she repeated, giving my shoulder a gentle nudge.

A smile curled my lips, but I didn't open my eyes. "What time is it?"

"Midnight."

Letting out a groan, I hooked an arm around her middle and dragged her on top of me. "Woman," I mumbled, burying my face in the curve of her neck. "I am barely an hour into my post-orgasm coma. There is no way you can be ready for round two already."

She giggled and trailed the tips of her fingers over my pecs. "No, baby, it's *midnight*."

"So you've mentioned." I scrubbed a hand over my face, trying to wipe away the exhaustion. I had no idea why she was up, but if she was awake, I was awake. Too much of our lives had already been wasted.

That was my fault. All of it. But I had big plans to spend forever making it up to her. If that meant dragging my sated body out of hard-earned REM at midnight to listen to her ramble about whatever was on her mind, then that was what I was going to do.

"You want the light on or off?" I asked.

Her answer was to roll over and click on the lamp.

My eyes stung as they adjusted to the brightness, but the pain was nothing compared to the punch in the gut I felt when I finally pried my lids open and caught sight of her tear-stained cheeks.

Bolting upright, I grabbed her shoulders and brought her up with me. "What's wrong? What happened? Are you okay?"

The blanket became trapped between us, and as though it had somehow offended her, she tugged it out of the way before straddling my lap. "Relax. I'm fine."

Relax wasn't a word in my vocabulary when it came to her. I was working on it. I really was, but Thea Hull Stewart was my undoing. Overreacting was something of a full-time job for me.

"Why are you crying?"

"Because it's midnight, Ramsey." She lifted her wrist to glance at her watch. "Well, actually twelve-oh-one now, but you get the point."

My girl had something of an obsession with time. The day we'd met over twenty years earlier, she'd been counting the minutes, so I was going to need a little more than just a reading from the clock.

"I can honestly say I *don't* get the point. Talk to me. What's going on? Is something wrong?"

She smiled. "No, baby. Everything is very, very right for once. It's over." She grabbed both sides of my face and planted a hard kiss to my lips.

I inhaled as if I could somehow absorb her. God knew I'd been trying for the majority of my life to no avail. My heart began to slow, and with the panic ebbing from my system, my brain was finally able to catch up.

It was midnight.

Midnight.

Twelve-oh-one.

It was over.

Sixteen years, one month, two weeks, four days, and twelve hours after this nightmare had started, it was finally fucking *over*.

My parole was done.

Thea and I had been talking about that moment for three years. Spending day after day, plotting and planning our future together. And we had big dreams, so it was no easy process. However, earlier that day, neither of us had brought up that it was the final day of my sentence.

It was too surreal.

Too fragile.

Too perfect.

I was worried I'd jinx it. Thea, well... She had just been worried about *me*.

It had been a normal day. Quiet—just the way we liked it. I'd fallen asleep not even an hour earlier, after making love to my wife, knowing that the next time I woke up I'd be a free man. After sixteen years, freedom was an abstract concept; it seemed like the impossible.

But here we were, fucked up, in love, and free.

"It's midnight," I stated, needing to hear it again.

"Twelve-oh-two now." She rested her forehead on mine. "You're free, Ramsey."

I sucked in a sharp breath and gripped her hips. I had no words. There was no combination of syllables that would do justice to the magnitude of relief swirling inside me.

Thea knew it. We were two halves of one soul; she could feel my emotions building sure as she could feel the beat of her heart in her chest.

Like a nervous tick, I switched my gum from under one side of my tongue to the other. "Stop looking at me like that. I'm okay."

Her eyes flashed wide and my loving wife disappeared. A witch straight out of a horror film took her place. "Is that gum in your mouth?"

Oh fuck. Fuck. Fuck. Fuck.

"What? No."

She leaned in close and sniffed my mouth. "You liar! You reek of watermelon."

I adamantly shook my head. "I have no idea what you're talking about."

"Nu-uh. No way." She snapped her fingers and held her palm out. "Spit it out. We agreed after the gum-in-the-hair incident last month that you wouldn't sleep with it in your mouth again. My hair is still uneven from where you had to cut it out."

Yeah. It was exactly as terrible as it sounded. No, peanut butter hadn't worked to get it out. Baby oil, either. It had been as if I'd been chewing concrete when I'd fallen asleep that night.

No matter how much your wife loves you, if at any point she wakes up with gum in her hair—gum that fell out of your mouth in the middle of the night because you have a slight obsession—there is going to be hell to pay.

Luckily, my wife loves me a fuck of a lot, so I got off with a warning. I had a sneaking suspicion that she wasn't going to be so gentle this time.

Given that I had a healthy respect for my life, I fought to suppress my smile. "I can't help it. It's like having a cigarette after sex. It relaxes me."

She glared, all pissed off and sexy. "Right, and I wouldn't be okay with you burning the house down with a cigarette, either. Chew your gum. And then spit. It. Out."

"What if it still has flavor?"

"Ramsey," she warned.

"Isn't that wasteful?"

"Ramsey!"

Unable to contain it any longer, I barked a laugh. "Okay, okay. No more gum at night." I didn't spit it out though. Leaning forward, I brushed my lips over hers. "You're not allowed to be mad at me today. We're free, remember?"

She instantly melted, her whole body sagging against me. "Let's go somewhere. Right now. Let's just get in the car and go."

"Where to?"

She nipped at my bottom lip and ever-so-subtly rolled her hips. "I don't care. Take me anywhere, Ramsey."

God, did I want that. It was everything we'd dreamed of when we were younger. And everything we'd lost the day I'd been convicted of killing the boy who had assaulted her.

After three years of being tied to an invisible ninety-mile chain, I thought getting the hell out of town would have been the perfect way to kick off the end to this godforsaken chapter of our lives. But it wasn't exactly like I'd been miserable the last few years. There was something to be said for the comfort and conveniences of home. Like the fact that Thea slept naked, ready for me any time I wanted to roll over and slide into her from behind. We had a lot of years to make up for. At least that what she'd told me each night as she rolled over and climbed on top of *me*.

And luckily for us both, in our bed, I slept naked too.

So, currently, while relief and freedom ricocheted inside my chest, it was my wife naked and straddling my lap, my cock thickening against her slick core, that demanded my focus.

"If we leave in an hour, we could be at the beach in time to see the sunrise."

The tips of her nipples grazed my chest as she replied, "It won't take me an hour to get dressed."

All at once, I turned, flipping her to her back. She let out a squeak and then a loud laugh that may as well have been the soundtrack of my childhood.

"You won't be spending that hour getting dressed, Sparrow." I kissed her hard. Our tongues tangled in a fluid rhythm, and her legs fell open in a silent invitation. I did not delay in settling between them.

Yeah. Home was a fucking beautiful place.

She purred as I kissed my way up her neck. "Why are we waiting an hour to leave? No offense to your sexual prowess or anything, but I'm pretty sure round two is not going to take that long."

My head popped up and I shot her a glare that held no heat due to the fact that I was smiling like a fool. "Wow. You are hell on a man's ego. You know that?"

"What?" She feigned innocence. "I said no offense."

She was busting my balls. It was her favorite pastime, and because it was Thea, it had quickly become my favorite pastime too.

"Well, offense taken. My sexual prowess is thoroughly insulted."

Her breasts pillowed between us as she wrapped her arms around my neck. "I just meant that if we had sex in the shower and left in fifteen minutes, we could stop and pick up a bottle of champagne on the way." She shot me a sly grin. "As a free man, you can finally drink alcohol. What do you say we get a little tipsy and have round three on the beach?"

"I'd say that my first legal drink in my entire life is sure as shit not going to be champagne, and how about you don't get me arrested for indecent exposure less than twelve hours after I finally became a free man."

She giggled. "Fair enough. But I still don't think we need an hour. We could stop and get beer or something."

"Fuck the beer. And trust me, we are going to need all sixty minutes of that hour." Holding her gaze, I inched down her body, peppering kisses across her breasts. Her nipples peaked and I all too willingly answered their pleas for my attention.

She arched off the bed as I licked and sucked, alternating between gentle flicks of my tongue and rough nips with my teeth.

"Ramsey," she breathed as I continued my descent down her torso, worshipping every curve on my way. "Please," she whispered, thrusting her hand into the top of my hair, urging my mouth between her thighs.

But just like always, no matter how much it frustrated her, I stopped and rose to my knees.

"No," she hissed. "Not now. Please, Ramsey."

Oh yeah, she hated this part. Eventually, she'd love it. Though even I could admit that working her up only to stop and stare was cruel. But I needed those seconds to drink her in, to remind myself that she was really there.

When I'd decided to let her go so she could have a better life without the confines of my choices imprisoning her too, I'd never in my wildest dreams thought I'd get a second chance. When you tell yourself something for long enough, it eventually becomes a cold, hard fact.

Most days, it was still hard to believe that what I'd accepted as fact was actually fiction. But seeing her bare before me, her cheeks pink, and her long, brown hair splayed across the pillows while my name sat on the tip of her tongue as she begged to come against my mouth, I allowed my mind to differentiate between the two.

I licked my thumb and lazily trailed it up her slit, circling at her clit before sliding back down. "I thought about you," I confessed while continuing to stroke her.

"Ramsey," she moaned. "Don't."

I couldn't stop myself. "When I was behind bars, I used to think about this a lot. Being free. Being with you. Being us again."

Circling her hips off the mattress, she pleaded for more. "Stop talking."

"I didn't want to. I fought like hell, convincing myself that it was wrong. But I thought about you just like this. So wet and beautiful. So eager and ready. It nearly killed me every time the images floated through my mind because I was never the man between your legs."

Her body stiffened, and her sad gaze locked with mine. "There never was anyone else. It was always you."

"I know. But these were my nightmares, Thea. I didn't have to be asleep for them ruin me."

Suddenly, she tried to sit up. My sparrow was always there, ready to take care of me when the world became too much. Warmth filled my chest, desire to let her wrap me in her arms warring with the need to watch my wife come on my hand before I fucked her long and hard.

Need won out, and without warning, I sank two fingers deep in her heat.

"Oh God!" she cried, falling back against the pillow.

Her mouth open, ecstasy flowing from the perfect O shape of her lips, she arched off the bed, screwing her eyes shut as I began a frenzied rhythm of thrusts and circles.

My fingers became almost as urgent as my words. "I'm here now, Thea. It's not a nightmare. It's not a dream. I'm here, and I swear to God, for the rest of my life, it's me and you. Forever."

"Forever," she panted, reaching for my hand. She wanted to touch me, and fuck, I wanted that too.

Her nails bit into my bicep as I continued to work her. Between the sounds of her moans and the hypnotic view of her breasts swaying, I could barely breathe. Dropping my head to kiss her collarbone, I allowed my gaze to linger on her flat stomach.

Thea and I had talked about a family a million times. The current timing was shit, what with our plans to tour the world and all. But as images of her stomach swollen, my baby growing inside her, flashed in my head, settling down when we were done playing nomads sounded more exciting than ever.

"I want a baby," I whispered, resting my palm just above her belly button.

Her body stilled, and her eyes suddenly popped open. "Ramsey...I..."

"Not right now, crazy." The side of my mouth hiked up. "But one day."

She smiled back at me, love burning her cheeks. "As many as you want."

I had no idea what that number looked like. I had zero experience with kids besides my little sister, so the "couple" we'd discussed might as well have been a dozen. It was all the same to me. I just wanted a family.

No. Strike that. I just wanted a family *with her*.

"I love you," I whispered.

The final syllable hadn't cleared my lips before she replied, "I love you too, but I *really* want to see that sunset on the beach."

I laughed. Yep. That was my wife. It was a wonder I got her to slow down every night long enough to sleep. But if she wanted to be at the beach, a man could find it in his heart to hurry.

She gasped as I guided my length to her entrance.

And then she cried out as I drove inside.

She held me tight as I worked her hard and fast, a sheen of sweat covering us both by the time she fell over the edge of ecstasy.

And then, in true Thea Stewart fashion, she flipped me, her long legs straddling my hips, her slick heat surrounding my cock. As she rocked and circled, riding me with her hands resting on my chest, her eyes locked on mine and time officially started again.

But in a way, time became irrelevant.

Thea was still the girl I'd been in love with before I'd known what the word truly meant.

I was still the kid who would do whatever it took to give her the life we'd never had growing up.

The only real difference was that midnight hadn't only freed me.

It had freed us both.

As my release tore through me, leveling me in its wake, the only words that mattered slipped from my lips.

A gasping promise that I would follow her to the ends of the Earth.

First stop: the sunrise on the beach. And yeah, I'd probably even agree to the champagne too.

Next stop: "Forever, Thea. Forever."

———————

Thank you for reading. To continue in this world, try Release by Aly Martinez.

CHANGING TIDES

A SANDCASTLE COVE SHORT STORY

AMBER KELLY

CHAPTER 1

Why the hell not?

That's the question I ask myself as I open the Tiffany-blue suitcase on my bed and begin to cut the tags off of the pile of new vacation clothes I purchased last week.

I toss them inside, along with my favorite white bikini and pineapple-print cover-up.

Conrad and I planned this vacation for over a year. Painstakingly searching websites for the best accommodations, food, and excursions. I saved every penny earned from my part-time job of waiting tables at a bistro near the University of Georgia campus so we could afford to splurge on anything we wanted to do or buy while in Honolulu on the island of Oahu.

Looking forward to a week of baking in the Hawaiian sun and drinking all the tropical cocktails with my favorite guy was the only thing that kept me going through the all-night study sessions, finals and months of long seven-day workweeks.

Once everything is packed, I snatch the pair of airline tickets from the nightstand and sit on the end of the bed.

Two first-class round-trip tickets for Avie Carrigan and Conrad Sullivan.

Nonrefundable.

I swipe at the warm tear trickling down my cheek.

Pull it together, Avie.

I tuck the ticket with my name on it inside of my purse and tear the one with his name into tiny pieces.

Asshole.

Conrad and I had been dating for almost three years, and stupid me thought maybe he was planning to hide a ring away in his luggage to surprise me on this trip.

It was always the plan. Once I finished school, we would move to the city and begin our life together.

Instead, he took me to dinner last night and professed how much he loved me at the same time he was breaking up with me.

Dumped. The night before the trip of a lifetime.

He said we needed a breather.

I asked, "What the hell does that even mean?"

He explained that his dad's best friend had offered him a job at his architectural firm in New York.

A job that starts next week.

He accepted the position, and he is moving this weekend.

When I asked why the news meant that we needed a breather, he said he wanted to concentrate on work and that a long-distance relationship would be too much of an emotional drain.

"Look, the job is a summer internship. I need to be focused in order to prove myself. After that, I'll know if it's what I want to do and where I want to be. Then, we can revisit our situation and see if I want you to move to New York or if I should move back here to Atlanta."

What he wants to do and where he wants to be?

I stood up as calmly as I could muster, told him he could go fuck himself, picked up the glass of red wine I had been drinking, and dumped it in his lap before I made my way out of the restaurant.

When I made it home, all of his things were gone from the apartment we shared. His clothing, toiletries, laptop, and even the expensive gaming system I'd bought him for his birthday last month.

The jerk had packed up his things while I was on campus. Before bothering to tell me he was moving out.

I will not cry again.

My phone chimes from the dresser, and I stand to see the message that my Uber driver has arrived.

I sling my purse over my shoulder and grab my suitcase.

As I pass the full-length pedestal mirror in the corner of the room, I admire my tanned shoulders peeking out of the top of the gorgeous palm-print maxi dress. I place a wide-brimmed straw hat on my head and pull on my new aviator sunglasses before slipping into the white sandals by the door.

Glancing back at the apartment one more time before shutting and locking the door, I head to the elevator.

The driver takes my suitcase and loads it into the back of the car, and I open the door to the back seat, where I find my best friend, Amiya, waiting.

"Hey, chica. I'm ready to get this tropical party started," she cries as she scoots to the left to make room for me.

Thank God she was able to get off work at the last minute to join me. The romantic getaway I planned will now be the girls' trip of a lifetime. And the best part is that it's being partially funded by the douche formerly known as the love of my life.

"I've been looking at the resort's website," She taps her phone screen and begins to read, "*Welcome to your own private paradise. Our property prides itself on being an exclusive getaway experience, curated just for you. Where you can disconnect from the stress and worries of life, connect to a dream landscape, and enjoy exceptional service with your own personal butler. At The Stanhope Grand Resort, we are all* ohana."

She looks up from the device and at me. "That means family."

"I know."

"The pictures are insane. I can't believe we get to stay there," she squeals.

Her enthusiasm is infectious, and I find myself getting excited about the trip.

The driver drops us off at the airport, and we make our way to the Delta counter to see if I can get the ticket Amiya purchased upgraded.

"I'm totally okay in coach. Just send me back a free cocktail or two," she says.

"It can't hurt to ask if they can move you beside me. It's not like anyone else will be sitting there."

"But I checked last night, and the cost difference is astronomical," she informs.

I reach into my bag and pull out the American Express card that has my name on it.

"I don't want you to pay for it either."

I grin. "I'm not. This is Conrad's account. He gave me a card with my name on it to his account a while ago so I could pick up his dry cleaning, grab takeout, and fill his car up with gas on the occasions he was working late. I think the least he can do since he left me with an apartment that still has five months left on the lease is pay for your upgrade."

"Oh, it absolutely is the least he can do," she agrees.

After I explain the situation to the lady at the ticket counter she changes Amiya's seat, and we quickly make our way through security.

We grab a bite to eat and a couple of beers at Phillips Seafood while we wait for boarding.

Amiya flirts shamelessly with our barely legal server as I incessantly check my phone.

Once our glasses hit the table, Amiya reaches across the table and snatches my phone from my fingertips.

"Hey!" I quip.

"Hey nothing. You're not going to keep staring at this thing, looking for a text from him or cyberstalking his social media accounts while we're in Hawaii. In less than twelve hours, we're going to be draped in leis and frolicking in paradise. Conrad fucking Sullivan is not going to ruin this trip any further. Got it?"

I nod.

"Let me hear you say it," she insists.

"Conrad fucking Sullivan is not going to ruin this trip," I affirm.

She opens the top of her bag and drops my phone inside. "You'll get that back when we return home."

"Fine," I huff.

She smiles, picks up her glass, and leans in. "There will be an incredible amount of beautiful men there, and we're going to find one to occupy your time. You'll forget all about what's his name before we return. Here's to a wicked holiday affair."

I raise my glass and clink it against hers. "Cheers."

CHAPTER 2

We land at Daniel K. Inouye International Airport and disembark. After claiming our baggage, we are greeted by a couple from the car service Conrad hired, receiving one of the warmest welcomes I've ever encountered. The two are waiting with a sign that reads *Mr. Sullivan and Miss Carrigan*.

I inform them that Conrad was unable to make the trip and introduce them to Amiya.

"Aloha! I am Kiana, and this is my husband, Makoa. We are happy to welcome you to our island," Kiana says as she presents us with colorful necklaces full of blooms, which she places around each of our necks. "This is a fresh flower lei, which is a Hawaiian symbol of aloha, and love," she explains.

I inhale the fragrance of the beautiful flowers and smile. "Thank you."

Makoa takes our bags and loads them into the back of the car, and then they whisk us away to the private luxury resort.

When we walk through the sliding glass doors, a hotel employee presents us with a tray filled with pink cocktails in fancy glass flutes.

"Aloha," she says as she smiles brightly.

"Aloha to you too," Amiya says as she takes two of the offered glasses.

She follows me as I make my way to the reception desk to check us in.

"Aloha, Miss Carrigan, and welcome to The Stanhope Grand Resort. We have you booked in one of our seaside bungalows for seven nights," the front-desk attendant states.

"That's correct."

"Excellent. I have a key card for you in addition to your mobile access. Please allow Nalani to guide you to your home away from home. A member of our staff will deliver your luggage to you shortly."

She hands me the card, and Amiya and I accompany the young lady who explains the layout of the resort as she walks us down a lit path to the breathtaking bungalow. It has a wall that opens to the beach, allowing us to sleep while exposed to the Pacific breeze and the sound of the crashing waves.

"Wow," Amiya says as we make our way onto the teak deck that leads to the large king-size bed with rose petals sprinkled on top.

A bottle of champagne is chilling in a silver bucket on a tray by the pillows.

She turns to me and raises an eyebrow. "So romantic."

I laugh. "Right?"

Nalani gives us a brief tour of the bungalow and explains how all the gadgets work. There is a remote that lowers the wall and draws the shades and a telephone that can reach our butler directly. An outdoor shower is located on the deck and a small sauna room off the bath.

"This place is amazing. I might never want to leave," Amiya declares as she plops onto the bed and lies back.

"If only we were independently wealthy," I quip.

Before excusing herself, Nalani informs us that Wednesday's luau begins at six and we can follow the signage on the footpath to the left of our deck to find it.

"What is a luau exactly?" Amiya asks.

"It's a celebration where we feast and drink on the bountiful offerings of the unique crops from this tropical paradise. It is a cuisine you won't find anywhere else in the world. There will be music and dancing, joy and laughter in abundance," she tells us.

"We look forward to it," I declare.

A young boy arrives with our bags ten minutes later. Amiya tips him generously, and he beams as he runs off back to the main part of the resort.

We quickly unpack and change into our bikinis before calling the butler, Pika, to arrange our afternoon of sunbathing on the pristine Waikiki Beach, which is steps from our terrace.

When we arrive, our umbrella-covered loungers are prepared just out of reach of the flowing shoreline. Two luxurious, large towels are folded on each one, and sitting atop a table between the two is a plate of fruits and cheeses, along with two cocktails served in coconut shells, adorned with small paper umbrellas.

Pika greets us and asks if there is anything else we need.

"If you keep these yummy coconut concoctions coming, you won't hear another peep from us today," I assure him.

"Yes, ma'am," he promises with a smile before excusing himself.

I lather my body with sunscreen before parking it in the lounger and grabbing my drink.

"So, other than the luau, what's on the agenda for the week?" Amiya asks.

"Tomorrow is the Pearl Harbor tour," I begin.

"Pass," she interrupts.

"What? Why?"

She rolls her eyes. "I know Conrad liked all that history stuff, but I'm on vacation. In Hawaii. I can learn about World War II from a book."

I sigh. "Fine. Tuesday, we're taking the Dole Plantation Tour, and don't you dare say pass," I say as I point at her.

She shrugs. "I'm down with the pineapples."

"Wednesday, we are going snorkeling before the luau. Thursday, we have the island circle bus tour that takes us out to Waimea Valley to see the waterfall, and Friday is the glass-bottom boat dinner cruise. And Saturday is our last full day, so we can just relax on the beach," I continue.

"That's cool," she replies.

"So, we're good for everything, except Pearl Harbor?"

"I'd prefer to lie on the beach all day, every day, working on my tan, and enjoy doing nothing at all but napping, eating, and drinking, but I am here for you, so we'll do all the nerdy, touristy shit that you're excited about too."

I shake my head. "Thanks."

She slides her sunglasses from the top of her head onto her nose. "You're welcome. I'm such an awesome friend."

I laugh. "Yes, you are," I agree.

We both fall silent for about an hour while we soak up the sunshine.

Pika checks in with fresh cocktails in hand.

I take the shells and thank him.

"I could get used to this," I murmur as I pass one of the drinks to Amiya.

"Girl, I could get used to *that*," she utters, tilting her head toward the water.

My gaze follows hers to the sight where three men with washboard abs, sun-kissed skin, and long, dark hair are sitting astride colorful surfboards.

Oh my.

"You and me both," I mumble.

"Perhaps the best way to get over Conrad is to get under one of them," she suggests.

"Amiya!" I gasp.

"What?" she says with a shrug. "You're young, attractive, and single. I think a hot Hawaiian fling is exactly what you need."

"They're strangers."

"Precisely. We don't know them; they don't know us. We're like ships passing in the night. No commitment. No expectations." She cuts her eyes to me. "No shared apartment leases. Just temporary adult fun."

That does sound tempting.

"For all we know, they could be here with their wives or girlfriends or boyfriends," I say.

She sets her cocktail aside and stands.

"Where are you going?" I ask.

"We'll never know if we don't ask."

"You're going to ask them if they're single?"

She nods.

"Don't do that. Please," I say as I reach up and grab her wrist, tugging her back to the lounger.

She falls back. "Fine, I won't, but I'm serious. I think a hot and heavy summer fling is just what the doctor ordered," she insists.

"I've never had casual sex before," I confess.

"Never? No one-night stand or quickie in the bathroom at a college frat party?"

"No," I say, feeling the blush hit my cheeks.

"Maybe it's time you did."

"Maybe," I whisper.

She grins, and we bring our straws to our lips as we watch the beautiful boys ride the large waves to the shore.

CHAPTER 3

Monday and Tuesday are a blur.

I canceled the Pearl Harbor tour, as Amiya had requested, and the two of us spent a blissfully lazy day at a quiet spot on the beach, where we played in the warm water and bathed ourselves in the sunshine. On Tuesday, we spent most of the morning and afternoon on the Dole Plantation Tour, which included a bonus stop at an amazing Arabica coffee tree farm, where I had the best cup of coffee I'd ever tasted, and then we spent the evening on the beach with a bottle of wine as we watched the sun set over the ocean.

Today, we are on a boat, heading out to snorkel and take in all the amazing sea life and coral off the coast of Honolulu.

"Is this okay?" Amiya asks.

I turn to see her standing in the hallway in a teeny-tiny purple bikini. She's wearing gold hoop earrings with a thin gold necklace, two chunky bangle bracelets, and a pair of gold stiletto sandals. A sheer lavender wrap is tied around her waist.

"We're going snorkeling, not yachting with the Kardashians," I quip.

She takes in my outfit—a pair of frayed blue jean shorts, a white bikini, and dark leather flip-flops—and frowns.

"It wouldn't hurt you to add a little pizzazz to your ensemble. Besides, you said we would get back in just enough time to make it to the luau."

We are, but we don't have to get dressed up for that either.

"Haven't you ever watched a movie set in Hawaii? We could run into a handsome singer with soulful eyes at this luau. We have to look our best."

"A handsome singer with soulful eyes?"

She shrugs. "I might have watched *Blue Hawaii* during our flight."

"Trust me, Elvis isn't going to be at our table," I state.

"Maybe not, but that doesn't mean other handsome Hawaiian natives won't be. Jason Momoa lives here."

I roll my eyes. "Jason Momoa is probably on some set in Hollywood."

"Will you just change?" she huffs.

"Relax. I brought a couple of gorgeous tropical maxi dresses. I plan to slip one on before dinner, but seriously, you can't wear those shoes on the boat."

She goes to the bedroom and returns, sans jewelry and wearing a pair of flat pearl-white sandals.

"Better?"

"Much," I reply.

———

When we arrive, the boat *Coral King* is waiting in slip B-3 at Huaka'i Basin Boat Harbor on Waikiki.

After a short safety presentation, we are all fitted with life jackets and equipment before boarding the craft. We set sail for a snorkeling site in Turtle Canyons, where Hawaiian green sea turtles congregate above the reef.

"Do you think one of them would give me mouth-to-mouth if I were to drown?" Amiya asks as her chin lifts to the crew in red swim trunks, seated across from us on the boat.

One is helping a small child strap on the flippers the excursion provided.

"I knew I should have worn my sexy shoes," she whispers.

I elbow her side.

"You are," I say as I raise my right leg and wiggle my foot, which is wrapped in orange rubber.

She starts to giggle when her eyes go wide. She does her best ventriloquist impersonation when she speaks without moving her lips. "Oh my God, one's coming over here."

I turn my head to see one of them approaching us, and I start to greet him when my long brown hair is caught in the breeze coming off the cerulean water and obstructs my view. By the time I have it contained by a ribbon, he has passed by and taken a seat next to the tour guide, Alex, at the back of the boat. He is staring in our direction, and his lips lift in a sexy half smile.

"I'm so glad you made me do this," Amiya says.

When the engine comes to a stop, Alex stands and instructs us all to create a single-file line.

With my snorkel gear in hand, I feel a tingling mix of excitement and anticipation as we follow the others who drop from the steps of the vessel into the ocean, one by one.

I adjust my mask and fins, and my heart races when it's my turn to leap.

Taking a deep breath, I close my eyes and drop. I keep them closed until I feel the cool embrace of the sea enveloping me and kick my way to the surface just as Amiya takes the handsome crew member's hand and lets him help her down.

Once she is by my side, we swim to the others who are skimming the water.

Alex explains what we will see and the boundaries we are to adhere to as he makes his way into the center of the group. Then, we have forty-five minutes to explore the roped-off area on our own.

Amid the vibrant coral formations and the kaleidoscope of colorful tropical fish, the giant green sea turtles swim so close to us that we can almost reach out and touch them.

I am in complete awe.

My only complaint is that the crowd is so large, and as other boats come close to the reef, their parties join us in the water.

We are literally elbow to elbow by the time the last vessel anchors.

I am skimming the rippling water, watching a spinner dolphin playing just outside the ropes when a figure catches my eye.

A man with a muscular back and a mop of unruly, dark hair is swimming effortlessly through the water. I watch as he gracefully navigates around the other explorers, his movements fluid and mesmerizing. When he surfaces, I recognize the playful blue eyes behind his mask. It's one of the guys who was surfing the day we arrived.

My attention is pulled from him as a flying fish emerges and crashes back down in front of me, and I let out a surprised scream.

"Avie, are you all right?"

I hear Amiya's concerned voice, and I turn to see her wading with Alex and his coworker.

"I'm fine," I shout.

I'm about to swim to them when a voice interrupts my movement.

"Looks like someone wants to be friends," the man says with a chuckle, his eyes crinkling at the corners as he grins.

The little fish flies out of the water again and splashes salty liquid in my face as he lands by my chest.

"Well, he's an awfully persistent thing, isn't he?" I reply playfully.

He laughs, and it echoes through the sea as we tread it's surface.

"Absolutely. But I can't say I blame him. Showing off for a pretty girl."

My heart skips.

He paddles toward me and stops once he reaches my side, water droplets glistening on his skin.

"I'm Sebastian, by the way," he says, extending a hand.

"Avie," I reply, shaking his hand with a smile.

"Didn't I see you on the beach the other day?" he asks.

"I'm not sure. Maybe," I lie. "My friend and I arrived on the island on Sunday."

"Where are you staying?" he asks.

"At The Stanhope Grand Resort on Waikiki."

He grins. "Yeah, I'm sure it was you."

"We did notice some guys surfing. Was that you?"

He bites his lip and nods. "Yep, my buddies and I are here to catch some waves for a few days before heading back home."

I open my mouth to ask where home is when a whistle sounds, drawing our attention to Alex standing aboard the *Coral King*.

"I think that means my time is up," I mutter, disappointment in my voice.

I slide my eyes back to his.

The sun has dipped lower, casting a warm amber glow over the water.

"It was a pleasure to meet you, Avie."

"Same," I say.

He kicks his feet and begins to float away on his back.

"I hope we run into each other again," he bellows, and a flutter of excitement dances in my chest at the sound of his deep voice.

"Maybe we will," I call back.

I swim over to the boat and take Alex's hand as he helps me climb aboard. I grab a towel from the basket on the right and wrap it around myself. I pluck the fins from my feet and walk to the bench seat where Amiya is chatting with the hot crew guy.

"Hey, I lost you out there," she says as I take a seat.

"Did you have a good time?" I ask.

She leans in and wraps an arm around my shoulders. "The best," she squeals.

"Me too."

CHAPTER 4

When we step onto the sandy shore and navigate the footpath, the distant sounds of drums and laughter are carried by the ocean breeze.

I can't help but feel a sense of excitement as Amiya and I make our way toward the sounds.

We showered after the snorkeling excursion and took a long nap in the hammocks on our deck before dressing for tonight. I skipped makeup, except for swiping on some lip gloss, and spritzed on a moisturizing mist. Then, I pulled my beach-wave hair into a long ponytail and slipped on a strapless, vibrantly colored maxi dress and sandals.

The Hawaiian luau is in full swing when we make it to the venue.

We take a few moments to mingle with the crowd and take in the enchanting music and festive dancers.

The tantalizing aroma of grilled food fills the air as we take a spot at a communal table.

We settle in and watch the fire dancers mesmerize the gathering.

That's when I notice him.

My eyes meet Sebastian's across the crowd, and he and his two friends make their way over to us.

He stops across the table and smiles.

"Hi. Sebastian, isn't it?" I ask.

"Yes. It's nice to see you again, Avie."

We stare at one another for a long moment when a throat clears.

I look over at Amiya's expectant face.

"Oh, this is my friend Amiya. Sebastian and I met while snorkeling this afternoon," I explain.

She raises an eyebrow.

"And this is Parker and Anson," Sebastian introduces.

"Mind if we join you?" Anson asks.

Amiya extends her arm to the empty seat across from us. "Not at all."

The three of them sit down, and with the rhythmic beat of the drums in the background, we strike up a conversation.

"What brings you fellas to Oahu?" Amiya asks.

"Work," Parker says.

"Work? I thought you guys were just catching some waves for a few days," I say to Sebastian.

"That too. We work on a couple's personal yacht in the summers, traveling from California to Hawaii. I am the captain, and these two are part of my crew."

"You sail a yacht from California to Hawaii?" I say.

"Yep, every summer for the past four years. They have a house on the island, and they bring friends and their kids on vacation."

"How long does that take?" Amiya asks.

"It takes two weeks at sea to get here. They usually stay two to three weeks, and then we sail them back," Sebastian explains.

"So, your entire summer is bringing them here and taking them back?" I ask.

"Pretty much, but they pay us very well, and we get to stay on the yacht for free while we're on the island. So, it's a sweet deal," Parker replies.

"Damn, that's a cool gig," Amiya says.

She looks at me. "It sure beats waiting tables all summer."

"Where are you ladies from, and what brings you to Oahu?" Anson asks.

"We're from Atlanta, and we both attend the University of Georgia. We'll be graduating next spring," Amiya answers.

Parker leans back in his chair. "I knew it. I knew I heard a sweet Southern accent."

We fall into an easy conversation as we are served a delicious feast of poi, fish, roasted kalua pig, limu, breadfruit, sweet potatoes, lau lau, opihi, and a selection of fresh fruits and haupia.

As the night wears on, we find ourselves on the dance floor.

Our laughter mingles with the music as Amiya and I try our hand at hula dancing, following the instructions of the locals.

The boys join us, and before I know it, Sebastian and I are moving in harmony, our bodies swaying to the melody. In that moment, it feels like the crowd has faded away, leaving only the two of us.

As the luau reaches its end, we steal away to the shoreline with our bellies full of wonderful food and cocktails in our hands.

The moon's soft glow illuminates the waves, casting a magical spell upon the beach.

Sebastian and Anson build a fire, and we sit and enjoy the night breeze and the sound of the waves meeting the sand.

Parker receives a text from a girl he met earlier in the week, and he and Anson talk Amiya into accompanying them to the tiki bar a few miles down the beach.

"You sure you don't want to come? It's still early," Amiya asks.

I shake my head. "Nah. I just want to stay and enjoy the moonlit beach a while longer," I say.

"I'll stay and keep her company."

Her eyes slide to Sebastian, and she smiles.

Then, she turns back to me and leans down to whisper in my ear, "Remember what I said about getting under a hot stranger."

I push her away, and she winks at me.

"All right, you two kids have fun. Don't do anything I wouldn't do," she says as she follows the guys, and I watch them fade out of sight.

"They'll take good care of her. You don't have to worry. Trust me," Sebastian assures.

They should be the ones worried.

I turn back to him and smile. "I do."

And it's true. I just met him, but for some reason, I do trust him.

It's probably the cocktails.

"What do you say to a night swim?" he asks.

"I do have my bathing suit on under my dress," I muse.

He stands and offers me his hand. I take it, and he helps me to my feet.

He watches intently as I shimmy out of my dress, letting it fall to the sand.

Then, I take off running toward the water, and he gives chase.

I dive into the dark depths of the ocean, and when I surface, Sebastian is at my side.

He wraps an arm around my waist and tugs me close.

Before I have a chance to overthink, I bring my lips to his.

His hands slide down to my ass, and he hoists me up onto his hips. My legs wrap around him as his teeth nip at my bottom lip, and I moan.

Taking the opportunity, he deepens the kiss, and my fingers slip into the wet hair at his nape, holding on.

When we finally come up for air, I drop my legs and release him. Then, I slink back into the water and take off under the rushing waves.

He catches up to me in minutes, and when he reaches out to clasp my waist again, I twist and kick, splashing water in his face. Squealing, I attempt to edge past him, but I can't escape his firm grip.

Finally, I give in and slip my arms around his shoulders.

"You're beautiful, Avie," he whispers against my skin.

I rest my forehead against his and let him hold me.

An electric current runs between us, and I can feel his cock twitch as my heat brushes against him.

I gasp, and his eyes widen slightly as his lips part.

I can feel the loud thump of my heart beating in my chest as my breath quickens.

I can hear Amiya's voice in my head. *"A hot and heavy summer fling is just what the doctor ordered."*

I go still as the water laps around us.

"Avie?"

I bring my eyes to his, and my legs tighten around him, my core nestling against his erection.

That's all it takes.

He brings his lips to my shoulder and peppers a trail of kisses to my collarbone as he walks us back to the shoreline.

I toss my head back to give him better access, which causes my chest to press into his.

The thin, wet fabric of my bikini leaves nothing to the imagination.

He marches us up the steps to the dock that leads to the yacht as he cups one breast with his hand and gently kneads it.

I close my eyes and moan, and we walk aboard the yacht and down a hallway that leads to a small bedroom.

He kicks the door shut behind us, and we fall onto the tiny double bed.

He lets go of me long enough to reach around, undoing the straps tied at my neck, and pulls the white fabric down.

Plump pink nipples greet him.

"Fuck," he groans.

He sucks one between his teeth and gives it a rough tug. I buck off the bed, and he releases it, licks it gently, and blows across it. It tightens to a hard peak, and he wraps his lips around it once more.

My hips start to rock into him, and as soon as I find the contact my body is searching for, I hasten my movement.

The friction feels so good as I slide up and down on him.

His mouth moves to the other breast and sucks it as I continue to glide against his eager cock.

When I can take no more, I reach between us and into his trunks.

He bites down on my nipple, and I gasp.

I wrap my fingers around him and pull him free.

"Give me your mouth, Avie," he commands.

I lean in and do just that.

Our tongues wrestle as I continue to caress him.

His hand shimmies down and brushes across my core.

I bite my lip, and my body trembles as he guides a finger inside my bottoms, where he finds my entrance wet and ready, and begins to pump it in and out slowly.

His head falls to my shoulder, and I take all of his weight as I lose myself to the pleasure.

"Oh God," I groan.

I release him, hook my thumbs into the band of his shorts, and tug them down.

He bears up so I can skim them down his legs, and then he kicks them onto the floor. Then, he shimmies my bottoms down my thighs.

He takes hold of his cock and guides it to my opening, and his eyes come to mine, searching for permission.

I raise my hips to meet him, and he slides inside of me.

It feels so damn good as he thrusts forward, picking up the pace and going deeper and deeper until he fills me completely.

My muscles start to tighten around him, and I scream his name as he finds my clit and circles it with his thumb, applying just the right amount of pressure I need.

I rotate my hips and move more urgently, seeking the release my body wants so badly.

My legs tense around him, and I begin to shudder as I get closer.

"Look at me, Avie," he commands.

My head snaps up, and he watches as I lose the battle and shatter around him.

My cries fill the cabin and echo against the walls.

Then, he stiffens atop me, and his cry mingles with mine as I milk his orgasm from him. It's the guttural sound.

His head stays buried in my neck as our breathing calms.

When he finally looks up, he asks, "Are you okay?"

I nod.

He brings his hand to the side of my face and cups my cheek.

Then, he leans down and kisses me gently.

"That was incredible," he whispers against my lips.

Then, he falls to the side, tugs me into his chest, and pulls the covers over us.

Before I can even wrap my head around what just happened, I hear the rhythmic panting of his breath in my ear, and I know he has fallen asleep.

Carefully, I untangle myself from his arms and climb quietly from the bed.

I gather my suit and tiptoe out into the hallway of the boat and shut the door gently.

Then, I make my way back to the beach to gather my dress and sandals and head back to my bungalow.

CHAPTER 5

I awaken to the sound of the covers rustling and the feel of Amiya climbing in bed beside me.

I peek over at her.

"What time is it?" I ask.

"Six in the morning," she mumbles.

I blink against the sunlight bathing the deck and sit up.

"Are you just coming in?" I ask.

"Yeah, I ran into the hunky crewman from the *Coral King* at the bar, and the two of us took a bottle of rum and a couple of beach towels to the shore and made good use of it all. I woke up with a pounding head and sand in all the wrong places," she grumbles.

"That's going to cause some uncomfortable chaffing," I say as I plop back and pull the duvet up to my chin.

"Worth it," she says.

"We're not going to make it to the waterfall today, are we?" I ask.

She opens an eye and looks at me. "Nope."

I shrug. "I'm good with that."

The truth is, I'm exhausted. Deliciously so.

We snuggle in and drift off to the sound of the light rain that has begun to fall on the deck.

And I dream of sailing the open seas on a yacht with a beautiful stranger.

I awaken to ringing coming from somewhere in the bungalow.

I roll over to see Amiya is still dead to the world.

The chiming stops, and I sit up and swing my legs over the edge of the bed.

Standing, I make my way to the bathroom.

The ringing begins again, and I follow the sound to the coat closet in the foyer beside the door.

I open it as the sound halts and then starts once again.

I find Amiya's bag and fish the phone out just as it stops again.

The screen illuminates, and the wallpaper of me and my parents smiling stares back at me with a notification of six missed calls.

All from Conrad.

What the hell does he want?

I turn off the ringer so it doesn't wake up Amiya and carry the phone into the kitchen with me.

I debate on whether or not I should return the calls.

What if it's an emergency?

The thought crosses my mind just as a text comes through.

I read it and freeze at his words.

Amiya emerges from the bedroom, yawning and rubbing the sleep from her eyes.

"I need some hair of the dog," she mutters, stopping short when she sees my face.

Her eyes fall to the phone in my hand.

"What's wrong?" she asks.

I burst into tears.

She rushes to me and wraps her arms around me.

"I think I made a mistake," I whimper.

The phone slips from my hand, and she reads the message from Conrad.

"Fuck me," she hisses before dropping it to the counter.

She lets me cry into her chest for a few more minutes, and then she leans back.

"Let's go get some breakfast and talk about it," she suggests.

"Okay."

I sniffle, and she wraps an arm around my shoulders and leads me to the bedroom to get dressed.

I let Amiya talk me into taking the rest of our days in Hawaii to get my head together and decide what I want my future to look like.

Since I was a little girl, it has been my dream to graduate with a degree in marine science and apply for a job as an aquarist at the Georgia Aquarium.

Is that still what I want in life?

She doesn't leave my side as we take the glass-bottom boat and dinner cruise tour.

I stare down at the natural beauty at our feet.

This is what I love. The ocean. The sea life.

We spend our last day on the island on the beach with Pika serving our breakfast, lunch, and dinner in our cabana.

I decide to stay at the bungalow and spend time in the sauna as Amiya gets dressed and attends the final party at the resort.

I don't want to risk running into Sebastian. I wouldn't know what to say to him. I snuck out that night without even leaving a note.

It was for the best.

We hadn't exchanged phone numbers, and we don't even know each other's last names. Our night of passion will forever be a beautiful memory of my time here in paradise, but that's where it needs to stay.

In my memory.

When Amiya returns, she informs me that there was no sign of Sebastian or the other guys, so I guess he feels the same way about our brief tryst.

The next morning, we pack and say goodbye to our cozy bungalow as Pika comes to help us with our things and loads us into a car.

"Thank you for everything," I tell him as I wrap him in a tight hug.

"You're very welcome, Miss Carrigan. I hope your life journey leads you back to Oahu one day," Pika says as he returns my embrace.

"Me too."

The driver whisks us away to the airport, and we get checked in for our flight and make our way to the waiting plane.

I take my seat beside the window and stare out at the island as Amiya holds my hand.

Goodbye, palm trees and blue seas.

We were only here for a week, and yet it felt like a lifetime. I'm not the same girl who boarded the plane in Atlanta.

This island changed me.

I fish my phone from my purse before tucking it in the back of the seat in front of me as Amiya chats away with the gentleman across the aisle.

Tapping the screen so I can place it into Airplane mode, I pull up the text from Conrad one more time.

Conrad: I miss you so damn much. I'm sorry. I fucked up. Please come to New York.

New York ...

Thank you for reading. To continue in my world check out my popular series, Balsam Ridge and Poplar Falls.

A MERMAID AND HER STAR

ANGELINA M. LOPEZ

Marina Torres didn't know how she got here.

She floated cheek-down on the paddle board, her toes trailing in the water as the gentle sun warmed her back and the tender breeze wandered over her skin. She didn't think she'd ever felt anything as delicious as a Hawaiian summer day.

She opened her eyes. Across the expanse of teal blue water, a voluptuous green-blue she couldn't believe was real, she stared at the Mokes, twin tiny islands of sand and yellow grasses, rising out of the water like the undulating humps of a sea monster. In the 21years of her life, this was the farthest she'd ever been from her hometown of Freedom, Kansas. But there was nothing scary here.

How in the world, she thought again as she dabbled the fingers not holding onto the paddle through the water, did she end up here?

She knew the steps. She'd filled out the application last fall for the Medina-Esperanza Internship Program, which connected talented citizens from billionaire Roxanne Medina's hometown of Freedom with paid, temporary opportunities in her global organization. Marina got her reply while she was still at KU finishing her fall-semester finals: She'd been invited to use her soon-to-be degree in journalism with a minor in music to create social media and content for rock star Aish Salinger, Roxanne Medina's brother-in-law, who would be recording an album that summer at the world-famous Island Sound Studios in Honolulu.

Marina had cried, nearly thrown up, called her mom, then her Grandmo Loretta, then been bombarded by calls, texts, Instagram DMs, and SnapChats from everyone in her family. She'd responded to the invitation and accepted the position.

Over the course of the spring, she'd received the plane ticket, location of the huge beach house where the whole team chronicling the making of the new album – including Aish Salinger and his wife, winemaker Princesa Sofia – would be staying, and suggestions on what to bring for their two-month stay on Oahu. In Hawaii.

Hawaii!

Physically, she knew how she'd gotten here. A week ago, she'd stumbled out of the plane after a nine-hour flight, bumping her guitar case into everything before a flight attendant had steadied her and then slipped a flower lei over her head. They'd driven across the island from the airport, through the lushest green with the world's tallest, most-terrifying cliffs, to emerge on the other side in front of the world's longest, most beautiful shoreline. It was her first cliffs and her first shoreline, but she was certain she was right. The driver had driven them until the road ran out at a gate. When the gate rambled back, it revealed two, many-decked beach houses separated by a bridge of black lava rocks, a stretch of sand, palm trees hanging over the water, and the Mokes. Their little corner of paradise came with tiny islands.

How in the world did she get here?

Today was her first day off after three days chronicling Aish in the studio and while she wanted to explore Oahu, she figured she would spend the day drowsing on the paddle board that she'd gotten pretty good at as a first-timer and adjusting to the fact that she was hanging out with a rock star and a princess. When was someone going to pinch her and wake her up?

Her board bumped into the black, jagged lava rocks that made up the jetty between the beach houses that were in sight of each other but far enough away to provide space and privacy. A shadow fell over her.

"You're trespassing on my beach," a gruff voice said.

She yelped with surprise, dropped the paddle she'd been hanging on to, and scrambled up on her hands. Above her, a man stood on the levee outlined by the sun like Poseidon risen up from the water. He was a solid shadow, but the perimeter of him showed turquoise board shorts, well-defined biceps, broad brown shoulders, a trim black scruff over a square jaw, and a thick swoop of black hair as he looked down at her.

She should be inoculated to shocks by now, but she still felt little spots around the edge of her vision. There was no way it was him. But it was him. She knew that outline like the back of her hand.

She saw she had bobbed further over to the other beach house's side of the cove than she'd realized. "Sorry," she coughed out through her shock, pushing herself fully up and straddling the board. She began to pull the paddle back to her with the line strapped to it, anything to avoid looking up at him and full-on freaking out. "We were told the other house was empty."

"It isn't," he said, low and growly. Her toes curled in the warm water. "I'm gonna have to call security."

"What?!" Now she did look up at him. "Why?"

She wanted to point out that there were no private beaches in Hawaii, but she swallowed that along with her crushing disappointment. He wasn't a sexy, avenging sea god. The man whose picture was her screensaver and whose hit show she'd bought Blu-Rays of every season, even though she didn't have a Blu-Ray player, was an asshole. "I'll just go back to the house and let Aish and Sofia know—"

"You're with Aish and Sofia? Shit. Well now I'm going to have to kick all of y'all out."

"What?!" she screeched. Javier Campos wasn't a good guy or a laidback Texan, no matter what all the co-stars and charitable event organizers and the head of his foundation said. He was a big stupid jerk she'd spent way too much of the last five years adoring. He was no better than the farmer who'd called the cops on her and her cousins for picking blackberries out of the thorny ditch on the edge of his property. "That's ridiculous. You're going to evict us because I touched your side of the ocean?" God, how would Aish and Sofia take it when they discovered their intern got them kicked out of their summer house? Javier Campos was screwing with her life. "There has to be something I can do!"

He stayed quiet as he continued to lord over her. She'd jammed her paddle against the levee to keep from scraping against it; the only sound was the lap of the water against her board and the black, sharp rocks. He slid his hands into his shorts as he watched her. Prickles rippled over Marina's skin.

Without warning, he squatted down. Now she could see his face fully. She was a yard away from Javier Campos, staring up into the face she'd spent hours staring at, and helplessly her eyes wandered over his dark summer scruff, his bossy nose with that slight ding to the left, his overlong black hair moving in the breeze, until they looked into hazel-gold eyes as unreal as the ocean and as bright as seaglass. Those eyes, as intent as an oncoming storm, were looking right back into hers.

She prayed he didn't notice what was happening in her bikini top.

"You could sing me a song," he said without a hint of a smile.

The easy waves rolled beneath her, sending her closer to the rocks. "You heard me?" she asked, like a girl responding to a voice in a seashell.

There was a deck across the road from the beach house, and every night since she'd arrived, after spending the whole day surrounded by people, Marina had taken her guitar to the deck and sung to the sea and the endless stars and the dark outline of the Mokes. She'd minored in music because she wanted to go into music journalism. But the music, her music, was only for her.

He nodded, making his straight black hair fall across those golden eyes as he squatted there. "I've started drinking my whiskey outside to listen." The slight drawl that never showed in his voice when he played a 32nd-century space detective, the drawl of a 26-year-old man from the oil fields of West Texas, sounded weirdly familiar. He sounded like the boys she'd grown up with. "I woke up on the porch this morning. You lullabied me right to sleep." He pushed his hair back, showing off that incredible face. "You could be a mermaid lurin' me into the ocean. I should kick you out just for that."

He was as bad as her cousins or the boys on the playground who'd chase her, pull her ponytail, then wonder why she didn't chase them back.

She shook her head, trying to make what was happening align with a world that made sense, but didn't look away from him. "I can't believe you were just screwing with me," she said as the board rolled on a wave and her bikini-ed body rolled with it. His eyes flicked down before they met hers again. "You should know better than to screw with people with less power than you."

She couldn't believe *that* was what made him smile. It was a big smile, as bright-white as the sun and crinkling his cheeks, and it made him look less hot and so much sweeter. He seldom smiled in pictures.

"Want to call my mama and tell on me?" He pushed to standing and, without warning, dove over the front end of her board into the water. Astonished, she watched the ripple and eel of him in the perfectly clear Pacific water as he swam away then back. He popped up at her knee.

"She'd like you," he said, sleeking his hair back from his broad, strong forehead as he floated there. "Want to talk to my mama?"

TV star Javier Campos—his face wet and strong and handsome, his shoulders brown and sleek and muscular, his body naked except for turquoise shorts—bobbed in the Pacific Ocean half a foot from her left knee. Every centimeter of skin from her knee to the edge of her black bikini felt like it was sizzling like a sparkler.

She tucked her drying, short, brown curls behind her ear so she could look her fill. "Your mom should know that her son who owns fancy beach houses and fights book banning and has two Emmys is still a big jerk."

He smiled at her like she'd pull down her black bikini top. He smiled at her like *he* was about to pull down her bikini top. "Oh yeah," he said on a drawly laugh. "Now *I'm* starting to like you. What's your story, Ms. Mermaid?"

"No way," she said. "You first. Aish and Sofia said the other house was empty."

Although he still smiled, the tease in his face went down by a lot. He gave a huff like nothing was funny. His eyes wandered away then settled back on her. She wondered what could make him look that way in the middle of paradise.

Finally, as he tread in the teal-blue water, he said, "I walked off set a week ago. That's where I was supposed to be for the summer."

She couldn't believe it. The big-budget film, with its acclaimed director, amazing co-stars, and super-cool mystery-noir plot, was going to be Javier Campos's launch into movie fame. He'd had offers before, but had always said in interviews that, as the highest-paid Latino in television, the role had to be just right. That he'd walked away from such a well-publicized moment was actually harder to believe than the reality that she was sleeping in a beach house he owned.

"I'm so sorry," she said. "Here..." She leaned carefully back on the board. "Grab onto the nose." When he did, she adjusted her weight so the paddle board was balanced as it carried them both. She was glad to see his shoulders relax as he watched her curiously, the sun gleaming in his sleek, black hair.

"I thought mermaids wanted to drown their vics," he said.

"That's one way to make sure you don't kick us out."

They floated quietly and Marina marveled that the same water moving over his naked body flowed over her calves and between her toes.

He ran his teeth over his bottom lip. It made her lick hers.

"You're the first person I've talked to who hasn't asked why I quit," he said.

Marina thought of NDAs and lawsuits and unnamed sources. She thought of the noise of his phone and email and social media, and his beach house on the tip of Oahu that was so quiet a woman could be heard singing down the road.

She wondered if this wealthy, much-watched man felt as small as she did in this big ocean. "Although you're a jerk in person, you've always seemed like a pretty decent guy on paper," she said. "I'm sure you had your reasons."

His face as he stared at her stole the rest of her words.

Marina's parents had divorced when she was young and they'd both married again quickly into okay relationships. Still, she'd always felt the only benefit of coupling up was that it made it easier to raise kids and buy a house. That was until she'd gone home post-graduation and visited the family's bar on Milagro Street to see her favorite cousin Alex, who was back in town. When Marina walked in, there'd been a huge white guy sitting at the bar with floppy dark hair and glasses and a button-up shirt tucked into jeans that were ironed. The way he was looking at Alex...Marina felt like she'd walked into their bedroom. She would have snuck back out if the cowbells over the door hadn't given her away.

Javier Campos had just looked at her with a hint of the way that professor had looked at her cousin. It made Marina feel like a miracle and a gift and puzzle all at the same time.

Just as quickly, Javier Campos shifted to stare at the Mokes. Marina heard the caw of island birds above them.

"I didn't know they were gonna expect me to speak with an accent," he said, his voice coming out from way down deep in his chest. "They insisted it was more 'realistic.' I didn't know they were going to have me eat salsa and give me a throw-away line about my sister's quinceañera without any respectful Latinidad in the rest of the story." His knuckles flexed where they gripped her board. "It's so easy for them to look through white. But they behave like melanin is a fucking force field—the more there is, the harder it is for them to see the person and the actor." He sounded exhausted by battle. "I couldn't..." He shook his head then looked cautiously back at her. "When we get it right, they pat us on the head. But when we get it wrong.... Man, do they remember." He ran his hand over his eyes then scrubbed it over his head, making his black hair stand in wet peaks. "I wasn't going to fuck this up for every Latine actor who comes after me."

With no other person in sight and without a peep from civilization—no planes roared overhead, no boat sped across the water—they could have been the last two people on earth. It gave her the strength, the imperative, to do what she was about to do.

She leaned forward on one arm, reached out her hand, and touched Javier Campos. She combed her fingers through his thick hair, settling it down where he'd made it wild, smoothing it as she gently raked her fingernails over his scalp, then combed her fingers around his ear. When she ran her palm across the scruff of his cheek, the sandpaper shush of it lit up her arm. "It's okay to take a break so you can keep fighting," she said softly. "You'll remind us all to fight."

He looked at her like she'd shoved him under the waves. "Fuck," he said, grabbing her hand and dragging it to his mouth. Staring at her like she was keeping him from drowning, Javier Campos kissed her palm then pressed the hot tip of his tongue to the exact center of it, tasting her.

Her hand spasmed around his hard jaw as her pussy squeezed. He lifted his chin and freed his mouth. "Why does your sweetness make me want to take a bite out of you?" he asked, his eyes like lightening.

"That's my job," she said, running her thumb over the divot in his chin, now that she had free rein of it. "I lured you into the water. Now I get to eat you up."

Was that *her* talking?

"Fuck," he spat again, his black brows scrunching together. "Let me up there with you."

She nodded fast and desperate because if this was all a dream, she wanted to get to the good part before she woke up. "Just..." She leaned far back onto her elbows as he pushed down on the nose, tested it, then popped himself up and straddled the board, never taking his eyes off of her. Sunlight sparkled in the water dripping down his brown skin and taut muscles and she started to push up so she could grab him before he disappeared.

"Wait," he rushed out, stopping her. His eyes raced over her and she saw herself through them—girl stretched back on the board, skin just as brown as his, thighs and tummy and breasts offered up with only little scraps of black bikini to interrupt the view. He reached out then hesitated, squeezing his hand into a fist before he stretched it back out and pressed it to her stomach. "You're real," he said, like there'd been a doubt.

She sucked in at the sensation of his hot hand covering her from waist dip to waist dip.

"I can't believe you're real," he said, and they both stared as his hand moved with her breath.

This was a fantasy, but not a dream.

Still back on an elbow, she pushed his hand down until his palm held the heart of her. "I'm real," she said. "I want you."

He groaned like she was electrocuting the water and he pressed his palm between her thighs, shoving just right, and Marina's head fell back on a moan-gasp as she widened her thighs and rolled her hips to meet the pressure, the board helping her as the water lapped over her thighs. An orgasm usually took intense mental concentration and half an hour and enough friction on her clitoris to start a fire, but since it also usually involved Javier Campos's face, she was already half there.

When he growled, "Pretty girl," deep and low, Marina whimpered and that was before she felt him tug her bikini bottom to one side and stroke two fingers between her folds, grunt at how juicy she was for him, then twist his hand to pet her clit with his thumb. Her stomach jumped at the sensation. "Jesus, you're pretty."

He gently pushed those two fingers inside and Marina gritted her teeth and whined through them at the pleasure.

She forced her head up on her neck so she could watch. This brown, sun-soaked man had his hands between her legs, was staring where he was holding her suit to one side while his fingers pulsed inside of her and his thumb thrummed over her clit. Her thighs were trembling against the water, and his cock was a thick rod in his turquoise swim trunks.

He looked up and caught her staring at it with open-mouthed pleasure on her face. Trapping her in his gaze, he let go of her suit and gripped his cock through his shorts. He stroked it slowly. Then he gently pulled his fingers out of her body, raised them to his lips, and slid them into his mouth. His eyes closed and he clenched the head of his dick as he sucked them clean.

"Oh my God," she cried, feeling the want of her rush out, a tidal wave of welcome. None of this could be happening. "Oh my God, I need you inside me."

She shoved up as he grabbed for her and the board beneath them rocked dangerously but then he lifted her and slung her thighs over his and she clung to his biceps and he shifted to the center of the board, steadying it even as her brain exploded into a million stars as she realized she was pressed skin to skin, pussy to cock, to this beautiful man. Javier Campos met her eyes then bit her chin then her bottom lip then, eyes still open, pushed his tongue into her mouth and Marina drowned in him.

He tasted like the whiskey he'd talked about. He tasted like seawater and man. She never wanted anything else in her mouth as Javier Campos squeezed her ass and ran his hands over her naked back and shoved down a bikini cup so her nipple pressed against his chest then clenched her head so he could fully own her mouth. The whole time, she was grinding and grinding and grinding against his hard, hard—

"I'm gonna—"

"Like hell you are." He lifted her up, off the ridge of his cock, and leaned slightly back to keep them steady on the paddle board as she trembled. When she saw the tensed muscles of his abs, however, she gave up restraint and eagerly rubbed her pussy against that washboard. He smacked her ass, so loud it echoed over the water, and she squealed as the board tilted precariously and they were almost tossed into the drink.

She laughed as he squeezed his thighs around the board to steady them then moaned when he slipped his hand between her legs from behind to pull her bottoms to one side.

Below and above, he teased her lips. "How much are you going to hate me if I tell you I brought a condom?" he asked against her mouth.

She sighed in relief as he pushed a finger inside. "How could I hate you?" she breathed. "Who wouldn't want to have sex with a mermaid?"

She wasn't a mermaid. A week ago, she'd never even been in the ocean. She was just Marina Torres from Freedom, Kansas, a newly-minted college graduate who was in the middle of a fever dream, but when Javier Campos growled, "Get my cock out," before he sucked on her tongue, she felt like a mythical creature as she reached into his suit, stroked her hand down hard, hot skin before she pulled him out, long and thick in her hand, then snatched from him the condom packet he'd taken out from the back pocket of his trunks. She ripped it open with her teeth, pulled the latex out, then, as he kissed her and got her ready with his fingers, she slid the condom over his cock.

She bit his nose when he chuckled at her for sliding the torn wrapper in the bikini cup still covering her right boob. "No one's littering in my ocean," she said.

He stopped laughing when his mouth wandered over to her left nipple, heaving there right in front of his face, and she stopped chiding when he lifted her and slowly lowered her down onto his cock. She rocked her hips to ease the way, but being filled with him felt like the inevitability of the water meeting the sand.

When she was fully settled against him, when he was fully inside her, they both stilled. He panted against her breast. Her lips pressed into his hair. She could feel the wet bunch of his swimsuit beneath her, the corded muscles of his hips against the give of her thighs, the sculpted body his job demanded supporting hers. Floating in the Pacific Ocean with a man inside her shouldn't have felt like coming home.

"Sweetheart," he whispered against her skin. She heard him swallow, and then he kissed her nipple. "Sweetheart, you feel so good." He rubbed his thumb over the small of her back like he already knew that was one of her most sensitive spots and she full-body shivered and he deep-belly groaned then she squeezed him inside her.

They moaned in unison.

She was instantly, desperately hungry and so was he by the way he buried his hand in her curls and dragged her mouth to his, claiming it as he lifted her up with an arm around her hips then pushed inside as he let her back down, demanding and urgent. She dug her nails into his shoulders and back, clinging with the muscles inside her, gripping as tightly as she could to give pleasure and to demand it back. The water churned around him as they kissed and grabbed, both selfish and desperate and generous, and the foaming water felt like it washed them clean, washed away the TV star and the mermaid and left two skin-and-bone souls who had the incredible luck of finding each other.

He fucked her so good. When she started to vibrate on top of him, when she felt like nothing but ecstasy from her mouth to her toes in the warm water, he pulled her head and stared into her eyes.

"Do I call you my mermaid?" he said between gritted teeth, shoving in and holding her so close.

She was blinded by pleasure and his gorgeous sunset eyes. "Marina," she moaned out. She might never see him again. She didn't care. "Your Marina."

Her orgasm was volcanic and, dimly through the explosion in her own brain and body, she heard him give a sob of surrender and relief, like he was throwing himself into her fire. She shook on top of him, surely evaporating the water around them for miles.

Minutes later, wrapped around him and holding him close, her feet up on the board and heels resting against his bare butt, she began to cry.

"Hey, hey," he said, rubbing her back, and squeezing her even closer. "Hey, what's wrong, I—"

She raised her head from the crook of his neck so he could see her smile as tears dripped into her mouth.

"I just..." Joy throbbed in her tear-choked voice. She motioned at the islands, the water, the endlessly blue sky, and then down at their laps, where he was still inside her. "Look at where we are. Look at what just happened." She wiped at her cheeks and for the rest of her days, her tears would taste like this ocean. "This is the most magical moment of my life so far."

She focused on his impossibly handsome face. "Thank you for being here for it," she said. "Thank you for sharing it with me."

She saw again that mystified and amazed look flash across his face as he stared back at her. His fingers flexed into her hips, like he was keeping her from swimming away.

Finally, he said, "I like that. The most magical moment of your life 'so far.'" He gave the dimple in her left cheek the softest kiss. "Thank you for giving me magic, too. I needed it."

He kissed the dimple in her other cheek before he said, "Want to go for a swim?"

Without warning and still inside her, he tipped them both over into the water, used himself as her paddle board for a few strokes, then finally slipped out to deal with the condom, which he shoved into his zippered back pocket along with the wrapper. When she began to rearrange her bikini top, he asked for it as a souvenir, so then she demanded his trunks, which he gladly handed over because of its "gross DNA pocket", and soon, they were two naked people paddling around after each other in the Pacific, with no destination or goal, no background or consequences, simply a mermaid and star who didn't know how they'd gotten here, but who both wanted to make this fantasy last as long as they could.

A nighttime, a summer, or a lifetime all seemed like very real possibilities.

Thank you for reading. To continue reading more of my work, start with my *Washington Post* best romance of 2022, After Hours at Milagro Street by Angelina M. Lopez.

MOVE
BRITTAINY CHERRY

MARIE

He was late.

I'd been praying for the past fifteen minutes that he'd be late, because if he was late, it would give me an excuse to leave. I should've never come in the first place.

My heart pounded at a speed that I couldn't comprehend. My palms were sweaty as the sun beamed down overhead. I tried my best to shake off my nerves, but said nerves were pretty much choking me.

What am I doing here? Why was I in Maui, Hawaii, wearing a wetsuit, holding a surfboard in my hands? Bradley would've thought I was crazy. Or, really, really cool. It was hard to tell sometimes what my son would've thought of me, and he hadn't been around for a while to express his thoughts.

His father, Frank, on the other hand, was loud and clear about what he thought of me.

"You're not going to get on the dang plane. You're scared straight. And even if you did go, you'd stay cooped up in your hotel the whole time."

Nothing like an ex-husband to tell you about yourself.

Half the reason I'd showed up on the trip was to prove him wrong. The other half was because Bradley wanted me to go on this trip. It meant something to him. And anything that meant a lot to him meant even more to me.

Maybe I was going through one of those midlife crisis things.

As the waves crashed against the shore, my stomach repeatedly flipped.

Oh, my goodness, I was going to vomit any second now. I felt so out of my element and uncomfortable with…everything. I was pretty sure that the wetsuit was wedging up in places that wetsuits weren't meant to wedge. Gosh, I felt like a penguin in that dang suit. All I had to do was waddle a little and the transformation would've been completed.

I glanced at the time on my phone once more.

Six-thirty-two in the evening.

This instructor was beyond late.

Two minutes, to be exact.

That was it! I was done waiting. I was going to pack up my things, get on a plane, and head straight back to Maine, where quiet and somberness existed for me.

And loneliness.

There was a lot of loneliness back in Maine.

Frank said the lonely part was my fault, because after Bradley's health issues, I'd refused to put myself out there anymore. Yet there I was—putting myself out there. In a bizarre way, nonetheless. That was exactly the reason I somehow ended up across the United States, on a beautiful island that pictures never did justice, thinking I could be brave enough to try surfing.

At my ripe age of fifty.

What's wrong with you, Marie? You are not a surfer. You're hardly a knitter, for goodness sake.

As I bent over to pick up my surfboard to drag back to the rental booth, I heard words that made my heart skip a few beats.

"Aloha, madam."

Madam?

When did I become a madam? Gosh. I felt old. The gray hairs on my head showcased that fact, too. Smile lines, gray hairs, and cellulite all over my body. I never really minded any of those things, though. That was until a person called me madam. Ugh. The nerve.

As I straightened myself, I turned around to find the person who caused the offense. I was more than ready to give him a piece of my mind until I locked eyes with him. Those green eyes and wild, curly brown hair. His top half was exposed as his wetsuit was zipped down, hanging around his hips. Toned was an understatement for him and that body. Oh, my goodness, *that body*! That man had a rock-hard body that looked as if it was chiseled by one of the greatest sculptors in history. I wouldn't have been surprised if there was a 'Made by Michelangelo' tag hanging from his chin or something.

His smile was remarkably welcoming. To the point that I almost felt harsh for snapping at him.

Almost.

"You're late," I barked as I placed my hands against my hips. "I paid for a six-thirty start time, and it's six-thirty-five."

He didn't react to my bad attitude, instead he kept smiling and approaching me. "Sometimes, we have to let go of the restraints we set on life and learn to go like the ocean."

"What does that mean?"

He gestured toward the water. Water that was bluer than my mind could've imagined. I understood why Bradley loved coming to Hawaii so much. It had a calming feeling to it.

"Go like the ocean," he repeated, "go with the flow."

"Yes, well, I'm a bit more of an uptight type of person over a flow-er kind of person."

"And yet here you are," he said, sliding his arms—and biceps—into the sleeves of his wetsuit. "Looking to learn how to flow."

I grumbled under my breath before I narrowed my eyes and shielded them from the sunbeams shooting my way. "Maybe I'm too old for this. I could break a hip."

"Or maybe you're just young enough to start living." He laid his surfboard down and then walked over to me. He held his hand out. "I'm Makoa."

"Makoa," I repeated, shaking his hand. "Nice to meet you. I'm Marie. Sorry about my attitude. I'm just nervous."

"Not a problem here. I'm just happy to be able to teach you. I do want to ask, though. What brings you to Hawaii?"

The question wasn't meant to be deep, but it stung at the back of my eyes. I blinked away my emotions as I tried to shake off the feelings boiling up within me. "My son loved coming here to surf. He came five-six times each year. He always begged me to come, but I was too afraid to even leave my house. I'd been afraid my whole life of what could happen outside of the walls of my home…"

"Ah, an introvert?"

"A scaredy cat," I corrected. Introverts simply liked to choose to stay home often. A scaredy cat was too frightened to leave. "I never been on a plane before this trip. Too afraid."

"What made it happen now?"

"Well…" I swallowed hard. "My son booked this trip for me last year. He was sick and booked it before he passed away. He wanted me to not sit at home and mourn him. He wanted me to find him in the waves."

Makoa smiled. It was the kind of smile that made a person feel safe. A smile that felt like the biggest hug in the quietest kind of way. "What was his name?"

"Bradley."

"And how old was he?"

"Thirty. Too young to die."

"Yes. But it sounds like he's lived, too?"

"Gosh, yes. Bradley was the opposite of me. Adventurous. Brave. Courageous in the most terrifying ways. He got that from his father, I was certain. I don't even know how I birthed such a kid."

Makoa grinned and took a seat on his surfboard. "What parts of him are like you?"

I arched an eyebrow, curious to know what he was doing. "Aren't you supposed to be teaching me how to surf?"

"We'll get there. I want to know about you first, though."

My chest felt tight and I took a seat. "I'm not paying you extra for conversation."

"I have no other plans for today except to speak to you," he explained, shrugging his shoulders. "We can have the whole afternoon to learn to surf. Plus, we have more lessons tomorrow and the day after. We can move slow, like the sunsets. Colors slowly melting into one another to make a new, unique sky photograph to never be repeated the same again."

"You talk like art."

"Thanks, I think."

"You're welcome, I think."

He smiled again. I wasn't sure he'd ever stopped grinning. "So, again, what parts of him are like you?"

I wanted to argue more about him wasting my lesson time, but I also wanted to talk about Bradley. Gosh, I missed talking about him. Frank told me I had to stop bringing him up because I always ended up choking on my tears, but speaking about my child made it feel as if he was still around me. And overtime, people stopped asking about him. They let their mourning come to an end. Still, I lived in the land of wishing and missing. Wishing he'd come back. Missing him every second.

"He was smart," I stated, then I paused and held a hand up. "I don't mean that in a cocky way, I just mean he was well studied. He also was able to get a deal on pretty much anything he bought. A good haggler."

"That's how you got me to take fifty bucks off your service." Makoa chuckled.

"To be fair, you were late."

He tossed his hands up. "Touché." He leaned forward and moved one of my loose curls from out of my face and combed it behind my ear. His fingers brushing against my cheek made my cocoa skin heat slightly. I couldn't remember the last time someone did something so intimate toward me. I couldn't remember the last time a man touched me—even if ever-so-slightly.

"Thank you," I muttered, trying to figure out why butterflies were swarming in my stomach from this younger man's fingers slightly caressing my cheek.

"Of course." He bent his knees and rested his arms against his kneecaps as he looked my way. "He had your eyes, too," he said matter-of-factly.

I arched an eyebrow. "What?"

"Brad. He had your eyes."

I snickered and shook my head, confused by his words. "Don't be silly. How would you even know that?"

"Marie," he whispered, his words low and hoarse, and so *so* tender. "He had your eyes."

My heartbeat picked up speed as I stared into his eyes. "You knew my son."

He nodded. "I knew him well. He always talked about his mother being bigger than life. Powerful, gentle, and kind. So very kind."

I shut my eyes for a second and took in a deep breath. "You knew my son," I repeated, trying to gather myself so I wouldn't burst into tears.

"He was one of the best people I knew, and he had your eyes."

The moment I opened my stare, I found Makoa still staring my way. My hand fell to my chest and I blinked back my tears. "Thank you, Makoa."

"No, thank you. It feels good to see him through you. That's a blessing."

I didn't know what to say. I didn't know how to feel. But I *was* feeling. Something I hadn't done in so long. "I'm sorry. I just...I'm surprised he never mentioned you. He mentioned all of his friends to me, I thought."

"Ko," he replied. "He called me Ko. Well, everyone called us Bradley and Ko, because wherever he went, I was there with him as his sidekick."

"Ko!" I expressed, tossing my hands up in the air in shock. "Oh, my goodness, you're Ko?"

He held his hand up. "Guilty as charged."

Without thought, I darted over toward him and wrapped him into a hug. I didn't know if the hug was for me or for him, but for some odd reason, I thought we both needed it. I held on for probably too long, but he held me back. He held me tightly. He held me as if he would've held me for the remainder of the night if I'd asked him to do so.

"Oh gosh, I'm sorry," I expressed, pulling away from him. I wiped away the tears falling from my eyes. "I'm a mess."

"You look pretty perfect to me," he replied, making my cheeks heat.

I waved him off. "You're just saying that because you're my son's friend."

"No," he replied. "I'm saying that because it's true. I knew you were beautiful, Marie, because of how your son spoke about you, but I didn't know you were this remarkable."

Remarkable?

Me?

He was just trying to flatter me. I was certain of it. To make me feel better.

"You don't have to do that," I said, moving to the left side of his board and sitting comfortably. "You don't have to be so...extra with the compliments."

"I'm just speaking the truth. You are the kind of woman I would love to take out to dinner."

I laughed and waved a dismissal hand his way. "Yeah, right. You're young enough to be my son."

"But I'm not," he said with a sly smirk, brushing his leg against mine. "I'm not your son. And I'm fully grown."

The butterflies in my stomach intensified. Makoa's smile stretched wider and I couldn't pick up on if he was hitting on me or if maybe people in Hawaii were extra nice.

"Besides," he shrugged, "I was ten years older than Brad."

"How old are you?"

"Forty-one."

I narrowed my eyes. "I'm in my fifties."

"I love older women."

I laughed out loud, blushing, and full on flustered. "Maybe we should start this lesson sooner than later."

"Whatever you'd like, Marie," he replied, standing to his feet. He held a hand out toward me to help me up. I took his hand and felt a wave of heat shoot throughout my whole system. He pulled me up and pulled me closer to him. So close that our chests slightly brushed against one another. My heart pounded against my ribcage at his closeness. The sun was slowly starting to fade in the distance, yet it felt as if time had frozen right then and there. Just like I'd been. *Slow like the sunsets.*

"What are you doing, Makoa?" I whispered, as his hand fell to my lower back.

He pulled me closer. And closer. *And closer.*

My hands fell against his chest and I should've moved them, but I didn't. I should've left that beach, but I didn't. I should've been getting nervous, but I didn't.

He smiled my way. "Why did you come, Marie?"

"What? Because, well…because…" I took a breath. I shook my head in confusion, trying to gather a good reason. "I had a list."

"Yes. Brad told me about it. Tell me more."

"A list of adventures. Of things I thought I could and would do in my life. I wrote it when I was sixteen and naive. I thought I was going to take on the world. But I didn't."

"He showed me the list," Makoa explained.

"You saw it?"

"Yes. And dancing near the ocean was one of the things," he said as he stepped off the surfboard. "You used to dance?"

"All the time." I couldn't stop looking into his eyes. It was as if he had me in the strongest trance, and I would've been a maniac to tear myself away from those eyes that seemed so welcoming.

"Will you dance with me?"

I quietly chuckled. "It's been a long time since I've danced. And besides, there's no music and—"

He began to hum.

I began to melt.

Oh, Makoa.

I couldn't recall the last time a person made me feel so okay with not being okay.

He wrapped his arms around me and began to sway underneath the setting sun. I didn't know how long we swayed, but he hummed a dozen different songs as the sky grew dark. He held me as I rested my head against his shoulder. He held me as I closed my eyes. He held me as I fell apart with an overwhelming number of emotions on his shoulder.

And then he held me some more.

Suddenly, this stranger to me didn't seem so foreign. Something about him felt so familiar, so welcoming. I could have stayed within his arms until the sunrise began over our heads.

We didn't surf that evening, but I did find the gentleness of the waves. I lost track of time and allowed Makoa to make me feel like waves. Free. Comforting. Able.

Once we finished dancing, he asked me if I'd join him for dinner.

"We'll surf tomorrow, I swear," he said, "But I made us a reservation at a restaurant that turns into a nightclub with salsa lessons."

"Oh! I always wanted to take salsa lessons."

He smiled.

He knew.

I sighed as I stared at him. "Why do I feel like Bradley is setting me up with you?" I asked. That would be very on brand for Bradley. He was always playing matchmaker for people. I'd never thought I'd be one of the ones he set up, though. Especially after he'd crossed over.

"I'm not complaining." Makoa shrugged his shoulders. "Plus, I just think he wanted you to be able to do one thing when he left his place for his journey to calmer seas."

"And what was that one thing?"

He took a step back, unzipped his wetsuit, and pulled his arms out. I studied his arms and smiled as I saw him point out the tattoo on his forearm. It read '*I mua*'.

"What does that mean?" I asked.

"I mua means 'move forward'. That's all Brad wanted for you. He didn't want you to sit in your sadness and lose more years of your life. He wanted you to start again, to really start living and go on your adventures that you'd put on hold to raise him. He wanted this next chapter of your life to be about you and your list. He wanted you to live, Marie. So, please, let's start living."

I couldn't stop feeling as if Bradley had given me the greatest gift by sending me to Hawaii. I had two weeks left on my trip, and Makoa told me he had every single day planned for us to explore, for us to try new things, and for us to dance beneath the sunsets.

Makoa took my hand into his and kissed it gently before we picked up our surfboards and headed off to return them for the night. I didn't know what the next few days entailed, but all I knew was I was going to live them to their fullest potential for Bradley. Not only for him, but for me, too.

Because I was going to do it.

I mua.

Move forward.

Thanks for reading. Check out the rest of Brittainy Cherry's books at bcherrybooks.com.

ONE NIGHT IN PARADISE

BRITTANY HOLLAND

CHAPTER 1 - CAMILLA

Music fills the salty night air as I step under a blanket of stars. My work is done. The bride has changed into her reception gown, and the party is in full swing. The day went off without a hitch. Pleased with myself, I slip out of my heels and walk barefoot into the lush patio of flower-wrapped pergolas and hidden alcoves.

This is my favorite time of night. The adrenaline from the day is starting to crash, the rush of knowing I was a part of someone's forever. That I helped a bride feel like a goddess in a gown I designed and made with my own two hands. I'm a long way from that lost little girl growing up in the Atlanta suburbs, bouncing from home to home with a black trash bag of worn belongings and my secondhand art kit. Even then, I never gave up on happy endings. *I just haven't found mine yet*.

I'm far enough into the garden that moonlight replaces the firelight but still close enough to hear the celebration. I sink onto a cushioned chair in one of the alcoves looking over the ocean, and my bare feet find a resting place on the balcony.

"Shoot! I forgot to grab cake," I mumble, too tired to pry myself from my hiding spot. Hearing the waves crash is a wonderful sound—one I could get used to. So peaceful, so different from the noise in Atlanta.

As if on cue, my phone vibrates.

Briar.

My best friend, roommate, and business partner.

"Hello?" I feel the need to whisper in my private little paradise.

"Camilla? Why are you whispering? Wait—are you with a guy?" Her voice squeals through the phone, and I'm pretty sure the whole island just heard her. "Is it one of the groomsmen?"

"What—no! Are you insane? I'm working! So are you! This isn't Girl's Gone Wild Maui—Destination Wedding Edition."

"For starters, I just photographed the bride and groom cutting the cake. Two, didn't say it was. But you've been single for how long again?"

A deep sigh escapes my chest. "Briar, I told you I'm not looking for anything right now. Not long-term. Not one night. Not. At. All. I'm so grateful to your aunt Opal for bringing me on as head bridal designer at Enchanted—I can't let anything get in the way of that. This job is all I have."

"You have me." She lowers her voice.

"I know. And love you." She's the first person in a long time who has let me be myself—no judgment or expectations. Growing up a foster kid I always felt on display and tried to be my very best, but my best wasn't enough. I never found a permanent home and aged out of the system at eighteen with no family. Now Briar is my family. And Aurora Hills is my new home.

"I just know this is the part of the night where you sneak off and think about...*stuff*."

My heart twinges with sadness. She's not wrong; she knows me too well. It always hits me hard, after the happiness wears off, seeing all the families together. Sure, I see myself doing this one day—being a bride. The white gown, carrying my favorite flowers, starting a life with someone...but then I think about walking down the aisle alone. No mother to fix my veil, no father to take my arm and give me away.

"Oh, gotta go. She's about to toss the bouquet. If you hurry, you can make it in time for the garter, and all the single guys will be in one place. Fish in a barrel."

"If you say so. I'll be in soon. Save me a slice of cake." I laugh.

"Already did." The call ends, and I start to imagine what kind of dress I might design for myself. I do this often, and tonight is no different, but I can never actually see it. I can sketch a dress for everyone...except myself. I don't want to linger on what that means. I'm sure my therapist would have plenty to say about it.

Movement out of the corner of my eye startles me. A dark shadow storms to the other end of the balcony, gripping both hands on the railing. In the faint lantern light, I make out a tall, well-built man—dark suit, tapered waist, wide-set shoulders. As a seamstress, I notice these things. *Right...that's the only reason.*

Or maybe it's that glass of champagne I had during the toast.

He turns toward me, and I freeze. There's no way he can see me, hidden in the shadows, but when he looks my way, my knees go weak. The light illuminates his face...and he's gorgeous in a movie star kind of way. Strong jaw and nose, golden hair, curly on top and cut short on the sides. His full lips appear to be set in a scowl as he continues to look in my direction before casting his gaze back out toward the Pacific Ocean.

My curiosity increases as I watch him. His shoulders stiff, he pulls at his hair in frustration. Maybe he's a heartbroken ex of the bride who came to convince her to take him back.

I shake my head at the thought. I've been reading too many romance novels. Besides, he doesn't look like the type of man a woman would let go of. *I know I wouldn't.*

And...that's my cue to leave. I'm not sure if it's fatigue or the bubbly talking, but if this is how he makes me feel across a dark balcony, I can't imagine what being up close and personal would be like.

A loud ringing fills the air as he reaches into his pocket and pulls out his cell. "What?" he barks, and I feel sorry for whoever is on the other end. "The deal is off. You broke the contract, and no amount of whining is going to change that."

He pauses, listening. "Go. Tell them all. And watch your family's precious empire crumble. Guess you didn't read the fine print. You also signed an NDA, but you were too busy trying to weasel your way in you didn't bother to see who it was you were crawling into bed with." I swear, I can feel the anger radiating off him. It reaches across the darkness, drawing me to him. Watching him from afar is one thing, but overhearing something obviously private seems wrong.

Now, if I can just figure out how to sneak past him and back to the reception to get my cake. This whole creepy stalker thing isn't really my style. Dipping down, I pick up my shoes. But backing up to leave, my foot catches on the chair, and the metal grates on the stone, echoing in the silent night air. I freeze.

Busted.

Turning, I look up to find his gaze locked on me, and it's murderous. He's clearly angry I interrupted his privacy. Well... that makes two of us.

CHAPTER 2 - CARTER

"What are you doing out here?" My voice comes out harsher than intended, and her gorgeous green eyes widen at the bite in my tone.

"Excuse me?" she finally speaks as I close the distance between us.

"You heard me just fine." Now, I'm just being a dick, but I can't help it. There's something about seeing her caught off guard. Women aren't typically shy with me because it's not really me they are after; it's what they can get from me. Carter Brooks, from *the* Charleston Brooks.

"So?" I challenge her, stepping closer. She remains frozen, her eyes wide. Crossing her arms over her chest, she takes a step back, and it's such a shame. Chocolate-brown hair cascading over her pale, creamy shoulder makes me ache to run my fingers through it.

My eyes sweep up to find hers narrowed, and she gives a defiant lift of her chin, obviously aware of me checking her out. "I'm sorry. I'm not trying to be an ass, and I certainly didn't mean to startle you, but you're lucky it was me who caught you out here and not one of the groom's security guards."

She opens her mouth to speak, then closes it, her full, heart-shaped lips resting in the perfect pout. The more I watch her, the more I find her irresistible.

"And what exactly do you think you've caught me doing?" she challenges.

"Wedding crashing," I throw at her, waiting for the embarrassment to register in her cheeks, but the moment never comes.

"Unbelievable," she mutters under her breath.

"So, I'm wrong? You are a guest?"

"Yes, no—ugh, not exactly." She worries her bottom lip, eyes darting around. I shouldn't keep toying with her, but I'm not ready for her to leave.

"Camilla!" someone calls in the distance.

I stalk closer, but she holds her ground, refusing to be intimidated by me. *Feisty little thing.* I instantly like that about her. "Didn't your mother ever teach you it's impolite to crash weddings? Bad luck even."

She draws back as if I just smacked her. Something passes over her face, but anger takes its place before I can decipher what it is.

"Camilla! Where are you?" The voice sounds closer, and she looks toward the main tent, then back to me, eyes now full of fire.

"Not that it's any of your business, but no, my parents never 'taught' me that. I'm not sure it was a high priority to explain wedding crashing etiquette to a six-year-old before they were killed by a drunk driver." Her mouth twists into a scowl, her delicate posture rigid as she unleashes on me.

Regret slams into my chest. She's still talking, reading me the riot act, her arms flailing out by her sides, and I take it. I deserve it.

"Cam-ill-a." A tall blonde singsongs as joins us on the patio and shares a look with who I'm assuming is Camilla. But Camilla throws her hand up to gesture for her to wait a minute. I could stand here all night watching her talk, her plump lips pressing together as she thinks about what she's going to say next. That passion and tenacity is hot as hell, and I love that she didn't throw herself at me instantly. In fact, she seems to really dislike me. *Game on.*

"Furthermore, I'm a guest here, the same as you, but I'm also working with the bride. You remember her, right? The one wearing white? So, it seems I'm needed here, while I'm guessing, based on your lack of coordinating tuxedo, that you are an obligatory invite and not a member of the wedding party."

My tongue is heavy in my mouth, lost for words. Blonde girl clears her throat, and Camilla and I whip our heads her way. "Um, so…we need you." My eyes snap to the camera in her hand, then back to Camilla. She must be her assistant.

"Excuse us. Have a great night." The photographer grabs her arm and urges her back toward the resort, but the look they share tells me they're less like a boss and employee and more like partners in crime.

"So, not alone after all?" the photographer whisper-shouts as they walk away.

"It was nothing," Camilla defends.

"Didn't look like nothing. And you know you can't talk like that to the guests." She laughs.

"I wouldn't call him a guest... more like a pompous ass."

As they get farther away, the waves and music from the party drown out the rest of their conversation, and my body, which was wired up from my interaction with her, is now disappointed by her sudden departure.

"What the actual hell was that?" I laugh to myself. I'm not used to being caught so off guard by a woman, at least not intellectually. She was something else. She had a contagious fire about her, a little bit like flying too close to the sun. A woman like that could burn, and I'd like to find out just how hot. And that mouth on her...

My phone beeps in my hand, distracting me from my salacious thoughts.

AJ: *We can figure this out.*

Me: *Nothing to figure out.*

AJ: *Sure about that?*

AJ: *<Click to download incoming image file>*

I don't need to open it to know what it is. So freaking predictable. I shove my phone in my pocket and head back to the party. There is something to figure out, but it has to do with a curvy brunette and how to get her alone again.

CHAPTER 3 - CAMILLA

"Pompous ass, huh?" Briar repeats just to mess with me as she pulls me aside, a shit-eating grin on her face.

"I didn't stutter," I point out.

She keeps smiling. "I just didn't know you had it in you, Camilla. I mean, I had faith deep down, but I've never seen you go full-blown postal on a stranger."

"Rude stranger," I interject.

She waves me off. "Whatever you say. All I know is what I saw, and he is H-O-T—hot!"

My cheeks heat. "Was he? I hadn't noticed," I say, trying to play it off, but she knows me better than that.

"Bullshit," she coughs. "I saw sparks flying between you guys."

"Okay, yes, I'll admit it, and I was ogling him like some creepy stalker until he caught me. Then he opened his mouth, and the trance was broken. Satisfied?" I offer.

"And?" She is relentless.

"And... he accused me of being a wedding crasher, then brought up my parents. Mood killer," I explain.

"Yikes. I'm so sorry." She moves in to hug me, and I let her. When I break away, tears prick my eyes, and my throat does that closing-up, tickling thing.

"I know, I know. Okay, whew… Why were you looking for me?"

"The bride wanted to make sure you had her ceremony veil back in her dressing room. She couldn't remember," she explains.

"Yeah. I have it put away," I tell Briar as I look back to the reception.

"Beautiful, isn't it?" She follows my awestruck gaze around the candlelit room, dripping in tropical flowers.

My chin lifts to nod. "Are they all this lavish? All the ones you've seen so far?"

"Mostly. Opal has very exclusive clientele. She's the best at what she does." She bumps my shoulder. "And now, you're part of that."

"Thanks to you," I remind her.

"Let's hit the bar," she suggests. "I want to see if the pilot from the rehearsal dinner is here."

"Wait, is that professional?" I ask. This is my first high-profile wedding "I don't want to blow it by committing a faux pas before I've even begun." I move to follow her, the stone cool beneath my feet. *How did I forget my shoes?*

Briar sees me looking down, and I lift the black chiffon, wiggling my bare feet. "Missing something, Cinderella?" she teases.

My hair tickles my shoulder as I shrug. "Who knows."

"We're officially off duty. The bride and groom have made their exit. Just a couple drinks, then I'll whisk you away before you turn into a pumpkin…or make a huge fool of yourself," she goads me.

"Oh, look who's practicing for open mic night," I joke.

"Okay, *Cindy*, just for that, shots it is. I heard they have this amazing coconut-infused tequila." Her wicked smile is back. This could be trouble.

CHAPTER 4 - CARTER

What's one more drink? The amber burns as it goes down.

I glance down at the sexy black heels on the stool next to me, and yeah, I definitely need it now.

I've been watching her across the dance floor for nearly half an hour, maybe more, swaying to the music, dark hair escaping and falling over her bare shoulders. Standing, I adjust myself, down the rest of my drink, and grab the heels before heading toward their owner.

The bride and groom are long gone, along with most of the bridal party. It'll be winding down soon, and I'm about to lose my chance. A slow, soulful pulse starts — old-school, like something my grandparents used to listen to.

She's moving to the beat, her back to me. Her friend's eyes widen as she sees me approach, and I lift my hands in a silent prayer, pleading for her not to give me away. She nods, and I set the heels down before falling into rhythm behind Camilla. Placing my hands on her hips, I grip the fabric and pull her closer. At first, she tenses, but I hold her tight. "Shhh, I've got you," I whisper into her silky hair. It tickles my nose, and the smell is incredible, like cotton candy and flowers.

Between her scent surrounding me, the pulse of the music, and the way she's pressed against me, I need to get her alone. But I already know she's not that kind of girl. It would be so much easier if she were. For the first time that I can recall, it's more than a physical attraction. Of course, I'm attracted to her, but when she put me in my place earlier, it jolted me to my core. Then, when she broke about her parents and her anger barely covered her sadness, she chipped away a little of my armor.

The tempo picks up on the chorus, and I squeeze my eyes closed. Graceful arms lift, reaching behind my neck, holding me where she wants me. Nails scrape the sensitive skin behind my ears, fingertips working their way to tangle in my hair. Her body tenses, arms falling away, and my eyes blink open.

Pulling away, she whips around. "You!"

I throw her my best smirk, the one reserved for panty melting. "Hey, Crash."

"You have got to be kidding me." She looks around, and her friend, who appears extremely amused, waves at us. She also seems to be filming our exchange on her iPhone.

"Can't we finish the dance, at least?"

"The song ended," she informs me, looking back for her friend, who seems to have made her escape.

"I hadn't noticed," I reply, tucking my hands in my pockets to keep from reaching for her.

She keeps staring like she wants to say something, or maybe slap me, I can't tell for sure. But she has to feel this pull. I can't be the only one.

Another song starts, and I raise my eyebrows in question.

My stomach falls when she shakes her head and turns to walk away. "Wait," I say. She turns around to face me, and I bend to retrieve the shoes she left behind.

"You ran off and left these." I hold them out to her.

"Um, thanks." She blushes, looking everywhere but at my eyes.

"For what it's worth, I'm sorry about earlier," I try to explain. "I'm not usually such a pompous ass," I add.

"You heard that?" she gasps, her hand flying to her mouth, pink tinting her cheeks.

"Yeah, no worries. It was warranted." I clear my throat, "Can I get you a drink?"

"No, thanks. I really need to go," she says as her stomach growls. "Kill me now," she mumbles.

"Something to eat, maybe?" I quirk a brow in question.

Her green eyes narrow, scrutinizing me. "I don't know if that's such a good idea."

"After all those shots, I'd say it's a great idea." My smile drops when I realize what I've said. *Oh, shit.*

Her emerald eyes widen. "You were watching me?"

"If I'm not mistaken, you did it first," I say, trying to recover from my slipped confession. The pointed look she shoots me lets me know she's still not convinced. "Look, it's not a marriage proposal. It's just food."

She smiles, nodding. I can't believe she didn't make me work harder.

"Okay," she replies, and I take her shoes back to carry them for her.

"Let's do this," I lead her back to the alcove where I first saw her. She's quiet as she sits on a chaise. "Wait right here."

Turning, I rush back to the banquet tables. Most of the food has been cleared away—what now?

"Pssst, Romeo!" I turn to my left and see her blonde friend. "Go for the chocolate groom's cake." She motions to the dessert table with her head.

"You sure?"

"Definitely," she replies, smiling like she's let me in on a little secret.

"She's a chocolate lover?"

"Something like that. Treat her right, or I'll cut your balls off, okay?" she states.

"Understood, thanks." *I have other plans for my balls tonight.* Grabbing the biggest piece of chocolate cake I can find, a fork, and a couple of bottles of water, I head back to her, hoping she's still there.

CHAPTER 5 - CAMILLA

Sinking into the soft chaise, I draw my legs up and wrap my arms around myself, remembering the feel of his hands possessively holding me close, his breath on my neck... I wish he had leaned in a little closer and pressed his lips against my skin.

He smelled incredible, like the ocean but spicy. Shivers run through me at the thought of being close to him again—which should worry me, given my history with men, but the way he held me was...protective.

Which is insane. I don't know this guy. And our first encounter left me thinking he was a major jerk, but something changed during that dance. Something I can't pinpoint or explain. There was an energy pulsing around us, making the rest of the room disappear.

While I am a romantic, I'm not naive enough to think there's a Prince Charming waiting to sweep me off my feet the minute our gazes collide across a crowded ballroom. No damsel in distress here. But there was...something.

And to be cherished, held, adored...loved by someone—that, I could get used to. I lie back on the cushion and close my eyes, trying not to overthink whatever it is that's about to happen.

A hand brushes my shoulders, and my eyes snap open.

He's back. *My mystery man.* The thought makes me shiver.

"Cold?" he asks, laying his jacket over me. My cheeks heat as I stifle a yawn and sit up.

"No, not anymore. Thank you," I whisper, though the shivering had nothing to do with being cold and everything to do with him. I meet his eyes again, and the look I find makes me not so tired anymore. It's a look of want, and it mirrors what I'm feeling.

He motions to the table beside us. "I brought reinforcements." Taking a seat next to me, he grabs the plate and holds it between us.

My eyes land on the biggest piece of chocolate cake I've ever seen, and I can't help the little moan that escapes my lips. My hand flies up to cover my mouth, mortified at my outburst.

He reaches up, his strong hand pulling mine away from my face and holding it in his. "Keep moaning like that and I'll be eating more than this chocolate cake." He nips at my fingers before letting go.

Equal parts shocked and turned on, I stare into his blue eyes, tempted to make the sound again just to see what he will do.

I'm no prude, but I'm also not this bold, and it makes me wonder whether it's him or that coconut-infused tequila that has me practically falling into his lap.

"Plus, I usually save that kind of dessert for the second date," he adds with a wink as he digs in and lifts the fork to my mouth.

"This isn't a date—" I start, but the rich chocolate taste silences me, and another tiny moan passes my lips. Eyes widening, I look up just in time to see him set the plate down and reach for me.

"I warned you." His hands touch either side of my face as he leans in. My breath hitches at the contact, and I prepare for the rush of his mouth on mine, but it doesn't come. Instead, his warm tongue traces along my bottom lip from one corner to the other. He pulls away slightly, looking at me as he licks his lips. "Chocolate, my new favorite."

Leaning back in, he repeats this process with my top lip. A thousand shock waves crash through me as our thighs press together and his hands move to tangle in my hair. As he increases the pressure of his tongue dancing against my parted lips, I reach up and grip his shoulders, strong and solid under my touch.

Needing more, I run my hands up his firm chest and grab his collar, pulling him closer to me, sinking my lips into his. Warm, wet, and soft, our lips part, and I sweep my tongue out in search of his.

This seems to urge him on. Gripping my hips, he pulls me so I'm sitting on his lap. His jacket falls to the ground, and my dress bunches up around my waist as I straddle him, his hard length pressing against my core. I'm a little self-conscious about being so exposed, but his lips distract me from all reasonable thought. He kisses me with such passion, it's all I can focus on.

I rest my hands on his shoulders to steady myself and rock back and forth, my need for him building.

As if sensing this, he begins to roll his hips, and our bodies find a perfect rhythm, as if we've done this a thousand times. He grows harder beneath me, and our lips increase the tempo to match our bodies.

Breaking away, he begins to lick his way down my neck, and tiny fires ignite along my skin. His hands run up and down my arms, caressing me.

Pulling my dress straps away from my shoulders, he drops the fabric enough to show the black satin cups barely containing my aching breasts. Electricity follows in the wake of every single place he touches.

Lips taste the sensitive skin at the base of my neck, and teeth nip my shoulder before he moves to my collarbone. My body aches with need. His hands are everywhere, a combination of slow and hurried as I continue to grind against him.

Reaching down between us, his hand traces up the inside of my thigh, finding the edge of the wet lace and breaching the barrier to stroke my clit. My hips buck, desperate for more.

"You like that?" he rasps out, withdrawing his hand.

"Come to my room." His lips brush against my ear, and hearing his voice brings me from my lust-filled haze, and the doubt seeps in.

"Camilla, please look at me," he pleads.

The impulse to run hits me hard, but my sudden awareness of how exposed I am has me pressing my face farther into his shirt and willing the ground to open up and swallow me. Gathering my wits, I breathe him in one last time, knowing this won't happen again. It can't. Guys like him don't pick girls like me. I have a business to worry about, and...

"The reception, the guests."

"No one saw anything," he offers.

"Thank God," I blurt out. I can't believe I let this go so far.

His chest rumbles beneath me as he laughs, which causes me to draw back and finally look him in the eye.

"What's so funny?" I ask, but it comes out as more of a challenge.

"There she is. The fiery girl. I wondered where you had gone." He has the nerve to smirk at me, and I narrow my eyes.

"Seriously, we could have been seen. I have a reputation to uphold. And it's not one of slamming shots and mauling wedding guests. Stupid Briar and her coconut-infused tequila," I mutter under my breath.

He watches me cautiously. "Are you done?"

"Excuse me?" I bite my lip. I've never been in a situation like this and have no idea how to handle this...predicament.

"If you're done scolding yourself and overanalyzing, I'd like to continue whatever this is back in my room. Possibly with more cake and some of that tequila." His smile should be illegal.

I slide backward to get up and feel his hard length on my thigh. I want him more than I've ever wanted anyone, but old insecurities threaten to surface. *Deep breath.*

"It's crazy, but I know you feel it too. Please stay with me. For the night," he adds, reaffirming nothing more will come from this. *For the night.* My stomach drops in disappointment, though I should feel relieved.

Like Briar said, I need to get back out there. Why not this guy? It's not like I'll have to see him again. We're in Maui, a long way from Aurora Hills, Georgia, and I've already made an ass of myself. He rubs against me, as if I need convincing, and my fuse is lit again, encouraging me to throw all caution to the wind.

I tease, standing and pulling my dress back into place as he leans down to grab his jacket.

Picking up the cake, he swipes his finger into the fudge icing and spreads it across my lips before leaning in to kiss me, our tastes combining with the chocolate. He deepens the kiss and licks every bit of the icing away before stepping back. "Your wish is my command."

I grab my shoes, forgoing putting them on, and take his free hand. As we walk back toward the resort, he squeezes my hand.

"I'm Carter, by the way."

Looking up at him, mouth open in shock, I realize I never asked his name. Not only is it rude of me, but he just made me come on a balcony, in a public place, a place I was working only hours ago. And I didn't even know his name.

Classy, Camilla. Real classy.

Deciding I could let the reality of the situation mess up the rest of the evening or just go with it, I opt for keeping it light.

"Hmmm, Carter. It suits you, I guess. Personally, I thought pompous ass was a fitting name," I laugh, and judging by his reaction, I'd say it was the right call.

He stops and pulls me in for a quick kiss. "That's just what my friends call me. But Carter is my real name, so you'll know what to cry out when we're in bed." He presses into me, further proving his point. If he keeps this up, we'll never make it to the room.

"Here we are." I look up to see a beautiful stone building with a large wooden door.

"Private villa, huh?" I tease as he unlocks the door and holds it open for me.

"I like my privacy. Plus, now you can be as loud as you want." He winks and I'm certain about to lose my panties.

CHAPTER 6 - CARTER

The door closes, and the lock clicking into place causes her to jump. I set the cake on the entry table and drop my phone and key card next to it.

Reaching out, I pull Camilla into my arms. We could barely contain ourselves a few minutes ago in the open, but now that we're in private, I don't know where to start. "Would you like a drink?" I pull away and look down at her.

"No, thanks," she replies, breathless.

"How about a bath?" Walking farther into the room, I throw my jacket over the back of a chair and turn on the lamp. That was random. *Shit.* She probably thinks I'm just trying to get her naked right away. Which I am, but I want her to relax, not take advantage of her.

"Um…well, I thought—I dunno." She twists her hands at her waist and I wonder what she's thinking. I can almost see the wheels turning.

"Come with me." Taking her hand, I lead her to the sofa and ease her down before taking a seat across from her on the ottoman. "We don't have to do anything you don't want to do. But I'm not going to deny that I want you. I don't know what it is about you Camilla, but I've never felt this way about a woman after just meeting— hell maybe never."

Her gaze flicks to mine, and I hear her quick intake of breath.

"Tell me what you want, Camilla. Don't be afraid."

I don't want her to feel pressured. I'm used to doing this type of thing—one-night stands are kind of my MO since my last relationship imploded—but I have a feeling this isn't something she does.

I can tell the moment Camilla starts to lose control, she reins in it. I want to help her unleash that. The best part is she has no idea who I am. No preconceived notions of Carter Brooks, the playboy. The son of the ruthless East Coast real estate tycoon.

"Tell me," I urge her.

"You." The word is barely audible, a whisper.

I search her face to make sure.

"You," she says louder, slightly more urgent. "Tonight."

Standing, I scoop down to throw her over my shoulder and carry her to the bedroom. "That's good to hear. I want you too."

She giggles at my reply. "Plus, I seem to remember being promised chocolate cake," she teases, and I'm glad to see her humor has returned.

"Oh, I've got something sweet for you." Setting her down at the foot of the bed, I start to unbutton my shirt, and she joins in. The light scrape of her nails against my chest as she fumbles with the buttons makes me so hard I'm worried I'll embarrass myself any second.

My shirt falls to the floor, and I give her time to explore my chest, but my restraint is slipping. She runs her silky palms down to my abs and back up again. When she tentatively reaches out to kiss my chest, I take her hands in mine to still them.

"Did I do something wrong?" She looks at me through dark lashes.

"Not at all. It's just that I want this to be amazing for you, and if you keep touching me like that, this will be over way too soon. What I have planned for you, baby, is going to take all night."

Her mouth widens in shock, forming a perfect O, and I imagine those lips wrapped tightly around me.

"Turn around," I need to get her out of this dress. She follows orders, in the bedroom at least, and that's a major turn-on.

Bringing my hands up, I slip the straps off her shoulders, then reach for the exposed silver zipper, sliding it slowly down her body. Creamy white skin exposed with every inch makes my mouth water to taste her.

So, I do. Pushing her hair out of the way, I lick my way up the column of her neck. She leans her head back against my chest, her moans the only encouragement I need.

She stands before me, clutching her dress against her front like a shield. Wrapping my arms around her, I tug her hands, and the soft, dark fabric pools around her feet. She looks like a goddess—all curves, pale skin practically glowing against the contrast of the lacy lingerie, long, dark hair spilling around her shoulders. I walk around her, drinking her in, and she watches me, eyes wide.

"You look better than any cake I've ever had. I can't wait to taste you," I warn her.

She rewards me with a smile. Reaching up, she unclasps her strapless bra and lets it fall to the floor, revealing perfect full tits. "What are you waiting for?" she asks, toying with me, and I toss her back on the bed.

"You'll pay for that, you little minx." She giggles as she scoots up the bed, and I crawl my way up her body, kissing as I go, causing her giggles to turn into moans.

Calves. *Moan.*

Knees. *Moan.*

Thighs. *Moan.*

Belly. *Moan.*

Positioning myself between her legs, I prop up on my elbows, careful not to crush her, and draw lazy circles across her stomach with my tongue. She covers her chest with her arms, and I tsk, wanting her to open up, to let go. "Hands above your head, and keep them there." She complies, her chest now arched and in my face.

I take my time licking around her breasts and sucking them into my mouth one at a time. She begins moving against me, and my body falls into rhythm with hers as she grips and claws at the sheets.

Sitting up, I tap her hip so she lifts and tug her panties down her legs before tucking them into my back pocket. I spread her thighs wider, holding her legs open as I bite and nip my way up. She bucks, and my mouth finds its intended target.

Forget chocolate, Camilla taste is one I'll never get enough of. One swipe of my tongue and her back arches off the bed. Then another. And another. I replace my tongue with a finger, teasing her clit. I've barely touched her, and she's drenched. "You're so wet for me."

"Carter!" she cries out as I continue to massage her, alternating between my mouth and fingers. "Please!" Her hands break their hold on the sheets, and her fingers thread into my hair, gripping, holding me in place.

She rides my face, taking what she needs, and I increase my tempo, sending her almost over the edge, her legs wrapping around my shoulders and clamping tightly.

I want to make this last, but I'm painfully hard for her, so I make her come with my mouth first. I feel it as it takes hold. Her body begins to shake, and her moans get louder and louder. I lap up everything she gives me. Her legs relax and fall back to the bed, arms thrown carelessly over her head. I like seeing her like this: relaxed, sated.

While she's still coming down, I sit back on my heels and grab a condom from my wallet.

Feeling the shift of the bed, she sits up, kneeling to face me, our knees touching. She looks incredibly sexy—naked, flushed, hair all wild.

Sliding back off the bed, I stand to remove my pants and boxers. She never takes those hungry green eyes off me. I run my hand over my shaft, once, twice, then tear the foil and roll the condom on, more than ready to be inside her.

Climbing my way up her body, I lay her back and settle between her thighs. I grip her sides, dragging my hands down her ribs before coming to rest on her hips and scooting her closer to me.

Lining up at her entrance, I look down at her, wanting to lock away the image, and edge into her. Her eyes flutter closed as she moans, "Carter."

I press deeper, and she stretches for me. So tight. "You feel so good." Inch by inch, I fill her up and pause, allowing her time to adjust. She lifts her hips, so I rock into her, giving her the friction she's looking for.

Taking her hands in mine, I tangle our fingers and settle them on the pillow above her head as I pull out slowly and push back in, adjusting my angle to reach deeper.

Our bodies find a natural rhythm, and it doesn't take long for a slow burn to start in the pit of my stomach. A light sheen of sweat covers my skin as I climb toward climax, not even caring that it's coming so fast. "Come with me, Camilla. Now," I growl, driving into her harder and harder.

"Carter, yesss!" she screams.

On command, her body releases, walls tightening as she milks my orgasm from me. Waves of pleasure crash through my body, and I open my eyes to find her looking right at me.

What passes between us is way more intimate than anything we've done this evening—a look that both terrifies and excites me.

Our movements still, and I free my hands to cradle her face. Without breaking eye contact, I kiss her, my lips lingering across hers, worshipping her. She sighs into my mouth, and I close my eyes, resting my forehead against hers. Because I've never felt his intensity with someone before, and definitely not someone who was only supposed to be one night.

CHAPTER 7 - CARTER

After cleaning up, I grab us water and climb back into the bed, pulling her against me. I slide the chilled bottle over her side and hiss when she jerks back, rubbing her ass along the hardness that's already returned. "Insatiable, are we?" she teases, and I grip her hips, stopping her.

"With you, it would seem so," I admit, placing a kiss to the back of her head.

"That was...uh..." She trails off.

"Incredible," I finish her thought, squeezing her tightly. "Do you need to let your friend know you won't be coming back to the room? Let her know you're safe?"

She rolls over and looks at me as if I have two heads. "You want me to stay?" Her eyes watch me, full of questions.

"Do you want to stay?" I raise a brow, giving her a get-out-of-jail-free card—the only one I'm going to offer.

When she doesn't answer, I lower my mouth to her shoulder.

"You're making it a little hard to concentrate," she accuses as she nuzzles closer.

"That's the whole point." I run my tongue along her skin, and a breathy moan escapes her lips.

"So, you want me to stay?" She wraps her arms around my neck as I roll her onto her back, pushing myself up so I can look down at her.

"Well, I thought that was implied. How rude of me to assume," I tease as I thrust between her legs.

"You know what they say about people who assume." She grins.

"Touché. And I'd hate to add presumptuous to my title. Pompous already takes up so much room on my nameplate."

She laughs, a genuine belly laugh, and it's my new favorite sound. Well… a close second behind hearing her cry out my name while coming.

"It's settled, then. You're staying." I end the conversation with a sweet kiss.

"Okay," she murmurs against my lips. "But if we can pause for one second, I really need to use the restroom to freshen up."

Reluctantly, I roll off her and walk to my suitcase. Grabbing a fresh pair of boxers, I slip them on and snag a T-shirt.

"Here." I offer her the shirt so she has something comfortable to put on and run my hand through my hair before resting it on my neck. The whole after part of sex is new to me, and being out of my element has me unsure of what to do next.

She stays still on the bed, the sheet draped over her, inspecting the worn gray shirt. "Harvard?" she asks, brows raising.

Clearing my throat, I shrug. "Yeah."

When she remains quiet, eyeing me for a moment, my back tenses, waiting for the part where she asks about my family or career. Women typically equate Ivy League schools with money and a name. But the question never comes.

"Thanks. Looks comfy," she says with a smile before hopping off the bed and walking to the bathroom. This girl continues to surprise me.

I stare at the closed bathroom door for a moment before swiping a hand down my face. I was so sure there would be questions I don't know how to handle the fact that there weren't. My eyes roam over the room before landing on the cake I left by the door. With a smirk, I grab the plate and crawl back into bed to wait for her.

When she walks out, my eyes widen. How hard she got me in that sexy black dress is nothing compared to what seeing her in my T-shirt does. The worn cotton straining over her full chest, the hem barely hitting her thighs...

"Like what you see?" she taunts as she climbs back in the bed. Licking my lips, I nod.

"How about you?" I lift the plate of chocolate cake.

"Very much." It's her turn to lick her lips as I lift a forkful to her mouth. Closing her mouth around the fork, she sucks away any remaining icing, and I nearly groan. I've never been so jealous of flatware.

Another little moan, and her eyes open to see me watching her. "What, haven't you ever seen a woman eat chocolate cake before?"

"Yes. I've just never seen one enjoy it so thoroughly." I reach up and brush away some stray crumbs from her lips with my thumb. "It's sexy."

Her eyes light up at my confession as she sucks my thumb into her mouth, and the cake is once again forgotten.

———

A pulsing beep wakes me. My eyes adjust to the dark room, and warm breath tickles my bare chest. Looking down, I see the gorgeous brunette, and last night comes flooding back.

The wedding.

The angry phone call.

Finding Camilla on the balcony.

Her calling me a pompous ass.

Watching her dance.

Dancing with her.

Kissing her on the balcony.

Bringing her back to my villa.

Countless orgasms.

Chocolate cake.

Her falling asleep in my arms.

Continued beeps drag me from bed. Careful not to wake her, I grab my phone off the nightstand and head to the bathroom.

"This better be good," I answer, annoyed this couldn't wait until daylight.

"Son, nice to talk to you too."

"Spare me the pleasantries, Dad. Why are you calling so early?"

"It's not so early in New York. It's nearly lunchtime. But I didn't call to discuss time zones. If it weren't important, I wouldn't have called. It's AJ. There's been an incident."

Christ. Running a hand through my hair, I release a ragged breath. "What do you mean an incident?"

"AJ showed up drunk at the country club where your mother was having brunch with one of her committees and started making wild accusations that upset your mother. Went so far as to threaten her. You need to get home and fix this."

I sigh. "I don't know what you want me to do. I can't control AJ. You know it, I know it—hell, AJ knows it." My mind replays the phone call from last night.

"Well, you better figure out how to handle your business. We can't afford any blowback on the company over this. I'm out here trying to close this deal. I don't have time to clean up your mess." His dig stings. It's his fault there's a mess in the first place, but I bite my tongue and choose my words carefully.

"I'll be on the next flight." The words stick in my throat as the gorgeous girl asleep in my bed skirts across my mind. The last thing I want to do is walk away, but with all this shit going down with AJ and my dad playing the family loyalty card against me, I don't have a choice.

"No need to book a flight. I've sent a plane for you. Just get your ass home and fix this. Prove to me you're the man I raised you to be, who will someday run this company. Not Carter Brooks, the playboy." And with that, the line goes dead.

Anger washes over me. Setting my phone on the counter, I gather my toiletries, throw them into my travel bag, and splash cold water on my face, my palms scraping over a day's growth of scruff.

I send for a car, then move around the room in a quiet rush, packing my stuff. I hate having to leave her, but I know she'll hate me enough for both of us when she wakes to find me gone.

I watch her for a moment, smiling at her soft snores as she sleeps so peacefully. Taking out my phone, I snap a picture. She's breathtaking, and she doesn't even know it. Chocolate crumbs catch my eye as I move the covers over her, and my smile widens as an idea strikes.

Grabbing her phone, I set the wheels in motion, then press a gentle kiss to her lips, taking one last taste before turning and walking away from the girl I'm pretty sure stole my heart—a heart I wasn't sure I even possessed.

CHAPTER 8 - CAMILLA

"This dream is too good. I don't want to wake up," I murmur, pulling the fluffy blanket around me, covering my head.

"I don't need to hear that shit." Briar's voice invades my peaceful slumber.

Cracking one eye open in an attempt to locate her, I'm blinded by the light flooding the room, so I squeeze it back shut. "Do I even want to know how you got in here?"

Caught between sleep and awake, I can't decipher between what is real and an incredible dream—a dream that left me sore, but in a good way. Stretching my arms over my head, my hands brush cool leather, and I freeze.

"In three...two...one!" Briar gives commentary as I throw back the covers and open my eyes, looking around. Carter. It hits me all at once. Sleepy and confused, I look around. *Where is he? If this is his villa and he's gone, why am I still here?*

What time is it?

I look to her, realizing I've asked nothing aloud. She just sits on a chair next to the bed, smiling her crazy-ass I-know-a-secret smile. "Morning, slut!"

I toss a pillow at her head, which she dodges. "I'm not a slut!" I yell as she just sits there sipping coffee. *Mmmm, coffee. Need coffee.*

"Says the woman sitting naked in a strange man's bed." A quick peek reveals I am, in fact, naked.

"How did you know I'm naked?" Crossing my arms over my chest, I stare her down.

"Seeing as how your dress is over there on the floor, along with what looks like a bra...I took a wild guess. Unless you're wearing only panties." She smiles, unfazed by my scowl.

My face turns red, and I keep my mouth shut. Not only am I not wearing any, I have no idea where they are.

"Figures. Looks like Cinderella lost more than her shoes last night." She laughs and motions to the other coffee she brought. "Come on out here and get your drink, sleepyhead."

My eyes dart to the coffee as the gray shirt I wore last night catches in my peripheral. Snatching it up, I bring it to my nose and breathe in. It smells like him, like the ocean and a masculine musk.

"Hey, Lassie, if you're done sniffing the evidence, let's eat. I'm starved!" she complains.

Pulling on the shirt, I head for bathroom, flipping her the bird as I go.

"He's not a strange man," I call out.

"He's a man and he's a stranger, therefore, he's a strange man. A gorgeous strange man, I'll give you that."

"He's not a stranger!" I poke my head out the bathroom door.

"What's his last name?" she throws back.

"What?" My eyes go wide. How could I not know his last name?

"Drawing a blank? Hmmm. Nothing? I'd say that's stranger danger!" She laughs, and I slam the bathroom door.

Bracing my hands on the polished stone counters, I study myself in the gilded mirror. My cheeks have more color than usual, and there's a light in my eyes I haven't seen in a long time. Pulling my hair back, I twist it into a knot, noticing red marks along my neck. Whisker burns. I run my hands over them, recalling how alive he made me feel. My thighs clench, my core aching from our incredible night of passion, and I can't help but smile.

In less than twelve hours, he turned my whole world upside down. The way I was with him, I never knew it could be like that—never knew *I* could be like that. And now he's gone. My chest aches at the thought, and tears sting my eyes.

My gaze falls to his shirt. Harvard. So many things I meant to ask him, but I thought we would have more time. I don't even know his last name. I wrap my arms around my waist and grip the worn gray fabric, holding on to all I have left. A lone tear escapes, and I wipe it away.

He gave me what I asked for—him, for a night, nothing more, nothing less. I'm sure he's used to that sort of thing, and as much as I tell myself I'm okay with it, I'm not normally that kind of girl. But not one thing about last night was normal.

Splashing water on my face, I wash away the tears and hopefully any traces of sadness. Time to get back to reality. I have a job to do. An amazing job I'm lucky to have. I need to focus on that.

"You about done in there?" Briar calls from the other room. "You might wanna get out here."

"Coming!" I yank open the door and freeze, my eyes landing on a table full of decadent desserts. A chocolate fudge cake, double chocolate muffins, cupcakes, chocolate chip cookies and pastries. I walk closer, taking in the incredible smell, and spot a silver carafe of coffee.

Still in shock, I turn to Briar, who is snapping pictures of everything on her phone. "What did you do?"

"Me? This wasn't me. I just answered the door." She motions to the room service cart across the room. "Good thing one of us was dressed, huh, Harvard?"

Before I can sit, ringing across the room sends me in search of my phone. Looking at the caller ID, my brows furrow.

Pompous Ass.

My hand flies to my mouth. "Briar, it's him! How?"

"Who knows, but answer the damn phone and thank the man for the goods so we can eat."

I swipe to answer. "Um, hello?"

"Hey, sleeping beauty. I take it you got my little surprise." His voice is deep and sexy, even over the phone. I walk into the bedroom to sit on the bed.

"You did this? How?" I ask, baffled.

"I have my ways," he says, his tone coy, and I can't help but love his playful side.

"I see. Well...thank you, Carter. It's a very sweet gesture, pun intended."

"I wish I could have been there to see you in person, to feed you the cake. I'm really sorry I had to take off." His voice seems genuine, but maybe this is a grand gesture blow-off.

"Why did you, then?" My words come out harsher than I intended.

A heavy sigh fills the line. "I had a family emergency. I want you to know I would have never left you sleeping in my bed if I could have helped it. It took everything I had to walk away."

"Oh no. I hope everything is okay." My stomach fills with dread at the mention of his family. Losing my parents at such a young age, I can definitely understand needing to put family first.

"Yeah, it's nothing I can't handle. I'm just working out some stuff. It's more business related, honestly, but with my dad, the two are synonymous."

"Well, I'm glad everyone's all right," I offer, even though I have no idea who his family consists of. There's so much we don't know about each other.

"They will be. Thanks. Listen, I'm getting ready to board a flight. I'll be gone a couple days, but I'd like to see you again." His voice is gravelly, almost a whisper. "I know we didn't talk about it. There's a lot we didn't get to say, and I'd love to have the chance."

"Really?" I blurt out the first thing that comes to mind.

"Yeah, really. I'd like to take you out on a real date."

My heart slams into my rib cage, pounding at the thought of seeing him again. This is so sudden, and I need to focus on the shop, but it's just one date...though I find it hard to believe anything with him could ever be just one.

"You still there?"

"Yeah. Sorry. Just thinking."

"Don't overthink this. I know it seems very sudden—warp speed, really—but I'm just asking for a chance to get to know you. We can talk or text. You have my number, so ask me anything. Then we'll get in *touch* once I'm back home."

My knees go a little weak at the way he emphasized "touch." It's a good thing I'm sitting down.

"Wait, how did you get my number?" We never exchanged contact info. Or last names.

He laughs. "I called myself from your phone. I hope you don't mind. I kind of panicked when I had to rush out and didn't want to wake you. I could barely leave as it was. Then I programmed myself into your phone."

"I see that, Mr. Pompous Ass."

"Curious to know what I programmed you into my phone as?"

"Wedding crasher?" I tease.

His laughter comes over the line, making me smile. "No, but that would have been a good one. My mind wasn't on the spitfire I met on the balcony. It was on the gorgeous girl sleeping in my bed. When we hang up, I'll send a screenshot."

"Okay," I whisper, not knowing what else to say. I seem to lose my ability to form complete sentences around him.

"I look forward to hearing from you soon, Camilla. Enjoy your breakfast, and tell Briar thank you."

Briar. Breakfast. Right. I completely forgot I wasn't alone. Looking over my shoulder, she smiles and lifts her mug as if she's toasting me. I get up, the smooth wood feeling cool under my bare feet as I begin to pace. "Uh, wait," I say, not ready to hang up yet. "You said when you're home. Where's home?" I ask, biting at my thumbnail. What if it's across the country? How can this work?

"Charleston." His answer calms my fears. That's only a couple of hours away.

"Oh. Wow. That's, um...perfect." I sound like a stumbling fool, but I can hardly contain my excitement.

"I know. Only a couple hours away, less if I fly," he agrees.

"Wait, how did you—?" I stammer.

"Camilla Lacey, from Aurora Hills, dress designer at Enchanted." His voice drops low. "You'll find I'm a very resourceful man when there's something I want."

My mouth forms a perfect O, and a silent gasp passes my lips.

"Talk to you soon, Camilla."

"Goodbye, Carter," I whisper and end the call.

"Shit, I could use a cigarette after that call, and I don't even smoke." Briar's voice startles me.

"You couldn't even hear what he was saying." I walk back over to check out the feast Briar's already dug into.

"Didn't have to. Your umm-ing, oooh-ing, and stuttering pretty much let me know whatever he said was hot. Takes a lot to tie your tongue."

My face flushes. She's right, and he probably thinks I'm a total moron. "Crap! I meant to ask his last name." *Ugh!*

She just shrugs.

"Well, Ms. Tequila Makes My Clothes Fall Off, how was he?" she asks, holding a chocolate long john to her mouth while making inappropriate gestures.

"You're insane. You get that, right?"

My phone dings with an incoming text, and I open the screen, seeing a picture of me sound asleep in his bed. My chest tightens. I look so peaceful, and thankfully, I'm not drooling. I swipe to reveal the next message. It's a screenshot of my contact info.

Sleeping Beauty.

If you enjoyed reading about Camilla and Carter's one night in paradise, watch for their full length novel coming Spring 2024!

JUST ONE FANTASY

A "JUST ONE DARE" STAND-ALONE SHORT STORY

CARLY PHILLIPS

CHAPTER 1

Aurora Dare had a plan. A sexy plan to get her husband away and alone on her brother-in-law's island retreat, away from the hustle of everyday life. And from their children whom she loved dearly but oh, she needed a break. Her pseudo-mom, Melly Kingston, had offered to take the girls for the long weekend. Aurora had packed while Ellie napped. All she needed to do was bring the kids to Melly and head to the airport where her brother-in-law's private jet hangar was located.

She stood outside the elementary school, waiting for her older daughter to walk out the doors. Other parents crowded around and not for the first time, Aurora wished the school had a better system for pick-up that didn't have her jostled between anxious moms and dads. A security guard waited to the side, just one of the modern-day necessities and Aurora was grateful for it.

An annoyed squeak sounded in her ear, and Aurora lifted seven-month-old Ellie higher on her hip. "We're waiting for your sister," Aurora said, automatically rocking the baby before she grew fussy.

What felt like an hour but was only minutes later, Leah's precious face came into view. "There she is!" Aurora lifted Ellie's chubby hand in hers. "Leah's coming!"

"Bah!"

Aurora laughed. "Not bah, Leah."

"Mommy!" Leah rushed out to her. "You'll never guess what happened today."

"Hi, sweetie. Let's go to the car and you can tell me all about your day." Though the weather wasn't too cold for early December, Aurora had a cap on the baby's head and wanted to put her in the warmer vehicle as soon as possible.

She grasped Leah's hand and they walked to the SUV. As they made their way, Aurora smiled at the other moms, all the while listening to Leah babble about the boy who got in trouble during lunch for deliberately spilling his milk on another girl. Aurora was so grateful for these little moments, from her seven-year-old daughter still allowing her the privilege of hand-holding to having a happy, well-adjusted child who liked to share everything about her world.

Aurora's mother had dumped her as an infant on her grandmother's doorstep and after the older woman died when Aurora was five, she'd been sent to foster care. Not long after she'd aged out of the system at eighteen and moved into a back room of the diner where she worked, she'd met Leah's father. A vacation fling for him, an escape from life for her, they'd never exchanged last names and she'd had no way to find him when she realized she was pregnant. Until one fateful day, fate and a movie premier had brought them back together.

"Mommy, it's Friday. What are we doing this weekend?" Leah asked once she had both kids settled in the car and she was behind the wheel.

"You and Ellie are going to stay with Grandma Melly." Aurora hadn't told Leah ahead of time so she could keep her surprise for Nick.

"Yay! I'm going to ask grandma to take me to the movies. I want popcorn!" Leah began to ramble about all the way she'd run Melly ragged this weekend.

Just the thought had Aurora stifling a yawn. With Ellie teething, she and Nick rarely got a full night's sleep these days. Just one more reason she needed this long weekend away. All Aurora wanted was the beach and Nick.

"That sounds like fun," she said to her daughter. "Will you help grandma with Ellie?"

Leah nodded. "I'm a big girl. I know where the diapers are and how to give her a bottle."

"I know you do, sweetie." Aurora glanced in the rearview mirror and smiled as her oldest patted her sister's little hand. She started the car, pulled out of the lot and onto the street.

Aurora raised the volume on the music. A song from Frozen, which was still Leah's favorite movie, played through the speakers from the playlist Aurora had made. Leah immediately began to sing along.

Her daughter was adorable, precocious, exhausting, and Aurora loved every second of being a mom. When she'd been pregnant and alone in Florida, she'd had no way to imagine the life she now lived. Had no way to know her wealthy half-brother, Linc Kingston, would soon find her and bring her north to a family that wanted her.

Every day since, Aurora made sure her child had all the love and security she'd never experienced growing up. And when she fortuitously ran into Nick five years later, her life had changed for the better yet again. She not only had security but the love of an amazing man who'd done everything to convince her to take a chance on him a second time.

And she never forgot how fortunate she was or where she'd come from. These days, Aurora juggled running a foundation she'd founded to support foster kids, giving them the skills for when they aged out of the system. To give them the ability to find jobs and places to live instead of hot, sweaty rooms behind a diner. She also had great assistants to hold down the fort when she was with her kids.

Instead of driving them home, Aurora dropped her daughters and the suitcase she'd already packed, off at Melly's. Then she headed home to surprise her husband.

CHAPTER 2

Nick wrapped up his work at the Meridian Hotel, the main office from which he ran the other luxury hotels his family owned in various large cities across the United States. He'd had a rough day, the sous-chef in New York quit and Martin, the head chef, was taking his frustrations out on the rest of the staff. It had taken his sister, Jade, who he called the Martin-whisperer, to calm the man down. Nick had called Max Savage, who was married to his cousin, Lucy, and owned the restaurant, Savage in Soho. Max had given him some names of chefs who might be able to step in on short notice.

After that fiasco, he'd decided to call it a day. He shut down his computer and rose to his feet as his brother, Asher, walked into the room.

"What are doing here? Everything okay?" Nick asked. Asher ran the Dirty Dare Spirits company and had no reason to show up at the end of a workday without notice.

"Everything is fine. I'm here to take you to my jet. Your wife has a surprise for you."

Nick raised his eyebrows. "What kind of surprise?"

"If I told you, I'd have to kill you." Asher chuckled. "Just get your ass into my car. We're going to the airport."

With a groan, Nick rose to his feet. "I'm fucking exhausted. Can it wait?" The baby was teething and he liked to help Aurora at night so she didn't have the entire burden on her.

"Nope but trust me, this will help whatever is bothering you. Exhaustion included," Asher said.

"Where am I going?"

Asher strode over and slapped a hand on Nick's back. "Think. Where does everyone in the family go when they need to get away?"

"Aurora wants to go to the Bahamas?"

"What she wants, is to be alone with you, and she took steps to make it happen. You're a lucky man. Now let's go so she doesn't think I fell down on the job."

An hour later, thanks to rush-hour traffic, Asher dropped him off at the private terminal and he walked up the steps to the large jet. Since they had a large family, the Gulfstream could accommodate eighteen people. He'd never get used to the plush interior that he knew his brother allowed only because their cousin Lucy, an interior designer, went all out.

No sooner had he walked onto the plane than the door behind him closed. He strode to the back of the aircraft, hearing the curtain close behind him. Obviously, his wife had given the pilot and crew specific instructions for privacy.

He found Aurora in the last set of seats in the back, wearing a flowing flowered skirt and a pale gold tank top that dipped low to reveal a tantalizing tease of flesh. She'd kicked off her sandals and was sitting barefoot and comfortable.

"Hey, gorgeous."

Aurora smiled up at him. "Hey, yourself."

He loosened his tie and undid the top two buttons on his shirt, before sitting in the seat beside her. "This is an amazing surprise." He slid his hand over hers and pulled it into his lap.

"I thought we were due for some alone time." Her beautiful blue eyes twinkling with happiness.

He grinned. "I wish I'd thought of it. How long are we staying?"

"Melly said she'd take the kids through Monday night. She'll get Leah to school on Tuesday, you can go to work and I'll pick Ellie up early that morning and Leah in the afternoon."

He stretched his legs out in front of him, feeling the movement of the plane as it began to taxi down the runway. The faster the movement, the more he relaxed. "I think we owe *her* an island vacation after she has our kids for four days and five nights."

"I was considering buying her a spa package at the hotel."

"Good idea." Nick raised her hand and kissed the top, his lips lingering as he took in the strawberry scent of her hand cream. "I can't wait to get you alone." With a six year old in the house and a teething baby, their time together was limited. Not that he didn't adore his girls and making up for all that lost time of being Leah's dad.

But he has just as much time to make up with Aurora. From the moment he'd laid eyes on her during his Miami break, she'd burrowed her way into his heart. If there was such a thing as love at first sight, he'd felt it for her. They'd just been too damned young. And stupid, not exchanging last names.

He waited until the plane leveled off and the pilot informed them over the speaker they could remove their seatbelts, to unhook his and turn towards her. Cupping his palms around her face, he pulled her to him and sealed his lips over hers. Her taste never failed to arouse him and just knowing she'd arranged this getaway for them made him want to give back to her any way he could.

Starting now. He slid his hand to her soft skirt and began pulling the material up until he could slip his hand beneath the silky material.

"What are you doing?" she asked against his lips.

"Thanking my wife for thinking about us." He clasped her thigh in his hand, letting his thumb stroke over her damp panties, finding her soaked already. He let out a hiss. "Fucking wet," he muttered.

"I have been since I sat down on the plane to wait for you. And when I saw you walk back here in your suit?" She trailed her fingers over the bulge in his pants and he grasped her wrist with his free hand.

"Nope. This is for you. Now sit back and enjoy. But let me see those eyes when you come." Ever since they not only reconciled, holding her gaze calmed him. Let him know he wouldn't lose her again.

He could tell she was wearing thin lace panties and he pulled hard, ripping one side and easily removing them. She gasped but grinned as he slipped them into his pocket.

"I heard this expression once, start as you meant to go on. And I mean to keep you naked and coming all weekend." He moved his hand over her sex and easily played with her clit, letting his thumb brush over the sensitive bundle of nerves.

She moaned. "Harder."

He pressed the bottom of his palm against the exact place he knew she needed pressure to come, while slipping his finger inside her.

"More, Nick." She bent her knees, placing her feet on the seat for leverage and pushed forward, sucking his finger deeper into her body.

He pulled out, adding a second and thrusting in and out until she was writhing with need. God, he loved to make her come.

"Eyes, baby."

Her desire-laden blue gaze met his and he curled his fingers inside her, rubbing in just the right spot. She held his stare but as he applied more pressure on her G-spot with his fingers, her eyes rolled back and her lips parted. Before she could make too much noise, he leaned over and kissed her, swallowing her screams, her body bucking as her orgasm consumed her.

When she finally relaxed back in her seat, obviously spent, he removed his fingers and brought them to his mouth, licking each, one by one. "Delicious as always."

And as always, she blushed, and he chuckled. "And gorgeous, too." He adjusted her skirt, pulling it down until she was fully covered. "I'm so grateful you made sure we could get away and have time alone."

She grasped his hands and smiled. "There's nothing I wouldn't do to keep the spark alive and well and us close."

"No matter how busy life gets, that's one thing that is never going to change." He leaned over and kissed her again.

CHAPTER 3

Aurora's legs were still trembling hours later when they landed and drove to Asher's incredible home. The place might as well be like a hotel, it was so grand when the SUV pulled up. For a girl who'd grown up with her things in a garbage bag, prepared to move from foster home to foster home at a moment's notice, she still found herself getting used to the Kingston and Dare wealth. No matter how much time had passed, she was still overwhelmed and filled with gratitude for all she had.

Once they arrived, she'd had visions of a romantic dinner on the veranda with her husband and making love all night long. Instead, she was shocked when she woke up in the morning, still dressed in yesterday's clothes, laying on top of the bedspread. Nick snored softly beside her. She rolled over and he, too, was fully dressed.

"Honey?" She wriggled closer to him. "Nick?"

"Hmm?" His long dark lashes fluttered open. "Morning. What time is it?"

"After ten and we fell asleep in yesterday's clothes. And we missed dinner. I'm sure Maggie is upset," she said of the housekeeper Asher kept on staff full time.

Nick shook his head. "Maggie never gets upset when things don't go according to plan." He reached a hand out and cupped her cheek. "I think you're the one upset. What's wrong?"

"I had a whole romantic night planned and we slept through it all. It's no different than being home." A swell of disappointment filled her at the thought of one night in paradise wasted.

Nick sighed. "We're parents, we work, it makes sense that we're exhausted. But we have all day today and tomorrow alone together and that's because of you. So don't be upset and let's enjoy these couple of days. Deal?"

She pulled herself to her knees, leaned over and kissed him full on the lips. "Deal."

An hour later, they'd showered together, making the most of the coconut scented bodywash regularly stocked in each bathroom. Breakfast was on the veranda outside, fresh fruit, homemade pastries, and delicious omelets, and mimosas. Nick was usually a harder whiskey guy but first thing in the morning, champagne and orange juice would do.

He lay beside his wife on a double recliner with a plush cushion, sand beneath the lounge chair and the pristine ocean in the background and blue sky above. The best part was how relaxed Aurora now seemed to be. He hated seeing her so stressed.

"This place could be a resort," she said with a happy sigh, as if reading his mind.

"It could but luckily it's in our family and we can escape any time someone decides to plan a surprise." Reaching beside him, he squeezed her hand. "Look at me." He rolled to the side and she did the same.

He let his gaze slide over her, taking her in from head to pink painted toes. She wore a high cut bikini that covered her belly, one he knew she was sensitive about after having his kids, but he found her sexy no matter what.

"I'm really glad you arranged this for us. I know how busy our lives have been and I always want us to make time for each other. But more than that, I need you to know, that I love you. I love our kids and most of all I love our lives together. Don't think that because we miss out on one night of romance or sex means I want you any less."

She lifted her sun glasses and he caught the sheen of tears in her eyes. "Nobody said juggling life would be this hard."

He pulled her onto his side of the lounge. "Well, the one thing you never have to worry about is me and how I feel about you."

Her smile was brighter than the sun. He rolled on top of her, letting his cock settle against her sex. "What are the chances I can make love to you right here?"

"Oh, I'd say about one hundred percent," she said and wriggled beneath him until she moaned, obviously finding the perfect spot to give her the friction she needed.

He raised his hips and between them both, they got rid of her bathing suit bottom. He followed by standing and shucking his. Then he climbed over her and braced his cock at her entrance.

Without him asking, her gaze locked with his and he pushed inside her, sliding in slowly, feeling every soft, tight inch. She was wet for him and he bottomed out quickly, his entire body lighting up with need.

"Nick." She wrapped her arms around his neck. "I love you."

"I love you too, sweetheart." He made love to his wife, slowly, without the worry of being interrupted by their kids or rushing due to time constraints.

She bent her knees and thrust deep. She immediately arched up, rubbing her pussy against his pubic bone, in total sync with his thrusts.

His balls drew tight and he was on the edge. "You're everything to me," he said in a gruff voice, his entire body on the precipice. He tunneled in and out, his gaze never leaving hers.

"Yes, Nick. Right there." He shifted his hips and gave her what she needed, sliding his hand between them and rubbing her clit.

He saw the moment she tipped over, her cheeks flushed, her eyes unfocused. "Oh God. Harder."

He drove into her over and over until her shaking subsided and he let himself go, falling into everything that was Aurora.

They cleaned up and redressed.

Hand and hand, they went into the ocean, ending up back on the lounge where they both fell asleep side by side, her hand tightly in his.

Aurora woke up and glanced at her phone. To her surprise, the entire day had passed. It was four p.m. From the way her body felt, napping the day away under the Caribbean sun without reapplying sunscreen hadn't been a smart move.

She glanced at Nick who still dozed beside her and smiled. He was right. It didn't matter what they were doing or where. They were connected and always would be. But she was glad she'd arranged this short trip away. As parents, they needed time alone.

"Nick." She woke him, pressing her lips to his.

"Is everything okay?" he asked, his gorgeous eyes focused on hers.

She nodded. "It's time to call Melly and check on Leah."

With a grin, he sat up in the seat and she pushed herself up too. "I hope she's been good."

"If that means running her grandma ragged, I'm sure she has."

She hit the FaceTime button on her phone and instead of Melly, her daughter's sweet face came into view. A reminder of how far she'd come from the lost, lonely girl she'd been. She had Nick, her daughters, and a life most could only dream of. She would always be grateful to be both a Kingston and a Dare.

If you enjoyed the sneak peek into the lives of Aurora and Nick Dare's Happily Ever After, read more Kingston ~ Dare standalone stories by Carly Phillips in Just One Dare.

SWEET STUD

CARY HART

CHAPTER 1 - MIA

"Maddie, get your ass up." I fling open the curtains.

"Go away." Maddie yawns. "And take the sun with you."

"No can do, little sis."

"Please—" she whines. "I've had a rough day."

Maddie is a masseuse at one of the most luxurious hotels in NYC. Some days she only has a couple of clients and other days it's filled with some of the bitchiest high maintenance women who run her ragged. Luckily for her, their husbands cover the bill—tip included.

"But I have a surprise for you." I make my way over to the closet.

"What kind of surprise?" Maddie rolls over on her back, eyes still closed.

"Open your eyes to find out?"

"So dramatic…" She mumbles.

"Hey!" I clap. "Time to wake up."

"Jesus, Mia! I'm awake… just resting them one at a time." Maddie peers out of one eye before she switches to the other. "See? They're taking shifts."

"You don't have time to be tired." I unzip the bags. "We have a party to go to."

"Did you say party?" Maddie's eyes pop wide open. "What's this madness you're talking about."

"You heard me." I take out the black puff-sleeve belted mini dress with a plunging V neckline. This dress screams Maddie. It fits in all the right places, and with its asymmetrical hem, her legs are sure to be a showstopper.

"Holy hell, sis." Maddie rolls out of bed, snags the dress, and holds it up to her tiny frame. "Please tell me I get to keep this one."

"That's a negative."

"Seriously, what good is being a blogger if you don't get to keep *everything* they send you?" Maddie holds out the little black number. "Just take it. I'm kind of tired anyway."

"But I need you to take pictures tonight."

"Ohhh…" she sighs, "it's a *work* gig. Definitely not going then."

"Maddie," I plead.

"I'm going to take a long hot bath."

"For the party, right?"

Maddie pads her way to the bathroom. "If by party you mean me sitting in bed eating takeout and binge-watching Netflix, then yeah."

Okay, this isn't going as planned. I reach inside another bag and pull out my secret weapon. "Could these convince you?"

"Mia, give it up already." Maddie spins around, looking annoyed—until she sees the recognizable brown box. "Oh! My! God!" She darts over to stand in front of me. "Are those what I think they are?"

I nod.

Her eyes tear up. "Please don't tease me."

"I'm not." I flip open the lid, exposing the cherry red dust bag.

Maddie gasps.

I win!

"Are these mine?" She carefully extracts one of the bags and slides out the matte black heel with the signature red bottom.

"All yours."

"Ahhh!" Maddie lets out the breath she was holding. "Thank you, Jesus."

"There's only one catch."

"I knew it!" She holds the heels to her chest. "There's always a fine print."

I chuckle. "You just have to let me take some shots of you strutting around at the fundraiser event the Klayton-Ellis Foundation is putting on tonight."

Maddie freezes. "Are you serious?" Her emerald eyes shine with excitement. "The party you want me to go to is the Krown Kandie's Sweet Stud Auction?"

"Um…yeah."

"Why didn't you say so?" She glances at the alarm clock. "Shit! Mia, you're wasting time. We only have three hours to get ready."

"I take it that's a yes?" My lips curve into a smile.

"It isn't just a yes—it's a hell to the yes!" Maddie strips down and steps into the shower, peeking her head back out. "Weird. All of a sudden, I'm craving something sweet." She winks.

Oh lord, what am I getting myself into?

CHAPTER 2 - MIA

"We're almost there," Maddie practically bounces out of her seat.

"I'm nervous."

Maddie swings her head around, her face twisting in confusion. "Why? You do these things all the time."

"I know, but this is different."

She's not wrong. My calendar is full of celebrity events and club openings, but this is the first time I'm attending a fundraiser where almost everyone is here because they have deep pockets. And it's the first time that I'm actually asking my followers for something in return... money. It's a little intimidating when you think about it.

"How?" Maddie narrows her emerald eyes. "What aren't you telling me?"

There's no use. I can't keep this a secret any longer and once she follows the hashtags I'm sure she's bound to find out one way or another.

"I don't know how to say this without getting your hopes up." I try to drag out the inevitable.

"Spill it."

"Fine." I drag in a deep breath and spill the beans. "All the bloggers are in a contest. The influencer who raises the most money for the charity, wins a trip for two to Hawaii."

"Ex-excuse me?" Maddie holds a hand up to her ear. "I don't think I heard you correctly. Did you say Hawaii?"

"Yeah..." I lean back into the seat and rest my head against the leather.

"Hawaii... as in beautiful, picturesque islands, surrounded by the Pacific Ocean, lush tropical rainforest, active volcanos, cascading waterfalls, luaus, and getting laid the moment you arrive? One of the most beautiful places on earth... that Hawaii?"

"That's the one."

"And you're just now telling me this?" She throws her hands up in the air. "You should have led with that. Now what do we have to do to get that trip? Because you are going to win it and I'm going to be your plus one."

"See..." I wag my finger in her direction. "This is why I didn't tell you."

"Because... I make things happen?" Maddie winks. "I want this trip and I'll do whatever it takes to get it."

It's not so much about the trip, like don't get me wrong, I would love to win, but what if I can't pull in the money like some of the other blogs?

"Oh hell no." Maddie leans forward and taps the side of my head. "Get those intrusive thoughts out of there."

I sigh. "I can't help it." I glance down at my phone. My nine-hundred and fifty-nine-thousand Instagram followers stare back at me. "Sure, I have a lot of followers, but some of the bloggers coming tonight have millions of them."

"And?" Maddie doesn't seem to be following.

"We are given an affiliate link and those links report live on the event page. Everyone will see the funds I'm pulling in. What if I fail? What if me coming here was a mistake? What if I took a spot of someone who could have raised way more money? What if everyone thinks I'm a fraud?"

Maddie rolls her eyes. "Okay, so let me just clear this up so we can get our party on. You are not a fraud. And you don't need them to donate big money. You just need them all to donate a little money. And if they all do that then it will not only benefit the charity, but it will win us a trip to Hawaii."

"I don't care about the trip."

"Seriously?" Maddie arches her perfectly sculpted brow.

A smile tugs at the corner of my lips. "Okay—so maybe an all-expense paid trip to Hawaii wouldn't be so bad."

"Okay... now that's what I'm sayin'." Maddie takes the bottle of champagne out of the bucket of ice. "This will take the edge off."

I hold up my hand. "I'm not sure. I've already had one. And if we are going to do this I need to be totally sober."

"Oh, come on." Maddie forces the crystal glass engraved with the Krown Kandie logo into my hand. "If they didn't want you to drink it, they wouldn't have sent us a car with a fully stocked bar."

"I guess." I tilt the glass to my lips. The bubbles tickling my nose.

"Here." Maddie takes my phone. "Do that again." She leans back to get a fully body shot, snaps a picture, then flips the phone around to show me. "This is why you're here."

I set the glass down and take the phone, examining the picture. My blonde waves are braided back into a low-hanging, loose chignon bun, showcasing my baby blues. I went with more of a natural look of nudes and pinks, highlighting my cheekbones with a rose gold shimmer, and tinted my lips with gloss.

My dress…it's fun and flirty. Perfect for an event like this. It's the prettiest shade of cotton candy pink. Not the darker shade when it's packed down or wet, but the light and airy pink when it's first spun. My sleeveless tulle bustier tea-length dress has a sweetheart neckline and a full pleated skirt. The corset boning on a sheer bodice plays peek-a-boo with my faded summer tan. I absolutely love it.

Maddie's right. I'm here because I shared the hair products I used on my hair. I'm here because of the one-hour makeup tutorial I gave while getting ready. I'm here to showcase a dress for Ava Livingston, a rising NYC fashion designer. I'm here because somewhere down the road, people give a damn what I have to say. They trust my brand… they trust me.

"Holy shit. We're here." Maddie reaches over and grabs my leg. "They live in a freakin' castle!"

"I know." I don't bother looking up. "Their house was featured in one of those design magazines a couple months ago."

"Mia—I can't even."

"It's not a big deal. If you've seen one big house, you've seen them all." I add the affiliate link to my post and a cute caption.

"Hurry! Get ready."

"Stop it!" I smack her hand away. "Red carpets aren't my—holy shit."

I add the picture to my story and tag Krown Kandies. "We have to go live."

Maddie scoots closer to the window. "Right? I think we've been transported to a different universe. How do I look?"

Maddie is gorgeous, favoring our mother with her green eyes and light brown hair. She may only be five-five, but she's all legs.

"Absolutely sinful." I hand her the phone. "How about me?"

"Totally yummy." Maddie winks.

"Let's take a selfie." I angle me face toward hers. "Make cute kissy lips."

Maddie reaches her arm out, snaps the picture, and posts it right before our car comes to a stop.

"Crap. We need to switch places so I can get your reaction as you get out." Maddie climbs over me.

"Good thinking."

"Ms. Matthews." The driver comes over the intercom, startling us both. "We're next. As soon as the door opens, please exit the vehicle promptly."

"It's showtime." Maddie whispers.

"You ready?"

"Sure am." Maddie holds up the camera and signals when it's live.

"Hey, guys! Mia Matthews here. If you've been following my stories, then you know exactly where I am. That's right. We are about to walk the red carpet of one of the most talked about events of the year." I glance out the window, eyes big, mouth hanging open for more of a dramatic feel. "Scratch that. This is hands down the event of the decade!"

The door opens.

"Ms. Matthews." The doorman offers me his hand. I look over my shoulder at camera and waggle my brows.

"Why thank you, kind sir." I step out of the vehicle and quickly turn around to make sure Maddie's able to get out of the car without flashing her goods.

She runs a hand down the back of her dress as she steps toward me, still filming. "Holy gumballs! This is epic."

I spin around. The crowd clears.

Unbelievable.

Maddie nods for me to go on. "Guys, do you see this?" I step onto the red carpet that isn't red at all. "The Klayton-Ellis estate has morphed into Candyland." I wave toward the carpet, which is a replica of the board game. "Red, purple, yellow, blue..." I step on each block. "I feel like Princess Frostine making her way to the Candy Castle—or, in this case, the Krown Kandie Castle." I wink at the camera. "Do you guys see this? Valet ropes of licorice, gumball theater lights, and lollipop signs guiding us where to go."

"This is..." I twirl in a circle, holding my arms out wide, "ah-mazing! All this is put on by the incredibly tasty Krown Kandies and the Klayton-Ellis Foundation, which is raising money for the local children's hospital. One of the events will include a bachelor auction of some of New York's Sweetest Studs."

Maddie motions behind me.

I twist around to see five banners strung from the top balcony. Each one representing one of tonight's bachelors.

"Ladies and gentlemen..." I wave my hand like Vanna White, "tonight's bachelors. Well…all but one. You see the solid black one in the middle? They're keeping him a mystery by saving the sweetest stud for last." Reaching over, I take the camera from Maddie, bring it in for a close-up, and whisper, "Pretty hot, right? If only you guys at home had a chance to bid on one of these guys…" I raise my finger in the air. "Oh wait! You can. All you have to do is go to the Krown Kandies link below and click on the Sweet Stud banner on the homepage. Not only will someone here win a date, but you at home will too!" A smile stretches across my face.

Maddie comes up behind me and rests her head on my shoulder. "Sign me up. I'll take one of each."

We both laugh.

"If you want a chance, all you have to do is donate a dollar. One. Single. Dollar. Or donate more, it's totally up to you. However, the more you donate, the more entries you receive. Kind of cool, right?" I glance over my shoulder. "What do you say, Mads? Think we should enter?"

"Of course."

"Well, that's my cue to go." I blow a kiss. "Make sure you follow @Me_Time_With_Mia because this party is just getting started!"

"Bye-eee," we say in unison.

I end the live just as we hit the waiting line for the step and repeat.

"I think that went well. It's been a while since I've been live at an event."

"You do realize that you are worried for nothing? All you have to do is promote those bachelors and your followers will keep the money flowing."

"I guess you're right."

"I know I'm right." She grabs me by the hand. "So—who would you marry, fuck, kill?" Maddie blurts out.

"What?" My face twists in confusion.

She points to the banners. "I would marry Damon, fuck Nash, and kill Chase."

"Oh!" I ponder her question. "Hmmm…I don't know."

"Well, Damon is obviously hubby material. He's a pediatric heart surgeon which means he's practically a superhero! Nash, a sexy country singer. Not from here, but he can lay me down and play me like his guitar any day. Chase? Well…Chases suck. The end."

I shake my head. "You're crazy."

"You never know, Mia. Yours could be up there too!"

Yeah, I don't think so.

CHAPTER 3 - MIA

"You won't believe this." Maddie slides up to the candy bar.

"You got married in Ice Cream Mountain?" I fight back a smile.

"Let's forget the marriage thing for now." She scoffs. "Dr. Damon was a no-go."

"That stinks." I pick up a bowl. "Peppermint?"

"Don't mind if I do." A deep voice vibrates behind me, causing all the tiny hairs on the back of my neck to stand at attention and my sister's eye to widen.

"I think that's my cue to leave." Maddie gives her a nod of appreciation. "Plus, I'm meeting Logan McGregor, bachelor number four, in the storage closet for a little game of seven minutes in heaven." She pops a mint into her mouth before walking away.

I'm going to kill her!

"Peppermint?"

He's still here.

"No, I'm good." I set the bowl back down, hoping he takes the hint.

He reaches across the table and grabs the striped candy.

"Listen—" I spin around, coming eye-to-chest with a wall of a man. "Holy shit."

"Everything okay?" I don't have to look up to know he's smirking. It's probably one of those sexy, make-your-clothes-fall-off kind of smirks.

Don't look up, Mia.

"There's nothing much here." I pat around on the table and grab the first thing I find. *A Twizzler!*

"So..." he rasps out, "are you just going to stand there looking at my chest?"

"I'm not looking at *your* chest," I choke out. This man is making me nervous and I'm not sure why. I don't feel threatened in the least. There's something about his presence that has me wanting to strip off all my clothes and go skinny dipping in the chocolate river.

"What would you call it then?"

"Eating a Twizzler."

"They wouldn't have Twizzlers at a Krown Kandie event." He mock scolds me.

Shit! Why didn't I think of that?

"Looks to me like they do." I tease, taking a bite off one of the ends to hold it up.

Big mistake.

Because my vision betrays me and glance up to meet some of the sexiest hazel eyes I've ever seen.

"Hello." His gaze glistens with mischief.

"Hey." I can't seem to form any other words.

"How's the licorice? I actually prefer it to the brand I shall not mention. It has more of a natural strawberry flavor don't you think?" His full lips curl into a wicked grin.

Stupid lips.

"Did you know if you bite off the ends it doubles as a straw?" I blurt out before flipping the licorice stick upside down, showing him step by step. "See?"

Palm to the face!

"Interesting. Give me a minute." He walks off, leaving me standing there holding a straw formally known as a Twizzler.

Get a grip, Mia.

I'm being ridiculous. I came here to do a job—and that's what I'm going to do. I pull out my cell phone and flip the camera around.

Candy bar selfie time.

Maybe if I distract myself with work, I can drown out the urge to hunt down Mr. Hazel Eyes and drag him back here so I can...*what? Ravage him?*

This is stupid. There are only so many pictures you can take without it being overkill. My followers don't want me ogling over chocolate, they want the bachelors—which is exactly what I'm going to give them.

Standing on my tiptoes, I peer over the crowd, trying to get a glimpse of one of the studs in their signature pink bowties when I see him...Mr. Hazel Eyes.

This man is more than just eyes and lips. He is perfection with his slicked-back hair, devilish eyes, and sinful smile.

He catches me staring.

Great. He looks like a million bucks, and I look like a stalker.

No. No. No.

He's coming back this way, looking like James Bond with two flutes of bubbly, one in each hand.

"Champagne?" He casually extends a glass my way. "I couldn't help but notice you couldn't take your—."

"I wasn't staring." I blurt, before downing the drink to settle my nerves.

Smooth. Real lady-like.

I mean, what if I was practically one step away from humping a giant sucker on the way to Lollipop Woods.

"I was going to say camera. I saw you taking pictures." He winks, downing his own drink before raising the empty glass.

"Another." It's more of a demand as he grabs two more flutes from the passing waiter.

"Time to test out your theory." He grabs a Twizzler and bites off one end, then the other.

Oh! My theory.

He watches me as he places the licorice in my glass. "Try it."

Is this man nuts?

"I don't need to. I *already* know it works."

"Well, just think how much more fun for you to show me."

I roll my eyes.

His mouth twitches.

"Fine." I wrap my lips around the makeshift strawberry straw and suck, draining my glass...for a second time. "See! It works. Are you happy?"

"Very." He cocks his head.

"What?" What is it with this man? He's driving me insane.

"I was wrong about you, Ms. Matthews."

"Ex-Excuse me?"

"How rude of me." He holds out his hand. "Klayton Ellis."

Holy hell!

How did I not recognize him? As the face of Krown Kandie he's practically plastered on every billboard... and gossip magazine. His mom Kandace Klayton-Ellis approached me to promote this event and the new candy line Klayton is marketing.

"Oh!" I take a step back to put some space between us. "I'm sorry. I didn't recognize you..."

Without your flavor of the week hanging off your arm.

"Really?"

Crap! Did I just say that out loud?

Klayton reaches for my arm and spins me around.

I'm going to get tossed out. My reputation will be ruined and my IG status gone.

"I don't know, Mia...do I look different?" He stares at our reflection in the mirrored walls of the Ice Palace. His eyes rake over my body.

"No," I choke out.

There's something about this man that has me feeling things I've never felt before.

Need.

"Good. You can't always believe what you read." Klayton turns toward me. "What *you* see right now—it's exactly what you get." He runs his tongue along his bottom lip, shaking his head. "But can you say the same? Are you that quirky, quick-witted girl who trembles at my slightest touch?"

"I don't—"

He runs the back of his hand along my bare arm and I shiver. "You were saying?"

"They must have kicked up the air." I point toward the Ice Palace sign. "You know, to set the mood."

"Is that right?" Klayton closes the distance between us. "Because I think your body knows exactly what it wants."

Traitor!

"It doesn't. It's all this damn chocolate." I wave my hand around the room. "You know...it's an aphrodisiac."

Klayton throws back his head and laughs. "Try again. I haven't seen you eat a single piece."

"You know there are like a hundred candy bars here, right?"

"Fifteen actually," he corrects as he steps forward, wraps his arm around my waist, and pulls me into his chest.

"I'm going to ask you nicely." I plead, bringing my hands up between us. "Please don't. I'm not something you can play with."

He lowers his face, breathing me in. "You've had champagne, strawberry licorice, and something a little sour, but no chocolate."

"Okay, fine." I push off him. "You're my chocolate, but the joke is on you. I hate it. It's too messy for me."

Klayton brings his hand up to his chin, narrowing his eyes. "So, I'm chocolate?"

"Yes, follow along. You're bad for me. You're sticky and temperamental."

"But if it tastes good, isn't it worth it?"

Yes!

"No!"

His smirky smile is back. "Two can play this game." He holds up his finger, telling me to wait as he walks over to the table and grabs a bag of cotton candy.

"What are you doing?"

"You're cotton candy." Klayton reaches into the bag and pulls off a little section. "Looks amazing, light—almost transparent." He takes a bite of the pink fluff. "Tastes fucking amazing." He pulls off another piece and pops it into his mouth. "It's addicting."

"Whatever."

Klayton brings his fingers up to his mouth, licking them one by one. "It's a little messy, but fun to clean up."

I gulp.

He notices.

"Mia—"

"Klayton!" someone calls out. "There you are." A petite brunette comes strolling up. "I've been looking for you." She wraps her arm around his waist.

"Cassie." He says her name. Not a *hello* or *what do you need?*—just her name as his eyes remain fixed on me.

"They need you backstage for a moment," Cassie coos, leaning into Klayton.

I don't know what it is about this girl, but I don't like the way she's looking at me while draping herself all over him.

"I'll be right there." He runs his hand down her back.

"You know what?" I hold up my phone. "I have to get to work anyway."

"Come on, Klayton. Let the *help* get back to work."

I slide the phone to life and open the camera. "But first, a picture of Krown Kandie's finest with his *girlfriend*."

"Oh yes!" Cassie giggles, striking a pose. "This is nice. Isn't it, Klayton?" She glances up to him, but his eyes are on me.

"Perfect! See you guys around." I walk over to the candy bar and pour myself a cup of M&M's or Krown Kandie's version of the chocolate coated candy.

"Hey!" Klayton calls after me.

I spin around. "Yeah?"

"I thought you didn't like chocolate."

"Like I said, chocolate is messy, but these have a protective shell." I pop a few into my mouth, then hold up my hand. "Melts in your mouth, not in your hands."

"We're not done here," he calls after me.

That's what I'm afraid of.

CHAPTER 4 - MIA

"We're in the lead." Maddie rushes over to my side and holds her phone in front of my face. "That trip is so ours!"

"Shh!" I pull her over to the side. "Someone may hear you."

She rolls her eyes. "You're so dramatic." She waves her hand around. "No one here cares except for the other bloggers who are too busy snapping pictures and perfecting their posts."

"This isn't about the trip."

She flashes me her screen again. "We have raised almost two hundred and thirty thousand dollars! That's huge, sis. And it's all because of you and your followers. This is why they had you here." She motions to all the guest and bloggers who are roam around the castle. "It's why everyone is here and it's also why they decided to give away a trip to Hawaii as an incentive. There is nothing to be ashamed about. That trip is well deserved for someone who is giving so much and putting in the work. So, why not us? Why can't we be excited about going to one of the most beautiful places on earth?"

It's not so much that I don't want to win the trip. I do. I just don't want to make a scene about it. That's all I need is for someone to get us on video celebrating too early or make some kind of accusation.

"You're right. We do deserve it, but let's try to contain our excitement for when we do when."

"Now, that's what I'm talking about." She does a little hula dance before she spins around and runs into one of the bachelors on the banners.

"Hello ladies." A drop-dead gorgeous man with piercing blue eyes saunters up to us.

"Chase fucking Carmichael." My sister mumbles turning her back to bachelor number one.

I'm sure there's a story there that I'll have to interrogate her about later.

"Maddie." His voice is laced with amusement. "How have you been?"

"Good." She doesn't bother to turn around until she stuffs her mouth full of caramels.

I can't help but notice the way he's eyeing her up and down like she's on the menu. "Looking more beautiful since the last time I saw you and I wasn't sure if that was even possible."

She shrugs nervously and points to her mouth that is in overdrive working the extra chewy candy.

"Well... this is awkward." I give Chase an apologetic smile. "Do you care if I pull you over here to do a quick live for my viewers?"

Maddie shoots me a look that could kill before she spins around and darts out of there.

"Maddie's your..." He watches her walk away.

"Sister." I cut him off letting him know exactly who she is and that she's off limits of any discussion. "So, anyway... how about that live."

Chase straightens his pink bowtie before coming to stand next to me wrapping and arm over my shoulder. "Let's do this."

No doubt Chase is an attractive man but being in close proximity to the pretty playboy does nothing to my heartrate—not like when I'm near Klayton. With him it's not warm and fuzzy, or even butterflies, it's a powder keg and a match just itching to be struck. I know I would love the burn, but it's the aftershock that would ruin me.

Focus!

"On the count of three." I plaster on a smile and mentally count down.

Three... two... one.

"Hello everyone! I'm live at the Krown Kandie charity event with one of tonight's sexiest most eligible bachelors, Chase Carmichael." I turn my head and give Chase an approving glance from head to toe. "So, ladies... how much do you think bachelor number one will go for?"

Chase winks at the camera and chuckles when he reads some of the comments.

@bookish_girl101: I'd be his for free.

@net_diva21: It's the eyes for me!!!*sigh*

@sweettooth: I'm hungry for something and it's not Krown Kandies!

I glance over my shoulder and flash them Ice Cream Mountain. "Whoa... ladies. How about some of you take a minute to cool down, then click the link in my bio and take your chance on bidding on Mr. Blue Eyes here."

"I'm ready and waiting." Chase gives the camera his best smoldering look. "Every single dollar tonight goes to the children's hospital, the patients and their families." Chase pulls me in for a big squeeze. "So, let's show them what Mia's followers can do and get those bids in. For every dollar you donate, I'll match it."

He smiles down at me, and it's genuine. Not just for the camera.

"Wow! That's amazing. Thank you, Chase." I lean my head on his arm. "Who knew this big guy had an even bigger heart?"

"So, what's going on here." Klayton squeezes in between us and takes my phone. My followers go crazy with their comments. He's obviously their favorite bachelor. *No surprise there.*

"Are you guys really falling for this guy's nice-guy act?" He gives his audience what they want and flashes them his signature panty melting smile. "Or would you rather bid on someone you know who will show you a good time?" He pats his chest. "What you see is what you get." Klayton brings the phone closer. "Not all those reports are fake news." He waggles his brows, and the comments continue to flood in.

Is he...

"Nice try, Klayton." I tug on his tie. "Ladies... he isn't wearing the pink."

His deep rumble vibrates sending tingles down my spine. "Good eye." He nudges Chase out of view.

"Hey." He mutters flipping Klayton off out of view before walking off.

"I'm not wearing the pink tie, but why don't you bid on New York's very own McDreamy, Dr. Damon. He's not only one of the most eligible bachelors here, but he's also a pediatric surgeon at the children's hospital that this event is raising money for. So, let's show Dr. Damon and his hospital what we can do."

"We?"

"Yes, Mia... we." As if to prove a point he pulls me twice as close as Chase did, and I definitely feel something. "For every dollar @Me_Time_With_Mia raises I'll triple it."

I'm speechless. My heartbeat pounds in my ears like a steel drum.

"Better hurry up. The bidding ends in..." He looks down at his gold vintage Rolex. "In fifteen minutes."

"Well—ladies and gentlemen. You heard him. Time to go out and bid on your favorite bachelor. You know what to do. Stay tuned because the live bidding starts soon, and bachelor number five will be revealed." I bite my bottom lip. "Comment on my post on who you think it may be. The winner will have a chance to win my swag bag from tonight." I wave at the camera and hit end.

I can't believe that just happened. Did Chase and Klayton just have a pissing match, on my live, worth possibly millions of dollars? I don't know what is going on here, but I'm not sure if I like it.

Maddie ran off and Klayton lingering around has me distracted.

"Looks like trip to Hawaii is about to be yours." Klayton's voice pulls me back.

I sigh. "Don't you have a thrown of candy to perch on?"

He laughs and damn if it isn't sexy on him. Maybe I should insult him some more just so I can get the same reaction.

What is wrong with me?

This is *his* event that I was invited to, and this is how I thank him? I need to get my shit together before I ruin it all with my emotional whiplash.

"I'm sorry. That was uncalled for." I breathe out. "It just rubbed me the wrong way. Everyone assumes I do this for the incentives."

Klayton cocks his head to the side and just stares at me. His eyes are so intense right now I would swear he has x-ray vision. I have never felt so naked as I do in this moment. It's as if he can see my every thought and I don't like it. Especially, since I have no clue what is racing through his own mind.

"What?" I stumble back. His gaze throwing me off balance. He reaches forward, catching me by the elbow.

"Steady." He drops my arm reluctantly. "I'm just surprised that's all. Why else blog?"

I hate this question because the answer isn't a simple one. I wish it was, but it's not.

"There are so many blogs who are paid to advertise their products. Which fine... I get it. We are walking, talking billboards, but I wanted to be the person they could trust. Everything I do is because *I choose* to do. Sometimes,

I get something for free, but I usually give it away to my followers, family members, friends or charities."

He nods.

"So, you can't be bought?" Klayton bites his bottom lip, and my eyes follow. "Everyone has a price... like Hawaii."

"Unbelievable!" I throw my hands up in the air.

"Hey!" Klayton holds his hand up in surrender. "I'm not your enemy. I'm just curious. I hear what you are saying, but at the same time you are the front runner for the trip. My company hired you to sell the event to your followers. And you're doing that, killing it I might add."

"I could care less about it." I bite back. "I wanted to use my following for good. I knew I could raise money for the event and your parents did too. I worked my ass off to get where I am and it's all because people trust me. Can you say the same?"

Klayton steps forward, hands in his pockets looking like a cocky S.O.B. "Hmm—see that is the difference between me and you. I don't care if anyone trusts me. What they say... it's not true and I don't feel the need to convince them otherwise."

I gasp.

"That's not what I meant." I spin around as he catches my hand.

"Wait." He pulls me pack to him. And there goes my heart again, working overtime being inches away from him. "That came out wrong."

"You think."

"I have lived my whole live trying to avoid the spotlight and you want to throw yourself in it. I'm curious... that's all."

Is he joking right now? This man oozes attention whore. If there is a camera, he will find it and make it his bitch.

"I don't believe you. They don't find you, Klayton. You find them." I pull away.

He arms fall to his side.

"Looks can be deceiving, Mia. If someone is going to invade my space, I refuse to give them the satisfaction of knowing I care. I'm just being me, but they twist it into something that sells. It's the price I have to pay for being in the public eye. I've learned I can't trust anyone. Not even my family."

"That's sad

"It's life." He clears his throat. "So—this Hawaii trip—it wasn't why you agreed to do the event?"

A part of me wonders if this isn't a set up by Krown Kandies to vet the bloggers invited tonight. Rumor has it they are looking to partner up with a team of influencers for their social media campaign. And then there is a part of me that thinks he's just a guy trying to get to know a girl.

"It wasn't. I'm not going to lie... it's an amazing opportunity to grow my brand, but I mostly did it because it's raising money for a great cause. My cousin died of leukemia when we were in kindergarten."

"I'm sorry." His hand rest on my arm gently, genuine concern shines in his eyes. It's not just another robotic sentiment.

"Thank you. I know it seems like I'm just another blogger, but I'm not."

"I can see that."

Being here, in this literal palace with my sister, living my dream, and now having him looking at me like he is, a mix of admiration and desire... it's too much. Tonight, is so much more than views and dollars, candy and hot guys. It's about the next step in my brand and making a real difference. Then there is the trip...

"My sister is obsessed with Maui. Our parents met while vacationing there with their families. She's convinced that her very own love story is waiting for her on one of the islands."

He watches me, searching my face. "And you?"

"Truth?" I fight back a smile and confess a secret. "I used to think Hawaii was a magical place where couples went to fall in love."

"Magical huh?"

"When my friends used to say they wished their parents loved each other as much as mine did I told them to go to Hawaii." I cover my face. "This is crazy, and I can't believe I'm telling you this." I shake my head.

He pulls my hands away from my face. "Don't be embarrassed. It's cute." Klayton gives my hands a squeeze before pulling away. "Plus, it's just getting good. Go on."

"I know I'm going to regret telling you this. Anyway, I was so convinced couples would fall under a love spell or something that when my ex-boyfriend wanted to surprise me with a trip to the Big Island, I pretended to be sick because I knew he wasn't right for me, and I was afraid I would fall under his spell and be lost to him forever."

I can't stop the blush I feel creeping into my cheeks at my confession.

Klayton fights back a smile. "I've been to Hawaii plenty of times and I can honestly say I've never been bit by the love bug."

"Maybe you just haven't went with the right person." The words are out of my mouth before I can take them back.

"Noted." He winks. And my ovaries just exploded.

"Mia!" Maddie pushes her way through the crowd. "Mia—we did it. Chase paid up and now we are just waiting on this guy's match." She nudges Klayton in the side. "Pay up there is only a couple minutes left."

He gets the biggest smile on his face, and it's directed right at me. "It's about the charity, right?"

"Of course." My blush deepens.

He hits a few buttons on his phone before sliding it in his pocket. "Done."

My phone goes crazy with notifications, beeping erupts around us. Maddie swipes up just as I hear someone cheer *Aloha!*

"You asshole!" Maddie spins around and shoves her phone screen in his face. "How could you? You made a promise."

"I promised I would match your funds— and I did."

But he didn't.

I grab Maddie's phone so I can see what happened, unable to believe my eyes. "You did."

"He sure in the hell did. He donated a shit ton of money but using someone else's link. Not yours Mia!"

"Hey!" Klayton takes a step back. "I just saved you from a spell that could lead to a lifetime of misery and heartache. You can thank me later."

He flashes me a cocky smirk and walks off. Maybe he's not who I thought he was...

Or maybe he is.

CHAPTER 5 - KLAYTON

The look, Mia gave me, was like a knife to the chest.

I know I did the right thing, but then why does it feel so wrong?

Impulsive. That's what my mother would say. And maybe it was but the decision behind it wasn't. For the first time in a long time, I'm thinking clearly, about someone other than myself. And it terrifies me.

I need some air. Loosening my bowtie, I step past a rope made of candy bearing a restricted sign. One minute I'm in *Candy Land* surrounded by people and cameras, and the next I'm walking down a pristine, white marble hallway to my private balcony.

The click of heels echo. So much for privacy, damn Cassie can't take a hint.

I turn to find Mia storming behind me. I halt dead in my tracks.

"How did you get back here? This area is restricted—" I regret my choice of words as soon as her gorgeous eyes narrow on me.

"Really! That's what you want to lead with?" She stops right in front of me and looks up with anger.

"Mia. No, I— look I know you're upset."

"Upset? No, you listen here you Prince of Peach Rings! I'm not upset... I'm furious!" She enunciates each word as she pokes me in the chest.

"I thought you said the trip wasn't important." I stand my ground.

"This isn't about the trip. Yes, my sister would have loved to win it. Yes, it would've been great to go where our parents fell in love." Mia huffs and lets out a deep breath. "But this isn't about the trip. It's about my reputation. It's about the fact that you used my own followers—*my followers,* against me and then humiliated me by supporting somebody else."

Well shit. I didn't think of that.

"Mia, it wasn't like that. I didn't do it to hurt you." I reach out to comfort her and place my hands on either side of her arms.

"Oh no, you don't." She pushes me away.

"Look, if this is about the social media campaign, and you're worried about securing a spot I can assure you, you have nothing to worry about."

"Oh, because I'm so lucky to have met Mr. Krown Kandie himself. Is that it? Just because we shared a moment over a bowl of peppermints, and I told you about my parents you can "hook me up with a spot." If you were listening to me at all tonight, you would know that's not who I am. That's not what I'm about. I wanted to win, fair and square, on my own terms. Not because you liked what you saw, or my cotton candy dress caught your attention."

"Would. You. Please. Just. Listen. To. Me." I step toward her until her back brushes the cold marble, and she's caged between my arms.

Her blue eyes widen in shock, but she doesn't back down.

Mia lifts her chin defiantly, looking me in the eye, our lips just inches apart. "How would you like if I bid on... oh—I don't know—maybe Chase?"

Fuck that.

The thought causes me to see red and I do the only thing I can think to shut her up, I take her cheeks in my hands and seal my mouth over hers in a searing kiss.

I expect her to push me away, but she does the opposite, her hands reach up and tangle in my hair.

I deepen the kiss, and she moans pressing tighter against me. She tastes sweet, just like I knew she would. What I wouldn't give to take her to my room and blow off the rest of the evening.

My phone vibrates, breaking the spell between us, and when I step back, she's looking at me like I just slapped her.

"I can't. I'm sorry." Her face falls. "My reputation.... your girlfriend—"

"Girlfriend?" I ignore the buzzing of my phone.

"Cassie, your girlfriend." She raises her eyebrows at me, her tone clipped.

"Cassie—is not—my girlfriend. She's my ex-girlfriend and a close family friend."

"You two sure looked pretty cozy earlier." she counters.

"It's complicated." I sigh, running a hand through my hair.

"I'm sure it is."

My phone keeps buzzing and I wish I had more time to explain.

"That's because I have to play nice with her due to family business, but trust me, there's nothing between us anymore, although Cassie seems to have trouble grasping that."

The buzzing turns to ringing, and I finally answer my phone. "I'll be right there.."

She watches me, and I can see the wheels turning as I end the call.

"Mia, I'm really sorry but I have to go. They need me—"

"Sure, it's fine." She turns away from me.

"It's not, but it will be. Just promise you'll give me a chance to explain." I plead.

She nods, and it kills me to walk away.

"Oh, and Mia..." I call out over my shoulder. "This isn't over."

"That's what you keep saying..." She smiles.

"Well, I'm about to make you believe it."

CHAPTER 6 - MIA

I haven't been able to find Maddie all night, and when I finally do, Klayton has her pinned up against a wall whispering sweet nothings in her ear—just like he was with me moments ago. What a jerk. He totally is chocolate. Actually, he's chocolate syrup. The generic kind. Looks like the real thing but tastes like shit. I can't believe I fell for his bullshit lies.

"Slimy asshole," I mumble.

Shoulders back, chest out, I lift my chin, putting one foot in front of the other, and head to the ballroom where the auction is taking place.

"Mia!" Maddie notices me and motions for me to hurry. "Bidding has already started."

I pick up my pace. "Sorry, I had to use the restroom," I lie. "I got lost."

Maddie shakes her head. "Yeah, I haven't explored more than the supply closet, but I can tell you it's huge and the shelves are pretty sturdy." She hugs her body and pretends to make-out with herself.

"You're a mess." Finally making my way over to her, I grab her hand. "Come on. We have seats reserved for us in the front row."

We bob and weave our way through the crowd, trying to get to our seats before bachelor number two comes on the stage.

Maddie taps my shoulder. "Look for Mr. Mint."

I spin around. "What?"

"Logan said to look for Mr. Mint. He'll take us to our seats."

I stop walking and spin around.

Maddie bumps into me. "Hey."

"Don't hey me. First it was Damon, then Logan, then Klayton, and now it's back to Logan?" I grip her shoulders. "Make up your damn mind."

"Klayton?" Maddie scrunches her nose. "I'm not interested in Klayton."

"Didn't look that way." I give her my best *I'm your older sister and you can't lie to me* look.

"What way?"

"He had you pinned up against the wall, whispering in your ear."

She places a hand on my shoulder. "For one, we were at least ten feet away from the wall, and two, they had just started bidding on the first bachelor. It was loud, and I couldn't hear him."

Oh my God!

I can't believe I just accused my sister of cheating with my non-boyfriend who cheated on me with his old slash ex-girlfriend or whatever she is. I'm losing it.

"My bad." I try to hide my embarrassment as we work our way through the rest of the bidders.

"You know he likes you, right?" Maddie confesses.

"Look! Mr. Mint." I point to the tall guy dressed in head-to-toe red and white stripes.

"Go ahead. Ignore me."

"I will." I wave at Mr. Mint, who directs us to the two empty seats. "Let's get a quick selfie, then a picture of the stage, and then we can sit back until they reveal the mystery bachelor."

"First, let's get one of just you." She bends over and pulls something from under her chair. "With this." She hands me the paddle. "Ready?"

"Where did you get this?" I hold up the glittery gold paddle with a black sixty-nine on the front. "Seriously?"

She shrugs. "It's an auction." Leaning back, she holds up the camera for the perfect angle. "Say Sweet Stud."

"Sweet Stud!"

We sit there for almost an hour watching the bidding war between a little old lady and a divorcee battling it out over Damon, the pediatric heart surgeon.

"I can't believe he went for over a fifty thousand dollars," Maddie whispers.

"I know. That's crazy."

"Get ready." Maddie grabs my knee. "The mystery bachelor is up next."

I pull out my phone and go live. "Ladies, we are about to find out who Sweet Stud number five is. Who's ready?" I turn the camera on me and waggle my eyebrows. "The suspense is *killing* me." I flip the camera back around.

"Ladies—get your paddles ready," Dr. Feelgood, host of New York's Hotline Hookup and tonight's celebrity host, teases the crowd. "This bachelor has been a little naughty."

Everyone goes nuts. The women carry on while their husbands are on standby with their credit cards in hand.

"This Stud is the Prince of Sweetness. He loves traveling, volunteering, and long walks on the beach..." Dr. Feelgood pauses. "Is this for real?" He tosses the card to the ground. "I know this guy. Whoever wrote that was laying it on thick." He rests his head in his free hand. "I mean, come on—his favorite sweet is cotton candy."

It can't be.

"This Sweet Stud adorns a *Krown* of *Kandie* and is one hell of a sweet talker. If you don't believe me, read the tabloids. That's right. He's in them *all*. If you don't know who I'm talking about, you should ask yourself why you're even here."

The crowd starts to chant his name. "Klayton! Klayton! Klayton!"

He walks out dressed in a white traditional tux with a black button-down shirt and hot pink bowtie, swinging around a bag of cotton candy.

"You guessed it—Krown Kandies very own, Klayton Ellis! Let the bidding begin at thirty thousand."

Paddles raise everywhere. When one goes down, another goes up.

"Fifty!"

"Fifty-five!"

"One hundred!"

A very familiar voice shouts, "Three hundred thousand!"

Cassie. *Old girlfriend my ass.*

"Wow—" Dr. Feelgood's jaw drops. "Ladies, this beautiful brunette in the middle here isn't playing around. If you want a date with this playboy..." he clasps Klayton on the shoulder, causing him to hang his head in laughter, "you have to up your ante."

Klayton turns around to put on a little show and grabs the mic. "Did he mention the date takes place in Maui?" Klayton's hazel eyes land on my blue. "Now let's see those paddles." Klayton winks.

Dr. Feelgood points to Cassie. "Going once, going twice…"

Klayton twirls the cotton candy cotton in the air.

Maddie raises her paddle. "Three-twenty."

"Maddie!" I shout, forgetting I'm still taping. I quickly turn the camera around on me. "Surprise! It's Klayton Ellis. Make sure you follow @Me_Time_With_Mia and click on the link in my bio for your chance to win your very own date with one of these studs. Bye-eee!"

"Three-twenty to paddle sixty-nine." Dr. Feelgood pretends to cover the mic. "Nice."

"Maddie, what are you doing?" I try to take the paddle from her, but she tugs it away.

"Stop it."

"Maddie! Listen to me!" I look my sister in the eyes. "It's three hundred and twenty *thousand*!"

"I know!" She laughs. "Isn't it crazy?"

"Three-fifty," Cassie chimes in.

Everyone goes silent.

"Three-fifty. Going once—going twice…"

"Paddle sixty-nine," Dr. Feelgood teases, "looks like Klayton has a special show just for you."

My eyes dart to his left where Klayton already has his tie off. He sways his hips back and forth while he slowly unbuttons his shirt one agonizing button at a time.

"Ladies, how about a little window shopping?" Dr. Feelgood steps back to reveal Klayton ripping off his shirt to expose a solid blue tee.

"No way!" My hand flies up to my mouth. "He didn't." I really should get this on video, but something about this seems too personal to share.

Klayton takes the microphone from Dr. Feelgood. "I melt in your mouth, not in your hands."

I don't even bother looking at Cassie. I can only imagine her face right now. The smug smile *thinking* she's won.

Not today, Satan!

I take the paddle from Maddie. "Four hundred."

Cassie fights back. "Four-ten."

Maddie leans in. "She's running out of money."

Oh my God!

"Maddie, what am I doing?" I throw the paddle down. "We don't have that kind of money."

"Do we have four-twenty?" Dr. Feelgood calls out.

Maddie picks up the paddle and raises it high in the air. "Five—hundred

—thousand—dollars! Booyah! I win!" she exclaims, dropping the paddle to the ground like a mic.

Oh my God! Oh my God! Oh my God!

I pace back and forth. Thank God for marble. If this was carpet, there would be a hole burned in it.

Maddie grabs me by the shoulders. "Mia, calm down. Breathe with me."

Inhale. Breathe in.

Exhale. Breathe out.

"What are we going to do?" I start calculating everything we have. Even if we sold the house, it's still not enough to make a dent in this. "We don't have the money."

"But I do," a voice whispers in my ear.

I spin around.

Klayton.

In his blue cotton shirt, hands tucked into his white tuxedo pants, he looks as yummy as ever.

"I can't believe I kept this a secret." Maddie clasps her hands as she eyes us both.

"Wait! What?" My eyes bounce between the two of them. "Oh my God, I'm such an idiot." I laugh out.

"Well, that's my cue." She winks. "I've got my own bachelor to find."

"Thank you, Maddie!" Klayton calls out.

Maddie doesn't turn around; she just raises one fist in the air and follows the path through Gummy Hills. Her mission accomplished.

"So—?"

"So what?" Klayton rocks back on his heels.

"What about Cassie?"

"What about her?"

"She seemed pretty invested for being an ex-girlfriend."

"Mia, our families have been conducting business together for years. Her little scene back there was a simple business deal between families."

Something tells me Cassie doesn't see I that way, but he's standing here with me not her.

"Interesting." Heat rises to my cheeks, embarrassed I let myself get worked up over a misunderstanding.

"Do you want to know what I find interesting?" Klayton closes the distance between us. His smile is beyond sinful. It's downright criminal...and I like it.

"What's that?"

"You claim M&Ms melt in your mouth, not your hands." He wraps his arms around my waist. "Care to find out how true that is?" He lowers his mouth to mine.

"Uh-huh."

"Kiss me," he breathes into my mouth, his words a plea. "See if I melt." I can feel his smile.

My heart races and my legs tremble as he swipes his tongue over my bottom lip, inviting me to open.

I do.

Our tongues tangle. Slow to hot and perfect. Just like him.

Klayton takes a step back and offers me his arm. "You ready?"

"For what?" I glance around, waiting for gummy bears to start raining from the sky or some crazy shit.

"Our date."

Oh?

"What date?" I play dumb.

"The date you just paid half a million dollars for." He gives me a sickly-sweet smile.

"You mean the date *you* just paid half a million dollars for."

Mic drop!

"Worth every penny."

"It's a great cause."

"Oh, the children, yeah, for sure. But I was talking about you—best money I ever spent."

"And to think I've always been called a cheap date."

"There is nothing cheap about you." His eyes drink me in from head to toe. "Ready? I have a jet waiting on us?"

"A jet?"

"Have you ever been to Hawaii?"

"I can't say I have."

"I heard it's a magical place."

"Well, I heard it all depends on who you're with." He pulls me into his arms resting his forehead against mine.

"Lucky for me, I'm going with you."

"I don't think luck had anything to do with it."

The night may not have gone as planned. But I still ended up with a trip to Hawaii… and the sweetest stud.

Mia and Klayton's full-length novel will be released in the summer of 2024. Check out Cary Hart's other stories in the Hotline Hookup Collection.

GOLDEN AMBITION

PREQUEL SHORT STORY, TANGLED DESIRES: BLOODLINE MAFIOSOS

CATALINA SNOW

CHAPTER 1

I lean against the worn fence that encases my family's meager plot of land; my eyes fixed on the horizon. The *pueblo* stretches out infinitely, yet it confines me and stifles my dreams. Beside me, Rafael's eyes sparkle with the same restless ambition.

"You ever think about what's beyond that ridge, Toño?" Rafael's voice sounds like a serene blend of excitement and fear.

"All the time, Rafa. All the time." His nickname tastes like freedom on my tongue. "And I know exactly how to get there."

Rafael turns to me and widens his dark eyes. "You mean...?"

"To the *Norte*. The United States," I say, my voice firm, filled with conviction. "There's opportunity there. We can make something of ourselves."

Rafael's eyes narrow as he considers the proposal. "It's dangerous. The journey, the crossing, the life there. What if we fail?"

"We won't." I nod, and my voice carries unbreakable confidence. "We're strong, and we're willing to work hard. There's a better life waiting for us, Rafa. I can feel it."

We spend hours that day talking about our dreams and our plans. We will leave together two young men barely eighteen, fueled by the promise of a new beginning. With my best friend at my side, the possibilities become endless.

Days turn into weeks as we prepare, each stolen glance at the horizon fueling our determination. Our families do what they can with what little they have to support us, bidding painful farewells to our families, the *pueblo*, and the only life we've ever known.

With our meagre belongings packed, I look back at my mother's tear-filled eyes. "I'll make you proud, Mama," I whisper, embracing her.

"I know you will, *mijo*," she replies, her voice breaking. "Just come back to me safe."

I nod, my throat too tight to speak, and turn to Rafael, who taps his fingers against his leg but still shows a wide grin on his face.

"Toño, are we doing this?" Rafael's voice trembles as he runs a hand over his clean-shaven face.

I stand tall. "We are, Rafa. We're going to change our lives."

We set out, two dreamers chasing a vision that seems almost unattainable.

The desert is alive with the whispers of those seeking a new beginning. Under The Coyote's watchful eye, Rafa, me, and fellow travelers navigate the treacherous path toward the border.

The Coyote, a wiry man with eyes that betray no emotion, barks orders, treating us like cargo rather than human beings. "*¡Apúrense!* Hurry up! And keep quiet unless you want to be left behind!" he spits, glancing back with a sneer.

Rafa leans closer to me, his voice barely a whisper. "I hope this is all worth it."

I nod, my throat tight with determination. "It will be. You'll see. If others can do it, so can we."

As we near the border, The Coyote's commands grow more urgent, and his demeanor becomes more unpredictable. "Down, all of you!" he hisses, pushing us to the ground. "Stay silent and follow my lead."

Hearts pounding, we huddle together, and the harsh reality of our undertaking settles in. In the distance, the glow of headlights approaches, and a murmur of fear ripples through the travelers.

My eyes widen as I notice a U.S. Border Patrol vehicle slow down. The agent inside locks eyes with The Coyote. A subtle nod passes between them, a silent acknowledgment of corruption that leaves a bitter taste in my mouth. I've always believed the U.S. had no corruption. After all, they are supposed to be the land of law and order. But I quickly shake the thought out of my head. Even at a young age, I understand that power and greed have no borders.

The vehicle moves on, and The Coyote's voice cuts through the tension. "Get up! Now! And move quickly."

We obey. Desperation and hope fuel our pace. The ravine looms ahead, and as we begin our descent, I notice a young woman struggling to keep up. Her child's cry pierces the night.

"We have to help her." I keep my voice low but insistent as I gesture back to her.

Together, we grab the woman's arms and help her to her feet.

The Coyote glares at us. "Leave her behind! Anyone who is too slow can't come! Get a move on."

I shake my head and glare at him. "I'm not leaving her behind. She needs our help!" I ignore him yelling at me and help the woman as we rush forward after the others.

"*Gracias.*" Her dark eyes glisten.

We continue our journey. Each obstacle we face becomes a test of our will, and each step confirms a commitment to our dreams. Finally, on the other side, as the sun begins to break the horizon, we know we have crossed more than just a physical boundary.

Rafa clasps my shoulder, and his voice thickens with emotion. "We did it, *hermano*. We're here."

I look back, knowing that the journey is far from over, but we have taken the first step on the path to a better life.

CHAPTER 2

The lush landscape of Northern California is a sight to behold for Rafa and me, a stark contrast to the arid lands of our hometown: the evergreens, snowcapped mountains, and ample lake sparkle with promise.

"Look at those houses!" Rafa exclaims, his voice filled with wonder as he peeks out the window of our car. The Coyote's men transport us in a passenger van from Los Angeles to our new home in Northern California. "And those yards! It's like something from a painting."

"It's incredible." I share his awe.

We arrive at the home of José, an acquaintance from our *pueblo*, who quickly pays the men and waits patiently while they count. As soon as the money is accounted for, José welcomes us with open arms. His house, surrounded by a well-tended garden, looks charming. The comforting smells of home-cooked meals wafts throughout the home.

"*¡Bienvenidos, muchachos!*" José greets us. "Welcome to your new home."

"Thank you, José." Rafa clears his throat and looks sheepishly down.

As we settle down to a hearty meal prepared by José's wife, Maria, the conversation flows naturally to life in this new land, the opportunities, and the challenges we might face.

"You'll find work soon," José assures us. "There's a construction site nearby that always needs strong hands."

Rafa and I listen attentively. Our faces reflect the hope and determination that have brought us this far. But I know we need to tread lightly. After all, we are illegally in the United States, and the risk of being caught is too costly.

I nod, and my voice comes out firm. "We'll do whatever it takes."

The construction site bustles with activity as José guides Rafa and me through the maze of equipment and workers. He leads us to a grizzled, stern-looking white man with a hardened expression.

"*Señor* Mitchell, these are the young men I told you about." José looks as smooth as he sounds, and his voice remains steady. "Antonio, Rafael, this is the site supervisor."

Mitchell grunts and his eyes size us up as he nods in acknowledgment. "Go find Ivan. He's your lead," he barks, his English thick with an accent that I struggle to comprehend.

"*Vayan con Ivan, él les dirá lo que tienen que hacer,*" José translates for us, his voice gentle. "Good luck, *muchachos.*"

"*Gracias,* José." Rafa grins and his eyes look bright.

As we make our way toward the workers, a young woman peers through a window of a house on the building site. Our eyes lock. There's a sparkle in her eyes as she curiously tilts her head. A smile quickly follows. It's a connection, and I feel it too. Something's caught her attention as she shifts her gaze and quickly ducks away, leaving me puzzled but intrigued.

"Come on, Toño," Rafa calls, and I focus back on our mission—work.

We find Ivan, a sturdy man with rough hands and a welcoming smile. "What do you know how to do?" His Spanish accent sounds thick.

I meet Ivan's eyes. "We grew up on a farm. We can do hard labor, and anything else, we'll learn."

Ivan's face brightens at my response. "Good. Help those men carry the lumber." He points to an area bustling with activity. "Be safe and don't argue or fight. The boss has no patience for quarreling."

The work is grueling, but Rafa and I fall into a rhythm quickly as our bodies are already accustomed to hard labor. Again, I glimpse the mysterious woman in the house a few feet away. Her eyes meet mine before she turns away. I can't shake the intrigue she has ignited in me.

Rafa gazes at me, clearly noticing my distraction. "What are you looking at?"

"Nothing." I shake my head, though my mind still focuses on the woman who has vanished from sight.

The sun bears down on us, and one of the other workers reminds us to grab hard hats. Rafa goes to fetch them, leaving me to work faster. My body aches from the effort.

"Don't hurt yourself, or you'll get fired," another coworker warns. "And without papers, there's no workers' compensation."

I don't fully understand my co-worker's meaning but sense the warning's gravity.

Rafa reappears, grinning as he hands me a hard hat. "I think I met my future wife," he teases.

"That's all great, but you need to get back to work," I scold, my mind still on our goals. "We're here to work, make money, pay back José, and help our families."

Rafa's grin fades, but he nods, knowing our purpose is clear.

We work late into the day. Our bodies feel tired, but our spirits undaunted. The mysterious woman lingers in my mind, a puzzle I can't solve, a story I can't read. But there's no time for distractions, only the path we've chosen, and the future we're building.

And yet, I can't shake the feeling that she will be a part of it, a piece of the intricate puzzle of our new lives in this foreign land.

CHAPTER 3

A few months have passed since Rafa and I started working at the construction site. The days feel long and hard, but we settle into our new life. The local *cantina* has become our regular spot to unwind without worrying about being carded.

I push through the *cantina's* door, and lively music and chatter greet me. I scan the room, and my eyes land on Rafa and his girlfriend, Sonia, kissing passionately in a corner. Sonia, the mysterious girl from the construction site, our coworker, has become an inescapable presence.

My eyes hungrily rove the couple, and an unfamiliar longing gnaws at my insides. I can't help but be drawn to Sonia's deep brown eyes, luscious laughter, petite features, and the curves that threaten to spill out of the confines of her clothes. My heart pounds in my chest as I imagine her nipples tauntingly hidden underneath her garments that beg to be ripped off. I know she's well aware of her effect on me—she flaunts it like a siren, pushing her chest out just a little further each time, daring me to take what she offers. I sigh heavily, trying to stifle all thoughts of her. She's with Rafa, my best friend... my brother. Those forbidden desires are not meant to be acted upon here.

I reach the bar, since my throat is parched, and order a drink. As I wait, a nicely dressed man approaches me with sharp and calculating eyes.

You're Antonio, right?" the man asks, his voice smooth. "I'm Emilio. I've seen you and your friend around here quite a bit."

My heart skips a beat. Emilio. Rumors swirl about this man, linking him to the local Mexican cartel. I try to keep my face neutral as I respond, "Yes, that's me. Do I know you?"

Emilio's lips curl into a smile that doesn't quite reach his eyes. "Not yet, but I think we could be useful to each other. I've heard you are hard workers, and I might have some opportunities for you to make extra money on the side."

My mind races. This is the last thing I want; entanglement with a man like Emilio. But I need to tread carefully, to navigate this conversation without offending or arousing suspicion.

"We're doing fine with our current jobs." I pause to choose my words cautiously. "But thank you for the offer."

Emilio's eyes narrow, but his smile remains. "Think it over, Antonio. The offer won't be on the table forever. And in this town, it's wise to have friends in high places."

I feel a chill run down my spine as I realize the veiled threat in Emilio's words. I nod, forcing a smile. "I'll keep that in mind."

Emilio claps me on the back and moves away, leaving me to my thoughts. My drink sits forgotten on the bar.

I glance back at Rafa and Sonia, only Rafa isn't at her side, and I lock eyes with her. My eyes widen in a mix of surprise and arousal as I see her hair over her shoulder, inviting me in. As her chest draws my eyes, I lick my lips out of an involuntary response. Her hand drops slowly, enthralling me with its movements, as her fingers trace the center of her chest in a slow, tantalizing motion before swooping over her breast. She bites her lip suggestively before allowing her hand to slide down the front of her jeans. I tense at the deliberate provocation, desperately wanting to take over for her. I can't take my eyes off her as she shamelessly massages herself between the legs. She throws her head back and breathes hard as she feels herself, her hand racing, giving herself pleasure. Finally, she brings her fingers to her mouth and licks them clean, never breaking eye contact with me, teasing and smiling. She's a minx. I gulp down my drink faster than ever and push it forward for another serve, all while enduring a pleasure I've never known.

The bartender distracts me with another pour, and when I turn back, Rafa slides into the seat beside her.

The show ends, and a strange sense of foreboding settles in my gut when Emilio joins my friend and Sonia. I want to rush to Rafa and yank him out of this place, putting as much distance as possible between us and Emilio. But it's too late. I can see the look on my friend's face. It's filled with an eagerness, a desire that many people like us yearn for—a better life. Our lives have changed so quickly, but I can't shake the feeling that we're standing on the edge of something dangerous that could consume us all.

I sip my drink. The bitter taste fills my mouth, and my thoughts become a whirlwind of uncertainty and desire as I look back and find Sonia staring at me. I raise my glass, drink the last drop, and escape before I do something rash.

CHAPTER 4

I lie in bed, and my mind feels like a whirlwind of thoughts and fears. Beads of sweat break across my shirtless chest as I toss and turn. It's late, and Rafa isn't back. The clock on the wall seems to mock me; each tick is a reminder of the uncertainty that gnaws at me.

The converted garage that serves as me and Rafa's shared studio feels stifling. It's a temporary refuge we can afford for now. I pace back and forth. My bare feet slap against the concrete floor as my mind grapples with what to do next.

A distant sound catches my attention, and my heart leaps into my throat. The faint rumble of an engine creeps closer, growing louder until it reaches the driveway in front of the house, right outside my window.

My breath catches as I jump up and peek through the blinds. Rafa gets out of a slick, luxurious truck that seems entirely out of place in our modest neighborhood. His animated voice carries through the glass, filled with cheerful thank yous and goodnight farewells.

My eyes narrow, and I cross my arms over my chest as I try to understand what I see. Rafa enters the room, and his face lights with a smile that could brighten the darkest room.

"Where've you been?" My voice tightens with worry.

Rafa laughs, and his eyes dance. "Well, *Dad*, if you need to know, I met a man who will bless us beyond our wildest dreams."

My heart sinks as he confirms my fears. "No! Not him. That man, if it's who I think it is, is Emilio. He's trouble, Rafa. We can have no association with him. Come on. You have to see that that is a world we don't belong to."

Rafa's eyes narrow, and his smile fades. "You know, you could at least hear his proposition. It's not that bad."

"Not bad?" I snap the words as I shake my head, and my voice rises. "I'm sure it's not good either."

Rafa stands square to me, and I pull myself to my full six feet one inch, towering over Rafa. The room seems to shrink around us as our conflict fills every inch of space.

Rafa's tone is low and deliberate, and his eyes never leave mine. "If you want to work as a construction laborer for the rest of your life, that's your choice. I see this man is handing us a way out, and I'd be a fool not to take it."

The words hang in the air, a challenge, a rebuke. My mind races, torn between fear and desperation, knowing that any decision will change everything.

CHAPTER 5

The air in our tiny garage studio feels stifling, thick with tension that's been building for weeks. My relationship with Rafael strains to the breaking point. Every interaction is tinged with an undercurrent of suspicion and resentment. Rafael's comings and goings, at all hours of the day and night, are a constant reminder of his chosen path. Emilio's gift of a midsized SUV to Rafa only deepens our rift.

"Come on, bro, take a ride with me!" Rafael's eyes brighten with excitement.

"No, Rafa." I glare at him and keep my voice icy. "I want nothing to do with that truck or anything else Emilio has given you."

We've become roommates in every sense of the word. Our brotherhood has been replaced by distance and distrust. Sonia's absence from the construction site only adds to my worries, feeding my fear that she, too, has been pulled into Emilio's dark world.

On a record-breaking hot, oppressive day, as my ride drops me off from work, I find Sonia sitting on the steps leading into the garage. Her eyes widen, her breath turns ragged, and a sense of dread settles in my stomach as I rush to her.

"*¿Qué pasa?*" I ask, my voice filled with concern.

"Rafa... detained," she stammers, gulping for air.

My heart freezes in my chest, and my mind races as I move her aside to open the door. I guide her in, toss my belongings to the ground, and secure the door behind me. I struggle to breathe beyond the scorching heat in the garage, but my focus is on Sonia. I pour her a glass of water from a filtered pitcher. Her shaking hand takes it, and she sips.

I want to press her for more details but wait to give her the needed time. When she finally meets my eyes, they fill with fear, raw and unfiltered.

"It's Rafa." She swallows deeply, and her voice trembles. "The police picked him up. They've detained him, and I can't go there. I don't have papers. *¿Qué pasa si empiezan a hacer preguntas?* What if they start asking questions?"

My mind whirs the long hot day on the job site, a distant memory as I grapple with the situation. I move to turn on the AC unit, pacing as I try to make sense of it all.

"*¿Qué estaba haciendo?*" I finally ask. It's essential to understand what he was doing to be detained.

Sonia takes another sip, and her eyes fill with tears. "We were on an errand for Emilio. But he didn't have anything on him. We'd already delivered the package."

"*¿Dinero?*" I press.

She shakes her head. "No. I have the money in my purse." She grips it tightly. "He'd gone into a convenience store to grab us some drinks when patrol cars circled him. I escaped through the driver's side door, away from the action, and ran... I hid in a laundromat, and then I walked here. I've been waiting."

My mind reels. The reality of the situation crashes down on me. The money needs to get to Emilio and quickly, because you don't keep men like Emilio waiting. The consequences can be grave.

"I need to shower, then we'll find a way for you to get that money to its rightful owner, and hopefully, he'll have some ideas." My voice comes out firm.

She nods, and her eyes follow me as I move into the bathroom, leaving me with the heavy weight of responsibility and the knowledge that Rafa, my best friend, has just complicated our lives.

I close the door behind me. My heart pounds erratically. Quickly, I tear off my clothes as a million questions race through my mind. I step into the shower, turning on the faucet in the hopes of hiding from reality, but no matter how hard I try, nothing can wash away what's about to happen. The water pressure in our dingy makeshift studio is almost undetectable, but at least I have privacy. I feel the droplets of grime and sweat wash away under the scalding stream as I stand still while the entire world moves around me. I squeeze shampoo into my hair and reach for the soap, only to feel a pair of hands wrap around me from behind. Sonia's body presses firmly against mine as she lathers bubbles over my chest. Her hands move up and down feverishly. Is this happening? Sonia is Rafael's girlfriend, yet she is naked in the shower with me. Should I push her away or give way to temptation? I don't know what to do and can't move—paralyzed by an unbearable mix of guilt and joy.

My rage boils as I've watched Rafa drift further and further away, sucked into a downward spiral of careless business decisions. My desire for the woman I've been enamored with was almost too powerful to resist—until she turned her attention to Rafa.

My heart gallops in my chest as her hands slowly inch up my body, leaving an electric current that shoots through my veins. My arousal is irrefutable evidence of how deeply she has ensnared me, but it's too late—she has me all to herself now. The water cascades down our bodies, washing away the soap, allowing me to finally see with my eyes what my imagination has tried to show me all this time, and it's even more beautiful than I imagined. She has won me over, ultimately.

I yank her toward me. Her body smacks into mine as the soap slips from my grip. My lips collide with hers in a passionate kiss as my arm coils around her waist while my other hand roves over her curves. My fingertips graze across her nipples, making them harden, and she moans against my mouth. I take one of her breasts in my palm and, urgently needing to consume her, my tongue flicks out and tastes every bit of it. She gasps again as my hunger grows, and I switch arms without skipping a beat to lavish attention on the other breast. My breathing matches hers as I carefully ease myself inside her warmth. Though inexperienced, every move of mine is laced with the knowledge learned from all the fantasies I have imagined about this moment. She welcomes me deeper as we move together. With every movement, a moan of pleasure escapes from Sonia's throat and drives me further on, faster and harder, until I feel flooded with overwhelming desire. I've never been this close before, but I know exactly what to do; Sonia has ensured that. She guides me eagerly, rocking against me in an ecstasy of mutual hunger. Everywhere we touch feels hot, and the searing lust threatens to consume us both.

She grabs my shoulders and pulls me against her body, pressing her dripping wet skin against mine. She lifts a leg onto the tub's ledge and guides me to what we both crave. My fingers spread her delicately apart as my tongue explores every inch of her. She moans louder in pleasure as I tease her nipples with my fingertips and send her over the edge with flicks of my tongue on her clit.

I spin her around with a quick jolt. My fingers are like claws as they tangle into her hair. My mouth descends upon her eager breasts, biting and sucking in wild abandon until she's ready to scream out with reckless desire. She leans forward, desperate for my touch, as I surge into her from behind, pushing myself deep inside her. My thrusts become powerful and relentless. Our moans escalate in intensity, in unison with our fervent cries. We reach the apex of pleasure and scream out in blissful release. We cling together.

The water cleanses away all traces of the moment together, yet I embrace her tightly. Her body trembles against mine. As our lips meet, an insatiable hunger stirs between us, and we hold onto one another, mouth meeting mouth with a passionate desperation far from finished.

After another feverish round, I finally break the silence with a husky growl. "I want to do this until the sun comes up and never stop." I kiss her lips passionately. But the thought of Rafa snaps me to attention. "Rafa," I say.

Her eyes widen in surprise before she melts into me, blushing as she remembers why she's there.

"Of course," she murmurs when we finally pull apart.

As I watch Sonia exit the shower, my eyes linger hungrily on the curves of her body as she towels off. She dresses in skimpy panties and a sheer, low-cut bra that can barely contain her voluptuous figure; no wonder my body always yearns for her. Now, I will never be able to erase or forget what she tastes like... or how electric our connection feels when we're together.

She quickly disappears, leaving me alone with just the steamy mirror. I wipe away the fog with my hand and see my reflection. The boy has now become a man.

As I step out of the bathroom, partially clothed, my thoughts stay a whirlwind. I'm met with a violent punch to the face. I stumble back, scrambling to keep my footing, my eyes widening in shock as I find Rafa, eyes wild and face red with rage, roaring at me again.

"*¡Traidor!*" Rafa screams, his fists clenched.

"Stop, Rafa!" I dodge another swing. "I don't want to fight you!"

But the fury in Rafa's eyes looks unquenchable, and I have no choice but to charge back. We fight, fists flying, pain and betrayal fueling our movements as Sonia screams in the background.

"*¡Cállate!*" a male voice snaps, and my heart stops as I realize who else is there.

With a mighty shove, I send Rafa stumbling to the ground, my eyes widening as I catch sight of Emilio standing there with a cold smile.

"*¿Qué haces aquí?*" I snarl, my chest heaving.

"I bailed him out while you screwed his girlfriend!" Emilio grins. "Oh, yes. We arrived in time to hear the excitement."

My mind races. Did *we really make that much noise?*

"Some friend you are!" Rafa spits at me.

I throw my hands forward. My voice fills with anger and frustration. "Stop. Yes, that happened. No, it was not planned, and you know what? I don't regret it. Because maybe if you'd been more careful, she wouldn't have needed to come find me."

Rafa's face twists with rage, and he's about to charge again when Emilio's voice cuts through the air. "*¡Basta!* Enough!" He commands, and Rafa obeys. His compliance only infuriates me more.

My eyes narrow as I see the lost cause my friend has become. Emilio steps forward, his voice smooth as silk as he offers me two choices. "You can leave and return to Mexico with a little money. Or you can join me."

My response comes immediately, with defiance in my eyes. "What if I do none of that?"

Emilio's smile is sinister as he brings a finger to his throat, making a slitting motion. The terror on Rafa's face is a confirmation. My gaze shifts to Sonia, who stands near the window, her expression inscrutable.

A decision settles in my mind. The *Norte* is suddenly a place I want to leave behind. "I'll go back," I say, my voice filled with resignation. "But I never want to see any of you again."

"Very well." Emilio pulls a wad of money from his pocket. "One of my men will drop you off in Tijuana. From there, you're on your own. I don't ever want to find out you're on this side again or else."

The room fills with heavy silence, and the air thickens with the weight of betrayal, loss, and a chosen path. My heart feels broken, but I've made the right choice. The *Norte* has cost me everything, and I'm ready to leave it behind.

CHAPTER 6

I stare out the window of my tiny apartment in Guadalajara, my mind drifting back to memories of my *pueblo* and friend Rafa. The *Norte* has changed me, hardened me. I'm no longer that naïve young boy, full of dreams.

I've heard Rafa ended up in prison for a short time before being deported, but he quickly returned and finally started anew. A smile tugs at my lips as I think of Rafa finding happiness. The ache of our broken friendship still lingers but knowing that Rafa is doing well gives me peace.

"Antonio? Are you thinking about the past again?" Luciana's gentle voice pulls me from my reverie.

I see her standing in the bedroom doorway, and her eyes flash with understanding. She is everything to me—beautiful, compassionate, and my refuge from the shadows of my past.

"*Sí*, Luciana. I was just thinking about Rafa, my old friend. He's doing well now, found a new life and a woman who loves him."

"That makes you happy, doesn't it?" Her slender body moves slowly to me.

"It does. But not as happy as you make me." With a smile, I take her hands in mine.

Her family resisted our relationship from the start. They see me as a plebe beneath their daughter's status. It's a challenge and a painful reminder of all the barriers I've faced.

As if reading my mind, Luciana clears her throat. "Antonio, you need to ignore what my family says or thinks. They have an idea of what they want for me. So much so that they forget this is my life, not theirs." Luciana leans into me. Her passionate voice and sweet scent calms my anger.

"I know, *mi amor*, but it's hard. They don't see me for who I am. They see where I come from, what I've been through," I confess. My shoulders slump, but the frustration is still in my voice as I move closer to her.

"But I see you, Antonio. I see the man you are, the man you've become."
Luciana squeezes my hands as her eyes shine.

I pull her into my arms, feeling the warmth of her love, and gently press
my lips on hers, grateful for our paths crossing. "I don't deserve you, and not
because of what they say, but because you are an amazing human being."

"You deserve all the happiness in the world," Luciana whispers against
my lips. "And I'm going to make sure you have it."

I kiss her deeply, tasting a future of hope and possibility. I will sacrifice
anything to make sure we can be together, and our lives are made even better
with each moment that passes.

Her arms slide around my neck, pulling me closer as she presses her lips
to mine. "You have no idea how amazing you are," she whispers breathlessly
against my mouth. Her fingers tug at the belt loops of my trousers, slip into
them, and release the button. She yanks them off and kneels between my legs,
taking in the sight of me. Taking me deep into her mouth, she pleasures me
with a skill I've never felt before, as if she commands the laws of nature to
bend to her will—my blood thrums in anticipation of what comes next.

My desire reaches a fever pitch when Luciana removes her panties and
positions herself atop me, pushing deep into her tight center as we move
together. Every sensation sends pleasure radiating through my body; I never
want this moment to end.

My eyes widen with pleasure and anticipation as I thrust faster and harder,
and my body trembles with each movement. As the intensity rises, I remove
her soft summer dress in a flurry, leaving her exposed and vulnerable to me.
Her full breasts and pink nipples gleam in the light as I hold her close and
begin to suck gently yet hungrily on them. With each pull, her nipples harden
while she gasps for air, and her body vibrates from the onslaught of sensations
caused by my movements.

I feel the power of the man I've become coursing through my veins as I
hold Luciana closely in my arms. My body feels electrified by her touch and
burns with desire for her. I'm euphoric as she gives herself to me, like a
precious offering from the gods. Her beauty is mesmerizing, her scent
intoxicating, and every kiss feels like an explosion of emotion deep within my
soul. Making love to her is all I live for; never ending and always pure bliss.

Luciana gasps as my lips find her erect nipples. My tongue flicks and
teases them into shivering submission. She quivers in anticipation as I push
myself further with each thrust, bringing her closer to pleasure as she lets out
a passionate moan.

Her hands sensually explore her body, massaging and caressing her
breasts. I can see the pleasure radiating through her as my fingers pleasure
her. Every curl of my finger sends electric shocks of delight throughout her
body.

I surge forward, snatch Luciana, lift her swiftly, and lay her on the bed. I
part her legs and plant my tongue onto her, savoring the sweet flavor of her
arousal that fills my senses. Luciana gasps as I move my tongue faster around
her, sending shocks of pleasure coursing through her body. I add two fingers

to the mix with a smirk and swirl them around her swollen bud while thrusting deep inside her with another. Her muffled screams are music to me as they drive me madder with desire; I want her to come first to find rapture together.

Her back arches, and her knees quake as I enter her. My strong arms hold her tightly against my body, thrusting with an insatiable hunger. My sweat mixes with hers as our pleasure gradually increases. She moves hard against me, fueling the raging fire within us to the point of combustion. My lips find her breasts, and I suck ferociously on her nipple, biting and releasing in a hypnotic rhythm.

"Harder!" she demands, and I drive into her more profoundly than ever, pushing past her limits until we are both rendered breathless with pleasure.

Afterward, we lay entwined, our bodies a testament to the love we shared. I watch Luciana drift off to sleep as her naked body wraps around me. The steady rhythm of her breathing gives me comfort, but something more profound stirs within me.

An understanding settles in my heart as I lay with the woman I love. I know what I want more than life itself.

I gently nudge her awake. "Luciana," I whisper, a nervous edge to my voice. "Luciana, *mi amor*. Wake up."

Her eyes, barely a sliver, find my gaze. She smiles sleepily. "Yes?"

My heart pounds as I take her hand. "Marry me."

Her eyes fly open, disbelief turning to joy. "For real?" Tears well as she pushes onto me. "Tell me you're not joking?"

I smile, and love swells within me. "I'm not joking. I don't have a ring yet. But I promise you I will get you the ring you deserve. So, tell me, Luciana Portillo. Will you be my wife?"

Tears spill down her porcelain-like face as she throws her arms around me. "Yes!" Her voice breaks with emotion, and she presses her full lips against mine.

We make love, and empty our souls into each other. There is no lust—just pure intimacy and passion.

Her soft breasts, the smell of her hair, the feeling of skin on skin, the sound of our breathing, the taste of her—it is so beautiful. It is deep, and it is meaningful and soul-searing, passionate love.

I vow in silence that I will create the best life for her. Luciana will want nothing.

I've struggled mentally and emotionally for weeks, losing sleep over my next moves. There are not many opportunities for an educated young man like me in Mexico. My meagre earnings are barely enough to make ends meet. I already work extra hours and pick up odd jobs for extra cash to take Luciana out.

My brain is constantly buzzing with ideas. I can't shut it off.

And there, like a sinister whisper finding its way to me at all hours, the opportunities of the underworld with a cartel. My innards twist in reaction to the idea. *I can't*, I say to myself. Yet, I'm unable to push the possibility away. *How else?* I hear that voice in my head. *How else are you going to give Luciana the life you want for her? How else are you going to prove to her family that you are capable?*

At twilight, when my world is finally still, my heart pleads but my brain silences it. It's decided. I'll do what I can for a short period of time. Long enough to make quick money and get out.

I start to connect with people from the darker side of business, exploring opportunities that are not strictly legal. The lure of easy money tempts me. I feel the pull, the desire to give the woman I love everything she deserves and, once and for all, silence her family.

Luciana becomes the stabilizing force in my life. She is my moral compass, even as I start to step into the shadowy world of cartels, I feel cleansed every time we are together.

I work hard, and the recognition abounds. The *jefes* reward me with money, and lots of it, as I slowly climb the ranks, utilizing every skill and knowledge at my disposal.

My slithery yet lethal ways earn me a nickname, *La Serpiente*. The serpent. Because I can slither my way in and out of almost every situation, escaping death and cutting golden deals.

Oblivious to what I am genuinely involved in, Luciana announces she is pregnant, and we feel happy. But the fairytale wedding I want to give my bride will not be, not even a honeymoon to Hawaii that I've fantasized about. Instead, we have a small quaint gathering, and exchange our sacred vows before God, in a small *capilla* on one of her family's properties, *Hacienda La Luz*.

Luciana's parents take me to the side, and condescension drips with every word. "Antonio, this place…" Luciana's dad spreads his arms spread wide. "Now passes on to my daughter and you. This is our wedding gift. A place to call home and somewhere decent our grandchild can grow up in."

I seethe. Despite my love for his daughter and her carrying my seed, every word that oozes out of the man proves they still think little of me. I nod and walk away. I'm not about to thank Don Portillo. Sure, it's the mature thing to do, but I'm not allowing the man to believe *I* need to be grateful for marrying into his family. My child will be a Cervantes, a surname to be proud of.

The weeks pass, and the agitation from my status in the Portillo family's eyes grows. I refuse any of their invitations and appreciate that Luciana respects my decisions. But she makes it abundantly clear that just because I won't visit her family doesn't mean she will not. She's not wrong.

In the field, my reputation as *La Serpiente* grows. My bodyguards, Roberto, and Luis, and two others with hand-selected night watches always stay by my side.

"*Jefe*." Jorge, my driver, pulls my attention away from the newspaper I'm reading.

I meet the man's gaze, and he stares at me through the rearview mirror. "The boss wants to see you."

There's no fear in me, despite the look on my driver's face. I nod. "Go there at once," I instruct, returning to my paper. My conscience is clear. I've done nothing to offend the man nor double-cross him. I'm a loyal soldier, doing his bidding quite well, if I say so myself. Despite what I told myself when I entered this dangerous role, I've learned quickly how to pivot and anticipate the bosses' needs. His recognition always comes with a monetary bonus; money I've become addicted to as I elevate my family's lifestyle and my standing in the cartel. The truth is, it's not just the money, it's the power that I'm becoming drunk with.

CHAPTER 7

The car grinds to a halt outside a building that's an odd mixture of warehouse and office. My heartbeat accelerates, a natural reaction to the tension in the air. Roberto and Luis, my bodyguards, exit the vehicle behind me. Another one of my men rushes ahead, opens the door, and checks the path.

We enter the building, and the receptionist glances up from her desk with a forced smile. "The boss is waiting in the warehouse office, Señor. Antonio," she stammers, and her body trembles.

I nod, but a nagging feeling deep in my gut tells me something isn't right.

I lift my fist, motioning for my men to stop, and quickly move to the side, taking cover behind a stack of pallets. My hand points to Roberto and Luis to follow suit. My heart pounds and my ears strain to listen.

Crash!

The sound echoes through the warehouse. I lock eyes with Roberto, and a silent understanding passes between us. This is a setup, or someone got to the boss before us.

Roberto dashes ahead, finding shelter behind a stack of boxes, while Luis stays close, flanking me. We move forward, slow and stealthy, every sense attuned to the environment. The scent of dust and oil fills my nostrils.

Glancing back at the receptionist, I notice her eyes have widened, and her hand presses to her mouth as she dips behind her desk. She knows something, but I'm unsure whether she's part of this or a frightened bystander.

But one thing is sure: we're walking into something dangerous.

The feeling in my gut grows stronger. Whatever awaits us is not going to be pleasant. Yet we continue to move, ready to face whatever comes next.

I slowly draw my gun. Its familiar weight feels cool and deadly in my hand.

I quiet my mind as we approach the door to the office. Roberto presses against one side of it while Luis crouches on the other.

Taking a deep breath, I nod at them both before opening the door with an explosive burst of energy.

The onslaught of bodies leaves no question. We're under attack. The boss lies dead on his desk, and blood soaks his white shirt. My eyes dart around frantically, scanning for signs of who may have done this or if they're hiding out of sight.

There's no sign anyone else is here except for us. Whoever did this ensured nobody could get near him without being noticed first.

That realization sends a chill down my spine. It's an expert job—a professional hit.

And we've just walked into it.

"Clear," Roberto calls out after checking under tables and behind boxes piled high along the walls. We stand cautiously and survey everything happening around us.

We walk back toward the reception area when– gunfire thunders loudly throughout the building. Shortly afterward, cracks and snaps pull our attention indicating more damage as we shift our line of sight.

The smell hits me next: a sharp metallic tang mixed with something sweetly sickening—the unmistakable stench of death drifting down the corridor outside toward Pallet 12B, housing chemicals lethal enough to kill large animals by simple inhalation. But it's much more than that. I believe it to be a compound used to create weapons of mass destruction. It was something I questioned myself over quietly, upon learning of the dangers of this job. Could I live with myself knowing I have a hand in it all? If there truly is a God, which I believe there is. Am I redeemable? I've already killed. If I continue down this path, there's no question that I will kill more. My eyes focus on the pallet. I may not be a chemist, but the instructions are grave yet simple. The chemicals, under no circumstance, can be allowed to leak or be exposed to extreme temperature changes. I push my moral compass to the depths of my being. *I'm already going to hell.*

I motion for Luis and Roberto to follow me toward the source of the gunfire. My heart races with each step, fearing what we might find around the corner.

My finger tightens on the trigger as I round the corner, and a figure jumps out from behind some stacked boxes. The semiautomatic in his grasp glints menacingly in the light. Only one conclusion reaches my brain—*fire!* I pull the trigger without hesitation, every muscle tight with anticipation, praying that this shot will save me.

The bullet finds the center of the man's head, pushing him back, then crashing to the ground. I can already tell he's dead as I stalk past his body toward the lethal chemicals.

A string of gunfire is unleashed on me, but I dive and roll out of the shooter's line of fire.

Finally, at Pallet 12B, we come across armed men guarding the chemical containers.

An enraged man screams "¡*Atras!*" incessantly in broken Spanish as his troops close in. They point their guns at us with deadly intent. There's no going back now; too much hangs in the balance.

Realization slams into me: this shipment is being hijacked. We are likely dealing with a rival cartel. The whys of getting their hands on these chemicals leave little to the imagination. But I don't have to time to rationalize it. We're only hired guns for a job that evidently was doomed from the start. Gunshots in the distance tell me some of our team still live. Fighting. I must act fast.

Luis yells, "Take cover!" moments before, multiple explosions rock through the buildings nearby. Massive, billowing smoke rises into the azure sky. My eyes leave the broken windows above and scan for my men.

Roberto darts forward, pulling a grenade pin from his belt, likely to create a makeshift path between us and the rival cartel determined to kill us.

I watch in horror as Roberto throws the grenade. Its explosion throws me back and deafens me momentarily. Through blurred vision, our rivals fly through the air like rag dolls. We exploit this momentary gap and race toward Pallet 12B.

But we're not quick enough. Those left standing catch up with us. A hailstorm of bullets rips through my clothes as I dive for cover behind a container filled with toxic chemicals.

An acrid cloud surrounds me from a punctured drum, and another explosive discharge sounds nearby. My thoughts turn dark. *Is all this worth it?* The promised money won't return anyone from the dead or repair relationships ruined by this bloody trade war, making cartels rich off innocent lives. I'm already neck deep; I doubt there's any going back to the status quo. But the boss is dead. *Can I walk away? Is this that sliver of an opportunity to get out if I make it through this battle?*

I see danger encroaching on Luis, as a man springs in the air to attack him from behind.

Right there, I decide: *Heads will roll for crossing our turf!* My heart pounds loudly as I military crawl and ambush a man. He's not expecting me, and surprise is on my side as I put a bullet through his forehead. Brain matter splatters and blood flows freely. My breathing comes out labored, but adrenaline keeps me going even though I know I'm injured. I pull a switchblade from my holster. My next victim fights back, but my height and relentless drive help me slash through his throat. The gurgling doesn't even make me cringe as I drop him to his knees without a second thought. The sound of gunfire slows down as pain sears through my abdomen. My lungs burn, probably from the chemical exposure. My body's on the verge of giving up.

Then, Luis grabs onto my arm and pulls us both forward. "Let's go," he says urgently.

My mind snaps back into focus; I have a purpose—a child. My child is soon to be born, and Luciana, my beloved wife needs me. Racing adrenaline fuels each movement as I allow Luis to lead me.

We fight like never before, using whatever weapons we find against the enemy in pursuit. We block their passage. We battle fiercely, fire repeatedly, and exchange blows without relent until it's over.

Roberto surfaces and tries to catch his breath. "We need to get *el jefe* to the doctor, STAT!" he yells, kicking away whatever litters our path—bodies, boxes—to him, it's all inconsequential.

As we exit the building, Jorge awaits with the door open, and the second SUV stands idly by. I lose count of the number of SUVs that pull up. I study the men, making brief eye contact with Roberto and Luis. I know them. They're with us.

"He's gone," Roberto says. "They all are. We barely made it out with our lives."

One of the other men steps forward. "Clear the way so we can get Don Antonio to the doctor. Now!" he yells.

And just like that, I hear it. *Don*. Our cartel isn't massive. We move different types of contraband and have yet to face opposition until now. The stakes are higher, but I have ideas. Many of them. But first, I must survive.

CHAPTER 8

The aftermath of my choices leaves indelible scars. As I stand before the bathroom mirror, staring at the stranger in my reflection, I realize the boy from the *pueblo*, brimming with dreams of a better life and simple joys, is gone. In his stead stands a man who embraced darkness for power, success, and money.

An image of Rafa flashes through my mind, and I quash it immediately. I've become everything I feared for him and worse.

I splash cold water on my face. The shock momentarily cleanses my thoughts. My past is sealed, locked away by irrevocable decisions.

Luciana's soft footsteps approach from behind me, and she places her gentle hands on my shoulders. "Are you okay, Antonio?" Her voice laces with concern. I've already burdened her with too much. The terror of not knowing if our unborn child would have a father was palpable as she willed life into me, whispering, "Survive. You must survive," when I awoke from a medically induced coma.

"I'm fine, Luciana," I assure her, though the words ring hollow.

Her eyes, wells of understanding, meet mine in the mirror. "I love you."

I nod, touched by her unwavering support. Yet I'm aware of my dangerous path. I kiss her forehead, feeling the warmth of her unblemished love.

"We must be strong, Luciana. For what's coming next," I say, my body rigid with determination, yet masking the entire truth.

Luciana is patient and wise, her silence and never prying into my work, gives me the physical and emotional space needed to cope and carry on. Her caring for me, sustains the part of me that needs loving nurture that only she can provide.

She nods and resolve flashes in her eyes. "We *are* strong."

My thoughts weigh heavily as we leave the bathroom, but my purpose becomes crystalline. The naïve boy is long gone, supplanted by the hardened resolve of a man who's seen too much. I am now the founder and head of a new criminal organization. A mafioso. Antonio Cervantes. La Serpiente Dorada. The Golden Serpent.

My heart thunders in my chest as the nurses shove me aside. "What's wrong? Please, tell me. Is my wife going to be all right?"

An experienced-looking woman pulls me out of the way. "Yes, she will be fine. But we need to move her quickly into the delivery room. It appears the baby is coming now."

Luciana awakened me in the middle of the night, folding over in pain. Her tear-filled eyes blinked back tears as she fought to control her breathing to tell me, it was time. Thanks to her preparation, we soon drove to the hospital. Now, I find myself chasing after her and a team of medical professionals as they rush her down the hall of the private hospital. According to our plan, Roberto has the grounds covered and my men on high alert.

We arrive at the labor and delivery suite. Staff members quickly push her bed into place and hook her up to monitors. "What's all that for? Is it necessary?" I ask, my ignorance on full display.

Luciana reaches for my hand, a soothing presence. "Calm down. Everything is going to be fine. Trust the process."

How can she remain so calm? I force a smile. "Of course, *mi amor*."

The doctor rushes in with a lighthearted demeanor that grates on my nerves. "So, I hear we have a baby on the way."

Luciana grimaces through another contraction, and my fists clench as I glare at the doctor. I want to make him take away her pain.

"Hold it," he instructs as a nurse counts, and I fidget impatiently, urging her to count faster.

Finally, Luciana is allowed to breathe, her wail tears at my heart. This process continues, each moment an agonizing eternity, until a cry pierces the silence.

"It's a boy!"

Tears spring to Luciana's eyes as she welcomes him into her arms. I'm awestruck.

"Would you like to cut the cord?" The doctor asks.

I comply, for Luciana's sake, and soon I gaze at our perfect son.

A nurse attempts to take the baby away, and I block her path as my protectiveness flares. "You're not taking my son out of my sight."

"It's protocol, *señor*. I assure you." The nurse's eyebrows furrow.

"Don Antonio," the doctor interjects, using my formal title. "If you'd like to accompany her, you are welcome."

I nod, instructing Luis to watch Luciana as I follow the nurse to the nursery. Seeing her gently cleaning and swaddling my son brings a rush of emotion. She hands him to me, and I'm filled with fearful reverence.

He's so tiny. What if I break him?

The nurse guides my arm, and I feel a connection as his eyes open, locking onto mine. "Gabriel," I whisper. "Your name is Gabriel."

A profound realization washes over me: *I may be many things, but I am now, first and foremost, a father and a husband. This is my family. And I will kill anyone who dares hurt them or come between us.*

I hope you enjoyed Gabriel's story. To continue reading try book 1, Silken Chains by Catalina Snow.

PUCKING MARRIED

CRYSTAL PERKINS

For Kawehi (Lauren), Rose, Cel, Laury, and all my friends who are from
Maui. My heart is always thinking of you while I'm here in the Ninth Island.

CHAPTER 1 - LAUREN

Why am I here again, waiting around in an ice rink in Henderson, Nevada, when I could be comfortable in the finally warm weather at home? Oh yeah, I have to convince billionaire Luke Griffin that my family's company should be a sponsor for his new AHL team. The one that's located back in my hometown, Williston, North Dakota. Since their season is over, Luke's here to watch the Stanley Cup Final in neighboring Las Vegas. Vegas is the city where Luke has lived for the past decade or so, but now that he's bought the first NHL and AHL teams in North Dakota, he's been splitting his time between the two places.

As for the man himself, he's ignored emails and calls from my dad, brother, and older sister. For some reason, they think I can change his mind. Not in a sexual way—my family wouldn't ask that of me, I wouldn't do it, and well, he's also happily married and like ten years older than me, so just no. They think I can convince him because I'm a teacher, and so is he.

Honestly, though, I think that's all we have in common. My family has millions, not billions. I just graduated from college, and he's been teaching for many years. He's married, I'm not. Oh, and from what I've seen from afar, he's outgoing and friendly. Me? I'm shy and reserved unless I'm talking to kids.

Yet, here I am, doing my family's bidding because despite in their disappointment in me not wanting to join in the commercial farming business, or maybe because of it, I still want to please them.

"Mr. Griffin," I call out as I see him walking my way.

He stops in front of me, and smiles. "Hello."

"Hi. I'm Lauren Sandberg, and I was hoping to have a few minutes of your time."

"Sandberg?" he asks with a frown. "From Williston?"

"Yes."

I see his expression shutter, and know I'm losing my chance.

"Please, sir."

And, his smile is back. "Sir? My students only call me that when they are in trouble."

"Mine only call me ma'am when they are in trouble, too."

"You're a teacher?" he asks, and I nod. "Okay, you've got five minutes."

AXEL

I'm not supposed to be here. Not in Las Vegas, but in the AHL. I was a top player in Sweden, playing in the SHL. I was signed by the Grand Forks Bobcats, not the Williston Bison, but here I am. Or will be. The AHL season is over, and I'm here on a "team bonding" trip to Sin City to watch the Golden Knights try for the Stanley Cup. Our team owner is a fan since he lives here half the time, but he swears to the media our teams are now his priority.

Regardless, we're here, and honestly, there's been no sinning on my part. I had one drink last night at a club, and that was enough. I know my limits, and they are as hard as the ice I skate on.

"Jonnsy, lighten up and have fun," my new teammate Kit tells me, skating past me.

Fun? I haven't had fun on a sheet of ice in years, and I'm not about to start on a borrowed rink that I'll soon be back on as an opponent. Fun would be skating with my nieces and nephew back in Stockholm. No, this is just torture masquerading as a fun and friendly free skate.

Still, I paste a smile on my face as I catch up to him and fake it. "What are the plans for tonight?"

"Drinking, women, table games, women. Maybe not in that order," he tells me with a shrug and a smirk. "You in?"

"Yeah, I'm in," I tell him, knowing I'm stuck with him right now, and I have to fake being happy about it. Hell, everything in my life is pretty much fake right now.

"Alright. Let's gear up and scrimmage," he yells, garnering cheers from our teammates.

I'm cheering on the inside, too. It's going to be a lot more fun to show these idiots what I've got than just skate laps on this rink. Game on.

CHAPTER 2 - LAUREN

Well, I didn't get a yes from Luke Griffin, but I didn't get a no, either. He expressed his worry that my family is too conservative to be a sponsor. His plans are for both his teams to be inclusive and really embrace the "Hockey Is For Everyone" philosophy. Historically, other members of my family have voted red, but I assured him not for the last two elections. We're hard workers, and my father is definitely conservative, but social justice is important to all of us.

"You've given me a lot to think about, Lauren. I'll be in touch," he tells me at my car, which he insisted on walking me to as the sun went down while we were talking.

"Thank you for your time and consideration."

"Please don't be this formal when you're hanging out with me and Liv. I should be the one thanking you for all the info on Williston, and letting me take more than five minutes of your time."

"I'll try," I promise.

I blow out a breath before calling my dad on Bluetooth while I pull out of the parking lot.

"I hope you have good news," he says, because of course he has to get right to his point.

"Hello to you too, Dad."

"Dammit, Lauren, stop being so sensitive, and tell me you got me that sponsorship spot."

"He's going to think about it."

"I shouldn't have sent you there."

"No, Dad, you shouldn't have," I tell him, trying and failing to keep the hurt out of my voice.

"When will you be home?"

Never. That's what I want to say, but despite his disappointment in me, I love my town and yes, I love him too.

"I'm not sure. I think I'm going to take a vacation while I have the time."

"Selfish."

He mutters it, but I still hear it. "Goodbye, Dad."

I hang up, and decide I need some fun in my life. I need at least one night to let loose and this is the exact place to do it. No one here knows me, and I can be whoever I want to be tonight. First stop needs to be the mall down the street from my hotel.

AXEL

I should've just gone back to my hotel. The music in this club is too loud. I can only imagine what it would be like if we hadn't all chipped in for a table. At least I can sit down, and not have to fight my way to the bar.

"Have another drink," Simon, our goalie tells me, picking up the bottle of vodka from the ice bucket.

"Why not?" I tell him, holding out my glass.

The liquid is cool down my throat, reminding me of home, and I can barely feel the burn. The next three go down even smoother. And that's when the trouble begins.

The DJ starts playing "Dancing Queen" and I suddenly think I know how to dance. I'm fumbling around with another glass of vodka in one hand when I bump into something, or rather, *someone*. And holy hell, she's a smokeshow.

Long, dark hair that's curly and untamed, tanned skin that doesn't look fake, and curves for days. She's a little on the short side, making me think about carrying her around everywhere.

"Uff da, you're a Viking. Hello, sexy Viking," she says, squeezing my right bicep.

"My eyes are up here, *sötis*."

She steps back, her blue eyes blazing. "So tis? What did you say? Is that supposed to be cute?"

"Yes," I answer honestly. *Sötis* means cutie, after all.

"Well, damn. You've got a Viking accent too."

That's the last thing she says before jumping up and climbing me like a tree. Her hands are on my shoulders, her legs are wrapped around me, and her mouth is on mine. I don't know how this all happened, but as I set my drink on the closest surface and wrap my arms around her, I realize I really don't care how we got here. My dick and I are more than ready to keep going.

CHAPTER 3 - AXEL

I wake up with a warm body next to me, not remembering how we got here. Cracking my eyes open, I recognize my hotel room at Circa, where Luke booked us rooms. He said we needed to experience Vegas, and not just the Strip, which isn't really in Vegas. Whatever. It's great to have a room to myself, and this is a nice one.

Turning, I recognize the woman lightly snoring on the bed next to me. I just really don't know how we got here. I remember drinking and making out. There might have been some mutual hand jobs, but after that, nothing. I've never gotten so drunk I couldn't remember my night. At least I woke up with boxers and a t-shirt on, so maybe we didn't take it further.

Right now, I just know I need to take care of morning business, and then wake her up to see what she knows. Her. Because I don't even know her fucking name.

After I do what I need to do, I walk back toward the bed. Photos on the nightstand stop me in my tracks. "What the fuck?"

"Huh? What?" the woman asks, jacknifing up into a sitting position.

Yeah, I was loud, because I needed to be. Because these pictures just sealed our fate.

"We got married," I tell her, and watch her pull the comforter up to her chin, despite her clothes being on her body.

"We most certainly did not."

"Pictures don't lie," I respond, holding one of us in chapel up for her to see. She's got on a veil with a bouquet in her hands, and we've both got huge smiles on our faces.

"This can't be happening," she says before jumping from the bed and running to the bathroom.

I follow, and hold her hair back while she throws up, because that's what you do for your wife. Even if you can't remember her name.

LAUREN

How is this even my life? I'm apparently married to a Viking whose name I don't even know. He held back my hair when I puked, and I woke up clothed, but none of that makes this situation any better. Hell, the only thing I know for sure is we don't have a prenup, which might be the worst part of all of this. I have a lot of money, and while I don't use it, I'm not about to give it to some random dude.

"What's your name?" we both blurt out at the same time.

Well, shit, he doesn't know mine either. This is a cluster.

"Lauren."

"Axel."

Axel? Even his name sounds badass. Is it bad that I'm freaking out about being married to someone whose name I didn't even know, but yet I still want to climb him like a tree?

"So, we're married. I guess we can get it annulled or something?"

"Or we could get to know each other and see where it goes," he says, looking as shocked as I feel by his words.

I'm shocked, but also intrigued. I don't think we got much further than making out last night, and for once in my life, I don't want to be sensible. I already wanted to avoid going back to North Dakota right away.

"We could go on a honeymoon. Hawaii has been on my mind lately."

"Oh, Hawaii would be cool. But I don't exactly make a ton of money," he tells me, rubbing his hand through his longish blond hair. Hair I want to run my fingers through again.

How am I going to say this to him without either offending him, or making him think he hit the jackpot?

"I have some savings. We can use it for a honeymoon." He starts to speak, but I hold up my hand. "I was already wanting to go, so it's not like I'd be getting an extra room or anything. You can buy me a meal if you can afford it."

"Oh, I can afford some meals. This is unexpected, and I'll have to tell my boss, but yeah. Let's go to Hawaii."

CHAPTER 4 - AXEL

"What you're telling me isn't possible. They do not issue marriage licenses to people who are drunk. It's why us locals roll our eyes at all those stories about people waking up married," Luke tells me.

"Maybe we got it before being totally wasted? We have pics."

I don't know what else to tell him. I don't want to be here in his house, explaining why I'm leaving early.

"Go to Hawaii with this woman, but email my brother, Scott, the pictures. He's basically a genius, and I'm going to have him look into this. Something isn't right. You don't even have a copy of the license. I don't know who you married, so I'm hoping to God she's not some bunny hoping to hit it big."

"I don't think that's the situation here."

I really don't, and that's why I didn't give him her name. She offered to pay for the trip, our rideshare dropped her at the Four Seasons, and she seems as freaked out as I am. Guessing she's not a bunny, but I also guessed I'd wake up single today, so there's that.

"We'll see. Go have fun, and we'll get your gear back to Williston. Oh, and I had $10,000 deposited into your bank account as a wedding present. There are lots of great free things to do in Maui, but there's also some pricey experiences you may want to try. The salary cap is a bitch, but gifts for weddings are allowed."

"Thanks."

I don't know what else to say. This was unexpected, but not unwelcome. Luke just nods and claps me on the back before I walk out his door. Time for me to head to the airport and see what the future holds.

LAUREN

I splurged and bought us first class tickets. You only get married once, right? Or at least black-out drunk married once, because I'm not sure this first marriage of mine is going to last. I didn't know Axel's name when I woke up, I don't know if he's just in the U.S. for the business trip he said he landed in Vegas for, and yeah, I just basically know nothing about this man I somehow married.

"Should we play twenty questions to pass the time?" I suggest once we're in the air.

"How about ten questions, and we can opt out of any. I'm not ready to give away everything right now."

Compromise. Marriage is about compromise, right?

"Okay, ten. I'll go first. What do you do for work?"

"I'm in sports," he says, after a slight pause.

"What does that mean? Are you part of a staff, a player? And what sport? Or did you mean more than one?"

"That's four questions. Are you sure you want to waste all of those?"

Dammit. He got me there. "No."

"Good, now it's my turn. What is your job?"

"I'm a teacher."

"Respectable."

"Excuse me?" I ask, more than a little pissed. Who is he that he gets to decide what's respectable, and why does it matter.

"It's good that you have a job that is well-respected. There is nothing wrong with me thinking that."

"Asshole," I mutter under my breath.

"Was that a question?" he asks with a smirk.

"Are you going back to wherever your Viking life is, or staying in the States?" I ask through gritted teeth.

"Viking life? I am from Sweden and nothing about my life has to do with Vikings. I will be staying in America, yes."

"That's good. I wasn't sure how this would work if you were going back home. And you're still a Viking to me."

"Noted. Now, my turn."

We go on, talking about favorite colors, movies, music, and other superficial things. We seem to have an understanding that neither of us is ready to dig too deep, because it's too soon. But, too late at the same time since we're already married.

CHAPTER 5 - LAUREN

We arrive at Kahului airport, and as we're making our way to baggage claim, I see someone holding a card with our names. I hadn't ordered car service, since we'd decided to drive ourselves around.

"Aloha," the woman tells me, placing a beautiful purple and white lei over my head.

"Thank you," I tell her, running my hands over the velvety orchids on mine, while she places a Ti Leaf one on Axel.

"I'm glad you like them," Axel says, his hand on my lower back guiding e to our baggage carousel.

Looking around, I notice not everyone has one. "Did you do this?"

"I did. I thought it was something you'd like."

"I love it," I tell him, wrapping my arms around him for a hug. "We need a picture."

He takes out his phone, pulls me in close, and snaps a selfie. We look so happy, and I can't help but wonder if we can make it work.

Once we grab our bags and have retrieved our rental car nearby, we are on our way. Axel is driving, but slams on the brakes when I yelp a short time later.

"Are you okay?"

"Yes, I'm sorry. I just saw a restaurant I had on my list to try. Are you ready for lunch?"

"I can always eat, but please don't yell again unless you need help."

Tante Ma'alaea is just as good as I'd heard. We both have the Hawaiian Lu'au Plate, and Axel also gets Oxtail Soup. I convince him to share some Dinuguan off the Filipino menu, not telling him what it is. My friend back in Williston, Velma, makes it sometimes and being an adventurous eater, I gave it a try and loved it.

I have to try the Blue Hawaii drink, since I watched that Elvis movie with my mom growing up, and Axel has a pear and green apple Sake. We talk about the other drinks that look good, but agree to wait for more alcohol until we're at our hotel.

The drive to the Grand Wailea is even more beautiful than I expected it to be. And the hotel is simply stunning. I've stayed in luxury hotels before, but the ocean and palm trees and just everything are magical. I chose a deluxe king room, and not a suite or villa, because I want us to explore this island I've dreamed of visiting, and not feel like we never want to leave the room.

"Good choice," Axel tells me, his eyes on the bed.

"Don't get ahead of yourself, Viking. We can share a bed without having sex."

"But can we?"

Yes. No. Maybe. "Yes, we can."

"Fair enough," he concedes. "Do you mind if I go work out for a couple of hours?"

I eye him up and down, taking in this shirt fighting to hold in his muscles. I remember his arms holding me up without straining in the club, and how round and high his ass is in his jeans. Did I mention his strong thighs? His body really is perfection.

"Not at all. It would be a shame for you to miss leg day."

"Glad you approve. I won't be too long."

"Good, because I made dinner reservations for later. It's another place that sounds amazing."

"After lunch, I totally trust you to choose our meals," he tells me, pausing in his walk to the door.

He comes back to where I'm standing, picks me up so our mouths are level ith each other, and kisses me senseless. Like I can't even remember my name while he walks out the door. I am in so much trouble with this new husband of mine.

AXEL

I can't miss a day of working out, even though it's the off-season, but I had other reasons for leaving that hotel room. Namely my smokeshow of a wife and that bed. One big bed that's going to feel like the smallest bed in the world once we're both in it. I have no reservations about consummating our marriage, would've done it the moment we walked in the room if she'd been down for it. But she wasn't, so exercise it is.

I push myself almost to my limit with crunches, pullups, curls, and yes, leg presses. Then, I add in the treadmill with the steepest incline available. I'm dripping in sweat when my watch alarm tells me it's been two hours, and I'd told Lauren it would be just two.

A quick shower just to make myself presentable, a stop by the concierge desk to ask Kawehi at the desk for some tips and help, and then I'm in the elevator back to our room. My relaxed state disappears the moment I walk in and see Lauren curled up on our couch, wearing a slightly gaping bathrobe, and snoring softly with her e-reader hanging loosely in her hand. Damn, she's beautiful — and so much more.

I want to kiss her gain, but in a completely different way than earlier. This time, I would kiss her slowly, teasing her awake. I can only imagine how soft she would be, waking up to my hands caressing her. But she didn't give me permission for that, and I already took a kiss without asking. I won't take more.

My dick didn't get the message and is hard as a rock once again. Time for another shower. I grab my clothes for tonight and head into the bathroom. I don't bother to close the door, because I don't care if my wife sees more of me.

Once in the shower, I can't stop myself from taking my cock in hand. I moan louder than I meant to when I get flashbacks of Lauren's hands on me. It was only last night, and although I don't remember everything, I remember how good that felt, how right.

I feel the cool air on my back before I register the shower door opening. Lifting my head, I see Lauren drop her robe. Fuck me sideways. She's all curves and soft skin, and I have a primal urge to rail her into the wall.

"I know I said we weren't going to have sex earlier, but I was lying. I was dreaming of your cock in my hand. Or maybe it wasn't a dream. I think you fucked my hand last night. But that's not enough. I want you to fuck me. Fuck my pussy, and make me scream. Do you want that, too?"

"Hell, yes," I tell her, letting go of my cock and reaching for her.

I lift her into my arms and after shutting off the shower, carry her out of the bathroom and onto the bed. I need the space and time to explore all of her.

"What time is dinner?" I manage to growl.

"Seven."

I glance at the clock. "Three hours is not enough time, but it'll have to do."

CHAPTER 6 - LAUREN

Axel starts at my feet, showering each one with little kisses. Then my ankles and calves get some attention, too. By the time he's lifting my legs and flicking his tongue over the back of my knees, I'm writhing on the bed and murmuring pleas for his cock. I remember holding it but seeing it in his big hand in the shower almost made me come right then and there. It's long and thick, and my pussy wants it.

"Such a pretty pussy dripping for me. I know you want my cock in there, but I have to eat it first and make sure it's ready for the taking. Because, make no mistake, Lauren. I'm going to take it and make it mine."

"Yes."

His mouth sucks and nibbles on my thighs until I've nearly lost my mind. And, then he's there. He licks me up like I'm his personal treat, before sucking my clit into his mouth. His tongue darts out to flick the bud while he sucks, making my hips fly off the bed. My hands land in his hair. I pull on the strands and rake my nails over his scalp when he slides two fingers into me. When he quickly removes them, I whine in protest.

"You're coming on my mouth this time, *Älskling*. Then, once you feed me your sweet cum, I'm going to fuck you with my fingers until you scream."

"Oh my God."

"No, I'm your husband. Now, be a good little wife and let me get back to work without interrupting me again."

I nod and pull his head back where I need it as he chuckles. It only takes seconds for him to have me coming on his tongue. I remember what he told me, and I need those fingers next.

"Lick it all up," I order, pushing his head lower. "Take it all."

"Dirty woman, and no, I'm not complaining," he insists, licking my pussy and then my thighs clean. "You want my fingers, *Älskling*? Tell me."

"Get your damn fingers inside me, Viking, or I'm using my own."

I know I just came, but I am still on edge. I meant what I said. I'll take myself over if I have to.

"Nej. No. The next one is mine."

He shoves his fingers inside me again, his thumb playing with my clit. He knows what he's doing, and while I should be nervous about that, all I can think about is the orgasm barreling down on me like a runaway train. This one is so intense, I scream.

"Perfect," he tells me.

He leans over to kiss me, and while I taste myself on his tongue, I feel his hard cock bouncing on my leg.

"Can I have him?" I ask, reaching out to lightly stroke his length.

"Let me grab a condom, and he's yours."

"I thought you were taking my pussy," I tease.

"We take each other, Lauren. When and where we want. Agreed?"

There's only one answer for that. "Yes."

AXEL

I'm so horny and hard for this woman, I can barely walk to my suitcase to grab the condom. She's a sexual dream already, and we haven't even fucked yet. I already know it's going to be amazing, though. She's free, expressive, and as dirty as me.

Once I've sheathed myself, I make it back to the bed. Lauren's lying there with her legs spread, eyes glazed over in pleasure, and a smile on her face.

"I want you to feel every inch of me, so you're going to go for a ride," I tell her.

"I'm down for that," she tells me, scooting over, so I can lie down.

I put my hands behind my head as she climbs over me, straddling my thighs with her own. She stops before sliding onto my cock, and I raise my eyebrows.

"Problem?"

"I was hoping you'd like my tits and want to play."

"I love your tits, *Älskling*."

I do love them. They're high and round, and more than even my big hands can hold. But I want her to tell me what she wants. What she *needs*.

"Then play, Viking. If you can't suck and lick, then grope and pinch. Show me you love them as much as I love your chest."

She leans down and nips at my nipple for emphasis before using one hand to explore the ridges of my pecs down to my abs. Her nails come into play, and I growl at her.

"Get on my cock, and maybe I'll do your sexual bidding."

She smirks, licks her lips, and lowers herself down. Inch by inch, she takes me in. She's tight and hot, and I force myself not to thrust into her yet. Once she's settled all the way down, she arches her back in pleasure. It has the added effect of giving me her tits, and I take the bait.

My hands knead and pinch, causing her to start moving as she moans. It's fucking hot, and gets hotter when I sit up, letting go long enough to pull her legs forward while I bend her back far enough that she's now grabbing my calves for support. I latch my mouth onto one nipple while thrusting into her. I truly meant for her to ride me, but right now, I'll take her orgasm however I can get it.

I feel her pussy start to clamp on my cock right as she pushes up and moves me back. My mouth pops off her nipple and she quickly takes it with her own, kissing me fiercely. She's riding us toward where we both want to be, and I can't be even a little mad that she took control of the situation. She yells, curses, and screams again while milking my cock for every last drop that ready to go. I let go of her hips and grab the comforter because I'm afraid I'll bruise her as I come harder than I ever have.

"Damn, Viking. I hope you'll be ready to go again after dinner, because I'm pretty sure I'm addicted to your cock."

"No worries, *Älskling*. Stamina is definitely not an issue for me," I promise.

CHAPTER 7 - LAUREN

After that sex-a-thon aka make Lauren a sex addict, I am a mess. Hair sticking up everywhere, sticky from sweat and my own body fluids, and barely able to stand up. But, I know I also need food if we're going to do this all night. He promised he has the stamina, and I have the need for him.

We shower separately because we know what will happen if we try it together. I'm blow drying my hair when he emerges in just a towel. My mouth literally starts watering.

"Stop looking at me like that, or we'll have to order in."

I momentarily consider it, but no. I want to try this restaurant and lust is not enough to make a marriage work. At least, I don't think it is. Right now, I just want to lick the water droplet sliding down the middle of his pecs.

"I want to go out, but I also want to lick you."

"I guess I have to be the mature one here. Out I go," he says, rushing past me out to the bedroom and closing the door. "I'll tell you when I'm dressed."

"Won't help," I yell back.

He says something in Swedish, and I'm pretty sure it's swear words. I can't help it if I'm a shameless hussy for his body. He made me this way.

But he's right to do this, and leave me be so we can go to dinner. I finish my hair, grab my dress from the hook on the bathroom door, and put on some mascara and lip gloss. I think I look good, but I'm also always my biggest critic.

Once he yells he's ready, I open the door to see him in a dark red suit with a white shirt and no tie. Damn.

"You look beautiful," he tells me, taking in my flowered red dress that hits just above my knee.

"So do you."

He pulls me to him and kisses my forehead, before leading me out the door. We hold hands down to the lobby and only let go to get into the car. Our drive to the restaurant takes about 40 minutes, which is a lot for me coming from where I live, but it's not much for Axel, who tells me he likes to drive an hour or two outside of Stockholm for weekend trips when he's there.

Mama's Fish House does not disappoint. We share appetizers of Crispy Fish Collar and Maui Octopus. There are five types of fish dishes, and when I can't decide, Axel orders them all. Each lists the fisherman who caught it, and they are all beyond delicious. Mahi Mahi, Ahi, Ono, Toothfish, and Kanpachi with lobster and crab. I take a few bites of each, and Axel finishes them off, deciding he also needs to try the Blue Crab.

"Where do you put all of that? I know you're huge, but damn."

"I burn a lot of calories working out, and well, you helped me burn more," he tells me with a shrug.

I can't say no to the Coconut Chiffon Cake, and he gets the Kuau Chocolate Pie. We share, but again, he eats way more than I do. Again, we limit ourselves to just one drink, mine fruity and his with whiskey.

This time, we also talk about family and I'm not surprised to hear his is more supportive than mine. I don't go into too many details, because they hurt to talk about, but I can tell by his pursed lips that he's gotten the general idea.

He holds my hand on the ride back to the hotel and takes it again when we walk inside. I'm surprised when he walks us outside and not to the elevators. When we're close to the beach, he kneels down to take off my shoes, before standing to toe off his own.

"I think the beach is closed," I tell him.

"We won't go far; I want to look out at the waves while I hold you close."

AXEL

I'm falling for my wife. I know it's fast, and I would like to say it's just lust, but it's not. She didn't say much about her family, but it's more what she didn't say than what she did that made me want to hold her. I have a wonderful family, who I could talk about and spend time with anytime, anywhere.

We're only on the beach a few minutes, before security comes by to let us know the adults-only pool is still open, but we can't swim in the ocean as it's not safe at night. We assure him we're not going in and promise to not stay out here long.

"Thanks for just holding me. I know I promised you more. We can go back to the room now," Lauren tells me about twenty minutes later.

"I'm happy to just hold you once we get back up there."

She turns in my arms and kisses me softly. "I'm lucky to have you for a husband."

"And I'm lucky to have you for a wife."

We walk back up to the hotel, and head upstairs. Once inside, I draw her a bath and tell her to relax for a bit because I finally looked at my phone and saw a voicemail from Luke. I promise to join her once I give him a call.

"Hey, Luke, I saw you left a voicemail but thought I'd just call you," I say once I'm standing outside on our deck.

"So, you didn't listen?"

"No, what's up?"

"I had my brother look into your photos, and well, you're not married."

"What? I am. There are photos."

"Fake wedding photos. A couple of chapels here are doing fake weddings and photos. I'm guessing the two of you stumbled on one and thought it would be fun, then got even drunker and forgot."

"No," I tell him, dropping onto the chair next to me.

"You don't sound happy."

"I'm not. I'm falling for her, and I wanted this to be real."

"You can still make it real," he reminds me.

"Maybe."

Would she still marry me again? Does she feel the way I do? She called me sweet and asked me to join her in the bath, but is that just lust?

"Well, do what you gotta do. I'll see you soon."

I hang up and join Lauren in that bathtub. I don't say a word to her about what Luke told me. Not then, and not when I'm making love to her all night. I know I should, but I'm too afraid to lose her.

CHAPTER 8 - LAUREN

We spend the next several days doing all kinds of fun things. At the hotel, I stumble through hula lessons, try some Hawaiian bracelet making, and lounge in a cabana while Axel is exercising. We've been to Hana to see the breathtaking waterfalls, visited Iao Valley, which I never wanted to leave, went snorkeling at Molokini, and took a drive to Ho'okipa to see the surf and the turtles. We've also tried local food from places like Ramen Bones and Isana's, and had another upscale meal at Hali'imaile General Store. Plus, a pineapple plantation visit, and shopping. And let's not forget the lovemaking every morning, afternoon, and evening. Maybe I'm jumping the gun by not calling it just sex, or fucking, but it feels like more.

Today, on our last day, we did some conservation work through the hotel with the Hawaii Land Trust. It was meaningful and beautiful. We are finally doing the hotel's Grand Luau tonight, and then we fly home late in the afternoon tomorrow.

We've talked about important things, but not about where we live or what happens when we leave this island. Or even how we feel about each other. I know we need to talk, but I'm just as chicken as Axel is about bringing it up.

"I love this dress," he tells me later in the day, when we're done getting ready for the luau. It's a dress I bought when we were out shopping. A long crossover dress that ties behind my neck and has a big slit.

"I'm glad you approve," I joke.

"I approve of you in anything, or nothing."

"Keep talking like that, and you might get lucky tonight."

"I hope so."

"You know I'm a sure thing," I remind him.

"I will never take you or your consent for granted," he assures me.

That sound right now? It's my heart jumping from my chest into his hands. Yep, I think I'm in love with my husband.

I think I fall even more in love with him when we both get pulled up to dance at the luau and he awkwardly goes along with it. Or when he kisses my forehead while stealing some pork off my plate. Or maybe it's when he enthusiastically introduces me as his wife to some of his gym friends.

The falling is sealed when he surprises me in the middle of the night. Not with sex, but with a drive to Haleakalā to see the sunrise. It's truly magical and couldn't be a better end here on this island I never want to leave. This is where I feel too fast, and too hard for the man I accidentally married. I wouldn't change a thing right now, except for the fact that we have to go home. The people, the places, the feeling of knowing we're somewhere where the heritage needs to be protected and not taken over by developers are all things that will never leave me.

AXEL

A week ago, we landed back in Vegas and went our separate ways. We both pretended that some time apart was needed to decide what we really wanted. I didn't need that time. I know I want Lauren. But I pretended to go along with it because I need her to want me back.

It sucks not talking to her, touching her, making love to her, and hell, even knowing where she lives. We just kissed passionately and walked away from each other. We didn't even exchange numbers, just made a WhatsApp chat. Who even does that?

I just have to be patient and get my own shit together here in Williston. That starts with talking to Luke.

I knock on his open door at the new ice rink he built for us by the old airport. He looks up and smiles.

"Good to see you, Axel. I have a meeting in a few minutes, but we can chat if it'll be quick."

"I just have one question," I tell him, walking in and leaving the door open because I'm sure what I'm about to ask isn't a secret.

"Go ahead."

"Why am I not on the Bobcats team?"

"You need to get used to American play. Once you're ready, we'll see about moving you up."

"What can I do to get there faster?"

"Play your best, and show me and everyone else you're ready for the NHL."

I knew he was going to tell me that, but I still had to ask. It's frustrating to be so lauded in my own country, and then be told I have to work harder here. I understand in some ways, but in others I don't. I just want to play and make a salary that matches my play. I have Lauren to think about now, too.

"Okay. I will do it and prove it to you."

"I have no doubt. While you're here, what happened with that fake marriage of yours? You never told me what happened when you told the woman what Scott found out about the places that do fake weddings."

"What the hell? Our wedding was fake, and you knew about it?"

I turn now to see my worst nightmare come to life. Lauren is standing behind me, and if looks could kill, I'd be dead now. Maybe twice. I think she could find a way to kill me a second time.

"*Min kära*, I wanted to tell you, but I didn't want to lose you before we even began."

"Wait, you fake married one of my players? This better not have been part of your family's plan."

"You've lost me now," she tells me, before turning to Luke. "As for your insult, I didn't know he played hockey, much less for you. And my family had no idea I thought I was married. So, back off."

I'm in shock, replaying her words over in my head. She said I've lost her.

I know I deserve it, but it still feels like someone's stabbed me in the heart. Maybe a combination of looks and words can actually kill someone.

"I apologize, Lauren. I just had to be sure since I called you here to tell you I'm going to let your family sponsor the team, but only if you ran point on everything. I've done my research and I find you're rather impressive."

"Damn right, she is," I tell him.

"None of your business, Viking. Stay out of this."

I hold my hands up in surrender and walk out the door. I know when to walk away from a fight I can't win. Doesn't mean I'm giving up on the war.

CHAPTER 9 - LAUREN

I put on a brave front for Axel, acting tough and angry when I found out he'd lied to me. And then, I fell apart. Right there in front of Luke Griffin. He rushed over to catch me as I literally started to fall and helped me to the couch in his office. Once my tears had dried, he implored me to give Axel another chance.

I've ignored that, and also the messages on WhatsApp from the man himself. I want to be stronger than I am and delete our chat, but I can't. I'm so hurt and angry, but I can't break my last connection to him.

Who am I kidding? This town is small enough I'm bound to run into him. It's a wonder I didn't in the week before I saw him in Luke's office. The last few days, I've been hiding out at home as much as possible. I needed some comfort Culvers, so I ventured out today.

I'm pulling out of the drive-thru when I feel my right tire blow. I manage to get my car into a parking spot before banging my head on the steering wheel. I just wanted a good burger, cheese curds, and a custard sundae. Why is that too much to ask?

Before I can get out of the car to change the tire, an identical Subaru SUV pulls up next to me. And of course, it's Axel who gets out of it.

He seems as shocked as I am when he gets to my driver's side window. "Shit, I didn't know it was you. Do you want me to leave and call another teammate who is in town to help you? Or Luke?"

"What makes you think I need help? I grew up on a farm, for God's sake."

"I did not know."

No, he wouldn't unless he asked Luke more about me. It hurts a little that he didn't.

"Well, now you do. You can go on along and hit a puck around the rink or whatever it is you do."

"I am a goalie, so I catch the pucks, *min kära*."

I want to know what those words he says to me mean, but I don't know how to spell it. He used to call me "*Älskling*" and then one day in Maui he changed it to this. I'm too scared to ask him, though.

"Okay, well, be on your way."

"Your custard will melt even more if you get out to change your tire. Maybe I can take you home and you can eat it. Then, I can bring you back."

Or, I could just eat it here and then change the tire. When I look into his eyes, as grey and stormy as the sky is right now, I know his option is the better one. A storm is coming, and not just the one between us if we ever get the guts to really talk to each other. A raindrop hits his nose, and I'm done.

"Okay, let's go."

I close my window, grab my food, and make a run for his car. Once I'm inside, I gag.

"Oh my God, what is that smell? Did you kill someone? Is that why you wanted me in the car with you? You want my DNA, don't you?"

"Calm down, *Älskling*. It's my gear. That's what hockey smells like. And yes, I want all your DNA, but not to escape prison time."

"Ew, gross. And this hockey smell is gross too. Why is it like that? And why didn't you leave your nasty stuff at the rink? I'm sure Luke can afford to clean it."

"The gear is against our skin, and I've been told it's bacteria as well as sweat and other fluids that make it smell like it does. Luke has a cleaning team, but it's the off-season, so they aren't there often because we are in charge of our own cleaning right now. I'll wash and sanitize it and it won't be so bad until I practice with it on again."

"I think there wouldn't be any puck bunnies left if they got a whiff of this."

He laughs. "Do you want me to hold your nose while you eat your custard?"

I contemplate it but decide if I could deal with the smell of manure on the farm and not be put off dinner, I can deal with the smell of gross hockey gear.

"No, I'm good," I tell him, taking a big bite.

I guide him to my house, which is just outside of the city limits. It's a modern house that's too big for just me, but I liked the look of it.

"This is nice. Very modern. It would fit right in back home."

"Thank you," I tell him, gathering my stuff and preparing to run inside.

"Do you want me to park in the garage, so you don't get wet?" he asks.

"Oh, okay. I need to call and tell them not to tow my car. I almost forgot it wasn't in there."

I can open my garage with an app on my phone, so I do, and he drives us inside. I immediately open my window so I can comfortably breathe again.

"Even if it was, I think I could fit in your three-car garage," he teases.

"You don't have to be a smartass."

"I'm sorry if I offended you."

"You didn't offend me!" I practically yell. "Stop being so formal with me. It's like you're walking on eggshells and I don't like it."

"I don't like it either. I am trying not to upset you, so maybe you will invite me in to talk."

"I don't know if I'm emotionally ready for you. You hurt me," I admit.

"I know."

"Can I ask you one question?"

"You can ask me a million questions, *min kära*."

"What does that mean? That's what I want to know. You call me that, and the other word I would mangle if I tried to say it, and I want to know what they mean."

He swallows hard, but nods. "*Älskling* means darling. Well, that and some other endearments, but that's what I mean when I say it to you. *Min kära* means 'my love' and I've called you that since I realized I was falling in love with you."

"You can't. It's too soon. We barely know each other."

"All of that is true, but me loving you is also true."

In Maui, those words would've been all I needed to hear. *Wanted* to hear. But now, they're too much.

"Stop. I can't do this. Thank you for the ride."

I practically jump out of the car and run inside. I lean against the door until I hear his car leave, and then I'm just a puddle of emotions, sliding to the floor. Why can't I forgive him? Would I have even done anything differently than he did? I was so scared that what we had wasn't real enough to survive life back here, so would I have told him we weren't really married if I knew? I don't know, and that's what scares me the most.

Can I really be angry and keep my distance from the man I fell in love with when I might've done the same thing? We talked, laughed, and loved in Maui, and I knew things would be different once we were home. But, I thought we'd still be together. I'd be lying if I said I didn't want a future with Axel. I just need a little more time to wrap my head around, well, everything.

AXEL

It's been a month since I dropped Lauren off at home. I've seen her around town, but always from a distance. I always honor her by going in the other direction or making sure I'm not seated facing her if we're eating at the same place. Williston isn't a big city where we can hide from each other, but I can do my best to not make her uncomfortable. Although, the few times I wasn't quick enough and our eyes met, I swear I saw her face light up for a moment. Maybe I am getting a tiny bit closer to winning this war for our love.

Today, I don't have the luxury of pretending I don't see her. I'm the only player on the team who's still in Williston, as everyone else headed up to Grand Forks to get ready for Development Camp. I can't bring myself to leave, and that means I somehow got roped into a big picnic at Lauren's family farm. Luke said it's good publicity, but I know he's tired of me skulking around all sad and shit.

"Hello, big boy, and welcome to the farm. I'm Liesel," a woman accosts me when I get out of my car. She looks a little like Lauren, but she is not my *Älskling*.

"What are you doing here?" Lauren asks when we walk to where many people are gathered.

"Lauren, I know you were actually born in a barn, but you can pretend to have manners. Jonsson here is one of the players we'll be working with. You should play nice for once," the older man standing next to her admonishes her, and I'm not about to let that stand.

"She can play however she wants with me."

"Hey, I saw you first," Liesel complains.

"You most certainly did not," I tell her, removing myself from her clutches and going to stand in front of my love. "How are you, *min kära*?"

"At the moment? I've been better. I didn't mean to sound so harsh when I saw you. I was surprised, and you were with my sister."

"You are allowed to be upset at seeing me. I was not *with* your sister, though. She grabbed me when I exited my car."

"You are pretty hot, Viking."

"For you, *Älskling*."

"Oh, for funny. That was too cheesy," she tells me with a laugh.

"You like cheese."

"I *love* cheese."

"I'm sorry to interrupt what seems weirdly like flirting, but do you two know each other?" the man asks us.

"Yes, Dad. He's my husband. I guess I should've told you I got married in Vegas and honeymooned in Maui, huh?" She hasn't taken her eyes from mine while saying any of this, and I love to see the sparkle back in them.

"What? Did you at least get a prenup? AHL players make much less than your inheritance."

"Nope, no prenup. I trust Axel with my heart, soul, body, and my money. He loves me, and I love him."

She holds out her hand, and I take it. We ignore the chaos behind us as we walk into a barn close by. I let her lead me up into a hay loft with blankets over a couple of the bales.

"This is my favorite place on the property. I like the calm up here. I've come up here to think a lot over the last month, and I'm sorry I was so harsh with you."

"You're sorry? Oh no, you do not say those words to me, please. I was wrong to keep the truth about our marriage from you. You were right to be angry."

"I was angry, and betrayed, but I'm not sure I would've done things differently. I fell in love with you on that beautiful island, and I wanted our marriage to be real."

"It still could be," I tell her, dropping to one knee before her.

I take out the ring I bought in Maui. It's a pear-shaped diamond with rows of smaller diamonds crisscrossing around it. I've had it in my pocket whenever I wasn't on the ice or in the gym.

"Really?"

"Really. I love you, Lauren. I wanted to give this to you in Maui and ask you to be my wife for real, but you're right, I was scared. I'm not scared of marrying you, or of falling for you so soon. I'm scared of losing you. I promise to do my best not to make that happen again. Will you marry me?"

She hesitates, only for a moment, but it feels like hours. I understand we haven't figured everything out yet, and I'm asking way too soon. But, we've done everything fast, so why slow down now?

"Yes. We both made mistakes, and we have things to still work out, but I want to spend my life with you."

CHAPTER 10 - LAUREN

Two days later, I'm walking down the aisle on Luke Griffin's arm to meet Axel. We're in the small chapel at the Grand Wailea, where our favorite concierge, Kawehi, helped this all come together.

We had a short amount of time before Development Camp started, so Luke offered his jet. He and his wife, Olivia, are my only guests. My parents were livid when they realized what was going on, and I refused a prenup again. Luke actually pulled the sponsorship. I'll have to see them around town, but I don't have to do their bidding any longer.

Axel's family is here with us, and they are just as wonderful as he described them to me. Loving, and supportive, and so happy for both of us.

My simple white dress sways in the white breeze when we reach *min kära*. My love.

"You look beautiful."

"So do you, Viking."

Vows are said, inappropriate PDA is shown, delicious food is had, and I am happier than I ever have been in my life.

AXEL

I'm married for real this time, and nothing could be better. Well, maybe playing in the NHL. I know that's coming though. Right now, I'm just going to enjoy this night we have together before I have to start working toward my other dream.

"I'm sorry I couldn't get us another sunrise reservation this trip."

"I don't need a sunrise, Viking. I just need to wake up to you in the morning."

"You start teaching next month. We haven't talked about what happens if I get called up to Grand Forks."

"I'll hire a private plane to take me back and forth when you're there."

"I forgot I'm married to a millionaire."

"I expect to be soon as well, so don't get used to me paying," she teases me.

"Never."

We laugh, then kiss some more before clothes and inhibitions are once again lost. We've found each other, and that's all that matters.

Thank you for reading! If you enjoyed this short story, find more of Crystal's work www.crystalperkinsauthor.com.

GROUPIE
DEE LAGASSE

CHAPTER 1

"Forced family fun."

That's what my father called this vacation when my parents gifted my sister and I plane tickets and room reservations to the resort we'd been staying at with the entirety of my mom's side of the family for the last six days. All thirty-seven of us.

We basically hostilely took over the entire third floor of the hotel. *Okay, maybe it wasn't a hostile takeover.* There were a lot of credit cards on file in the resort's database, but I somehow doubted the employees would be sad to see us leave tomorrow.

I realized to anyone that didn't know me, I came off an ungrateful brat. A free vacation to Hawaii?! Poor Wren. And it wasn't the island itself. Maui was breathtaking. Between the bright sunshine, the warm crystal blue water, and the welcoming resort staff, the experience itself has been a complete dream. I mean, my sister and I freakin' snorkeled with green sea turtles yesterday. The resort is all-inclusive and we have everything we could possibly need right at our fingertips.

Including the unlimited fruity cocktails my mother has taken full advantage of since we got here.

Every day, by noon, she's three sheets to the wind and asking me why I haven't settled down. Depending on her mood, she either insisted it was time for me to get a "real job" or find myself a husband. Because, at the ripe old age of twenty-fucking-six, I was practically a spinster.

My older sister married her high school sweetheart at nineteen. At twenty-two, she had the first of her three kids. Two boys and a girl. I failed to see the reason I needed to marry the first eligible bachelor that looks my way and have his children. Which was verbatim what my mother suggested yesterday.

Our first flight homeward bound was at five o'clock tomorrow morning. That meant there was only one more day of endless frozen daquiris. I just needed to get through today. Then, I could go back to only getting badgered weekly during Sunday dinner.

Just one more day, I reminded myself as I walked up to the tiki bar my mother perched herself at with two of her sisters. If I didn't think I might fall on my face from dehydration, I'd walk back to the resort hotel for water. We'd been playing hard for the last forty-five minutes and the shakiness in my legs told me I needed water A.S.A.P.

"Bambina!"

My mother hopped off her barstool and began to walk toward me as I approached the bar.

"Hello Smother," I sighed knowing damn well how much she hated it.

My sister and I secretly called her "Smother" for years before I slipped and said it to her face when I was about nineteen. Once the cat was out of the bag, there was no shoving it back in there. I could not care less now. I used it more than "Mom." The best part was she still got just as offended as she was the first time that I called her it. But, if the shoe fits....

When she reached me, she leaned in for an air kiss. In our family, it was normal to greet each other with a quick double air kiss. Cheeks pushed against each other for two seconds, a quick kissing motion, done. Simple.

Not drunk Smother though. Drunk Smother did everything in a loud dramatic fashion. With both hands gripping my shoulders, and holding me in place, she leaned in and made the loudest "mwah" sound as she planted two kisses directly on my face. I offered her a tight-lipped smile as I stepped back.

My mother's theatrics captured the bartender's attention, so I seized the moment and asked for a bottle of water before I turned back to her.

"Where's Pops?" I asked.

I knew the effort was futile, but I still tried like hell to keep the conversation basic and light.

"He's off bird watching with your grandfather," she said with a roll of her eyes.

That was another thing that bothered me about my mom. My dad was the kindest, gentlest, most supportive man I'd ever met. While some men liked expensive cars or golf, Dad loved birds.

You didn't become an ornithologist or name your daughters Sparrow and Wren without having a passion for feathered flyers. Smother didn't mind that it was his profession that allowed her to stay home and kept her in the designer clothes she loved so much. Yet she took the opportunity to belittle his profession any chance she could. I truly did not understand how my father stayed with her.

"Are you going to the concert tonight?" my Aunt Cecilia piped in.

Tomorrow was going to be a long day of traveling back to Massachusetts.

The only thing I wanted to do tonight was pack my suitcase and lay in bed with room service.

"I'm probably going to call it early," I told her. "God knows I don't want to have bags under my eyes while going through multiple airports tomorrow. You never know… I might be seated next to my future husband."

Both of my aunts caught my sarcasm, but my mother was either completely oblivious to the fact I was being a smartass or she chose to ignore it because she didn't skip a beat.

"That's what's makeup is for, Wren," she huffed with such exasperation. "Are you even trying to meet someone? You aren't going have this beauty forever, you know."

What little patience I had for her dissipated with the last dig.

"Alright, Donna" my aunt Rosaline began, gently pulling my mother backwards. "I think that's our cue to get you out of the sun for a little bit."

Aunt Celicia mouthed "I'm so sorry" to me before they walked away.

Everyone knew she was out of line, but no one ever said anything to her because my mom was the baby. The only person that ever stood up to her was my brother-in-law. He was the best husband to my sister and filled a protective older brother role when it came to me. Jordan never hesitated to have our backs. It was to the point that Sparrow and I didn't need to say anything anymore. He just knew.

If I ever settled down, I needed someone like Jordan. Someone who would be willing to go into battle with me. Someone who could combat the smothering voices that echoed every awful thing she ever said to me. It was a lot to ask. No one wanted a girl with mommy issues. Not for anything longer than a night or two anyway.

"And I thought my mom was bad," a voice chuckled from the other side of me.

Warmth flushed over my cheeks when I realized a complete stranger heard my mother berate me about my lack of ambition when it came to finding a husband. When I turned, the heat of embarrassment covered my entire body. Because, of course, it had to be the hottest man I'd ever seen staring back at me.

He looked like he walked right off the Abercrombie & Fitch bags I kept to hang on my walls as a teenager. Disheveled wavy brown hair was tousled in a perfect mess on top of his head. The cutest little dimples settled in his cheeks as he flashed me a cheeky grin. Under his perfectly kissable lips, he had a sharp, defined jawline… based on his appearance alone, he checked every box I could ever want in a man.

I'm pretty sure I counted *eight* defined ab muscles. I wasn't entirely convinced I wasn't suffering from heat stroke, and he was a figment of my imagination. When I collected enough confidence to look him directly in the eyes, amusement danced in the specks of golden browns and greens.

And, god, he was tall. Maybe six feet, give or take an inch or two. Tall enough that I could still wear heels and look up at him. And he was walking over to me right fucking now.

"I do agree with her on one thing though," he continued. "You're *beautiful*."

The way he emphasized beautiful made my knees go weak.

Physical based flattery rarely caught my attention. It was lazy. Sure, every woman wanted to hear they were beautiful, but without a single shred of arrogance, I knew I was blessed in the looks department.

I heard it my whole life. I was in diaper commercials before I could sit up on my own. My mother stuck me in beauty pageants as soon as I could walk. A wall of the crowns I won over the years still hung in my parents' house. They meant nothing to me. They were my mother's trophies more than they were mine, so I let her keep them all. I stopped competing as soon as I turned eighteen.

It wasn't just Smother though. My grandfather called me his "bellissima bambina" which translated to "beautiful baby" in Italian. My uncles all called me "bella" which also meant beautiful. The only people who didn't seem to give one iota about my appearance were my dad, my sister, my brother-in-law, and their kids. Somewhere along the way being called "beautiful" lost its luster.

It didn't matter that I made straight A's all throughout high school or that I was the student class president all four years. Being captain of the volleyball team and taking our team to state didn't matter when I wasn't named prom queen. Something I couldn't have cared less about.

"And at the risk of sounding like a creep," he kept going. "I was watching you out there. You're a badass. You've got a mean spike."

"Thanks," I said, before awkwardly sticking out my hand. "I'm Wren."

"Even your name is pretty." He flashed me another smile as he took my hand in his. His grip is firm, but still gentle enough it doesn't hurt. "It's so nice to meet you, Wren. I'm River and I think you should reconsider going to the concert tonight."

"Oh? And why is that?"

"Because I'll be there," he answered. "And I really want to see you again before you leave. You got a last name, Wren?"

"I sure do," I laughed. "But I don't make a habit of telling it to complete strangers I just met on the beach."

I expected him to try to persuade me into telling him anyway. Most guys didn't seem to understand subtly.

"Okay," he started. "Wren with No Last Name, you just head to VIP and tell them River put you on VIP list. Feel free to bring a friend or two."

With that, he flashed me one last smile and began to jog in the direction of the hotel. I wished I hadn't stared at him as he moved, because he turned back and I was caught gawking at his backside. Since there was no sense in denying it, I decided to be brave. I blew a complete stranger a kiss. Without hesitation, he held his arm up and pretended to catch it. It was the cheesiest and cutest act I've ever witnessed.

Well, fuck. Smother was going to get her wish because I had no choice but to go to that damn concert now.

CHAPTER 2

By the time we made it back down to the beach, it was packed with people. Mostly females. The range was wild. Preteens and grannies alike filled the crowd.

The moment I saw the banner with the band name on it, I understood why. Saint James was a band of brothers from Boston. A few of my cousins were obsessed with them.

They must not know they're the band playing tonight because there is no way I would have made it down here without them if they did. Not after Sparrow not so casually dropped the fact I was going to the concert because I met a cute boy at the beach at dinner. My mother was thrilled, and Jordan was all too quick to offer to "man the hotel room solo" tonight so Sparrow could come be my wing-woman.

The energy was contagious. I might only know a handful of Saint James songs, but I was fucking excited. As we move in and out of the hordes of people toward the VIP area, the opener hyped the crowd.

"Who's ready for Saint James?" the lead singer asked the audience. She was immediately answered by a roar of applause and cheering. "Us too! Us too! We have just one more song for you tonight. This one's called Lotus Flower and it goes a little something like this…"

Butterflies fluttered in my stomach as we stepped to the barricaded VIP area. I looked around unsure of what to do next. It wasn't like a club with one security guard standing out with a list.

"Excuse me," I called out to a member of the event staff. "I know this is going to sound crazy, but I was told to let someone know River put me on the list?"

The man quirked his brow at me but went over to a petite woman at the front of the barricade. She glanced over and nodded before saying something back to the man.

"Can I have your name, ma'am?" he asked, and I felt every flutter come to a full stop.

This was it. We were about to get thrown out. How dumb could I have been? This man from the beach, whoever he was, must be having himself a good little laugh at my expense right now.

"Wren," I sighed.

"You got a last name Wren?" He tilted his head forward as if he was giving me a major hint here.

I laughed. "Nope. No last name. Some people might even call me 'Wren With No Last Name'."

"Just you two?" he asked as he glanced between me and Sparrow.

After I nodded, he let us through. Once we were inside the barricade, he handed us both an All-Access lanyard.

"Those will get you anywhere you need to be tonight," he said. "Enjoy the show!"

Once we were in, my sister grabbed my arm and gave a quiet excited squeal. I couldn't remember the last time Sparrow and I went and did something just the two of us. I loved being the fun aunt. The trampoline park and too much candy was my jam, but there were times I missed getting to hang with Sparrow in a setting that didn't involve screaming children. I wasn't sure if tonight counted as a night without screaming children, but it was a night without children that were her responsibility.

"Holy shit." Sparrow said under her breath as she squeezed my arm. "Be right back. I'm going to get us a couple drinks while we wait for your mystery man to appear."

As soon as Sparrow stepped away, the woman from the front of the barricade excused herself from the conversation she was having and beelined toward me. Her style reminded me of my mother's. Very chic. Very expensive.

As she got closer, there was an unexplainable familiarity about her. As hard as I tried to place where I could know her from, nothing came to mind.

"Hello Wren," the woman greeted me.

"Hi," I replied wishing I had as much confidence in who she was as she did in knowing who I am. "Do we... do we know each other?"

"I don't think so," she said. "Not yet anyway."

"Oh, good," I laughed. Her brows quirked in confusion as I continued. "It's just that you seemed to know exactly who I am. I thought maybe we met at some point this week. It's been nonstop so I wouldn't have been surprised."

"Oh, no," she reassured me. "This is definitely the first time we have met."

"Okay, good. I already feel a little silly because I'm pretty sure the guy who told me to come meet him is standing me up."

I looked around again. Still no sign of River.

She pulled her bottom lip in as her body shook with silent laughter. I had no fucking clue what was going on, but clearly, this woman found my situation amusing.

"River didn't stand you up, honey. He's getting ready to get on the stage." She grinned. "I'm Meadow St. James, but most people just call me Mama SJ. I'm River's mom."

With every word she spoke, I began to process what she was trying to tell me. River wasn't just some hot guy I met at the tiki bar. He was River St. James. A world-famous musician. My cousins had his posters on their walls. His songs played on the radio at the bar all the time.

"Wait." Small droplets of perspiration began to bead in the palms of my hands as my stomach tightened. "You're telling me, the boy, I'm sorry, man, I met this morning..."

"Is River St. James?" Meadow finished for me as the music stopped and the lights went out. "See for yourself."

Despite being in the open air, the screaming around us was deafening. A heavy drumbeat filled the speakers and as the guitar joined in, one by one, the three men sprinted onto the stage.

Sure enough, with a white electric guitar strapped across his body, there he was. The Cali surfer vibes from the beach had been traded for a pair of ripped jeans, a mostly unbuttoned Red Sox jersey and a backwards white snapback hat. The confidence radiated off him as he effortlessly played riff after riff while singing along with his brothers.

"I don't wanna be a buzzkill, but where is this guy?" Sparrow shouted from the side of me after half a dozen or so songs.

She was on her second or third drink, but unlike our mom, the fruity cocktails just made her dance badly and sing louder. I was so swept up, I forgot to tell her that I'd found River.

"Um," I said as I pointed to the stage. "He's the one in the white hat."

Her eyes went as wide as saucers as she whipped her head back and forth between me and the stage where River was playing.

"Shut the fu-" she stopped short of cursing, but the effect was not lost on me. Sparrow never swore. She was the good sister. The proper and well-behaved sister. Not that I was wild, but I appreciated a good f-bomb more than the average girl and I sure as hell wasn't in bed at eight every night like Sparrow was. "You really didn't know?"

River hadn't so much as hinted he was in the band. As I recalled our short, but memorable interaction, there wasn't a single cue I missed that could have led me to believe he was a St. James.

"You girls should go watch from the side stage," Meadow suggested while one of River's brothers talked to the crowd about a new album coming out.

My sister answered with a yawn. "You should go. I'm probably going to head back to the room."

Meadow frowned at Sparrow's answer. I thought it was because she felt offended that my sister was going to leave until she flagged down a member of the St. James security team and asked them to make sure Sparrow got back to her room safely.

Before she left, my sister pulled me into a hug.

"Love you. Be safe. Make smart choices," she said, mimicking what our dad used to say to us as teenagers. "And have so, so much fun."

I didn't have a fucking clue what I was doing, but the likelihood of something like this happening again in my lifetime was slim to none. If nothing else came from tonight, I would have a fun vacation story to tell when I got back to work.

Once Sparrow was on her way, Meadow gave me directions to the side stage entrance. I assumed she was coming with me, but she stayed behind in the VIP area. Despite having the All-Access pass hung around my neck, a small flicker of panic jolted through my body when I reached the security standing in front of the steps on the side of the stage. There was no hesitation to let me pass, but I let out a breath of relief once my feet touched the top step.

Shit. Where do I stand?

I've been to a lot of concerts, but never up on the side of the stage while someone was performing. I had no idea how chaotic it was. From the techs running back and forth switching out guitars to the handful of people standing at the ready by a clothing rack, I could tell it was a well-oiled machine. I didn't want to be the person that threw a wrench in the performance.

"Are you lost, ma'am?"

My saving grace came in the form of a muscular, bearded man covered in tattoos from the neck down speaking in an accent I would recognize anywhere. This man was from Boston. I grew up in Southern New Hampshire, so I didn't have a thick accent myself, but most of my family lived right outside of the city. Being so far from home, it brought me a weird sense of comfort to be in the presence of a fellow New Englander.

As he got closer, I noticed it said "Head of Security" in the corner of his black short-sleeve polo.

"Kind of?" I told him. "Meadow told me I should watch the show from here. I just don't know where to stand. I don't want to be in anyone's way."

"You're Wren," he said.

It wasn't a question, but I confirmed anyway. "I am and you're from Mass." When his brows quirked at my response, I pointed to myself. "New Hampshire."

"Ahhh, okay, New Hampshah," he chuckled. Reaching into a little container on a small table, he handed me two ear plugs. "First, take these. It's a lot loudah up heah," he said. "Now, follow me."

CHAPTER 3

Before he left, Max properly introduced himself and told me to ask anyone for him personally if I needed anything. St. James wasn't messing around when it came to their VIPs. I felt like someone had rolled out the red carpet for little unknown me.

"Hey, nice dress!" the only other woman standing on the side shouted before I could introduce myself.

I wouldn't have been able to pick out any of the St. James siblings before tonight, but I recognized Scout LAST NAME. She was the runner up on the first season of my favorite reality tv show, Design School. I was bummed when she didn't win. The disappointment didn't last though. Within a few months of the finale airing, my favorite boutique back at home was carrying her clothing line Rock Chic. The black baby doll dress I wore tonight was from her latest collection.

I almost told her I knew who she was but opted to just say "thanks!" instead. If she wanted to be fawned over, she would be down in the crowd. Though, I would be lying if I said I wasn't intimidated standing back here with her. There was no shame in being a bartender. I had my own apartment. All my bills were paid. There was just something about being in the presence of a Fashion Week icon that made me feel a little "less than."

"Oh." Scout let out a laugh. "I should probably introduce myself. I'm

Scout. Sorry, I'm still kind of new to all this." She waved her hand, motioning to everything around us. "Well, not to St. James," she added. "But being a St. James girlfriend."

I didn't have to wonder for long which St. James she was dating because the one River had introduced as "Arrow" came running over to steal a kiss from her as soon as the song they were playing ended. River glanced over and as his brother ran back and the double take that he did when he saw me standing next to Scout made my heart burst. His smile was ear-to-ear as he made his way over to us.

I sure as hell did not expect him to wrap his hand around the back of my neck and pull me into a kiss. My body stilled, frozen in shock, for a second before I allowed myself to melt into him. It ended as fast as it came. Before I could say anything, River was back center stage.

"Okay, spill!" Scout yells from the side of me. She tugged at my arm and pulled me into an area behind the stage that was set up like a living room. There were couches and a big monitor that showed the band playing. "I've known those boys for a long time, and I've never seen River kiss someone like *that*."

For some reason, that comforted me. I didn't think I was going to be the love of his life, but I sure as hell didn't walk into this concert with the intention of leaving a River St. James groupie either.

"We met this afternoon," I told her. Any nerves I had in her presence had already melted away. Maybe it was the cocktails or the adrenaline from River's kiss, but I didn't hold back with her like I normally would upon first meeting someone. "He overheard my mom giving me a hard time about not trying to find a husband and invited me to the concert. I had no idea who he was."

"He didn't tell you?" she asked. The corners of her lips curled into a smirk when I shook my head no. "That sounds like Riv."

"So, I'm going to be totally honest here," I began. "I'm way out of my league here and have no idea what the hell I'm doing. I'm just a bartender from -"

I didn't get to finish before she cut me off.

"I'm going to stop you right there," she said. "I waited tables all through college and I would never do it again. That was the most physically demanding and emotionally draining jobs that I've ever done. Their mom, Meadow, worked at a diner in the town we all grew up in. No one here is going to look down on you because you're a bartender. If anything, they'll respect the hell out of you for it."

As someone who got told all the time by her parent that she needed to "grow up and get a real job," Scout's words overwhelmed me. I swallowed, fighting the tug of emotions bubbling at the brim of explosion. I was just about to thank her when she grabbed my hand.

"The guys are about to come off stage," she said as she guided me back to where we started.

We made it back just in time to see them stand in a line, grab hands, and take a bow with the rest of the band. A tech was waiting to take River's guitar just off the stage. Once his hands were free, he walked right over to me. With every step he took toward me my heart beat faster.

"Bye Wren," Scout called out before she walked off stage, hand in hand, with Arrow.

"Later, Scout!" I waved.

I doubt I will ever see her again after tonight, but I will never forget the kindness she showed me. Especially after I eventually admitted I knew exactly who she was.

"What do you say we get out of here?" River asked, sliding his hand in mine.

I answered with a nod. I might not have come with the intention of leaving this concert a River St. James groupie, but after watching him sing and play guitar for almost two hours, I wasn't opposed to the idea either.

Behind the stage was a line of dune buggies. Each one was guarded by a member of the security team. River walked to the one in the front of the line and told the man we were going back to the villas. He handed River two bandanas as he tied one over own nose and mouth.

"This is Paul," River explained as he gently secured the bandana around the back of my head. "He's going to get us back to the villa. I'm usually solo after shows, so you're gonna have to sit on my lap for the ride."

As soon as River was situated in the passenger seat, he extended his hand for me to take. I hadn't sat on someone's lap since I was a young child. This was different. Intimate. He wasted no time wrapping his arms around me once we were secured by the lap belt that he pulled over the two of us.

The drive to the villa was less than five minutes, but it was long enough to feel the hard twitch of River's cock against his jeans. The black baby doll dress I was wearing barely covered my ass when I sat down. I spent the drive clutching my legs together, hoping Paul couldn't tell I was fighting the urge to wiggle my ass all over River's lap.

"This is us," River said against my ear as we stopped in front of a small cottage.

His breath against my skin sent a trail of goosebumps against my body. With the arm wrapped across my body, he unbuckled us. While I stood, he thanked Paul for the ride. The moment his feet touched the ground below, he grabbed my hand and walked us to the front door. A security code unlocked the door and the moment it closed behind us, my back was against the wall, River's body pressed against me.

"Are you okay with this?" he asked as one hand wrapped around the side of my neck and the other gripped my hip. "We don't have to do anything you don't want to. I can get someone to bring you back to your room if you want to leave."

"I'm okay with this. I'm more than okay with this."

Feeling bold, I covered the hand that gripped my hip with my own and guided him under my dress. His eyes bore into mine as I brought my hand back out and allowed him free reign. Moving my panties to the side, he cursed when he trailed a finger over my clit teasingly before he kept going.

"So wet for me, baby." He smirked as he slipped a finger inside of me. My back ached as he bent down and tipped my head back, branding my lips with a hot kiss. With every pump of his finger, River pushed in deeper. I was at the brink of combusting all over his hand when he broke our kiss and said, "I want to taste you."

He withdrew his finger and used his hand to pull my underwear off my hips. It fell to the floor, settling by the heels of my Converse. One by one I lifted my legs and stepped out of them. When River saw the black lace thong on the floor, he growled in satisfaction, then, used both hands to spread my legs apart before dropping to his knees in front of me.

I swear I saw stars as his tongue slowly swept against me. It was like he was trying to savor every single second. I'd only had one other guy do this before now and it felt nothing like this. Much like I guided him earlier, he took my hand and placed it on his head, giving me permission to grab at his hair.

It didn't take long for him to figure out exactly what I liked. Every time I pulled him closer or pushed my body up to him, he moaned in pleasure. There was something so sexy about a man getting turned on by me reacting to what he was doing to me. When I looked down at him, I felt like a goddess. River St. James was on his knees worshipping me.

The build up in my core intensified and I pulled River back.

"I'm so close," I told him. "I don't want this to be over just yet."

"Baby, we're just getting started." He grinned. "I'm going to make you cum till you can't anymore."

CHAPTER 4

River was a man of his word. After coming undone on his tongue, he carried me to his bed, where he fucked me not once, not twice, but three times. After we finished, he insisted on running me a warm bath. In the sweetest, most caring way, he washed my body and wrapped me in a big fluffy white towel before carrying me back to the bedroom.

He rifled through an open suitcase before handing me a t-shirt that said Cape Cod on it. Can take the girl out of New England, but apparently New England followed her all the way to Hawaii. I giggled at the thought.

"What's so funny?" River smiled.

That's when it dawned on me that I just let this man put me on all fours and I *begged* him to fuck me deeper and harder, yet we knew next to nothing about each other. I had never been a participant of a one-night stand. With River's lifestyle, I couldn't imagine tonight would amount to anything more than that.

I was officially a St. James groupie.

"I'm from New Hampshire," I told him. "It's just kind of ironic that I came all the way to Hawaii and the one guy I hook up with on vacation is from New England too."

"You say it like this is the last time we're going to see each other," he said.

"Isn't it?" I questioned. "I don't expect you to pretend this is anything more than what it is. I'm not some delusional fan girl, River. Not to bruise your ego, but I had no idea who you were or what you did when we met this morning. Or is it yesterday morning now? Shit. Maybe I should go. We have to leave in like three hours and I need to get some sleep."

"I won't stop you from leaving if that's what you want to do." His words stung. I guess I was wrong. I did hope it would be more than this. "But I would be really happy if you stayed. Don't worry about your flight. I'll make sure you get home."

The butterflies from earlier returned tenfold as he continued.

"I don't want to presume anything, but we leave for tour in a couple days," he said. "You should come with us."

"Yeah," I laughed. "I'll just join you on tour."

When I caught his stone-faced response, I stopped mid-laugh.

"You're serious?" I asked.

He closed the space between us. "I don't know what's going to happen, but I know I'm not ready to say goodbye just yet."

"Me either," I whispered.

"Is that a yes?" The hope in his voice was all I needed to hear to solidify my decision.

"That's a yes."

The End... for now.

River and Wren's story will continue with Pop Star – a full length romance coming in early 2024. Follow Dee @deelagasse on social media for updates!

SHOOTING STARS

DIANA PETERFREUND

Elliot North had spent nearly every season of her life with her feet planted firmly on the ground. It was the only way to survive on the North estate, where land and labor were plentiful but her father cared little for the welfare of either. Someone needed to remain practical, to dream of only what might help the people of her land get through the next winter.

She reached her toes out over the edge of the net, nothing but stars and sea visible beyond her soles. No longer. The North estate was finally in good hands, and she was free to dream as much as she liked.

The *Argos* sailed through the night, piloted by those who best knew how to read the stars. The giant solar sails were drawn now, but gossamer nets still stretched out in all directions from the deck, and this was where Elliot preferred to spend her evening hours, where she could smell the sea air, and feel the sea breeze, and listen to the soft murmurings of Kai and his co-pilots.

She'd gone years without the sound of his voice. She did not intend to miss another moment. Kai's presence was more soothing than the rocking of the boat among the waves.

At some point in the night, he slid onto the hammock beside her. She always awoke when he came, and pressed a soft kiss to the nape of her neck and curled his body around hers.

"The Innovations don't like that you sleep out here. They're afraid you're going to get knocked overboard and no one will know in the dark."

"The Innovations, of all people," she responded, "should know I'm in no danger when you're on duty."

"I never said I agreed with them," he murmured into her hair. Kai's hand traced the outline of her body, down the length of her arm, meeting her hip just below the elbow then curving in across her forearm to her wrist, until their fingers intertwined. Elliot remembered another night, another time their hands had touched, and her entire world had opened up like a flower reaching toward the sun.

Now, he lifted their intertwined hands against the night sky. All Elliot could see was the indistinct outline of their limbs as they blocked the light of a few stars. Again and again, she wondered what it was that Kai saw instead.

"Do you ever get bored of the stars?" she asked.

"You know me better than that," he said, and brought her hand to his mouth. "I never get tired of being with the things I love."

With the stars above and the sea below, it felt as if they two were the only solid things in the universe, floating alone in a big blue sphere. Dimly, Elliot knew their quest was important, but she couldn't help but feel it would be fine if this night never ended, and she could stay right here with Kai forever.

The years that he'd been gone now seemed like nothing more than a half-remembered nightmare. The months after he'd returned, when neither of them could bring themselves to acknowledge the truths they still held in their hearts, even more unlikely. Perhaps she would never have his extraordinary eyes, but she knew they still saw the world the exact same way.

At once, Kai let go over her and sat up, his attention shifting away and across the water.

Elliot sat up too. "What is it? Do you see something? Do you hear something?"

Even in the darkness, she watched him narrow his eyes. "No — I thought for a second — but no."

———

The next morning, Elliot stood at the prow of the ship and looked out on the ocean, straining for some glimpse of whatever had captured Kai's attention last night.

The salt wind nipped her skin and the spray misted her skirt, but still she stood. By day, this was her favorite spot on the ship. Here, Elliot was the farthest away from home, the first to enter into... whatever it was they were bound to find.

The overcast sky cast a slate-gray pall over the waves, like the dull drab coveralls she used to wear on the farm. She liked the water best when it was the deep, ponderous blue that matched the color of Kai's favorite coat.

He'd seen something last night. She knew he had. And this morning, he'd acted like it was nothing. But why? Elliot thought they were done trying to keep secret from one another.

On the railing, a pair of hands covered her own, and a split second later, she felt Kai at her back, heard his voice in her ear. "It's good I always know where to find you."

She leaned back into him, pushing until his hands left the rail and encircled her waist. "Trying to beat me again, I see."

He chuckled, and his breath stirred the fine hairs at her temple. "I wouldn't dare, Chancellor Boatwright. Wherever we're going, you're going first."

Elliot stretched her fingers out over the waves, where the sharp prow of the ship sliced into the untamed sea. "Oh, I get special treatment because I'm a Luddite Lord?"

"No," he said. "It's because this way, if there are cannibals, I'm safe."

She whirled around to face him, strands of her hair whipping in the wind. "You look like Medusa."

"You're just digging yourself deeper, Captain Wentforth," Elliot replied, trying to untangle herself with little success.

Kai did the job for her, sweeping her long dark hair back and away until they could see each other clearly again. As always, his eyes were black, glimmering dimly with odd facets and reflections that were the only outward signs of the genetic enhancements he'd illegally received.

"Allow me to make it up to you." And now she noticed the tinge of excitement in his voice, the boyish grin he could hardly contain. "Today we're going out on the gliders."

So he *had* seen something! Or at least, suspected it enough to do some further investigation. Though Kai had shown her the gliders the first day she'd boarded the ship, they'd remained strapped to the side of the hull for the entire voyage thus far. She'd yet to see them unfolded, let alone in flight.

"Is this because of last night?"

He cocked his head. "Trust me, if the Innovations weren't happy about you sleeping on the nets, they're going to be livid about this one."

"That's not what I meant—" she stopped. "Wait, what *you* mean?" Elliot stared at him in wonder.

"Elliot," said Kai, shaking his head. "I said *we* were going out."

Unfolded, the gliders took up the entire deck of the *Argos*. Like the sails of the solar ship, the glider's wings were a shiny gold, ready to catch the rays of the sun in order to power their flight. Between each elegant, curving wing was a slim, light body containing an open-air cabin with two seats—one in front of the other.

"You'll sit in front, of course," Kai said. "So you can be first."

A shiver ran through Elliot's limbs. Flying. *Really* flying. Once, on this earth, people flew every hour of every day. But though she'd spent her childhood folding and flying paper gliders with Kai on the shores of their little island, she couldn't comprehend going up in the air herself.

She ran her hands along the body of the glider, feeling its smooth sides, squinting as the gold panels on the wings snatched a bit of the intermittent sunlight and caught fire. Kai hadn't merely imagined flying. He'd made it happen. While Elliot was folding paper and doing simple cross-grafts with wheat strains, Kai was recapturing mankind's mastery of the skies. He'd built the sun-carts, he'd designed the ship, he'd made these gliders. Every single thing he'd ever imagined as a child, it was all right here in front of him, his dreams made solid.

How could she ever compare?

As many of the crew as could fit on the deck were standing around, checking the gliders and preparing the tilted launchpad that would propel them into the air. There was Felicia Innovation and her husband, the Admiral, standing near Ro, who looked vastly confused by their animated gestures explaining what the machines were built to do. Felicia was making bird shapes with her hands and Nicodemus was waving his arms in the air. Elliot saw the exact moment her Reduced friend understood—the girl's face almost split in a smile as bright as glider wings. Nearby, Andromeda Phoenix was bent over the second glider, buffing a few marks on the shimmering surface as they readied for departure.

Kai surveyed it all, an understandably self-satisfied look on his face. Elliot swallowed. So far the journey had been idyllic—easy weather, happy companions, the company of new friends like the Innovations and old friends like her darling Ro, and best of all, the knowledge that every day would start and end in the comforting circle of Kai's arms. But it was clear no one here had forgotten their mission to find other lands. When it came to that, Elliot felt like she had nothing to add. She was a passenger, a tourist, on an expedition built entirely out of the dreams of the man she loved.

She looked down at her hands, clasped tightly in front of her, and tried to force back her emotions. Whatever fear and doubts she faced, it was too late to go back now. She'd cast off everything and boarded this ship. She had to make the best of it. As she raised her eyes, something on the wing caught her attention. There was a tiny inscription etched into the gold.

The real voyage of discovery consists not in seeking new landscapes but in having new eyes.

She raised her face to Kai's steady gaze.

"I see you found it," he said softly, as if they were the only two on deck. "It wouldn't be a glider of mine if it didn't have a message for you."

Elliot laughed. "For me? Hardly. My eyes are just the normal kind."

He shook his head. "No, Elliot, they aren't. These words were written by an ancient writer named Proust. He didn't know anything about ERV. We're discoverers, you and I, even if we never find a thing out here. We're discoverers because we're looking. We're willing to see things in new ways. We fought for a world we knew we could make exist. I put these words on the wing to remind me of that. If there's nothing out here, we haven't lost, because our true discovery is that we can make the world what we want it to be."

"You can make things," Elliot pointed out, spreading her arms. "Look at all you've made."

"Look at all you've made, back on your estates," Kai said. "And don't think you weren't a part of this, too, Elliot. Every line of this glider belongs to you." He came close and slipped his arms around her. "Just like I do. Years ago, you promised me that if I built a glider, you'd come with me to see the stars. Are you ready to keep that promise?"

"It's daytime."

"Details."

As the sun dappled the deck of the ship, Elliot closed her eyes and breathed Kai in. His lips were soft on hers, but his hands pressed firmly against her back.

There was an unsubtle cough from somewhere beyond. "If you two are quite finished, some of us have actual work to do." Andromeda's voice was dry and as Elliot, her cheeks darkening, turned toward the other captain, the older girl rolled her eyes. Kai merely shrugged and grinned.

"No one said that bringing her along meant dealing with *this* nonsense all the time," Andromeda grumbled as she wheeled the glider away and into position on the launching pad.

"It's not *all* the time," Elliot argued to Kai. Besides, they had a lot to make up for.

He nodded in agreement. "No apologies, Chancellor."

Hand in hand, they approached the glider. The launchpad had tilted the machine up and forward, and a tightly wound spring at the back of the contraption was responsible for shooting it into the sky. Kai helped Elliot up into the cabin then climbed in behind her. As they buckled themselves in, Elliot noted that the controls looked very much like the ones Kai had built on the sun-cart—which in turn were copied from the design of the tractor Kai had spent his childhood maintaining on Elliot's estate.

At last they were strapped in tightly, Kai's thighs on either side of her own, her back against his chest. His hand pressed hard against her stomach. "There's going to be a bit of a jolt when we take off, so brace yourself."

Elliot nodded.

The force of the takeoff shoved her hard against Kai, and her heart leaped into her throat. Angled as they were, she could see nothing but sky and clouds. She had no sense of how high they were hurtling, no idea how much higher they could even go. The air chilled around them and there was nothing but wind in her ears.

After what seemed like forever, the plane began to level, and her stomach flipped for a second as Kai found purchase among the wind currents, engaging the fans to help push and lift the little glider through the air.

"Should I look down now?" she shouted over her shoulder.

"That's sort of the point," he cried back.

Gingerly, she leaned to the side and glanced down. Beneath them, the ocean seemed flat and unremarkable, the giant swells she knew so well from their voyage reduced to wrinkles. She couldn't even see the *Argos*, but she feared stretching out any farther to try to catch a glimpse.

Kai tapped a mirror near the edge of the cabin. "It's there," he said, as if reading her mind.

It was a pinprick of gold against the expanse of sea. Were they mad to be doing this?

Soon enough, Kai found his footing in the sky and, just as he did with the sun-cart, started having fun—rising and dipping with the wind currents, hooting and hollering, and laughing out loud when she squealed and clutched at his legs.

"Just you wait until I'm the one flying," she said. "I'll do loops."

He handed her the controls, and she thought better of it. But it was still fun to fly, to let the winds lift you higher and lower in turn.

"I probably should have asked this before," she shouted back at him, "but how do we land on the ship?"

"I probably should have thought of that, too," he said, which earned him an elbow in the ribs. "There are nets, Elliot. And if we miss . . . well, it floats. I hope."

"Kai!"

"I *think*," he added, and though she couldn't see him, she knew he was grinning.

"So . . . what are we doing up here?" she asked. It was time for him to come clean.

"Oh," Kai said vaguely, "I thought it would be good for us to practice with the glider from time to time. It gives us a new perspective on the seascape. And when we reach land, we can send a small party out on the gliders ahead of the ship."

When, not *if*, Elliot noted. For Kai, land worth finding was a certainty, despite all they'd been raised to believe about being alone in the world. And his belief had been strong enough to carry them all out to sea, and even up into the sky. "If we land somewhere," she asked, unable to speak as definitively as he had, "how would we take off again without the launcher?"

Kai nudged his foot against something built into the side of the cabin. "There are two rockets in there. All we'd have to do is get the glider on some sort of tilted platform, even with stones or a log, and it should be fine."

"*Should* be?"

Kai laughed again. "You trusted me to first sail, then fly off into the unknown, and now you question my methods?"

"I'm curious," she corrected. "Not questioning." And he must know it. She'd go to the ends of the Earth with Kai in any contraption he dared to build. She already had. Who could have guessed, all those years ago, that the boy from the barn could have made his dreams come alive? Who could have foreseen, even a few months ago, that she would be sitting with the love of her life in a golden machine in the middle of the sky? Not Elliot North.

But here she was. The real voyage of discovery consists of having new eyes, indeed. Elliot closed her eyes, letting the wind buffet her face, letting it wash over her and around her and into her. *Flying*.

It wasn't only Kai's dreams that had come to life today.

For a long moment, she stayed like that, eyes shut, enjoying the warm, solid feeling of Kai's body at her back, even as everything else floated away.

No matter how many times they'd pretended they were the only people in the world, this time it was true. Here, up and away, they were all there was—no water spray, no smell of salt, no noise at all but the rushing wind.

And when at last she opened her eyes again, Elliot saw the world anew. The sun broke through the clouds, turning the sea a bright blue. The sky on the horizon was clear, the expanse broken only by a single set of puffy, low-hanging clouds in the far distance.

"Elliot," came Kai's voice in her ear. He sounded breathless, shaken. "What do you see?"

"Water," she said. "Sky. Clouds."

She could feel his heart pounding against her back.

"Anything else?"

"I'm not the one with the inhuman eyes."

Kai raised his arm over her shoulder, pointing, and she followed the direction as far as she could. "That cloud over there?" It hung low on the horizon, and its underside had an almost greenish cast.

"Yes." Then he lifted his hand higher, and she looked again. Up, deep in the bowl of the sky, she saw a bird circling.

"A bird?" From this distance, she couldn't tell what it was. They'd seen several albatross on their journey already, though such far-ranging seabirds signified little. Kai could probably see well enough to tell, though.

"And down there?" Again his arm shifted toward the surface of the ocean. She followed the line down to where the ripples that were probably huge swells seemed to have shifted some.

Three signs. She caught her breath. Heedless of their balance, Elliot turned in her seat to stare at Kai. "*Why* did you bring me out here again?" she cried, a tone of mock accusation entering her voice.

"Because you stand at the front of the ship," he whispered. His voice could hardly be heard over the sound of the wind, but she had no trouble understanding him. She knew his heart. "Because you always pushed your toes out over the cliff. Because you wish you could see as far as me. Because I built this glider for you, so you can see what I see. Because I know you know what it means."

Elliot twisted around in her seat and stared at him. single word thrummed though her blood like her own heartbeat.

Land.

"If we were going to find the rest of the world, Elliot, I wanted to do it together."

She kissed him, there in the sky, as the sun rays shone on the wings of the glider and the fire in their souls took flight.

Find out how Kai and Elliot came here in For Darkness Shows the Stars. Learn where they're going in Across a Star-Swept Sea.

REBOUND
EMMA LOUISE

CHAPTER 1 - NORAH

Standing at the window, I watch as the florist finishes setting up the flowers that line the aisle that I'm going to be walking down in less than an hour. Looking around, I take in how beautiful it looks. My dream wedding day is coming together just like I'd planned for so long. Rows of white chairs stand on lush green grass, white roses and peonies everywhere.

People start to wander out from the cocktail area, the women in pretty gowns, the men in smart looking suits. Well, most of them anyway. Jake's friends look good, most of the men in my life are either hockey players or related to hockey players and the majority of them look like they picked up their suits from their closet floors after their last road-trip.

Holy shit, it's my wedding day.

The day I've been dreaming about for as long as I can remember, yet the ball of anxiety that formed in my stomach late last night just won't seem to shift and the nagging voice in the back of mind is saying one thing on repeat, *you need to see Jake.*

I know it's just jitters and every bride gets them, but I also know that traditions are silly and if I want to see my soon-to-be husband before we sign that bit of paper, then I damn well will. Glancing around the room, looking for my maid of honor, Kallie. She's been like a guard dog all morning, even the mention of me seeing Jake earlier today was met with her threatening to lock me down until the ceremony starts.

"If you're looking for Kallie, she had to go fix some emergency with one of your brothers and his tux!" Ella, one of my bridesmaids calls out. Why am I not surprised at that? I love my brothers, but they only seem to only be happy in sweatpants and workout gear. Getting four overgrown hockey boys into tuxedo's has been one of the biggest challenges I've faced this weekend.

Seeing my chance at escaping for a few minutes, I don't hesitate to take it. Hiking up the layers of tulle that make up my skirt, I slip out of the room and make my way to the staircase that leads up to the honeymoon suite Jake and I will be sharing from tonight.

Luck is on my side because I get to the door of our room without being spotted. Twisting the handle, I push the door open and slip inside, all the while praying that the rest of the groomsmen are all downstairs already. When he'd last texted me this morning, Jake had said he was going to skip getting drinks with the guys like they'd planned so that he'd have a clear head to remember every second of today. Part of me thinks that it's really because he knows my brothers will be there and he hates that they act like they hate him.

Well, I'm almost certain it's an act anyway.

My shoulders slump as I look around the quiet room, it seems like he's changed his mind because it's empty. I can't even call him to meet me here because the stupid dress I'm wearing has no pockets and I've not seen my phone for hours now. He probably won't answer from the unknown caller ID, but I decide to take a chance and call him from the room phone anyway.

Making my way to the bed, I'm stopped short by the sight of the bed sheets in complete disarray. One pillow is on the floor, the others pushed up into the headboard. I'm pretty sure I can see grip marks there. The blankets are a twisted mess, the corner of the bottom sheet pulled back to expose the bare mattress underneath. Unease twists my gut, that ball of anxiety turning to a heavy acidic weight. Jake is the most serene sleeper I've ever known. It's almost eerie, like he's a machine that simply unplugs at night. He can get up in the morning and the bed doesn't even look slept in.

Maybe he couldn't sleep just like you couldn't? I try to reason with myself. It might have worked if it wasn't for the stains on the sheets that look a lot like smeared lipstick and the empty condom wrapper on the nightstand.

"Jake? I need to get back downstairs before Norah notices..." The words die a gargled death on the lips of my so-called best friend, as she steps out of Jake's bathroom, reaching back to zip up the maid of honor dress that we spend weeks looking for. The very same maid of honor that had a small emergency to deal with, giving me enough time to sneak away to see my soon-to-be dead fiance.

"Norah," Kallie gasps, "it's not what it looks like-" she says immediately,not even attempting to lie. I've no idea if she says anything else because I can't hear her over the thundering sound of the blood that is now rushing in my ears. I stand there frozen, watching her lips move but not hearing a word from her.

I think I might be dying, there's no way my heart can beat this hard, this fast and it *not* kill me.

Flashes of memories slice through my mind. The times I'd come home from work to find them in my apartment together. Never in compromising situations, but I'd still been a fool to ignore the gigantic waving red flags. The looks, the jokes. Her hand on his arm. His hand on her back. All the times he would offer to drive her home when she was tipsy. I'm a fucking idiot.

"Are you sure he's the one?" she'd asked me over a bottle of wine just last night. And like the fool I am, I'd said he was the love of my life.

The space where my heart was just a few seconds ago twists painfully in my chest. I need to get out of here, I want to escape this nightmare. I *need* to escape it, but none of my limbs are co-operating.

The door to the room swings open behind me as Jake strides in, the cocky smirk on his face sliding clean off when he sees me there, Kallie in the doorway to the bathroom. His eyes dart between us, flick to the nightstand and back to me again. I can see him trying to work out exactly how much I know, how much I've seen, and I can see with a newfound clarity the mask he wears slipping into place. The fake smile that doesn't reach his eyes, the calculated look he adopts.

Has all of it been fake? A lie?

"Norah, baby, what are you doing here? You know it's unlucky for me to see you." I take him in, his jacket off, hair in disarray. Did he fuck her in his wedding suit? My stomach lurches at that thought.

"Jake,-" Kallie croaks, the tears evident in her voice.

"Kallie, did you find the groomsman gifts you were looking for?" he cuts her off with words sharp enough to snap me out of the fog I've been trapped in. I watch with morbid fascination as he approaches me, I can almost see his mind working overtime, scrambling to come up with a believable story for what the fuck is going on here.

It's not until his clammy hand closes around my elbow and he leans in for a kiss that I'm finally able to move. Twisting free, I sway to the left to dodge his advances. Before he can reach for me again, I do the one thing my brothers always taught me to do when a boy was coming on too strong. Gripping Jake's shoulders tightly, I bring up my right knee and slam it into his balls as hard as I can. I don't take the time to feel any satisfaction watching him crumble to the ground, writhing in pain. I get no joy from his breathless whimpers, choosing to walk away instead. I get to the doorway before turning back to get one last look at the two people I never want to see again after today.

Yanking the damned diamond ring from my left hand, I heave it with all my might, watching as it flies through the air before landing on a now prone Jake.

Then, I take off running as fast as my wedding dress allows me to.

CHAPTER 2 - NORAH

The warm afternoon sun beats down on me, the faint sound of music coming from the swim up bar, the slight but very appreciated breeze that drifts over my heated skin all combine to send me into a much-needed slumber. The three Mai Tai's I had after lunch may also be contributing to that.

I try to convince myself to pick up my stuff and go back to my room, but something about being in what should have been my honeymoon suite very much alone & unmarried, doesn't seem appealing right now.

My mind wanders back to memories of the chaos that had occurred on my should-have-been wedding day. The almost brawl that had broken out when I'd ran out of Jake's room and straight into my brother, Maverick. I'd been passed from brother to brother, Maverick passing me to Finn when I'd told him what I'd just seen. The same had happened, Finn passing me to Ward, he in turn passing me to Riley as each of them had the story relayed to them. I adore my brothers, and in that moment, I had to appreciate that I was the baby of the family and my professional hockey playing siblings would hopefully teach Jake a lesson.

Did it make me a bad person to hope they'd afflict real pain on him? Maybe, but I'd debated myself on that over multiple cocktails over the ten days I'd now been in Hawaii, and I'd still not managed to feel any kind of guilt over it. Instead of dwelling on what they were all doing in that hotel room, I had charged upstairs, stripped out of my dream wedding dress, thrown on my pajamas, called an Uber and headed straight for LAX. It had cost a small fortune to bring my flight forward a day, but that was going to be Jake's problem since I'd used his credit card.

It wasn't until I was in the air that I let the tears fall. I gave myself those few hours to let it all out. I'm sure I looked more than a little crazy, my wedding hair still in place in an elaborate up-do, the pj's that had BRIDE emblazoned across the back and over the pocket on my chest. The beautiful bridal make-up that had taken an hour to do running down my face as I cried a river of tears. The hostess had kept a steady stream of alcohol coming my way along with plenty of pitying glances, but somewhere over the pacific, I'd stopped caring. Anger set in; the tears dried.

My heart hardened as I came to the realization that love is a scam. It's a cruel joke. It's an illusion.

It's something I'll never put myself through ever again. I'd always prided myself on being a good person, I run a charity that helps sick kids get their dying wishes fulfilled, I nursed both my parents through horrific terminal illnesses, sacrificing my college education to do so. How does karma repay me? It lets my fiancé fuck my maid of honor on my wedding day, that's how.

Although, I highly doubt that was the first time, they were probably at it for months, if not our whole relationship. I wonder if they're together now? My mind starts to fill with the what if's that have plagued me all week. The answers I know I'll never get because I'll be damned if I ever speak so much as one word to those two assholes ever again.

My phone had rung off the hook that first day, both Jake and Kallie sending me a barrage of messages and voicemails. None of which I'd even considered opening. It only took one quick call to get my number changed and just like that, blissful silence. Well, except for the daily check-ins with each of my brothers, all of whom were and still are furious on my behalf and baying for Jake's blood.

"Hey Miss Norah." A soft, melodic voice says from above me, pulling me from my spiraling thoughts. Cracking an eye open, I find Koa, one of the many staff that have looked after me since I arrived, grinning down at me. "If you're not careful, you're going to sleep through your excursion." I can tell he wants to add on an *again*, but his good manners win out and he keeps it to himself.

"Thank you, Koa, I'll be there this time. I promise." Feeling bad that he's tried to get me to leave my spot at the pool so many times and I've been too stubborn to. The plan when I'd decided to come on my honeymoon solo, had been to wallow in self-pity, not to join in on all the activities we'd pre booked. It was a plan that had been working well until Koa had found out why I was here alone. Since then he'd been on a mission.

"There's more to Hawaii than just Mai Tai's, getting a tan and feeling sorry for yourself, Miss Norah. I want you to see it before you leave tomorrow."

We share some small talk, ending with me pinky promising to be ready for my pick-up time later, before I head back to my room to shower and pack my things ready to leave tomorrow. I'm probably not ready to face reality, but I'm damn well ready to pretend like I am.

It's later in the evening and I'm very much regretting that of all the excursions I've made it to, it's a romantic evening of stargazing from the top of Mauna Kea.

Thankfully, I'm not alone. There's a small group of us. There's a couple of newlyweds whom I've managed to avoid through both the chaperoned drive here and the picnic meal that was waiting for us earlier. Then there's the older couple that spent most of the night alternating between bickering and holding hands and acting like they've just met.

And then there is Reed.

The silent, broody guy who looks about as happy to be here alone as I probably do. Outside of being introduced to one another by our tour guide, I've not said more than a word or two to anyone else, but even that is more than anyone has gotten out of Reed. He's probably around my age, but the perma-scowl he's sporting on his obnoxiously handsome face makes him look older. Not that it takes away from how good looking he actually is though.

He must be at least 6 ft 4, with a bulky, athlete's body that could easily put my brothers to shame. Unruly dark hair that you can just tell he never wastes time on but always falls oh so perfectly. And I've not gotten close enough to be sure, but I'm pretty certain he's got blue eyes to round out the romance novel level of gorgeous that he is. Fortunately for me, his good looks do not matter because I've sworn off men for life, so I allow myself to indulge in a few furtive glances his way, it would be a shame to waste that level of eye-candy after all.

We've just got done watching the sunset from Pu'u Kalepeamoa, and the experience can only be described as humbling. From the drive up through cotton candy clouds, to watching the sky turn from a serene blue, to a warm orange with slashes of pink, fading into a haze of inky black as the sun descended seemingly into the dormant volcano we were sitting on. I've never experienced anything so breathtaking in my life.

It had left me with a reminder that I'm just a tiny blip on this earth, and that meant that Jake and Kallie, they were nothing but blips too. Tiny, insignificant in the grand scheme of my life, blips.

After watching the life altering sunset, the tour guide takes us back to the observatory and we get to look at the stars and planets, and our guide gives us a detailed history of Hawaii. It's left me in awe of the place and feeling more than a little silly that I chose to come here for my honeymoon just so I can lounge in the sun for a few weeks. I'm already planning on coming back here for our annual summer vacation but actually appreciating the history of the place instead.

"You were supposed to bring something warm to wear." A deep, gruff voice says from behind me, right before I feel the weight of something being dropped on my shoulders. A soft waft of fragrance hits my senses, a mix of fresh sea air and something darkly masculine wraps around me, reaching up I feel the warm material of a well-loved sweatshirt.

Leaning back, I see Reed staring down at me, scowl still in place, but a resigned softness there now too. I had been shivering slightly, but not enough that I'd thought anyone would notice. After all, it's my own fault for not reading the itinerary before being picked up from the hotel.

How was I to know that after wearing not much more than bikinis and cover ups for days, I'd need to wear winter clothes. I'd been lucky to have some running tights and a long sleeve top with me. I'd been given a jacket to wear along with everyone else, but it wasn't quite enough to stop the evening chill from seeping in. I'd obviously not done a good job of hiding how chilly I've really been.

"Thank you, but I'm not that cold-" I try to hand him back the sweater but instead find my hands full with a paper cup filled with hot cocoa instead.

"Just put the damn hoodie on." He practically growls at me right before he slides his huge frame into the seat next to me. I'm suddenly very aware of just how close that seat is when I feel the heat of his thigh pressed tightly against my own. I open my mouth to argue, but once again he stuns me into silence by plucking the cup from my hand, placing it on the ground at our feet, and maneuvering me out of my jacket and into the hoodie like I'm some kind of unruly toddler.

"What in the-" I start to ask but the words on my lips die when he has the sheer audacity to shush me. "Did you...did you just *shush* me?"

"I'm trying to listen." He grunts, pointing to where the tour guide stands a few feet in front of us, continuing with his detailed history of the big island. A talk I'd been avidly listening to until he'd so rudely interrupted.

I scoff in indignation, ready to give him a piece of my mind, but the people around us start to stare, our discussion not being as quiet as I'd have liked. Instead of pushing it, I decide to let it go until we're away from the prying eyes and ears of the group. Instead, I cross my arms over my chest, sinking deeper into my seat and glaring daggers at the side of Reed's head.

It's fast approaching 10pm by the time we're being driven back to the hotel and after so many restless nights, I'm having a hard time not letting sleep win me over. The gentle hiss of the breaks is enough to wake me, but the warm pillow I'm leaning on is so freaking comfortable, I really don't want to wake up.

As my senses slowly creep awake, I realize it's not a pillow, it's a very muscular chest.

A muscular chest that I seem to have drooled over while asleep. Pushing myself back, I look up to find an amused Reed staring down at me.

"What on Earth?" I manage to engage my brain enough to ask.

"You were falling all over the place, I came over here to wake you up but as soon as my ass touched the seat you were all over me." he says, giving me a cocky grin.

"I highly doubt that." I refute vehemently, knowing that I probably did exactly that. I'm a notorious full contact sleeper.

"You most certainly were, sweetie." The older lady stops by our seats as she moves off the bus, giving me a knowing look before she turns her alarmingly hungry gaze on Reed.

"Although, I can't say I blame you, If I was a few years-"

"Okay, that's enough out of you." her husband appears at her side, taking her arm and pushing her towards the doors. He looks at Reed and I with an amused look on his weathered face. "Enjoy the rest of your night kids." he winks before looking down at where my hands are still resting against Reed's impressive chest.

They both disappear down towards the front of the now deserted bus, leaving me alone with the man that I really should probably be doing a better job at avoiding.

CHAPTER 3 - NORAH

Leaning on the porcelain sink, I stare at my reflection in the restroom mirror. My eyes are slightly glassy from the alcohol I've been drinking, and my cheeks are flushed a light shade of pink.

But, I look...happy? It feels like a lifetime since I felt anything except sadness.

How the hell did I get here?

Thinking of the man waiting for me at the table just outside those doors, my stomach clenches in excitement. I'd been stunned when Reed had asked me to have a drink with him after I'd finally peeled myself away from him on the bus. I had tried to get out of it, I really did, but he'd put one warm hand on the small of my back and ushered me to the small beach hut bar.

One drink had turned into three. That had turned into us ordering food and yet more drinks, but now the plates are long gone and we're on our second or maybe third bottle of wine now and somehow we're still here.

The conversation has flowed between us effortlessly for hours and it's been so good to just forget the rest of the crap going on in my life and speak to someone new. Someone that doesn't have any idea of what I ran away from.

I'm just Norah, girl on vacation, not Norah the poor jilted bride.

I've never felt a connection to a stranger like I've felt with him tonight. There's an ease between us that is new for me, a level of comfort that I didn't know I could feel. It's the strangest feeling, but it's exciting nevertheless. Especially when you add it to the insane attraction I have to him. I don't recall ever being so in lust at first sight before.

Pushing down my nervous excitement, I decide to do something I've never really done before. I decide to take a risk. I'm here for one more night and I deserve to enjoy it. That's exactly what I plan on doing.

When I make it back to the table, I find the place is now deserted and Reed is standing there waiting for me. The butterflies in my belly take a dive when I see he's ready to leave. Looks like the night is over. I'm hit by a wave of disappointment. I'm not ready to say goodbye, not ready for tonight to be over.

He watches as I approach, a small smile flirting with the edge of his full lips. Lips I've found myself watching a whole lot tonight.

"You wanna get out of here?" He asks. The softness of his tone belies the heat that flares in his eyes as he stares down at me, waiting for my answer. I shock myself, and judging by the way his eyes flare, he is too when I reply.

"Let's go back to your room."

Stepping out into the warm night air, I realize I have no idea if he's even staying at the same resort as me, I assume he is seeing as we were both picked up from here earlier. What the hell did we even talk about all night?

I'm about to ask him to come to my room instead when he grabs my hand and swings me around so I'm facing him. "I need to do this now. I can't wait one second more." He announces right before he kisses me.

It's nothing like any first kiss I've ever experienced. His full, warm lips devour mine. Raising up on my tip-toes, I give myself over to the riot of sensations he elicits from me. My hands grip the front of his t-shirt so I can pull him even closer. His hands frame my face, moving me exactly where he wants me, tilting my head to the side so he can slide his delicious tongue further into my waiting mouth.

He dominates me and I cannot get enough of it. He groans from somewhere deep in his throat, the sound sending a rush of desire straight to my belly.

"You're sure about this?" he asks without taking his lips off mine. My response is nothing more than a guttural moan. It must be the only confirmation he needs because the next thing I know we're on the move, my hand clasped tight in his as he all but drags me away.

CHAPTER 4 - REED

The door to my room slams after I kick it shut. I'm too busy trying to get Norah out of her clothes to care if I wake up the whole damn resort. Now that I've touched her silken skin, taste her sweet mouth, I'm not planning on stopping any time soon. We leave a trail of destruction from the front door all the way through to the bedroom and we've barely come up for air.

Letting my fingers run down the expanse of her exposed back, I feel the shiver that runs through her. Reaching down, I lift her from behind her thighs. Wrapping her legs around my waist, I carry her the last few steps to my bed before gently laying her back. Fuck. She's the most beautiful thing I've ever seen. Her long, wild hair is splayed across the crisp white pillows. Her lips are red, swollen and there's a faint blush on her cheeks. I'll never forget this sight as long as I live.

"You're so fucking beautiful." I allow myself to say the words out loud.

"And you're still wearing too many clothes." She says coyly, moving so she can start to strip at a slow, agonizing pace. She slips her shirt over her head exposing smooth tanned skin, she reaches back to take of her bra but I can't stand the torture of watching her for another fucking second.

Moving in, I drop my lips to her shoulder, taking one strap down, I kiss a path over her collarbone and do the same with the other strap before taking the whole thing off. My dick practically weeps at the sight of her full, lush tits. Tit's that I have visions of fucking later.

Next to go are her skin-tight jeans.

Choosing to save time, I take her panties at the same time. My breath actually fucking stops at the vision before me. She's perfection. Tanned, smooth perfection from head to toe.

From the moment she stepped onto that bus tonight, I'd been taken with how fucking pretty she is. Her long reddish hair caught my eye, but it was her curves that kept them on her. I've never been the type of guy to have a type, I love women of all shapes and sizes, but after seeing Norah and her dips and curves laid out for me like this, I think that may have changed for me.

As soon as I can shake myself out of the lust filled daze she's left me in, I get rid of the rest of my own clothes and join her on the bed.

I want so badly to shove her legs open and bury my face in her pretty little pussy, but I know I just won't last if I do. I need to be inside her.

Now.

She opens her legs to give me room and I take the invitation eagerly. There are fireworks between us as soon as we're fully skin on skin. Her hands are all over me, touching every part of me she can reach. I go straight for her mouth, already missing her taste even though I had my tongue in her mouth mere seconds ago. My aching cock begs for me to slide home, but I'm not ready for this to be over, and I already know it's not going to last long enough.

No amount of time is going to sate my hunger for the siren I've got in my bed.

"Reed." She moans as I let my tongue slide down her neck, finally getting to kiss that spot that's been calling to me all night long. I can't resist letting my teeth drag over the harsh thump of her pulse. Judging by the way her hips fly up to grind against mine, she likes it almost as much as I do. The wet heat of her against my bare skin has me cursing out loud.

"I need you." She begs softly, head thrown back, eyes closed.

"You have me, beautiful." I murmur against her skin, feeling the goose bumps that spring up across her in the wake of my breath.

"I need more." She breathes out harshly, raking her nails down my back. Who am I to deny her what she wants? I keep moving down her neck, making my way to her tits, the ones that have been teasing me all night long. At the same time, I let my fingers make their way between her thighs. My cock practically weeps with joy when I feel how wet she is. My fingers slide through her folds, up and over her clit in slow swipes. My lips close around her tight nipple, pulling and sucking gently to match the rhythm I've set between her legs. Her hips start grinding again, reaching for more contact.

"I can't wait to feel you come." I say when I let go of her tit. Her eyes are on me, her mouth open as she pants. My fingers continue their assault on her pussy, speeding up then stopping to pay more attention to her clit on each sweep.

"Please." She begs hoarsely.

"Tell me what you need, baby."

"You, Reed. You inside me. Now." My name on her desperate lips does something to me, makes something happen inside my chest fucking spasms. Sliding my fingers downwards once again, this time I press forward with first one finger, then two.

She's so damn hot, so wet. I almost blow my load and have to think of work, stats, the shit I have to deal with at home, anything to stop from embarrassing myself.

"Fuck." I groan, slamming my mouth down on hers again. One of her hands comes up to grab my shoulder, the other goes south, wrapping around my length. Even lying in bed, I feel my knees go weak at the feel of her gripping me. Pulling her hand away, I shift so I'm positioned ready to push inside.

"Look at me." I say, the need burning inside me makes my voice a gruff bark. Her eyes flutter open, the darkest blue orbs burning up at me. "I want to see your eyes when I make you mine."

I don't know if her gasp is because of my words or the feeling of my cock driving deep inside of her.

All I know is that right here and now, I've found something I had no idea I was even looking for. Something I have no intention of letting go of. *Ever*.

CHAPTER 5 - NORAH

"I want to see your eyes when I make you mine." My entire body clenches at the memory of his words. Rolling over in bed, I bury my head in the mountain of pillows and let out a frustrated scream.

It's been two months since I woke up in Reed's bed.

Two months since I freaked out about how much he'd made me feel.

Two months since I'd crawled out of his bed in the weak early morning light, gathered my clothes and snuck out of his room.

I'd known I was making a mistake before I'd left. Standing next to the bed, looking down at his gorgeous face relaxed in sleep, I'd known that I'd regret leaving. I don't even know why I did it. The whole time I'd been doing the walk of shame back to my own room, I'd fought with myself over going back.

But, how could I? It's not like I could just knock on the door and ask him to let me back in. Instead of doing what my heart was telling me, I'd listened to my head, grabbed my bags and once again I'd run to the airport to escape.

I'd made my choice and now I'm stuck dealing with the consequences.

Consequences I'm going to be dealing with for a long time to come.

A lifetime.

The nightly dreams aren't helping. Every time I close my eyes, I'm assaulted with memories of the things he'd done to me. The way he'd dominated my body and wrung an unfathomable amount of pleasure from me has been on a near constant loop in my head all this time.

The sound of my phone ringing from somewhere in my apartment breaks me out of my little self-pity party. Throwing off the blankets, I go in search of my phone. I can't stop that little seed of hope that blooms. Hope that it's Reed on the phone. That's never going to happen because we were too busy ripping each other's clothes off to get silly things like each other's contact numbers. Or last names for that matter.

By the time I find my phone it's gone silent. Seeing Mavericks name on the screen, I'm glad I missed the call. I love my eldest brother dearly, but he just won't leave me alone since I've gotten home. I see him multiple times a week for work, it's his foundation that I run after all, and ever since I got back from Hawaii, he's been on my ass all the time trying to arrange family dinners for us all. He thinks I'm not getting over the wedding fiasco, none of my brothers do, but they don't know that the reason I'm not ok is that I can't stop thinking about Reed.

Or the souvenir I've brought back from our too brief vacation fling.

The phone in my hand rings once again, this time showing Finn calling. That's only a fraction better than it being Mav seeing as he's also a protective, overbearing brother, but I answer anyway. It's the only way to get them to leave me alone.

"Hey Finneus."

"Why you ignoring Mav?" he says by way of a hello.

"I'm a grown adult with a job. I don't sit around waiting all day for my darling brothers to check-in with me." I say, getting an unamused grunt in return.

"That stuff we were supposed to drop off? It's gonna be late." He drops the bad news on me.

"Finn! No!" I whine like a child. That stuff he's talking about is signed jerseys and pucks for the hospital visit I'm making today. The perks of having brothers that play in the NHL is getting signed shit off them all the time. "Mav promised he would get that to me two days ago, why can't you bring it to me?"

"Nor, it's been crazy here today. Can you come down here and I'll get it ready for you?" He offers, surprising me that he's trying to be helpful for once.

"You promise it will be ready?"

"Scouts honor." he lies, both of knowing he was nowhere near well behaved enough to have been a boy scout.

———

I don't make a habit of coming to the arena very often unless it's a game night and I'm bringing some kids and their families along. Some of the guys on the team must have taken a few too many punches to the head because they'll hit on me unashamedly, despite the death threats they get from Mav and Finn. They both play for the team here in LA, Ward is playing in Vancouver and Riley is in Tennessee.

I assumed that it would be quiet here today as the season doesn't start until next week, but there seems to be people everywhere, a buzz of excitement filling the corridors.

I don't waste time looking around too much, I know my siblings well enough to know they'll either be in the gym, or they'll be shoveling copious amounts of food in their mouth somewhere. I'm proved right when I walk into the weight room to find not just my brothers, but what looks like half the team standing around staring up at the huge screen, sports center on.

Nobody notices me coming in, they're all too busy concentrating on the breaking news banner that is running across the bottom of the screen.

NHL champions LA Vipers sign Reed Hayes in a record breaking deal.

And then he's there. My Reed. In full, glorious color, right in front of me on the TV screen. His gorgeous face has its customary frown in place as he's shown battling his way through a crowd of reporters and fans.

My one night of lost inhibitions.

The one that I thought I'd never get a chance to see ever again.

The father of the baby nobody knows I'm carrying yet is going to be here, in my town, working with my family, close enough to touch.

All too soon, there will be no escaping him and the surprise I'm about to drop right in his lap.

———

Thank you for reading, keep an eye out for an all new hockey series by Emma Louise, starting with Norah & Reed getting their HEA, coming soon-ish!

HERE ALL ALONG

EMMA SCOTT

This is very intensely inspired by my family's love of Maui, Lahaina in particular. I can't write of Maui without sharing that my first daughter Izzy's ashes were placed in those dark blue waters in 2018. We visit the island every year as a kind of pilgrimage. Maui gives us a sanctuary of peace. We were there a week before the fires. I can't give back to Maui a fraction of what it has given me, but this little story is dedicated to the island and its people whom will always hold a place of deep love and endless gratitude in my heart.

CHAPTER 1 - LUNA

"I had a really nice time tonight," I said.

Okay, so that was a lie. I spent the entire date listening to Brad talk about himself, chew with his mouth open, and be rude to the waiter. Now we were outside the restaurant on Hollywood Boulevard, a few blocks from my apartment. He had that look on his face. The look a guy wears when his experience of a date is completely different from reality, and he's expecting it to continue well into the night.

No chance, bro.

"So anyway, thanks for dinner…" I said and took a step back.

"Whoa, hey, hold on. Where are you going so fast?" He gripped my wrist, squeezing hard enough to make the bracelets dig into my skin.

I glanced down at where he gripped me. "Are you freaking for real?"

"I'm super real." He pulled me close. "Do you want to go back to my place? I have a Hockney."

"A Hockney," I said flatly. "Whose paintings routinely sell in the tens of millions."

I wanted to add that a systems analyst at a mid-level marketing company wasn't going to get his hands on a Hockney unless he stole it, but my parents taught me better than that. And hell, I taught art to little kids at West Hollywood Elementary; I was light-years from Hockney territory myself.

Brad shrugged with a self-satisfied laugh. "Okay, it's a copy, but who cares? We won't be looking at it much anyway." He grinned and leaned in. "Because I don't keep it in my bedroom."

I don't know which was more gag-worthy, that line or the whiff of the carbonara he'd had for dinner. I twisted my arm out of his grip and took another step back.

"Yeah, I'm going to call it a night."

Brad frowned, perplexed. A little incensed. I'd offered to split the bill, but he wouldn't hear of it. Now he wanted payback.

"I thought we had a good time," he said.

"Right, I just feel like…maybe not."

He reared back. "*Maybe not*? What the fuck does that mean?"

"I'm doing this thing where I want to be honest all the time, and I'm not really feeling it." I offered a smile. "It's just a vibe thing."

"A vibe thing," Brad's lip curled. "You aren't *vibing* with me."

"Look, I—"

"No, it's fine." He put up his hands. "Eighty dollars for dinner, but sure, whatever. See you." He turned to go, then whipped back around. "No, you know what? I'm *doing a thing* where I want to be super honest too." He pointed at my chest triumphantly. "You have small tits. And I was willing to overlook that."

I cocked my head. "My hero?"

He stormed off which was the best part of my night so far. I wasn't even insulted. I was twenty-six and had been dating for roughly ten years; pretty sure I'd seen it all.

I walked the few blocks to my apartment. It was early yet, and all of my roommates were gathered in the living room, playing music and talking. Carter was in his favorite puffy chair, sipping wine. Dean and Claudia sat tangled up on the floor together, finishing each other sentences and laughing as usual. Mateo—tall, dark, brooding Mateo—was at the end of our couch, a beer hanging in his hands between his knees.

Carter arched an eyebrow at me as I came in and hung my patchwork sweater by the door. "It's not even eight o'clock on a Friday evening. That doesn't bode well."

"You have no idea," I said with a tired laugh.

"No love connection?" Claudia raised a brow.

"'Fraid not." I poured a glass of red from the kitchen that faced the living area. "You got the last good one," I said with a nod at Dean

"The tea, please," Carter said. "Spill."

"He's not worth any more of my energy." I sat on the floor near Mateo's booted feet and smoothed my flowing dress around my knees. "I don't know, guys. I think maybe I need to take a dating hiatus before I lose my faith in humanity."

"I hate when that happens," Dean mused.

"Anyway, tell me how you guys are doing." I glanced at Mateo behind me. "You had a day off from the bar, yeah? What did you do?"

Mateo lifted one muscular shoulder in a shrug. He had a habit of wearing tight-fitting T-shirts, usually in black, that left very little of his impressive physique to the imagination. Or maybe just enough.

"Not much," he said in his low, gruff voice and abruptly put his beer bottle on the table and got up.

"Where are you going?" Claudia asked.

"Out," Mateo said, grabbing his leather jacket from where it hung next to my sweater, like samples from a craft store and a biker shop.

He shut the door behind him.

Carter rolled his eyes. "Under the dictionary definition of *emotionally unavailable*, we'll find a picture of our sweet baby Mateo."

"He's a mystery and an enigma," Claudia said and gave Dean a kiss. "I'm a lucky gal."

"They make me sick," Carter said to me. "The cuteness…"

"Agreed," I said with a wink. "I'm going to bed. Good night all."

"Good night, darling."

I gave Carter a peck on the cheek and headed down the hall with my wine. On the way, I passed Mateo's closed door. It was always closed. He never let anyone in.

A fitting metaphor, I thought as I went to my room that was half bedroom, half art studio.

I set the wine on the nightstand, sat cross-legged on my bed, and picked up my sketchbook and pencil. I had no plan or agenda. I just let my hand go and was surprised to find, after twenty or so minutes, I had drawn heavy brows over rich dark eyes, dark hair, square jaw. A full mouth in a perpetual grimace.

I smiled at Mateo. Such a grouch. The opposite of me or so I've heard. The eternal optimist. I set down the sketchbook with a sigh. That optimism was quickly waning. I was beginning to think I'd never find something like what Dean and Claudia had. I wanted someone I could just burrow into and feel safe, yet who knew I could take care of myself.

But I wouldn't mind taking care of someone else, too.

CHAPTER 2 - MATEO

Lucky 13 was seeing the tail end of a Saturday night rush when Luna walked in. Like a fucking comet streaking across the darkened bar. A guy got up off a stool just as she approached, and she slid gracefully onto it. Dozens of bracelets slid down her slender arms as she set her elbows on the bar, hands folded under her chin. Every finger wore rings of silver and turquoise and was smudged with paint. Her blond hair had a few random braids and poured down her back like honey.

How many times had I imagined running my fingers through that hair? Grabbing a fistful and tilting her head up to mine...

Luna shot me a friendly smile, but her eyes were direct. Everything about her was direct, except which direction her own damn heart was facing. I just knew it wasn't aimed at me.

"Pretty happening in here," she said.

"Typical Saturday," I said, tossing a coaster in front of her. "What can I get you?"

"Nothing," she said, her smile tilting. "I came to see you."

"Me?" I said, practically shouting over the noise of the bar like a dope.

"I wanted to see you in your natural environment," she said. "I have to say, you look very commanding. *In command* of this establishment."

Is she flirting with me?

A cold sweat broke out down my spine. I shrugged one shoulder. "That's why they pay me the big bucks."

Luna's smile dimmed a little as she traced a paint-smudged fingernail over the bar. "It's just that we've been roommates for a month now, and I haven't gotten to know you as well as the others."

"I've been busy," I said. "I'm busy now."

Nice one, asshole.

Her face fell a little, but Christ, I could pick up any woman at this bar and take her home with a look. Which I did. Frequently. But Luna? I had no fucking clue how to talk to her.

"Busy, okay," Luna said. "Look, I know you don't like me much—"

"Why would you say that?"

She looked amused. Seeing through bullshit was one of Luna's superpowers.

"How about, when I walk into a room, I can start a countdown of how fast you'll walk out." She arched a perfect brow at me. "I think our record is twenty seconds."

"I don't know what you're talking about."

"You rarely make eye contact with me, and when you do, it's one of those smoldering grimaces you're so good at."

Shit.

I crossed my arms over my chest.

"And you cross your arms over your not-unimpressive chest whenever the roomies and I are talking about basically anything that pertains to me."

A guy a couple of seats down was making impatient noises.

"Hold that thought," I said.

I took care of the guy with a fresh beer, practically shoving it at him, and came back to Luna.

"And I know what you're going to say," she said before I could speak.

"Yes, it seems like I'm awfully self-absorbed and taking all your mannerisms personally. But if that's not the case, how come we don't hang out?" The eyebrow arched again. "Too busy with your houseguests?"

She was referring to the parade of women that came in and out of my bedroom. What was I going to tell her? That they were distractions to keep me from pounding on her door instead?

"Maybe I don't like you much," I said with a hint of a smile.

"Impossible," she said, not missing a beat. "I'm fucking delightful."

"We're on different schedules, I guess."

She narrowed her dark blue eyes at me. "You sure? It seems like you've never warmed up to me since I took over Barry's room. Were you guys close?"

"Close?" I smirked. "It was against his religion to do dishes, and the Cockroach Infestation of 2022 can directly be connected to his collection of half-eaten pizzas under the bed. No, we weren't close."

Luna's smile brightened. "That, my friend, is the longest sentence you've ever spoken to me."

"You're welcome."

She laughed. "Hey, look at that. We're bantering. See, I'm not so bad." She reached across the bar to touch my forearm. "I'm glad we cleared the air, Mateo. Don't be a stranger, now."

I watched her slide off her stool with mounting alarm.

"You're not staying?" I asked, praying to every god alive my voice didn't sound half as desperate to her as it did to me.

"I've got plans."

"Another date?" I couldn't help but ask.

Another date with another loser who didn't know what he had sitting across from him.

"Yep," she said. "I have a hot date with my canvas and a fresh tube of paint. I'll see you at home."

And then she was gracefully slipping between bar patrons on her way to the door.

"Yep," I said to myself. "See you at home."

I watched her go until she was out of sight. Luna Davies was fucking luminous, and the only reason I wasn't trying to be that loser sitting across from her was because I had no clue what I had to offer. Sex, definitely. That I could do. But she liked long conversations that had depth. *She* had depth. She was an artist and knew exactly what she wanted. I was a college dropout, still trying to figure my shit out.

She'd been right about everything tonight—I could barely stand to be in the same room with her. The sweetest torture for the simple fact she wasn't mine.

CHAPTER 3 - LUNA

That night, sleep eluded me. I tossed around until one in the morning. Finally, I got up and turned on the light. The first thing I saw was my sketch of Mateo staring broodingly at me from my nightstand.

Why did I draw him? I wondered, tracing my finger down the square line of his jaw.

"I'll eventually sketch all of my roommates. I just started with him, that's all," I told my empty room.

I got up to go to the kitchen for a comfort-food snack to get me back to sleep. Pop-Tarts usually did the trick. I was rummaging in the cabinets, trying to be as quiet as possible, when I heard a woman's muffled moan coming from Mateo's room.

"So he took someone home after I visited him at the bar. So what?" I murmured, ignoring the strange twang in my heart.

I was about to scoot back to my room when his door opened. My roommate came out wearing nothing but plaid flannel pants. No shirt. Hair mussed. We're talking postcoital by *minutes*. He stared at me with a peculiar look on his face. As if he were both glad to see me and sort of horrified at the same time. Then the moment passed, and he slipped on a mask of granite.

"Hey," he grunted and reached for a water glass.

I realized I'd been loitering far too long, my eyes drawn to the perfection of his chest, the muscles cut and defined…

"Welp! Have a good rest of your evening."

I didn't wait for an answer but headed back to my room and shut the door. It was then I realized I didn't have my Pop-Tarts, but there was no chance in hell I was going back to the kitchen.

Or back to sleep.

Three weeks went by as October bled into November. The energy in the house had changed somehow. Carter, Dean, and Claudia were the same as always; I don't even think they noticed it. But Mateo had stopped bringing women home. And while my dating app sent me notifications, I didn't have the slightest interest in looking at them.

When Mateo and I passed each other in the hallway or were together in the small kitchen, I could feel electricity or heat or both radiating off him. It was like my body had somehow become attuned to his frequency because all I could pick up was him. He had infiltrated my thoughts. And I never did get around to sketching anyone else in the house.

What the heck is going on?

He's super-hot, so of course I'm attracted to him, I assured myself. But we lived together. Investigating the mysterious vibration could wind up being a disaster of epic proportions.

"I am not moving again this fiscal year," I told my empty room.

I realized I was talking to myself a lot, which wasn't like me. But many things about me that I thought I understood, I suddenly knew nothing about.

"Gather around, everybody. It's time to play." Dean stood in the middle of our living room, holding a stack of index cards like a game show host.

"Play what?" I asked from my usual seat on the floor in front of the couch. The coffee table was littered with our roommate-only monthly dinner. Claudia had made empanadas, Mateo brought the beer, and Carter had baked a chocolate pie from scratch. I—possessing zero culinary talent nor interest—provided the chips and guacamole.

"We're going to play roommate trivia to see how well we know each other. First person to answer a question correctly gets a point."

"Someone's been watching too much *Friends*," Carter said from his chair. "Is this why you've been peppering us with endless personal questions lately?"

"Indeed."

"It's not exactly fair since you and Claudia have known each other since the dawn of time and probably share toothbrushes."

"Which is why I'm asking the questions," Dean said. "I've leaked no answers to Claudia, scouts honor."

"I think I'm at a distinct disadvantage," I said. "Being the newbie and all."

Dean smiled. "It's all in fun."

"Nonsense," Carter said. "What's the prize? I want a prize."

"Fine. The person with the highest point total doesn't have to help clean up tonight's dinner mess."

I glanced at Mateo, sitting behind me on the couch. I wondered why he didn't beg off. This kind of wholesome stuff didn't seem like his thing, but he was a few beers in. Maybe they loosened him up.

Not that I could tell.

"Are we ready?" Dean shuffled through his cards. "I'll start with something easy. What is Carter's favorite color?

"Blue!" Claudia exclaimed.

Dean hesitated and I jumped in.

"Robin's egg blue."

"Correct!"

Claudia made a face. "Oh, come on. Blue is blue."

"I beg to differ," Carter said, shooting me an appreciative smile. "Tiffany boxes only come in one color, and it's not merely *blue*."

"Truth!"

Claudia rolled her eyes at us and laughed.

"Next question: How long has Mateo worked at *Lucky 13*?"

Carter perked up. "Two years."

"Correct! Luna teaches art to what age group?"

"Kindergarten," Carter said, clearly pleased with two in a row. But his face fell when Dean said, "Incorrect."

Mateo's deep voice came from behind me. "It was kindergarten up until last June. This year, it's first grade."

"Correct!"

The other roommates exchanged impressive sounds. I glanced back a Mateo. "You've been paying attention."

His lips quirked up in what might've been his smile, and he took another pull from his beer.

Dean flipped a card. "What is Claudia allergic to?"

"Playing *Enya* at top volume," Carter said.

Claudia frowned. "What? I love *Enya*."

"Oh, right," Carter said. "That was my wishful thinking."

"Ha, ha."

I jumped in. "Scented fabric softener."

"Correct! What is Luna's dream vacation?"

Carter squinted. "Shit, she told me once and I can't remember..."

"She wants to go to Maui sometime between November and February so she can see the humpback whales," Mateo said into the quiet.

"That's correct," Dean said. "Mateo's on a roll."

I felt a strange tingle go down my spine. I vaguely remembered telling Carter that over breakfast one morning when I'd first moved in. Mateo had been in the room, but I couldn't have imagined he cared enough to remember. The game went on, and there was a lot of laughter and jokes, but it didn't escape me that when a question about me came up, Mateo was first to answer.

"Final one," Dean said. "Who in this house gets up the earliest and what time—?"

"Luna. At 6:15 am," Mateo said before Dean could even finish.

Dean lowered his cards. "Correct."

The apartment grew quiet. Mateo was in the process of taking another pull of beer when he realized everyone was staring at him. He didn't look embarrassed or angry, but he didn't look at me either. He set his empty bottle on the coffee table and went to the door.

"We're out of beer," he said, and then he was gone. The others looked to me.

"What?"

"This is just like *Love Actually*," Claudia said.

Carter tilted his head back. "Oh my God, of course."

"What are you talking about?" I looked between them almost desperately.

"Andrew Lincoln was in love with Keira Knightley but acted like he could barely stand her," Carter said.

"But then his wedding video was all her," Claudia said.

Dean nodded. "Mateo only answered a question if it was about you. And he got them all right."

I sat back. "That's...stupid."

Carter raised a brow. "Is it?"

Dean and Claudia wore soft, knowing looks.

I jumped to my feet. "Okay. I don't know what's going on, but I can't...I have to...I'll be right back."

I hurried out the door, a hundred different emotions bubbling up in me: exhilaration, denial, and something deeper that was thrilling but scary as hell.

CHAPTER 4 - MATEO

Footsteps sounded from behind me on the sidewalk.

Shit.

Before I could turn around, Luna spoke, her voice sounding watery and uncertain. Completely unlike her.

"How do you know all that about me?"

I turned. In the streetlight, her dark blue eyes were wide and shining. Her arms were crossed.

"I listen."

"That's it? That's the only reason?"

I sighed. "What do you want me to say, Lu?"

"I want you to tell me what...what you..."

"Want?" I moved closer. "I want to take you to Maui. I want to put you on a boat and take you out to see the whales. I want to watch your face as one of them breaches the surface. That's what I want."

A tiny gasp fell from her mouth, and she took a step back.

"But I'm not that guy," I continued. "I'm a bartender with mountains of debt from the college I dropped out of. I can't go back unless I want to be more in the hole, and even if I went back, I don't know what the hell I'd do."

"Mateo..."

"Go home, Luna."

I turned and kept walking, half expecting her to follow me and demand better answers. She didn't. The disappointment cut like a knife, but what did I expect? We were too different. She'd grow tired of wanting more from me, and I'd die a slow death that I couldn't give it to her.

CHAPTER 5 - LUNA

I did as Mateo said. I went back to our apartment and regretted it immediately. As soon as I saw my sketch, I realized it'd been a mistake to let him walk away.

"This is stupid," I said to my empty room. "A ridiculous *Love Actually* theory? Am I that suggestible?"

Then I had a flash of that moment at the bar. When the way Mateo was looking at me changed for just a moment. A flash of...something that had escaped his dark gaze, making me warm.

I waited until I heard Mateo's heavy, booted steps come through the house. He was alone. No eager young woman whisper-giggling on the way to his bed. There still hadn't been any. Not for weeks.

My heart was in my throat, but the not knowing was unsettling. This rearranging of all my insides had to stop. I had to know.

I padded out into the hallway in my oversized T-shirt and sleep shorts. I tapped on Mateo's door.

"Yeah?"

I peeked my head in. He was in bed, on top of the covers, and wearing those same flannel pants but with a V-neck undershirt. He shut off the TV that had been quietly playing ESPN and started to speak.

"Don't say anything." I closed the door behind me and crossed his room. It was simple but clean. The usual masculine decor scented by his cologne. But all I could see was him and his brown eyes that darkened as he watched me approach.

"Luna…"

I moved over him, bracing myself on either side of his pillow.

"What are you doing?" he whispered gruffly.

I silenced him with a kiss. His mouth was hard, but his lips were soft. He stiffened at first, and then his mouth opened against mine. My heart crashed somewhere to the bottom of my chest, plummeting like how it does on a roller-coaster ride when the drop begins. Then he took over the kiss, capturing my mouth with deep, demanding sweeps of his tongue. His hands went to my hair, gripping, holding me to him. My arms started to shake on the pillow.

I pulled back to catch my breath. "Oh God, I'm in big trouble."

"Why?" His voice was thick with want, ready to take me again.

"All those dates," I said. "All those guys. I was searching and searching…"

He swallowed hard. His combination of sexual potency and vulnerability made me dizzy. "And now?" he asked.

"Now I know it's you."

His brow furrowed. "Luna, I don't know—"

I put my finger to his lips. "Don't give me any crap about how you have nothing to offer, Mateo. I don't have my shit figured out, either. In fact, I'm kind of a mess. Maybe we could be a mess together? Like finger paints. You mix it all up and let it go and see what happens." I shrugged with a small smile, my own vulnerability making me feel weak and strong at the same time. "Sometimes you get something really beautiful."

Mateo watched me in the dimness for a moment, then rolled me onto my back. He held my face with surprising tenderness.

"You are something really beautiful."

His words washed over me like champagne, bubbly but potent. The start of something new. Before I could catch my breath, his mouth was on mine, taking it in a moan-inducing kiss. It felt as though he was plundering me but at the same time, filling me with sensations and emotions I'd begun to wonder if I'd ever feel.

"God, Mateo," I said, breaking away for air. "If I'd known you could kiss like that, I would've come to your room a lot sooner."

"I wish you had," he said. "I've wanted you since the first fucking moment I saw you."

And then he was kissing me again. His hands were on me and mine on him, first his torso and then around to his back, discovering him. Learning what his warm skin felt like, how hard his muscles were, the power of his body on top of mine.

And his hands felt like they were creating me, as if his touch was bringing awareness to every part of my body for the first time.

He reached behind his head to grab the collar of his shirt and tore it off with one yank. In the dimness, I took him in. His chest, the bunched muscles of his shoulders, the contours and cut lines of his collarbone, the hollow of his throat where his pulse pounded.

"You are a sculptor's dream," I whispered.

"I don't know what to say to that," he said, his mouth blazing a path of hot kisses down my neck. "Thanks?"

"You're welcome," I moaned and then bit back a cry as his large hand found my small breast, covering it completely.

I had a brief moment of self-consciousness, Brad's words coming back to me. But Mateo removed my shirt, and the way his eyes raked over me, dark and heavy with desire, erased all hesitancy.

"You are so fucking beautiful," he growled. "I imagined, but I never..." He shook his head, words falling away as he kissed me again.

We stripped each other out of the rest of our clothing. I could feel Mateo's desire to explore every part of me. I wanted the same, to take my time getting to know him, but we were both in too much of a hurry. Both too greedy and wanting each other too badly.

He left me long enough to put on a condom and then was back.

"Luna..." he said, a question in his eyes.

I pushed him onto his back and straddled him, to erase any doubt that this was what I wanted. I reached between us, to the huge hardness of him. I'd get more acquainted later, but for now, I just needed him inside me.

I slowly slid down on top of him, impaling myself, feeling him stretch and fill me. He gripped my hips while he watched me take him. When I had all of him, he made a sound in his chest—animal need, mixed with something else. Relief.

I began to move, our eyes locked. His jaw was tense as he watched me undulate on top of him, using his hands to bring me down harder while he drove up into me.

"Oh fuck, Luna, I can't..."

Another curse and he flipped me onto my back. I let out a cry that our roommates—not to mention half the building—had to have heard.

The perfect happiness and pleasure of Mateo inside me stole my breath. I was no blushing virgin and not prone to romanticism, but I'd never experienced anything like this with anyone. The perfect harmony of physical need and a rightness that *this* was the guy. I don't know how but I felt safe and secure while he relentlessly fucked me. His cock pistoned in and out until the pleasure grew into a crescendo, his mouth just as insistent with hard, heated kisses. When the wave crashed, I pulled him to me and bit down on the slope of muscle between his neck and shoulder. His body shuddered a moment later, his orgasm coming on the heels of mine. An ecstasy so powerful, it left us both panting and glistening with sweat.

Mateo collapsed on his side and immediately held me close against his chest. His lips pressed on my forehead. His fingers pulled through my hair.

"So that just happened," I said, my breath still shaky. The aftershocks of the orgasm moved through me like warm ribbons of honey.

"Regrets?"

"No," I said. "You?"

I felt him shake his head against me. "Absofuckinglutely not."

"It's just that we live together," I said. "It's like Nick and Jess on *New Girl*. They were perfect until they weren't."

Mateo pulled me closer. "Then let's just stay perfect."

EPILOGUE - MATEO - FIFTEEN MONTHS LATER

The schooner bounced over the ocean waves and swells that were the craziest shade of dark blue I'd ever seen, trimmed with little pearls of white. That's how Luna described it, anyway. We'd left that morning from the marina in Lahaina. A historic town on Maui, it had once been the seat of Hawaiian royalty.

Luna told me that, too, while we kissed under the huge banyan tree in the town center. She knew everything there was to know about the island and told me all of it as she pulled me into different galleries and shops. We shared a frozen pineapple slushy that was even sweeter after I kissed it from her mouth.

I'd been saving for this trip for over a year, working extra shifts. Luna, of course, wouldn't let me foot the whole bill, but took extra work giving private art lessons. We couldn't afford one of the fancy resorts, but it didn't matter. It was enough to be on Maui. There was something about the island that made all the things that rattled around inside me feel calm and settled.

Or maybe that was just Luna.

I watched the wind catch her hair and blow it from her face as the boat went farther out in search of a whale.

It was late February, the tail end of their migration, according to my girlfriend. I was beginning to think she was never going to see one, when suddenly, Luna let out a gasp. Her small hand gripped my arm. I looked to where she pointed, off the port side of the boat, just in time to see a whale breach the water.

And not just the dorsal fin or the tail. It was the whale's face, its eye seeming to take us in before slipping beneath the waves again. I saw it, but more importantly, Luna saw it. If I could draw like she could, I would've drawn her. She was so beautiful in that moment, full of awe and respect and love.

Like me, looking at her, because I loved her too.

She turned to me and smiled, her eyes the same color as the sea off the shores of Maui.

"Did you see that? Wasn't it incredibly beautiful?"

"Yeah," I said, brushing a stray lock of hair from her cheek. "The most beautiful thing I've ever seen."

Emma Scott is the *USA Today* and *Wall St. Journal* best-selling author of *Full Tilt* and *Between Hello and Goodbye*. Visit her at www.emmascottwrites.com.

A PATH FOR THE LOST

ERIC R. ASHER

Vicky sat on Rivercene's back porch, wind catching her fiery hair as the trees shifted across the yard, and one thick trunk stepped forward. She watched the creature move, a terrifying sight to most, but this was a gathering place of the Green Men and the Forest Gods. Though one was sorely missed there.

The old Victorian mansion felt emptier without the Innkeeper, but time and violence could change a great many things about the world. The Innkeeper might be gone, or at least changed, but the mansion was still cared for.

Of course, Rivercene was never empty, not really. Ghosts still roamed the old halls, and magic thrummed in the spells and wards laid down to protect the place. The tree grew closer, though in truth the creature was anything but a tree. Even the Green Men bowed before the Forest Gods, and Dirge was one of the oldest.

"What troubles you, child?" The Forest God's voice didn't boom. It creaked and groaned like a gale ripping through the woods.

Vicky hesitated. They'd been through a great deal in the past months, pulling Damian back from the edge of oblivion, releasing the Old God Gaia upon the earth once more, facing down the Mad King of Faerie. And not all of them had come out unscathed.

Not all of them had come out alive.

Despite all that … there were things in the shadows, and there were new tragedies every time she looked at her phone. "The world is burning, Dirge. And I don't feel like I can do anything to stop it."

Dirge let out a long breath and looked away, the dim glow of his eyes rotating in the violent gashes of bark that formed his face. "It would be better for you to speak with Stump, but I suppose he is not here. I have heard the stories from the northern gods and those across the great oceans. There is little we can do to stand against these things."

"Can't Gaia stop it?" a voice squeaked from above them.

Vicky startled on her bench, looking up to find the snow-white face of a death bat hanging in the rafters. Luna could have been a large cotton ball if it wasn't for her flat yellow nose and wide ears. She dropped to the bench and flopped down beside Vicky, lacing her clawed fingers together before adjusting an aged Green Day hoodie.

Dirge focused on Luna for a time. "It is not so simple as that. There is always balance in the chaos, child of Camazotz. It may be disrupted from age to age, as the Mad King showed in the east. Gaia will not be so brash as that."

Luna clicked her claws together and glanced at Vicky. "But we fight to keep people safe. We fight to keep our friends safe. All those families, Dirge. They're just ... they've lost so much. Camazotz used to tell me stories about Hawaii. I always wanted to see it."

Dirge frowned at Luna, his face oddly wooden as he contemplated her words. "There will always be darkness, but however long it may be, darkness will always end, child. What replaces it may be different, may be unrecognizable to those who knew it best, but it will heal in time, as we all must."

Vicky wondered how many of Dirge's words were directed to Luna, and how many spoke to his own experiences. Did Forest Gods even think like that? Like mortals? Or did they simply have a keener sense of empathy?

What an odd thing to think about Dirge. Vicky had seen him storm the battlefield against vampires and Fae alike. Empathy he might have, but it was tempered by ruthlessness.

Dirge looked away for a moment. "There is something you both should see. A place I know well, and one that has seen tragedy in its time. And if our friend is still visiting, perhaps you may find some other enjoyment in it."

"What friend?"

Vicky exchanged a glance with Luna when Dirge didn't respond. He walked away, clearly expecting them to follow. And so they did, making their way through the yard, following the Forest God behind an old barn where an arch of vines waited.

Something warm and furry grabbed Vicky's ankle, and she glanced down in time to see Jasper, the dark gray ball of fur that was a dragon in disguise, climbing his way up her leg. He settled in on her shoulder, unblinking black eyes watching the Forest God.

Dirge reached out to the arch, and the air shimmered between the brilliant green vines. It reminded Vicky of a portal to Faerie, only without the violent reds and purples that often accompanied it.

"Come." That was all he said before vanishing through the shimmering gateway. Luna followed close behind.

Vicky sighed and rubbed the patch of fur between Jasper's eyes before stepping through after the others.

It wasn't like the violent shifts of the fairies' Warded Ways. It wasn't like the dizzying exit so common when they walked the Abyss, either. There was a brief flash of color, like oil spilled across brilliant greens, and then they were out, feet landing on soft grass as the world resolved around them. Vicky recognized Old Greenville. A lost city that had become something else. Something more.

But the peace of that place was soon broken by a shriek.

Dirge led them away from the portal, past a screaming family who apparently didn't know what lurked in Old Greenville when they'd pitched their tent. Luna waved and smiled at the terror-stricken adults, but it was only a child who waved back, a small plush dragon clutched to her chest.

Jasper took that as a cue to show her a *real* dragon, exploding into his full-sized form, looming over everything in that field except for Dirge himself. A gray behemoth that should not have existed, even when the veil between the Fae and the Commoners had fallen.

The father fainted on the spot, and while the mother tended to him, their child sprinted forward, arms wide as she charged the scaly snout adorned with long silver teeth.

Dirge paused and watched.

"Don't you dare scare her, furball." Vicky patted the dragon's nearest leg.

Jasper chuffed a moment before the girl plowed into his snout, hugging the beast's face as best she could before patting him on top of his nose.

The girl's mother finally noticed where her child had gone before she screamed and started forward. A shimmer in the air stepped around Jasper, slowly forming into the ghost of Terrence, a musician who had died centuries before and now often dwelled near the old city.

"I'll address this."

Dirge raised what amounted to an eyebrow.

The woman fainted mid-stride, passing directly through the ghost and slamming into the ground.

Vicky winced. "That's going to leave a mark."

"I'll get one of the Fae to heal her." Terrence put his hands on his translucent hips. "What a mess."

"Mommy's funny." The girl laughed and patted Jasper again before heading over to her father at their trailer.

"Is that kid insane?" Luna whispered.

Terrence sighed. "Aren't they all? Go on, I'll take care of them."

Vicky felt a little guilty leaving them behind, but she followed Dirge as Jasper snapped back into his round furball form and rolled after them.

The Forest God led them to the ruins of Old Greenville. A town that had flooded and vanished beneath the water, only to be torn down and moved a few miles away. They walked a long-abandoned street, now overgrown and flanked with leveled foundations and aged stairs that rose into nothing.

"Fire is not what took this city, but water did its work. Gaia may have influence over these things, but you must understand that nature is a force beyond any of the Old Gods. Fulvus and those like him may have dominion over the magma within the earth, but not even they could stop the most violent eruptions. Not even they, with such influence over flames, can calm the heat that scorches the forests, and nor can I spare the trees and beings consumed by it."

Vicky had never heard Dirge speak so many words at once. She wondered what her questions had prodded in the Forest God to have him open up so widely.

He turned and settled in beside another campsite that appeared to have been rapidly vacated, as a cooler and cast-iron pan still sat on a modest fire. "I had a dream once, about the dark."

Vicky slid into a camp chair at the side of a firepit when Luna gestured for her to join them, the death bat pulling her own seat closer.

Dirge looked toward the cemetery behind him before glancing away from the river and focusing on the forest. "Spring comes in the end, child. Never forget that. Life is only one change after another—experiences you will overcome or endure, as you have already done. But spring comes in the end."

Vicky sank back in her chair. She'd heard similar words after tragedy and loss and when friends had fallen in battle. Her question was almost a whisper, one she hadn't fully intended to speak out loud. "Why do they always say we'll be stronger for it?"

Luna's clawed hand reached out and squeezed Vicky's arm while Dirge pondered her words.

"They are not wrong, child, but they do not wish to embrace the sorrow in these moments. Do not fault them for it. All grieve."

"It's Dirge!" a familiar voice shouted. "And Vicky? And Luna?"

Vicky craned her neck around to see long blonde hair cascading over the shoulders of the water witch. No, the *Queen* of the water witches. "Nixie?"

She heard a brief shout followed by a wet splat before an angry necromancer cursed at great length. A moment later, a rather muddy Damian climbed up the bank to stand beside Nixie.

"Mud. Mud everywhere."

"Oh no, the lovebirds are here." Luna said it like it was the worst thing in the world, but Vicky didn't miss her sly grin. "I thought they were on a second honeymoon. Or third honeymoon? Whatever, they're adorably annoying sometimes."

Nixie held her hand out, and a wave rushed up from the river below, concentrating into a funnel before hitting Damian with far too much force. He might have been clear of mud, but the way he rag-dolled down the hill toward them on a wave of water was probably going to leave him with a few bruises.

He slid to a stop not ten feet away before raising his head slightly. "Ow."

Nixie cringed before starting after him. "Sorry, I was distracted!"

"Still alive." Damian slowly gave a thumbs-up before climbing back to his feet and wincing as he stretched.

Vicky's brow furrowed. "I thought you two were still in Puerto Rico?"

Something roared and another burst of water shot into the air.

Nixie glanced back before turning to Vicky. "We were, but Damian was trying out his Abyss walking, and the Guardian sneezed and, well, we came to visit Dirge instead."

"The … Guardian?" Luna slowly asked. "Do you mean the mosasaurus that guards Atlantis?"

A huge flipper rose over the ridge before slapping back down into the river below.

"Oh my gosh, that's amazing!" Luna squeed and took off for the river, sprinting past Damian and Nixie without another look.

"Don't get eaten!" Damian shouted after the death bat.

"Join us, please," Dirge said, gesturing to a hollowed log that had been whittled into a bench.

Vicky was ninety percent sure it hadn't been there a moment ago.

Damian dripped some water into the cast-iron skillet, and it fizzled away immediately. "That's just about perfect. Time to make some rice balls!"

"Musubi," Nixie said.

Damian harrumphed. "Rice rectangles."

Their brief exchange told Vicky it wasn't a random campfire he'd led them to. The Forest God had led them straight to their friends.

Nixie pinched the bridge of her nose and muttered under her breath. "I'll prepare the rice and the sauce. You do the rest?"

"Yes, My Queen."

Dirge sat up a little straighter. "Have you established a proper relationship with the necromancer, Queen of the Undines? Ruler of Atlantis and all who dwell there?"

Nixie let out a sigh. "No, Dirge, that's just Damian being a sarcastic ass."

"I am allowed sarcasm after getting thrown down the hill without a Slip 'N Slide, thank you very much."

A small giggle escaped Vicky, but she bit her lips when the pair cast a glare in her direction. She half expected to see a box of chocolate or marshmallows, considering Damian ate worse than anyone she'd ever known. Instead, he pulled out a few bottles for Nixie, some seasoning jars, nori, and … "Less sodium Spam?"

"It's the best on these," Damian said. "The regular stuff gets a little *too* salty for my taste."

"There isn't much Damian has good taste about, but his opinions on food are generally well thought out." Nixie walked over to the fire and checked the lid on a pot, picking it up without so much as an oven mitt. Steam hissed and billowed from her grip, but she didn't seem to mind. Water witches were a strange bunch, and Vicky still felt like she was in the dark when it came to some of their abilities.

"Rice is almost done."

"Spam filets are going on." Damian dropped several thin slices of Spam onto the pan. Vicky would have called them *anything* other than filets. "Did I see Jasper running toward the river with Luna? How is the furball?"

"Good. He's good. He introduced himself to the kid over there." Vicky hooked her thumb toward the other campsite where the family was still sitting with Terrence. Two small fairies stood nearby, likely the healers Dirge had mentioned.

Damian squinted at the scene. "Who is that?"

"They camp here from time to time," Dirge said. "Their child has run through my woods on many occasions."

"What about the fairies?"

"Ah, they moved here from Falias with Gaia's guidance. They still find it odd to interact with the humans, but the days have grown strange for us all."

Nixie focused on a series of ingredients, blending together soy sauce and brown sugar and a few more things Vicky didn't catch. That done, Nixie opened the package of nori, one Vicky recognized from her dad's obsession with the stuff.

Nixie gestured to the Forest God. "Dirge, could you raise the rice so it cools faster?"

Dirge sank a trio of thick branches into the earth as easily as sand. He hooked the handle of the pot over the center, keeping it elevated from the ground.

Nixie smiled. "Thank you."

"What are you and Luna doing here, anyway?" Damian asked as the Spam cuts sizzled in the pan.

"Dirge brought us. He was telling us about Greenville and how it flooded here bad enough that they moved the town."

Damian narrowed his eyes and glanced at the Forest God.

"They are concerned for the world, necromancer." Dirge gestured to the ruins closer to the woods. "They have heard tales of the tragedies that are being endured, and it weighs on them. They wonder why Gaia does not rail against nature itself."

"I mean, that was a lot of words," Vicky said under her breath. "But that's kind of it, yeah. You broke my bond to the Destroyer. We saved you from the Abyss. We pulled Graybeard out of the Burning Lands. Why can't we do ... more?" She didn't mean for the words to come out in such a rush. She didn't want to feel the tightness in her chest. It reminded her too much of the darker days. Days that were not so far behind her.

Nixie folded her hands together and smiled at Vicky. "Even the most powerful of us can't stand against nature. Floods and fires, earthquakes and hurricanes. They reshape the world."

"But you're an undine. You can move water. You could fight an inferno like no one else! Maybe Dirge and Gaia would catch on fire, but what about the water witches?"

"Damn, kid." Damian turned the Spam over and gave her a sad smile. "You're talking about things that *change* the magic around it. A forest doesn't just burn. The ley lines themselves redirect, strengthening in some places and dissipating in others."

"Everywhere but a nexus is like that," Nixie said. "But even the flow to a nexus can grow weak. I might raise water here, in this place, but without enough ley line energy, I would burn as surely as the driest tinder."

Vicky glanced down at the crackling campfire. "I didn't know that."

"Maybe Drake needs to hand you over to Koda for a bit." Damian winked at her. "The whole real-world experience of coming back as a ghost, becoming the Destroyer, and then getting stuck with the powers of a necromancer doesn't always make up for learning from a good book."

Damian slid the skillet off the flames, keeping it close enough to stay warm, but it would cool in short order. "We fight when we have to, kid. We help when we can." He winced and looked at his now-swollen finger. "I'm pretty sure that's broken."

"Would you like me to lick it better?" Nixie asked.

Damian and Vicky both blinked at that.

Luna burst into laughter as she walked back into the circle around the fire, Jasper perched on her shoulder. "That's not what they say! *Kiss* it better, not … oh, I shouldn't have said anything. I should have just taken pictures. Imagine the blackmail."

"Kiss it better?" Nixie asked before frowning. "How on earth would kissing a wound make it better? There is no exchange of energy, is there? No fluids to channel—"

"Okay, we're good," Vicky said in a hurry. "Let's focus on the food."

Damian leaned forward and pointed at Vicky. "Tell you what, why don't we look into the charities who are helping? I've had a good month at the shop. We can donate some extra to whoever you want to help the most."

"Don't say it like that!" Luna recoiled. "That's like saying pick who you don't want to fall off the cliff."

Damian blinked at the death bat.

Nixie laughed and shook her head. "I will offer some of our fortunes as well. It is a good lesson for the undines who have dwelled too long in the waters. They must be reminded there is more to our world than the sea."

Damian reached out to take Nixie's hand. She eyed his swollen finger, then wrenched it violently to the side. Something popped audibly, and the necromancer let out the tiniest screech.

"It was just dislocated. You'll be fine."

Damian stared at her with an expression that fell somewhere between awe and absolute betrayal. "At least I won't have a co-pay."

"There isn't a co-pay with the fairies," Luna said.

Damian scoffed at that. "Luna, they have the worst co-pays of all. Endless supplies of Irish whiskey, constant raids on the fudge shop. It adds up."

Nixie spooned rice into a rectangular box before inserting what at first appeared to be a lid, but she pressed it down to compress everything inside. That done, she dragged a cut of Spam through her freshly made sauce and added it to the rice.

Vicky wasn't the biggest fan of nori, but she watched in fascination as Nixie turned the assembled block of rice and sauce and Spam out onto the sheet. Nixie rolled it like a square chunk of sushi before starting the entire process over again.

It wasn't long before they were each holding a rectangular serving of musubi, and Vicky had to admit it smelled amazing.

Dirge frowned at the block of food carefully pinched between his knobby thumb and long, gnarled forefinger. "And this is more than one bite for the commoners? Fascinating. It seemed a great deal of work for so small a thing."

Damian let out a low laugh.

"What?" Nixie asked.

He leaned in conspiratorially. "We're feeding a Forest God musubi. Like, it's kind of weird, right?"

"Damian, you were dying in the Abyss less than a month ago, and *this* is what you consider … weird?"

He pursed his lips. "I mean, I guess our date on the back of the mosasaurus was weirder, but still, yeah, a little bit."

Vicky took a bite as the pair bantered some more, and any reservation she'd had about the new snack melted away. The nori was subtle, just a hint of the sea before everything gave way to the rich salt and fat and sugar of the Spam and sauce. Sweet notes played across her tongue, and the rice grounded everything.

It was a perfect bite, there in a place that had seen so much darkness. And she understood in that moment why Dirge had taken them to Greenville. The city had been inundated, destroyed, and even the ruins had seen a war with the dark-touched vampires and given rise to a Harbinger.

But they were there in a different time. They were there now with friends. With family. With some of the people who meant the most to her, and while the history of that place might always have a weight to it, a darkness, the people she loved would always carry the light.

"What do you think, kid?" Damian asked.

She didn't trust herself to answer. Not with the pressure behind her eyes. Instead, she stuffed the rest of the musubi into her mouth and hopped around the fire, reaching out to embrace the necromancer who'd saved her life.

"It's because of the sauce," Nixie whispered.

Vicky burst into laughter, squeezed Damian a little tighter, and then almost tackle-hugged the undine. "I'm so glad you're all here."

Something thudded behind her, and when she released Nixie, she found Terrence sitting on a log by the fire.

"I think that family will be fine. I told them they may see some strange things around Old Greenville, but they'll always be welcome here."

"A song, perhaps?" Dirge asked.

Damian raised an eyebrow. "Can you still pick up a guitar? I thought that magic would have worn down by now."

In answer, Terrence took the guitar when Dirge offered it. The Forest God studied the musubi in his other hand as Terrence started to play. While Vicky couldn't be sure if Dirge was smiling, he did finish the musubi in two quick bites.

They stayed until the sun went down and the fireflies lit the woods. Only when the snores of the mosasaurus threatened to bring down the cliff did they say their goodbyes. But it wasn't like so many before that, when they didn't know if they'd ever see each other again. This was a goodbye for now, with an unspoken promise they would all be together again. They would stand side by side, and they would do what they could to bring some small light into others' darkness.

Featuring characters and creatures from the Vesik series. Listen to the first audiobook for free at ericrasherstore.com.

MAUI FOREVER

HEIDI MCLAUGHLIN

CHAPTER 1 - LIAM

The door to the studio, which is in the same office space as Elle's business, opens. I expect to find Elle or Quinn coming through, but it's Eden and Rush. My eyes widen in surprise. "Hey," I say to them. "What are you doing here? More importantly, does your dad know you're in the city?" I give Eden a pointed look.

"Yes." Eden and Rush come farther into the studio and let the door shut behind them. Thankfully, I'm not recording—not that I would mind if she interrupted me. "I need your help."

My heart does a double bounce before it settles into my stomach. I can approach her statement in one of two ways. Be the adult she needs me to be or send her to Josie. Or Elle, who is in the other room. I clear my throat and before I can say something incredibly adult-like, she holds her hand up.

"I shouldn't have led with 'I need your help' because you're probably thinking Rush and I are in some type of trouble—"

"You're not?" Finally, my heart returns to its rightful place in my chest. "That's great." It's really more than great, but eloquent words fail me. "So, what's up?"

Eden looks at Rush and then back at me. "You've heard about the fires in Maui, right?"

I nod. "The entire world has. It's devastating."

"It is. I was supposed to go there for a competition next week and, as you can imagine, it's been canceled."

"Makes sense."

"But here's the thing," she continues. "The island depends heavily on tourism, and the surfing comps bring in a ton of people, sponsorships, and money to the locals. With the event being canceled, that means the parts of the island that didn't succumb to this disaster are losing out."

"I agree, but I'm not sure what you're getting at."

Rush takes a small step forward and smiles sheepishly. I like the kid. So does Harrison. JD's on the fence, which I get. I'm the same way when it comes to Betty Paige and Mack. While I know there's something there, I don't allow it to build while he's living with us.

"Sir, if I may."

I laugh and shake my head. "You can call me Liam. I've told you this before." A-plus for manners. I've met his parents, Irina and Abraham Fenimore. They weren't starstruck, which was nice, and we've done a couple of family gatherings with them. We'll also meet up again this winter when Rush competes for a world championship. Honestly, these two are lucky to have each other. With Eden being a surfer and Rush being a snowboarder, they're always available to support one another.

"Right, Liam." Rush smiles again. "What Eden is trying to say and failing miserably at . . ." Eden elbows Rush in his side. He flinches, but never wipes the smile off his face.

Aw, young love.

"Can you hold a benefit concert, Uncle Liam? I've seen old home movies of you doing one for the twins after their dad died, and I just think with your following, the band could raise a lot of money. I thought about asking my dad to pose for a calendar, but my mum says that'll go right to his head and his ego is already too large for the house."

I crack up and am very thankful I don't have a mouthful of anything, otherwise I'd have a mess to clean up. After I gather my wits, I nod. "I think that's a great idea, Eden."

She claps her hands and launches herself into my arms. "Thank you, thank you, thank you."

"On one condition," I tell her.

"Oh, I'm not singing or anything."

"No, nothing like that. The band doesn't have a problem doing this, but the money only goes so far and is controlled by the government once we donate it. So, why don't we do a drive of sorts? Let's ask people to bring new blankets, clothes, or gently used items. Things we can fly over to Maui to help the residents. The money will help them rebuild, but they can't rebuild if they're not clothed."

"What if we do a silent auction as well?" Rush suggests. "We can get items donated and auction them off."

"That's fantastic," I say. "Tell you what, I'll work on the venue and get that set up. I think we'll need somewhere big—some place outside. I'll ask some friends to perform. We'll make it a day event. I'll have Josie work on vendors for food, bathroom facilities, security, and whatever else we'll need. You two get donations. Betty Paige and Mack will help."

"We can do that." Eden beams at Rush.

"Don't be afraid to use your name, Eden," I tell her. "Tell people who you are, sell your story, and if they don't budge, tell them who your dad and uncles are."

"I think I can get the snowboarding team to donate. Even the ski team," Rush adds.

The door opens and Elle walks in. "What's going on in here?"

Eden and Rush turn to look at her, and smile.

"They just sold me on hosting a fundraiser for Maui," I tell her.

"That's what I came in to ask. Plum wants to do something, and I thought we could do a joint venture."

"We'd love to have them," I tell Elle. "What about Talking Til Dawn?"

She nods. "I'll ask, but they're usually game for whatever."

"Do you think Sinful Distraction will play?" Rush asks.

"Without a doubt," Eden says as her cheeks flare. It's no secret Eden used to crush on Quinn. It's harmless and while she says she doesn't, she can't hide the evidence. I used to tease JD about Eden liking older men, just to rile him up. It's not like Quinn or Eden would ever look at each other as anything but family.

"That's four bands," Rush says.

"That's more than enough," Elle says. "Venue?"

I shrug. "I think some place outside?"

"I'll make some calls. We want something with facilities because rentals are such a hassle. There's the new amphitheater out toward my parents' place. It faces the water. It might be kind of cool to have it there."

"Do you want me to contact them?" I ask Elle.

She shakes her head. "I'll take care of it."

"Then what am I going to do?" I ask, throwing my hands up.

"I don't know," Elle says as she heads toward the door. "Sit there and look pretty?"

Eden and Rush laugh.

"Elle . . ."

She laughs. "What's the point of knowing a manager who can handle all of this for you?"

"When she's my niece—"

Elle laughs. "Love you, Uncle Liam," she says as she walks out.

"We have a list of things to do, so we're going to take off," Eden says as she approaches me. I pull her in for a hug. "Thank you."

"It's my pleasure. If you run into any problems, call me."

"We will. See you at dinner."

"We'll be there."

As soon as the door shuts, I tap the screen on my phone and open the app that allows me to video chat with Harrison and JD at the same time.

Harrison answers first, but before I can say anything, JD's face pops onto the screen. "Ooh, three-way. This is saucy," he says, causing us to laugh.

"Are you ever serious?" Harrison asks him.

JD scoffs. "Pffft, what's the point? Being serious sounds boring, mate."

JD's not wrong. I think there was a time in his life when he would've changed, but then he was shot and ever since he's lived life to the fullest. There's never a dull moment when he's around.

"So, what brings us all together?" Harrison asks.

"Well, moments ago, my niece and her boyfriend approached me, asking if we'd be willing to hold a fundraiser for the people of Maui."

"Ah, so that's why she wanted to come and see you," JD says. "She wouldn't tell me the reason."

"And we agreed?" Harrison asks.

"We did, and then my other niece took it a step further and said all three of her bands will perform as well."

Harrison laughs. "Does Quinn know?"

"Nope, I'll leave that up to his sister."

"So, what's the gist? What do we need to do?" Harrison asks.

I clear my throat. "With Elle managing the logistics of it all, I think we spread the word, find people to donate, get some advertisements going. I sent Eden and Rush to find donations and told her not to be shy about telling people who she is."

"Good luck there," JD says. "I tell her all the time that she needs to be all 'Do you know who my dad is,' but she won't."

"That's because no one knows you," Harrison blurts out through laughter. To make matters worse, he adds a "ba-dum tsh" drum sound, which only infuriates JD.

"You know, after all these years, I wonder why I stick around. The amount of disrespect." JD shakes his head.

"Because we're family," I tell him. "And you know damn well we'd do anything for you."

"Yeah, yeah," JD continues to shake his head. "Someday . . ."

"Someday, we'll retire, and then we'll be three guys who sit around, fiddling with our instruments while reminiscing about the good ole days. Until then, we're a band about to have a charity concert because our resident surfer needs her family to help her friends out."

"I'm going to send a tweet," JD says. "Or X, or whatever the hell it's called now."

"I'll go live on TikTok once I have a date from Elle," I add.

"How's that going—the Love Line with Liam?" Harrison asks.

"Good. It's fun answering questions. People seem to dig it."

"That's good. I thought about doing something similar, but each time I pick up my phone, Ollie wants it and we're not putting him on social media."

"I don't blame you," JD adds. "We hired someone to manage Eden's. She needs it, but doesn't have the time between competitions, practice, and school."

"That's probably for the best," I add. "Okay, I'm going to check in with Noah. I'm sure some of his teammates will do something."

Harrison scrubs his hand over his face. "I'll reach out to some peeps once we have a date. Rehearsal?"

"Yeah," I say, sighing. "Tomorrow?"

They agree, and we hang up. I hadn't planned my visit to California to be taken up with a fundraiser, but it is what it is. I text Josie quickly and tell her I'm heading back to the house and ask if she needs anything. She tells me no and reminds me we have dinner plans with my mother later.

CHAPTER 2 - HARRISON

As soon as I hang up with Liam, Quinn's voice rings out, asking if anyone is home. I sit up and pull my legs off the coffee table while Oliver runs toward the door, yelling, "Win!" When Quinn enters the room, he has Ollie on his hip.

"Have you spoken with your sister?" I ask him.

"Nope. Why?"

"You didn't even ask which sister?"

"Well, since I haven't spoken to either of them, saying no seemed like the logical answer."

"Smart ass," I mumble under my breath.

"Ollie, did you hear what Daddy said?" Quinn asks the toddler on his lap. Katelyn started a swear jar and if she catches me, or anyone for that matter, saying things we shouldn't, she tells us to pay up. It's for Oliver's college fund. Not that he needs one because we've already started a trust for him.

"Daddy pay. Daddy pay." Oliver claps his chubby hands in excitement only because that's what my lovely wife taught him to do.

"Where's Mom?" Quinn tickles Oliver, who giggles uncontrollably.

"With your aunts."

"Josie's in town?"

I nod. "Liam and the kids are as well."

"Noah's pre-season game is at home. Why are they here?"

"We're working on new music."

"Ah." Quinn nods. "So, back to one of my sisters?"

"Elle volunteered Sinful Distraction to perform at a charity event 4225 West is hosting."

"Yeah, I know," he says. "Eden called and asked if we'd do it."

"Wow, and you're okay with it?"

Quinn rolls his eyes and sets Ollie down. "You make it seem like I don't like performing. I do. I don't enjoy touring. There's a vast difference. Besides, Eden asked, and it's important to her."

I place my hand on his shoulder and squeeze. "I guess growing up on a tour bus ruined you, huh?"

Quinn shrugs. "It's not that. I don't like leaving Nola for long periods of time. She wants to work, and I respect that. Plus . . ." Quinn trails off.

"Are you afraid of Alicia?"

He nods. "I always wonder if she's lurking out there, somewhere. It's like I love singing, writing music, and being with my band, but then I think about her and then I don't want to leave my house."

"She can't hurt you if you don't let her."

"She can't hurt me or Nola, or you and Mom, as long as she's not hiding behind someone."

I sigh heavily. As much as I want to regret ever meeting Alicia Tucker, I can't imagine my life without Quinn. He was my missing piece. My entire reason for living. That was until I met Katelyn and the twins. Then my life became about the four of them and giving them all the life and family they deserve. Life became better when we added Oliver.

"Is there anything I can do?"

Quinn shakes his head. "Nah. It's my demon."

While that may be, it's not one I want him to tackle alone. "I'll make sure security is tightened at the event. We won't take any risks of someone getting backstage."

"Thanks."

For a long moment, he's quiet. I don't pretend to understand what he goes through when his mind wonders about the woman who left him on my doorstep. I always said if Alicia came back, I'd encourage Quinn to form a relationship with her. That was until she did some sneaky, underhanded shit. I've never thought about harming another person in my life until that moment.

Before I can say something profound to my son, the door opens again, and the high-pitched squeal of Evelyn rings out. "Grandpa!"

"Evelyn . . . oof." I groan as she tackles me. On the outside, Miss Evelyn Jameson Ballard is a sweet little girl. But on the inside, she's a holy terror, determined to cut me down at my knees.

"Sorry, Grandpa," she says "grandpa" with a snicker thanks to Liam. He thinks it's funny that I have this moniker because I'm older than him. I keep reminding him his time is coming, and if he's not careful, I'm going to teach his grandchild to call him something ridiculous, like pewpew.

"It's okay, love bug."

I stand and give Jamie and Ajay hugs and rub my hand over James's hair. He's too busy playing with Oliver to say hi. "What are you guys doing here?"

"Katelyn called and told us to come over," Jamie says. "I brought chips and dips." She holds up a grocery bag before taking it into the kitchen. I look at Ajay and then Quinn. Both shrug.

"Don't look at me," Quinn says. "I came to hang out while Nola's doing her thing."

I pull my phone from my pocket and walk out to the patio, with Evelyn hot on my heels.

"Can I talk to Grandma?"

"Yeah, let's call her."

I sit and bring Evelyn onto my lap. Holding the phone out, Evelyn presses the video button next to Katelyn's name. After two rings, she answers.

"Hi, Grandma!"

"Hi my sweet girl. Are you at my house with Grandpa?"

Evelyn nods. "Are you coming home soon?"

"I'm on my way."

"Okay, I'll wait for you."

Evelyn climbs down and heads back into the condo. "Hey, wanna fill me in?" I ask.

"I'm assuming you've spoken with Elle?"

"Liam, but not Elle."

"Well, this is an all-hands-on deck situation. I invited everyone to come over for dinner."

"Everyone?"

Katelyn nods. "Yes, except our son. He's not answering." I look over my shoulder to find him and Ajay deep in conversation.

"He's on the couch, and any mention of free food will keep him there."

She laughs. "Everyone should be there shortly. I called in an order for some barbecue, which I'll pick up along the way. I think what you guys are doing is really commendable. Elle told me all about it, how Eden had the idea."

"You know I'm game for whatever. By any chance, did Elle tell you when it is?"

"This Saturday."

"Oh wow, so not much time to plan."

"No, which is why everyone's coming over. We're going to divvy up some responsibilities so no one takes on more than they can. Chandler is going to watch the kiddos while the adults work."

"All right. What can I do here?"

"Send the boys to get drinks. I don't think there's enough in the garage. Liam and Josie are bringing dessert, and they're bringing Bianca, too. They were supposed to have dinner with her tonight, but she'd rather plan the shindig. Oh, and make sure you have the laptop set up. We'll need to call Peyton later. She's going to get the team to do something. They can't attend because of Noah's game, though."

"I figured."

"Okay, I'll be home after I stop to pick up the food. I love you."

"Love you more." We hang up and I go back inside to find Quinn on the floor with the boys, and Evelyn on his back, trying to get him to act like a horse. "Okay, just got off the phone with the boss. We're having a family gathering and by family, I mean everyone. Mom needs you boys to stock the fridge in the garage."

"On it," Ajay says as he stands, as does Quinn with Evelyn, who's still attached to his back.

"Can I go, Daddy?" she asks Ajay.

"Yes, but you can't get a piggyback ride in the store. Quinn will need his hands."

"Okay." While Evelyn agrees, she doesn't make any attempt to get down.

The boys leave and I round up the toddlers and take them into the kitchen with me. It's not ideal, but leaving them in the living room by themselves isn't, either. This is where I find Jamie, busy putting out an assortment of chips in bowls.

"I can do that if you want to take these guys," I say, as they both try to wiggle out of my arms.

"Nope, I'm good."

Bamboozled.

I sigh heavily and as dramatically as possible, but to no avail. Jamie ignores me, which leaves me no choice but to take these two into the other room to keep them busy.

"All right, Thing 1 and Thing 2, let's head up to the playroom."

When we get to the playroom, I finally let them out of my hold. They both rush to the toy boxes and, within seconds, the floor is no longer visible. I sit in the rocking chair, the one Katelyn bought when we brought Ollie home, and watch them. Every so often, Oliver brings me a toy to hold—not to play with, though—until he's ready for it.

As soon as Katelyn appears in the doorway, I no longer exist. I watch our son make his way to his mama and reach for her. She scoops him up in her arms and he nestles into the crook of her neck. From the day she met him, their bond has been strong. It's like Oliver was meant to be in the hospital where Katelyn volunteered.

"Channy," James says as Chandler walks into the room. I've never been so happy to see her in my life. As much as I love having the babies around, I like adult time, especially when my wife has been gone all day.

Katelyn hands Oliver over to Chandler and I motion for her to head down the hall to her office. I lock the door behind us and turn to face her. The energy in the room shifts. The dull static of the day turns to radiant power. I will never, ever tire of looking at Katelyn. Each day, each moment, she takes my breath away.

In one long stride, one hand cups her cheek while my other hand finds its place on the small of her back. Our breathing becomes synchronized, becomes one. I lean in, our eyes flutter closed, and press my lips to hers. What starts out as sweet turns quickly into fervent passion. I do my best to tell her, to show her all the love and desire I still feel for her after all these years together.

Katelyn presses her hand to my cheek and holds it there for a moment. "I love you."

"I love you. Did you have a good day?"

"I did. I miss not having Josie near me every day, but I get it. I'm really hoping they'll move here after Paige is done with school."

"They own a lot of property there, and other businesses, too."

"I know." She leans into me and I wrap my arms around her.

"We could always move there."

Katelyn steps back and looks at me.

I shrug. "I've thought about it now that we have Oliver. And with Elle and Ben spending more time there, it makes some sense."

"But Peyton and Noah bought a house here."

Nodding, I add, "And we'd still own the condo. There's nothing saying we can't go back and forth. Beaumont's your home. If you want to go back, we can."

"We can discuss this later," she says. "Right now, we're about to have a house full of people and a lot of planning to do."

I kiss the tip of her nose. "Yes, ma'am."

"Come on, let's go plan the biggest charity event we can." She takes my hand in hers and leads us to the door.

"I'm right there with you," I tell her as I follow her out of the room.

CHAPTER 3 - JIMMY

I stand next to Eden and look out at the crowd. How we ever pulled off this fundraiser will be one of life's greatest mysteries. It's been five days since it was first discussed and in that time, my friends and family took my daughter's request and turned it into a mega event.

"How many people?" Eden asks.

I look down at the text message Elle sent me. "One hundred thousand," I tell her.

"How much have we raised?"

My daughter is far from incompetent, but in this moment, I don't mind providing her with an answer. "In just ticket sales, twenty million."

When we set the ticket price, we wondered if it was too high and too expensive for some people. The weird thing about charity or a natural disaster is that people come out in droves when needed. At last count, three semi-trucks had been filled with non-perishable supplies. We asked for clothes, toys, school supplies, and blankets. Items people need to restart their lives.

Eden looks at me with tears streaming down her face. "Thank you, Daddy." She wraps her arms around me. "Thank you so much."

"I wish I could take the credit for all of this, Little One. But I can't. You did this. You, your cousins, your family, Rush and his family. It's what we do when one of us is in need."

"But without you—"

"Nah, let's not go there. We're a team. One unit. You asked, we helped."

Eden stands tall and wipes her tears away. "How will we get everything to Maui?"

"Planes. As many as it takes. Liam thought about a cargo ship, but it'll take too long. We'll charter some planes and take everything over next week."

"Can I go?"

I nod. "Of course. Now, what do you say?" I nod toward the center of the stage. "Why don't you go introduce yourself and get this party started?"

Rush joins us and smiles at my daughter. I want to hate the kid. I really do, but it's hard to. He's got great parents, a good head on his shoulders, and makes my daughter happy. Still, I think they're too young to be this serious. At their age, I was all about having a good time and not settling down, but then again, if it wasn't for Jenna, I'd probably still be using Twitter to find chicks.

They walk hand-in-hand to the center of the stage. Liam, Harrison, our wives, and the rest of our family join me at the side of the stage.

Eden taps the microphone. "Can you all hear me?"

The crowd roars to life.

"There are a couple of things I need to say before we get started. First and foremost, thank you for coming out today, for spending your hard-earned dollars to support this fundraiser. Today, I'm supposed to be in Maui, competing against some of the strongest women surfers I know, but a fire ravaged one town, and they canceled our event and many others. People changed their vacation plans and instead of going to Maui, went somewhere else, leaving others to feel the brunt of lost tourism.

"When the fire broke out, I called all of my friends who live there. I'm still waiting for one to call me back." Eden pauses and collects herself. Losing her friend hasn't been easy on her. Jenna and I are doing everything we can to help her cope.

She clears her throat and continues. "I needed to do something and thought, what do I have at my disposal—4225 West?" The crowd erupts and Eden looks over at us. I wave while Jenna blows our daughter a kiss.

With Eden still looking at our group, she speaks to the crowd. "I asked my Uncle Liam if he could help me—help me help my friends in Maui. He said he would, but didn't know how. I asked if he'd be willing to hold a benefit concert. He's done them before, and I thought having 4225 West perform would be pretty rad. However, my cousin came into the room and took everything one step further." Eden wipes at her tears again. "I'd like to introduce you to the person responsible for today, Elle James."

Eden claps and steps aside as Elle comes onto the stage. They hug for a long moment and Elle whispers something in Eden's ear. When Elle steps up to the microphone, the crowd quietens down.

She clears her throat. "Thank you for coming out and helping us raise money for Maui. What happened in Lahaina is truly a travesty. Our family's thoughts and prayers go out to everyone. However, none of this could happen without these two coming up with the idea." Elle turns and claps for Eden and Rush. "Now, enjoy the show."

Rush steps up to the microphone. "We proudly present, Talking Til Dawn."

Once again, the crowd erupts into boisterous cheers. Eden and Rush walk towards us and Eden's arms are spread wide. Jenna and I engulf her in a hug.

"I'm so damn proud of you, Little One."

"Thanks, Daddy."

Jenna releases Eden and welcomes Rush into our fold. The dad in me wants to be angry and tell the kid to bugger off, but he's earned a spot with us. Still, I don't trust him. I'll never trust any man with my daughter.

Hours later, we sit in our makeshift green room, which is a camper donated by the local RV dealer, and wait. Liam sits in one chair, strumming his guitar and muttering the lyrics to the new song we wrote this week, while Harrison sits opposite him, drumming on his thighs. My fingers are idle.

There's a knock on the door and Elle comes in. She's all business, wearing a headset and carrying a clipboard. She speaks to whoever is on the other end and then looks at us. "Are you ready?"

"Born ready," Harrison says as he stands. He goes to her and kisses her forehead.

"Eden and Quinn will join you on stage for your third song."

"What are you talking about?" I ask her.

She looks from me to Liam and widens her eyes. "Seriously? Do I have to do everything around here?"

Liam laughs.

"What the fuck is going on?"

Elle sighs and Liam stands, making the trailer feel even smaller than it is. "Quinn came up with the idea of having Eden sing. They worked on a song in their spare time," Liam says.

"So, why not sing it during Sinful Distraction's set?" I still don't fully understand what's going on here.

Liam places his hand on my shoulder and gives it a good shake. "Come on. We have a show to get to."

He, Harrison, and Elle leave me there, literally in the dark because my niece turned the lights off on her way out. I mutter a string of obscenities as I make my way to the stage. Last one to know anything and the last one to arrive.

We open with "Wake Up" the song Liam wrote about Josie when he was eighteen. It's one of my favorites to perform, probably because I have the luxury of starting it off. My fingers glide over my keyboard as I play the opening bars, then Liam and Harrison join in.

> *Can't take my eyes off of you*
> *I'm a man that's speakin' the truth*
> *This love could make mountains move*
> *Hope you feel the same way I do*
> *I wanna be holdin' you*
> *When the dawn is breakin' through*
> *As yesterday fades with the moon*
> *And forever fills up this room*
> *I wanna wake up with you*

Liam strums his guitar and looks off to the side, where his wife sways to the music. He never takes his eyes off Josie. When the last note finishes, he says, "I love you, Jojo."

Instantly we go into "Painkillers", another song he wrote for Josie, although it has a much different meaning. It was his way of apologizing for the ten years he missed.

Arms of a stranger, a warm blooded kiss,
trying to fill the void, of the one that I miss.
Perfume whispers, lashes and lace,
but I can only hear your voice,
I'm so out of place.
All these painkillers, that's all they are.
Painkillers.

My anxiety skyrockets as the last note fades. The crowd erupts when Quinn and Eden come onto the stage.

"Ladies and gentlemen, I give you Quinn James and Eden Davis," Liam says as he steps to the side.

"Good evening," Quinn says. "Eden and I have something special for you, and with the help of our uncle, we'd like to play it for you."

Eden steps up to the microphone, turns, and looks at me. "Daddy, this is for you."

Liam and Quinn begin the melody, while I stand there, waiting to see what my daughter is about to do.

In the warmth of your embrace, I found my place,
An anchor of love, a memorable face.
From every childhood dream to grown-up days,
You've guided my ways.

Through every wave, through every crash,
You stood by me, strong and tall.
Because of you, I found my strength,
A bond that time can't stretch or length.

Oh, Daddy, you're my guiding star,
No matter how near or how far.
Through every laughter, through every tear,
Your love's the constant treasure that I hold near.

It's probably a good thing I didn't know about this song because I would've never made it through the whole thing, while she sang it to me. I don't know what spurred her to write this for me, or how it came about, but I'm a blubbering mess because of her.

When the last chord is played, I rush to the front of the stage and embrace my daughter. I've never been so thankful for her and her mother for saving me. It hits me then, I probably don't thank Jenna enough for loving me, or giving me our daughter.

I walk off the stage with Eden and into Jenna's arms. "Our daughter is amazing," she says in my ear.

Stepping back, I look into her eyes. "Thank you."

"This wasn't me," she says.

I point to Eden and then to my wife. "Wifey, this was *all* you. You didn't have to give me a chance, but you did, and I will be forever grateful for you, and for Eden." I kiss Jenna deeply, and then hug both my women before heading back onto stage.

"Well now that JD's back, what do you say we finish this show," Liam says to the crowd. They're in agreement with how loud their applauses are.

"For Maui!"

Thank you for reading. For more information about my work, including Forever My Girl, now a major motion picture, find me at www. heidimclaughlin.com.

SWEET CELEBRATION
A LIES, HEARTS & TRUTHS SERIES NOVELLA

HELENA HUNTING

CHAPTER 1 - BJ

"I need your help." I snatch the remote control and hit pause on the pre-recorded episode, grab a chair, spin it around and plunk my ass down so I'm blocking the TV.

Rose, my roommate and longtime family friend, is sitting in the middle of the couch. Lovey, my best-friend, is cross-legged on the floor between Rose's parted legs, having her hair French braided. Lacey, Lovey's identical twin sister, and my other roommate, Quinn, flank Rose on either end of the couch. River, my half-cousin, and his boyfriend Josiah are snuggling in the lounge chair.

Quinn closes his textbook, his brows pulling together in a concerned furrow. "Everything okay?"

"Yeah. Everything is fine." I check the time. My girlfriend, Winter, will be home in less than twenty minutes. Getting everyone together in the same room without Winter present is nearly freaking impossible these days. Not that I'm complaining. I love that she's been absorbed into our makeshift family. But it's hard to plan shit when she's in the room.

"Winter's birthday is coming up."

Lovey claps her hands excitedly. "We're throwing her a party, aren't we? Tell me we're throwing her a party."

"We are totally throwing her a kickass party," Rose announces. "And stop moving, Lovey, or I'll have to start all over again."

"Sorry. I'm just so excited. We're going all out. A big, knock your socks off party," Lovey declares.

"That's exactly what I was thinking." I knew I could count on them.

Winter's life has been hard. She's grown up never really having enough. Not enough money, food, freedom, opportunity. I want to make this birthday special and one to remember.

"I'm in charge of decorations," Josiah declares. He's in drama and designs sets for the school productions, so this is right up his alley.

"I'll help Josiah," River volunteers. "And I'll be in charge of flower arrangements, if there are any flowers to arrange." River looks like he stepped out of a nineties emo video. Despite his black-on-black ensemble, and his almost permanent scowl, he's a wizard with greenery and plants. There's always something blooming in the gardens, even in the middle of Chicago winters. He's recently developed a mild obsession with hibiscus, which would appreciate Hawaii's climate a whole lot more than our current fluctuating temperatures. He potted all of the outdoor ones and brought them inside as soon as the idea of fall arrive.

"We definitely want flowers, even if it's just for centerpieces." I give them the thumbs up.

"So, a dinner party? Someone needs to take notes," Lovey says.

"On it." Quinn trades his textbook for his laptop.

"We need a theme," Josiah says.

"Hockey, obviously." Rose rolls her eyes.

"We should rent out an arena and have a catered dinner. The whole thing should be hockey themed," Quinn adds.

"We'll have some ice time, some fun games where we can shoot on net and win prizes and stuff, and then the serious players can take the ice while the rest of us watch," Rose suggests.

"And after, a buffet dinner and vanilla cake, we should see if we can get some Boones fritters because they're forever Winter's favorite," Lovey adds.

"Oh! I can see this coming together! We'll have twinkle lights and snowflakes decorating the arena," Josiah declares.

"Is there enough time to have jerseys made for everyone? We'll have to invite her hockey team. What day of the week does her birthday fall on?" Quinn asks.

I pull up my calendar to double check. "Saturday, which is perfect."

Quinn cocks a brow. "We should look at Kody's schedule." Kodiak Bowman was my roommate until this year, when he was called up to play for the NHL. He's having a hell of a rookie season. We've been friends since we were kids. He's also dating River's twin, Lavender.

"Oh. Now that would be amazing. Especially if he could bring a couple of the other players along. She has a Grace jersey," Lovey says.

"Really? I didn't know that." Grace has been playing for Philly for the past few years.

"I think she may have tucked it away because of our allegiance to Kody," Lovey explains.

Winter plays for the college team. She's met Kody a few times. She's low-key obsessed with his career. She never misses a Philly game. If she can't watch, she'll record it and avoid listening to sports updates until she can watch the game.

"I'll text him." I fire off a message and we resume our planning.

We're in the middle of talking through the dinner menu, highlighting all of Winter's favorite foods, when the front door opens. We have enough time to tuck lists away and close the laptop before Winter appears in the doorway.

"Hey, what's going on?" she asks.

"Nothing!" Lovey all but shouts. She's a terrible liar. And it's made all the worse when she bites her lips together and tries to sink into the floor while her face turns red.

Winter's brow arches. "Soooo...that's a load of bullshit right there, huh?" Her suspicious gaze swings to me.

"Hey babe, how was practice?" My attempt at changing the subject is weak at best.

"Good. My wrist shot is around sixty miles an hour, which is kickass. Why does it look like you're having some kind of house meeting?" She makes a circle motion with her finger.

I pull my hair tie free, trying to buy myself some time. I should be able to concoct an easy lie, but feeding Winter bullshit kind of sucks, even if I want this to be a cool surprise for her.

"We wanted to plan a birthday dinner for you, but we're having trouble narrowing down your favorite foods. I know you're a fan of pizza, but that you don't love the takeout stuff and prefer when we make it here. When we go out, you always get fries, but at home you're way more likely to go for salad. So, your input would be awesome," Rose declares.

"Oh. You don't need to make a birthday dinner for me. It's not a big deal," Winter waves a hand around.

"It is so a big deal. You're turning twenty. And it's the first time we get to celebrate you." Rose flips open her notebook. "Favorite foods, no thinking, just say the first thing that comes to your mind."

"Boones fritters."

Lacey grins. "We all knew that."

"Give me more." Rose makes a go on motion.

"Uh, chicken parm." Winter tips her head to the ceiling. "And Caesar salad, but the kind Lovey makes, and that lavender lemon ice cream from The Creamery."

"Oh my God, we should go there now. What time is it?" Rose asks.

"Like seven-thirty," I say.

"What time does it close?" Rose asks.

"Eight."

She hops to her feet. "Round 'em up! Let's go!"

And just like that, Rose saves the day. And the surprise.

CHAPTER 2 - BJ

"Delivery for Randall Ballistic." The UPS guy's brown truck is a giant beacon in the middle of our driveway. "I have four more boxes like this." He taps the one on the landing. It's huge. Big enough that Rose could comfortably sit in it.

One thing I didn't account for was the sheer amount of stuff we'd be ordering for this party. Is it over the top? Absolutely. Is it also necessary? Again, absolutely. If anyone deserves an over-the-top birthday party, it's Winter.

But the timing of this delivery couldn't be worse. Winter is coming over in the next few minutes for communal dinner—we join houses several nights a week for family-style meals where everyone contributes something to the potluck—and if we can't hide the delivery fast enough, the whole surprise will be blown. We're less than a week out from the party and we've managed to keep it quiet up until now. It'd be great if we could make it to Winter's birthday without her finding out.

"Rose, Quinn, I could use some help!" I call out.

Rose comes bouncing around the corner. She's wearing an apron covered in a dancing hotdog pattern. Quinn appears a few seconds later, drying his hands on a dish towel.

"What's...oh. Did the jerseys arrive?" Rose jumps up and down, while clapping.

"Yeah, which is awesome. But Winter and the gang will be here in a couple of minutes. We need to hide these boxes." I motion to the UPS truck.

"Shit." Rose makes a face to match her one-word reply.

"Yeah. Quinn, you got any room left for these?"

Quinn runs a hand through his fire red hair and makes a cringey face. "We can put them on my bed for now and figure out what to do with them later?"

"My closet is stuffed." Rose bites her fingernails.

My room is off limits because Winter sleeps at my place about fifty percent of the time. And Rose's room is problematic because they're friends and they sometimes hang out up there. Quinn's room is the only safe place to store things and it's already pretty full.

A white windowless van pulls up in front of the house. The kind used for deliveries, or kidnapping, context dependent. "That better not be more stuff, or we're screwed," I groan.

A familiar dark-haired figure comes around the side of the van carrying a foil covered pan.

"Laughlin? What are you doing here?" Laughlin is Lovey and Lacey's older brother, and the only dark-haired member of their family. He's also the most antisocial of the bunch.

"I came for the potluck. I brought bacon-wrapped water chestnuts and vegan meatballs, but I can't attest to the awesomeness of the latter because I've never made them before."

"I invited him," Quinn mutters.

"Why are you driving a murder van?" Rose asks.

Laughlin arches a dark brow and nods toward the UPS van. "Because my car is in the shop. Also, I saw Quinn's room last week and assumed you'd need a place to store deliveries, so when they offered me an SUV or this beast, I chose this." He thumbs over his shoulder.

"That was unusually thoughtful of you, Dracula," Rose says, almost reluctantly. She and Laughlin have a love-hate relationship that leans heavily toward strong disdain.

"That almost sounded like a compliment, Rosebud," Laughlin replies with zero inflection.

Rose ignores him and grabs my arm. "Go distract Winter for a minute."

"What?"

"Go distract her. Give her an orgasm or something. Just keep her from coming over for five minutes so we can get this stuff in the back of the van without it raising suspicions."

"Oh, right. Yeah. I can totally do that." I bust it down the front steps and sprint down the sidewalk. Winter lives two doors down. I don't bother knocking. "Where's my sexy girlfriend at?" I call out as I open the door.

"In the kitchen!" Winter calls back.

I toe off my shoes and head toward her voice. The kitchen is bustling with activity. Josiah and River are sliding a casserole dish into a giant insulated warming container. Lovey and Lacey are topping their fresh salad with halved cherry tomatoes, and Winter is checking on whatever is in the oven.

"Smells good in here." I tuck my hands into my pockets and try to act natural, instead of like I'm hiding shit from my girlfriend. Which, over the past couple of weeks, I've discovered I'm really fucking bad at. "I thought I'd come give you a hand."

"I think we're good." Lovey's smile looks forced, and her eyes keep darting to the phone on the counter. I assume Rose texted them.

"My buns just need a few more minutes," Winter says.

"Your buns are perfect, babe." I wink at her.

"I could have predicted those words coming out of your mouth," River rolls his eyes.

"It's not an inaccurate statement. Winter wins the ass of the year award." Lovey's still wearing that odd grin.

"We'll bring the salad and casserole to your place and help set the table." Lacey elbows her twin. "You two take your time."

With that, Lovey, Lacey, River, and Josiah file out of the kitchen.

Winter watches them leave. It isn't until the front door closes that she turns to me. "Is it me, or has everyone been really weird lately?"

I frown and work to maintain eye contact. "How do you mean?"

"Three times this week I've walked into the living room and everyone goes silent. And Lovey has been…off? Sometimes it feels like she's avoiding me on purpose." She rubs her temple. "I don't know. Maybe I'm being hypersensitive. I've never had roommates before, so maybe this is normal and I'm reading into things."

I need to give her a nugget of truth to put her at ease. As much as I want this party to be a surprise, it's no good if Winter feels as though she's purposely being left out. I blow out a breath and give her a sympathetic smile. "I'm going to tell you something, but it has to stay between us."

Her eyes flare. "Is everything okay?"

"Yeah. Everything is fine. Lovey's being weird because she's been working on something for your birthday." I hold up a hand when she starts to protest. "It's nothing outrageous." This is true where Lovey's gift for Winter is concerned, so it's not a lie. She, Rose, and Lacey are doing it together. "But she wants it to be a surprise and you know how bad she is at lying."

Winter's nose wrinkles. "Yeah, she's not a good liar at all, although she's good at evading answers so she doesn't have to hurt someone's feelings."

"Yeah. She is." Lovey is a wizard at dodging questions she doesn't want to answer. Or she'll suddenly be busy with something. I imagine that's been her strategy with Winter. I step into her personal space. "Did you think you'd done something wrong?"

She shrugs and runs her hands over my chest and links her fingers behind my neck, her eyes on my chin. "I don't know."

"Babe." I tuck a finger under her chin and tip it up. "Were you worried?"

She rolls her eyes. "I don't know. Maybe. Yes."

"The only secrets people are keeping are the good kind." I brush my lips over hers.

She tips her head and parts for me. I slide my hand into her hair and deepen the kiss. Winter hums into my mouth and presses her body closer.

I break the kiss long enough to ask, "How much time do we have before your buns are ready?"

She grabs her phone from the counter and shows me the timer.

"Let's see how close I can get you to an orgasm before it goes off."

She grins. "You're always good under pressure."

I hook my fingers into her athletic pants and panties and drag them down her thighs. She steps out of them and I lift her onto the counter, drop to my knees, and part her thighs with my shoulders. I run my hands up the back of her calves and kiss the inside of her knee, slowing it down.

Winter bites her lip as I kiss a path up the inside of one thigh, then the other. She slides her fingers into my hair and tries to guide my mouth, but I'm all about taking my time now that I have her to myself for a few minutes.

"The clock is counting down and you haven't even put your mouth on me yet," Winter says breathlessly.

"I'm getting there. How many minutes left?"

"Two and a half."

I hook her legs over my shoulders and nuzzle into her sex.

Her fingers tighten in my hair. "Stop teasing me."

"Stop rushing me," I counter.

She laughs and drops onto her elbow, lip caught between her teeth as my gaze lifts to hers. I kiss the juncture of her thigh, mere inches from where she wants my mouth.

"You're killing me, you know that, right?" she groans.

"So impatient, Snowflake. Don't you trust me to make it good for you?"

I wait until her annoyed gaze meets mine before I lick up her center.

"Oh, thank God." She exhales a relieved moan.

I lap at her, circle her clit with my tongue and suck gently. Enough to bring her close to the edge, but not enough to tip her over. Her hips roll with every stroke of tongue. Just as her legs start to shake, the timer goes off.

She grips my hair with one hand and slaps around on the counter for her phone. "Don't stop, I'm close!"

"If we burn the buns, everyone will know what happened in the kitchen." I chuckle, and she groans.

"They'll already know! I wear my orgasm bliss on my face like a flashing neon sign."

"I'll finish you off while the buns cool," I bargain.

"Fuck! Fine." She releases my hair.

I grab the closest oven mitt and quickly pull the buns out of the oven. I flick one, testing for doneness before I set the tray on the cooling rack and turn back to my girlfriend. She's replaced my tongue with her fingers. Her gaze darts to the front of my joggers. There's no hiding what's going on behind the fabric.

"I want you in me when I come," she declares.

"I love it when our genitals communicate telepathically."

We both grin and she beckons me forward. She pulls my shirt over my head so I'm naked from the waist up, then slides her hand into my joggers. Winter's warm fingers wrap around my length, stroking once before she frees me from my fabric prison. Her thumb slides over the piercing at the tip before she drags her hand back down and guides me to her entrance.

Our gazes meet and then drop as I push inside. I pause when the piercing disappears.

"God, I love the way that feels," she murmurs.

"I love the way you feel." I drag my eyes back to hers as I push in deeper.

"Same. So much same." Winter wraps her legs around my waist and curves a hand around the back of my neck, pulling my mouth to hers as she takes me inside.

It doesn't take long for my easy, slow thrusts to quicken, or for Winter to tip over the edge. Her legs tighten around me and her body quakes with the first orgasm. "Going for two," I tell her.

"We'll be so late for dinner."

"Yeah, but totally worth it."

"Absolutely worth it."

I kiss her again, shifting in time with her hip rolls. I hold off until she tips over into bliss a second time before I pull out. Despite being in the middle of an orgasm, Winter wraps her hand around my length and grabs for the paper towels. She tears a handful free and uses them to contain my orgasm.

We laugh and I drop my head to her shoulder. "Nice reflexes."

She kisses my temple. "I'm quick when it matters."

We clean up, wash our hands—and I wash my face—then load the fresh buns into a basket and head back to my place for dinner.

Everyone's already gathered in the kitchen when we arrive.

"Why is there a murder van parked out front?" Winter asks as she toes her shoes off.

"It's mine," Laughlin replies. "My car is in the shop."

"Oh, well, as long as the back isn't full of candy, I guess that's fine."

Everyone laughs and Lovey excuses herself to the bathroom.

Another near crisis averted.

CHAPTER 3 - WINTER

On the morning of my twentieth birthday, I wake alone. Which is not what I expected. At all. I anticipated waking up with my boyfriend wrapped around me, offering pre-breakfast orgasms. Instead, the space beside me is empty. Although, to be fair, it's going on ten-thirty. I rarely sleep in because of classes and hockey practice.

I roll over to find a bouquet of blue flowers on the nightstand. It's my favorite color. It eases some of the disappointment of waking alone. I've never had the kind of boyfriend who would go out of his way to leave flowers beside my bed on my birthday, let alone ones in my favorite color. I pluck the card from the bouquet and flop back against the pillow. I free the card from the envelope and flip it open.

Morning Snowflake,

Happy 20th Birthday!

I'm sorry if you wake up and I'm not beside you, but I promise today will be unforgettable. There's something special waiting for you in the kitchen.

Love, BJ

I throw off the covers and shiver as the cool air hits my skin. I sleep in a tank and shorts no matter the time of year and add comforters for warmth. I grab a hoodie and pull it over my head as I rush down the stairs. My housemates' doors are open, but no one seems to be in their rooms. Maybe they're part of the surprise in the kitchen. But when I reach the kitchen, it too, is roommate free.

There's a fruit bouquet on the counter, though. One of those awesome ones with chocolate dipped strawberries and pineapples in the shape of unicorns. I pluck the card free and flip it open, smiling as I read the note.

Happy 20th Birthday Winter!

We can't wait to celebrate you today.

Lots of love,

River, Josiah, Lacey, Lovey, Rose, Quinn, BJ, and Dracula

"Am I supposed to eat this on my own?" I muse.

The sound of the lounge chair footrest being closed draws my attention. I'm halfway to the living room when a figure appears in the doorway.

"Mom?"

"Happy birthday, honey!" She smiles and does jazz hands.

I pull her in for a hug. "I thought you were coming up tomorrow because you had to work today!"

She pats my back. "I know."

When I pull back, confused, her smile widens. "I wouldn't miss your birthday, honey."

"But you suck at lying!" It's something she and Lovey have in common.

She laughs. "Well, originally I was on the library schedule for today, but I had my shifts changed around."

"How did you even get here? Did you have to take the bus? Are you staying the day?"

"I got a ride in. And yes, I'm staying the day. I thought we could go for breakfast. BJ left us his Jeep and said he'd be back a little later but had a few things to pick up."

"Was he here when you got here?" My ears are turning red. Which is silly. My mom isn't an idiot. I'm sure she's aware that BJ and I have plenty of sleepovers.

"He was dropping off the fruit bouquet."

"I'll put that in the fridge." We'll demolish it in one sitting if everyone comes over later. I don't even have to make space for it because someone has already gone to the trouble.

"BJ mentioned a pancake house. Maybe we could go there," Mom suggests.

"That's perfect." Usually I would walk, but my mom had a fall in the summer. She's getting around okay these days, but it's probably better to drive. "I'll just throw on some clothes and I'll be right back down." I kiss her cheek and rush upstairs to change.

I grab my phone and notice it has blown up with birthday wishes from my roommates, friends, and my teammates. I scroll until I find one from BJ.

BJ: Morning Snowflake. Enjoy breakfast with your mom. We'll be stealing you soon enough! *kissy face emoji*

Winter: I love that she's here! Looking forward to whatever's in store.

I bite my lip. I have a distinct feeling there's more happening than I realize, but having my mom here is one hell of an amazing gift. In the past, she often had to work on my birthday, regardless of the day of the week. And celebrations were always low-key in our house. Most of the time I'd end up at the diner where my mom used to work. We'd have dinner there so we didn't have to cook, and meals were half price for employees. They'd always give me free cake and ice cream.

This year is so different, though. Mom doesn't work at the diner anymore, and for the first time in my life, the fridge is always full of fresh fruit and vegetables. I don't have to worry about not having enough. It's amazing, but sometimes it's hard not to give in to the worries that it will all just vanish. The longer I'm here though, the more I trust in the security.

I rush back downstairs, wearing a pair of jeans and a hoodie. Mom slides her phone into her purse. "Would you like to open your present before we go?"

"You being here is more than gift enough, Mom."

She gives me a wry smile and pulls a small box out of her purse. "It's just a little thing."

"Thank you." I take the wrapped box from her and peel the small card off the top. It's handmade, as all our cards were in my house growing up. It was out of necessity, but now I do it because it means more. Flowers line the border of the card.

Inside it reads:

Winter,

Happy birthday to my one and only. It's such an honor to be your mom. I love you with all my heart.

xo
Mom

I hug her, already all emotional.

"Get to the good part." She taps the box.

I peel the paper off and need scissors to remove the tape. The contents are nestled in bubble wrap. I free it and smile. It's a hand-painted mug with my name on it. "Did you make this?"

"I went with Clover and some of the other women to this place called The Pottery Palace and we got to paint our own mugs. I thought it might be nice to have your own. And you can put it in the dishwasher."

Growing up in a house where money was always in short supply, we had to get creative with gifts, and this one is perfect. "I love it so much, and it means so much more that you made it for me." I hug her again. "I'll use it every day. Thank you." I put it in the cupboard with the other mugs and nab the keys for BJ's Jeep.

We hop in and make the short drive to the local pancake house.

I usher my mom inside first and come to a grinding halt as soon as I spot the long table near the back. Which contains my housemates, friends and, of course, BJ.

"You were totally in on this," I say.

She shrugs. "I just had to get you here, they did the rest."

I'm swarmed by my boyfriend and my friends. The only people who aren't here are Quinn, who's teaching hockey lessons this morning, Rose, who has some kind of tutoring emergency, and Laughlin, who sometimes shows up to things and sometimes doesn't.

Birthday breakfast is awesome. My friends adore my mom. Afterward, we head back to the house and jump in the hot tub for a soak. I lend my mom one of my bathing suits. She's shorter than I am by a few inches, and she doesn't have my thighs or hockey butt, but we could usually trade clothes, even if mine were sometimes a bit baggy on her.

Mid-afternoon, Rose and Quinn arrive. We make quick work of the snack tray and fruit bouquet, and then we're off to the arena for skating. Mom rides with me, BJ, and Quinn.

"I can't believe you guys got ice time. This is like the best birthday ever." I squeeze Mom's hand and she squeezes mine back.

"We wanted it to be fun for you." BJ winks at me in the rearview mirror.

The arena parking lot is busy, so BJ parks around the back, along with Lovey and River and the rest of the crew. Once we're inside the arena, Mom tells us she'll meet us at the rink. She can't skate because of the accident, but hopefully she won't be too bored.

I expect BJ and I to part ways when we reach the locker rooms, but he follows us inside. I stop short when I see the jerseys hanging from the hooks. They're blue with black and white stripes and they read WINTER'S SQUAD across the front with a white snowflake in the center.

"Oh my gosh." I slap a palm over my mouth and shove BJ's shoulder. "What did you do?" I'm not big on tears. Not the emotional kind, but this is way more than I ever expected. "Did you seriously have jerseys made for my birthday?" I scan my friends' faces. Everyone is smiling. "You were all in on this? This is what you were planning?"

Oh yeah. I'm totally going to cry.

"We love you. You're part of our family now and we do birthdays big. We wanted to celebrate you the way you deserved to be celebrated," Lovey says.

I do that terribly girly thing where I wave my hands in front of my face and try to will the tears not to fall, but it's pointless.

BJ wraps his arm around me and suddenly my friends converge on me. I'm enveloped in a giant group hug. I can't stop smiling, or keep the happy, overwhelmed, grateful tears from falling. Eventually, I get myself together and we all change into our gear. The special jerseys have our names and numbers on the back. The hockey players get their regular number and everyone else gets to pick their favorite, or their birthday.

I don't think it can get any better until I leave the locker room and clomp down the hall to the rink. "Oh come on, seriously? The jerseys weren't enough? When did you have time for all of this?"

The arena has been transformed. Twinkle lights hang from the boards. There are snowflake decals on the plexiglass, along with a banner from one end of the back wall to the other that reads HAPPY 20TH BIRTHDAY WINTER!

The rink is already full of my teammates, and my coaches from Pearl Lake are here too. It's where we all live during the summer months when college isn't in session. But it's not just my coaches, one of which is my boyfriend's dad, his mom Lily, who I adore, has come too. My entire extended hockey family is here.

"This is unreal. I can't believe you pulled this together. For me."

"Hold on to your helmet. Your mind is about to be blown." BJ kisses me on the cheek.

I notice Lavender, River's twin and BJ's cousin, sitting with her mom and mine. She lives in New York right now and designs costumes for an off-

Broadway theater company. Everyone is wearing jerseys, but I notice there are two variations. Because obviously we're going to scrimmage. I'm surrounded by former professional hockey players. Like me, they won't miss a chance to shoot the puck around.

I almost faint as I step out onto the ice and Lavender's boyfriend, one of the most sought-after rookie players in the league, skates up to us. I've met Kodiak Bowman before. More than once. I still get a little starstruck. I figure it's an exposure thing. But then Connor Grace appears beside him, and I lose my ability to speak.

I grab BJ's arm and make a horrible, squeaky sound. I'm going to embarrass the hell out of myself.

Kody gives BJ a hearty back pat. They were roommates up until this year. And they've known each other their whole lives. Then he turns to me. "Hey, Winter. Happy birthday."

"Hey. Hi. What is even happening?" Yeah. Embarrassment is coming for me.

He laughs. "I have it on good authority that you're a Connor Grace fan. I invited him to come out for a visit and to play a little hockey."

I tuck my gloves under my arm. My hands are sweaty and I'm breathing like I've just done speed laps. I wipe my palm on my jersey and shake his hand. "It's so amazing to meet you. In person. Hi. Your career is amazing. You're such a smart player. I need to stop." I release his hand. I'm going to die.

"I've heard amazing things about your skills on the ice. I'm looking forward to playing with you tonight," Connor says with a wide smile.

I'm grateful when BJ's dad and his uncle come over, as well as Kody's dad, Rook. It's helpful that Connor is just as starstruck as I was a minute ago. I get it. I felt the same way when I met them all over the summer and got invited to play on their women's team.

Before we scrimmage, we play games for prizes so everyone can participate. There's an on-ice photo booth set up and we cram as many of us as we can in there, taking a ridiculous number of pictures.

When the games are over, the non-players take a seat off the ice and eat popcorn and snacks while we scrimmage. It's so cool to be on the ice with my teammates and my Hockey Academy coaches, as well as two pro players. I'm on the same team as Connor, which means I'm playing against Kody. Those two run circles around us, but it's so much fun.

After ice time, we all shower and change and head up to the arena restaurant. The back half has been transformed into a party space and half of my friends and hockey family are already there. A huge buffet is set up against the back wall. I grab BJ's hand and squeeze. "Seriously, this is a completely unbeatable birthday. It's the coolest experience ever. I can't believe you got Connor Grace to come."

"His sister is a freshman here, so when Kody suggested it, he was happy to make it work. Plus, he's seen a few of your college games, so he's a fan, too."

"I love you. I can't wait to show you how much with my warm, soft parts later."

He throws his head back and laughs. "Fuck, Snowflake. You're my favorite." He cups my face in his palms and kisses me. But he doesn't make a move to deepen it. Probably because my mom, his parents, and a bunch of his aunts, uncles, and hockey family are all here watching.

Even the restaurant has been decorated. I find out the centerpieces were designed by River, who not only has a green thumb but also a talent for flower arranging. Everything is decorated like my name. It's unreal.

Dinner is literally all my favorite foods. All of them. Everything I mentioned weeks ago when I walked into what was clearly a planning meeting for this incredible birthday extravaganza is on the menu. There are even mini cheese toast appetizers. I try not to overdo it, mostly because I know there will be cake, and if the rest of this day is anything to go by, it will be over-the-top and ridiculously delicious.

I am not even a little wrong. The cake is a hockey rink, and the pucks are mini apple fritters from Boones, my favorite bakery and place of employment when we go home for the summer.

I honestly don't think this day could get any better, but during dessert, Rose, Lovey, and Josiah cue up a video on the massive wall of flatscreen TVs. I almost lose my mind when Kody's entire team wishes me a happy birthday on video. And then come the wishes from friends back home in Pearl Lake. All the people who couldn't be with us today send their love. I get emotional all over again when my high school hockey coach appears on the screen and says she knew I was destined for great things and that she's so glad the Hockey Academy helped me get where I am.

I'm still struggling to keep it together as BJ kisses me, then pushes his chair back and moves to stand at the front of the room. Rose hands him a microphone.

"It's a good thing I don't wear mascara, or I'd have a real problem." I use my sleeve to dab at my eyes.

Lovey slides into the seat beside me and threads her fingers through mine. Mom does the same on the other side.

"We could be here all night talking about how amazing Winter is, and we have a two-hour video that you can watch at home where every single one of the people in this room tells you exactly what you mean to them. But in the interest of letting all the old-timers get home before midnight—"

That earns him some heckles, and a bun thrown at his head. He catches it out of the air and sets it on the table beside him.

"As I was saying, in the interest of time, I was nominated to speak on everyone's behalf." His gaze shifts to me and his smile softens and warms. "Winter, you came barreling into my life out of nowhere."

"Literally since you almost hit her with your Jeep!" Rose yells.

That gets some startled gasps from the parents, and my mom gives me a questioning look.

"Rose is being dramatic. I was coming out of the trail, and he was turning left at the T."

"A roll through?" Mom asks knowingly. Everyone does it.

I nod.

"Thanks for taking that to the grave, Rose." BJ gives her a thumbs up.

She shrugs. "I thought it was common knowledge at this point. And she's here, so obviously you didn't actually take her out with your Jeep."

"We'll be talking about this later," his dad calls from the other side of the room.

BJ blows out a breath. "Anyway. You, Winter, are the most amazing badass I know. You're kind, you're patient, you're a demon on blades, and damn sexy."

"Keep it PG for the parents please!" Lily, his mom, shouts.

BJ rolls his eyes. "Every single person in this room is blessed to know you, Winter. We're all better people for having you in our lives. I'm so damn grateful I get to love you and have you as part of my every day. Happy Birthday, Snowflake." He bends, disappearing for a second. When he straightens, he's holding an exceptionally long box. "We have loads of gifts for you, but you can open them later. This one is from everyone here." He motions for me to come up to the front.

My palms are sweaty as I make my way to him. His smile lights up the room.

"This is way over the top, BJ," I say when I reach him.

"I know. You deserve all the over the top in the world." He kisses me on the cheek and presents the box. It's wrapped in blue paper with thick silver ribbon and a huge sparkling snowflake. "I'll hold it while you open."

I bite my lip as I pull the ribbon free and drape it over his shoulders. His smirk gets laughter from our roommates. Once the ribbon is untied, I peel off the paper and pry the lid off the box. "Oh, no way." My gaze lifts to his, my mouth agape. "For real? It's signed. Oh, it's signed!"

I lift the custom hockey stick from the box and run my hand lovingly over the blade. It's black carbon fiber, lightweight, sleek—stunning. But what makes it special are all the names scrawled in white, silver, and metallic blue marker.

"It's all your coaches and the legends you know, plus Kody's teammates and a few others we know you love," BJ explains.

"This is just…" I'm speechless. And on the verge of tears again. I take a deep breath and try not to lose it before I can thank everyone. I hug the stick to my chest and take in the sea of smiling faces. "This family, found and otherwise, is so incredible. I am so blessed to be part of your world. So thankful for every one of you." I turn to BJ. "Especially you. Thank you for making sure I took all the chances and for being so damn charming."

Everyone erupts into applause, and I spend the next hour thanking each guest for being here. BJ's parents and the other people who came up from Pearl Lake say their goodbyes, since it's an hour and a half drive back. BJ's parents are taking my mom home with them.

"I'll come up for another visit soon, but you should enjoy the rest of your night with your friends. Be safe. I love you."

"I will. I love you, too." She squeezes me and I squeeze her back.

Once the last guests leave, we pack up what's left of the cake—there's a lot and we'll be eating it for days. Everyone pitches in to load the gifts into Laughlin's murder van.

"Is your car really in the shop?" I ask as he and Rose carefully stack boxes like a pair of Tetris geniuses.

He grins. "Yeah. This thing isn't entirely fashionable, but it's been helpful."

"Seriously, it's been a lifesaver on more than one occasion." Rose swaps out two gifts, so they fit better.

Once the truck is loaded, I hop into BJ's Jeep with him, the twins, and Quinn and we head home. With everyone's help, we get all the gifts into the living room in less than ten minutes.

I stand in front of the pile with my hands on my hips. "This is ridiculous."

"Ridiculously awesome." Rose pats me on the shoulder. "You should open this one first, though." She points to one in the corner of the room, leaning against the wall. It's huge, and square.

BJ grabs us all drinks—now that we're home, we crack wine coolers and beers—and everyone settles in to watch me open gifts. It reminds me of bridal showers and the mountain of gifts rivals one.

I open the card first. It's a gift from Lovey, Lacey, and Rose. I tear through the paper and reveal a collage of photos artfully arranged in the frame. It chronicles our friendship, from my first day working with Rose at Boones, my first ever hockey game playing for the Hockey Academy in Pearl Lake, the day we moved into this house, my first college hockey game, to me and BJ cuddled on the lounge chair in this living room. All our adventures are here, with dates and thoughtful little quotes. BJ has something similar in his bedroom back in Pearl Lake and I've always loved looking at it.

"How did I end up with such amazing friends? This is so awesome."

"We'll help you hang it tomorrow," Lovey says as I'm enveloped in a group hug.

I open more gifts, overwhelmed by the generosity of my friends and this hockey family I'm part of.

It's well past midnight by the time I'm done with the pile of gifts. I have lots of new hockey stuff and school supplies, as well as some gift cards that I can use at my favorite restaurants and stores. We're all exhausted from the amazing day. I hug and thank my friends before BJ and I climb the stairs to my bedroom on the third floor.

"I have something for you," BJ says once I've closed the door.

"You already bought me flowers and arranged a huge party, and I got to play hockey with my favorite professional player. You really didn't need to get me anything else," I tell him.

"It's just a little something." He laces his fingers with mine and guides me to the bed.

"Is it orgasms? It's orgasms, isn't it?"

His eyebrows dance. "I'll give you a few of those too, but first..." He produces a small box from his pocket.

I carefully peel away the paper and flip open the box. Nestled inside is a pendant on a silver chain. I bite my lip and stare at the gorgeous, sparkling snowflake, overwhelmed all over again.

"I know you're not a huge jewelry wearer, but I thought it might be nice for special occasions and formal hockey events," BJ explains.

"I love it. And you, so much." I throw my arms around him. I've never had the opportunity to be a jewelry girl. Mostly because if there was extra money, it went toward food and necessities. There was never enough for something like this. And if my dad found it tucked away in a drawer, it would go straight to the pawn shop to feed one of his shitty habits. But now that my mom has left him, everything is different. She's different. Our whole life is.

"Are you sure? It's okay if it's not your thing," BJ says.

"It's my thing now. Will you help me put it on?" I lift the delicate chain from the box.

My fingers are too shaky to manage the clasp, so BJ does it for me, sweeping my hair over my shoulder. Once it's fastened, he presses a kiss to the nape of my neck. The snowflake sits perfectly in the hollow of my throat. It's so much more than a gift, it's a talisman.

"Thank you for today. Thank you for making it so special."

"Anything for you, Snowflake. You know that."

He cups my face in his hands and presses his lips to mine.

This is what I've been waiting for all day. Time with him.

An opportunity to show him how much he means to me.

We undress slowly, taking our time getting to the good part. I thank him with kisses and touches. Love him with my body and words. I'm wrapped in him. In the safety and decadence of his love.

And like he promised, my birthday ends with the sweetest bliss.

NYT and *USA Today* bestselling author, Helena Hunting, writes contemporary romance and romantic comedies, and when she wants to dive into her angsty side, she writes new adult romance under H. Hunting. Follow her at www. helenahunting.com.

I CAN'T LOVE YOU

J.L. BALDWIN

CHAPTER 1 - LORA

"Oh, come on, Loralie! You know he has been dying to go to Hawaii for years. You also know his parents never took him as a kid because they could not afford it. I do not know why the fuck you're making such a big deal about it!" If Logan could look any more ridiculous right now, he would probably have smoke blowing out of his ears. I sighed and shook my head.

"First of all, I hate when you use my full name. It's why I insisted upon all my professors using Lora in my classes. And second, who gives a shit what he does? I certainly don't!"

Logan groaned and paced my bedroom some more. It was bad enough we shared an apartment together which meant I saw his best friend, Mack, more often than I cared to admit, but that also meant he followed us everywhere.

Literally everywhere.

When my parents came up with a family vacation to Hawaii, I jumped at the opportunity. I was on break from my Ph.D program and needed a little getaway. And what better vacation than the beautiful island of Hawaii? I couldn't think of a better place to relax and get some reading done.

"You know he needs to get away from Sophia. She's driving him fucking crazy."

"Then he shouldn't have stuck his dick in her. Repeatedly. Or is that a lesson he can't seem to learn?"

Logan grabbed the chair to my desk and spun it around until he was sitting in it backwards. "Lora, sis, come on. I know you don't want him to go because it will bring up old feelings."

I scoffed at that. "That's crazy."

He raised an eyebrow in a challenge. "Is it though?" No. Yes. I honestly didn't know anymore.

Logan crossed his arms on the back of the chair and just stared at me, the larger muscles of his arms dwarfing the back of the small desk chair. It was easy to tell us apart. Brown hair, brown eyes, and a dark complexion. Thanks to our Polynesian side. But where we might have looked alike, that's where our similarities stopped. On the inside, I'm a bookworm and my brother is a gamer. Two completely different ends of the spectrum. It paid off for both of us because I'm getting a Ph.D in English Literature and my brother founded a huge tech company that could rival some of the biggest companies out there. My brother may not have had the best grades in English or History but when it came to Math and Science, he was a certified genius.

Mack also worked alongside my brother and he has developed some popular games.

"You know Mom and Dad are going to be thrilled to have him go, right? Your argument is pretty much a moot point."

I glared at him as my eyes cut into slits. "I hate you."

Logan's smile lit up his whole face as he grinned. "You love me. And I know you love Mack, even if you don't want to admit it."

My whole face lit up on fire. "That's wrong. Besides, I don't want to be someone's sloppy seconds. Or thirds. He's been around the block quite a few times and I didn't want to catch a disease."

Logan rolled his eyes. "Stop being childish. He doesn't have a disease. I'm sure he gets checked regularly."

"It doesn't matter. Not like I'm sleeping with him anyway."

Logan smirked. "You keep telling yourself that, sis. We all know you turn into a puddle whenever he's around."

I stomped my foot down on the floor hard, like a child. "I do not!"

"Since you're throwing a temper tantrum, I'm assuming you do?" The whole situation was fucked up, to say the least. The last thing we needed was Mack Danvers tagging along on our family vacation. I hated the idea, but knew our parents would take Logan's side because they do love Mack. Logan and him have been friends since they were thirteen and bonded over some dumb video game that was popular that year. They've been thick as thieves ever since.

I sighed, and pinched the bridge of my nose between my thumb and forefinger. "Is he bringing any of his floozies along for the ride?"

Logan grinned then reached into his pocket and pulled out his cell phone. He pushed a couple buttons and a few seconds later, Mack's gorgeous face lit up the screen. "Why don't you ask him for yourself?"

I gaped at him and I didn't know who I was more angry at right now. Logan or Mack. "You had him on the phone?"

He shrugged like it was no big deal. "Knew you would throw a fit about it so I brought in reinforcements."

Mack chuckled, the smooth sound sliding over my skin like silk. He was dangerous for my health. I hated him so much, but the shiver that shot down my spine at his voice was proving to make a liar out of me.

"What's wrong, Lora? You don't trust yourself around me?"

What the hell? "Do you just assume that every girl wants you? Is that how you sleep at night?"

Mack chuckled, then raked his hand down his face in a not-so-oh-my-god-why-was-that-so-attractive-way and shook his head. "No, but sooner or later, they usually cave. They all do. No matter how *stuck-up* they seem to be."

He emphasized the word stuck-up like he was implying something. "What are you trying to say?" I spoke angrily. He was really beginning to get on my nerves and we left for the airport in less than six hours.

"Nothing, sweetheart. Just wondering why some girls are the way that they are."

Sweetheart. Fuck. Why did he have to go there?

"I'm not your sweetheart so stop calling me that."

Mack smiled, and damn if it didn't light up his face. Mack was very much the typical country boy. He had a little bit of a dad bod, but it looked good on him. You would never think he was a smart tech genius like my brother. He liked his trucker caps, his family farm, and going out to the field on a Saturday night for a bonfire.

He loved his calm, relaxing life outside of work. And that was something we always had in common. Doesn't mean we get along, because I still hated him.

"Would you like me to stop calling you that if I brought somebody else with me?"

"You are not bringing anyone else on our family vacation! You're lucky we're letting you come."

"See, Mack? Told her she'd let you come."

"Logan, buddy, I could make such a fucking inappropriate joke about coming, but I would hate to have your sister think any less of me than she already does."

I rolled my eyes then bent over so I was level with the phone and plastered on my best smile because my next words were going to hit below the belt. Literally.

"Mack, I bet if you have a problem telling the joke, then I bet you have a problem performing the act. Plane leaves at five." I pressed the end button on the phone but not before seeing his mouth drop open and I smiled triumphantly.

"Well, this is going to be fucking fun. Any chance of you guys leaving me there?"

I scoffed and smacked his arm. "With any luck, I'll push both of you into a volcano as a sacrifice to the Hawaii Gods."

"That's a bit harsh."

"Don't mess with Texas, bro."

CHAPTER 2 - LORA

We were two, maybe three hours from landing on the island of O'ahu and I had about an hour left of the podcast I was listening to. I felt someone poke the side of my arm and I knew without turning that it was Mack.

"Hey."

I sighed.

He poked again.

"Hey."

I silently plotted his death. Multiple times.

Poke.

"What?" I whisper yelled, whipping the earbuds out of my ears and turned to face him.

Mack smirked, then straightened up in his seat. "What ya listening to?"

"A podcast. Now hush."

Before I could place the bud back into my ear, Mack grabbed it and placed it into his right one. I should be grossed out about sharing an earbud with someone, but for some reason, I wasn't.

He reached over to my phone and pressed play. The sounds of the author filling my ear made me relax back into my seat. I kept sneaking a peek out of the corner of my eye and seeing how he reacted to the podcast. When it was finally over, I slipped my phone back into my bag.

"Did you enjoy that? I hope you learned something."

Mack nodded, then straightened up in his seat. "Thought maybe you were lying at first. Maybe you were listening to one of those dirty smut books you women like to read."

I rolled my eyes. "Romance, Mack. Maybe if you took the time to read one, you'd know how women behave and what they want in a relationship." Thank God I wasn't listening to one of my romance novels. I would have died a thousand deaths of embarrassment if he had caught on. I was conveniently listening to a brother's best friend story and it was getting hot between the hero and heroine. They were fucking in the locker room at the gym and were moving into the shower to avoid getting caught. But he kept fucking her, even after people started coming in.

The idea of public sex should not make me hotter than hell, but fuck if it doesn't.

"What has you so red in the face?" Mack asked in his low, country voice. Great, now he caught me thinking about that damn book.

"Nothing. Nothing at all."

Mack eyed me suspiciously, then turned his attention away and picked up his phone. Thank God. Logan came walking back from the bathroom at that exact time, pulling Mack's attention away even more when Logan started talking to him. I wanted to kill my parents for putting Logan, Mack, and me all in the same row.

"Hey, man. You catch the game last night?" Logan asked, pulling out his phone to check the football scores probably.

"Nah, been too busy working on the farm. My grandparents are thinking about selling it and they want to get it up to par before looking at any potential buyers. I'm really going to miss that place."

"Why are they selling it?"

Mack shrugged. "Guess it's becoming too much for them. I'm thinking about buying it from them, but I know they won't take my money."

"Maybe I will. I spent just as much time there as you did. I wouldn't mind having a place out in the country."

"You hate the country," I said, speaking up and interrupting their conversation.

Logan glared daggers in my direction. "Doesn't mean I don't like the escape every now and then. I'll call them tomorrow and see if they'd want to sell it to me."

"Man, I would love that. It would be nice to still have it around."

"I'll let you know what happens," Logan replied, putting in his own earbuds. The sound of heavy metal could be heard and I shook my head. It's a wonder he wasn't deaf by now.

Leaning my head against the seat, I stared out the window as the clouds rolled by. Flying has always given me a sense of peace and contentment. The ocean below was as blue as ever, and I felt the sun's rays against my skin from outside the small, round window. A gentle poke against my arm brought me out of my serene moment as I slowly turned and met Mack's piercing gaze.

He stared at me, and for the first time ever it seemed like he was seeing through me. The way his eyes flickered as the sun passed over them. Mack was beautiful, I'm mature enough to admit that. He had the typical country boy look. And it worked for him. The dark hair, scruff along the jaw that was turning into a full beard, and the way his eyes twinkled when he smiled and talked about something he loved.

Whoever was lucky enough to capture his heart would get one hell of a guy. I already hated the woman who would manage to tie him down.

As much as Mack got on my nerves, I wasn't blind. I saw what other women see in him. I always have. It's just that when he opened his mouth, annoyance came out. He was one of the people who had the looks, but the attitude didn't match. From the outside, he looked like one of the good ones. Hell, maybe he was and I was just so far out of the loop, I wasn't sure who was actually 'good' anymore. The books I've read proved that the 'good guy' isn't as desired as the asshole with morally gray intentions. Mack didn't have a morally gray bone in his body, and I liked that about him. For all intents and purposes, he was as close to the 'good guy' as one could get.

"Want to join the mile high club?" Just like that, the tender moment of me thinking Mack was a good guy was ruined. Shattered. I scoffed at him and shook my head. "Are you crazy?"

He shrugged like it was normal to partake in airplane sex surrounded by a couple hundred people. "Maybe. But it would be something of a first for me."

"I find that hard to believe. It's disgusting, immoral, and I'm pretty sure illegal." Then why did the possibility of sex in an airplane bathroom make my insides quiver? Clearly, I needed psychological help. Get your shit together, Lora. You are on your way to a Ph.D. You can't be getting distracted.

"Maybe if you got rid of some of that stuck-up attitude, you'd have fun once in a while. Maybe even get laid more often too."

"My sex life is none of your business, thank you." He was really starting to piss me off.

"Awe, now don't be like that sweetheart. It's not like you're a virgin or anything."

When I didn't say anything in response to that, Mack sat up straighter and put all his attention on me. And I wanted to push so far back into the seat as far as I could to avoid his gaze. The gaze that up until a few minutes ago was annoying the hell out of me.

"You're not a virgin, are you, Lora?" He grinned wide, like he was uncovering the biggest secret known to mankind. I wanted to jump out of this plane and into the deep blue ocean. Nothing would have prepared me for that question. Technically I was not a virgin, but the one time in my undergrad year with my on and off again boyfriend was such a horrible sexual experience, I have avoided it ever since. With the exception of my handy vibrator, of course. A girl does have needs.

"Dude, did you just ask her if she was a virgin? Don't make me sick." Logan visibly gagged for emphasis and I flipped him the bird.

"Both of y'all are gross. And leave my sex life out of your mouths."

"Duly fucking noted," Logan said, returning to his music.

Returning to looking out the window, I felt his eyes on me the rest of the flight. I didn't dare turn to look because I couldn't take his scrutiny. Let him think I was a virgin. It was less humiliating than him finding out the truth. Or worse off, making him rehash a past trauma that I would rather stay buried regarding that particular topic.

10 YEARS AGO - LORA

Senior prom was the rite of passage for any girl. It was a night I had been dreaming of my entire life. Second to my wedding day, of course. I wanted everything to be perfect. It was going to be one of the best nights ever.

"Honey, you look beautiful. I can't believe you're growing up and you'll be off to college soon." My mom wiped a tear from her eye and clasped her hands together under her chin, looking me up and down. I beamed and looked back into the mirror at my reflection. The dress was baby pink with so many sparkles. Spaghetti strap with sheer cuffs that hung off to the side, and it dropped just below my knees. I had the perfect silver heels to match. The whole look was elegant, and gorgeous.

"Thanks, Mom. I'm so thankful for this night. I can't believe it's finally here." I had spent many years saving up by helping tutor kids to get the money for my dress. When it came time to buy it, my mom insisted upon taking the money and putting it into a savings account for me for when I'm

away at college and buying the dress herself. It was her little last gift before I left next year.

"Is your date here yet?" she asked as she dried her tears. My dad brought her a tissue and she blew her nose loudly. I shook my head and picked up my matching silver clutch.

"I'm meeting him there."

"He's not picking you up?" my dad asked in a stern voice. "That's not very gentlemanly of him. I will want to have a firm talking to about treating you like a lady."

"Daddy! It's fine. It's how dating is nowadays. Don't worry so much. Logan is driving me. He's meeting his date there too."

Logan came barreling down the stairs just then and he stopped when he saw me standing there.

"You look beautiful, sis!"

"Thank you." I blushed. "You look pretty handsome yourself."

"Come on, let's get a picture."

Logan wrapped his arm around my waist and pulled me against him. I smiled and shook my head. "You know, I hope when we're old and gray and have lost our memory, we don't look back on this and think we're each other's dates."

Mom snapped a few pictures and Logan and I made silly faces before he spoke. "Dating me wouldn't be all that bad. Think of Flowers in the Attic."

I gagged. I never could read that book, despite how all my friends raved about it. "No thank you. Not gonna happen."

"I was joking. But we're going to be late if we don't get going."

We told our parents goodbye and when we were in the car and on our way, did Logan finally say something.

"You didn't tell them you don't have a date?"

"God no. They'd want to set me up with one of their co-workers' sons. I was not dating a trust fund baby." Someone who had everything handed to them their entire life. No way. I wanted a guy who worked hard and was still sweet as apple pie to the woman he loved.

Someone like Mack, Logan's best friend. He worked on his family's farm and it showed. Even at seventeen, he was so much larger than boys our age. And the girls flocked to him.

Me included.

We got to the dance and Logan kissed me on the cheek before he went in search of his date. I couldn't remember her name, but it was pretty. Just like her. We got along and for once, I didn't hate one of his girlfriends. I walked across the dance floor and smiled at a few of the book club members. They waved me over and before I took a step, a strong hand wrapped around my wrist and tugged me roughly against a hard chest. I gasped and stumbled, but caught myself by bracing both hands on this stranger's chest.

"Whoa, there. Careful, darlin." That voice. I looked up and my stomach plummeted to my feet. Mack towered over me at six foot two.

All I could do was squeak out a measly, "What's up?"

"Thought maybe you'd want to dance." The smooth baritone of his voice sent shivers down my spine. I nodded, and waved apologetically to the book club. When an insane upbeat song came through the speakers, Mack spun me around and we danced together. It felt like a dream. I was dancing with the boy I had been crushing on for four years.

Only he wasn't a boy anymore, and I wasn't a girl.

He was a man, and I was very much a woman. Who wanted to do what I have heard for years.

Mack wrapped his strong arms around my waist and pulled me until I was flush against his body. My soft to his hard. It was a perfect mixture of pleasure and suspense. I felt his rough callused fingers press firmly into my lower back and the distinct hardness of his dick pressed against my thigh.

Holy shit. Was Mack turned on by me? No, it couldn't be. I gasped and Mack seemed to have picked up on the cue because he stepped back. The look on his face changed from fun and flirty to sorrow in an instant.

"Shit, I'm sorry, Lora. I didn't know... I can't control it sometimes."

I reached for him, eager for him to put his hands on me again. "No, no. It's okay. I, um..." Maybe we should take this somewhere more private. "Follow me." I grabbed his hand and led him out of the gym and into the night air. The chill in the air did nothing to cool down the heat that was radiating throughout my entire body.

Mack regarded me curiously, then rubbed the back of his neck nervously. "What's going on, Lora? Look, I think you're really pretty and I think that you're awesome, we have a lot in common and I guess I got caught up in the moment..."

Before he could say anything else or possibly risk ruining this amazing moment, I just blurted out what had been on my mind for a while now. "I want you to take my virginity."

Mack's whole body froze. He dropped his hand and took a step toward me. I stood there and waited. Agonizingly waited for him to say something, to confess something. Of what, I had no idea. I just felt like there was something there that was not one-sided.

"Loralie," he whispered, closing his eyes and letting out a sigh. Oh, no. Whenever he used my full name, knowing I hated it, was never a good sign.

"I... I can't, Lora."

My emotions came flooding out as I let out a sob. "Why? I thought you liked me?"

We had been more flirty than usual, and I thought it meant we were starting something. I knew Logan wouldn't care as long as we were both happy. But maybe I was wrong about this whole thing.

He took two strides and cupped my face, wiping my tears away with his thumbs. "Lora, baby. Sweetheart, it's not that I don't want to. You are so beautiful, and any man would be damn lucky to be your first." He dropped his hands, and it felt like the last piece of my broken heart fell along with it.

"But that man is not me."

"But, why? I just want to know why."

Mack sighed, and raked a hand through his hair, pulling on the strands. "Because I'm not a relationship type of guy."

"What's that supposed to mean?" It made no sense.

"I don't want a relationship, Lora. I don't want to be tied down to one woman. And I would hate to be your first then turn you away."

My lips parted as my eyes stung with unshed tears. "You'd do that to me?" Surely he was just messing with me and he wouldn't actually hurt me like that. Logan would kick his ass.

"Yes." He didn't even hesitate. The first tear fell down my cheek and hit the top of my dress, just above my heart. The one that has now shattered into a million pieces. Reaching down, I picked up my clutch that had fallen to the ground and pulled out my cell phone.

"Lora, what are you doing?"

"Texting Logan. I want to go home."

He snatched the phone from my hand and shoved it into his pocket. "No, I am not going to let you ruin your prom night because of me. You are going to go back in there and find somebody who is fucking worthy of you because it sure as fuck ain't me. You got that?"

Trying one final time to get my phone back, he stepped out of my way. I held the clutch to my chest as more tears started falling.

"Fuck you, Mack Danvers. I hope you never find a woman who is worthy of you because she doesn't exist."

I ran back into the school, bypassing the gym completely and ran straight into the girls' bathroom and cried my eyes out for the rest of the night.

CHAPTER 3 - MACK

Every straight man in a fifty-mile radius would be tripping over themselves if they had the kind of view I had right now. I tossed the football back to Logan while periodically making sure he didn't toss it back to me while my attention was focused elsewhere. Long tan legs meeting up with an already too small yellow bikini. I swallowed and turned my head at the right time that the football came hurtling toward me.

"Dude, pay attention!" Logan yelled then chuckled when it almost smacked me upside the head.

Lora didn't even give us a second glance. She had her head buried in whatever book she was reading. Periodically, she would kick her legs up and down. It was such a carefree motion, that you wouldn't think she was as stressed out as she was. From what Logan has told me, school was kicking her ass and I hated seeing her so stressed out.

"Boys and Lora, we're going in to make some lunch. Be inside in fifteen minutes," Logan and Lora's mom, Mindi, said. Her and her husband, Harry, gathered their beach towels and put them into their bags.

"Sounds good," Logan said.

"Yeah, be in shortly," Lora said, turning back to her book.

When their parents had gone into the house, Logan jogged over, grabbed the football, then without warning, tossed it toward Lora. The football bounced off one of her butt cheeks and landed beside her a few feet away. I laughed as she whipped around, but the image of her butt cheek jiggling like that will forever be burned into my brain.

"Stop being so immature, Logan!" She yelled and picked the ball up and tossed it back to him angrily. I chuckled and shook my head. "Whoa, what an arm. You could have made quarterback at some point with a throw like that."

"Why don't you put that book down and join us? Do something other than read for a change." I couldn't help but goad her. It was, after all, our thing.

She scoffed, then put the bookmark in her book and slammed it shut. Lora turned and glared in our direction before standing up and wrapping her towel around her tiny waist. "For your information, I like to relax and enjoy myself while I'm on the beach. Too bad you can't do that for five minutes."

"We actually like to have fun. Not waste our time by reading, Loralie." At my remark, she flipped me off then did the same to Logan. Something about her anger really got under my skin and made my blood boil, but it was sexy as hell.

"Both of y'all can just get a life. Jesus!"

With that, she stormed off toward the house and left Logan and me alone. He laughed and tossed the ball to me. "You really have to stop giving her such a hard time. You know she had that crush on you."

"Yeah. But it's kinda fun."

"You're such a dick sometimes."

It was just like that whenever she was around. She got under my skin and made me say things I wouldn't normally say. Hell, maybe I was being too harsh on her. I held up a hand at Logan then jogged toward Lora and caught up with her before she could make it to the house. I got to her just in time by wrapping my hand around her elbow.

"Hey, wait." She turned around and leveled me with a scrutinizing glare. "I'm sorry for being such a dick."

She scoffed, and hiked her bag further up onto her shoulder. "Yeah, sure you are. Which is why you keep doing it."

I ran my hand down my face. "What can I do to make it up to you?" Reaching down, I clasped her hand in mine. "Come on, darling. Don't be mad."

Lora's cheeks reddened and she looked away. She sighed, then turned her head back to me and glared at me with those chocolate brown eyes. They were the same shade of brown as my best friend's, but on her, they were so much more beautiful.

"You can start by leaving me alone. I think you've done enough damage for a lifetime."

Before I could ponder what she meant, she stormed away and Logan's timing couldn't have been more perfect when he yelled, "Why don't you two just fuck already and put everyone out of their misery?"

Lora stopped dead in her tracks and whipped her head around and glared at her brother. She flipped him off again then screamed out in frustration and stormed into the house. I stood there and watched the sway of her hips as she ran up the stairs.

The whole conversation was playing over in my head. What did she mean by damage? I wanted to ask her but Logan jogged up beside me and tossed the football into the chair beside the pool. I followed him inside the house and the cold air conditioning hit me and instantly cooled my sun-kissed skin.

"Kids, well, not kids. Anyway, just letting you know that Harry and I have reservations for a romantic dinner tonight on the beach so you'll be on your own for dinner. I'm sure you won't burn the house down." Mindi laughed at her joke and handed each of us a sandwich she had made. I took mine and sat at the bar in the kitchen. Lora sat at the opposite end and Logan sat between us.

"I'm sure we could find something to do," Logan said, not looking up from his sandwich.

"Well, I have to study, so I'll be busy," Lora replied, popping a grape into her mouth.

"Studying on vacation? Even that's a bit much."

"Not like you would know anything about that, now would you?"

I could tell the second the words came out of her mouth she instantly regretted it, but I did my best to not let it show it bothered me. She muttered a whispered 'sorry' before going back to eating her sandwich.

After high school, I never went to college. Didn't need to since I was working the farm. And I never regretted it once. Until now.

"Loralie Jane! You apologize to Mack, right this instant!"

I held up a hand, smiling gently. "No, it's quite alright, ma'am. I know I didn't go to college and I'll have to live with that. Not all of us have the kinds of smarts required for college."

Lora's eyes locked on me and we had a whole silent conversation with those looks alone.

Sorry.

No, I'm sorry.

Let's apologize to each other by fucking our brains out.

Okay, maybe that last thought was mine. But I hoped she had the same one. Lora finished her sandwich and tossed the plate into the trash. She walked over and gave her parents each a kiss on the cheek. "Have fun at dinner tonight. I'm going to turn in early and get a jump-start on that studying."

Leaning up off the chair, I wanted to say something to ease the tension. I hated having this tension between us, but this was how it was between Lora and me. We fought constantly and it never ended well.

"Dude, just let it go. She'll cool down and be fine tomorrow."

What if she wasn't though? We fought but we never, not once, made it personal. That was off-limits. So, something changed. I just wish I knew what.

CHAPTER 4 - LORA

No matter how hard I tried, I could not fall asleep. I thought reading would relax me, and get me to stop thinking about Mack's lame excuse for an apology, but it did nothing. I sighed heavily, then threw the covers back and sat up. The clock read nearly two in the morning. Great, that's just fantastic. Leaning my back against the headboard, I picked up my phone and scrolled through my notifications. Various social media icons stared back at me and zero desire to open a single one was making itself known.

Damn it. Double damn it.

I knew the reason. I knew exactly why I couldn't sleep. Two words. Two lazy smiled, panty melting, drop dead gorgeous words.

Mack Danvers.

Triple damn it.

He was so hot and cold, I couldn't figure him out. One minute he was giving me shit then the next he was apologizing. Or at least attempted a half-assed apology. I shook my head and scooted up and out of bed. Maybe some time on the beach will give me some clarity. I grabbed my blanket and my phone, and walked outside and found a spot on the sand. It was warm still, but cool enough so I didn't sweat without doing anything.

"What am I doing?" I muttered, pulling my knees up to my chest and just watched the waves. The sound of the ocean was always calming and relaxing. Something about the waves breaking and leaving, then turning around and repeating the same thing over and over again. Maybe waves were like snowflakes. No two were the same. It sounded a lot like my life. No matter how hard I tried, I kept repeating the same patterns over and over again.

"No, seriously, what the hell was I doing?" I muttered again, hoping someone out in the universe would hear me and give me an answer.

A low chuckle caught my attention and a warm body settled in beside me. "Well, talking to yourself for starters. Second, you might not want to do that in the middle of the night where people might think you're crazy."

I scoffed. "Yeah, crazy. What are you even doing down here, Mack?"

"I was up and saw the light from your phone light up your face so I thought I'd join you."

"Couldn't sleep either?"

"Nope."

My lips twitched with the barest hint of a smile, but I pulled it back. "Do you have any idea why we hate each other?" I asked, deciding to just say fuck it and throw caution to the wind.

He whipped around to look at me, shock and confusion written on his face. Or what I can make out of it in the darkness. "I don't hate you, Lora."

"Could have fooled me," I replied.

"What makes you think I hate you?"

A million different reasons flashed through my head at that single question. What could I say to make him not hate me? We bickered constantly and I hated it. Sometimes I wished we could get along just once, but I knew that was never going to happen.

"You seemed to always try and pick a fight."

He smirked. "I think you got that backwards, sweetheart."

I gasped. "I do not! I think you're mistaken."

"Ding, ding, ding. We have a winner. You just proved my point."

My mouth opened and closed like a fish. I shook my head and looked away, angry at myself for even entertaining this ridiculous conversation. "You're insane."

"Nah, I'm pretty normal."

"You're also extremely annoying."

"Not a word women would usually use to describe me, but okay."

"Ugh. You're insufferable!"

"And you have anger issues."

"I have anger issues? Pray tell."

He waved a hand in the air in a circular motion. "Just like that. You say shit like 'pray tell.' Who says stuff like that?"

"I do! It's supposed to be said by someone who has a college education."

Oh, shit. I felt the shift in the air no sooner did the words come out of my mouth. His whole face hardened and he pulled back a few inches, putting way more distance between us than I would have liked.

"Mack, I..." I started to say, but before I could get the word out, he stood up and picked up his blanket. Shaking it angrily, he slung it over his shoulder. Before he walked away, he looked down at me with the coldest stare I had ever seen from him.

"You know something, Lora? I don't know why you feel the need to keep throwing the fact that I don't have a college degree in my face. But you keep sitting on your fucking high horse all you want if it makes you feel better. I never regretted choosing not to go to college, not once. I like my life on the farm, but clearly that's not good enough for you. I don't expect you to like it or hell, even accept it. But I've made peace with it and love my farm life. So, have fun out here on the beach with your thoughts and I'll see you later."

"Mack, I'm sorry, okay!" Standing up, I ran until I caught up with him and grabbed his hand. "Please, I'm sorry. I don't know why I keep saying it. I just...I don't know. I'm sorry." I was crying now and tears were streaming down my face in waves from the guilt. Hurting Mack was a low blow that I constantly took. It made no sense, but it seemed to be the one that I always went for.

"Lora." Mack growled, then he dropped his blanket and lowered his head then shook it. "Fuck it."

He turned around suddenly and brought his hands up and cradled my face between them and brought his lips down onto mine, capturing them in a brutal kiss. I gasped in surprise, parting my lips slightly which only made him kiss me deeper. He swallowed my gasps and kissed me passionately and without mercy, he left me with no other choice but to grip his waist and pull him closer. This was what I've wanted since I was thirteen years old.

Mack. Kissing me.

Mack. Making me his in every way.

Giving into the feelings I suspected he shared with me since we were teenagers.

He broke the kiss and trailed his lips down my jaw until I was a panting mess of goo right there on the beach. Mack nipped my earlobe and the slight pain shot all the way down to my core.

"Mack," I whimpered his name so softly, I didn't think he heard it.

"You drive me so fucking crazy, Lora. First you piss me off, then you turn me the fuck on with your sass."

I smiled despite the erotic emotions he was pulling from me. "It's a gift."

Mack chuckled then pulled away and rested his forehead against mine. He sighed then closed his eyes against the onslaught of emotions that were shared between us. I felt them. I'd hoped he felt them too. There were a million reasons why we shouldn't work, but another million why we should.

Seventeen-year-old me would be over the moon if she could see us now.

I wanted him to pull me back to his lips and lay me down onto the beach and own me completely.

But I knew those dreams were fleeting because when he sighed and muttered "shit" then pulled away, I felt him pulling away more than just physically. He was pulling away emotionally too. I was losing him, right when I thought I got him.

"I like you, Lora. I know it's insane, but I like you. I said it before on your prom night and I'm saying it again. I'm not right for you. I won't commit to you. I won't commit to any woman. I'm not a one-woman man, darling. I'm sorry."

The memory of prom night came flooding back instantly, and the feelings that were swirling around earlier left just as soon as they came. "You remembered?"

He nodded. "Of course I do. I'll never forgive myself for hurting you that night. But I meant what I said back then, and I still mean it. I'm not right for you, baby. You're better off with someone who actually can commit and stay loyal to you."

"Then why did you kiss me?" I pressed my fingers against my swollen lips, the kiss forever branded on them.

He sighed, and looked positively destroyed by what he was about to say next. "To remind myself of what I'll never be able to have."

"It doesn't have to be this way, Mack." I knew he felt the passion we shared in that kiss. There was no way he didn't feel the intense chemistry between us. I *wanted* him to feel it, then maybe, just maybe, he'd want to stay.

He nodded. "It does. I'm sorry, Loralie. I truly am."

With those words, he turned around and walked back into the house, leaving me standing there with a head full of memories, and a twice broken heart that will never be the same again.

CHAPTER 5 - LOGAN

"Has anyone seen Loralie?" Mom asked as she walked through the house, looking all around. I walked into the kitchen to grab a bottle of water. I didn't see her at all this morning. Checking my phone, I saw it was nearly noon. Way past when she should have been up and about.

"She wasn't in her room?" I asked.

Mom shook her head. "No, I just went in there to wake her up because it's not usual for her to be sleeping in this late."

That's odd. And completely unlike her. What was going on with her? I went and tried to talk to Mack but he cussed me out and said he couldn't sleep last night so he was going to sleep in today. So he was out of commission for a while. I pulled out my phone and sent her a quick message, asking her where she was.

"She's been acting really strange lately. I hope everything's going okay with school."

I nodded. "I think so. She never complained about it." Other than being stressed out sometimes, she rarely complained. Come to think of it, Lora never complained about anything. She always seemed to be calm, cool, and collected. Except when Mack was around then it became an all-out war between those two. If the not-so-obvious sexual chemistry wasn't so thick between them, which grossed me out but whatever, I would have thought they actually hated each other.

My phone dinged with a text message and I recognized my twin's ringtone instantly. When I looked over the message, my heart fell to my stomach. "Shit," I muttered.

"What?" my mom exclaimed, running over to see the message but I read it out loud to her.

Logan— Tell Mom and dad that I'm sorry, but I wasn't feeling well and decided I didn't want to be sick on vacation so I caught a flight early this morning and came home. It was totally last minute and I didn't want it to happen this way, but please tell them I'm sorry for ruining vacation. Also, tell Mack what happened last night was fine. And to forget about it. He was right.

"She left. She said she wasn't feeling good and caught a flight back this morning."

"What?" Mom and Dad said at the same time. "I'm calling her," Mom said before she raced off to their bedroom and for sure was blowing the whole state of Texas up at this point.

"What's going on?" Mack asked with a yawn and scratched his stomach as he walked out of his room.

"Lora left this morning. She's on her way home."

"What the fuck?"

"She said to tell you that what happened last night was fine, and to forget about it. Also, you were right. What does that even mean?"

He ran both hands down his face and breathed out a huge breath. "God damn it, Lora."

"What did you do to my sister, man?" I stepped forward, ready to go toe to toe with my best friend if he hurt her. Dad stepped in between us just in time though.

"Hey, easy now." He turned to Mack. "What happened?"

Mack looked like he didn't want to say anything, but I guess the look I gave him made him talk. "Okay, well, last night we both couldn't sleep so we were on the beach, talking. Then we got into an argument and said shit we didn't mean. I kissed her."

Not at all surprised about that. It was bound to happen eventually. "Then what happened?"

"I brought up prom."

"You didn't?"

He nodded. "I did. And said the same way I felt then hasn't changed and I still won't commit to her."

"I'll fucking kill you. Don't you know she still cares about you, Mack?"

He rolled his eyes at me. "Don't you think I fucking know that? Even though she likes to throw the fact that I didn't go to college in my face, she drives me fucking crazy."

"She's hurting, you idiot! The only man she's ever cared about, possibly even loved, didn't want her and you confused her even more by kissing her." Dad was doing everything he could by keeping me from pummeling in my best friend's face. I wanted to knock his ass out right then and there, but I knew it would only make the situation worse.

"So, what do you want me to do, huh? Say I'm going to be with her and only her for the rest of my life? I can't do that."

"Oh, that's bullshit and you know it. She wanted you to be with her when we were teenagers and even ten years later, you still can't pull your head out of your own ass because I know damn well you feel the same. You can try and hide it all you want but I know better."

Mack sighed, then pulled out his phone and dialed Lora. He dialed over and over but she wasn't answering. "She's either getting no reception or blocked me. I don't know."

"You better figure it out and also figure your shit out too."

Mack nodded, then ran a hand through his hair. "I'll fix this, man. I'll try to fix it the best way I know how."

"For everyone's sake, I hope you do."

Hope you enjoyed reading this little short from me! I had a lot of fun writing this story! Want to stay up to date on what happens after Mack found out that Lora left Hawaii? Follow me at @authorjlbaldwin

BEACH, PLEASE!

JAMIE K. SCHMIDT

CHAPTER 1 - KAILANI

August 8, 2023

Kailani Nakamura stepped out onto the lanai, the warm ocean breeze fanning her heated skin. She paused to take in the postcard view—palm trees swaying, the sound of waves crashing on Ka'anapali's pristine shore. This was her happy place. It was only marred by the haze from the brush fires that had been burning since early this morning.

She closed her eyes and imagined herself underwater, weightless, with a tropical fish gliding silently beside her. The image was so real she could almost feel the cool water on her skin. No sharks in sight. In fact, there were no sharks anywhere, in the whole world. Kailani opened her eyes to stare out at the shimmering blue ocean. She had always been fascinated by marine life and longed to learn more about the mysteries of the deep. Ever since she was a little girl, she dreamed of becoming a marine biologist. But she was terrified of sharks.

"Kailani, table seven needs bussing," her supervisor Tia called from inside the bustling dining room.

Someday, she thought, *I'll be a marine biologist instead of a waitress. I just need to save the money for college.* Her dream felt so close here but also impossibly far away. Her family was struggling to make ends meet, and they needed the money from her job here. With her father unable to work because of his injuries, Kailani couldn't let them down, even if it meant postponing her own dreams.

Tucking a loose strand of inky black hair behind her ear, Kailani hurried back inside the resort. She wove between tables crowded with tourists enjoying the award-winning brunch at the Palekaiko Beach Resort.

As she cleared empty plates, Kailani overheard a family gushing about spotting sea turtles from their oceanfront cabana. She smiled to herself, knowing the green sea turtles liked to congregate near Palekaiko's rocky outcroppings. She had snorkeled a bit out there when she was feeling brave. Sharks seldom came in that close. But seldom didn't mean never.

"Order up!" The clatter of plates from the kitchen jolted Kailani back to reality. With a resigned sigh, she straightened her crisp white apron and headed back out to the dining room floor.

The next table over flagged her down after she delivered a large stack of taro pancakes topped with sliced bananas.

"Was everything satisfactory?" she asked brightly, already stacking their empty plates.

The man nodded. "It was excellent, thank you. We're here celebrating our anniversary—twenty-five years today." He smiled at his wife, who blushed.

"That's wonderful, congratulations," Kailani said. "Let me bring you a complimentary dessert for the special occasion."

As she walked toward the kitchen, Kailani ruminated about lasting love. She wondered if she'd ever find someone who looked at her the way that man looked at his wife. Shaking off her romantic musings, she retrieved a slice of lilikoi cheesecake and added an artistic drizzle of mango coulis. She carefully carried it back to the anniversary couple.

"A special treat for your special day," she proclaimed, placing it before them with a flourish.

"This is so nice of you, thank you so much," the wife said earnestly.

"My pleasure."

As she cleared more tables, Kailani's gaze was continually drawn to the ocean outside. She'd love to go for a swim, but there had been shark sightings recently. One of her best friends growing up had almost lost her arm when a shark mistook her friend's surfboard for a seal.

The dark plumes of the smoke in the distance worried her. The brush fires seemed to be getting worse. Poking her head outside, she could smell the acrid smoke. As calmly as she could, she went inside the lobby to see if there were any news updates.

Security Chief Holt Kawena was having an intense discussion with Amelia Kincaide, the resort manager.

"Those fires are getting close. We need to gather everyone inside," Amelia said.

"You're going to cause a panic," Holt warned.

"Not if we remain calm. I've already sent Hani and Makoa home to see about their families. You and Joely should get started rounding all the guests up. The Maui Emergency Management Agency has recommended we start sheltering in place for the next few hours."

"I can help too," Kailana said.

Amelia glanced up and smiled. "Thanks. I'd appreciate that. I'll let Tia know we've taken you away."

Kailani wondered how the authorities would evacuate all of the people safely. She thought of the families in Lahaina and the surrounding areas. The fires were brutal, and she hoped everyone would be all right. Despite her own nervousness about the encroaching flames, Kailani knew the resort had time to formulate a plan if the fire got worse.

She hurried to the beachside cabanas to alert the guests who were sunbathing and swimming. She spotted a family with two young boys building a sandcastle near the water.

"Excuse me, I'm so sorry to interrupt," Kailani said gently. "But we need everyone to return to their rooms for now."

The mother's eyes widened in alarm. "Are we in danger?" She turned to her husband. "Richard, get the boys!"

As they gathered their belongings, Kailani gave them a reassuring smile. "No, this is only a precaution. We'll make sure you stay safe. Just follow the staff's instructions once you're back inside."

After making sure the family headed indoors, Kailani scanned the shoreline. She noticed a young couple far out into the turquoise water, seemingly unaware of the danger.

Kailani's heart raced. She would have to go into the water to warn them. But her fear of sharks made her hesitate. What if one was lurking right now, waiting unseen below the surface?

"Please come back!" she yelled to the couple, waving her arms. "You need to come in."

At last, they heard her and began swimming back. She felt like a coward. She could have taken a zodiac out there. She didn't have to swim. But she had this stupid fear that a shark was just waiting for a chance to chomp on her, whether she was in a little inflatable boat or not.

As the evening went on, the air took on an acrid smell of smoke. In the distance, angry orange flames lit up the evening sky.

The fire was spreading faster than anyone had anticipated.

Kailani helped the staff guide panicked guests to safe areas. Suddenly, the power cut out, plunging the lobby into darkness. Cries of alarm erupted as the emergency lights flickered on.

NAKOA

The sunlight glinted off the turquoise water as Nakoa's father, Ikaika Mahelona, steered the boat away from the dock in Makena.

"Aloha, folks," his father greeted their passengers. "Welcome aboard the Island Breeze. I'm Captain Ike, and this is my son, Nakoa. He's just back from the mainland. We'll be taking you out to Molokini Crater today for some snorkeling."

Ike flashed an easy smile at the excited tourists, his brown eyes crinkling at the corners. He lived for days like this, out on the open ocean, sharing the beauty of Maui with visitors. After Nakoa checked that the passengers were settled, he signaled his father, who opened up the throttle. Ike was in his element out here, far from the stresses of land.

Nakoa, on the other hand, had been dying to get off the island all his life. Not that it wasn't beautiful. It was. He just wanted more opportunities and more choices than the island of Maui could give him. But life had other plans. The pandemic had eaten up all his savings, and his parasailing company in Marina Del Rey went tits up.

As Ike guided the boat around the southern tip of Molokini, the crescent-shaped islet famous for its pristine reef, a hush fell over the boat. Nakoa grinned, inhaling deeply. He coughed as he got a lungful of smoky air instead of salty ocean breeze. He glanced at the Maui coastline in concern. The brush fires from early this morning were still burning. The high winds on the island weren't helping matters.

He couldn't think about that now, though. He pushed down his unease, focusing on his job. Nothing he could do about those fires from out here. Time to make sure these folks had the snorkeling trip of a lifetime. Still, in the back of his mind, he couldn't stop thinking about the smoke darkening the horizon. After cutting the engine, Ike dropped anchor.

"First time snorkeling?" Nakoa asked a nervous-looking woman clutching the rail. She nodded hesitantly.

"Don't worry. Even though the water's a bit rough because of the wind, you'll see a lot of fish. You're gonna love it," he reassured her. "I've been doing this for years and still get a rush every time I jump in. It's like entering a whole new world down there."

The woman smiled, relaxing her white-knuckled grip on the rail. He pointed out a spinner dolphin pod in the distance and then got down to business of getting everyone in the water.

"All right, who's ready to get wet?"

They pulled on fins and masks and one by one took the plunge into the warm water. Nakoa divided his attention between his passengers as they swam around and the distant smoke steadily blowing west. He turned on his transistor radio and popped an earbud in so he could listen to the news. Roads were being closed, and there were reports of downed power lines. He squinted into the distance, but the smoke made everything hazy.

By the time everyone was back on board, dark smoke almost obscured the Lahaina coastline. He didn't like what he was hearing over the radio. He and his father exchanged worried glances.

"Hey, Cap, what's going on over there?" a passenger asked, his voice tinged with concern.

Ike hesitated, not wanting to scare anyone. "Looks like there might be some fires burning inland," he said casually.

His nonchalant tone belied the unease they both felt. Lahaina was a popular historic district, full of old wooden buildings. Nakoa thought of his friends, the restaurants he loved, the charming streets lined with art galleries. "Please let the firefighters get it under control soon," he prayed silently. As he pulled up the anchor, he heard over the radio:

"Major fires burning through Lahaina. People are jumping in the water to escape. The Coast Guard is en route, but it may be too late. We need any and all small crafts to assist."

Nakoa's gut twisted.

Without hesitation, Ike radioed back, "Coast Guard Maui, this is Island Breeze. I'm fifteen minutes from Lahaina Harbor with rescue gear aboard. I'm heading in to assist."

The passengers murmured anxiously, but Nakoa steeled himself. "Folks, change of plans. Lahaina needs our help."

Jaw set, his father pushed the throttle forward, and the Island Breeze bounded over the waves. As they approached the harbor, the true devastation came into view. Flames engulfed several waterfront buildings. Ash and embers rained down as panicked people splashed in the water. Nakoa scanned the scene, mind racing. A young couple flailed near the pier, about to go under.

"Over there," Nakoa said, pointing.

Ike steered toward them, the boat barging through floating debris. Nakoa winced at the scrapes and dings, but they'd deal with that later.

"Toss them the ring!" Ike shouted to him. Nakoa slung the life preserver into the water. The young couple grasped it, and he and some of the passengers helped pull them in. Once they were onboard, they wrapped them in towels and gave them some water.

"Thank you," the woman coughed out.

"There's more people trapped farther down," the man said.

Ike turned the boat back in that direction. Dark smoke made it nearly impossible to see, but as the boat inched forward, Nakoa leaned over the side, straining to see anyone they could reach. As Ike slowly navigated through the smoky haze, Nakoa could barely make out the shoreline. Flames engulfed palm trees along the beach, their fronds exploding in bursts of orange. The air was filled with the sounds of sirens, panicked screams, and the roar of the inferno.

Nakoa spotted a few people huddled on top of an overturned boat near the seawall. As they pulled alongside, he saw their terrified faces streaked with soot and tears. "Come on, let's get you to safety," he called.

A woman handed her toddler to Nakoa before climbing aboard herself. "Have you seen my husband?" she asked frantically. "He went to get our son but hasn't come back."

Nakoa's heart sank, but he tried to sound reassuring. "We'll find them."

He scanned the water, desperate for a sign of the missing father and child. Ike continued through the floating debris and swirling ash as they all called out for survivors. The roar of the flames drowned out his voice. Nakoa blinked sweat and tears from his stinging eyes, struggling to see through the haze.

Up ahead, a dark form floated in the water. Part of the dock. Two figures held on to it.

"That's him! That's them," the woman said, pointing.

The roar of the fire drowned out everything. Nakoa squinted against the swirling embers as Ike guided the Island Breeze toward the broken piece of the dock. Nakoa could barely make it out through the smoke. Then he spotted them—two heads bobbing among flaming debris.

"Dad, over there." Nakoa pointed.

Ike swung the wheel hard to port, bringing the boat alongside the struggling pair.

"Help us!" the boy screamed over the cacophony of the fire.

The passengers shrieked as a burning mast from an adjacent boat crashed onto the Island Breeze's bow. The boat shook, but the mast rolled off. Nakoa grabbed the fire extinguisher and put out the flames it left in its wake.

"Get the boy up," Ike said while steadying the boat. "We've got to get out of here."

Nakoa sprinted to the side of the boat. "I've got you, just hang on," he said, hauling the boy aboard.

The father thrashed in panic. "Hurry," he begged. It took Nakoa and two other men to pull him in the boat, but they did it.

Nakoa's heart pounded as Ike turned the boat away from the inferno. They were at maximum capacity. The boat had taken damage, and Ike didn't look so good. Stress like this wasn't good for his heart. Even though Nakoa knew they needed to get their passengers safely away, guilt gnawed at him for leaving.

His passengers huddled together, their eyes wide with shock.

"Everyone okay?" Nakoa called.

A few shaky voices responded in the affirmative.

When the passengers were mostly settled, Nakoa walked to the bow to assess the damage. The fallen mast had crushed part of the rail, and the embers had left scorch marks across the deck. They had gotten lucky.

"Shit," Nakoa said, turning to his father.

His father's face was sheet white, and he was sweating. Hurrying into the bridge, he had to pry his father's hands off the wheel and sit him in the captain's chair.

"Are you all right?"

Ike shook his head. "No."

Nakoa reached into the cabinet and pulled out a bottle. "Water or whiskey?" he asked.

"Both."

After giving his father the drinks, Nakoa pointed the boat toward Ka'anapali Beach, away from Lahaina. His hands trembled on the wheel, but he got everyone back safely.

CHAPTER 2 - KAILANI

One week later

Kailani stepped onto the warm sand of Ka'anapali Beach, her eyes scanning the shoreline for the boats carrying much-needed supplies. The bigger boats couldn't fit into the small dock outside of the Palekaiko Beach Resort, so they anchored out, and jet skis took turns going out to them and bringing the supplies back. The sun, high in the sky, cast a golden glow on everything it touched, but underneath that beauty lay a somber mood. The people of Maui had been through so much lately with the fire leaving many homeless and in need.

She eyed the small boats lining up to get to the dock, ready to unload their precious cargo: water, food, and other essential supplies for the survivors of the Lahaina fire. Her heart ached for those who had lost everything. Her family on the Big Island wanted her to come home until things were more settled, but the last thing they needed was another mouth to feed. And besides, this was her home and her community.

"Kailani!" a familiar voice called out, beckoning her toward one of the boats that had just docked. She waved back at her friend Joely, who worked at the Palekaiko Beach Resort with her. Joely was one of the maids, and they often worked the same shift, so they ate meals and hung out together. Joely had somehow managed to find a beach wagon with large sand wheels to make the unloading easier.

As Kailani helped her load up the wagon, her gaze drifted to a nearby boat. She was transfixed by a handsome stranger who was working diligently. He was strong and athletic, the muscles in his arms flexing as he lifted heavy water jugs onto the beach. His jet-black hair was tousled from the sea breeze, and his dark eyes sparkled with determination.

She'd never seen him before, but Joely waved eagerly.

"Who's that?" Kailani asked, trying not to gawk.

"That's Nakoa," Joely said. "He's new around here. He runs snorkeling tours, but he's been doing supply runs since the fire."

Kailani took a moment to admire him some more. He had an air of authority and confidence. People came up to him to ask questions. When he turned and caught her staring, she glanced away quickly. *Get it together,* she told herself. *Now's not the time for crushes.* There were people counting on them.

Soon she and Joely were swept up in the organized chaos, shuttling supplies back to Whalers Village and a waiting truck headed for the evacuation centers. As she worked, Kailani kept catching glimpses of Nakoa. His easy smile and carefree laugh made her wish she could forget her responsibilities for just a moment. There didn't seem to be a lot to laugh about right now. She had to keep her focus on helping the fire victims, not daydreaming about a cute guy.

She tracked Nakoa as he maneuvered his boat out of the docking area. He gave them a jaunty wave and another one of those devastating smiles before he headed off to resupply farther down the coast.

Kailani sighed, ignoring the thumping of her heart. There were too many people counting on her right now. But she still wished she had the courage to ask to go with him on the supply run. It would be nice to go for a boat ride and get away from things for a bit. She'd be safe from sharks in a boat that big.

Kailani's feet hurt from standing at her table, but she didn't mind. Being able to hand out necessities to people who had lost everything was worth every ache and pain. Out of the corner of her eye, she saw someone approaching her with a big box. She hoped it was more toiletries. They were running low.

"Hey there," Nakoa said, thunking down his box. "Thought you could use an extra hand."

"I'll take all the help I can get."

"I'm Nakoa." He gave her the shaka and started to empty the box.

"I'm Kailani." She tried to sound casual, but her heart fluttered at his smile. She busied herself by putting the sunscreen and sunglasses together and arranged the deodorant and aspirin in a shaded area on the table.

There wasn't much time to talk. Instead, they worked steadily side by side, handing out food and supplies to the long line of evacuees. Kailani was hyper aware of Nakoa's presence. The brush of his arm against hers as they both reached for more infant formula made her shiver.

During a respite, Nakoa handed her a bottle of water. "Hydrate."

"Thanks." She tried not to gulp it down, then handed him one. "Your turn."

Nakoa took a long drink of water, beads dripping down his chin. Kailani forced herself to look away from the flex of his throat as he swallowed.

"Are your family and friends safe?" She hoped the tremble she felt didn't show in her voice.

"Yeah, everyone here is accounted for. My family's from Makena."

Kailani closed her eyes in relief. "Same. Except my family's on the Big Island."

He clicked water bottles with her. "Maui strong."

"Maui strong," she repeated.

As the sun began to set, the crowds started to dwindle. Kailani and Nakoa kept working until they were the only ones left. The quiet sound of waves lapping against the shore was a welcome break from the chaos of the day.

Kailani leaned against the table, stretching her sore arms as Nakoa packed up the last of the supplies. She looked up to find him staring at her.

"What?" she asked, feeling self-conscious.

"You worked so hard today."

Kailani felt a flush creeping up her neck. "So did you."

"You're amazing."

"Right back atcha," she said, hoping she didn't sound as awkward as she felt.

Kailani wiped the sweat from her brow as she arranged the last of the donated canned goods on the folding table. The makeshift food pantry at Whalers Village was starting to take shape.

"Looking good over here."

She turned to see Amelia approaching, her face flushed from the heat. As one of the lead organizers, Amelia had been running around all morning directing volunteers.

"I think we're just about finished," Joely said from her table across the way.

"You guys have been a huge help today. Sam and I really appreciate you helping out."

Kailani smiled. "Of course. I'm happy to do whatever I can."

"There's nowhere I'd rather be," Joely said. "But right now, I've got to find Holt and make sure he's not working too hard. I'll see you guys later."

Just then, Sam appeared from the back room carrying a large cooler. He was dressed like a beach bum, even though he owned the Palekaiko Resort with his brother Marcus. Amelia was the only one who called him Sam. Everyone else called him Dude.

"All right, who's ready for a break?" He grinned, setting down the cooler. "We've got choke ono grindz back at Palekaiko. Break da mouth."

A cheer went up among the thirty or so volunteers. After a long morning of unloading supplies, everyone was eager for a bite to eat. As the smell of sizzling hit them, Kailani's stomach rumbled.

"I'm hungry too," Nakoa said. "Let's wrap it up here and head over."

"All right."

It didn't take long, and it was a short walk from Whalers Village to the Palekaiko Beach Resort. Volunteers were lined up with paper plates, bantering light-heartedly as they loaded up on the free food. For a moment, the horrible past few days faded into the background.

Kailani served herself a hot dog and a heaping dollop of macaroni salad. Finding a picnic table in the shade, she sat down and glanced around at the other volunteers eating together and taking comfort in the shared space.

"I don't think I've ever been so excited for a hot dog," she joked when Nakoa sat next to her.

"I know what you mean, but I'm a hamburger man, myself. Nothing tastes better after a hard day's work."

He took a huge bite of his burger, eyes closing in bliss. Kailani chuckled at his exaggerated reaction.

"What's so funny?" Nakoa asked, noticing her smile.

"Nothing, nothing." She waved it off. "You've just got a little something..."

She gestured to a spot of ketchup on his cheek. Nakoa wiped it away.

"Thanks for the heads up," he said with a sheepish laugh.

Their eyes met, and Kailani felt a flicker of electricity shoot through her. *Oh boy*, she thought, *I'm in trouble here.*

The smell of sizzling burgers and hot dogs wafted through the air, mingling with the sound of upbeat music playing from a nearby speaker. There was a sense of community and joy as people danced and talked. Ohana was reinforced and in some cases restored.

Nakoa nudged her playfully. "Do you want to join the kickball game?"

"Not me. I don't have that kind of energy. I'm not good at team sports."

"So what do you do for fun then?"

"I like hiking and going for bike rides. Just being outdoors. What about you?"

"Same," he said. "Especially anything ocean related. I could be on or in the water all day."

Kailani smiled. "I'm not surprised. You seem like a real island boy."

Nakoa chuckled. "Yeah, I guess I am. What about your family?"

Kailani's smile faltered. "My dad's not doing so well."

Nakoa's expression softened. "I'm sorry to hear that. Do you want to talk about it?"

Kailani hesitated. She wasn't sure how much to share with him. Sometimes, though, it was easy to be honest to a stranger. "My mom's a secretary, and my dad worked in construction until his knees and back gave out. It's a struggle to make ends meet, but I try to help out when I can."

Nakoa reached out and took her hand. "I'm sorry, Kailani. That sounds really hard."

"It's not so bad." The concerned look in his eyes made her feel uncomfortable. She didn't want him to feel sorry for her. There were so many other people worse off, especially now. She should have just said her family was fine. Maybe it was better to pretend with a stranger, to avoid all the awkwardness.

"What do you do here on Maui?" he asked.

Kailani froze. For some weird reason, she didn't want to tell him she was a waitress. It's not that she was ashamed of it. She just really wanted to impress him, especially since he was already feeling a little bit sorry for her because of her dad's accident. Straightening her shoulders, she bent the truth a bit. "I'm a marine biologist."

Kailani's heart sank as she realized the size of the lie she had just told. She wasn't a marine biologist, not even close. She was saving up to take classes. That counted, right?

"Wow." His eyebrows raised. "That sounds like an interesting job. I run a snorkel boat. The Island Breeze. Have you heard of it? I'm the captain."

"I don't do much snorkeling," she said. "At least not far from shore." The lie about not being a waitress had just slipped out of her mouth in a moment of panic. And now, she had dug herself a hole.

"I've always been fascinated by marine life," Nakoa said, oblivious to her inner turmoil. "What kind of research do you do?"

Kailani swallowed hard. How was she supposed to answer that? Here's where she should just come clean and tell him that she didn't know what came over her and she'd just lied to his face. Yeah, like that would really be a stellar first impression. So since she was already in the hole, she kept digging. "Uh, I mainly focus on coral reefs. You know, studying the impact of climate change and pollution on them."

Nakoa nodded, looking impressed. "That's really important work. I'm glad there are people like you fighting to protect our oceans."

"It's not as glamorous as it sounds."

Guilt gnawed at Kailani's stomach. She didn't deserve his admiration. But at the same time, she couldn't bring herself to come clean. She would have to if this went any further. But what was the harm in a quick little fantasy if she never saw him again after tonight?

Reaching over, he tucked a strand of hair behind her ear. "I think it sounds pretty glamorous. And you're beautiful, too. Like a mermaid."

Kailani felt her cheeks flush. She could feel the heat from his hand on her cheek. "Thanks," she murmured. "That's really sweet of you to say."

They sat there in silence for a few moments, just enjoying each other's company. Kailani felt a sense of contentment that she hadn't felt in a long time. Maybe, just maybe, everything would be okay.

Nakoa's gaze dropped to her lips, then darted away.

"Hey, Uncle," a little boy said, coming up to them. "Can you open this for me?" The little boy thrust a coconut into Nakoa's chest.

Nakoa cleared his throat and stood abruptly. "I'll be right back. Gotta show off my cracking skills."

Kailani watched curiously as he went over to the large pile of coconuts intended for the evening's dessert.

"You don't want that one, keiki," Nakoa said.

"Yes, I do," the boy said stubbornly.

Nakoa hefted a few coconuts from the pile, testing their weight, before selecting a massive one that drew impressed murmurs from onlookers.

"Stand back, folks, the master is at work!" Nakoa declared, shooting the keiki in front of him a playful wink. Squaring his stance, he held the coconut aloft like a trophy. With a mighty roar, he brought it crashing down onto a nearby picnic table.

The coconut didn't even crack.

Rubbing his reddened hand, Nakoa tried again on the corner of a concrete planter. Still not a budge.

Kailani pressed her lips together, struggling not to giggle at his comical display of machismo giving way to frustration.

A competitive glint entered Nakoa's eye. He began smashing the coconut with focused fury against trees, railings, boulders—even his own forehead.

The kids dissolved into laughter. The other volunteers chuckled at his antics.

"Come on, you stubborn little..." Nakoa trailed off into unintelligible grumbling as he grappled with the intact coconut.

Finally, he staggered back to Kailani's table and slammed it down with an all-mighty crack. Milky coconut water exploded outward, splattering them both.

Kailani met Nakoa's stunned gaze. A beat, then they both burst out laughing.

"I think you got it open," Kailani managed between giggles.

"Maybe a little too open," Nakoa chuckled, swiping the coconut milk from his face.

Their laughter faded, but their smiles lingered. Nakoa handed her half of the cracked coconut. When Kailani's fingers brushed his, it sent a little thrill through her.

"To victory!" Nakoa declared, handing his half to the little boy, who ran back to his parents with his prize.

"To victory," Kailani echoed. She took a sip of the sweet milk and sighed contently.

Nakoa wiped his face with his discarded T-shirt, then slung an arm around Kailani's shoulders. She shared her half of the coconut with him.

Looking out at the sun dipping low over the ocean, Kailani felt the world settle back to normal. It wasn't really. Not even close. But for these few minutes, it could be. With the salty breeze ruffling her hair and Nakoa's sturdy frame beside her, she wished this moment could last forever.

Nakoa leaned in, his lips hovering over hers. "Is this okay?" he asked, giving her an out if she wanted it.

She didn't hesitate. "Yes."

That was all the encouragement he needed. Their lips met in a tender kiss. Kailani melted into Nakoa's embrace, the sounds of the barbecue fading away. His arms encircled her waist as the kiss deepened. An exhilarating rush coursed through her.

When they finally parted, Kailani's cheeks were flushed.

"Wow," she breathed.

"Yeah. Wow," Nakoa echoed, looking delightfully dazed.

But then, her phone buzzed. It was a text from Tia, asking if she could come in early for her shift tonight.

Kailani's heart sank. She didn't want to, but she needed the money. She texted back that she needed to change first, but she'd be there in an hour. "I'm sorry. Something just came up, and I have to go," she said, standing up from the table.

Nakoa looked disappointed. "Is everything all right?"

Kailani nodded. "Yeah, just a last-minute lab report that needs to be done." Ugh, why was she still lying?

"I had a really great time with you today, Kailani."

"Me too." Kailani's heart fluttered as Nakoa leaned in and kissed her tenderly again.

"Will I see you tomorrow?" he asked.

"I'll be volunteering again in the afternoon."

"I'll see you then," he said.

Kailani hated deceiving him, but she couldn't bring herself to tell him the truth just yet. She had always felt like she wasn't good enough, and the lie about her job made her feel like she was. She knew she had to come clean, but she didn't know how or when. And maybe she didn't have to. After the crisis passed, he'd go back to Makena, and she'd be up here in Ka'anapali. It wasn't a great distance, but maybe while they were apart, she would become a marine biologist, and then it wouldn't be a lie anymore.

CHAPTER 3 - NAKOA

Nakoa hated seeing his father like this. Ike sat in his chair, glued to the news. He didn't want to step foot on the Island Breeze.

"Hey, Pop," Nakoa said. "You should come out with me tomorrow."

Ike shook his head. "No. You need to go get a real job. Volunteering is all right, but we need another income until the tourists come back."

"You could go around the other side of the island. See if the resorts need some snorkel tours."

Ike scoffed. "No. I'm taking a break from boating. So should you."

He would, but he'd just told the girl of his dreams that he was the captain of the Island Breeze. Nakoa supposed technically he was if his father wasn't on board. But that wasn't the impression he had given out. He had wanted to impress Kailani, and captain sounded a lot better than unemployed and living with his parents.

"Besides, I don't like how the Island Breeze sounds. Ever since the fire, she's been different."

Ever since the fire, Ike had been different too. But Nakoa didn't say that. "The boat seems fine to me."

"What do you know?" Ike grumped. "It's years since you've been on her. I know her. She's suffering. But I don't know what's wrong with her."

"Too bad you're not that intuitive about me," Nakoa's mother, Mei, said.

Ike waved his hand and scoffed at her.

"I heard the Palekaiko Beach Resort is looking for help," Mei said.

"I was just over there," Nakoa said. "They're doing a lot for the relief effort."

Maybe it was time to get a real job. One where he put in his hours and got a steady paycheck. The thought made his entrepreneurial spirit cringe, but his family had supported him when he had started out in his business. Now it was his turn. Swallowing his pride, he took the boat over to Ka'anapali. Nakoa didn't know what his father was talking about. It drove just fine. He left it anchored far enough away where he wouldn't get in the way of the supply boats and rode his zodiac into the Palekaiko Beach Resort area.

After getting an application, he sat at a bench overlooking the azure waters. Nakoa tapped the pen against his lip. He had to make this good.

Experience: He wrote about his helping his dad run tours when he was a kid and his three years running his own boat in California.

Skills: Navigation, CPR certified, boat maintenance, and repair.

"I just gotta get my foot in the door," he muttered. This wasn't his dream, but it would keep his family afloat. And who knew? Maybe he'd end up liking it. It would be a nice change of pace to have an expected amount every week instead of hoping for a party boat to turn the week around.

Nakoa walked back into the lobby with his completed application. He could do this. For now, at least, until the economy turned around. He handed in the paperwork to the receptionist.

"I guess you'll call me?" he said.

"No, let me get Marcus for you," she said.

Marcus Kincaide was one of the owners of the resort. Nakoa smoothed down his aloha shirt and wished he had run a better iron over his khakis. But Marcus didn't seem to notice. He shook his hand and then led him into his office.

"You clearly have extensive experience on the water and an intimate knowledge of the area," Marcus said.

"Mahalo, I've been boating here since I was a kid."

"Precisely why I'd like to bring you on board, even though we don't currently have an opening," Marcus continued. "Your skills are an asset I don't want to lose. Would you be interested in a truck driving position for us? Now, more than ever, we need someone we trust to get supplies from all over the island."

"I can do that," Nakoa said. "I even have use of a boat if that's quicker."

"Excellent," Marcus said. "When can you start?"

"I'm not doing anything now."

"Great, let's get you processed, and then I've got some supplies that need to be picked up from our sister resort in Hana."

"Hana." Nakoa fought to keep the smile on his face. It had been years since he'd driven those twisted roads.

"Will that be a problem?"

"Not all," Nakoa lied. It would be hard enough driving it with his small car, but with a big box truck... It was going to be an adventure. Maybe next time, he'd see if he could take the Island Breeze. But he wanted Marcus to know he could handle the Maui roads.

———

He survived the trip to Hana and back. It almost killed him. Literally. The roads were winding and narrow with traffic going both ways along hairpin turn after hairpin turn. Three hours down and three hours back. Nakoa needed a drink. Or a medal. He'd settle for a beer.

As he sat in the truck in the covered garage of the Palekaiko Beach resort, he tried to convince his white-knuckled grip to loosen from the steering wheel. Out of the corner of his eye, he saw Kailani. She must be heading over to the beach to help with the supplies from the boats.

His heart leapt at the sight of her—that long dark hair blowing gently in the breeze, her brown legs golden in the sunlight. Nakoa had to stop himself from waving or calling out to her from the truck.

No, he couldn't let her see him like this. Driving a resort truck, doing odd jobs instead of commanding his own boat. She thought he was successful, an accomplished captain. If Kailani knew he was barely keeping afloat, that he'd had to take this job just to pay the bills, she might think he was a loser.

Nakoa slumped down in his seat, hoping the truck's tinted windows would keep him hidden. His stomach twisted with shame and uncertainty. He wanted to tell Kailani the truth, to share his struggles with her. But the fear of losing her respect held him back. For now, he would keep up the façade. Nakoa just hoped that one day, he could reveal his true situation without jeopardizing everything. But deep down, he knew it wasn't right to keep hiding the truth from her. Kailani deserved to know what was really going on with his business and his life. Nakoa wanted their relationship to be built on trust and honesty, not appearances. If they even had a relationship after only knowing each other for one day.

After he had unloaded his cargo, he made sure to catch up with Kailani.

"I need your help," he said.

"You do?"

"Come and keep me company while I sail to Maalaea Harbor to pick up a load of medical supplies and propane."

Kailani looked back at the human chain that was bringing the supplies across the sand. "I could use a break."

"And I could use the company."

"Okay," she said, smiling. "Deal."

She paused at the zodiac. "Are you sure this is safe?"

"Totally." He helped her in and then pushed it into the water before hopping in it himself. He turned on the motor and headed back to the boat.

Her fingers were gripping the side of the little inflatable almost as hard as he had been clutching the steering wheel.

"You okay?" he asked.

"Sharks," she muttered.

"Where?" Nakoa didn't see any.

"They're everywhere," she said darkly.

"How do you become a marine biologist and be afraid of sharks?"

She gave a short laugh that had no humor in it. "It's not easy."

Nakoa saw her looking at the Island Breeze as he helped her aboard. He suddenly felt a little self-conscious at the boat's appearance. The scorch marks and warped metal on the bow were new, but it could also use a good paint job.

"How's the snorkeling business?" she asked.

"Slow. It's to be expected, but…" He shrugged. "It still sucks."

Nakoa smiled. But in the back of his mind, worries crept in. He thought about the repairs needed for his boat, the stacks of bills piling up at home. Money had been tight ever since tourism dropped off after the pandemic. Most days, he could push those thoughts away. But now, talking to Kailani, he felt a pang of insecurity.

"What made you want to be a boat captain?" she asked.

Nakoa looked out across the water, reminiscing. "I've always loved the ocean. My dad taught me to snorkel when I was young. We'd go out fishing and camping all around Maui. I wanted to share that joy with others. I could show you some of my favorite snorkeling spots a little later."

"No," she said, holding her hands out. "Sharks."

"Just don't swim at dawn or dusk," he said. "And it's the tiger sharks you mostly have to be afraid of. They're territorial."

She shook her head. "No, they're not. That's a misconception."

"Oh yeah?" He smiled at her. "I forgot this is what you do. Tell me more."

Kailana blushed. "They don't really have territories. They go where the food is, and sometimes, they think we're food because they don't see so well."

"Still," he said. "Shark bites are pretty rare."

"True," she said, "but once you see an attack, it's hard to forget. My friend almost lost her arm."

"I've swam with a few," Nakoa said. "They leave me alone, and I left them alone."

"Then you're fortunate," she said tartly. "And a little foolish. What would you do if your passengers were snorkeling and a shark swam up?"

"I'd get them out of the water without panicking them."

She snorted. "Good luck with that."

"I've got shark repellent on the boat too."

"Good." Kailani wrapped her arms around herself.

"You don't have to worry about sharks when I'm around," he said reassuringly.

"Is that right?" She gave him a small smile. "I don't suppose you're afraid of anything?"

"I'm not a fan of fire," he said, staring at the damage done to the bow of his boat. He was surprised when she slipped her hand inside his.

"No one is."

CHAPTER 4 - KAILANI

After they stocked up on infant formula, medical supplies, and a large load of energy bars from Costco, they brought the cargo back to the dock outside of the Palekaiko Beach Resort. Things were winding down as night was creeping up on them.

She was tired, but it was a good tired.

There was another get-together that night for the volunteers. The guests in West Maui had been encouraged to cut their vacations short while West Maui recovered. Some tourists switched their bookings to another part of the island or one of the other islands. But the Palekaiko Beach Resort, like many other hotels on the Ka'anapali Beach, was acting as a shelter and temporary housing for families who had been displaced because of the Maui wildfires.

Kailani had been up since dawn serving breakfast and lunch. And after an afternoon of volunteering and traveling on the ocean with Nakoa, all she wanted was a nap.

But the upbeat tempo of ukulele music and the sweet aroma of kalua pork on the grill welcomed Kailani and Nakoa as they arrived at the bustling community event perked her up a bit.

"Aloha, you two!" Joely emerged from the crowd, the grass skirt of her hula costume swishing as she pulled them both into an enthusiastic hug.

"Why are you dressed like that?" Kailani asked.

"Didn't you get my text?"

"No, I've been out on the water." Kailani took out her phone and shook it, but no messages appeared. Cell service had been spotty for days.

"That's okay. You're here now. That's what matters. Amelia asked us if we would join a hula dance that some of the evacuees wanted to do."

Kailani shot a quick look at Nakoa. If he wondered why Amelia wanted a marine biologist to dance at her resort, he didn't mention it. "I'm not a very good dancer," she said.

"Luckily for you," Nakoa said, "I am. My mother made sure I took lessons."

"I never did," Kailani said. She needed to get him out of here before someone outed her as a waitress. "Why are we doing this, anyway?" she asked Joely. "All our guests are from Maui. They've grown up with hula."

"Some of the aunties and uncles wanted to hear the ancient hula chants. It's a comfort, I guess."

"I've only seen modern," Kailani hedged.

"Just move with the spirit of aloha and you'll be perfect," Nakoa said.

"Easy for you to say," Kailani muttered as he slung his arm around her shoulders.

Joely led them to the grassy area, where other volunteers were talking to the musicians about what dance they were going to perform. She noticed a few more people who worked at the Palekaiko Beach Resort. Kailani greeted them warily, but no one said anything about her being a waitress. Nakoa went to change into a malo, and Joely led her to a tented area where she could put on a long tapa cloth wrap and a lei headpiece.

When the music started, they began with basic hip sways and hand movements. Kailani did her best to follow along. She stood in the back so any mess-ups wouldn't be as apparent. Nakoa, on the other hand, led the men with dazzling footwork set to the beat of the drums. He was in his element as he danced the history of their people with pride and joy.

The music swelled, and Kailani lost herself in the pulsating beat and the chants. Her movements grew more confident as she mirrored Joely's steps. When the song ended, applause erupted from the crowd.

Kailani clasped Nakoa's hand, exhilarated. "I didn't suck."

"Told you." He squeezed her hand.

Kailani breathed a sigh of relief as Joely and the other Palekaiko Beach staff headed off to. Her secret was safe, at least for now. She was going to have to come clean sooner or later because she didn't want this to be a quick hookup. Two days and she was smitten with Nakoa. But would he want her if she was just a waitress?

After they got out of their costumes and got dressed, they took a stroll along the garden paths. The encroaching night turned everything sultry and romantic.

"Look, a red-crowned parrot." Nakoa pointed up at a palm tree, where a burst of colorful feathers peered down at them. The parrot let out a throaty screech and fluttered its wings. "There's a bunch of them on Oahu, but this is the first time I've seen one here."

"He seems friendly."

"Like he's greeting us," Nakoa said, mimicking the parrot's call. His imitation was so absurd, she couldn't help giggling.

The light wrap she had wrapped around her shoulders fluttered behind her in the breeze. The parrot's gaze narrowed on it. Letting out an excited squawk, it swooped down from the palm tree to grab the shawl in its beak and claws.

She froze in place, startled by the parrot's tug on her shawl. It was clearly enamored with the vibrant pattern and colors.

"I think he likes you," Nakoa said with a chuckle.

"Or he just really loves my scarf." She gave a cautious pull, but it wasn't letting go of it. The parrot was bigger up close, with a mix of greens and reds in its plumage.

"He seems quite taken with you," Nakoa said. His lips quirked into a teasing smile. "I can't say I blame him."

Heat rose in her cheeks at the compliment. "Oh, stop."

"What?" He shrugged, the picture of innocence. "You can't help being irresistible."

Kailani's breath caught as Nakoa's lips brushed the sensitive skin below her ear. The parrot let out an indignant squawk at being ignored, but she barely noticed, lost in the sensations flooding her senses.

Kailani's lips parted slightly as Nakoa leaned in, his hand coming up to cradle her cheek as he turned her face toward him. Her eyelids fluttered closed as his mouth found hers in a soft, tentative kiss. Warmth flooded through her body.

Emboldened, Nakoa deepened the kiss, his tongue slipping past her lips. Kailani melted against him, fingers twisting into his shirt.

Nakoa's hand slid around to the nape of her neck, tangling in her hair as heat pooled low in her belly. They had shared a kiss before, but this was different—more intense, more passionate. Like they had both finally given in to the simmering desire between them.

Her scarf slipped off her shoulder, fluttering to the sand. The parrot shrieked in triumph and flew off, her shawl trailing behind him.

"Should I chase him down?" Nakoa asked wryly. "I think if I jump, I can get your shawl back."

The parrot flew up higher and ruffled its feathers, fixing them both with a baleful glare.

"No, if he wants it bad enough, he can keep it." She was sure that the parrot would get bored, and she'd find her shawl on the sand later. Hopefully, if someone found it before she did, they'd put it in the lost and found box at the resort.

"I can get you another one," he said softly.

The tenderness in his eyes made her breath catch. She curled her hand around the back of his neck, pulling him down into another searing kiss. The world around them faded away until there was only Nakoa. Her hands roamed over his shoulders, reveling in the feel of his bare skin beneath her fingers.

"You know, I was thinking..." he said after lifting his mouth off hers.

"Yes?"

"I was thinking maybe we could continue this back on the boat." His lips quirked. "If you want to, that is."

Her breath caught. The thought thrilled her—but it also made her nervous. They had only known each other two days. She hesitated, staring out at the rolling waves as she gathered her courage. If anything, these last few days had taught her was there were no guarantees in life. You had to take joy and pleasure when you found it.

She looked up to meet his gaze, desire flickering inside her. "I'd like that," she said softly.

A slow, devastating smile lit Nakoa's face. He leaned down, his breath warm against her ear. "Then let's go."

CHAPTER 5 - KAILANI

Intertwined together in Nakoa's bunk below decks on the Island Breeze, Kailani unbuttoned his shirt, greedy to slide her hands over his muscles. His kisses were slow and sensual. Kailani clung to him, craving more of his intoxicating touch. Pulling off her shirt, he kissed the tops of her breasts. She shivered at the contact, aching for an intimacy beyond kisses.

As his hands roamed over her, his lips explored her body. She arched into him, moaning softly. Nakoa kissed down her neck while he unbuttoned her shorts.

Kailani's heart pounded at the thought of being naked in front of him. Did she want this? Yes. Was it too soon? Also yes. Did she care? No. Her body tingled with anticipation as he slowly slid her shorts and panties off in one movement. Her shirt and bra soon followed. Trailing kisses from her neck down her body, Nakoa tracing each curve with his tongue.

Kailani whimpered as his lips found her nipples.

Nakoa lifted his head to gaze down at her, his eyes dark with longing. His thumb traced the line of her jaw in a tender caress. "You're so beautiful," he rasped.

His hand slid from her cheek to her waist, pulling her closer as he kissed back up to her mouth. As their mouths slid over each other, her nipples brushed against the silky, soft hair on his chest.

Nakoa's kisses grew more insistent, passionate yet tender. Kailani let out a soft moan, every nerve alive and tingling. She had never been kissed like this before. Like she was the only thing in his world that mattered.

Nakoa left feather-light kisses along her jaw. He slid his hand up her side, pausing to cup her breast. She jumped in surprise as his thumb teased her nipple, sending a jolt of pleasure straight to her core.

"Nakoa," she gasped.

He nuzzled her ear, the hand at her waist sliding lower. Kailani sucked in a breath as his hand ran over the curve of her hip. Slowly, he slid his fingers over her thighs.

Her heart pounded. Her breathing was ragged. Kailani was lost in the sweet sensations washing over her. His lips nuzzled her neck, while his hand continuing its slow exploration of her body.

"Do you want this?" he asked, waiting for her hurried nod.

"Don't stop." She closed her eyes in bliss.

He pushed his fingers between her legs, teasing her wetness. She let out a soft cry, her eyes flying open. Nakoa's face was inches from hers. She was captivated by the look of passion in his eyes. His fingers moved in slow, tantalizing circles, teasing her. He pulled back, kissing her deeply as he played. He stroked her again, this time a little firmer, and Kailani moved her hips to dance with his fingers.

Her whole body tensed as the pleasure built. Nakoa's thumb circled her clit, sending an electric shock through her. She moaned against his lips. She writhed, needing more.

Nakoa's fingers continued their tantalizing assault as he kissed her, his thumb stroking her to the brink. Kailani's back bowed off the bed. A crashing rush of pleasure swept through her as she came. She moaned as the pleasure washed over her in wave after wave of ecstasy.

Kailani's body trembled. Nakoa kissed her again, his lips tender and soft. She wrapped her arms around him, holding him close.

Nakoa pulled back to gaze down at her. He stroked a thumb over her cheek. "You're so sweet," he whispered.

She traced her fingers down his chest to the waistband of his pants, looking into his eyes for permission. Nakoa's eyes were dark as she undid his zipper. He sucked in a breath, watching her as she slid her hand inside.

Her eyes widened at the feel of him, hard and hot in her hand. The lightest stroke sent a wave of pleasure rippling through him. Kailani leaned forward, kissing him as she ran her hand over him again.

Nakoa's breathing grew ragged.

Kailani wrapped her hand around him, stroking him firmly as she kissed him.

His hips went tense as she gently gripped his butt with her other hand.

"Oh, God." Nakoa sucked in a breath as she stroked him, his hips jerking. Kailani felt a thrill of triumph as his pleasure built.

"You like this?" she whispered.

"You're perfect," he moaned.

His hips bucked as she pumped him. He gripped her hair. Kailani's body hummed with pleasure as she gave Nakoa what he wanted. She adored the look on his face as she stroked him to orgasm.

"I bet you're sweet too." Slowly, she lowered her head.

His body tensed as she touched her lips to his tip. Her tongue darted out, tasting the drop of pre-cum. She licked him again, tasting him. He shuddered when she took him into her mouth, her tongue swirling over him.

He groaned, his hands tightening in her hair. She wrapped her hand around the base, her mouth taking all of him deep. Kailani's heart raced at the rush of power. She wanted to feel him explode against her tongue. Her hand worked in rhythm with her mouth, kneading him hard.

Nakoa's body convulsed as he came, his head falling back. Kailani held him, loving the sweet taste of him. She was breathing hard as she sat up. Nakoa looked down at her, his eyes dark with passion as he shed the rest of his clothes.

"I want you so much," he murmured in her ear. His body felt strong and hard against her, his hands gentle. He rolled her over onto her back as he kissed her, his hand cupping her breast. His thumb teased her nipple as he kissed her throat, his head dipping to kiss the curve of her breast.

Kailani moaned with pleasure, her body aching for more. Nakoa suckled gently on her nipple, sending hot shivers through her. Her body arched into his touch, her legs spreading for him. She was on fire, her body aching for him.

Kissing down her belly, he pushed her legs wider as he settled between them. Kailani saw stars as he licked her with slow, loving strokes.

"More," she demanded, pulling on his hair.

He groaned against her core, sending little shock waves through her. He concentrated on her clit until her throat was hoarse with crying out. He licked her until she came, drenching his face.

Nakoa covered her with his body, his mouth descending on hers as she tried to recover from the earth-shattering orgasm he had just given her.

He slid into her with a smooth thrust. Kailani shouted his name, her body shuddering around him. Nakoa's mouth took hers as he thrust again.

Kailani's world dissolved into a blur of sensations, her body tightening around him. She could feel him, every delicious inch of him, the heat of him radiating against her skin.

She wrapped her legs around him, holding him tighter. Nakoa buried his face into her neck as he drove into her repeatedly. The feel of his cock, hot and thick, made her desperate for each thrust.

Kailani moved her hips against his. Her frantic cries mingled with Nakoa's hoarse ones as the pleasure built again to a crescendo. He continued to take her slowly and deeply until Kailani went over the edge. Nakoa went rigid as he came, his forehead gently touching hers. Afterwards, he collapsed next to her and kissed her softly as they caught their breath.

Kailani's heart was still pounding, her body humming with delight as exhaustion took her, and she drifted off to sleep.

CHAPTER 6 - NAKOA

Something was wrong.

And since he had just had the greatest night of his life, Nakoa shouldn't have woken up with that thought. Easing out of bed, he made his way up on deck. The stars were still out, but the boat was moving fast across the currents.

What the hell?

His anchor line had snapped. And now they were adrift and who knew how far from shore. He fired up the GPS and the motor.

"What's going on?" Kailani said, coming up to the bridge and stifling a yawn.

"The anchor is gone," he said. "We're a little past Lanai and heading toward Kahoolawe."

"Oh no," she said.

"It's okay. It's a good thing I woke up when I did."

"Are there sharks out here?"

"No," he lied. He was sure there were, but they wouldn't be bothering them. "I'm heading back to Maui." He hoped he had enough gas. He should have filled up when they came back from Maalaea, but he had been distracted by the kalua pork. And his gauge was showing full. But thinking about it, it had been showing full all week, and he hadn't filled up in a while.

Nakoa punched the motor, causing Kailani to jostle back and hang on.

"Sorry," he muttered. He wanted to get closer to shore if they were going to run out of gas. With one eye on the gas gauge, he plotted the most direct course back. But the Island Breeze was sluggish. There was something wrong.

"Shit," he muttered.

"What?" Kailani asked.

"We're not going to make it in."

"What do you mean?"

Nakoa could see she was trying not to panic. "We're going to run out of gas."

"Is that all?" she asked.

"I think so." *I hope so.* "Can you drive a boat?"

"Me? No." Kailani shook her head.

"Okay, lesson time." He pointed to the compass. "Keep the needle here. Look out there and don't hit any boats."

"I don't see any boats."

"Good," he said. "I'll be right back."

"Nakoa!" she shrieked.

"It'll be fine. Just yell if you see a boat or a rock."

"Oh, I'll yell all right."

Nakoa headed to the stern of the boat and looked at the engine. It was straining, but that wasn't the problem, although a spun prop might not be out of the question. Then he realized he was kneeling in water. They were taking on water. As calmly as he could, he flipped on the emergency water pumps. Nothing happened.

That wasn't good. He immediately got up and grabbed two life jackets. "Put this on," he said to Kailani.

"What? Why?"

After putting his on, he took over the wheel. "Just a precaution. We're taking on water."

"We're sinking?" she shrieked.

"It's a slow process," he said, reaching for the radio. He called in a Mayday on the radio and gave his GPS coordinates and his projected trajectory. He got confirmation that the Coast Guard would send out an auxiliary boat to meet them.

Kailani gripped his arm. "Are we going to be all right?"

"Yeah," Nakoa said. He wasn't sure if the Island Breeze was going to be, though. "I'm sorry for this. My dad said he thought something was off with the boat, but I didn't see it."

"Should I start to bail water or something?"

Nakoa looked over his shoulder. "Not just yet."

It was another fifteen minutes before the boat stuttered to a stop. They were either out of gas or out of luck. Possibly both. Kailani took a shuddering breath. "We're going to be okay," he said. "Look, here comes the rescue boat."

They walked back out on deck. The water was ankle deep.

"We're sinking," she said.

He took a moment to wrap his arms around her. "You're safe. I won't let anything happen to you."

Her tense body relaxed. "What if we go into the water before the rescue boat gets here?"

"We hang on to the boat and wait."

"Sharks?" she whispered.

"Come with me." He brought her back to the bridge and turned on the fish finder. "You keep an eye out here."

Images of fish swam by on the screen.

"If there's a shark out there, you'll see it." So far, the only thing on the scope were a few schools of small to medium fish. "Right now looks like some ahi and dolphin fish. So if you get hungry, let me know, and I'll grab the spear and get us lunch."

When she gave a sniffling giggle, he knew he could leave her alone for a bit. He looked out in the distance. The boat was getting closer, but Nakoa wanted to know why he was taking on water. It would kill his father if they lost the Island Breeze. He hoped it was just a loose drain plug.

But he had a feeling that it was something worse. In any event, they were going to have to pull the boat out of the water and check for leaks.

A large power boat was getting close, and Nakoa went back to see Kailani. She was nibbling on her lip worriedly, and he put his arm around her. "They're almost here. Do you have everything?"

"Yeah, I didn't bring much."

"I'm so sorry about this," he said, touching his forehead to hers.

"It's fine. It happens. I'm sorry about your boat."

He sighed. "Yeah, me too." He was more worried about being late to work, though. He didn't want to make a bad impression on his second day. But as the sun was just coming up, he thought he'd have time to make it to the Palekaiko Beach Resort by nine.

When the power boat pulled alongside, he said, "Let's get her on board. I'll stay here if you can tow me in."

"Nakoa, no," Kailani said.

"It'll be fine."

"Hey," one of the auxiliary coast guard men said, "you're Nakoa, right?"

Another of the coast guard held out his hand to Kailani as she stepped up on the boat side to transfer over.

Kailani looked up and seemed to recognize the man who spoke. "Hani?"

"Nice! Dude and Marcus will be so stoked. We rescued two Palekaiko Beach Resort employees today," Hani said.

"What?" Kailani and Nakoa said at the same time.

And then a rogue wave hit, and Kailani's hand slipped out of the coast guard's hand. She wobbled for a bit, caught with one foot between the two boats, and then she fell in.

KAILANI

The water was a shock, but not as much as Hani's words had been. Hani was a bellhop at the Palekaiko Beach Resort. He knew she was a waitress, and now so did Nakoa. But what had he been saying about Nakoa being an employee too? The resort wasn't doing snorkeling tours at this time.

"Grab the net," Hani said, holding out a long pole with a net on it. The current was strong, pushing her farther away from the boats, but her life jacket was keeping her above water.

Nakoa dove into the water after her.

She swam toward him, but then something caught the corner of her eye. Was that a fin?

"Nakoa," she shrieked, pointing.

A dark shape slid through the turquoise water, slicing a V-shaped wake. Kailani stiffened, squinting against the glare. A dorsal fin. Oh God, it was heading straight for them. What was she supposed to do? Punch it? She immediately stopped flailing her legs. Nakoa was swimming strongly toward her.

"Get back," she said. "It's a shark."

Except it wasn't. As it sliced through the water toward her, it turned and headed off.

"Turtle," she gasped out. "Sea turtle." It had been swimming on its side and just came close enough to see what was going on.

Nakoa was suddenly there. He wrapped his arms around her.

"Hey, I don't mean to be a buzz kill. But some of us have to get back to work."

Kailani stiffened. Work.

"Nakoa," she started to say.

"Later."

They swam back to the Coast Guard auxiliary boat and climbed in.

"Thanks, brah. I was starting to worry we'd get swamped out there," Nakoa said, giving them the shaka.

"No problem, brah," Hani said. "Couldn't let our favorite waitress go down with the ship."

Kailani froze, mortified. She had wanted to be the one to tell him, but she had waited too long.

"Waitress?" Nakoa asked in surprise.

Kailani cringed. Her cheeks flushed hot with embarrassment as her lie was exposed.

She risked a glance at Nakoa and saw the surprise register on his face. His eyebrows raised, and his mouth opened slightly. She quickly looked away, unable to meet his eyes.

"You're not a marine biologist?" Nakoa finally said.

Kailani shook her head, her throat tight. She tried to swallow her mortification. "I'm so sorry I didn't tell you. I was afraid if you knew, you wouldn't..." Her voice trailed off. Wouldn't what? Want to get to know her? See her as an equal? She had wanted Nakoa to like her for who she was, not what she did.

"Hey, it's okay," Nakoa said gently.

"Yeah, it's okay," Hani said, watching the two of them as if he wanted a bag of popcorn. "He drives a truck for us."

"A truck?" Kailani asked. "But the Island Breeze…"

"Is my dad's boat. I was just helping out until I found a job."

"And he did," Hani said. "With us." Hani gathered them up in an awkward hug. "We're one big family."

"I guess we both stretched the truth a little," Kailani admitted.

"Yeah," Nakoa sighed.

"Are we gonna tow you or what?" Hani asked. "Because I've got a nine a.m. shift."

"Me too," Nakoa said.

Nakoa secured his boat to the bigger one and went back over to the Island Breeze to bail water and check the bilge. Slowly but surely, they made it back to Ka'anapali safe and sound. Kailani wrapped the coarse Coast Guard towel around her and thought of the sea turtle. Seeing one was supposed to be good luck. She hoped it was because they all could use a little luck right now.

CHAPTER 7 - NAKOA

He hated seeing the Island Breeze out of the water. Even more, he hated that he couldn't afford to tow it back home. Luckily, the Kincaides allowed him to store it in their boat house while he worked on it. He was searching for holes, but so far, he hadn't been able to find any. Ike was beside himself, but Nakoa's mother said it was a good thing. It might be the impetus he needed to get his butt out of his easy chair and get back to living his life.

"You look troubled, dear."

Nakoa jumped at the lilting voice. An elderly woman stood there in the doorway of the boat house, her salt and pepper hair billowing in the breeze. Dangling earrings framed her deeply lined face.

"I'm Zarafina," she said. "I read palms here."

Nakoa blinked in surprise. Zarafina was a local legend at the Palekaiko Beach Resort. She was renowned for her psychic abilities.

"Let me guess...relationship problems?" She raised one silver eyebrow knowingly.

Nakoa sighed, too exhausted to deny it.

"Come." Zarafina gestured toward her nearby hut. "We'll get it all sorted out."

Though reluctant, Nakoa allowed himself to be led away. If anyone could unravel this mess, it was Zarafina.

Inside the candle-lit pavilion in the courtyard of the resort, the air was thick with the sweet aroma of incense. Zarafina settled onto a pile of embroidered pillows and gestured to the space across a low table from her.

Nakoa sat down hesitantly.

"Now then," Zarafina said, "tell me what troubles you."

Haltingly, Nakoa explained about the boat, his father, and the lies between him and Kailani. "I know we've only known each other a short time, but I think I'm falling for her. What if she's different? What if she thinks I'm different?"

Zarafina listened intently, her dark eyes filled with compassion. When Nakoa finished, she took his hands in her wrinkled ones.

"The heart wants what it wants, no matter the circumstances," she said gently. "This woman cares for you, that much is clear. Don't let fear and shame rob you of happiness."

Nakoa looked down.

Shuffling a well-worn deck of tarot cards, Zarafina placed a spread of three cards on the table in front of them.

"Your father will recover. In fact, he's on his way now."

"The cards can tell you that?"

Zarafina paused as if for a moment she was going to take credit for it. "No, he called the resort, and Amelia sent me to tell you."

Nakoa smiled, feeling a little lighter inside.

"The boat is another matter. I sense there will be greater things coming from this." She tapped the cards. "And as for Kailani, go to her. Be honest about who you are and what you feel. That is the only way forward."

Her words resonated with him.

"I will," he said, rising from the pillows. "Thank you, Zarafina."

The old woman smiled. "Anytime, dear. Now go get your girl."

Nakoa left the pavilion, his heart lighter than it had been in days. He found Kailani sitting alone on the beach, gazing out at the shimmering ocean. His pulse quickened at the sight of her.

"Hey," he said softly.

She turned, eyes widening in surprise. "Oh. Hi."

"Can we talk?" Nakoa gestured beside her.

Kailani nodded, a hesitant smile touching her lips. Nakoa sat down, taking a deep breath.

"I owe you an apology," he began. "I wasn't honest about my situation. I just wanted you to think I had it all together. But I don't. The truth is, I'm barely keeping things afloat. I didn't mean to deceive you. I just...I really like you and didn't want you to see what a mess I am."

Kailani was quiet for a moment, processing his words. "I'm sorry I lied too," she said finally. "I have my own insecurities. About not being smart or accomplished enough."

Nakoa turned to her in surprise. "But you're incredible. You're strong, kind, beautiful..."

Kailani flushed, smiling shyly. "You're incredible too. I like you for you, not what you own."

Nakoa took her hand, interlacing their fingers. "I'm looking forward to us to really getting to know each other."

"Me too." Kailani leaned her head into his shoulder.

Nakoa kept his hand entwined with Kailani's as they sat together on the beach, the setting sun casting a warm glow over them.

"Can I tell you something I've never told anyone before?" Kailani asked softly.

Nakoa nodded, giving her hand a supportive squeeze.

"I've always dreamed of being a marine biologist," she confessed. "Ever since I was a little girl. But I never thought I could do it. My family always said I wasn't smart enough for college."

"That's ridiculous," Nakoa said adamantly. "You're brilliant, Kailani. If it's your dream, you should go for it."

Kailani looked at him uncertainly. "You really think I could?"

"I know you could," he said with conviction. "I'll support you in any way I can to help make it happen."

Kailani's eyes misted over with tears. "You really believe I can do it?"

"I absolutely do," Nakoa said. "I believe in you, Kailani."

Overcome with emotion, Kailani pulled Nakoa into a passionate kiss. As their lips met, the rest of the world melted away. All that existed in that moment was their love and the future they would build together.

The End

Can't get enough of the Palekaiko Beach Resort? Check out Jamie K. Schmidt's Hawaii Heat series, which opens with Amelia and Dude's story USA Today bestselling story, Life's A Beach.

CRAZY LITTLE MEET CUTE

JANA ASTON

CHAPTER 1

My name is Georgina Reeves and there are three things you need to know about me.

One, my ex-boyfriend is getting married.

Two, the bride-to-be is my stepsister.

Three, the wedding is today.

Four, I have a slight, teeny-tiny problem with procrastination.

Five, I don't have a date to the wedding.

Six, I RSVP'd a plus-one.

Seven, I've already told everyone his name is Ben.

Eight, I've also told them that Ben's very successful, wildly handsome, and entirely besotted with me.

Nine, Ben does not exist.

Ten, my poor counting skills are not the reason my ex and I are no longer together.

The way I see it, I've still got options. Option A, I find someone in the lobby of the Ritz-Carlton in Maui to impersonate my non-existent boyfriend, Ben.

Or option B, I admit defeat... and tell my family that Ben's appendix unexpectedly ruptured so he missed his flight to Maui.

Obviously option B requires a plethora of additional lies on my part, but I think I'm up to the task. Poor Ben though. He was definitely looking forward to this trip. It'd have been impossible for him not to have been. A week-long trip to a tropical island. Perfect weather, gorgeous scenery and a lot of sex. Loads of it. It's probably how he missed all the signs that his appendix was about to call it a day, distracted as he must have been thinking about all the creative ways I was going to thank him for coming with me to this thing.

Lies and delusions are also not the reason things ended between me and my ex.

At least not lies and delusions told by me.

Since my ex-boyfriend is marrying my current stepsister, I think you can do the math on that one.

Anywho.

A date. I still need one.

Yeah, yeah, finding one in New York and bringing him with me would have been the practical thing to do. The logical thing. And I was going to. I absolutely was going to find a date, months ago. Early enough so that we'd be exclusively dating by the time this wedding rolled around. Early enough to book his ticket on the same flight, in side-by-side seats. I. Was. Going. To.

That's the important part. My intentions were good. It's just that dating is so stressful and, frankly, annoying. And I was distracted shopping for the perfect wedding gift. One that said, ever so subtly, You're marrying my leftovers. Congratulations. I hope you're as happy as you deserve.

I bought them a composter.

No gift receipt.

Anyway, the point is, I was busy.

Time crept away on me. At some point I made up Ben, with every intention of actually meeting him, but once I'd made him up I conveniently decided that what I'd done was manifest him and the Universe would deliver.

Thus, I was free and clear to ignore the entire wedding situation and binge-watch a few seasons of Grey's Anatomy on Netflix. By a few, I mean the first fifteen seasons.

Look, I had the best of intentions. I bought the composter, didn't I?

And I did look, but it's harder than you'd think to find a single man named Ben, in his thirties, living in Manhattan and working in finance. The finance part wasn't super important, as I'd had the foresight to be pretty breezy with those details when I made him up. Finance, accounting, trading. Who the fuck cares. He looks good in a suit and my stepsister's mother can fuck right off if she doesn't believe he's real and that he has selected the fish on the RSVP.

Obviously at this point I'm aware that I'm not going to find Ben. The universe has not provided. It's fine. Some other guy is just going to have to deal with being called Ben for the next week. As soon as I find him and convince him to agree to it.

I scan the hotel lobby, ignoring the mild panic fluttering in my chest. I am really, really cutting this one close. To be fair, I'd had the best of intentions of finding a fake date last night. I'd even gone down to the hotel bar after checking in with the sole purpose of finding someone. Anyone. It's just that the hotel bar is on the beach and I'd been distracted by a cat walking along the sand, which led to me googling whether cats can catch fish, which led to me researching if I could bring a cat with me on the flight home, which led to me looking up patio lights on Amazon. I have no idea how I made the jump to patio lights, I don't even have a patio in New York.

In my defense, there wasn't a single unattended man in the bar. It was all couples. Or families. Kids drinking fourteen-dollar non-alcoholic cocktails with little paper umbrellas while I sat alone researching cat carriers for Mr Darcy.

The evening wasn't a total waste, however, as the bartender took pity on me when I told her my tale of woe and let me know that the hotel was booked solid this week due to a convention checking in the following day. The convention being—wait for it—an international conference on gambling law. It's not finance, but close enough. I'm sure the law nerds dress well and I can pass one off as Ben.

Boom.

Mic drop.

Clearly the universe was telling me to wait another day to deal with the date situation, and who was I not to listen when the universe spoke?

Which brings us to now. I'm lingering under a banner welcoming the legal conference to the resort. All that's left is to find someone and bring him up to speed on the shortest love story ever told.

I can do this. Exhale.

It's going to be fine.

Who wouldn't want to skip a boring conference to attend the wedding of a couple they've never met? With a woman they met twenty minutes before the wedding started?

Yeah, I'm fucked.

Ben has definitely ruptured his appendix. Or is it torn? Leaked? Burst? I open a browser on my phone to read up on appendixes while heading in the direction of the wedding ceremony when I plow right into something.

Not someone.

I am not caught by a strong pair of arms and yanked to safety after nary a delicate wobble on my feet.

No.

I'm on my ass in the lobby of the Ritz-Carlton.

CHAPTER 2

"Are you all right, love?"

Oh, my God.

He's tall, dark and handsome.

And British.

I will never question the universe again.

The man extends a hand to help me up. I slip my hand into his and we live happily ever after.

Just kidding. I'm looking for insta-love, but he's going to have to woo me just a little. Like an iota. Like, if he smiles at me that will seal the deal for me.

"You should really watch where you're going," he murmurs, no longer looking at me. "You could have dented my suitcase."

Charming.

Not.

Still, I can make this work. I'm sure of it.

"I'm fine." I make a show of brushing myself off and ensuring I'm not in the midst of a wardrobe malfunction. Not that he'd notice, busy as he is examining a non-existent scratch on his stupid bag.

"Brand-new Tumi," he gripes, now rotating it to ensure the wheels are working to his satisfaction.

Chivalry really is dead.

"My ankle is fine," I offer, hoping to refocus him.

"I'd imagine so, since you fell on your arse."

This is… not going to plan.

"Indeed I did." I offer him my friendliest smile. "Nonetheless, thank you for coming to my rescue. I'm Georgina."

"Harvey," he replies, barely sparing me a glance, his gaze now focused over my shoulder in the direction of the convention area. The conference lanyard looped around his neck confirms he's here for the conference.

Luckily for him, I'm about to spare him the boredom.

"Look, Harvey, I'm having a bit of a rough day and I fear we've gotten off to a bad start."

That catches his attention, lines forming on his forehead as his eyes narrow. "Do I know you?" he questions, looking thoroughly confused. To put it nicely. Annoyed would be another way to look at it, but I'm sure it's the language barrier, what with him being British and all. It's adorable, honestly. One day I'll tell this story to our children and we'll all laugh and laugh.

"Not yet." I grin and give him a little wink. "But you're about to."

"No." He shakes his head and starts to move around me. "No, thank you."

I exhale.

The universe is really trying me. I can't see this relationship working if he's going to be this difficult over every little thing, but whatever. It's fine. I don't need to marry the guy, I just need a date for this wedding.

"Listen, Harvey. Hear me out. How would you feel about doing me a favor?"

That stops him. He steps back a full foot, as if I'm about to pick his pockets. He pats the breast pocket of his jacket, as if to reassure himself his wallet is still there, then crosses his arms across his chest and stares at me.

"A favor." He repeats the word back and it leaves his mouth as if it's idiotic. "What a ludicrous idea. Why would I want to do a favor for you, a clumsy, inconsiderate woman I've only met moments ago?"

That did not sound better in a British accent, in case you're wondering. It sounded worse, actually. Like being chastised by a posh headmaster, and not in a 'sexy fun times' way.

"Yes, a favor. You know a small kindness that humans sometimes do for one another. Also, I am neither clumsy or inconsiderate," I snap, then, for reasons unknown to my brain, I add "Sir," to the end.

You'd think that would be the moment sparks would fly. His eyes would flash and there'd be a tiny hitch of his lips as he imagined the potential between us. My pulse would race and heat would simmer low in my belly.

But no.

He checks his watch.

I sigh.

"You're pretty clumsy. You just plowed into me because you weren't watching where you were going. You could have injured someone, or damaged my property."

I can't believe I ever thought about sleeping with this guy. Granted, it was three minutes ago before I knew better, but ugh. Never. What a waste of an accent. And a perfectly good sexual fantasy in which I'm detained by Scotland Yard for being very, very naughty. Wasted.

"If you must know," I say, still desperate to salvage this in some way, "I was having an emergency."

"Do tell." He twirls a finger in the air in that universal gesture to continue, boredom covering his face.

"Well, my boyfriend's appendix exploded," I say, and then, in a moment I will replay in horror for the next decade, I make little explosion movements with my hands as the word leaves my mouth.

Harvey stares.

I nod my head slowly. I'm in too deep. "So I was texting him, to see how he was feeling. Because," I stress the word, "I'm considerate."

We stare at each other.

Silence.

I make another hand explosion, mouthing the word 'boom,' but in my head I'm mentally booking my next therapy appointment. It'll need to be via Zoom, before I even get off this island, clearly.

Harvey tilts his head in a single nod. "Let's have it then. What's the favor?"

Oh, right. I'd nearly forgotten.

"Okay, so, my stepsister is about to get married." I glance at my watch before waving my hand towards the direction of the beach where the wedding is minutes from starting.

"Mmhmm," Harvey murmurs.

"To my ex-boyfriend."

Harvey runs two fingers across his forehead, as if the beginnings of a headache are developing.

"Obviously, I can't show up to the wedding alone." I shrug, indicating how impossible that would be. "And I've already told the entire family that my new boyfriend, named Ben, would be coming with me."

Harvey's eyes widen.

"But then his appendix," I add, my voice nearly a whisper. "So if you could just—"

"No."

Harvey doesn't even wait to see if I'm going to add anything else. He's already four feet away, his suitcase gliding beside him as he takes off without so much as a backward glance, his spare hand moving to once again reassure himself he still has his wallet.

Asshole.

I mean, I get it, but still.

Fuck the univer—

"I'll do it."

The words come from behind me, the voice a low rumble. Sexy. The hairs on my arms stand on end, my entire body is at attention and I haven't even seen him yet.

Do not get ahead of yourself. He's probably not even talking to you. He's probably a clown. Like an actual clown hired for the legal conference, or my stepsister's wedding.

I'm aware that neither scenario makes any sense, but I am who I am.

I exhale and turn.

I take him in and yes, he is indeed sexy. And he is, in fact, talking to me. And I know, without a shadow of a doubt, that I will someday retell this story.

Our story that is beginning right now.

He's... beautiful. Perfect. At least half a foot taller than me, if not more. Thick brown hair, trimmed to perfection. Strong jaw and a nose that might have been broken in some childhood stunt gone wrong. I want to press my thumb to his bottom lip to see if it's as soft as it looks, right before I press my own lips against them. His eyes though, those are his best feature. Warm. Brown. Small laugh lines at the edges. Completely focused on—and amused by—me.

And he smells good. That cannot be understated. It's a very important detail. His hair is ever so slightly damp, and I imagine him using the hotel-provided shampoo without giving a shit if it's scented to smell like the beach. I want to lean in and sniff him, but I've made this weird enough already.

Focus, Gigi.

"You'll do what?" I ask, a smile threatening my lips.

"I'll be Ben." He's already stuffing the conference lanyard into the pocket of his suit coat.

"You heard all that?"

"Every word. I wasn't even pretending not to listen. You'd have noticed if you hadn't been so wrapped up in selling that atrocity of a story." He pauses, then whispers, "Boom," while making the explosion gesture with his hand.

Then he winks at me.

Winks, for crying out loud.

With one of those perfect brown eyes, like this is all so amusing. Like he heard my entire insane story and, instead of being horrified, was amused. Because he took it for what it was meant to be, a lighthearted attempt to rescue myself from a shitty situation. And he's all in. Along for the ride.

Lord help me.

Still… it would behoove me to clarify.

"You're willing to skip your conference to help me?" I rest my weight on one hip and tilt my head to the side, as if I have all the time in the world for his answer. I don't. The wedding really is starting in a matter of minutes.

"The conference is bullshit. You think we actually come to Hawaii to discuss gambling law? It's a tax write-off for a week on the beach."

"Are you sure?" I press, sure this is too good to be true. That he's too good to be true. "Harvey seemed pretty intent on attending," I deadpan.

"Harvey's a fucking loser."

"Hmm." I eye him. I want to believe I've had a change of luck, so very badly. "What's your name?"

"Ben," he quips, a playful smirk on his face.

"It's not," I reply, snaking my hand into his jacket pocket to nab his lanyard.

He doesn't stop me.

"'Lawson McCall,'" I read out loud. "'International Gambling Law Conference, Attendee.'" I stuff the lanyard back into his pocket and stare at him for a moment longer as if I'm thinking this over.

I'm not. Not really. If I procrastinate any longer I'll miss the wedding. And I didn't fly to an island in the middle of the Pacific Ocean just to let everyone think I was too brokenhearted to show my face at the wedding.

Fuck. That.

"What's in this for you?" I ask, brows raised, as if I'm in some position to negotiate. I appreciate that he's playing along though.

"The privilege of doing a good deed."

I glare.

He laughs. "How about this? You'll owe me a favor. To be called in at some point in the future."

"I'm not sleeping with you," I tell him. That's a lie. I definitely might.

"Of course not," he agrees, shaking his head as if the idea hadn't even crossed his mind.

He better be lying.

Then he places his hand on my lower back, like it's the most natural thing in the world, and we slip into the wedding moments before the arrival of the bride.

And I know without a doubt I'm exactly where I need to be.

Loved my meet cute? Try my other books at www.janaaston.com.

NOT MADE TO LAST

JAY MCLEAN

CHAPTER 1 - OLIVIA

Standing over the lifeless body, I nudge it with my toe and watch it shift an inch.

I'm being dramatic.

Obviously.

So is the person I just hit with my car. *Hit* would be a slight exaggeration. I tapped it.

Him.

Not *it*.

But, going by how he's lying on his side in the middle of the road, completely silent and unmoving, you'd think I ran him over with a semi at full speed. I was rolling to a stop when he came out of nowhere—dressed in all black, in the middle of the night—and now that I think about it... I'm pretty sure *he* hit me.

"Are you okay?" I ask, waiting a few seconds for a response that never comes. "I'm sorry." I hunch down with my hands on my knees for a closer inspection. The headlights on my still-running truck illuminate the space around him, but I can't see much of anything with his hood over his head the way it is. He's tall, built, and that's all I can make out from his fetal position.

I take a moment to calm my thoughts, stand to full height, and look around. We're in a part of town that I often frequent, not because I'm invited, but because my second job brings me here. I'd just delivered a pizza to a house a block away—the most lavish home I've ever come across. I'm sure if I looked up the address online, it would be described as an *estate*, whatever that means. Either way, it's pretty clear that my beat-up old Toyota Tacoma and I—we don't belong.

Here, I'm surrounded by the rich.

Not rich.

Wealthy.

Big difference.

Not that any of it matters. If my eighteen years on this earth have taught me one thing, it's that at our cores, we're all the same. We're nothing but flesh and bones and organs; entire bodies that are overworked, minds that overthink, and hearts that have the potential to break.

We wake up every day with goals set, hoping for that tiny piece of joy we obtain when we achieve them—all the while knowing in the back of our minds that we have absolutely zero control over this shit-show of a thing called *life*.

Pessimistic? Maybe. But it's also the truth. And it's not as if I share these thoughts with anyone, because that would be horrible. Life is crappy enough —there's really no need for the reminder. Besides, people my age are made to believe they have the world at their feet. *We can achieve anything*, so we've been told, and I'm sure as hell not going to be the one to break it to anyone.

I heave out a sigh and blink back the fog, forgetting momentarily about the possible dead body by my feet.

He still hasn't moved.

I feel like I've been standing here for an eternity. In reality, it's likely been less than a minute.

Squatting down, I gently settle my hand on his arm. "Where are you hurt?" I ask.

Nothing.

"Can I do anything?"

Still nothing.

"Do you need me to call an ambulance... or take you to the emergency room? I..." I don't know what to do here, and now I'm starting to panic because maybe I did *hit* him.

The body moves.

Groans.

Progress.

I release the breath I'd unknowingly been holding and attempt to refocus.

"Ohana?" Max calls from the back seat of the car. "What's happening?"

Shit.

Shit shit shit.

At the sound of Max's voice, the figure moves again, and when his face comes into view, my panic doubles.

Triples.

"Ohana?" Max again.

I keep my gaze on the confused gray eyes in front of me and, not knowing if I'm lying, say over my shoulder, my words aimed for Max, "It's okay, buddy. Everything's fine."

It takes a moment for my victim to roll to his back, tilt his head up, then speak. "Drive much?" he croaks.

All the air rushes from my lungs at the sound of his voice. I used to spend hours imaging it, then, later, re-watching whatever clips I could find of him online. But I'd never heard it in person.

Until now.

Rhys.

Thank fuck I don't whisper his name out loud like I do in my head.

Rhys. Rhys. Rhys.

As in *Rhys Garret*—co-captain of the St. Luke's basketball team and, of course, the most popular and *powerful* guy roaming that school. Or at least he was. From my understanding, he graduated a few weeks ago, and I... I know way more about him than I should. Especially considering he has absolutely no idea who I am.

Nervous energy crawls through my veins, and thoughts fly through my mind faster than I can catch them. It sucks that the one thought I latch on to is: *please don't sue me.* "Are you okay?" I extend my hand, praying he's well enough to take it. "I'm sorry." *Sorry that he came out of nowhere and got in my way.*

Rhys accepts my offer, his large hand dwarfing mine as he slowly comes to a stand. I try my best to help him up, but with his towering height and nothing but muscle, I doubt I'm having much effect. Finally, he lets go of my hand and twists slightly at the waist, soothing his palm along his right hip. His low wince slices through the summer night air, and he states, "Yes."

I look from his hip to his hand, hanging lazily at his side, then up the length of his body until my eyes meet his. "Yes?"

"Yes," he repeats.

"Yes... you're okay?"

"Ohana?" Max calls out again.

I glance over my shoulder, through my car's windshield, and to the backseat, where Max's face is lit up by his iPad. "One second," I call out, then look back up at Rhys, my neck straining from our height difference—my 5'4" to his 6'3", and... I catch myself there, at the absolute peak of pathetic.

Look.

It's not as if I stalk the guy, but his height is listed on most websites that include his name, and it's *right there* beside his weight and a line above his birthday. Which, if I'm not mistaken, was only a few days ago. He just turned nineteen. All information which is completely irrelevant to our current circumstance. "So, you're good?" I ask.

"No, I'm not good." He shakes his head, eyes unfocused as he looks down his nose at me. "So, *yes*, take me to the emergency room." Without another word, he moves slowly to my car, a noticeable limp in his swagger, and all I can do is watch, frozen, wondering how the hell I got into this situation.

Because I offered to take him?

I didn't *mean* it. Not really.

Rhys opens the front passenger door, illuminating the interior.

Illuminating *Max*.

I rush to get in the driver's seat, my pulse racing, and glance from Rhys to Max and back again. My supposed "injured victim" sits carefree, legs kicked out, hands resting on his thighs. A slow smirk forms on his lips as his gaze switches between Max and me. Eyes the color of slate, he homes in on mine, his head tilting slightly. "You're not from around here, are you?" he murmurs.

I'm in denim shorts and a plain white tank, no makeup, my hair in a messy knot. My brow bunches as I glare at him. "I didn't realize my attire screamed *lacking financial wealth*." I should've hit the gas the moment I saw him.

He sighs, rolling his eyes dramatically. "That's not what I meant."

I don't care what you meant, I say. Not out loud. Just to myself. Because fuck him and his judgmental ass. I face forward, put the truck in gear, and begin the drive, waiting until I've rounded a corner to glance up at the rearview, at Max in the back seat, headphones on, eyes focused on his iPad. I'll be sure to check in on him later.

Rhys must sense my concern because he turns his entire body around, his injury seemingly forgotten. "You okay, kid?"

Through the rearview, I see Max look up and nod once.

Rhys extends his arm, his hand a fist, ready for knuckles. "I'm—"

"Timothy!" I cut in. *Timothy?* It was the first name I could think of, and I blurted it out before I could stop myself. Max doesn't need to know who he is. In fact, I'd *highly* prefer it that way.

"Right." Rhys draws out the single word. "*Timothy.*" The humorous lilt in his tone has me cringing. He's still facing Max when he asks, "And you are?"

Without thinking, I reach out, place my hand on the side of his head and *force* him to face forward. "He's... off limits."

CHAPTER 2 - RHYS

Off limits?

The fuck does that mean?

If this girl has a kid, then... it's whatever—no big deal.

Maybe she's ashamed of having a kid young, out of wedlock or whatever. I don't know. The things people are self-conscious about these days blow my mind.

Ignoring the dull ache pulsating from my hip, I glance behind me again. The boy's around five or six, dark-skinned, with thick glasses sitting crooked on his nose. Then, I focus on the girl behind the wheel. If I had to guess, I'd say she's my age, give or take a year. Dark hair piled high on her head, perfectly straight nose, and rounded cheeks—stained pink from her blush.

She's cute; there's no doubting it, but considering what's transpired the past few minutes, she might also be insane.

Just my type.

I peek over at the kid again. Maybe he's not hers, at least biologically. Not unless his dad's genetics are far stronger than hers. It's possible. Or perhaps she's just babysitting. But then why not just say that? Why attempt to shield us from each other? Also, why the fuck am I *Timothy*?

Hmm... now I'm intrigued.

And my intrigue never ends well.

"So..." I start, unsure where to go from here. "How are you?" Odd thing to ask considering what got us here, but what else is there to say?

"You mean besides hitting you with my truck hard enough that I have to take you to emergency?" Her eyes flick to mine, muddy brown beneath long, dark lashes. "I'm doing... *fine*..." The last word comes out as a question, and she focuses on the road again.

I focus on her.

On her teeth as they clamp down on her full bottom lip—worrying. On her eyebrows as they lower with each passing second. On her eyes as they continuously shift from me to the road and back again.

I bite back a smile, because she looks like a modern-day Snow White, only, unlike the fairy tale, this little princess wasn't wandering through a forest and stumbling across a cottage. No. Tonight, she was driving around in an old truck... and slamming straight into me.

Some might call it fate.

Kismet.

A series of unfortunate events.

"Everything okay?" she asks quietly, glancing at me quickly with her eyebrows raised. She just caught me watching her. Staring at her. Scrutinizing every damn inch of her.

Do I care?

Not even a little bit.

I've already decided that her cheeks are her best feature. At least on her face. I'll be sure to study the rest of her later.

"How bad are you hurt?" she adds, the softness in her voice conveying her concern.

"I'm all right." I shrug, trying to play it cool, but my eyes drop to her legs, all smooth skin and thick thighs, and sure, maybe an illicit thought crosses my mind, but now's not really the time to voice them.

Besides, she seems too nice for that.

Too pure.

Too... sweet.

Like a perfect little porcelain doll.

Breakable.

All assumptions, of course, because I don't know shit about the girl.

I know enough, based on her clothes and the car she drives, that she doesn't come from money, and I have no idea what she was doing in my neighborhood, and the more I think about it, the more the whole babysitting theory makes sense.

Am I being judgmental? Absolutely. But am I lying? Nah.

My phone rings, pulling me from my thoughts, and I quickly shove my hand into my hoodie pocket to retrieve it. I silence the call without ever fully comprehending who's calling.

"Was that your parents?"

I scoff at the thought. "No."

"Is someone looking for you?" she asks, the panic in her voice palpable. And now I'm starting to feel guilty for using her like this.

"Maybe," I murmur. Unlikely, though. I doubt anyone partying at my house even realizes I'm gone. At that thought, I'm reminded of why I left in the first place. Quickly shoving my phone back where it belongs, I stare out the window and re-evaluate my life choices.

The party had barely reached its peak when I determined I needed to get the fuck out of there. Granted, I was the one to invite them, but still…

Here's the thing: I live in an obnoxiously large house, and for the most part, I'm there alone.

Alone and lonely.

So, I throw these mini ragers on the fly, and people turn up. Lots of them. Most are nameless, sometimes even faceless, and it's only once they pack the place with bodies that my sense kicks in.

Somehow, amid the awareness of being lonely, I forget the not-so-insignificant fact that I hate people. Can't stand them, to be honest.

So, I leave.

Which is what I did tonight. I changed out of my jeans and T-shirt and got into sweats—black, to mix in with the night. I escaped through one of the guest bedroom balconies, jumping onto the roof of the first level, then leaped onto the ground like a stealthy fucking ninja. Then, I crept into the darkness of the woods surrounding my property and ran.

I had no real clue where to go, not that I ever do. I simply wanted to get as far away as possible, as soon as possible.

I wasn't looking where I was going or what was around me. I didn't even see the headlights. Just felt the impact. And I thought, as strange as it is, that getting hit by a car may be the best thing that could've happened to me tonight.

It was almost comical.

Until I felt the pain.

So, I lay on the ground, and I didn't move. Didn't even lift my head.

I didn't get up.

Couldn't.

Not because I was being a pussy, or because I hurt, or even because I didn't want to face the person standing above me.

I didn't get up because… sometimes, I feel as if this life, this world, isn't worth getting up for at all.

CHAPTER 3 - RHYS

I wait by the nurse's station at the emergency room while Little Miss Lead-foot stands just outside the entrance, phone held to her ear in one hand and the "off-limits" boy in the other. Carrying his backpack both shoulders, he looks up at her, his blinks slow. It's probably way past his bedtime, and that guilt from earlier returns, weighs heavier on my chest.

"Can I help you?" a female voice pulls my attention away, and I turn to the nurse behind the desk—a middle-aged woman with tired eyes and a forced smile. Her shoulders are hunched, her tone weary, and with a job such as hers, I don't blame her.

"Hi." I give her my most genuine smile and say, "I got hit by a car earlier."

The look she gives me shows her skepticism. After making her way around the desk, she stands in front of me and quickly examines me from head to toe. From the outside, I look perfectly normal. "It wasn't too bad," I mutter. "I'm just a little..." A little what? "Banged up."

The nurse—Marion—going by her name tag, hesitates. "Where exactly?"

"Uh... my hip. Thigh..."

Marion heaves out a sigh and makes her way back behind the desk. "Okay, so a banged-up body?" she questions, looking around the waiting area. There are at least twenty people here; a group of girls in one corner, but mainly guys scattered around, a few with obvious injuries. There's a kid with a clearly broken arm, and one dude has a blood-stained rag held to his temple. And here I am, able to walk, talk, and give Marion my details when she asks for them. At the mention of my last name, her eyes widen. Just a tad. "Garret?"

I nod.

"As in—"

My second nod cuts her off, and she smiles the biggest, *fakest* smile, her weariness from earlier completely diminished.

A few years back, my parents donated an entire wing in the children's ward at this very hospital and named it after my sister. The Isabel Garret wing provides temporary housing for kids undergoing treatment, with enough room for parents and guardians to stay with them.

My sister has never spent a day here. Ever.

I'm not saying it's a bad thing. I'd much rather their money go here than, say, my old high school—which they've done in the past—to bury whatever minor mishap or predicament I found myself in. It's just... it's hard to be a Garret in this town.

Poor little rich boy, right?

Even without my last name sprawled on the walls of this hospital, I'm almost positive Marion would have the same reaction. We're known around here, or at least my parents are. They're business owners. Venture capitalists. Philanthropists. Millionaires.

And they're not the only ones. Most of the people in my neighborhood have similar titles. The difference between them and us is that they come from old money—generational wealth.

My parents made theirs after Izzy and I were born.

"I'm sure we can have someone check you out right away," Marion says, typing away on her keyboard.

I glance around the room again, at the other people in far worse condition than myself, and then to the entrance as my forced companions make their way inside. "You know what?" I tell Marion. "Just add me to the end of the list." Seriously? What the fuck kind of asshole would I be if I expected preferential treatment on a medical issue just because my parents have money? Besides, the longer the wait, the longer it is until I'm forced to go home and face my living hell.

Marion glances at her colleagues working beside her, uncertain.

My smile is almost pleading. "Please?"

"If you say so…" She taps a few buttons on the keyboard before looking up at me. "We have all your details in the system." Then she motions to the waiting area. "Please take a seat, Mr. Garret."

I inwardly cringe at her words.

Mr. Garret is my father.

I'm merely his disappointment.

CHAPTER 4 - OLIVIA

"I hope you don't have any plans tonight," Rhys says as we approach him standing by the nurse's station. "We're going to be here a while." Without waiting for a response, he leads us to a row of seats where Max plops down on a chair, his eyelids heavy. I take the seat beside him.

Luckily, our minor incident didn't affect Max as much as I thought it would. But he's tired now. Beyond it. And honestly, so am I. I didn't expect my hit-and-stay victim to actually accept my offer to drive him here, and I definitely didn't expect to have to wait. Rhys is a *Garret*, and that means something.

Rhys is still standing, hands at his sides as he looks around the space. With his eyes busy elsewhere, I allow myself a moment to take him in.

To really, *truly* look at him.

I'd only ever seen pictures of him clean-shaven. Now, he's got the later stages of what I would call scruff. It's the same dirty blond as the short, almost crew-cut style that's on his head.

He looks older than his nineteen years.

Tougher.

And all the above is only magnified by the harsh overhead lights that create shadows across his features, highlighting the multiple tiny, almost inconspicuous, scars on his face.

The first time Rhys was brought to my attention, I assumed he was "troubled." The kind of problematic over-privileged kid who spent his free time getting off on using random people as punching bags for shits and gigs. Or, more than likely, to see if it would get his parents' attention.

I was wrong on all accounts.

As far as I know, he's never been disciplined for fighting at school, or outside of it, for that matter. In fact, the only time I'm aware of any reprimands handed to him by St. Luke's was for some bullshit prank that involved a child-sized dildo and some heavy-duty superglue on the front doors of the most prestigious high school in all of North Carolina—his own.

Unfortunately for him, his urge to pull such stupid antics hit right before the regional semifinals. It cost him a game and his beloved team a possible championship.

The day after the loss, a video of him being interviewed by a local news station circulated like wildfire, went viral on most social media. When asked if he regretted his actions, Rhys took a moment to respond, looking pensive, before asking the interviewer if he thought a hundred unarmed men could take on an adult-size gorilla.

To anyone else watching it, he came off as aloof, almost unsympathetic. It showed Rhys as just another fuckboy idiot who gave very little shits about his life, especially his team. But I knew better. I knew *him* better. His team was everything to him, though he'd never admit it to anyone.

Suddenly, Rhys's eyes flick down to mine, and I quickly look away, try to refocus on the present. On Max. He's holding on to my arm, his eyes half-hooded, fighting to stay awake. "Lie down, bud," I tell him, helping him kick off his flip-flops. He does as I say, while I grab his iPad and headphones from his backpack for him. When I look up again, Rhys is gone... back to the nurse's station. It's clear he asks something of them, because they nod enthusiastically at whatever he says, and one disappears through the large double doors, returning a moment later with a hospital issued blanket. Without a word, Rhys approaches and—wordlessly—covers Max with the blanket, making sure it surrounds his entire body. He stands to full height again before reaching behind him, and grasping the back of his hoodie. He lifts the hem higher, higher, exposing the tanned skin covering his flat, toned stomach and the smattering of hairs that lead to—

I look away.

Ignore the way my heart flies to my throat.

It's nothing, I convince myself.

This reaction?

Completely normal.

Rhys's hoodie feels warm on my bare legs when he unceremoniously drops it on my lap. Then he sits down beside me, his arm touching mine.

"Umm..." I look from the hoodie to him.

"You're cold." It's not a question.

"I'm fine," I lie. Truth is, the moment we walked into the building, the harsh air-conditioning pricked at my skin and turned my flesh to ice.

Rhys half turns to me, his gray Nike shirt shifting, pulling tight across his muscled chest. The heat of his hand circles my wrist, spreading through my bloodline. He's gentle when he lifts my arm, and I hold my breath, watching those cool gray eyes of his as they lock on mine. Then, slowly, he runs a finger across the length of my arm, exposing my lies as more goosebumps rise, crawl across my skin. "Wear the damn hoodie."

I glare at him.

He glares back.

And... I wear the damn hoodie.

It's way too big, or I'm way too small, but either way, it's nice. Warm. Smells *delicious*. "What is this?" I murmur, sniffing the neckline.

"A hoodie," he deadpans.

I contain my eye roll. "The smell, you idiot."

He chuckles. "I don't know. Body wash?"

I sniff it again. "Man, you must have some bougie-ass body wash."

He doesn't reply.

Minutes of silence pass.

Max sighs in his sleep.

Finally, Rhys leans forward to look at him, his lips ticked up on one side. "Do you just have the one?" he asks, settling back in his seat.

"One what?"

"Kid," he replies. "Is he your only one?"

I shift my eyes up to his and raise my eyebrows.

"Right." He nods once. "I forgot... *off limits*." He taps at his temple. "Timothy will keep that in mind." After a heavy exhale, he asks, "Is your name really Honor?"

Confused, I keep my head down and ask, "Honor?"

"Your kid or whatever—that's what he called you, right?"

"Ohana," I provide, shaking my head. "And no, it's a nickname. It's um..." I clear my throat, suddenly anxious. "...it's from *Lilo and Stitch*."

He shrugs, seemingly uninterested. "Never seen it." More silence passes, and he slumps lower in his seat, kicking out his legs and crossing them at the ankles. "So... are you going to offer your name, or should I just keep referring to you as my attempted murderer?"

"Shut up," I whisper, looking around the room to see if anyone heard him. "And it's Olivia."

"Olivia..." He seems to turn over each syllable in his mind—all while his gaze skims each of my features. "Suits you."

What am I supposed to say to that? *Thank you?*

"I'm Rhys, by the way," he offers, getting more comfortable. "You know... just in case you cared about the guy you almost killed." He smirks, and my stomach does this weird thing I haven't felt in years. "But you already know who I am, don't you?" It's not so much a question as it is a statement, and he says it in a way that's almost... teasing.

I admit the truth, however cringeworthy it is. "I know *of* you."

"Yeah, most people around here do," he mumbles, nodding slowly, before looking away and glancing around the room.

I stay quiet, but inside, my mind is racing, trying to come up with excuses to get the hell out of here.

"Hey, thanks for hanging around," he says, tilting his head toward me.

I lower my gaze, murmur, "Yeah, well, I'm kind of the reason you're here, right?"

"Not kind of," he's quick to respond. "You *are* the reason."

Ouch. And also: *fuck off.* "What the hell were you doing dressed in all black creeping around at night, anyway?" I'm defensive, and so I should be. He can't place all the blame on me.

He lifts his head, nose up in the air like he owns the air we breathe. "I fail to see why that matters."

Dick. "Oh, I'm sorry." My sarcasm is palpable. "Did I ruin your night of breaking and entering, burglary and debauchery?"

"Debauchery?" He laughs once. "And breaking and entering and burglary are the same thing."

Of course he's trying to outsmart me. "No, they're not."

"Yes, they are!" He pulls out his phone, taps it a few times, then reads aloud. "Burglary offenses are often referred to as breaking and entering or unlawful entry."

I roll my eyes. "You were practically asking for this to happen."

"You realize you hit me with your giant truck, right?" he almost yells.

I match his tone. "You realize I was going, like, two miles an hour. Right?"

He shakes his head, shouting, "You're unbelievable!"

"Right back at ya!"

"What's going on over here?" a man calls out, approaching us quickly. He's in navy scrubs and a white coat, his credentials visible by the hospital issued ID clipped to his breast pocket. Gripping the stethoscope around his neck, he stops only feet in front of us, his gaze shifting from me to Rhys, and back again. "You're Mr. Garret?" The doctor, a man close to retirement, asks.

Rhys slowly gets to his feet. "Rhys is fine, sir," he states.

Doc heaves out a sigh, saying, "Well, I was told I had to come out and see you immediately." Ah, so the Garret name does work like magic, just as I thought it would. "Besides feeling the need to have a shouting match in the middle of the waiting room, what seems—"

"We weren't—" I attempt to interrupt, but Rhys cuts me off.

"I got hit by a car."

I grimace.

"Did they stop?" the doctor asks.

Rhys is *too* quick to respond. "Nah, they bailed before I could get any info."

The doctor looks Rhys up and down for any obvious signs of injury. "Where are you hurt?"

Rhys looks around the waiting room before a slow smirk creeps across his features. It's so slight that I may be the only one to notice. Then, without warning or a second's hesitation, he grasps the band of his sweats *and* boxer shorts and pushes them down one side, past his hip, only stopping once he reaches the middle of his thigh. Clouds of red, green, and purple form over his skin, and I outwardly wince in response. And then I notice the other parts of him exposed: that smattering of hair again, the deep V that leads to the base of his—

Girls behind me break out in giggles, and I force my eyes away.

Jesus. I said that out loud. *Ah, shit.*

"You like that, huh?" Rhys murmurs, and when I flick my gaze to his, his eyebrows are raised, his teeth showing with his cocky smile.

Flames of embarrassment lick across my flesh, up my neck, to the tips of my ears. And, of course, it's not enough that I'm practically at eye level with forbidden dick, but now the doctor is inspecting his injuries and asking questions.

Lots of them.

For minutes that feel like hours, I sit ramrod straight, my heart racing, my blood simmering just beneath the surface. I stare at the ceiling as if Michaelangelo himself painted it. I don't think I take a breath. Not one.

Completely normal reaction, I try to remind myself, again, only it's getting harder and harder to believe.

Speaking of hard...

"You can pull your pants up now," the doctor says.

Thank God.

Swear, the girls in the corner audibly groan in disappointment.

"Aw, do I have to?" Rhys smirks over at them. "I think my audience likes the show."

Smug.

It's the only way to describe him.

Rhys Garrett is a smug motherfucker.

And I'm only just realizing it now.

CHAPTER 5 - OLIVIA

After getting advice from the doctor to ice his wounds, Rhys lifts Max into his arms and carries him all the way to my truck. Max never wakes. It's a thoughtful move—one I wasn't expecting.

I buckle Max into his car seat, making sure he's safe, and then get behind the wheel. Already in the passenger's seat, Rhys watches me, his arms crossed as if contemplating my next move. I start the car, and then... I just sit there because I have no idea where to go from here.

Literally and figuratively.

I have so many thoughts racing through my mind, and I push away all the forbidden ones first. "I'm sorry," I blurt out. "I honestly didn't think I hit you that hard, but it looks—"

"Worse than it feels," Rhys finishes for me. "I've had more serious injuries playing ball."

I nod, assuming as much. Though, I doubt he would've gone to the hospital for those, so why now? "Hey, why did you tell the doctor it was a hit-and-run?"

He seems distracted when he answers, "I wasn't sure if they had to report it to the cops. I didn't want to get you in trouble."

I never even thought of that.

He adds, "I'm not going to sue you if that's what you're worried about."

A giggle forms in my chest, but never escapes. "Not gonna lie, the thought did cross my mind."

He stares ahead as he shifts in his seat. "Of course, it did," he mumbles. But the way he says it—as if it's all he expects from the world—it's kind of... sad.

"I mean... if I recall correctly, I offered to take you even before I knew who you were, so..." I'm trying to console him, and I don't know why. "I would've done it, either way."

"Yeah, but would you have stayed?" he asks, his focus on me again.

Honestly? "Probably not."

"That's what I thought."

Silence stretches between us, and I don't know what else to do. What else to say. I put the car in gear. "I should probably take you home."

He releases a long, drawn-out sigh, his head rolling against the headrest. "What if..." he starts, then shakes his head.

"What if... what?"

Another sigh. "I want to ask you something, but I don't want you to take it the wrong way."

This can't be good. My hands grip the steering wheel tighter as I tell him, "Ask me anyway."

"You guys gotta be somewhere?" He pauses a moment. "I mean, do you have to get your kid home?" I don't get a chance to respond before he adds, "Because I'm thinking we drive somewhere and... hang out. We can sit in your car and just... talk."

"Um..."

"Or not talk. Just, you know, stare blankly at the space in front of us..."

"I don't—"

"I'll give you all the cash in my wallet."

"As if you carry cash." That was not what I meant to say.

What I meant to say was *no*.

As in... *hell* no.

"I do." His smile is almost wicked—as if he can somehow sense my temptation. "A lot of it."

"How much?" *Ugh*. I could do with "a lot" of cash, and I'm sure his standards of measurement are far greater than mine.

"You'll have to wait and see."

I can't believe I'm even entertaining this. "For how long?"

He pulls out his phone and, at lightning speed, sends out a text. Almost immediately, there's a response. "One thirty."

I check the time: 11:45.

I check my tank: empty.

"I'm low on gas."

"So go fill up. I'll cover that, too."

I take in a sharp breath, then rest my back against the door, eyeing him. He stares right back. But the flicker of light in his eyes is gone, and he's no longer the cocky boy who brazenly dropped trou in the middle of the waiting room. Now, he seems smaller somehow, less... confident, maybe? "You're really desperate not to go home, huh?"

His voice is quiet, almost a whisper when he says, "You could say that."

"Want to tell me why?"

He shakes his head, eyebrows lowering. "It's not anything that would warrant your concern."

I stare into his eyes and try to seek the answers there. He watches me back, his gaze moving from my eyes to my nose. My mouth.

"What do you say, *Cheeks*?"

"Cheeks?"

"I like your cheeks," he replies. "They're... pinchable."

Heat rushes to said cheeks, and I attempt to hide it with a scoff that sounds more like a snort. "You want to pinch my cheeks?"

"Why?" That cocky smirk is back. "You going to let me?"

Circles. That's what we seem to do every time we talk. Go around and around and around in circles. "No, I will not let you pinch my cheeks." I sound like an indignant snob.

"Fair call," he says, so nonchalant—and I don't know why it's getting under my skin. "So... what do you say? Feel like getting paid to spend the night with me?" He shakes his head, chuckling. "I didn't realize that would come out so creepy."

Surprisingly, I find myself laughing with him. "Until one thirty," I confirm. "And then I take you home."

"So that's a yes?"

I suck in all the air my lungs can handle, release it slowly. "I'll do it on one condition."

He blinks.

"You have to tell me why you don't want to go home."

"Deal," he's quick to say. "I'll tell you once we get there."

"Get where?"

"I know a place."

CHAPTER 6 - RHYS

Besides some small chatter at the gas station and me giving Olivia directions, we don't speak. Besides, I was too busy on my phone searching up *Lilo and Stitch*.

Lilo and Stitch is a movie about a lonely little Hawaiian girl who, along with her much older sister, loses her parents, thus making the sister her guardian. In order to bring some form of order into their lives, Nani (the sister) allows Lilo (the little girl) to adopt a dog (Stitch), who ends up being an extraterrestrial being from outer space. Spoiler alert: shit happens. A lot of it. But, through all of the absolute mayhem that occurs (which includes visits from a social worker), Nani never once stops fighting for Lilo. And through their love, faith, and a little Elvis, the trio never falters in their unwavering belief in *Ohana*, the Hawaiian concept of *family*. It's repeated throughout the movie that "Ohana means family, and family means nobody gets left behind"... or something like that.

Anyway...

I can tell Olivia's wary of where we are and who she's with, but she doesn't voice her concerns.

I'd be wary, too, I guess.

It's not every day a random stranger leads you to an abandoned rooftop parking lot in the dead of night, but here we are.

As soon as Olivia parks, I open the door and hop out. The cool night air hits my lungs, and I head right for the edge of the parking lot. The cement half-wall is low enough for me to lean my forearms on, and so I do and look down over the edge of the building. Where we stand is only four floors high, and at an average of 15.5 feet per floor, that would make us 62 feet from the ground. At 200 pounds myself, it would mean I'd hit the ground at forty-three miles per hour. The fall itself would take less than two seconds.

Give or take.

Thanks, fifth-period physics.

It's not that I've actually considered jumping. I just get curious about these things.

About death.

Not the finality of death or even the act of dying. More like... what would happen *if*?

At only four floors up, death wouldn't be instant, if at all. Unless you land directly on your head, you'll likely have a few minutes of pure agony before you suffocate on your own blood and bleed out through the holes made from all the broken bones you created.

Pretty damn interesting if you ask me.

Footsteps near, and for a moment, I'd forgotten I wasn't alone. "So... you come here often?" Olivia quips.

I don't turn to her when I say, "I do, actually." At least once a week. Twice if I feel like I need it.

Stopping next to me, she mimics my position and looks down at the alley between the two buildings. There's really nothing to see besides dumpsters and drainpipes. "Well, I can see why..." She pauses a beat. "This is some view...." The girl's got jokes, and usually, I'd be all about it. Right now, though, I can't bring myself to feel much of anything.

"Yeah," I murmur. "I don't really come here for the view." I come here for the escape.

Or maybe it's the opposite.

I haven't figured it out yet.

Olivia's quiet a moment, and I can only imagine the thoughts bouncing around that pretty little head of hers. "Are we currently committing what one would call burglary..." she says, and I finally turn to her, my head tilted, watching her profile as she takes in our surroundings. I wonder what it would be like to see this place from her eyes. To see it for the first time.

"Would that be a problem?"

"Well, yeah." She offers a smile, and I wish I knew what it meant. "I'm not, like, poor, but I don't have fuck-you money to throw around, and neither do my friends and family, so bail money? Kind of out of the question."

I've already decided that I like the girl. I like that she doesn't bow down to bullshit or worship whatever version of me she's admitted to knowing. I like that she pushes back, that she doesn't take shit she doesn't deserve.

Most of all, though, I like that she's present.

That she's *here*.

With me.

"I'd bail you out," I murmur, glancing over at her truck. It's only a few yards away with the parking lights on. Usually, when I come here, I sit in the darkness, the moon and stars my only source of light. Of life. I try to peer inside her truck to make sure her kid's okay. "Is he good in there?" I ask, stepping toward it.

Olivia follows me, saying, "The windows are open, and once he's out, he's out. Plus, I left the lights on so if he wakes, he can see us."

"Are you sure, because—"

She tugs on my arm, forcing me to stop, and I do, momentarily dazed by her touch. And not in a creepy Edward loves Bella way, but I don't know. It's surprising, is all.

I spin to face her, my lips instantly forming a smile when I see her standing there, hands on her hips, nose in the air, like an adorably annoying little brat. "I haven't forgotten," she says, and I have no fucking clue what she's talking about.

I tilt my head, confused. "Forgotten what?"

"That you owe me a truth."

My shoulders drop.

"Why don't you want to go home, Rhys?"

I shrug. "There's a party at my house tonight."

"Oh, yeah?" she asks, distracted by her phone. She taps it a few times, and when I peek over at the screen, I see that she's setting an alarm. *Great.* She can't wait to get the hell away from me. And me? I can't seem to get enough of her. Shoving her phone into her back pocket, she asks, "Who's hosting it?"

I move toward the basketball hoop I keep in the corner of the parking lot, and with my back turned, answer, "Me, apparently."

"Rhys!" she gasps. "How does that even happen?"

I shrug, shifting the weights off the base of the hoop before dragging it toward the middle of the lot. The entire time I keep my eyes on the kid in the truck, make sure he doesn't wake from all the noise I'm making. Olivia was right—he's out.

She waits in silence as I grab a ball from the same corner and dribble lazily to position. I take a shot. Sink it. Then finally answer, glancing her direction, "I was bored at home. Lonely. Big house, just me, you know? And so, I invited a bunch of people over. They invited a ton of other people, and the next thing you know…" I run a hand over my head as I jog toward the barely bouncing ball to retrieve it. "I was all right for a bit until I remembered that I hate most people there, and I wanted out, so I left."

"You *left?*" she almost scoffs, moving beneath the hoop.

She catches the next shot that goes through the net and passes the ball effortlessly back to me.

"Yep," I tell her after catching her pass. I hold the ball to my hip, adding, "And that's when you impaled me with that beast of a vehicle."

Her shoulders sag. "*Impaled* now?"

I crack a smile. "I'm milking this shit, Cheeks."

She rolls her eyes, and it's only slightly cute. "Where are your parents?"

"Colorado," I'm quick to answer. "My sister goes to college in Boulder. She's one of those people who are crazy smart but socially awkward, so she needs them more than I do right now." It's only half the truth, but it's all the information I'm willing to give. Anything more might literally send me over the edge.

Of this building.

And in under two seconds, I'd be nothing but mangled flesh and shattered bones, bleeding out onto the concrete.

"Can I ask you a question?" she asks.

I switch positions and score again, then wait for her to catch the rebound and return the ball to me. "Another truth?"

Her smile warms parts of me I keep hidden from the world. "Is college in your future?"

I give her what she wants and hope it leads nowhere. "I'd be the worst kind of jerk if I took a spot on a team when someone else could use it as a stepping-stone to better their lives. Their futures." Plus, I was never sure if the colleges that threw offers my way wanted me or if it was the money my parents could provide the program. "Besides," I continue, "I'm not passionate about the game so much as the discipline it provides me."

"What do you mean?" She's cute when she's inquisitive—all scrunchy nose and squinty eyes.

I take a moment to come up with a simplified explanation. "It's easy to push aside all other thoughts and everything going on around you when you obsess over something. Basketball's been my obsession for a long time, and with it came discipline. Self-discipline." And God knows how badly I needed that. Without waiting for her response, I throw the ball toward her, completely unsurprised when she catches it flawlessly. I step to the side, offering her my position. "Take your shot."

Olivia does as suggested, and I can tell the moment the ball leaves her hands that it's in.

"Nice form," I say, jogging to retrieve the ball. I face her, holding the ball at my side. "Now it's your turn."

Head tilted slightly, she replies, "I just had my turn."

I shake my head, stopping a few feet in front of her. "It's your turn to give me a truth."

She chews her lip, looking everywhere but at me.

"Did Dominic teach you to shoot like that?"

Her intake of breath is audible, and her eyes drop. *Busted.*

I hold my ground, stay silent.

Finally, she looks up, eyes right on mine. "I taught him."

I nod, slowly, watching every single emotion pass through her features. Fear, shame, something else I can't quite put my finger on.

Dominic Delgado: soon-to-be senior at Philips Academy—my school's rival. Like me, he, too, is the captain of the basketball team. Unlike me, he's a complete and utter dickbag. And I can't fucking believe he's Olivia's brother. Though, just like she and the kid in her car—they look nothing alike.

"How did you know?" she asks, her voice quiet, words trembling with each syllable.

I dribble leisurely around her. "You went into the gas station after I did and got a call from him. Your phone was still connected to the Bluetooth in your car, and I saw the name 'lil bro' and the number."

"And you know it was Dom, how?"

I shrug, lazy. "I typed the number into my phone to see if I knew him, and wouldn't you know it…"

"Of course you have his number."

Another shrug. "Keep your enemies close…"

Her eye roll is so dramatic, she must be seeing stars.

"I didn't even know Dom had a sister."

She steps forward so fast; I don't have time to get rid of the ball before she swoops it out of my grasp. "Yeah, that's kind of the point."

"Why?"

Her lay-up is fucking perfect, and I don't think I've ever been so turned on. Neither of us makes a move to retrieve the ball, and after a few seconds, she turns to me, her smile soft, eyes warm, and something switches in that moment. Something rare. Something… *easy.* "No more truths tonight, okay, *Timothy?*"

I laugh.

Because what else *can* I do?

After a good hour of playing ball and talking shit, none of which has to do with two specific boys in her life, we give up for the night and sit on the bed of her truck, my phone softly playing music she seems to enjoy.

"What a wild night," she says through a sigh. She'd taken my hoodie off while we were playing, and now she puts it back on, releasing her hair from its knot so she can slip the hood over her head.

For a long moment, we sit in silence, staring ahead, and surprisingly, it's not awkward or unbearable. I've always disliked people who need to speak just to fill the dead air with even deader words. So, this? Sitting quietly with her, it's almost… comforting.

She's the first to speak, saying, "So, I was thinking about what you said earlier, about the loneliness thing..." Swear, I hope she doesn't ruin the fucking moment. "I don't know if it's normal. If it's an unconscious choice not to let people in or whatever... but, I don't know..." She pauses, inhaling deeply, before adding, "You said you live alone in a big house, and I... I live with people in a small house, and I still get lonely."

For a full minute, the only sound that forms between us is the single, quiet clearing of her throat. She doesn't look at me, and I'm too damn afraid of what I'll feel when I look at her.

Maybe getting hit by a car wasn't the best thing that could've happened to me tonight.

But getting hit by a car driven by *Olivia* definitely was.

I release my breath, slowly, slowly, and I wish I could say *something*. Something to show that her words have meaning, that they're not dead like the air around us. Like the soul that wonders what it would be like to jump off the edge. Instead, I tell her, "Is that an invitation to come over?" I'm an idiot, but I don't stop there. "Because I could cure your loneliness real quick, Cheeks."

Olivia scoffs, but it's clear she wasn't expecting anything else out of me. Smart girl. "Oh yeah. Dominic would love that."

Right. Dominic. Or as his fans call him: *The Dominator*. Stupid name. So stupid, I almost forgot about his existence. "So, I take it you're not going to tell him about tonight... about me?"

"No," she laughs—as if the idea itself is ludicrous.

"Why not?" I ask. "It's not as if we planned it."

"Because if he knew it was you I hit, he'd tell me to one: hit you harder. Two: reverse and hit you again. Three: all of the above, then you leave there."

"Holy shit." It's my turn to laugh. "He hates me that much?"

She nudges my side with hers. "You stole his girlfriend, Rhys!"

My eyes widen, because just like his existence, I'd forgotten about that, too. But... hold up. "Is that where his story ends?"

"What's that supposed to mean?" she accuses.

"Look," I say, hands up in mock surrender, "I'm just saying, whatever history your brother and I have, it's got nothing to do with *us*—you and me."

"There is no *us*," she says, defiant, and *nah*.

Fuck that.

I grab my phone from between us, tap it a few times. "So... he wouldn't be too happy if I tagged him in a pic of us together?"

"You wouldn't!" She tries to grab the phone from my hand, but I hold it away from her.

"I wonder if he'd recognize you with your eyes covered," I murmur through a chuckle, trying to handle my phone with one hand while I tug down on her hood. It only covers half her face, so her mouth is still visible, and I shove down the urge to kiss her.

Just once.

Just to curb my curiosity.

I keep hold of the hood while I snap shot after shot of nothing, laughing at her panic every time the fake shutter of my phone sounds. "Don't you dare," she practically squeals. And then she's on me, trying to get the phone from my grasp, and I can't stop laughing. Neither can she. I fall onto my back and release the hood when she climbs over me, and I stretch out my arm, keeping it from her reach. The hood still covers her eyes, because she's too busy using both her hands to blindly search for my phone.

She's practically feeling me up—warm hands gliding over my stomach, my chest. She finds my shoulder and follows my arm up, up, up, and I'm shaking from withheld laughter because she's got the wrong fucking arm.

"Give it to me!" she almost growls, right in my ear, and I swear to God, I'm rock fucking hard.

How can I not be?

Those words? From her mouth? Not to mention that she's practically spread out on top of me, her breasts brushing against my face as she continues to reach up, her heated fingertips making their way up my arm.

I can feel the fire—their flames flicking through my bloodline, pulsating throughout my entire body, right down to my cock.

Her hand searches my empty one, and she groans in frustration.

I'm no longer laughing.

No longer breathing.

Her hands move again, searching for my other arm, and I grip the phone tighter because no fucking way am I letting her have it. Her hand's on my wrist now—so close to her end goal—and without thinking, I brace my arm around her waist and pull her away.

Pull her *down*.

Right onto my erection.

We freeze, our entire bodies locked.

Surrendered.

In the few seconds since she came for me, I hadn't realized that she'd practically straddled my hips, her knees on either side. That dull ache from the impact earlier? Completely gone, it seems. Now her pussy's pressed against my hardened cock, and I'm sure she can feel it because she—

She moans.

I exhale. Slowly. Silently. And I can feel the heat emitting from her center, can feel her short breaths against my chin. She attempts to lift herself up, but I tighten my grip, push her back down. This time, she shifts on me. Not a lot. Just enough to let me know she feels me too. My pulse pounds, vibrating across my flesh, and I can't seem to inhale enough air to satisfy my need for life. The hoodie still covers her eyes, but her mouth...

Her mouth is so close to mine, lips wet, parted. All it would take is a slight lift of my head... but, I wouldn't do that to her. I can't. Instead, I release my phone, let it drop on the metal beneath us, and then grasp the back of the hood, clearing her vision.

Her eyes are closed when they're first revealed, and they land right on mine when she opens them.

And those cheeks... stained pink from exertion, from lust.

She wants this as much as I do.

I lick my lips, and she does the same.

Gently, I thrust up, wanting to see her reaction.

Her breaths falter, her eyes widening just slightly.

And then she responds to my action with one of her own—a slight circling of her hips. I almost lose all control at the sudden pleasure that spreads through me—like a series of waves about to create a tsunami.

My hand is on her thigh—thick fucking thighs made for grabbing—and I don't know how it got there. I move up slowly, watching her every breath, her every reaction, until I find the bottom of her denim shorts, and I can't look away. I don't even want to blink. I go higher, higher, until my palm settles on the curve of her ass. I squeeze, pushing her onto me firmer, harder. I want her to know what she's done to me, how my body's reacted to her. How she so easily controlled me, possessed me. Every single inch of me.

Her head falls, lands on my shoulder, but she doesn't move.

Doesn't speak.

I keep one hand on her ass as the other bunches the fabric of the hoodie until I find the end, and then I reach beneath it. Her skin is flaming hot against mine, and I trace down her spine to her waist, memorizing the shape of her.

Her grinds are short, tiny circles, and I can feel the warmth of her scattered breaths through my T-shirt, spreading onto my chest.

Fuck, I'd give anything to be inside her.

"Liv," I croak, my throat aching with the single word that could possibly end this.

She lifts her head just enough to meet my eyes, and I don't know who kisses who first.

I don't care.

Her lips are soft, her movements slow, and I can't fucking get enough of it. The first swipe of our tongues has us both moaning into each other, and I don't know where to put my hands. I want to touch her, feel her everywhere, all at once.

Kiss her everywhere.

Everywhere.

I reach up and grasp a handful of her hair. Tug. The sound that escapes her is pure fucking pleasure, and I kiss down her jaw, her neck, sucking hard. Biting. I pull her hair again. Teasing. Testing. She turns languid in my arms, and I crack a smile against her flesh.

Liv likes it a little rough...

...and I'm all fucking for it.

She dips her mouth to mine, catching my bottom lip between her teeth and pulling it away before running her tongue along the length of it. I groan, my dick throbbing, pulsing, warning me of what's to come. "Fuck," I spit, holding her ass in place. The way she moves... the sounds she makes... it's too fucking much. "You're too fucking good. I can't—"

I don't get a chance to finish the sentence because her phone goes off— her alarm—and before I can stop her, she's off of me. Completely. The sound of the alarm shrills through the air and rings in my ears louder than the blood rushing through my body.

She jumps off the truck, and I stay on my back, looking up at the stars as I try to catch my breath. "I'm so sorry, Rhys," she rushes out.

Sorry?

The fuck?

"Please don't tell anyone about this," she cries. *Actually* cries. And I sit up just to witness her pain. To make it mine. She swipes at a single tear on her cheek. "I'm sorry," she repeats. "This was a mistake."

I push away the sudden sharpness of anger that flickers inside me.

Flick.

Flick.

Flick.

It's pretty fucking obvious what she's thinking right now. How she feels— regret, disappointment, *fear*.

In her eyes, this was nothing more than a fleeting moment of uncontrolled desire.

To her... I'm nothing more than a mistake.

But to me...

I crack the faintest of smiles.

Olivia just became my new sport.

My new discipline.

My new obsession.

And she has no fucking clue what she's in for...

Thanks for reading. Check out the rest of my books at www. jaymcleanauthor.com.

PICTURES OF HOPE

JESSICA ASHLEY

To those with hopeful hearts.

CHAPTER 1 - LILLY

Hope Springs hasn't changed in ten years.

I stand on Main Street, staring at the faded Hardware sign as it swings in the light breeze. *Hope Hardware* is printed in dark red lettering over the top of re-purposed driftwood. From here, I can't quite see the beach, but I can smell the ocean. The delicate salty scent that has always reminded me of a home I planned never to return to.

Yet, for all of my planning, here I am.

Now what.

A man with salt and pepper hair steps out of the hardware store and wipes his hands on fading jeans. His back is facing me as he locks the door, likely taking a lunch break, given that it's just barely noon. The red and black checkered flannel shirt he wears is tattered and torn from years of wear.

From here, I can smell his aftershave, and a warmth settles over me as I cross the distance between me and the store. This is why I came home. He is why I came back even when I swore I never would.

"Hey, Dad."

He whirls on me, confusion on his aging face. That is until he sees me, and that face splits into a wide smile. He rushes forward and crushes me against him. "You're really here."

"I am," I reply, hugging him right back.

After marrying my mom when I was seven, Felix Bishop embraced me as his own flesh and blood. He raised me, gave me the freedom to dream and space when I'd desperately needed to find my own way. He was my confidant and the one who convinced me that not all men were like my biological father.

I shove those thoughts away.

"Kid, I missed you like crazy."

"I missed you, too." A tear gathers in my eye at his embrace.

He releases me though he keeps a hold on both of my arms as he looks me over. "You look good. Are you good?" His brow furrows. "Is everything okay?"

"Everything is fine," I reply with a laugh. "I just missed home."

"This place? You were living in paradise, Lilly." He laughs. "I hardly think Hope Springs was a blip on your mind."

"But you weren't there." I smile, and his expression saddens as he realizes just why I've come back.

"You didn't need to come back just because of that, Lil. I'm okay."

"I know you are." Tears burn in my throat, but I don't let them fall. "It was a long ride from the airport; think we could grab some food?"

"Of course. I was actually just headed to get a bite. Let's get your bags inside first." He reaches down and lifts my bags then unlocks the door to the hardware shop again. I follow him through the center aisle, passing buckets upon buckets of nuts and bolts, screws, and plated washers.

Every inch of this place is branded into my memory from years of playing hide-n-seek in the stacks; then later working the store to help Felix out. I smile, feeling more comfortable than I have in years.

We ascend a set of stairs at the back of the store, and he unlocks the door to the apartment before stepping aside so I can enter. The place had been a one-bedroom when he and my mom met, but he'd worked tirelessly to turn it into a two-bedroom so we could move in after they were married.

As far as I'm concerned, *this* is the place I grew up. Not the large two-story in Boston where I'd suffered far more in my seven years than I should have. I close my eyes for a moment, taking a deep breath and shoving those thoughts down for the second time today.

"I'm sorry it's not clean." He sets my bags down then rushes around, gathering plates and sticking them in the sink.

"It looks great." I smile, and he stops to stare at me.

"I'm so happy you're home. But I'm so sorry you felt you had to come back. I really am doing okay, Lilly. It's been three years now."

"I know." I swallow hard. "It was time for me to come back."

He stares back at me then nods tightly and wipes his brown eyes. "Ready for some food?"

"Yes, please. I'm starved. I don't suppose *Hope Diner* is still open, is it?"

My dad grins at me. "That it is, kid. Let's go get some lunch."

We make our way out of the hardware store and down Main Street. As we walk, I take time to study the businesses around me. A floral shop, three antique stores, a pizza place, a seafood restaurant, a post office, and a bar make up Main Street. Small, quaint, and just the way I remember it. With it being close to Christmas, the town is covered in tinsel with the palm trees around us decorated so that, when the sun goes down, they will still shine brightly with multi-colored Christmas lights.

Hope Diner has been a staple in Hope Springs since the town was formed. Every single Sunday after church, Felix brought my mother and me here for lunch. We'd discuss the message, laugh, and plan our week.

It was a tradition that I looked forward to and one that I've long since missed.

The aroma of coffee and baked goods fills my lungs as Felix and I step into the familiar place. Christmas music drifts from the old familiar jukebox. Driftwood, an old anchor, fishing netting, and various photos cover the walls around the place, giving it a relaxed, beachy vibe. And yet, still classy even decorated for the visit of ol' Saint Nick.

Home.

The word echoes through my mind. The pull to return to my roots has been stronger than ever before recently, the voice in my head telling me to come home finally so loud that I couldn't ignore it anymore.

While I'm not entirely sure why I'm supposed to be here, I do know, without a doubt, Hope Springs is where I'm supposed to be.

That is until a man pushes out of the kitchen carrying two plates of food. He slides them onto a bar and says something I can't quite make out to the customers who'd ordered them. My heart hammers against my ribs, and my stomach twists into knots.

And when Alex Phillips looks up at me, the world tilts on its axis. He freezes in place, eyes widening, mouth falling slack as he stares back at me.

"He's back?" I choke out.

"Did I forget to mention that when we talked last?" my father asks, cheeks red. "He came back two years ago."

I glance over at him, betrayal in my gaze as he smiles at me. "No," I say. "You didn't mention that."

He wraps an arm around me and guides me over to a table near the window. "I'm sorry, I must have forgotten."

We both know it's not true. After all, how could he forget the return of the man I was supposed to marry? A man who broke my heart and sent me running from my home because I couldn't stand the pitied looks I received from everyone who crossed my path?

Looking as handsome as ever in a white t-shirt and dark jeans, Alex makes his way over to our table. He stops beside it and smiles at my dad. "Felix, good to see you."

"You, too, Alex. Did you see who came back? Fresh in town as of this afternoon."

Alex's bright hazel eyes shift to mine, and he smiles down at me though, even with the friendly grin, I can sense his hesitation. "Lilly. You look amazing."

"Thanks. You work here now?"

"I own it," he replies. "Bought it last year when the Greysons went into retirement."

"Is that so?" I ask, looking to my father.

He shrugs. "I must have forgotten to mention that, too."

"Seem's you have amnesia. We should probably have you checked."

He chuckles, and Alex's lips turn up in an amused smile.

"What can I get for you? Anything, it's on the house," Alex adds quickly. "A 'Welcome Home, Lilly' gift."

"You don't need to do that."

"I know, but I want to." The tension between us is palpable, the connection electric. Then again, it always has been. Since the moment Alex and I met back in elementary school, well before we knew what love was, we've shared something special. Or so I thought. Him choosing to join the military and leaving me forever certainly didn't support that belief.

"A water with lemon and a burger, please. Fries."

"Everything on it?"

"Yes," I reply.

"Got it. Felix?"

"Make that two of those," he says.

Alex smiles at me. "Be out soon."

As soon as he's out of earshot, I turn to Felix. "Really?"

He grins. "I wasn't sure you wanted to know about him."

"You didn't think I'd be interested to know that the man I was engaged to returned home?"

He shrugs. "Since you weren't here, it didn't seem relevant."

I take a deep breath and force myself to look back at Alex. His back is to me as he pours our waters, but I know every single angle of his handsome face like he's staring straight back at me. For years, I lived and breathed Alex Phillips. He was my best friend. It wasn't until our freshman year of high school that he kissed me for the first time.

After that, the rest was history.

He was my everything, and then he broke my heart.

CHAPTER 2 - ALEX

Lilly Bishop is back.

Seeing her standing in the doorway, framed by sunlight, had thrown coal on the still-burning flame I've carried for her nearly my entire life. She was my light when I'd struggled with losing my father. My hope when I'd felt like life had no meaning.

And the very reason I got out of bed every single morning. There hasn't been a single second of the day where I haven't thought about her and the love we'd shared once upon a time.

Honestly, I kick myself every day for leaving her behind to join the Army. But I knew, if I stayed, I'd have nothing to offer her. She deserved the best, and I was the son of an alcoholic, who had no money to go to college and no future.

I haven't spoken to her in over a decade. Not since I left a note on the door of Felix's hardware store, letting her know I was leaving for the military.

No apology. No explanation.

I'm an idiot.

I finish locking up the diner and head toward the church for the annual Christmas fundraiser meeting. Every year, the town gets together and raises money to help provide presents for the children living in Boston shelters. While we're just a small town three hours outside of the big city, our fundraiser has always been a wonderful success.

"Alex, good to see you." Pastor Redding reaches out to shake my hand as soon as I step in the door.

"You, too."

"Did you see Lilly is back?" he asks with a knowing smile.

I swallow hard. "I did. Saw her earlier."

"Really?"

"She and Felix came in for lunch."

He nods. "She looks as though Hawaii treated her well."

"That she does," I agree. Then again, there is nothing that could dampen the beauty that surrounds Lilly. It's more than surface deep. Goodness radiates from her. It always has. "Is the meeting in the Fellowship Hall?"

"It is. Head on in, and we'll be getting started soon."

"Thanks." I shove my hands into my pockets and do my best to avoid any and all conversations about Lilly as I make my way into the Hall. Unfortunately, as much as I'd hoped to avoid her, there she is.

Camera in hand, Lilly photographs the townspeople as they talk. Honestly, she moves so silently that I wonder if they even know she's there. Every moment she captures is one of purity, not tainted by forced smiles.

I'm struck once again by her beauty. Her long, silky, obsidian hair is braided down her back, and the white dress she wears compliments her tan skin as though it was made for her. But it's her eyes—a bright, crystal blue—that have always captivated me.

They hold such purity. Such kindness. Despite the upbringing that could have hardened her heart.

I clench my hands into fists at my sides as the memories of her confiding what happened to her slam into me. I tried so hard to bury those, too. To forget and keep myself from tracking down the man who fathered her and killing him with my bare hands.

Not great thoughts to have while in church.

God, forgive me.

She turns to face me, and the breath is stolen from my lungs. Our gazes meet, and a piece of me I thought had shriveled up long ago slides back into place. A warmth spreads through me. And even though I know I should probably keep my distance, I take the first step. Then another. Until I'm standing close enough to smell her delicate coconut shampoo. That's new.

"Hey," I say.

"Hey." Her response is clipped, pained. And I want to kick myself for coming over here in the first place.

"Listen, I'd like to talk. If that's okay. Anytime that works for you." Without thinking, I reach up and brush the hair from her shoulder.

She stiffens, and I let my hand drop despite the warmth that shot through me at the contact.

She pulls away. "I don't know if that's a good idea."

"Please?" I'm not above begging for a chance to explain myself. But I seriously hope she doesn't make me. "After the meeting? We can head over to the diner, and I can make us some coffee."

She chews on her bottom lip, and I fight the urge to lean forward and press my mouth to hers. The desire to capture her lips and make her forget I ever broke her heart is stronger than I'd thought possible. "Fine. One coffee."

"Thank you." Relief floods my body, but before I can say anything else, Felix crosses over and offers me his hand.

"Alex. I meant to ask you earlier; how's that project car coming along?"

"Project car?" Lilly questions.

I swallow hard. "I bought Jeoff Greyson's old Mustang."

"A car and a diner," she muses, her lips turning up in a slight smile. "How interesting."

"It has special memories for me," I tell her, knowing she'll remember the fact that we shared our first kiss in the front seat of that '65 Mustang. Back then, I'd worked as a busboy at the diner, and Jeoff had lent me his prized car before my first actual date with Lilly.

It had been a rough ride back then and broke down three years later.

Thankfully, he'd still kept it. And when I bought the diner, he'd thrown it in with the sale.

"How nice." She turns to Felix. "Should we grab a chair? Looks like they're about to get started."

An hour later, we're filing out of the Church. Lilly says goodbye to Felix, who waves at me as I reach her on the sidewalk. Without a word, she smiles tightly, and we start walking toward the diner. The tension between us is so thick one could slice right through it, but I'll still take it over the radio silence we've had since I left all those years ago. I'm hesitant to touch her again but desperate to feel her close to me.

After unlocking the door, I move inside and shut it again, leaving the main lights off so no one thinks I'm open. I cross over and press the button that will start a fresh brew of coffee as Lilly slides onto a barstool.

"Do you want something to eat?"

"No, thanks."

"You sure? I've been told my muffins are the best in Maine."

"No thanks," she repeats. "What did you want to talk about?"

Right to the point. It's always been her style. "I wanted to apologize. To explain why I left the way I did."

"Why do you need to? It's been ten years, Alex. I don't think it matters anymore."

"It matters to me."

She purses her lips and nods. "Fine. Go for it."

"After my dad lost the shop, I didn't think I had much of anything to offer you. I had no job outside of the diner, no money, no car, nothing to give you the life you deserved."

"The life *you* thought I deserved," she retorts. "I was just fine."

"You wanted to travel. To see the world."

"And I still did that without you."

"You did," I reply, running a hand over the back of my hair. The coffee pot finishes, so I pour two mugs and offer her one, not setting it on the counter because I'm desperate to touch her again.

She takes the mug, and her slender fingers brush my hand.

I swallow hard, and she sets the mug down as I slide an assortment of cream and sugar toward her.

She uses neither.

"Listen, was I angry when you left? Yes. Hurt? Absolutely. But I got over it." She flashes a smile that we both know is fake.

"I know you, Lilly. You still hate me for it."

She turns away and pushes up from the stool to cross her arms. "Fine. I do. You weren't there for me when I needed you. You bailed and left me to pick up the pieces all by myself. Do you have any idea how it felt? To face everyone in town each and every day? They looked at me with pity. Like I was pathetic. You were the hero who went to save the world, and I was just the girl who couldn't understand why you left." Tears fill her eyes, and my stomach churns in disgust for what I did.

"I needed to make something more of myself."

"And you couldn't do that with me? We couldn't do that together?" she demands. "When my mom died, you weren't here." Her bottom lip quivers, and I move around the counter to reach for her. She backs away. "I stood by your side through everything you went through with your dad. But when I needed you, *you weren't there,*" she repeats what she said only minutes ago, driving it home.

"If I could go back and do it over again, I would. You have to know that."

"Do I?" she asks. "Do I have to know that, Alex?"

"Will you please just give me a chance to prove it to you? I was young, stupid, and didn't see how I could give you the life that you deserved."

"The only thing I wanted was you." She speaks the words softly, delicately, but they carry the weight of a boulder crushing down on me.

"I cannot even begin to tell you how sorry I am that I wasn't there for you. When I found out about your mom, I tried to come back for the funeral, but they wouldn't let me leave."

"Wouldn't let you leave." She shakes her head angrily. "You wouldn't have needed permission if you'd never have left!" Tears flow freely down her face now, the façade she's worn all day melting away. "I loved you, Alex Phillips, and you broke my heart."

"I didn't mean to." But didn't I? I knew what would happen if I left, and I chose to go anyway. Nothing I say will fix that. Nothing I do will mend the brokenness I caused.

"You didn't mean to." She shakes her head. "I knew this was a mistake, Alex. I knew it, and I came anyway." She grabs her bag and heads for the door before I can reach her.

"Please don't leave. I want to know what you've been doing. I want to talk like we used to." *I want to show you that I'm still in love with you.*

"You lost the right to hear about my life ten years ago, Alex. I'm not leaving Felix alone again, so you and I will need to figure out how to co-exist in this town. But I want to make myself clear. I am not interested in being anything more than acquaintances."

I swallow hard, my resolve to change her mind cementing in my heart. "I am going to prove to you that I've changed. That I am worthy of your trust again."

"I very much doubt that." She turns and leaves the diner, her coffee still untouched on the counter.

As she disappears down the street, I send up a prayer. *God, please give me the strength to prove I meant every word.*

CHAPTER 3 - LILLY

Before I know it, a week has passed since I first stepped foot back into Hope Springs. I've spent my spare time editing photos from my time in Hawaii, working in the hardware store, and cooking so I can avoid Felix's constant push to have dinner at the diner.

His not-so-subtle attempts at getting me to face Alex have only grown more and more obvious over the last seven days.

I slip into a long-sleeved dress with hydrangea flowers printed on the skirt and pull my hair up off my neck. After securing my mom's old cross necklace around my neck, I slip into some short boots and step out into the living room. Felix is dressed in slacks and a nice shirt, his hair combed back.

"Ready to go?" he asks.

"I am." I move down the stairs and into the empty hardware store then step out onto the street and wait for Felix to lock the door. Because I can't help myself, I glance over at the diner. Its open sign is not illuminated, and I smile because it means Alex kept up with the tradition of it being closed until right after church each Sunday.

Even if he never found himself in a pew, he still respects the town's history, which, I suppose, is a notch in his favor. The late November breeze is chilly, so I pull the cardigan tighter around me as Felix and I make our way to the small church.

Most of the town has gathered inside, joining for coffee and donuts while enjoying happy conversations. I study their faces, feeling more at home each and every day that passes. Everyone here embraced my mom and me when we moved here. No one looked down on her for having been married once already, nor did they remind us of the fact that she and Felix met because we'd been living in one of the shelters they'd donated toys to for Christmas one year.

I'll never forget the look on her face when she saw him for the first time. Or the way he'd watched her like she was the most beautiful woman in the world.

After seeing how toxic the relationship between her and my biological father was, I hadn't had much belief in true love. But they'd changed that. And I'd always told myself that I wouldn't settle for less than what they had.

"Lilly!"

I turn as Mrs. Elodie Clementine, my fourth-grade teacher, comes rushing toward me. Before I can step back, she wraps both arms around me and pulls me against her body, crushing me until I cannot smell anything but her heavy floral perfume. She releases me with a wide smile, holding me back just enough that she can see me. "Mrs. Clementine, it's wonderful to see you."

"Girl, it is lovely to see you, too! Your daddy is so proud of what you've done. We all are. Photographing the world the way you have."

"Mainly just Hawaii," I correct her. "But thanks."

"Still. I think that Phillips boy bought every single one of your pictures. And I've got quite a few myself."

I stiffen. "Alex owns my photos?"

Her cheeks flood with color as she realizes she's clearly said more than she should. "Oh, I need to speak with Carlie. Excuse me." She rushes away as quickly as she arrived, so I turn to Felix.

"What is she talking about?"

He shoves his hands into both of his pockets. "Alex ordered all of your prints as they came out."

"Why?"

He arches a brow. "Do you really have to ask?"

As soon as he says it, my gaze rises, meeting Alex as he steps into the church dressed in his Sunday best. Slacks, a button-down, and a black suit jacket. "When did he start coming?"

"He's been coming since he got back. Every single Sunday."

I stare at him, his words from the other night running through my mind. *"I am going to prove to you that I've changed. That I am worthy of your trust again."*

Is it possible that he has changed?

But even as I consider the possibility, I shove it out of my mind. Alex broke my heart. Shattered it into a million tiny pieces and had me questioning everything I ever believed.

Letting him back in is an impossibility all its own. Regardless of whether or not he's changed.

Sunday lunch at *Hope Diner* is a tradition I really wish I could bring myself to change. But I can still see my mother sitting beside Felix, smiling with flowers in her hair. She'd been such a force of life. Such a happy, loving woman, despite everything she'd gone through.

And her memory is more important to me than my desire to keep space between myself and Alex.

My throat tightens. Today marks three years since my mother passed away. Three years since Heaven gained another Angel and I another crack in my heart. Even with the time that has passed, the grief doesn't lessen. Tears threaten to spill, so I clear my throat hoping to keep them shoved firmly back down.

I will not cry in front of Alex.

When I get home, I can let them free. But here, I need to keep it together.

"Hey," Alex greets as he approaches the table. "What can I get you both to drink?"

"Coffee," I say.

"Same," Felix adds.

"On it." Alex turns away, and I relax just enough that Felix takes note. He covers my hand with his.

"You okay?"

"Not really." Felix and I have always had an easy relationship. I've always felt comfortable sharing anything and everything with him, and never felt the need to pretend in his presence. When he doesn't press, I add, "I didn't realize how hard it would be to see him again."

"I am sorry I didn't tell you he was back."

I shrug. "It wouldn't have changed anything." And honestly, it wouldn't have. Had I known Alex was here, I might have given in to the pull to return sooner. Just so I could see him again.

My heart still aches for him. Something that has become painfully apparent over the past week as I did everything I could to avoid him. The nights have been restless and haunted with dreams of the past. While my days have been burdened with hopes of a future I swore I'd turned my back on.

"Is there anything I can do to help?" Felix asks.

I shake my head. "I need to grab some air, though. Do you mind?"

"Not at all." Felix releases my hand, so I slide out of the booth and step out into the cool afternoon air. I take a deep breath, then another, until finally, my heart begins to slow. Out here, where it's just chilly enough that no one is strolling the street, I let a few tears fall.

What would my life have been like if Alex wouldn't have left? I would have had more time with my mom because I never would have felt the desire to leave this place, sure. But is that really his fault?

Even a month ago, I would have continued adamantly blaming him for it.

But truthfully, it was my decision to leave just as it was his to do the same.

"Hey, are you okay?"

I turn, not at all expecting to see Alex standing just behind me, a mug of hot coffee in his hand. "What are you doing out here?"

"You looked cold." He offers me the coffee.

"I was going to come right back inside." But I take the warm mug, and my fingers brush his. The touch is welcome. Comforting. And I let my hands linger over his for a few heartbeats, our gazes locking.

Something passes between us.

The first hint of forgiveness thawing my heart. I pull my hand away.

"I figured as much. But I wanted you to be warm." He turns to leave.

"Alex?"

"Yeah?"

I study his sharp jaw and the stubble coating it. The way his eyes, though still the same hazel, hold a darkness that wasn't there before. Is it possible it's from the war? From what he saw overseas?

"Did you really buy my photos?"

He stares at me blankly for a moment then sighs. "Come with me."

I follow him back into the diner, offering Felix a smile and half wave, as I let Alex lead me up the stairs and into the apartment just above. He unlocks the door and pushes it open, remaining in the hall as I step into the studio apartment.

There's not much in the way of furniture. A queen-sized bed, dresser, nightstand with a worn bible on top. His TV is small and old and sits in what serves as the living and dining room.

But it's the wall décor that steals my focus. Nearly every inch of the far wall is covered in photos that I've taken. Brightly colored flowers, the ocean, sunsets, waterfalls that crash down into the pools below…he has them.

Tears blur my vision, and I quickly blink them away. Determined to shield the emotion welling up within me. That is until my gaze lands on a small picture on his kitchen counter. I cross over and set the mug down before lifting the photograph and running my fingers over the glass. It's a picture of him down on one knee and me crying as I accept the ring he slides onto my finger.

"Why?" I ask, turning to face him, my eyes full of tears once again. Only this time, I don't try to hide them. "Why did you buy them all? Why do you still have this?"

Alex looks about ready to bolt again, but he remains right where he is. "I wanted to feel like a part of your life. Even if I never thought you'd forgive me."

"Alex—"

"Please, Lilly. I came back to Hope Springs for you. Because, after they wouldn't let me take leave for your mother's funeral, I knew I couldn't stay away from you. I didn't extend my contract after that. I came home and have been trying desperately to build a life for you. For us. On the off chance you would understand and give me a second chance."

Emotion claws at my chest. It tears at my soul.

"You left me," I choke out.

Alex crosses toward me and reaches out, cupping my cheek with his hand, causing a jolt to move through me. "And I've hated myself every single day for it. There has never been another because it's *always* been you. I was so desperate to make something of myself because I'd felt so unworthy of someone like you."

I close my eyes, tears rolling down my cheeks. I press my hand over his, feeling the strength and warmth of the man I used to love.

"But I never stopped loving you, Lilly. Not for one second over the last ten years. I know we can't pick up where we left off. I know I can't make up for what I did. But if you'll just give me a chance, I'll prove to you that I can be the man you need. The man I should have been from the very beginning."

We have so much history. So much backstory between us. Which is what made it so hard when he left. I'd been betrayed, not just by the man I was going to marry but by my best friend.

"Please, Lilly.If there's even a chance you could fall in love with me again."

I open my eyes and stare up into his. The connection between us grows, and as I study his gaze for any hesitation, for any sign that this is not what he really wants, I hear the word *home* echoing through my mind again.

"I can't fall in love with you again," I tell him. "Because I never stopped loving you to begin with."

Alex smiles, and everything falls back into place. For a moment, I'm fifteen again, sitting in the front seat of an old Mustang as he toys with the ends of my hair before nervously pressing his lips to mine.

Which is what he does now. Tentatively, Alex leans in and brushes his mouth against mine.

Love slams into me like a freight train as he deepens the kiss.

My hands go to his hair, and he cradles my face.

Everything I ever felt for him comes back in a rush of heat, enveloping every part of my once-broken heart.

And when he pulls back and stares down at me, I see the future.

Marriage.

Kids.

A life together.

Everything I'd wanted from the time I was too young to understand what such a commitment meant.

All while a resounding *home* echoes through my mind.

Thank you so much for reading and being a part of something that will hopefully bring relief to those suffering in Maui. If you'd like to experience more of Jessica Ashley's books in Hope Springs and catch up with Alex and Lilly, then check out Pages of Promise.

A MATCH MADE IN MAUI
JIFFY KATE

CHAPTER 1

"Thank you," I call to the Uber driver as I climb out of the car with my carry-on.

"Safe travels," he replies, giving me a wave from the front seat.

The late summer heat is hanging on for dear life. The constant humidity in New Orleans makes it feel hotter than it actually is. And even though I'm trading one warm climate for another, just the thought of Maui's beaches has me smiling like I have a secret no one else knows.

I guess I kind of do.

The only people who know where I'm going are my mom and my sister, Brenn. Everyone else thinks I'm headed to Colorado to visit my grandparents. I didn't want them to know I'm going on a vacation I'd planned to take with my boyfriend... *ex-boyfriend*. That sounds pathetic. Not that traveling solo is pathetic. I think it's brave and adventurous, which are two of the reasons I'm going on this trip alone.

Hawai'i was always *my* dream. It's the only state I've never visited and at the tiptop of my bucket list, which is why I was the one who made all the travel plans. Dalton always said he'd pay me back for tickets and reservations as we got closer to the date, but he never did. I was a little miffed about it before the breakup, but now, I'm happy he didn't.

The only bad part is everything I have scheduled was originally booked for two, but I'll deal with that when I get there.

Up until a month ago, I was still going back and forth on whether I wanted to contact all the vendors and request a partial refund. But one morning, I woke up from a dream where I was on a beautiful beach watching the most gorgeous sunrise I've ever seen and I knew I had to go. It was a sign, and after I told my mom, she confirmed it, telling me to go. That I need this. I need the time away. I need closure. I need to move on. I need to pick up the pieces and start fresh.

I tried to convince my mom or sister to come with me, but neither of them had the vacation time. Plus, the elderly woman who lives next door to my mom, and relies on Mom for care, isn't doing so well.

So, here I am, traipsing through Louis Armstrong New Orleans International Airport heading for a Hawaiian vacation for one.

CHAPTER 2

After stopping by the ticket counter and printing my boarding pass, I make it through security with time to spare, so PJ's coffee it is.

"Excuse me," a gravelly voice says from behind me. "I, uh...left something behind."

I turn around and spy the most stunning pair of eyes I've ever seen. Classifying them as "hazel" doesn't do them justice but it's all I can come up with on such short notice. Realizing I'm gawking at this stranger embarrasses me and I barely manage to spit out, "I'm sorry?"

"My muffin." He points to the counter. "I forgot to grab my muffin."

Muffin? Is he being cheeky?

For goodness' sake, Shelbi, of course he's not. He just wants his baked goods.

Glancing behind me, I see a bag with the top folded over, a white sticker holding it closed that reads "blueberry muffin". I quickly grab it and hand it to him. "Blueberry is my favorite, too."

Why on earth did I tell him that?

He smiles politely as he takes the bag, mumbles "thanks," then turns and leaves.

Way to go, Shelbi. The first good-looking man you've interacted with in months *and you immediately creep him out.*

Not that it matters. This is an airport. The odds of seeing him again are a million to one. And besides, I'm not looking for a man.

Right?

Right.

No, yes. Absolutely.

This next week is about reconnecting with myself and figuring out what I want. They're about moving forward. Distractions in the form of a gorgeous hunky man are not on the itinerary.

CHAPTER 3

The wait for my flight to Dallas is uneventful. I barely get two chapters into the paperback I bought at the newsstand before they begin boarding. For once, I'm not dreading who I'll be sitting next to on my flights. Since I didn't cancel Dalton's ticket, I'll have an extra seat and I get the window on both flights. I'll be able to stretch my legs, take a nap, and not worry about some dude manspreading beside me and taking up all the elbow room.

How's that for living my best life?

One thing my breakup with Dalton has taught me is how to look on the bright side of things.

I'm not sad about never having anyone to eat meals with and instead I'm happy because I can eat cereal every night if I want.

Being depressed over not having anyone to snuggle up to at night has turned into embracing the fact I have an entire bed all to myself.

And I definitely don't miss traveling with a partner.

Especially when I struggle to put my suitcase in the overhead bin.

Nope, not at all.

Girl power.

Standing on the tips of my toes, I push on the wheels of my carry-on but it refuses to budge.

"Let me help you."

Oh, shit. Not the gravelly voice again.

I squeeze my eyes shut for a second, thinking he might be talking to someone else and maybe he'll move on by. But when a warm hand touches my shoulder, I peek over and sure enough, those damn hazel eyes are staring down at me.

My body flushes with heat and I mentally berate myself. If an innocent stare has me melting, I might need professional help.

"Thanks, but I have it."

Ignoring me completely, he reaches into the bin and shuffles the surrounding luggage, making a place for my bag to fit perfectly.

"You're welcome," he mumbles as he gives me a slight smile before turning and continuing his trek down the aisle, leaving me staring after him with a flushed face and racing heart.

What were the chances the man with the amazing eyes would be on my flight?

Settling into my seat, I pop my earbuds in and lean back. I need a nap and to not think about why my body reacted like that to a complete stranger.

CHAPTER 4

"Ladies and gentlemen, welcome to Dallas. For your safety and the safety of those around you, please remain seated with your seatbelt fastened and keep the aisle clear until we stop at the gate."

When the doors are opened and everyone begins to deplane, I can't help but glance over my shoulder to see if I can spot the hazel eyes I haven't been able to stop thinking about for the last hour and a half. The crowded aisle makes my search futile. For all I know, he's staying on board. I think this flight is continuing on to Denver, so maybe he's headed there for business... or to see his *girlfriend.*

Yeah, a girlfriend. Definitely a girlfriend.

Because a guy that hot isn't single.

See, there. That's better. He's taken and I would never make a pass at another woman's man. I would never be a willing participant in an affair. I'm not Dalton. I don't cheat and I would never be with someone who does. Just thinking about my cheating ex has my blood boiling and by the time I make it to the nearest women's bathroom, I'm steaming for absolutely no reason at all.

I'm over Dalton's betrayal.

I've cried all the tears I'm going to cry over him. I've lost all the sleep I'm going to lose. He's gone and good riddance, because he wasn't good enough for me anyway. Truthfully, I was more embarrassed than anything because his cheating was very public and we used to work for the same company. Plenty of my colleagues knew before I did, which means they were never my friends.

As I wash my hands, I study my reflection in the mirror, pleased to see a hint of the old me coming back. Before Dalton, I was carefree and adventurous. I loved going to new places and enjoyed new experiences. There was a time I liked doing those things with him. Then he ruined that. With his betrayal came so much loss and a lot of self-doubt.

I changed jobs and apartments.

I lost touch with all my old acquaintances.

The usual places I went to were off limits for fear of running into Dalton and his new girlfriend.

For a time, I became somewhat of a recluse.

I second-guessed everything in my life.

If I could overlook something as huge as my boyfriend of three years sleeping with a close friend of ours, what else was I missing? Was I that naive? Was I too trusting? Where did my gut instincts go?

After a few months of therapy, I can finally accept it wasn't my fault. I didn't make Dalton cheat. He did that all on his own and it doesn't reflect on me.

My only crime was wasting three years of my life with that asshole.

Once I've collected myself, I start looking for the closest food court. I'm starving and there are so many options in this huge airport, but thankfully, I have time to grab a bite before my next flight.

Or so I thought.

I not only chose the restaurant with the shortest line; I also chose the restaurant with the slowest employees. I mean, how hard is it to slap a burger patty between two pieces of bread?

With food in hand, I now have to race down the corridor to get to my gate on time. I arrive breathless only to find I've missed my boarding time and have to wait at the end of the line. And now I'll be one of those annoying people who bring their hot food on the plane for everyone else to smell.

It's irritating to be the last person to board but, again, I'm relieved that I'll have an empty seat between me and the other person on my row.

That relief quickly turns to dread as I spot my seat and notice a familiar head of wavy brown hair. My... no, *the* handsome stranger from earlier is sitting in the aisle seat of my row. He hasn't noticed me yet because he's reading a book, which only makes him hotter, and I can't help but wonder what his reaction will be when he realizes we'll be sharing a row for the next eight hours.

Will he be annoyed? Maybe.

Angry? I don't think so.

Aroused like I am? Doubtful.

"Excuse me. Can I put my food down here while I put my suitcase up?" I ask, motioning to the empty seat that will be between us.

He finally looks up from his book and when recognition strikes, he shakes his head while chuckling. "Why don't I just put your suitcase up for you like last time?"

Not the worst reaction he could've had.

I give him a relieved smile and pray it doesn't make me look too deranged.

Once we're both settled in our seats, me by the window, him in the aisle seat, and Dalton's empty seat between us, I try to strike up a conversation.

"So, what are the odds we'd meet at the New Orleans airport and end up traveling to Maui together?"

"Well, I'm no statistician, but I'd say they were pretty low. If I wasn't a gentleman, I'd ask if we were staying at the same resort to see if the trend continues."

"Good thing you're a gentleman then."

"Indeed," he murmurs, then turns back to his book.

CHAPTER 5

"I'm Shelbi," I tell him as the flight crew delivers safety instructions.

His eyes lift to meet mine and I see a hint of a smile there behind the neatly trimmed scruff outlining his full lips and sharp jawline. "Nice to meet you, Shelbi."

When he turns back to his book, I feel a twinge of something... disappointment, maybe. Normally, when someone tells you their name, you return the favor. I don't know why, or what it is about this man, but I want to know his name, among other things.

So, the fact he's not giving me anything to work with is a little annoying.

For the next half hour, I occupy myself as we taxi down the runway and ascend into the air. I eat my mediocre, mostly-cold burger and then use hand sanitizer and pop some gum in my mouth in hopes of not smelling like food for the rest of the flight. I take out my own book and try to immerse myself in someone else's life. But the pages don't hold my attention.

This might be the first time in a long time my life feels more exciting than a romance novel.

Here I am, over thirty-five thousand feet in the air on the way to a beautiful place that has always called to me. I'm flying solo, so I can literally do whatever I want for the next seven days. No one can tell me my ideas are stupid or rain on my parade.

It's just me and an adventure.

And a really hot guy who won't give me the time of day.

After another thirty minutes of silence, I can't stand it any longer. "Having an extra seat is nice," I say, when I realize he's set his phone down in the space between us. "I've always wanted to fly first class, in one of those cool pods, but I've never been able to justify the money. You know?"

He glances at where his phone is and then up at me. "Every once in a while, you just get lucky."

There's something about his words and the way he delivers them that makes my body tingle.

"My ex-boyfriend was supposed to be in this seat."

I don't know why I lead with that or why I'm spilling my guts to a stranger, but here we are.

"His loss."

Nodding, I pull my bottom lip between my teeth, waiting for the jab of pain that used to come with the reminder of Dalton, but it doesn't. I don't feel anything and that makes me smile.

"From that look, I'm going to take it you did the breaking up."

Chuckling, I shake my head and glance out at the clouds before turning back to my hot stranger. "I did, but it was because he cheated on me. So, I don't know if that counts."

"Hell yes it counts. It counts double, because you didn't stick around and let that douche have a second chance. You didn't, right?" he asks, his brows furrowing as he leans near, like he's invested in the conversation. At least he's shut his book.

"No, I didn't. I couldn't."

"Good girl."

Well, shit.

Why did I like that praise?

Stowing that thought away for later, I decide to change the topic and take advantage of this opening for a conversation. "Are you going to Maui for business or pleasure?"

"I think everyone goes to Maui for pleasure, whether working while there or not."

The way his eyes twinkle when he smiles is so enchanting. I could literally watch him do that all day long.

"True," I finally manage to say without sounding like a love-struck teenager who just ran into her newest crush. "I've never been, but always wanted to. It's the only state I've never visited... Hawai'i, that is. I've been to all of the continental United States, and Alaska."

Wow, word vomit much, Shelbi?

I want to roll my eyes at myself, but I refrain, giving him a tenuous smile.

"And you were supposed to take this trip with your ex?"

Instead of responding with words, which I seem to have no control over, I simply nod.

"Why didn't you cancel his flight? I'm sure you could've gotten a refund."

Swallowing, I avert my eyes to my lap and fidget with a loose strand on the hem of my t-shirt. "I don't know, actually."

"Were you hoping to reconcile?" he asks, one brow arched.

"No," I answer quickly. "The second I caught Dalton with his dick in someone else it was over." My cheeks warm as I glance around us, hoping I didn't say that in front of sensitive ears. "Sorry, but it's true."

He smiles again, shaking his head. "No apologies necessary."

There's a brief moment of us just sitting there staring at each other. Then he reaches over the seat and offers me his hand. "River," he says, in a tone that shivers through my body.

"Nice to meet you, River," I tell him, fighting back a stupid smile. His hand feels so big and strong, yet gentle. It does weird things to me and I'm reluctant to let go.

A moment later, a flight attendant stops by asking if we'd like a drink, breaking the bubble we were in. River orders a whiskey and coke and I order a vodka tonic.

I don't typically drink on flights, but this is a long one and if he's having a cocktail, it only feels right to join him.

While we wait for our drinks, I mull over his name.

River.

It's sturdy, maybe even a little rugged, but also a bit mysterious. With his towering frame, which I'm guessing is at least six-foot-three, maybe taller, and his long, lean muscles, his name suits him.

"I'm going to Maui for a bachelor's party. One of my best friends from college is getting married," he says, pulling me from my thoughts. "I'm arriving a day later than everyone else, due to work, but looking forward to getting away for a few days."

"Wow, Maui for a bachelor party, that sounds like so much fun. You always hear of brides and bridesmaids going to exotic places, but I love that you're getting together with all your dudes."

He laughs. "My *dudes*? Yeah, well, we've all been friends for a long time and the groom wanted to do something adventurous. We've all done the mountain thing—skiing, snowboarding, hiking. We've been to Canada and Mexico... you name it, most of us have done it. But we've never been to Hawai'i, so that's what he chose and we're all here for it."

"Sounds like my kind of people," I say with genuine intrigue. "I love traveling. I've been to all those places too. Where's your favorite?"

River doesn't even think about it. "New Orleans."

I expect him to laugh and change his answer, but when he doesn't, my face splits into a wide smile. "It's my favorite place too."

"No place like home."

"Were you born and raised there?"

He shakes his head. "No, I was born in Texas. My Dad's company moved to New Orleans when I was about ten. My family has lived there ever since."

"Same," I say. "Well, I was born in Colorado, but moved to New Orleans when I was thirteen. My dad's parents lived in Metairie. They were older. My grandfather had prostate cancer and my grandmother was diagnosed with dementia. So, we moved closer to take care of them. They passed away when I was eighteen and my dad died three years later."

"I'm so sorry."

"Thank you," I tell him sincerely. "I miss them every day. But they were all very adventurous people. My dad's dad had visited every continent by the time he was thirty and almost every country by the time he was fifty. He definitely lived a full life and had wonderful stories to share. I think that's where I get my wanderlust from."

River's eyes twinkle. "I love that."

For the next few hours, we exchange stories and I learn a lot about River Townsend.

He's the oldest of three brothers. They all work for their father's engineering firm, a family business started by his grandfather. They do consulting for civil, structural, mechanical, and electrical engineering.

A few years ago, he went on a three-month backpacking trip across Europe with his brothers after the youngest graduated from college.

Their family seems really close and hearing him talk about them is an adventure by itself.

I tell him about my mom and sister and my grandparents in Colorado. I even confess that my co-workers think I'm in Colorado right now.

He listens intently as I talk about my human resources job working for New Orleans' MLB team, the Revelers. It's still relatively new, but I love it so much and when I start talking about it, I can hardly stop myself. But River encourages me to continue, wanting to hear more.

"I know one of the players," he says when I'm done waxing poetically about how amazing my job is.

"What?" I sit up straighter in my seat, eyes wide. "How? Who?"

River chuckles. "You know how New Orleans is. It's kind of like a small town in a big city. Everyone knows someone who knows someone... It's like six degrees of separation, but fewer degrees."

I ponder that thought for a second, because he's right. It does feel that way sometimes.

"My brother, Reed, lives next door to Owen Thatcher. He's—"

"A relief pitcher, right hand, mean fast ball," I say, cutting him off.

His chuckle turns into a full-blown laugh and it's literal music to my ears.

"And you're going to think I'm lying, but I know his wife."

Now, it's his turn to be shocked.

"I swear," I tell him, turning in my seat and collecting my hair onto the top of my head, creating a messy bun before I use the scrunchy on my wrist to secure it. "We went to the same school. She was a grade behind me, but we had a few classes together. I ran into her at the stadium right after I started my job and we reconnected."

"Small fucking world."

Sighing, I lean back into my seat. It really is. It's also kind of crazy that we basically know the same people and have these odd connections. "What school did you go to?"

"Holy Cross and then Tulane. You?"

"Sacred Heart and then LSU."

River's eyes squint a little, like he's trying to figure something out. "Twenty-five?"

"Twenty-six. You?"

"Twenty-nine. I'll be thirty next month."

"So even if we didn't go to all-boys and all-girls schools, respectively, we still probably wouldn't have known each other in high school."

He offers me a small smile. "Probably not. But I sure would've liked to."

The butterflies that have been flapping around in my stomach take flight.

CHAPTER 6

When the flight attendant comes by to collect any remaining trash, I'm cracking up over a story River just told me about the time one of his frat brothers covered all the bedroom doors in their frat house with Vaseline-coated cellophane.

"It wasn't funny at the time," he says, fighting back his laugh. "Everyone was covered in the shit. We were so pissed."

"Is he coming on this trip?" I ask, wiping tears from my eyes at the visual of all these frat boys waking up and running into a wall of Vaseline.

"Yes, and I don't trust him as far as I can throw him. But he's still one of the best guys I know."

"Sounds like you have a really great group of friends."

One of the flight attendants starts instructing everyone to put their seats into the upright position and stow away any electronics. Apparently, we're already making the descent into Maui and I have no idea where the time went.

My heart lurches with the plane as we hit a patch of turbulence. "Whoa," I mutter, to myself more than anybody else, but I feel River's gaze turn to me as I tighten my seatbelt and lean back. I'm not a nervous flier, but I absolutely hate turbulence, even though I know it's normal and nothing to be too worried about.

"You're good," he says, in a low, soothing tone. "Just a little bump in the road."

River's words and voice calm my nerves, until we hit another patch and the pilot comes over the intercom to remind everyone to stay seated with their seatbelts fastened. I'm gripping the armrest when I feel a hand cover mine.

Turning my head, I see River watching me. "Got a funny story for me?"

"I had two imaginary friends when I was little. Fred and Elmer. They drove a brown Cadillac and listened to The Beatles."

A deep, warm laugh comes from beside me and causes a rush of heat to course through my body.

"My mom took me to the pediatrician because she thought I might need medical intervention."

He lets out another laugh. "Do you still have these imaginary friends? Is that who's sitting in this empty seat? Maybe the whole ex-boyfriend story was a cover-up."

"No, they retired to Hawai'i when I was in the first grade."

This has River laughing even harder. "So, that's the real appeal. You're on a mission to find lost imaginary friends."

Now, I'm laughing too and oblivious to the plane as it shimmies and shakes its way to the tarmac.

When we're on the ground, I let out a sigh, not of relief but of sadness. I'm not ready for this—whatever it is—to end. I'm not ready for River to be a fun memory I think back on when I remember my trip to Maui. It's on the tip of my tongue to ask him where he's staying when his expression turns serious.

"I really enjoyed talking to you," River starts. "But will you do me a favor and promise me you won't tell other random men you're on this trip alone? It's not safe. If anyone else asks, tell them you're meeting a friend or something, okay?"

Swallowing, I nod. He's right. It's the number one rule of women traveling solo, always seem like you're not. "I promise," I assure him. "I'm not normally that forthcoming. You just... I don't know." I shrug, struggling to explain how I'm feeling and how I've felt since the moment I bumped into him at the coffee shop.

"Yeah," he says. "Feels like we've known each other for a while."

That's part of it, but the other part is I'm wildly attracted to him. I just can't say that.

Can I?

"I know you have an exciting week planned and I have no doubt my schedule is jam-packed, so let's just appreciate this time we've had and if we're meant to see each other again, we will."

I nod as the plane eases up to the gate. "Okay."

I want to ask for his number or give him mine—at least find out where he'll be staying for the next few days—but I don't.

"It was nice meeting you, Shelbi Lewis."

"It was really great meeting you, River Townsend."

Once he helps me with my bag for the final time, we follow each other off the airplane and I head one way to the restroom and he keeps going to the arrivals gate. At one point, we both turn around and he gives me a final wave and I give him a smile.

His friends are waiting for him.

And I have an adventure waiting for me.

CHAPTER 7

Maui is everything I dreamed it would be and more, and that's not me looking on the bright side.

The people are so welcoming and friendly.

The food is so fresh and delicious.

The beaches are literal paradise and the weather has been perfect.

In the first thirty-six hours, I took a surfing lesson, joined a yoga session on the beach, and now I'm on a boat headed to Honolulu Bay.

The Ka'anapali coastline is breathtaking and worth the boat ride alone. Just a few minutes in and we've already passed beautiful resorts and beaches with a backdrop of the West Maui mountains.

Words escape me as I soak in the view and my thoughts turn to River. I wonder what he's up to today. Has he seen the island from this vantage point? Is he enjoying his stay as much as I am?

"Have you been here before?"

I glance over to see a lovely woman about my mother's age, smiling brightly.

"No," I say dreamily, still caught up in my feelings and emotions. "This is my first time. How about you?"

"Oh, I've been to Hawai'i a dozen times over the years. It's our favorite spot to get away from it all. But we've never been to Honolulu Bay, so I'm excited to see it. I've heard the marine life is exquisite."

My smile widens as I feed off her excitement, just thinking about the fun that awaits us.

"I love snorkeling and according to a few blog posts I read before booking this excursion, Honolulu Bay is the best around."

"Where is your partner? I noticed we're short one. I hope everything is okay."

The smile on my face falters, but only for a second. "They couldn't make it."

After explaining my situation to the surfing instructor yesterday, I decided I didn't want to rehash it every time someone asked or noticed I'm flying solo. It's easier to just say they couldn't make it and leave it at that. No need to bring down my mood or anyone else's and I definitely don't want people's pity.

Because I'm good.

I'm better than good.

I'm living my best life.

"Well, good for you for coming anyway. Some people would've let coming alone stop them, so I'm glad you didn't." She pats my arm in a motherly gesture and it makes me smile.

"Thanks," I tell her, turning my attention back to the amazing scenery. "I wouldn't have missed this for the world."

CHAPTER 8

"Dining alone?" the waiter asks, gesturing to the empty seat across from me.

Instead of eating in my room, I decided to branch out and try a restaurant close to the resort. With the open-air dining, a live band playing island music, and a beautiful ocean view, it was the perfect choice.

"Yes, it'll just be me," I tell him confidently. A few months ago, this would've bothered me. Actually, a few months ago, I probably wouldn't have been here. So, the fact I am and that I'm embracing every opportunity, makes me sit a little taller and hold my chin a little higher.

"I'll have a glass of your sauvignon blanc and the seared ahi."

The waiter smiles. "Great choices. I'll be right back with your wine."

While I wait, I take in the view. I've always known that the ocean spoke to my soul, but I never would have predicted how much it would heal it. This was exactly what I needed. Just a couple of days in and I already feel so refreshed and renewed.

The waiter comes back quickly with my glass of wine. When the first sip hits my tongue, I close my eyes and savor not only the wine, but the moment. I'm mentally cataloging the memory when a familiar voice catches my attention.

As I open my eyes, they drift across the restaurant to a long table filled with men. But it's one in particular that makes my stomach flip.

River's back is to me, but there's no mistaking that gorgeous head of hair or the gravelly voice I spent eight hours listening intently to. The group is laughing, not disruptively, but they're definitely having a great time, just like I'd assumed they would.

After hearing his stories, I kind of feel like I know some of them, even though I don't know who is who. It's hard to even pinpoint the groom.

For a while, I just inconspicuously observe.

He's magnetic, not just to me, but to the people around him. Even though he's understated and reserved, when he speaks, people listen. And when he laughs, good God, it's more majestic than the Pacific Ocean.

"Can I get you anything else?" the waiter asks as he sets my plate in front of me.

"Another glass of wine would be great," I tell him.

Prying my attention away from River, I turn it to the plate of seared tuna and vegetables in front of me and my mouth waters. After a day of adventure, I'm absolutely starving.

As I eat, my gaze is still drawn to the table across the patio. At one point, I think River is going to stand, but he just pushes his chair back to grab a bottle of wine that's down the table. They're all deep in conversations and occasionally their laughs filter over.

It makes me smile.

I'm happy that he's happy.

But the question that's plaguing my mind is, *do I say something?*

We agreed to go our separate ways, so I'm not sure what the protocol is for running into each other again. If I don't say something, I'm afraid I'll be full of regret and I don't want to live my life like that. If anything, these past six months have taught me to do just the opposite.

Seize the day.

That's what I promised my sister.

But half an hour later, when I've finished eating and paid my bill, I'm still so damn indecisive.

To go over there or not to go over there. And if I do go over there, what am I going to say?

Hi, River. Remember me?

Hey, River. How's this for a small world?

Gah, this is awful.

Grabbing my purse, I decide to leave it up to fate once more and head to the bathroom, but as I stand, so does the entire table of men. My heart leaps into my throat and then sinks down to my feet as River turns and our eyes meet.

I guess that's my answer.

His slow smile lets me know he's happy to see me too. Leaning over, he says something to one of the guys before walking my way. The rest of the group glances at me, but their gazes don't linger.

"Shelbi Lewis." The low timber of his voice shoots straight to my core.

"River Townsend," I reply, biting back a smile.

He runs a hand through his hair and then grips the back of his neck. "I promised myself I wouldn't seek you out, but it seems as though the universe has other plans."

"My thoughts exactly," I confess with a chuckle.

"And now, here you are looking so gorgeous. How can I possibly walk away?"

The compliment tangles with the existing heat coursing through my body that only River seems to elicit, and I feel my face begin to flush. It might be a combination of the wine and his proximity, but whatever it is, it's a heady feeling.

Words elude me as River steps even closer and I'm greeted with a deep, rich scent that can only be described as pure man. "Uh, ahem." I clear my throat as I try to regain my senses, but still, nothing comes to me.

"Would you care to join me for a walk on the beach? Are you staying close?"

His eyes bore into mine and I sway toward him.

"Or I can get an Uber—" he starts to suggest as he steadies me.

"No," I shake my head, regretting that second glass, because I want to be present for this. I don't want to miss a second with River. "I mean, no, I don't want an Uber. A walk on the beach sounds lovely."

His smile reaches his eyes and they do that twinkle thing that weakens my knees.

Shit.

I really need to hold it together.

Thankfully, River is a gentleman and he offers me his arm as he leads me out of the restaurant.

"Are you staying close by?" he asks once the ocean breeze hits us and we reach the sand.

I stop for a second, slipping my sandals off and River takes the opportunity to take his shoes off as well.

"I'm staying about a half mile from here. How about you?"

He shakes his head. "I think we might be at the same resort."

This entire situation seems unreal, but I can't say I hate it. "Wailea Beach Resort?"

River nods. "How have I missed you these past couple of days? Because, I admit, I've been looking."

"Me too," I tell him with a laugh, twisting my long skirt into a knot at the bottom to keep from stepping on it. "But I have been keeping myself busy."

"How are the adventures going?" he asks, sounding genuinely interested.

I tell him about surfing and snorkeling and the gorgeous fish at Honolulu Bay. We walk and talk for at least twenty minutes about how gorgeous the island is and he fills me in on what he and his friends have been doing—golfing, hiking, and also surfing.

We commiserate over how hard it is to actually get up on the board, but agree it's something we both want to continue to practice.

"I'm heading back out in the morning; would you maybe like to join me?" I ask. "My lessons are technically for two. But I know you're busy, so don't feel—"

"I'd love to," he says, making my heart beat double-time.

We've walked far enough that we have a little section of beach to ourselves. The moon is bright and is casting its glow on the water. Soft waves cascade onto the sand and it feels like we're in a postcard or movie.

"It's so beautiful," I whisper, not wanting to disrupt the moment.

"It really is," River agrees, but when I glance back at him, he's not looking at the water.

He's looking at me.

"I've been thinking about kissing you ever since I saw you in the airport. It actually pissed me off a little because I promised myself I was going to enjoy this trip with just the guys and not complicate things. Like you, I just got out of a pretty serious relationship and felt like I needed some time. Then you tried stealing my muffin and kept stalking me... and well, now, here we are standing on a gorgeous beach in Hawai'i and you look stunning in this smokeshow of a dress and I feel like I'd be letting down humanity if I didn't kiss you."

The laugh that escapes me is not exactly sexy, it's more a guffaw, and I should be embarrassed, but I have never been on the receiving end of a speech quite like this, and I can't help my reaction.

"I did not try to steal your muffin."

"Out of all that, you're stuck on the muffin?"

I feel the shift in the atmosphere around us—it's charged and alive. When

River reaches up to brush a strand of hair from my face, a current flows through my body, electrifying every cell in its wake.

"What do you say, Shelbi Lewis? May I kiss you?"

My eyes are trained on his lips as I nod my agreement. "Yeah, yes," I say, laughing at myself as I glance back up at those captivating eyes. "I would like that very much."

River takes my face in his hands and brushes his thumbs over my cheeks, and the world stops spinning as his lips descend to mine. At first, this kiss is soft and slow, but the second I open my mouth and invite him in, everything shifts.

The kiss.

His touch.

The way my body melds to his.

It all becomes more—more intense, more needy... more demanding.

And I love it.

When I feel his hardness against my stomach, my entire body becomes molten lava and I'm putty in his hands. If he wanted to take me right here on this beach, I would let him.

"You're going to be the death of me," River mutters against my lips as he breaks the kiss, resting his forehead against mine. "Fuck, Shelbi. I knew you'd be a great kisser, but I didn't expect that... I couldn't have."

Closing my eyes, I soak in this moment. The feel of his hands on me and his body pressed to mine. The smell of him enveloping me. The lingering taste of him on my tongue.

"I think that was the best kiss of my life."

CHAPTER 9

When I show up at the beach the next morning and find River standing there looking like a daydream, I have to remind myself to breathe. Now that I know what it's like to kiss him, it's all I can think about.

After he walked me back to my room last night, he kissed me again before saying goodnight and leaving me craving more.

Even after I got myself off and took a cool shower, my body was still humming and I had the hardest time going to sleep.

"Good morning," he says with that damn sly smile.

Shielding my eyes from the sun, I squint up at him. "Maybe for you, but I hardly got any sleep."

River bites his bottom lip and shakes his head. "Yeah, I slept like shit, too."

We're just standing there, sizing each other up and appreciating the view, when our surf instructor approaches us, boards under his arms.

"Hey, Benjamin," I say. "This is my friend, River. I told him he could join me this morning and take the extra spot."

"Absolutely," Benjamin says, giving River a nod. "Let me go grab another board. I'll be right back."

When he walks away, River smirks.

"What?" I ask, pulling my hair back into a ponytail.

He shakes his head, pulling up his wet suit that was hanging at his waist. "Nothing, except you didn't quite feel like my friend last night. I don't tend to devour my friends' mouths."

My face heats. "What else was I supposed to call you?"

"Friend is fine, for now. Later, I might have a better suggestion."

Did he just suggest what I think he suggested?

I don't have long to dwell on his insinuation and what that might mean for later, because Benjamin is jogging back to us with another board in tow.

"Ready to get wet?" he asks with a friendly smile.

River glances over at me and smirks.

Already there, Ben.

CHAPTER 10

After our surfing lessons, where River kills it, we dry off and grab some lunch from a nearby food truck and find a spot on the beach to sit while we eat.

He holds our boats of fish tacos and watches while I spread a towel out for us to sit on.

"Have I mentioned I didn't see this coming?"

I glance up, squinting against the sun, my wet hair hanging over my shoulder. "What? You didn't see yourself eating fish tacos on a beach after crushing some surfing lessons? Which by the way, I call bullshit on you saying you've never surfed before. You were way too good for this to be your first lesson."

"You didn't do so bad yourself," he says, gingerly sitting down on the towel while still holding both of our lunches. "And that wetsuit." He pauses, whistling through his teeth. "That was the real MVP of the morning."

"Shut up," I say, bumping him with my shoulder as I laugh. "And give me my fish tacos."

"There are so many crude jokes to be had, but I will refrain."

My smile is hidden with my first bite and I just shake my head at this gorgeous man sitting beside me. "I know what you mean," I finally say, after swallowing my food. "But I think some of the best things in life take us by surprise. It's like, if we had known they were coming, we might've ruined it with overthinking and preconceived notions."

River turns to me with a look of... I don't know. I hate to put a label on it because it sounds presumptuous, even in my head.

"You are the best surprise," he finally says with a bit of awe.

"Do your friends know you bailed on them to go surfing with a girl?" I ask, curious about how much they know.

He laughs, glancing out to the ocean. "They do. I kind of had to tell them because they weren't going to let me get by with it if I didn't. I told them we met on the plane and hit it off. I thought my chances of seeing you again were slim to none, which is why I didn't bring you up earlier in the trip. Besides that, I just wanted to keep that for me. When I said I enjoyed our conversation, I meant it. It was great getting to know you like that. Sometimes, when I meet a woman, everything happens so quickly. And I realize this is still quick, but I mean, really quickly. We meet for drinks and then bada bing bada boom."

"Bada bing bada boom?" I ask incredulously, fighting back a laugh.

"Yeah," he replies in utter confidence. "We fuck. She leaves. And we don't know shit about each other. This is different."

That shuts me up and I'm forced to swallow hard at the thought of River fucking me. After our kiss last night, it's not as far-fetched as it once was. I felt him as he pressed against me. It was that image that I used while making myself come last night.

Have I mentioned I haven't had an orgasm with another person in over six months?

"You're different," he continues. "I didn't want to ruin that, so I left it up to chance and for once in my life, chance came through for me."

"So, uh." I swallow again. "Where are your friends today? Are they waiting for you to get back?"

"They went on another hike... an all-day hike. I did that already, so I'm all yours."

Whoa.

That's, just.

Whoa.

CHAPTER 11

For the rest of the day, River and I walk the beach and go for swims. It's honestly the most relaxed I've been so far on this trip. Sure, I've been having fun and experiencing new and exciting things, but I haven't taken a day to just *be*.

"This is so nice," I say, relaxing back into River as we rest on the beach.

"It is," he agrees, brushing my damp hair to the side and pressing a kiss to my shoulder.

The small touches between us have increased throughout the day and it's felt a lot like foreplay. There have been moments I've wanted to drag him back to my room and have my way with him, but I love just spending time with him too, so I'm trying to be in the moment and not interfere with where the day takes us.

Fate has been kind to us so far.

But I know the clock is ticking.

"I hate that I have to leave tomorrow," River mutters as his lips brush my temple, taking the words right out of my brain.

I pull his arm around my waist and hold onto him.

The future for us is extremely unpredictable. What happens next? Does River *and* Shelbi only exist in Maui? Is he someone I'm only supposed to have for a moment... someone to remind me of what it feels like to be wanted and desired. Someone who reminds me of what it feels like to want someone in return. He's definitely brought me back to a part of myself that's been dormant for a while, and for that, I will always be grateful.

"When will your friends be back from their hike?"

River brings his wrist up to check his watch. "Soon," he says, placing a kiss on my hair. "I promised them I'd meet them for dinner on the beach. There's a luau tonight. You can come if you'd like."

I immediately shake my head. As much as I want to spend time with River, I also don't want to be *that* girl. "No, it's your last night with your dudes. I'm sure you have major celebrating to do."

"My flight leaves at noon tomorrow, so I'll have to be at the airport by ten-thirty at the latest. I don't have a bag to check, but I don't know what security will be like."

I wish I would've run into River sooner. We could've snuck away or scheduled a late-night rendezvous. But we still have New Orleans. Maybe we can exist outside of paradise.

"Promise me you'll come back here after I leave," River says, his voice taking on a rougher tone, like he's fighting with his emotions. "It's such a gorgeous spot and it deserves to be seen more than once."

My arm wraps tighter around him, trying to hold him here—trying to make this moment last forever.

"I promise."

CHAPTER 12

River insists on walking me back to my room, which gets no argument from me.

I'll take every second I can get with him, soaking him in and memorizing everything about him—the manly scent even the ocean couldn't wash away, the way his hand feels in mine, and the way his lips feel on my skin.

I want more, but I'll try to be happy with what I've got and appreciate it for what it's been.

When we reach my room, I want to invite him in, if only for a few stolen moments, but I know he needs to go. One of the guys already texted him before we left the beach, asking him where he was and making sure he didn't forget about dinner.

So, when I turn to tell him goodbye, I'm caught off guard by the intensity in his eyes and the way his gaze devours me like I'm his meal.

"I don't want to leave you," he admits.

"It's okay," I tell him, not wanting to make this a moment I'll look back on with sadness or regret, just happiness. "I had you to myself all day and I loved every second of it."

He gives me a lopsided grin. "It was a great day... the best, really. My favorite one yet, but don't tell my friends I said that."

"Your secret is safe with me."

River gives me a nod, swallowing hard.

"May I kiss you one last time?"

"You better."

His lips crash into mine, hands framing my face and we kiss like our lives depend on it. The scruff on his cheeks rubs against my skin, and his tongue dips into my mouth, causing me to moan in response.

As the kiss intensifies, he presses me to the door, his arousal heavy against my belly.

I want to feel every inch of his hard, taut body.

But before I get the chance to tell him, his phone rings, bursting the bubble we've been in.

River lets out a frustrated groan and his pained stare tells me all the things he wishes he could say—promises and proclamations. But this...us...feels too rushed, too soon. So, instead, he leans down and softly brushes his lips against mine.

"I think you're something special, Shelbi Lewis. And I'm terrible at predicting the future, so won't try. I'm just going to say if our paths cross again, I wouldn't hate it."

"I wouldn't hate it either."

This sounds a lot like goodbye, but I refuse to let my emotions get the best of me.

After a few more lingering kisses, he pulls away—giving me one final intense stare—and then he's gone.

I stand in the hallway for a while after he disappears, pressing my fingers to my lips. I don't want to ever forget how that felt or what it was like to kiss River Townsend.

CHAPTER 13

For the rest of the night, I try not to think about where River is or what he's doing. I convince myself it would be stupid to walk the beach in search of this luau he and his friends are attending. But I do allow myself to bask in the goodness of the day and do what I do best, look on the bright side.

I spent the day with the sexiest man I've ever met.

He made me feel amazing and beautiful.

I laughed and relaxed and savored every moment.

Those are things I'll hold onto for a long time.

And as wonderful as today was, I am still left wondering what it would've been like to have him in my bed, if only for one night.

But dwelling on what I didn't get to experience with River will only lead to frustration and I don't want that. I want to spend the next few days soaking up Maui and completing my last few adventures. It's what I came for and I'm not going to lose sight of that.

After I order room service for dinner, I take a walk in the gardens near my room before coming back and soaking in the tub. As the warm water soothes my sun-kissed skin, I'm plotting ways I could run into River before he leaves in the morning.

Once I'm out of the bath and dressed for bed, I finally feel like I'm relaxed enough to attempt to sleep, until I'm startled by a knock.

It's like my body knows as I approach the door.

The moment I look through the peephole and spot a familiar head of hair, my heart starts to beat out of my chest. When I swing the door open, he looks up and gives me the smile that makes my entire body turn to butter.

"What are you doing here? I thought—"

River pushes his way into my room and wraps me up in his arms. "I'm sorry, I couldn't leave without seeing you again. I just—"

"Have you been drinking?" I ask, catching a hint of whiskey on his breath.

"I just had a glass. I'm completely sober. And I came here to see if you're on the same page as I am. I want you, Shelbi, and if I was reading you right earlier, you want me too."

I nod fervently. "I do. I'm not typically a one-night stand kind of girl, like...I've never had a one-night stand, but I would be lying if I said I didn't want you... in every sense of the word."

His mesmerizing eyes dance in the dim light and his husky laugh sends shivers down my spine.

"I have ten hours before I need to be at the airport and I want to spend them with you."

With that confession, River and I don't waste any time discarding our clothes, but before he tosses his slacks, he pulls out a stack of condoms and tosses them to the bed.

My eyes go wide and he chuckles, reaching for me and pulling me up his body.

"One time will never be enough."

River's mouth devours mine and I let him. I let him take my mouth and my body, in any and every way he wants.

When he tosses me onto the bed, I revel in the way he handles me—gentle at times and with abandon at others. It's the perfect combination to have me needy and ready before he ever touches me.

As his hands glide down my body, his eyes never leave mine. And when he pulls my pajama shorts and panties off in one fell swoop, my stomach dips in expectation.

"I haven't had sex in over six months," I confess, the words tumbling out of my mouth. "So, if I'm not—"

"You're going to be perfect and I'm going to make this good for you, Shelbi. Don't worry. I've got you."

Oh, he does. He has me—body and soul.

Kneeling beside the bed, he pulls me toward him, my pussy level with his face, and I watch as his tongue darts out to wet his lips. That act alone has me writhing beneath him, begging for more.

I want to tell him that it's been even longer since someone went down on me, but I don't. I don't want to interrupt this moment or bring any thoughts of past failed relationships into this room or this bed. It's ours. This is just for me and River, no one else.

He parts my center with his fingers and then flattens his tongue against my clit, before sucking it into his mouth and sending a jolt of pleasure through my body. As I grip the soft blanket and curl my toes into the bed, he slides a finger inside me.

"Oh, God," I moan, biting down on my bottom lip to keep from crying out as he begins to thrust and suck in tandem. "You... ah... you feel soooo good. This feels so good."

River pulls his mouth away, but adds another finger inside me, curling them up to hit that magic spot that makes my toes curl and my body shake.

"You feel so good, Shelbi. Every gorgeous inch of you is pure perfection."

As I continue to ride River's hand, he dips back down to tongue circles around my clit, quickly bringing me to my head-spinning orgasm.

Once my orgasm subsides, I tug on him, silently begging for him to come closer. I'd love to return the favor and feel what it's like to have his cock in my mouth, but right now, I just need to feel him inside me.

"I need you," I finally manage to say.

Words are hard when your head is in the clouds.

"What do you need?" His question is somewhat teasing, but doused in a heaping dose of seduction, making my body quiver with his words.

"You, your cock... I want you to make me come again, but not on your hands or your tongue. I just need your cock."

River groans, gripping my hips. "Fuck, Shelbi. Keep talking like that and I'm going to come before I even get inside you."

Leaning over, he grabs a condom and rises to his knees to sheathe himself.

"That's only acceptable if you promise you can recover quickly," I say with a breathy laugh, brushing hair off my face so I don't miss the show.

River is a god. His chest is chiseled in all the right places, each dip and valley strategically placed. I've been ogling him all day, but there's something different about seeing him like this, completely nude and offering himself to me with nothing between us.

"I'd rather come inside you."

Scooping me up, he situates my opening just above his cock. This position, with us chest to chest, feels intimate, but it also feels right. With our eyes locked, he gradually lowers me down on his cock until our thighs meet and he's fully inside me.

I watch as his eyes close in pleasure and my breath gets caught in my throat. The fullness is almost more than I can handle, but it's perfect.

He's perfect.

With his hands on my ass, he leans in and captures my mouth with his, before pulling back to look at me again. "You okay?" he asks, brushing his lips against my cheek and whispering in my ear. "You feel so fucking good, but I can wait... tell me when you're ready."

I nod as the pinch of pain slowly begins to fade and I'm only left with pleasure. As I slowly begin to rock my hips, I feel a deep rumble reverberate from River's chest and his grip on my ass tightens.

"Yes, God yes," I cry out as he begins to thrust into me.

We come like that, me riding his cock as he fucks me into oblivion.

Later, I get on my knees for him in the shower, finally taking his glorious cock into my mouth and feeling like the most powerful, badass bitch when he comes loudly, his roar echoing against the shower tiles. And then he takes me against the wall, making me fall apart in his hands.

Then, sometime, in the wee hours of the morning, River wakes me with soft kisses to my stomach and thighs as he buries his face between my legs again, before taking me from behind. My hair tangled in his fist as he pounds into me, making me cry out his name... over and over.

When the sun wakes me some hours later, the bed is empty and there's a note on my nightstand.

Shelbi,

I'm sorry for keeping you up all night and I'm even more sorry for not waking you this morning.

You were sleeping so peacefully and looking so beautiful, I couldn't bring myself to wake you. Besides, if I had, I'm not sure I would've been able to tear myself away.

Last night was one of the best nights of my life and I will always think of you when I think of Maui.

Always,
River

CHAPTER 14

Days later, when I board my flight home and claim my window seat, a sweet little old man is sitting on the aisle. He greets me with a kind smile and I immediately notice his silvery white hair and the crinkles around hazel eyes that make me think of River.

My thoughts have been on him non-stop since he left.

We parted without exchanging phone numbers. I'm not sure if that was intentional or just a lapse in judgment. Our time together was so focused on the present, we didn't talk about what happens next, or if we'd see each other again once we're both back in New Orleans. So, exchanging numbers never came up.

But the idea of him being in my city and me not being able to reach out to him has my heart feeling sad and melancholy.

That, paired with leaving the most beautiful place I've ever visited, is enough to bring a few tears to my eyes. I quickly wipe them away, but the older man notices and reaches over to pat my arm.

"It's not goodbye forever, just for now."

He obviously misunderstands my sadness, but I give him a reassuring smile and nod my head in appreciation of his concern.

The flight home feels longer in some ways, but shorter in others.

When I make my connection in Dallas, I instinctively search the airport, looking for someone I know will not be there.

And when I arrive in New Orleans, I find myself doing the same, scanning every face as I make my way through the terminal. But when I step out into the area designated for ride shares and taxis, my heart leaps.

There, standing on the curb with one of those smiles that makes his eyes twinkle, is River.

"What are you doing here?" I ask, half chuckling, half crying—my utter dismay and immense relief at seeing him getting the best of me.

"I realized I didn't get your number."

My body collides with his and he catches me in his arms, picking me up and hugging me so tightly I feel like I might not be able to breathe.

And that would be fine.

Dying in the arms of this man seems like the perfect way to go.

"I would've found you," I tell him, my nose buried in his neck as I inhale him. "But I'm so glad you're here."

"There's no place I'd rather be."

———

Thanks for reading. Check out the rest of our books at www.jiffykate.com.

SILENT VOWS
EXTENDED BONUS EPILOGUE
JILL RAMSOWER

CHAPTER 1 - CONNER

"Give it to me. I'll let them know we aren't going to make it." I held my hand out for the invitation. Noemi just stared at me.

"We don't have any plans that weekend. Why wouldn't we go?"

I sighed as I prepared to beat my head against the brick wall of my wife's obstinate nature. It would have been so much easier to give in, but fuck that. I didn't want to go. I didn't care how stubborn Noemi could be. She couldn't make me go to a fucking baptism if I didn't want to.

"Because I hate that sort of thing."

"Family celebrations?"

"*Kid* things. The party after will be crawling with them. That stuff gets on my nerves when it's for my own family, let alone the Genoveses. I hardly know those people."

"*Those people*"—my wife arched a brow—"are family just as much as the Byrnes."

"Only in the technical sense." I might have been born with Genovese Italian blood, but I'd been raised among the Irish and would die loyal to my adoptive family.

"They've been there for you and your cousins lately. And besides, you won't get to know them—*half* of your biological family tree—if you don't spend time with them."

"Like we're going to spend quality time together watching a priest sprinkle water on some kid's head." I skipped over the part about the Genoveses being helpful because that part was true. They'd stepped up to help my Irish family in ways far beyond what our recent alliance would dictate. But I wouldn't concede that point unless she forced me to.

My wife's hands went to her hips. She was digging in for a war of attrition but could pitch a fit all she wanted. I. Wasn't. Going.

"It's a baby, not *some kid*. And it's a perfect chance to make an appearance with minimal obligation. A little chitchat. Some punch and cake. If it's awkward, we can leave whenever we want."

"How about we leave before it even starts?"

Noemi glared. It was fucking adorable.

"I thought you said the last time you and Mia talked, you left things in a good place?"

"We did."

"So what's the problem?" Her voice lifted with a note of exasperation.

I wasn't entirely sure how to answer.

I'd been taught to be suspicious of the Italians and other organizations all my life. I'd also wanted more than anything to prove my loyalty to my Byrne family. I was the only adopted kid in my generation and the adopted son of the only Byrne daughter, making me a Reid. I'd seen myself as an outsider by birth and name and had only ever wanted to prove myself worthy.

Finding out I was part Italian this year had been a fist to the gut. When I was asked to forge an alliance by marrying an Italian bride, I felt like I'd been kicked to the curb.

Those deep-rooted feelings I'd struggled with as a child didn't just evaporate, no matter how much I ended up loving the woman I chose to marry. How could I explain that to someone who'd never known what it was like to feel like an impostor?

"I'm sure they only sent the damn invitation to be polite. I'd be doing them a favor by declining," I grumbled, shifting my gaze to the city lights out our living room windows to avoid seeing the disappointment on her face.

Noemi's soft footfalls grew closer before she forced my arms to uncross and peered up at me. "What if I made it worth your while?" she murmured in a husky voice that had me and my cock at attention.

Don't take the bait, asshole. She'll have you by the balls.

"Oh, yeah? What do you propose?" I grazed my thumb across her full bottom lip.

Fuck. Too late.

"You know what you've wanted to do to me in the bedroom?"

"The clamps?" I asked in a breathless rumble that made me sound half feral. "Fuck, you'd let me clamp these?" I ran my thumbs over her pert nipples, already straining against her bra and shirt as if begging to be played with.

"I said it would never happen." She shrugged one shoulder and smirked. "That way, it's a compromise. We'd both be giving in."

"Yeah, but you'd like what I plan to do a hell of a lot more than I'd enjoy a *baptism*."

"I suppose we'll never know unless we try." Her palm cupped my erection, taking two slow strokes up and down the front of my pants.

Jesus. How could I possibly refuse?

"What if I promised to take you to Maui instead?" I whispered in her ear, my hands on either side of her face as I nipped her earlobe. "I could take you to Honolua Bay, where you have to walk through a forest of greenery that's almost too perfect to be real before getting to one of the best snorkel sites on the planet. There are even brightly colored chickens hopping around the rocky shore. You'd think you'd died and gone to heaven."

She stilled, and for half a heartbeat, I thought maybe my last-ditch effort had succeeded.

"Nice try, but no dice."

I growled, wrapping her legs around my waist as I lifted her into my arms. "*Fine*, but I want my payment up front." I kneaded my fingers into her ass cheeks, pressing her center against my aching cock.

Noemi dropped her head back with a laugh that sounded like goddamn sunshine. When she did shit like that, I couldn't even be angry that she was about to brazenly defy me.

"Baptism, then clamps. That's the deal. Take it or leave it." She leaned in and sucked my bottom lip between her teeth before releasing it with a pop.

"You drive me batshit crazy, you know that?"

She flashed a wicked grin. "Would a blow job help?"

I instantly dropped her feet to the floor. My wife kept her eyes on mine as she lowered onto her knees, then undid my pants. We'd been married for six months, and I still couldn't imagine ever growing tired of this view—her peering up at me from beneath a forest of lashes, golden flecks flashing in her green eyes as she took my cock in her hand.

"I still want my trip to Maui."

Before I could respond, she licked me from base to tip, then sucked me deep to the back of her throat. My lungs seized, making my breaths shudder.

Like I said, she's got you by the balls. Literally.

I didn't fucking care. The way my wife sucked me dry, I wouldn't just take her to Maui, I'd buy her the whole goddamn island.

CHAPTER 2 - NOEMI

"I thought babies were supposed to wear white to these things," Conner groused under his breath as the priest began the opening remarks to begin the baptism.

In the two weeks since we'd made our deal, Conner had made more than a few grumbled comments about how parents wrongfully assumed everyone was as enthralled with their spawn as they were.

His words, not mine.

The offhanded comments brought to my attention that we'd never talked about a family. Six months into our arranged marriage, we were still getting to know one another. At least, that was what I'd assumed. Now, I wondered if the subject hadn't come up for a reason, and the possibility worried me. I adored kids and couldn't imagine my life without them—whether biological or adopted.

We would need to discuss it, but not in the middle of a baptism.

Instead, I turned my attention to the handsome couple—Matteo and Maria De Luca—standing at the baptismal font with a raven-haired baby girl in a royal-blue dress. Maria had been a Genovese by birth—her father was the boss of the Lucciano family—and Matteo was the boss of the Gallos. Their marriage had been a huge deal in the mafia world. When two families made a marital alliance, just as our wedding had been, the impact could be felt far and wide.

We weren't invited to the wedding, and my father likely wouldn't have let me go even if we had been, but rumors prevailed about the event.

I leaned close to whisper in Conner's ear. "I don't think Maria's your average Italian wife. Pip said she heard that Maria wore a solid red gown to her wedding."

"Was it some kind of statement? I would have paid big money to see the look on all those scandalized Italian faces."

"No clue, but it doesn't surprise me that she'd buck tradition here as well." I tried to speak as quietly as possible, unsure who was seated around us. In a crowd of this sort, even the walls had ears.

I watched the beautiful woman with even more interest when the priest tried to take the baby from her, and she refused. Again, the balding man in ornately embroidered robes motioned for the little girl. Maria leaned in, her body shielding the baby, and whispered something to him. The priest visibly blanched.

My eyes darted to Matteo, wondering if he might try to persuade his wife to let the priest do what he needed to do for the ceremony. I could understand being protective, but I wasn't sure what she thought would happen. The man wasn't so elderly that he was at risk of dropping the little girl.

Her husband only smirked, more amused than bothered.

"I don't know what it is about children that make people lose all logic," Conner murmured, his head slightly cocked to the side as if mystified.

My head swiveled *Poltergeist*-style toward him. "You threatened to cut off the fingers of any man who touched me before we were even married. I couldn't have dancing at our wedding for fear of a bloodbath. Sometimes people are just irrational."

"That wasn't irrational," he grumped. "You were being secretive and unpredictable. I had no other choice."

The man was so damn absurd that I honest to God snorted in the middle of the baptism.

People around us shot annoyed looks our way. I took heed and kept quiet. Besides, I didn't need to refute Conner's statement. My snort had adequately conveyed my feelings on the matter.

Conner huffed petulantly.

We watched the remainder of the baptism in silence. When the congregation was dismissed, we filtered out of the main cathedral along with a couple of hundred other guests and made our way toward the event hall behind the church. As we walked, Conner took out his phone to answer a call. Taking my hand, he looked around with a thunderous expression, then led me to a nearby exit.

A million and one terrified thoughts raced through my mind. Had something bad happened? Was someone hurt? Having a life in the criminal underworld was terrible for a girl's anxiety.

However, the second the door slammed shut behind us, Conner slipped his phone in his pocket and sighed with relief. "We should be able to slip away now without getting backlash for leaving early."

I gaped at the breathtaking, infuriating man across from me. "You can't be serious."

"You said we could leave anytime we wanted."

"*After* chatting and cake." I crossed my arms stubbornly over my chest.

"I *did* chat when we came in, and we had communion—the wafer is sort of like cake."

I narrowed my eyes at him, pointing a finger at his chest. "If your imagination is good enough to pretend cardboard wafers are the same as cake, it's good enough to imagine me in clamps because that's the only way you'll see it happen unless you get back in there and freaking mingle."

Conner stepped closer, pressing his chest against the tip of my finger. His azure eyes caught the sunlight and sparked with liquid turquoise. "Or I could turn you around, press you against this wall, and fuck you until you forget how to stand upright because right now, that smart mouth of yours is making me too goddamn hard to go anywhere."

He was so damn good at throwing me off balance. The heat in his penetrating stare and the scrape of his ragged words across my skin eviscerated my thoughts.

What had I just said to him? Something about cake?

"We should … um, get back inside." I fought against the desire pooling in my belly, guiding a stray strand of hair behind my ear with a trembling finger.

My husband's hand came to my hip. I lifted my eyes to his as his hand slowly coaxed up my dress. When his fingers drifted around to my core, my silk panties a hapless barrier between us, my lips parted on a shaky breath.

"Ten minutes, Emi. Ten minutes before I take you home and get my reward."

It took every last brain cell in my head to remember why we had to wait ten minutes.

I nodded dazedly, hating myself a little when his hand fell away and left me wanting. Even more so when he brought his fingers to his nose and took a long inhale of my scent. The rumble that reverberated from his chest made my knees threaten to give out.

Sweet baby Jesus, we needed to get back inside.

I nodded again, this time to myself, then went back inside. The hallway had emptied, and the joyful chatter echoing from the event hall guided us in its direction.

"You go on in," I said when we spotted the double doors. "I just need to pop into the restroom for a second." I needed to collect myself.

"I'll wait for you."

"You're welcome to, but the sooner you mingle, the sooner we can go," I reminded him.

Conner shot me one last scathing stare, then strolled reluctantly through the double doors.

My shoulders sagged with relief. Finally, he was talking with his family, and I had a second to gather my wits. I wasn't sure why I felt it was so important for him to foster a connection with his mother and her family. My gut insisted he needed to do it. Had I been wrong?

As I pushed open the bathroom door, I wondered if I'd made a mountain out of a molehill.

"You're lucky you're so damn cute, or I'd be a little pissed right now." The female voice greeted my ears with an air of amusement.

Rounding the corner, I found Maria De Luca at the sink wetting a paper towel with one hand while the other clutched her daughter to her side. When she turned to see who had joined her, I was able to see globs of white goo trailing down her black dress.

"Perfect, a second set of hands. Can you take her for a minute?" She practically flung the baby girl in my arms. "She has reflux issues—spit up all over me. Who knew babies had reflux?"

I wasn't sure what to say, stunned that she'd been so casual about handing over the baby when she'd given the priest a death glare a half hour earlier.

"No problem. She's a cutie," I finally managed, smiling at little Gabby and getting an adorable baby grin in return. "We haven't officially met. I'm—"

"Noemi Reid. I know who you are. Fausto's daughter. I heard what happened."

My lips thinned as an awkward silence filled the small room. "I suppose that sort of thing gets around." When your father starts killing off family members, people talk.

She shrugged. "My family's a little fucked up, too. It happens."

I appreciated that she left it at that and realized that despite her dry demeanor, I liked Maria. Gabby squealed, patting her chubby little hand on my shoulder as though demanding my attention. I smiled at her and gave her my thumb to wrap her tiny fingers around.

"At least the reflux doesn't seem to bother her."

"Now that she's eating some baby food, it's not too bad. The problem is, you just never know when it's coming." She dabbed at the remnants of white embedded into the black fabric and grimaced. "Stuff stains like a motherfucker, though."

I fought back a laugh.

I definitely liked Maria—boss bitch vibe and all.

"Can I ask you something?" I said on a whim.

"Shoot."

"Did you really wear a red wedding gown?"

Her answering grin was lupine. "And a knife sheathed to my thigh."

My eyes bulged. "Why?" She said it with a meaning I didn't quite understand. Did she and her husband share some kind of strange knife kink? Oh God. I shouldn't have asked.

Maria shrugged nonchalantly. "I wasn't entirely sure I would let him live through the night." She said it without an ounce of false bravado. She was serious. She would have killed him had the mood struck. "It was sort of a secret, but our marriage was arranged. I *hated* him at first."

"*Really?*" I was stunned. They'd looked utterly in love in all the photos I'd seen after the fact. "That doesn't seem to be the case now, and you guys have this sweet girl. What changed?"

Maria tossed the towels she'd used into the trash. "Gabby—that's what changed. She wasn't exactly planned."

I couldn't help the frown that tugged at my lips.

"What's that for?" Maria asked.

"I'm not sure how much you know, but Conner and I got married six months ago in a similar situation. I thought we'd worked through our biggest obstacles, but I'm starting to worry that he doesn't want a family."

"He tell you as much?"

"No. It's just the little things he says."

"Have you seen him around any nieces and nephews?"

I shook my head. "He's an only child. We've gone to his family gatherings, but he doesn't really bother with the kids."

"I never did either. I didn't think I wanted any, but it's different when it's your own."

I wasn't sure how we'd strayed to this topic. Maria was the last person I would have sought advice from, but what she said sort of helped. Considering how intimidating she'd looked on the dais, she was surprisingly easy to talk to. Something about her straightforward manner put me at ease.

Maria's eyes glinted with mischief. "Maybe he just needs to see you in a different light. Come on, let's meet this husband of yours. He's my cousin, after all. It's probably time I introduced myself."

CHAPTER 3 - CONNER

I walked into the crowd, growing more pissed with each step. I could feel the curious stares like mosquitos swooping in for blood. I hated feeling like a zoo attraction. I hadn't come this far in life to be an outcast. Fuck that. I had a family and didn't need these people, no matter what I promised Noemi.

I looked toward the front entrance, intending to step outside to wait for my wife, when Mia made a beeline in my direction.

Just fucking great.

My birth mother was a kind woman. I truly didn't begrudge her for giving me up, but that didn't mean I wanted an invite to Thanksgiving dinner. Wasn't it enough that she'd learned who I was and that I'd been raised in a good family? Why did our relationship have to be any more than that?

"Conner, I'm so glad you could make it!" Her hands floundered in the air as though she wanted to hug me but thought better of it.

"It's good to see you, Mia. How have you been?"

"Good. Busy with all of this. And tonight is Valentina's nineteenth birthday. We're having dinner at the house." Her hand flew to her mouth. "I should have invited you—"

"No." I cut her off somewhat harshly. "You shouldn't. There's no need." Frustration coiled deep in my shoulders, stiffening my spine.

"I know I don't need to. I *want* to invite you. I want you to know you're a part of our family."

"But I'm not, Mia. And that's okay. I don't need to be. I already have a family."

"Oh … yes. Of course." Her gaze flitted to the vinyl floor. "I didn't mean to be pushy."

Shit, now she's upset.

I unleashed a heavy sigh. "It's not a problem…" I started just as Noemi approached with the De Luca baby in her arms.

"Hey, you two. Look who I found." She gave the baby a smattering of kisses on her cheek, making the little girl grin and coo. Over her shoulder, Maria took in the scene, her perceptive stare dancing from Mia to me with a jab of accusation. Mia was her aunt, and she wasn't thrilled to see the glassy sheen in her aunt's eyes.

"Maria," Noemi continued, oblivious to the tense undertones in the air. "This is my husband, Conner Reid. Conner, I'd like to introduce Maria De Luca, your cousin."

The curvy brunette took a step forward and shook my hand as I might a business associate, and somehow, it fit. Maria didn't strike me as the hugging type. And if the rumors were true, she was more likely to smother me with a pillow than love. I didn't know the particulars of the Lucciano family structure, but I'd heard whispers that Maria had been made since before she could drive.

"It's good to finally meet you," I offered respectfully. I had no desire to piss off the woman, regardless of her business affiliation.

Hell, I hadn't even meant to hurt Mia.

Truth be told, I just wanted to be left alone.

"Would have had the pleasure sooner if it weren't for this little hellion."

The wry way she said it summoned a smirk to my lips. I'd been wrong to assume she was a helicopter mom, hovering over the baby with adoring eyes. Maria was more like a lioness, just as likely to swat a misbehaving cub as she was to gut anyone who hurt her baby.

That little girl wasn't going to slip anything past that woman. Ever.

I almost felt sorry for her.

"She's a beautiful baby. You two must be very proud." Somewhat more at ease, my sense of diplomacy returned.

Maria shrugged. "She can be a handful sometimes, but she took to Noemi immediately. Your wife is a natural."

If I didn't know better, I'd have said there was a note of challenge in her tone, but I had no idea why. "More than I would be, that's for sure."

"Want to hold her?" Noemi quickly asked as though seizing the opportunity. I took an involuntary step back.

What the hell was going on?

"Not sure why you want to make her cry," I quipped, feeling like the clueless butt of someone's joke. I wasn't sure what these two were up to, but I didn't like it.

The little girl with short dark curls started to fidget. Noemi cooed at her, rocking her hips in a motion so damn natural I doubted she even knew she was doing it. She was great with children. Maria had been right about that. I'd seen the way she'd interacted with my cousin's kids.

"She's probably getting hungry," Maria explained.

Mia swooped in, motioning for the baby. "I'll take the little princess and get her a bottle. Come to Auntie Mia, sweet girl."

The baby readily accepted the swap, rubbing at her eyes with the back of her hands. Mia kissed the baby with a wealth of love in her eyes. She was a natural nurturer, too.

Like a bullet train racing through a station, it hit me out of nowhere just how hard it would have been for Mia to give me up. Knowing Noemi, she would have been utterly wrecked to have to give up a child. Mia would have been the same.

I looked at her, noting how I could even see a hint of the naive girl she'd been behind the warmth of her adoring grin. What sort of shame and regret had she suffered all those years ago? How long would something like that stick with a person?

If it had been my wife, she would have never forgiven herself.

Fuck.

I'd been such a selfish prick.

Mia had finally been reunited with the child she'd given up, and that baby had grown into a man who seemingly wanted nothing to do with her. That had to feel like a fucking cleaver to the chest, yet she kept a smile on her face and continued to try.

What the hell was wrong with me? Why had I been so reluctant to accept my Italian family?

If Mia hadn't defied her parents, there was no telling where I would have ended up. I owed her for that if nothing else.

I was twenty-nine years old. It was time to stop acting like a scared little boy.

My Byrne family hadn't changed their view of me. That was no longer a concern, which meant my insecurities were the only reason for my continued reluctance. I'd let my fears get the better of me.

Even as a terrified child, Mia had found a way to put me above all else in her world to give me the best chance in life. The least I could do in return was show the woman a scrap of gratitude.

"Mia, wait," I called as she began to walk away.

I'd interrupted Noemi, and she and Maria both turned curious stares in my direction.

"Yes?" Mia asked warily.

"Can I have a word? Privately?"

"Of course." She nodded, handing the baby back to Maria.

"We'll just be a minute," I told the other ladies, then placed a hand on Mia's back to guide her toward the banquet hall exit.

Once we were alone, I met her hopeful blue stare with a show of vulnerability I rarely exhibited. "I owe you an apology."

"It's okay, Conner, really," she rushed to say.

I lifted my hand to stop her. "No, it's not. I meant it when I told you I didn't harbor resentment over my adoption, but my behavior hasn't been consistent with that. I want to explain."

I had to pause for a second to find the right words. None of this was easy, but it was important to get it out there.

"When I was younger, a part of me felt unsure about my place in the Byrne family—because of the adoption and because I was a Reid, not a Byrne. When it was uncovered that I was Italian by blood, all those insecurities resurfaced, though I didn't understand it at first. I just knew I needed to distance myself from the connection. A need to make it clear to my Byrne family that my loyalties weren't in question."

Mia's hand went to her chest, her eyes softening with understanding. "I hadn't even considered what a tough spot that might put you in. I'm so sorry."

"I appreciate that, but the reality is that I was the only one with concerns. The Byrnes' opinion of me hasn't changed, which means it's time for me to get my head out of my ass. Connecting with my Italian roots makes me stronger, not weaker. I'm sorry for the way I've behaved, and that won't be an issue anymore."

My birth mother put a tentative hand on my arm. "I understand completely, and you have nothing to worry about with me. I'm just happy to know that you're happy and healthy."

I wrapped my arms around her and gave her the first genuine hug we'd shared. She released a shuddered breath that cracked open a reservoir of warmth deep in my chest.

Mia gave me one last squeeze, then pulled back and wiped at her eyes with a grin. "Okay, we better get back in there before they start to worry."

I returned her smile, a weight lifting from my shoulders. "Happy to. You lead the way."

CHAPTER 4 - NOEMI

After Conner and Mia returned from their chat, we only remained at the party for another twenty minutes. The surprising part was that I was the one who asked to leave. Conner seemed more at ease once he returned, but my mood had grown darker by the minute as I thought about how he'd recoiled from baby Gabby.

What if Conner didn't want children?

A life without a family would be a life half-lived for me. That wasn't the case for everyone. My cousin Pippa couldn't imagine ever wanting kids, but my heart would feel empty without them. It was just the way I was made.

How could I explain that to my husband? If he gave in and agreed to have a baby, would he resent me for it?

The depressing thoughts were lead in my veins, making me feel like I weighed ten tons as I stepped from the car back home. I made a quiet retreat for the bedroom but only got halfway through the living room when Conner grabbed my hand and stopped me. His large body radiated heat at my back, and his right hand circled around to cup my throat, holding me against him.

"Time to pay up." His dark command would ordinarily have thrilled me, but I could only muster a spark of desire that quickly fizzled out in my current state of turmoil.

I wouldn't refuse him, however. He'd held up his end of the bargain and had seemed lighter for it, just as I'd hoped. Now, it was my turn.

I nodded.

Conner didn't move.

When he finally did, he turned me to face him, his piercing blue eyes spearing me in place. "What's wrong?"

"It's nothing." I didn't know why I tried to avoid the subject. The determination set in his features made it clear that wouldn't happen.

Conner's biceps strained the fabric of his dress shirt as he crossed his arms. "Try again."

I sighed and turned toward the floor-to-ceiling windows. "Neither of us knew what we were getting into when we got married. That's nobody's fault. I mean, it's not like you can have intimate conversations about your hopes and dreams with someone you've just met, and our situation was infinitely more complicated than a simple arranged marriage."

"Emi, what the fuck are you talking about?" Conner barked, his confusion and frustration sharpening his words.

I turned and met his stare, my vision blurring with tears. "I'm starting to understand that you aren't crazy about kids. I get it—not everyone wants children—but I'm not sure I can be okay without them." Emotion choked back my voice to a hoarse whisper.

Conner's brows furrowed as he uncrossed his arms. "Kids? Is *that* what this is about?"

I nodded. "You've grumbled about them ever since we got the invitation to the baptism. I thought you were going to run screaming when I suggested you hold Gabby."

"Fuck, baby. You had me worried." He ran a hand through his hair, then closed the distance between us. "I'm *not* crazy about kids—*other people's* kids. I don't need someone else's baby snot on me. But that has nothing to do with us." Conner cupped my face, keeping my gaze locked on his. "I can't imagine anything more perfect than my child growing inside you. In fact, I'd plant that seed right now if you wanted."

He pulled my body against his as he kissed me, his rapidly hardening length proof of just how ready he was. My relief was voracious. I wove my fingers through his thick, dark hair and devoured his kiss. Our tongues teased and caressed, teeth nipping and claiming until we had to pull apart for air.

"You really do want a family?" Hope inflated my chest to bursting.

"Wouldn't have said it if I didn't mean it. Get off the pill, and we'll make it happen."

My grin was so wide it made my cheeks ache. "Not yet. I'm enjoying our time together, just us."

Conner's lids grew hooded, and the air around us thickened. I watched his deft fingers as he undid his cuff links, then placed them in his palm for me to see. I hadn't noticed them before. They were unusual—a sort of clip—each with a brilliant blue sapphire surrounded in white gold.

"Ready?" he asked pointedly.

Then it hit me.

These were the clamps. He'd been wearing them the whole time.

I took them from him and examined the beautiful craftsmanship. "When did you get these?" And where? They weren't something you'd have found at a standard sex shop.

"I went out the day we made our deal and had them commissioned with a jeweler. I liked the idea of knowing that after I see them on you, I can wear them to work and think of how incredible they looked on your perfect tits."

Air. I needed air.

"Oh," I said on a strangled breath.

"Now, my scheming little wife, you made a deal, and it's time for you to strip."

CHAPTER 5 - CONNER

Seeing Noemi slowly undress in the middle of our living room took me back to a pivotal turning point in our relationship. It was the first time she entrusted me with her body and soul. Every bit of the overpowering emotions from that day came flooding back to me. She was already my wife at the time, but that day, she truly became *mine*.

"On your knees." I used the same words I had that day, and I could tell by the fiery passion in her eyes that she recalled our exchange as clearly as I did.

With every inch of her perfect skin bared, Noemi lowered to her knees. She was far enough from the window that I didn't worry about anyone seeing, but just to be safe, I pressed the remote to close the automated drapes. The room darkened.

She still had the clamps clutched in her hand. I liked knowing she could feel their weight in her palm, the anticipation building.

Slowly, I rolled up my sleeves and slid the belt from my waist with purposeful intent.

"Arms up." I buckled the black leather around her wrists above her head. The rise and fall of her breaths at shallow, uneven intervals was intoxicating to watch.

Once her wrists were secure, I allowed her to lower them. "Spread your knees wider."

She obeyed my instructions flawlessly. Hair falling down over her shoulders, wrists bound and her legs spread for me, she was a fucking goddess. The wanton look in her green eyes frayed my control to the barest thread.

I held out my palm before her in a silent command. The metal clamps were warm from the heat of her palm. I dropped them into my pocket, then pulled the knot of my tie free, sliding the blue silk from around my neck before retying it on Noemi as a blindfold.

I allowed my fingers to trail from her jaw down her neck and onward until I gently kneaded her breasts in my hands. "Fuck, you're gorgeous. If it didn't mean someone else seeing you like this, I'd have your portrait painted." I pinched one pebbled nipple, making her gasp. "I suppose I could always kill the artist once the painting was done," I mused.

My wife smirked, slowly turning her head side to side in admonishment.

I lowered myself to my knees. "You're right. There'll never be anything as good as the real thing. And besides, I have better things to do with my time."

I took out the clamps and placed one on her right nipple. Noemi inhaled sharply, then relaxed into the sensation.

"That's my girl," I almost purred with satisfaction.

Jesus, she was almost too good to be true.

"How's the pressure?" I asked.

She nodded. "It feels good." Breathless with anticipation. Exactly what I wanted to hear.

"Mmm..." I positioned the second clamp, then admired my handiwork. The sight was even better than I'd imagined. I caressed my knuckles from the outer curve of her breasts down to the underside and back, then gave the clamps the slightest flick. They bobbed on her nipples. Noemi's head dropped back as she released a wanton moan.

If my dick got any harder, I was afraid it might fall off.

I circled behind her, then lowered myself to the ground. Lying on my back below her, I scooted my head between her thighs.

"Oh!" My wife's surprised gasp drew a smile to my lips.

I clasped her thighs and pulled her down. The second she made contact with my lips, I felt her legs flex to keep herself hovered above me.

"Em," I said in warning.

"I'm scared I'm going to smother you."

"I'm a foot taller and weigh a hundred pounds more than you. If you smother me to death, I deserved to die." I arched my neck and licked from her slick opening to her swollen clit. "Now sit on my face. I'm ready for my cake."

I licked and sucked and devoured, occasionally bringing my arms around to flick the clamps and tease a new wave of sensation from them. Only a few minutes in, and Noemi curved forward, her hands bracing herself on the floor.

"Oh *God*, Conner. It's too much. Being upright ... it's too much. The orgasm's too big—I can't..."

I released the clamps at the same time, causing her to arch back upright, then I fucked her relentlessly with my fingers and tongue. Noemi shattered on my face, her primal cry bellowing through the apartment. With her head thrown back and thighs squeezing my head, she could have been the Greek goddess of carnal pleasure—a deity too perfect to walk among humankind.

I gave her a handful of frantic heartbeats to recover before rolling her to her back and tearing off my clothes like they were on fucking fire.

With no barriers left between us, I dove back down and licked at her puckered red nipples. Emi moaned wantonly. It was enough to rob a man of his sanity.

I couldn't wait any longer.

I jerked the blindfold off and surged inside her, wanting to see the emerald spark in her eyes as I filled her.

"Jesus, *fuck*, you feel divine."

"*Yes*, Conner. Give me more. I need *more*." She hooked her bound hands over my head and clung to me as I began to pound inside her. Who was I to deny my wife when she needed to be fucked?

I buried myself inside her time and again, rutting like an animal on the living room rug. It was goddam perfection. When her inner muscles seized and spasmed around me, I couldn't hold back had I wanted to. Bolts of electric release shot from deep in my balls to my spine, then a flash flood of pleasure surged through my veins outward to every extremity.

Palms tingling and ears ringing, I glided in and out of her in measured, reverent movements.

"See, clamps aren't so bad."

"Mmm ... I suppose I could work on being more open-minded," she said in a raspy, sex-drunk murmur.

My hand drifted down her side and around to her ass. "There's all kinds of fun we can have with this if you're brave enough to try." I teased my fingers at the rim of the puckered ring of muscle.

Surprisingly, she didn't flinch or squirm.

"You'll have to come up with a hell of a lot more compelling incentive than a baptism for that."

I hadn't been sure how she'd respond, but the hint of amusement in her voice sparked hope.

"There's always Maui," I offered, a smile in my voice.

"Bigger. Maui's already a done deal."

Keeping her arms and legs wrapped around me, I lifted us up from the floor and set off for the bathroom to clean up.

"That's it?" she questioned. "You're not even going to argue?"

I snarled playfully, then grazed my teeth along her neck. "No need. This" —I snuck my finger back to her rear entrance—"will be mine, and you'll love every second of it. I have no doubt."

"Is that a promise?" she asked huskily.

"When it comes to you, there's a promise in every word I say. Always and forever."

Thank you so much for reading this extended bonus epilogue of *Silent Vows*! I'd been wanting to do a bonus scene for these two, and the Maui anthology felt like the perfect opportunity. I was in Lahaina in 2021 and have been heartbroken to see the devastation. I'm so thrilled that our book community has come together to help!

SHOPPING FOR A BILLIONAIRE'S COFFEE

JULIA KENT

CHAPTER 1 - SHANNON

"How's my little boy?" Declan asks as his hand comes around from behind me, smooth palm splayed so as much of his skin presses against mine. The murmur against my ear makes me smile, his lips warm as they kiss the soft skin at the nape of my neck.

"He's fine. His incubator is, too."

Declan's hand moves lower, to my aching thigh. "I was just about to make sure Madame Incubator's every need is met."

"Every need, hmmm? That's a tall order." I feel his smile against my shoulder as the heat of him against my back feels oh, so good. Morning beard growth is so sexy as he nuzzles me.

"I am a tall man. A big man." His hips nudge against my ass, the gesture making it clear what he means by "big."

"You are the best man."

"That sounds like I'm in a wedding."

"Maybe soon!"

"What?" He sounds nonplussed, hand halting. The strong scent of lavender from our sheets makes me sigh, burrowing back into him. Our bedroom is an oasis, a quiet place down the hall from where our four-year-old, Ellie, mercifully sleeps. Still living in our Boston condo, we're waiting for renovations to be completed on our Weston home.

"Home" is an understatement.

My husband is constitutionally incapable of doing anything within the range of average, so when he bought us our first home together, he purchased an entire conference center. Seventeen buildings, 118 acres, a working farm, six cottages, twelve suites. Two swimming pools. One large pond. A "modest" four-bedroom cottage larger than the house I grew up in can be our living space while a custom-designed home and office is built on the premises.

All abutting his childhood home, which is currently owned by his brother.

In other words: he out-competed him. Declan's home will be bigger, better, and more lavish than his childhood home built by his father, the one Andrew bought.

And lives in now.

Billionaires are so weird.

Dec pulls back, then peers over my side as I turn my head to look at him. Confused green eyes meet mine, and he has the worst case of bedhead.

Which means he's adorably rumpled.

I laugh. "My sister, Amy? Your cousin, Hamish? Remember them?"

"What about them?"

"You know he's going to propose soon. That means a wedding is coming." Alarm floods me. Oh, no. My mother planning another wedding. Poor Amy. As sisters go, she's wonderful.

As a bride? She's *screwed*.

"How did we get from meeting your every need to *their* wedding? Stay focused, honey."

His fingers do something that makes it impossible to focus.

Between moans and sighs, I manage to utter, "Ellie might come in here."

"I locked the door."

"She figured out how to pick it last week!"

"Only because Hamish taught her," he whispers between kisses. "You don't have to worry about Ellie. I bribed her."

"Bribed her! With what?"

The sound of Ellie's favorite video game music floats through the air.

I groan. Or maybe it's a moan. Hard to tell at this point as I roll over and kiss him deeply, my lungs working a little extra hard to take in air. I fully blame the occupant currently pushing up against them.

Our little boy.

Cupping my breast under my loose nightgown, Declan moves over me. He sleeps naked, so that makes morning sex easy. No matter how often we make love, the thrill of his chest against mine, our belly-to-belly skin contact, the feel of his coarse leg hair scratching against my legs – it's all so heavenly.

And his kisses are divine.

"I love your luscious body when you're pregnant," he says, looking down at me as he climbs off and helps me to stop being ridiculously overdressed. "Why do you wear anything to bed? I've asked you so many times to sleep naked, like me."

"I don't know." That's not a language placeholder. I really don't know. "It's just how I've always slept."

"Change is good for people, Shannon."

"Why don't you start wearing pajamas, then?"

Thick, dark eyebrows shoot up. "Why would I want to do that?" he demands, as if I've asked him to start a new crypto-currency or refuse a tax deduction.

"See? You have your comfort zone, and I have mine."

"But mine," he says in a low, predatory voice as he pulls my nipple into his mouth, "is so much more comfortable."

For the next five minutes, he proves himself right.

Yes, only *five* minutes. This is not our norm, but:

Minute 1: three text messages pinged on his phone, then four on *mine*.

Minute 2: his phone rang and he had to move his face from between my legs to throw the damn thing into a hamper filled with laundry.

Minute 3: the next-door neighbor appears to be doing a reno project involving a jackhammer and a guy from Southie with a voice like a mobster screaming, "Not ovah theya, Jacko!"

Minute 4: Declan was finally inside me, and things were looking up, up, *up*.

Minute 5: good enough.

We're spooning again because the watermelon pretending to be a baby makes any other position rough, and while Declan strokes my breasts and kisses my neck again, I just bask in the afterglow.

"We have to get away," he says, just as the construction dude next door screams, "DO YOU HAVE ONE BRAIN CELL RATTLING AROUND IN THAT MELON OF YAHZ, TOMMY?? IT'S DRYWALL, NOT FINE CHINA! PUT IT OVAH THEYA AND GETYA ASS TO THE YAHD!"

Ellie bangs on the door, shouting, "I can't find my tablet charger!"

I laugh hard enough that he falls out and turn to face him, stroking his cheekbone. Time has been good to my husband, laugh lines around his eyes an addition I'm proud of.

Immensely.

When I met him more than a decade ago, Declan McCormick was all business, and I mean *all* business. His face had the expressive range of a granite slab. The man never revealed his feelings, or thoughts. "Poker face" doesn't quite cut it, but it's close enough. He viewed the world through an intricate set of dynamic judgements about how to optimize for positive financial outcomes for his father's company, Anterdec, as if his life depended on it.

As if his sense of self were constructed one deal, one merger, one acquisition, one negotiation at a time, and the only way to have a soul was to *win*.

That makes him sound so cold, so clinical, almost sociopathic, but it's the opposite: his unique way of viewing the world, combined with family trauma, made him a force to be reckoned with.

Meeting him by accident with my hand down a toilet in one of the restaurants his family owned was kismet.

Teaching him how to accept my love and believe he is worthy of it is *fate*.

So those laugh lines at the corners of those gorgeous, sharp, moss-green eyes? *I* earned those. Every last one of them. If Declan's inner source of pride is achievement, mine is this.

Laugh lines made from my love.

And I cannot wait to put more on his face.

BANG BANG!

"Daddy? Mama? Where's the charger? And why is the door locked?"

Dec mutters a curse and climbs out of bed. "I did not anticipate *this*," he says in a tone that makes it clear he's sour about his own failure to strategize for every contingency.

"What did you bribe her with?"

"A $4.99 app from the Apple store."

"You value sex with me at *$4.99?*" I sit up and rearrange the covers, smiling at him.

"Don't even joke about that. If you force me to put a price tag on making love with you, I'll have to get her something outrageously decadent." His side-eye is full of mischief.

"Oh, no! Don't you dare! Do NOT buy her a yacht."

"A yacht? You think that —" he motions toward me " — was worth a yacht?"

"I'm guessing?"

"Priceless, Shannon." Dec crawls back into the bed, pressing his full body against mine, angling to give my belly wide berth. "I'd need to buy her the Mona Lisa. A seat on Blue Origin. The Red Sox."

"Now you're being silly."

"The priceless part is anything but silly."

Our kiss is interrupted with:

"I know what you're doing! Mama has a baby in her. Are you putting another one in? Is that how Uncadoo got twins? Grandma says when a mama and papa love each other the best, he puts a watermelon seed on her tongue and that's how babies are made, but Auntie Carol told Grandma she's full of – "

I wince. Yep. She said it.

"Shouldn't she be in school by now?" Dec mutters as he slides off me and walks to the bathroom, emerging quickly in a bathrobe.

"Maya's coming." Our nanny arrives promptly at 7:30 weekday mornings. I look at my phone. "It's only 7:22."

The doorknob rattles as he halts mid-step.

Our daughter's increasingly outraged voice pipes up through the thick wood. "Hey! Why can't I pick the lock? Ay-mish said 'e ken I'd 'ave nae trouble!"

Ellie's blur into Hamish's Scottish accent is simultaneously disturbing and cute.

Mostly disturbing.

Bzzz

That's my phone. It buzzes again. Then it *rings*. Declan throws his hands up in the air in frustration.

"Ellie first. I'll handle that call," I say, stepping in to triage the situation, suddenly in scramble mode. When I look at my screen, I realize my error.

Dave.

Dave, Dave, and more Dave.

A top notch, couldn't-ask-for-better executive assistant, Dave is extraordinary. But he's *Declan's* assistant, and if my husband sees the constant stream of messages between us, he's going to lose his ever-loving mind.

No, I'm not sleeping with Dave.

I'm *colluding* with him.

This is so much better than sex.

Blanton Jean-Pierre Koshigiri owns the premier Kona coffee farm in the world. There is nothing like the place he jokingly calls "Nui Ke Kālā" anywhere. Wholly unique and deservedly coveted by every billionaire on the planet, his farm receives a steady supply of offers to be purchased, most of them coming from my husband.

Because Declan wants to own the ultimate worldwide coffee chain *and* the ultimate coffee farm.

Not any coffee production facility.

The farm.

Eyeing Declan as he shuts our bedroom door and says something to Ellie I can't make out, I answer my phone.

"Skipper says we've reached the point where Declan needs to know," Dave announces with his characteristic, no-bullshit bluntness.

Years ago, on our freaking honeymoon, Dec spent a bunch of time cozying up to Blanton Jean-Pierre Koshigiri, but he was never given permission to call him by his nickname.

Koshigiri is Skipper to me, and when Declan finds out, he'll be pissed.

Or maybe not. Hopefully not. Because this house of cards I've been carefully protecting will all fall down at the same time, if I'm lucky. And when Dec learns I get to call the man Skipper, it'll be at the same time I tell him I've bought the Kona farm *for him.*

Two can play that game.

It's just like in 2004, when Mom got Dad a new weed whacker and Dad got her a ceramic straight-iron for Christmas, and they were able to one-up each other on Black Friday with the best deal.

Erm, maybe not *just* like that, but you get the picture.

I'm sneaking around behind Declan's back with his rival and his right-hand man, all to give Declan the biggest surprise of his life.

A deal he *didn't* negotiate.

"Shannon?"

Dave and Declan say my name at the same time, the sound in stereo, my neurons confused. In the doorway stands Declan, robe loose as he frowns at me. "Who's that?"

I am the world's worst liar.

"It's um, Mia."

Dec yawns, the stretch delicious to watch. "Mia? Is she late?" he says at the end, the words drawn out.

"I sound nothing like Mia," Dave says flatly in my ear. "You really are shit at lying. Declan always says so, but you're proving it."

"No!" I chirp at Declan, ignoring the insult machine on the phone. "Just asking to make sure Ellie has all the glitter she needs."

"Glitter." Shrewd eyes, narrowed into slits, meet mine. "Ellie does not need more glitter. I found some on my ass the other day."

"On your ass! Why would you have glitter on your *butt*?"

"I do not need to hear this," Dave grumbles in my ear. "Make it stop."

Dec glowers at me. "Good question, Shannon. Why did I?"

"You say that like it's my fault!"

"She thought it would be fun to use my razor on a glitter project. Something about shading it just right."

"Sha*v*ing, or sha*d*ing?"

A nonplussed look crosses his face.

"I don't know! But glitter got on my hands, and then it got *everywhere*. Andrew saw it when I was working out at the gym, and Vince started calling me 'Glowboi.'" He mutters a curse, turning on his heel to wander back to the kitchen.

I do not tell him Glowboi is an adorable nickname.

"Glowboi," Dave says into the phone with an evil snicker.

"You did not hear that!" I hiss into the phone. "Declan doesn't know I'm talking to you."

"Hear what? Other than the sound of a nice big raise this year?"

"You already get nice big raises."

"This year it'll be nicer and bigger."

"You help me close this deal with Koshigiri, and I'll help with that."

"Good news: he's here."

"Who?"

"Koshigiri."

"Here – where?"

"In Boston."

"What?"

"Something about being on business, headed to London. Wants to have lunch with you."

"LUNCH?" I gasp, the timing about as unfortunate as my mother overhearing me talk about going to her favorite thrift shop on ten-dollar fill-a-bag day.

"Mia wants to have lunch?" Declan asks as he drops his robe, walks into the bathroom, and turns on the shower.

"No. Done with that call. This is a new one."

"Who?"

"My mom."

Fastest way to make him lose interest, right?

"Oh." True to form, he closes the bathroom door.

"I am not Marie," Dave says archly. "First of all, my brain cells don't ricochet off the inside of my skull."

"HEY!"

"And second, fill-a-bag day is for amateurs. Just wait until thrift shops change over from one season to another and dumpster dive."

"What?"

A smug sound fills the phone. Dave makes a significant six-figure income as Declan's executive assistant, and he has an MBA from Wharton, but he's also a squatter living in an artist commune. The artisanal chocolate he makes from some special cacao he buys from co-ops in Central America. I know that working for Declan has given him more leverage in helping local people on cacao farms, which is fantastic, but the chocolate itself is extraordinary.

And the little boy growing inside me is probably seventeen percent built by Dave's handiwork.

"Dumpster diving," Dave says patiently, as if explaining how to use a computer mouse to a 104-year-old. "You wait until the thrift shop changes seasons. They throw out tons of stuff. Then you show up with rolling carts, a long-handled grabber, a step-stool, a flashlight, and plenty of cat food."

"Cat food?"

"Yes. Cat food."

"Why cat food?"

"Because cat food is your alibi."

"*Alibi?*"

"Excuse. Whatever. For when the cops show up."

"The cops? You… feed the cops *cat food*?"

"Of course not! You claim to be out there feeding the poor strays. Instant sympathy from the bastards."

"That's devious!" And a little sick. "Dave, seriously? You're going to risk dealing with the police over salvaged thrift shop clothing you could easily afford to buy and lie about feeding stray cats!?"

My own cat, Chuckles, wanders in as I'm speaking, gives me an extremely grumpy look, and shows me his butthole.

"The longer you're with your husband, the more judgmental you get, Shannon." Is he *tsking* me? That sound – *tsk, tsk, tsk* – makes him sound like Mrs. Hickey, the old librarian from my elementary school.

The one who smelled like moth balls and freshly baked child hearts.

"The longer you work for my husband, Dave, the more you sound like an asshole."

"Declan must be rubbing off on me."

I stay silent. Why interrupt someone hoisting themselves on their own petard?

"Let's change subjects," Dave says tightly.

"Yes. Back to Koshigiri. He's in town?"

"Will be. Today. Can you do a late lunch? He lands at noon in Bedford and can be at Consuela's by two."

"Isn't that risky? What if Declan has a work lunch there. Or Andrew?"

"I've booked Declan already for a Wisconsin dairy deal. Three-hour negotiation."

"I cannot fathom why he loves negotiations." I shudder.

"It's his version of Viagra."

"Dave."

"Sorry."

"No, I just mean – bad comparison. Viagra is what you take when you need a little... help. Dec doesn't need any assistance when it comes to negotiation." *Or in the bedroom*, I think – but do not say.

"He does with Koshigiri."

We share a conspirator's snicker.

"True! I cannot believe this is really happening. Skipper's selling to me."

"He is. Declan's fuming. He has no idea who the anonymous buyer is. Getting increasingly desperate."

"I know I'll have to tell him eventually." I drop my voice to whisper as the sound of the shower ends abruptly. "But not until after this lunch."

"Right. Consuela's, two p.m."

He hangs up just as Dec walks out of the bathroom, toweling off.

"Long call with Marie?" he asks with a tone that makes it clear he'd rather bleach the tile grout with a toothbrush and a cotton ball held by tweezers than spend five minutes on the phone with my mom.

"Yes," I sigh, pretending to be harried. "You know."

"What's her deal today?"

Oops. Now I have to invent something. Then again, this is a conversation about how annoying my mother is. I don't have to reach.

"She asked about Farmington Country Club for Amy and Hamish's wedding."

"They aren't even engaged yet! And I thought the wedding would be in Scotland."

"She says she got 'cheated' out of a full wedding at Farmington when we 'stole all the fun' out of our wedding." While I didn't just get off the phone with my mother, I have a memory bank of choice phrases she's used over time, so this part is easy.

"Again? Pulling out those old complaints?"

"Amy and Hamish's future wedding seems to have revived a bunch of hurt feelings."

"Then let her take it all out on them! Hamish is just a wall of ginger emotional Teflon. Nothing she says gets to him."

"I don't think that's quite true. She asked him if he knew anyone at the FAA and could get them to ground all helicopter traffic within a 50-square-mile radius around Farmington for their wedding."

We both groan.

"He didn't take that well," Declan adds unnecessarily as he searches for underwear in his closet, talking to me through the open door as he dresses. "Said something about stealing Amy away to Gretna Green for a good old-fashioned elopement."

"Gretna Green! Hah! Isn't that just in those historical romance novels?"

"No clue. It seemed to be code for 'screw Marie.'"

"Amy would never agree to that. She's way too attached to having a full wedding."

"But not a full Marie Jacoby wedding. And Hamish says his mom is basically the Scottish version of Marie."

"I remember. Amy laughed, but when he didn't a cold tendril of fear shot through me."

"*Fear?* You? She's not going to be *your* mother-in-law."

"Fear for poor Amy. Imagine having two versions of my mother? On two different continents?"

"No and no." Exiting the closet, he comes out wearing underwear, socks, and carrying a shirt, suit, and two ties. Declan points.

"Blue or purple?"

"Purple." Gray flecks mix in with fine black lines, navy accents, and a deep indigo that make the tie a perfect fit for his navy suit. "Why so fancy?"

"Video call. Have to look the part." Setting the clothes on his wooden valet, he heads for the bathroom, where an electric razor begins.

And my body screams *coffee time*!

The doorbell rings, then the front door beeps with a code being entered. Mia is particularly polite, though she's been Ellie's nanny for years, and will help with the new baby as well. She always rings before entering our home.

As Declan finishes shaving, I close my eyes and take a few deep breaths.

Renovating a conference center to be our forever home – and a new, boutique resort.

Negotiating a secret deal to buy an exclusive Hawaiian coffee farm.

Maintaining a somewhat-executive role at Grind It Fresh! until the baby's born.

Growing an entire human being with my body. *Again.*

Life is full.

So is my heart.

But you know what's empty?

My caffeine meter.

CHAPTER 2 - DECLAN

"It doesn't add up," I snap as Andrew spots me. Shannon left quickly this morning, and I decided to fit in a short workout – and another shower – before heading back to the office for my marathon negotiation call with a bunch of people who spend their days squeezing liquid from bovines.

"Business never does." A grunt, then I take in a deep breath and bench press it, feeling my core divert power through my limbs. Pumping iron is nothing like making deals and being a CEO.

It's bliss.

"No shit, Sherlock. I mean Koshigiri's behavior. Why is he dodging me?"

"There are five or six other billionaires in the world asking the same question."

One of the desk workers waves Andrew down. The motion catches my attention as I go for one more rep, arms screaming, shoulders begging for mercy, but *no* –

This is about powering through.

Being determined.

Never giving up.

Something in my neck turns to liquid fire, tendons turning into hot pokers, but I do it, racking the bar, making Andrew shake his head.

"Impressive, huh?"

"You?" He scoffs. "Hardly."

A whiff of funk and stinky canvas shoes hits my nose, sweat pouring down my brow as I wipe it with a white towel that reeks of bleach. As my heart rate goes back to something resembling normal, the blood rush feels nice and tight, as if all that power from lifting invades my cells.

Which means I succeeded.

Success begets success. Each layer builds on the next. A strong body fuels a strong mind and vice-versa. Andrew was smart to buy these basic, grungy gyms and find resilience.

"Fuck you," I mutter, but I don't have the heart to be angry. We're competitive. Always have been. Our dad pitted us against each other practically since Andrew's first breath. Our oldest brother, Terry, left the family business after our mother died, but he's got the killer instinct, too.

He just hides it under a lot of yoga and tie-dyed goofiness.

Buying Koshigiri's Hawaiian paradise would be a coup.

"You know, Dad tried to buy the Hawaii place."

My head snaps up.

"Quit messing with me."

"When he found out how much you wanted it, yes."

"I wouldn't put it past him. He probably outbid me."

"I don't know. Told him I don't piddle in little deals like that." His smirk makes me want to rip it off his face.

"As if this chain of gyms is Planet Fitness."

"It'll be better."

"Just like Grind It Fresh! I'm in eight more countries than you are. When will you go fro – oh, right. One country. You're only in one country."

"We have plenty of plans for Canada," he says flatly, hating the conversation.

Hah. Good. Means I'm winning.

"And besides," he adds, "Anterdec is still beating us all."

"And yet we all walked away from it."

We both sigh, staring out the gym's small window, feet passing us buy. The place is half underground, a basement-level space, the kind that feels like it's from a bygone era.

Which makes it so appealing.

I walk over to my water bottle and guzzle some before saying, "No new CEO yet. How are they managing?"

"The board is taking its sweet time finding someone."

"You mean *Dad* is taking *his* sweet time finding someone."

Andrew winces. "It's got to hurt to have all three of his boys reject the CEO spot."

"Dad would have to have an actual heart to feel hurt. He doesn't seem too destroyed in Greece right now."

"At least he waited until Jenna turned eighteen to take her on the yacht."

"He gets older, they get younger."

"Speaking of which, remember Katie? Katie Gallagher?" Andrew asks.

"The name rings a bell, but I don't know why."

"Dad's old girlfriend?"

"None of Dad's girlfriends are old. Ever."

"Former girlfriend. Owns that big wedding protection company?"

"Dad dated a bodyguard?"

"No, no. She was at my wedding. None of this rings a bell? Blonde, early 30s?"

"You're describing all of Dad's exes."

"Smart one? Clever eyes?"

"That narrows it. *Really* narrows it when you use the word *smart*. What about her?"

"Amanda ran into her at a bachelorette party. She handles celebrity weddings. They bonded over their disgust regarding Dad."

"I get the sense that's a powerful glue."

"We should know."

The door makes a sound, and I look up to find Gerald there. Good.

The real reason I'm here.

I give Andrew a shoulder pat and walk over to Gerald, who takes in a deep breath. Bald as a cue ball and the size of a small mountain, Gerald's been a bodyguard and chauffeur for Anterdec for years. He's also a sculptor and now – a father, as well. He and his wife, Suzanne, had a baby right around the time Andrew and Amanda had their twins.

"How's potty training going?" Andrew shouts to Gerald, who makes a face.

"You would think peeing on a Cheerio in a toilet would be exciting, but no. Paul thinks aiming for the cat is more fun."

We all make sympathetic noises.

Andrew looks around the room and pulls us closer as we get death glares. "Not everyone here is a dad, so let's cut the poop and pee talk." His phone rings and he wanders off, talking to his longtime assistant Gina.

"Hired him yet?" I ask Gerald quietly. He's dressed in a black suit, white shirt, and thick black shoes that barely pass as business casual but are great for chasing perps.

"On the job already. Koshigiri's just landing in Bedford."

"Bedford? Massachusetts?"

"Sure is."

"That asshole won't take a meeting with me even when I offer to come to Hawaii, but he comes into *my* territory and doesn't tell me?"

"You sure you want him tailed?"

"Do I ever waver when it comes to competitive advantage?"

Gerald grins. "No. It's why you're so fascinating to work for."

"I don't give a shit how interesting I am. I care about results. Following him will give me insight into his mindset."

"Or whether your dad is trying to snipe the Kona farm out from under you."

"Two birds, one stone, Gerald. Bottom line: have him tailed. I want pictures. If the guy so much as picks his teeth with his fingernail, I need images."

"That very specific."

"You know what I mean."

"What if he just isn't selling? And that's why no one can get him to talk to them? Maybe he just likes the Kona farm."

"Everyone has a price."

"Yes, but not everyone has a price at the same time you have a need."

The word *need* makes me think of Shannon, how it felt to be between her legs this morning, the way her belly swells with my son growing inside. Need is a funny word, isn't it? It connects to basic and primal actions that allow us to survive. Need implies you can't live without it, vs. want, which symbolizes desire.

I need Shannon as if it were desire. She's want and need all rolled into one.

Thinking about her makes me want to ditch my meetings, crawl back into bed with her, and hide from the world.

I could.

I really could. She reminds me, all the time, that my ambition is the biggest obstacle to having more of her. It's a double-bind I hate.

But my needs/wants are complex.

And having Koshigiri tailed will help me to understand any competitors for the thing I want/need most, aside from my wife:

That unparalleled gem in Hawaii.

"I want pictures and reports in real time. And no Dave on this one, right?"

"He has no idea." An uncomfortable look passes through Gerald's eyes. "You normally don't go 'need-to-know' with Dave. Why now?"

I glance at Andrew across the room.

Admitting this is going to hurt. Make me look paranoid. Make me look *stupid*.

So I'll just do what any intelligent, successful man would do.

Avoid the question.

I hold up my phone and wiggle it. "Gotta get that."

Skepticism fills his face as he snorts.

I walk toward the bathrooms and pretend to have a conversation with my wife until I don't have to continue the pretense. Between Dad and the CEO search, Koshigiri ignoring me, renovating the new resort that is also our home in Weston, and Shannon being six months pregnant, I've got more than enough on my mind.

Don't need to worry about what Gerald thinks.

I only need to deal with what his PI finds.

CHAPTER 3 - SHANNON

After kissing Ellie goodbye before leaving her in Mia's capable hands, I walked to work, knowing full well that my temporary elephant status will make that impossible soon.

Plus, once we move to Weston, no more city walking. No more city, period.

I enter our flagship shop from the back and go behind the counter to make myself a latte. One of the perks of owning Grind It Fresh! is that I can do that. When you own a store, you can do whatever you want.

And it still feels so weird.

"Shannon!" Gloria is the newest barista, from one of the vocational schools with a culinary focus. If she's seventeen, I'd be surprised, but looks closer to fourteen. Braces still on her teeth, she's all shy smiles and whip-smart competence. "What can I get you?"

"I can get it myself," I remind her. We've had this conversation before. Nervous eyes roam over my belly, which is impossible to hide. Not that I even try, but maybe today's electric-blue wrap dress wasn't so smart. I look like a giant blueberry.

"GLORIA!" Manuel calls from the back. "New shipment. Need unloading help."

Casting an anxious look at the door, she's uncertain.

"Go," I say, waving her off. "If someone comes in, I've got it."

"But – but – but you're a VP!"

In name only, I want to say, but Declan's warned me not to undermine my authority.

"And that means I need to stay in touch with the customers," I reply on the fly, impressed with my own slickness.

She shrugs and does as told.

Grinding fresh espresso, tamping and brewing it feels good. I'm only drinking one caffeinated cup a day now, so I save it for the office. Anticipation is hard to manage when you're pregnant and all your joints and skin are stretched out like a decaying rubber band, so every luxury, every small pleasure, needs to be perfect.

Like this latte.

I'm steaming my milk as the front door opens and a customer walks in, holding her phone.

"Hi there," I say. "Welcome to Grind It Fresh!"

She's young. Not as young as Gloria, but the way she squares her shoulders, as if reminding herself to be all business, is a young move.

The kind of move I'd have performed ten years ago, when I needed a confidence injection.

Her brow furrows and she almost looks at her phone, then seems to fight the glance.

Huh.

As she approaches the counter, her eyes scan the room, landing on my... chest? I pour my frothed milk into my insulated mug and dump one shot in it unceremoniously.

"You don't do patterns on the surface of the milk, um...." Her chin juts out at my shoulder. "I'm sorry." She gives me a tight smile, blinking rapidly. "You don't have a name tag, so I don't know your name."

My blood runs cold and hot at the same time, and suddenly, I have a flashback.

To my hand in a men's room toilet.

"Shannon," I say, trying to be pleasant and hold back growing laughter. A sip of my hot latte helps keep my mouth occupied before I say something ridiculous.

One eyebrow arches up. "Are you allowed to just make drinks and sip them at the cash register?" Her hand is practically screaming to touch her phone screen as she glances at the giant wall clock.

I take another sip and lean against the counter, too casual on purpose. I wink. "Sleeping with the boss gets you lots of perks here."

Her eyes widen, deep brown irises floating in white. "You – is that something you just tell every customer?"

Last year, Declan told me he wanted to hire a mystery shopping company to test customer service at our stores. After laughing so hard I nearly tore a calf muscle, which reminded me of all the gym shops Amanda and I did as I was dating Declan years ago, I told him it was a fine idea, but to watch out:

Because I can spot a mystery shopper a thousand miles away.

Turns out I was right.

"I only tell that to the nice ones," I reply, taking another sip of my coffee. "What can I get you?"

I already know what she's going to order.

"I heard you're having a special," she says in a sing-songy voice. It's clear she's memorized the stupid script the consultant suggested for this promo. The one I nixed.

Someone overrode my decision.

Someone's about to get in big trouble.

"I'd like a lemon-finished single shot of espresso and a piece of the fennel-saffron artisanal chocolate. And can I join your loyalty program?"

One of the issues I have with this script is that customers generally don't ask to join the loyalty program. Our baristas need to prompt them and be able to explain why joining is so valuable.

"Why would you want to join the loyalty program?" I ask as I drink more of my latte and reach under the counter for the tray of artisanal chocolates. Each one is a different shape, cut as if Dave created one large, flat bar and then took tiny arrowheads found on archeological digs in northern Ontario at sites presumed to have been settled by Vikings, and smashed the slick, hard surface.

Because he did.

As she stammers and searches for an answer, I slowly start eating the slivers. One by one.

I believe her eyeballs begin jiggling from pure stress.

"Are you – can you just eat all the chocolate you want?"

"Remember? I sleep with the boss."

"But that says the price is $215 per pound!"

"He thinks I'm worth it."

"This is the weirdest job ever," she mutters.

"Are you job searching? Because working here is the *best*."

She buries her face in her phone, but not well enough. The app she taps is a mystery shopping company.

Unable to keep this up, I lean in and say, "I know your secret."

"What secret?"

"You're on a shop."

Her face goes slack. "What's a shop?"

"Nice try. I used to be a mystery shopper."

"Good for you."

"It's a hard job. Always worried you'll blow your cover."

"Better than blowing your boss." She claps her hands over her mouth, then reaches for a sliver of chocolate, holding it up. "This and that lemon-finished espresso, please." Shoulders slumping in defeat, she taps in the app, probably answering timed questions.

I start making her the espresso and give her a break. "I'm not wearing a name tag because I'm Shannon McCormick."

Blank look.

Of course she has no idea who I am. When I was a mystery shopper, I had no clue who the owners of companies were. My job was simple. Clear. Dictated in the guidelines.

Rule #1: *never ever get caught.*

"What's your name?"

"Jane."

"Let me guess. Jane Doe?"

Her lips move up enough to show she's suppressing a smile.

"Don't worry, Jane Doe," I say as Gloria comes back to the counter, breathless. "I'll let my associate take over for me."

"ASSOCIATE!" Gloria gasps. "Since when is *the VP of the company* an associate of mine?"

Laughing, I take my latte, two more pieces of chocolate, and nod at Gloria while the mystery shopper gapes at me. "Can you inventory these and charge them to my account?"

"Yes, ma'am."

And with that, I go upstairs to my office.

Where I immediately encounter Dave.

Who *sniffs*.

"Fennel-saffron. My April 22nd batch." He frowns. "I should have added a pinch of Icelandic salt to it for balance."

"It's perfect."

"You're pregnant. Wax chocolate-covered circus peanuts are your idea of perfect."

"Would you make artisanal chocolate-covered circus peanuts for me? Because those would *sell*."

"That's like asking me to make money training AI chatbots."

"I don't know what that means."

"You're asking me to commit a crime against humanity that leads to the downfall of civilization."

"It's just chocolate!"

"You take that back!" he snaps, losing his cool in a rare display of disheveled fury. Dave is always calm and calculated Collected. A bit flat.

Robotic and sarcastic.

Apparently, I've hit a nerve.

"Take what back? You're comparing chocolate-covered circus peanuts to a mass-extinction event."

He runs his fingers through his thick, dark hair and glowers. "Eat enough of them and *yes!*"

"Did you come here to shame me about food choices or – " I drop my voice " – to help me with this Kona farm deal?"

"Both."

"Dave."

"Here." The folder he thrusts at me takes me by surprise. No one deals with paper anymore. Everything digitally signed. These days, it's a tablet that's pushed into my hands, not dead trees.

"What's this?"

"The terms. Koshigiri wanted everything laid out before your lunch."

"You mean *lei-ed* out," I joke.

"That's what I said," he deadpans.

I sigh and drink more coffee, rubbing my belly with my spare hand after I drop the folder on a pile of papers on my desk.

"Have we hit the limit?" I ask.

"I've hit mine." His tongue rolls around in his cheek.

Living with Declan has taught me that sometimes, people are angry for no reason at all. It's just a part of their personality, like having an aversion to mayonnaise or sucking air between your teeth.

Dave seems to need to hold onto his anger at my comments about chocolate, as if the chocolate itself is offended.

"At what point do we need to get Declan involved?" I ask, drinking more coffee, sad to realize I'm nearly at the end of my latte.

"I hardly think we need to go to that extreme."

"He'll be very upset if we don't ask his opinion."

"You think your husband really cares about your flagrant disrespect for quality cacao?"

"I meant the coffee farm!"

"Oh. Right. That." Smacking his lips once, he sighs and says, "Koshigiri hasn't confirmed. Wants this lunch." Dave's eyes slide over to his phone, where he stares at the screen. "A lunch that's just been moved up to... twenty minutes from now."

"What? Who lunches at 10:30? And I thought he was landing at noon?"

"Koshigiri, apparently. His assistant just confirmed. Said another important business meeting's been moved up and he's arrived early. Unlike your husband, he has his own private plane."

"Please," I groan. "Do not say that in earshot of Declan. You know how obsessed he is about the freaking private jet."

"He shouldn't stretch his capital buying conference centers and Kona farms, then." Dave makes a clucking sound. "Poor guy. So deprived."

"Dave."

"Right. Back to Koshigiri. Consuela offered more of a brunch for you two, including – " he squints at the screen. "That cannot be right. Tiramisu waffles?"

Consuela Arroyo is a celebrity chef and one of Andrew's old friends. She also knows I am six months pregnant, and the woman is a saint for offering the best combination of two things I love:

Sugar and carbs.

"I'll get there in twenty."

"With candied bacon," he adds.

"Can you teleport me?"

"If I could, I would, Shannon." Dave picks up the folder and hands it to me, then escorts me out of my office and down to the street where Gerald is waiting with a limo SUV. "All I can offer is second best."

"Hi there, Mrs. McCormick," Gerald says with a formality that makes me laugh.

"What are you doing here?"

"Subbing for Will." Will is Declan's newest driver.

I climb into the car and watch Dave's receding back, the end of our meeting abrupt as Gerald takes the wheel.

"You know where I'm going?"

"Of course. Happy to deliver you."

"Deliver?" I rub my stomach. "The only thing being delivered is this little boy in three months." I poke my own belly button. "In a hospital this time."

Gerald's hearty laugh is one of shared amusement. My precipitous first birth took place in an elevator, for God's sake, with my ex, Steve Raleigh, trapped in there with me. Declan had to break into the elevator like a cat burglar and help deliver our daughter.

For our son, I plan to check into the hospital two weeks before my due date. Everyone laughs when I say that, but I don't find it funny.

"How's Suzanne? And Paul?"

"Both are great."

"Potty training, right?"

"Why does everyone ask?"

"Because everyone in your life has little kids right now."

"Good point."

The rest of the drive is quiet. Gerald's not a big talker, but it's a pleasant silence, the kind you share with someone who is comfortable in their own skin.

Plus, the drive only takes twelve minutes.

"Easy traffic," he comments as he slides into a spot right in front of Consuela's.

"We got lucky. Thanks for the ride."

"Of course. It's my job," he says, getting out to open my door, but I'm already halfway out. As I finish exiting the SUV, my brain pauses.

Hold on.

This is all... weird.

The conflict with Dave. Gerald driving me. Koshigiri's sudden appearance. I don't know why, but it's not adding up. Has Declan been tipped off somehow? Is my secret no longer a secret?

Bzzz

My phone has a new message from a number I don't recognize:

On the rooftop – Skipper is all it says.

Okay, then. Here we go.

CHAPTER 4 - DECLAN

I'm working at my desk, checking slides before my big meeting, when my phone buzzes.

Message from Gerald:

Calling you now.

The phone rings and I pick it up, puzzled. "Why text me a warning that you're calling?"

"Making sure you're available, Look, Declan, this is a weird one."

"Koshigiri? The PI found something?"

"Yes."

"And?"

"I need you to brace yourself."

"For... what?"

"For a twist no one saw coming."

"You sound unhinged, Gerald." And he does. A catch in his voice makes my skin crawl. Gerald's always no-nonsense. Cool and collected at work. This doesn't bode well.

"Not unhinged. Troubled."

"Who the hell is Koshigiri meeting with?"

"It's better to send a picture. You ready?"

"Why the cloak and dagger crap?" A flush runs through me. "Is it Andrew? That asshole. Is he trying to buy the Kona farm out from under me?"

"Close. Not Andrew."

"Not that asshole Mullahy? From Central Coffee Holdings? The one I had to punch for coming onto Shannon? His wife muzzled him, and so help me, if that fu – "

"Not Mullahy."

My breastbone aches, throat going tight, mind racing. Who could be worse than Andrew or Mullahy?

Oh, no.

No, no, *no.*

"Not my father?"

"No."

"Cut the drama. Send the picture. Whoever it is has to be big. A major player. I can't think of anyone that powerful."

Instantly, an image appears in the text stream. It's Consuela's rooftop restaurant, Koshigiri at a table, fingering a wine glass filled with water. He's wearing a beige linen suit, white shirt, and a beaming smile.

A smile aimed at a very, very familiar brunette.

"SHANNON?" I bellow, as if her name were trying to exit hell itself. "What the hell is Koshigiri doing with *Shannon*?"

"It gets weirder," Gerald chokes out. "Because I'm here."

"Here? Here *where*?"

"At the restaurant."

"I told you to hire a PI! You weren't supposed to do the job yourself!"

"I didn't. Dave called me and asked me to fill in for Will. I picked Shannon up and brought her here. Paused outside to handle some business work on my phone. The PI sent the pictures while I was still sitting here."

"Wait there. On my way."

"Yes, sir."

He ends the call, but sends three more pictures, all of them Koshigiri and Shannon, one of them with her in mid-laugh, face stunningly beautiful, the wind blowing a strand of hair across her nose, eyes filled with a happiness only I should put there.

Me, and *only* me.

The bastard has ignored my outreach attempts for the better part of the last year, and he goes behind my back to meet with my wife? For what? There is no good reason for that SOB to get together with Shannon.

None.

Mind racing, I stand and pace, ripping my suit jacket off, flinging it onto the sofa. Hands in my hair, I scrub my scalp as if trying to file off the images I've just seen.

This isn't infidelity. Never in a million years would Shannon do such a thing.

Racing to the door, I run down the back stairwell, mentally calculating the distance. My phone's in my pants pocket and it buzzes.

Dave.

Ready for the call?

Cancel it, I type back.

And then I run.

Hailing a cab or finding a driver will take too long, the two miles easier to whip off. As I race through the streets, I ignore gawkers. Men in business suits don't go at six-minute-mile paces often, but I don't give a shit right now.

I just need to get there.

Get there and find out the *why* to this *what-the-hell.*

Shannon's meeting with Koshigiri. Is she persuading him to have a call with me? Working her charm to get him to crack? Why would the guy communicate with her and not me?

The uncertainty of it all makes my legs pump harder.

Gratitude floods through me, not for Shannon, but for Vince.

Yes, Vince, my personal trainer. That asshat forces me to run while carrying sandbags, and now I see the payoff.

I arrive at the ground level for Consuela's building in 10:51, which would normally be a nice accomplishment but my stomach's sour, hands so clenched they might be vises, and Gerald's at the door.

"Sir?"

"Quit calling me that!"

I race past him, up the stairs, and just as I reach the top, I realize I have no clue what to do next. Panting, I gather my thoughts as Dave blows up my phone.

What do you mean cancel?

What's wrong?

Are Shannon and Ellie okay?

Why are you doing this?

Ignoring him is easy.

Figuring out my next step is torture.

"I never thought of it that way!" I hear Shannon say, voice filled with happiness, as Koshigiri grins at her. I'm at the top of the building, hiding behind a small door, a window giving me a perfect view. To the left, I smell bacon and something sweet and doughy.

It's the scent of frustration and confusion.

"Declan!" Consuela's gasp makes me turn, sweat trickling into my eye as I hold a finger up to my lips and frown. She nods, ever discreet.

I point to my wife and my rival. "I don't want them to see me."

"You know espionage violates my extreme discretion policy," she says with a wink.

"When did he make this reservation?" I grunt.

"Just yesterday. Moved it up. He has another important meeting after this.

I've been ordered to have my finest porterhouse ready." She winks again, then leaves me to eavesdrop.

And then it hits me.

I know *exactly* why Koshigiri is having lunch with my wife. This is so much worse than I ever imagined.

"He's so committed to our family," Shannon says as she sips orange juice, looking over his shoulder toward the kitchen. Knowing her, the stomach orchestra has begun, starting with soft strings building to a crescendo.

Just then, Consuela walks out with two plates, setting one with a fruit cup and poached egg in front of Koshigiri, and a big platter covered with bacon and some ungodly pastry waffle thing in front of Shannon.

"Extra Nutella sauce," Consuela says, pointing to a small porcelain pitcher.

"I cannot believe you managed to combine my favorite four food groups," Shannon jokes. "Nutella, waffles, tiramisu, and bacon."

"It's how I serve humankind," Consuela says with broad smile, departing politely, leaving the two to eat. Shannon's comment about someone being committed to our family hangs in the air, leaving me waiting.

"Declan is a good man," Koshigiri says.

"An amazing man, Skipper," Shannon replies.

My jaw drops. Skipper? Did she just call him *Skipper*?

"Driven, loving, smart, kind – "

"You don't have to convince me, Shannon." They take bites of their food, leaving me on the edge of my nonexistent seat. Why are they talking about me? Not that I mind the compliments, but this isn't why they're having lunch.

"Oh!" she moans, the sound enraging me because that asshole doesn't deserve to hear her pleasure. Doesn't have a right to share space with my soulmate. He's brought her here to use her somehow, and my naive wife has been turned into a pawn by this sick bastard for some underhanded scheme she doesn't know about.

Hell, I don't know what it is, but I don't trust him one bit.

He taps a manilla folder on the table. "Once we finish this, there's no turning back."

As she chews, she smiles, a broad grin filled with so much contentment my heart squeezes out of the simple need to acknowledge her joy. "I know. And I appreciate all the ways you've helped me on this."

On *what*?

For the next two minutes, they chew, swallow, chew, swallow, drink, chew, and swallow.

While I fume, rage, fume, fume, rage, explode, fume, and rage.

Then: "I do think the proposition takes everything to a new level," he says, and that's it.

That's *it*.

"What in the hell do you think you're doing with my wife?" I bark at him as I come out from my hidden spot, Shannon looking at me in horror, dropping her laden fork, which falls to the ground in a lumpy, sad clang.

"Declan!" she shrieks.

"Declan," Koshigiri says with a pompous smile. "We were just talking about you."

"What the hell is going on here?" I demand.

"I'm popping your cherry," she says calmly, sadly eyeing her dropped fork, looking over my shoulder at the table behind me. "Would you ask for another fork? My tiramisu waffles are getting cold."

"Excuse me?"

"Fork, honey. Could you fork me?" she asks sweetly, batting those eyelashes.

"SHANNON!" I shout.

"Popping his cherry," Koshigiri says with a smirk.

"*Coffee* cherry," Shannon elaborates.

"And you call him Skipper!"

"She does. You don't," Koshigiri says, pushing his plate away. "I'm afraid my stomach's soured, my dear."

I block him in case he tries to leave. "What is this game?"

"Game?" Shannon reaches for the manila folder, suddenly nervous. "We, um, need to sign," she says to Koshigiri, who gives me another smug look.

"Maybe," he says to her. "Declan's intrusion has me second-guessing the sale."

"NO!" she gasps, leaping to her feet. "You're ruining this, Dec!"

"Ruining *what*? What could you possibly be doing here with him?" I point at Koshigiri, expecting more smugness, but it's Shannon who radiates....

Arrogance?

No. Worse.

Dominance.

She inhales slowly through her nose, extending the moment, her head held high, eyes canny, with a look I've never seen before.

And I've studied every expression my wife has ever shown.

Her words don't make sense, but she's damn proud of each and every one as she says, with so much satisfaction and delight that I almost don't register them:

"I'm buying Skipper's Kona farm."

That is not what I thought was going on here.

"You're *what*?"

"Buying Nui Ke Kālā ," Koshigiri says smoothly.

"Buying? *You*?" I point to Shannon, who spreads her hands on the table in a very familiar gesture.

It's one I use when I've won decisively.

"Me."

Thunder fills every neuron in my brain.

"You negotiated the purchase of the one place on earth I couldn't buy?"

They both grin at me, very different emotions pushing the change in their faces.

"YES!" she squeals, clapping once.

"Why sell? Why now?" I ask Koshigiri. *And why not to me*, I want to ask but to even posit the question would show me as weak.

I cannot do that.

His face turns contemplative, eyes focused at a spot behind me. "I have something bigger to move on to."

"Bigger? Bigger than your company? Bigger than Nui Ke Kālā?"

"Yes."

My scalp begins to tingle. The hairs on my arms stand up. Shannon's eyebrows meet in the middle, confusion evident.

"You told me you wanted to sell because I was so persuasive," she says to him.

He takes one of her hands in his, and that Cheshire cat smile only adds to my unease. "You are. As you said, Declan will be a very capable coffee farmer."

Farmer. *Farmer?*

"You said that about me?" I ask her.

"I didn't put it *that* way."

"The paperwork is a formality," he declares. "I've already initiated the major transactions behind the scenes. Shannon asked me to keep this a secret from you, and I did. McCormicks are wizards at keeping secrets, aren't you?"

His subtext only deepens my concerns. Shannon's not picking up on it.

"Funny you're here in Boston, of all places," I say to him. "Any specific reason for that?"

The sudden trip. The refusal to take my calls. Selling to Shannon. McCormicks keeping secrets.

Consuela ordering a porterhouse steak.

"Visiting friends," he says coyly.

"Dec," Shannon says, reaching for my hand. "I have a confession to make." Her hand lifts to my shoulder and she leans in, eyes on mine. Enchanted, all I can do is focus on her.

"I bought Nui Ke Kālā for you."

"You did?"

"You surprised me with the Weston conference center. My turn," she said, standing on tiptoe to kiss my lips lightly. "Surprise!" she says with a giggle.

Koshigiri has the decency to be amused.

"Surprise?" I echo as Shannon throws her arms around me in a hug, her belly to the side, her scent mingling with the shock of everything that's happened.

"Maybe I can get cleared by the doctor to fly and we can go to your new property!" she whispers in my ear. "Please tell me you're not upset."

I embrace her, my strategic brain caught in a vortex of pattern matching.

Until the ultimate pattern appears over her shoulder.

My father.

"It's a present for you!" she says with a giggle.

"And a lovely prize," Koshigiri says softly.

Prize. There's a vast difference between a present and a prize. Seeing my father here makes me realize quite clearly that Koshigiri used that word intentionally.

Nui Ke Kālā isn't a present.

It's a prize alright.

A consolation prize.

Suddenly, Shannon's kissing me, excitement radiating off my glowing wife as she says, "Isn't it amazing? We're going to Hawaii! You own Nui Ke Kālā. And I pulled it all off. What a coup!"

My dad starts golf clapping and mouths those same words.

What a coup.

Want more of Declan and Shannon? Start with *Shopping for a Billionaire*, the top-10 *New York Times* bestselling book that chronicles their "meet-cute," when Shannon's working as a mystery shopper and Declan finds her hiding in the men's room of one of his store – with her hand down a toilet. It was love at first flush. ;)

HOPE AND DREAMS

JULIE LETO

"I apologize, Mr. Jackson. It's going to be about ten more minutes until your favorite table is ready," Hope said, tapping the keys on the newly installed POS system. "Do you and Mrs. Jackson want to grab a couple of Mel's famous Maui Island Breezes from the bar or do you want to head out to the patio and check out the new water feature? We finally finished the remodel outside. It's very romantic,"

Mr. Jackson's familiar blue eyes twinkled. He was a "gray fox," as his wife, Glenda, liked to call him. The Jacksons were regulars at Sunsets Bar & Grille and Hope had seen them wait an extra hour to make sure they got their preferred table beside the stage.

"Can we do both?" he asked.

Hope grinned and waved over a server. "Absolutely. We will get a tab started for you and bring the drinks out to you when they're ready. Our system will text you when we have your table set."

Mr. Jackson pulled out his phone, which had just chimed from a text. "This is new."

His wife, Glenda, leaned around her husband to look at his screen. "How efficient! No more of those buzzy disks that people put who knows where when they have them. Hope, this was your doing, wasn't it?"

Hope shrugged. "Lu and Ben love to be on the cutting edge."

The Jacksons laughed in unison before Glenda said, "The only thing cutting edge about Lu and Ben Kapono is their decision to put you in charge. I'm so happy Sunsets survived the shutdown. What would we do on Friday nights without this place?"

"We will have to make sure you never find out. You both ordered enough take out during the pandemic to help us stay solvent," Hope said. "I'm glad you like the changes. We're proud of them."

"At least you haven't changed the menu. My sweet Glenda might not have bounced back so fast if not for regular deliveries of your saimin soup."

Hope hadn't eaten tonight, so her mouth watered at the mention of her favorite comfort food. The Hawaiian dashi broth and noodles had always been one of her favorites.

"It's medicine for the body and the soul," she said.

"And the heart," Mr. Jackson added.

He took his wife's hand and swiped a kiss across her knuckles before gesturing toward the hall that led to the outdoor space. Glenda exaggerated the weakening of the knees at her husband's gallant gesture, then winked at Hope as they disappeared out the double doors. Hope could not help but smile. No one would ever describe her as a romantic, but that didn't mean she didn't appreciate a good love story. Although just because love existed for other people didn't mean she was ever going to find it for herself.

Once, in what seemed like another lifetime, Hope Warren had thought she'd finally found a relationship as nurturing and solid as that of the Jacksons and her foster parents, Melelu and Ben Kapono.

Damn, had she been wrong.

Luckily, love came in many forms, not just the romantic kind. Since her break-up, she'd promised herself that she'd focus on those and only those.

She loved this restaurant. She loved the Kaponos, the family who owned it and who had taken her in as a foster kid when she was barely twelve. They weren't her family by genetics, but they had given her everything she had needed from her own blood relatives and had never gotten. Her father had bolted before she'd turned two. Her mother had ended up in prison, taking the fall for the last in a long string of asshole boyfriends, though that one had taken the cake by leaving her to take the fall for his crimes. Hope had bounced around foster care for years until she'd landed with the Kaponos, who'd taken her into their home and their hearts.

Thanks to them, she'd finally gotten the unwavering emotional support she'd craved all her life. And also thanks to them, she had an education and a career in restaurant management. The bar and grill a couple of blocks east of Venice Beach was her second home, where she was the newly minted general manager and, like tonight when an employee called out so she could study for a Trig exam, the hostess.

The Kaponos' natural-born daughter, Mel, a gifted mixologist, ran the bar and the food truck that went out to special events. The wait staff and line cook team were filled with former foster kids who'd come through the Kapono house on their way to reunions with their birth families or adoptions. But they always came home to Sunsets for a meal, a job, or both, grateful to the family that had given them shelter when no one else would. The Kaponos embodied 'ohana. They lived it every single day.

Her ex had been one of those kids, only once he'd left, he'd never come back. Not to end their relationship in person. Not to finalize the paperwork after the long, Covid restriction-fueled delay.

But not all men were as selfish or self-centered as Tyler Adams.

God, why was she thinking about him now? She didn't even realize how her ire had arced until it was zapped away by a buzz from her cell phone. Mel needed her at the bar. After enlisting a passing server to watch the host stand, she burrowed through the crowd in time to see her foster sister light the floater she'd just poured over a ceramic bowl filled with rum punch. It was kitschy and touristy and everyone whooped and applauded as it was passed to the group of rowdy bachelorettes.

"What's up?" she asked once she'd ducked under the divider and scooted carefully behind two of Mel's bar staff.

"We need more hurricane glasses and we're running low on cherries," she said. "The kitchen isn't answering my texts."

The back of house was managed by Mel's mother, Melelu. Normally, her father Ben handled host duties but as it was nearing time for live entertainment, he was busy setting up with the house band.

"Lu has a love-hate with technology," Hope said, sending another text to the assistant kitchen manager.

"Ma has a love-hate with everything, including my pops."

Hope rolled her eyes. "Lu couldn't hate anything about Ben even if he was a serial killer."

Mel snorted. "You've clearly forgotten the time he sent dry kalua pork to that last minute catering gig."

"That's what they get for not planning in advance," Hope retorted with a chuckle. The incident had happened shortly after Mel had dropped out of college, leaving Hope behind to study hospitality management on her own, an education funded by the family who could have cut her loose the minute she turned eighteen, but hadn't. The story of the sandpaper pork had been retold as many times as Ben had ended a set on stage with his rendition of *Aloha 'oe*.

"Glasses and cherries on their way," she said, "Anything else?"

Mel waved to a group of regulars who'd come in through the bar entrance that bypassed the restaurant. She reminded her staff of their drink preferences before they'd made it to the bar to order. Mel Kapono was a magician when it came to cocktails and customer service. Between the two of them, they'd raised the profile of Sunsets and broadened the appeal to the locals in Ventura, from young to old.

After greeting her new patrons, she turned her penetrating gaze on Hope. If she hadn't had vast experience with her sister's expressions before, she might have taken a step back. Mel was a terrible actress who wore her emotions on her face like a magenta plumeria *lei*.

"What?" Hope asked, not sure she wanted to know the answer.

"I was going to ask you that question," her sister replied.

She stared back, nonplussed.

"You look, I don't know, beige."

Hope scrunched her nose. Though everyone in the restaurant wore clothing Hope had sourced from a Maui-based fashion brand known for blending traditional island wear with the modern textiles, Mel jazzed up her look so that every eye in the building landed on her at least a dozen times over the course of a night. Her jet hair was cut with a blunt edge. Her illegally long lashes were lined in ocean green and her lips sported a signature lip color that matched her tequila sunrise.

Hope, on the other hand, had chosen earth tones for her uniform. Not because she liked blending in, but because she firmly believed that her staff should stand out. She was the player behind the scenes. Besides, with her dark blond hair, hazel eyes and *haole* complexion, she looked good in rustic caramels and mossy greens.

"Not all of us can pull off your colorful style."

"You don't need color," Mel countered. "You need sex."

Hope shoved one hand on her hip. Leave it to her sister to open them up to a lawsuit. She stared in disapproval and then backed out of the bar. "We're not having this conversation in front of staff," she said, lowering her voice. "Or worse, customers."

"You won't ever have this conversation!" Mel said, following.

Hope was blocked from escape by the arrival of one of the kitchen runners holding a large bin of clean hurricane glasses. She swung out of his way. Mel stopped short, but when she opened her mouth to keep her inappropriate workplace discussion going, Hope grabbed her arm and tugged her into the storeroom where they kept the kegs and mixers.

Mel squealed as Hope propelled her forward so she could shut the door.

"Hey! Watch how you manhandle the merchandise."

"Watch what you say in front of the customers."

"The only time I see you is in front of customers. Speaking of which," Mel said, sidling up suggestively. "I noticed a couple of cute guys sitting over by the front window. I think they're the lawyers who go to the food truck when it parks on Pacific. They do environmental stuff I think. Or maybe it's family –"

Hope cut her off. "I don't date lawyers."

"You don't date anyone."

"You say that like I hadn't noticed. It's a choice, Mel, not a chore. And why do we have to keep having this conversation? I have enough on my plate."

"Girl, your plate is entirely too full of entrees and sides. You need desserts and the sweeter the better, if you get my drift."

"Your drift is impossible not to get," Hope said.

Her sister's expression turned unexpectedly concerned. "Subtlety has never been my superpower. Look, why don't you and I plan a night out? Maybe Sunday night. We could try out the new small plates place over by the pier. I could call a couple of friends," she suggested, but Hope cut her off.

"No way," she snapped. "In your world, *friends* are code for exes and I'm not interested in anyone else's throwaways."

"You did not just call my exes throwaways. You know me. I'm a pack-rat. I don't throw away anything. Or anyone."

This much was very true. Mel was not seeing anyone in particular at the moment, but every one of her numerous romances had been hot and heavy–and short-lived. However, while subtlety wasn't her superpower, holding onto her connections to the various men and the occasional woman who had drifted into and out of her bed, was. Her relationships didn't end as much as they were moved from the front burner to the back, ever-simmering, always ready for Mel to stir the pot again.

It was admirable, she supposed, but to Hope it was also weird. She and her ex hadn't spoken since they'd ended their engagement. Not even via text. She had no idea where in the world he was now or if he was in a relationship. She only knew he was alive because she figured if he'd fallen off of his boss's yacht or flown too close to the sun on his boss's private jet–not that she'd fantasized about such things, of course–someone would have had the courtesy to let the Kaponos know.

It was better that way. No contact meant she didn't have to think about him, even when in reality, she somehow managed to do that every freaking day.

"Are we done? We have a full house and," she said glancing at her phone, "about ten minutes until the show."

"We will be done when you promise to go out with me on Monday. Tomorrow, we'll be slammed and Sunday brunch wears us both out. We don't even have to go anywhere with people. It's just been too long since we have had a real talk."

Hope tugged Mel into a quick hug, agreed to an outing on the restaurant's off day and then headed back to her station.

Mel was right about their lack of together-time. At the restaurant, they usually found a moment or two to chat or banter, but they rarely had time for the kind of deep-dish, late night conversations they'd had when they had quarantined during the pandemic. Or during middle and high school after Hope had joined the Kapono family as a foster kid, sharing Mel's room while the other fosters, all boys, had shared a separate room across the hall.

For some reason she'd never understand but would forever be grateful for, she and Mel had instantly connected. Hope had been prickly and standoffish, but Mel had wasted no time in thawing her out with her warmth and openness. She'd often wondered if that was why the Kaponos had never asked her to leave their family, even after she aged out of the system. She'd never asked. She would never question that particular gift horse. Never in a million years.

She would keep her promise to spend time with Mel on their one off-day on Monday. She just had to figure out how to do that without submitting to a deconstruction of her non-existent love life.

When she checked the time again, she realized the dinner rush had abated. Everyone had been seated and most tables had their entrees or were perusing the dessert menu. As if on cue, her foster father and his band emerged on the tiny stage in the corner and started tinkering with their equipment. The piped-in tropical-themed instrumentals that provided the background for dinner service would soon give way to live steel guitars, ukuleles and the melodious strains of Ben's magical voice.

"Will there be dancing tonight?" a male voice asked.

Hope spun around, her practiced reply already halfway out of her mouth before her eyes focused on who had asked the question. "We have dancing every –"

The word "night" clogged in her throat. She gasped, then popped her mouth shut so she didn't look like a hooked fish. Out of pure self-preservation, she grabbed the host stand to keep herself on her feet.

"Tyler." She gaped. "What the hell are you doing here?"

All at once, his expression morphed from hopeful to sheepish. He looked down for a second. Was he wondering how fast his feet could beat a retreat out the door in light of her instant and completely justified scowl?

When his intense gaze met hers again, however, she knew he wasn't going anywhere.

Not this time.

Not until he said things she already suspected she did not want to hear.

Tyler was a dick, and this was a dick move. He had no right to show up at Sunsets unannounced at the end of the Friday night rush and blindside Hope like this. But he'd shown up all the same. The minute his flight had landed at LAX, he couldn't stop himself from coming straight to where it all started and where it all might never have ended if he hadn't put his own personal ambitions ahead of his heart.

He acted like an asshole to her in every way that was possible. Up until a few weeks ago, he'd convinced himself that his actions had made things easier for her. He was certain Hope had been better off without him. His cold-hearted way of ending their engagement had made her hate him and wouldn't hate fuel her to move on faster, find someone new, someone who deserved her in all the ways he didn't?

He'd been cruel to be kind, he'd told himself.

Dick.

"Hey, Hope."

Her hands gripped the host stand so tightly, her knuckles turned white.

Behind her, the lights in the main dining room dimmed and the automatic spotlights swung toward the stage. His stomach dropped as he watched Mel's father, Ben, take to the stage with his band. He couldn't suppress a grin. Ben's act had corny jokes, authentic music and the kind of warmth and hospitality that Tyler had never found anywhere else in the world no matter how hard he'd tried to find it.

Dammit.

"Can we talk?" he asked, dipping his head as he leaned forward so she could hear him over the amplified sound.

"No," she replied.

She let go of the stand. Her hands dropped to her sides.

Behind him, patrons from the bar drifted over to the dining room to watch the show. They stood in the back, which crowded the lobby behind Hope. He chanced a glance over to the bar, but didn't see Mel. He wasn't sure if that was a good or bad sign. Knowing her, she was trying to sneak up behind him with one of Lu's cast iron pans.

"Please," he said. "I need to tell you–"

"You may *need* to tell me things, Tyler, but I have absolutely no *need* to listen."

Hope grabbed her phone, tapped out a quick message, then turned on her heel and disappeared into the crowd. He moved to follow, but his momentum was halted by a punch to the middle of his back.

"What the hell are you doing here?"

He winced and turned, unsurprised to find Mel on the other end of the fist that had probably left a bruise on his spine.

"I told you," he said, twisting to stretch out the sting. "I need to talk to her."

"You needed to talk to her three years ago," she said, poking his chest. "You *really* needed to talk to her before you ran off to be some fancy chef, left your newly engaged girlfriend behind and then broke up with her in twenty words or less when you decided you didn't want to come home."

Tyler opened his mouth to argue, but he and Mel had already debated this. He'd come to LA three months ago to investigate a new restaurant venture for his investor boss and had run into his former foster sister while she was out on a date. Not only had she slapped the hell out of his face before saying hello, she'd dragged him outside on a sidewalk and read him the riot act on how horribly he had treated Hope.

As much as he didn't like being told off by a woman who'd used to put ice cubes in his bed when he annoyed her, he couldn't argue with her. He had treated Hope like crap. Now, he simply wanted to apologize. Explain. Make things right. Help her heal her pain. At the time, he'd thought the cruel break would be best for both of them, but he'd learned from Mel that his callousness had resulted in the opposite of what he'd intended. Hope had not moved on. She carried her hurt and anger like an anvil. She'd become closed-off and lonely again, the way she'd been when they'd first met as foster kids in the Kapono home.

All because of him.

"I don't have a time machine, Mel. I can't go back and redo how I acted. I can only apologize to her now and try to explain and–"

"Explain what? How on earth are you going to rationalize abandoning your fiancee like that?"

Frankly, he had no idea. Per usual, he'd acted on his emotions. After meeting up with Mel, he hadn't been able to take his mind off of Hope. Truth be told, he hadn't stopped thinking about her since he'd first left to take a once-in-a-lifetime job opportunity as a private chef to one of California's most successful entrepreneurs. Like Hope, Tyler had grown up in the system. He'd never had anything he couldn't fit in a garbage bag to call his own. Now thanks to a generous salary and bottomless expense account, he had access to the finest of everything.

Unfortunately, the only thing he wanted was Hope–the one thing he no longer had a right to have.

He swung around and pushed past a couple more groups heading in from the bar and walked outside into the warm California night. He wasn't sure if Mel would follow, but she did. He could hear her foot tapping on the sidewalk.

"You shouldn't have come here," she said.

"I didn't have a choice."

She guffawed. "You've had a lot of choices, Tyler Adams. You always seem to make the wrong ones. If you have come here to unburden your soul no matter how much it tears Hope apart, then you're more of an asshole than I thought. And I'm not even sure that's statistically possible."

He was certain it wasn't.

"Do your parents hate me, too?"

He forced himself to turn around and face her. Mel Kapono had never been his biggest fan, a fact that rankled since she could make friends with a feral dog. She'd probably had to learn that trick to survive and thrive in her own house, with the constant flow of prickly foster kids living under their roof.

"Ben Kapono doesn't know how to hate anyone. As long as you send him the occasional text, which you do, he will always give you the benefit of the doubt. But I'm not speaking for my mom. She will tell you what she thinks on her own as soon as you grow the balls to face her."

Tyler shook off a chill. Melelu Kapono could be as warm as a Maui breeze or as chilly as a tundra, but she never made you guess about how she felt. And it wasn't her hate he feared. It was her disapproval. She'd provided the only maternal love he'd ever gotten in his life and he'd repaid her by breaking the heart of her most cherished foster child and cutting contact with the only real family he'd ever known.

"I need to talk to Hope."

"You *want* to talk to Hope."

"I have to apologize."

"Write her a letter."

"I owe her a chance to slap my face in person, don't you think?"

"I've done it," Mel reminded him. "It's not as cathartic as I'd hoped. And unlike me, Hope hates violence. I think that's because of the third house she was in where the foster parents beat her for taking an extra piece of stale bread at dinner. Or was that the fourth?"

Tyler pushed down the bile that instantly rose in his throat. He and Hope had both had horrible experiences in the system. Most kids did. They'd both found solace and home and love in the Kapono household. But where he'd been compelled to leave the first time he had an opportunity, Hope had chosen to stay. She'd become more than a former foster child. She'd become family. Just like she'd become *his* family when she'd accepted his proposal.

And what had he done? Thrown it away.

Dick.

"It was the fourth," he muttered, knowing Hope's history as well as he knew his own. "I don't know what to do, Mel, but I won't let things stand the way they are. You told me yourself that Hope was still hurting after all these years. You said she wasn't seeing anyone and does nothing but work and hardly sees friends. You said it was because of what I did and I believe you. How am I supposed to let that stand if I can do something to help her?"

"I'm not sure you can help her," Mel said. "I'm also not sure that helping her is your real motivation. Maybe you're just trying to help yourself?"

"Maybe I am," he said with a heavy sigh. "I've always been a selfish son-of-a-bitch, Mel. Haven't I proved it enough? But if I can help Hope, too, doesn't it matter if I finally earn a little absolution?"

Mel stepped up so close, it took everything in his power not to lean back. Her black irises bored into him with the intense heat of a laser. Then, in a brief flash, he saw uncertainty crossher face. Whatever sharp quip she'd been about to deliver transformed as she mulled the words over in her mouth.

"Honestly, Tyler? What happens to you doesn't matter to me at all."

Hope tore into the kitchen and grabbed the first solid surface she met, the top of a stainless steel work station that had already been wiped clean and disinfected after service. Though most of the meals had already been served, a couple of stations still buzzed with activity. Lu was supervising the plating of desserts, cutting her famous guava chiffon cake herself into perfectly square servings while one of the pastry chefs drew intricate designs on the plate with a thick lime coulis. For a brief second, she and Hope made eye contact. A half-second later, her foster mother was by her side.

"What's wrong?" Lu asked.

Hope shook her head. She wasn't sure she could even say his name out loud. What the hell was he doing here? Why had he come? It had been years. Years! She hadn't heard so much as a single word from him. He'd disappeared out of her life like a wraith. Like her father.

Her face flushed. The hot sting of tears burned her eyes and at the same time she shivered as if she'd been locked in the walk-in. Lu frowned, took Hope's hand, and led her to the office.

"*Ke kaikamahine*," Lu murmured, using the Hawaiian word for daughter that always tore straight through to Hope's heart. "What's happened?"

Hope hiccuped to hold back a sob. Her heart was too raw, too wounded, to survive even an unintentional wound. She wasn't Lu's daughter, but yet, she was. How could she not be? Lu loved her, cared for her, ensured her education and success. She'd celebrated when Hope and Tyler had gotten engaged, even though she'd had misgivings. They were too young. Too vulnerable. But she'd supported them.

And when Tyler had left, Lu had refused to say anything negative about his decision to leave Hope and his job as a Sunsets sous chef behind to take a job as a private chef. Even when he'd ended their engagement, Lu had tried to put a positive spin on the break up. Mostly now, she, like Hope, didn't talk about Tyler at all.

It had to be painful for her, too. He had been her protege and a son of her heart.

Hope shook her head. Tyler hadn't just hurt her when he'd left. He'd hurt them all.

"Hope, you look like you've seen a ghost. Tell me what is wrong right now or I will go get Ben."

Teardrops slid down her cheeks, but she laughed mirthlessly. "He's in the middle of a set."

"Since when has that stopped me?"

Never. It did not happen often, but Lu had no compunction about stopping the performance if she needed her husband for something related to their children. And blood relation or not, Hope was their kid. Trouble was, so was Tyler, no matter how much he'd hurt them all.

"Tyler is back," she said.

Lu's black eyes widened, then she spun to look at the door as if Tyler was going to materialize out of nothing, which he basically had. "Where? When?"

Hope sucked in a breath and forced it out slowly. She didn't want to cry or worse, sob uncontrollably. She'd wasted enough emotional energy on her former fiance. God, why did he have to show up now? Had her earlier thoughts about him conjured him from the ether?

No, that couldn't be it. If just thinking about him could manifest him, he would have reappeared every day since he left. The truth was that no matter how much he'd devastated her, she had never been able to force him completely from her mind.

"He came in a few minutes ago. I don't know where he is now. I ran away."

"No," Lu corrected, pulling her into a hug. "You ran *here*."

Hope allowed herself to melt into Lu's warmth. She didn't want to cry, but tears spilled out of her eyes in a silent flow. So maybe she hadn't entirely used up the tears allotted to Tyler. But the moment seemed to pass quickly and she was able to pull herself together.

"Why would he come here? Why now?" she asked as she stood and grabbed a tissue from Lu's desk, wiped her face and blew her nose.

"He had to come back some time," her mother replied.

"Did he? Did he really?" she said, her voice rising in volume. She pressed her lips together. Lu didn't deserve to be the target of her anger.

Lu pushed her hands on her thighs and stood with a grunt. She wasn't old or out of shape, but it had been a long day for all of them.

"This is his *hale*, no matter his reasons for leaving," she said softly. "I know he hurt you, Hope. He hurt all of us when he left. I'd always hoped he'd take over the kitchen here. He will have to ask for my forgiveness before I give it, but he must have a reason for coming back. Don't you want to know what it is?"

Hope shook her head without really considering the question. Tyler coming back meant she had to dig around in a well of hurt that she'd capped a long time ago. Or had she? She'd tried to, that was for sure. She'd thrown herself into anything and everything that didn't relate to her failed relationships and broken heart. She'd finished college. She'd worked at the restaurant, the website and finding the best point of sale system they could afford. She'd started the food truck. She'd partnered with a nearby culinary arts program to build their team. She'd helped her community during the pandemic. She'd read books and learned to knit and deepened her studies of Hawaiian history to better connect with the roots that she'd been grafted onto by the Kapono clan.

What she hadn't done was date or flirt or even entertain the idea of being in a romantic relationship again. That part of her had belonged to Tyler since they'd both turned sixteen. If she decided to explore that part of herself again, she'd first have to exorcize him out of that space to make room for anyone else.

And that would mean facing a whole lot of hurt. Facing it and even, if possible, forgiving it before she could move on.

Yeah, right, like it was just that easy.

"I can't deal with this right now," Hope insisted.

Lu put her hands on her ample hips. "If not now, when? If the past few years have taught us anything, Hope, it's that we have to live in the moment. Regrets from the past belong in the past, but you have to put them there. You haven't. You know you haven't."

Lu left the room, but she came back quickly with a plate of cake and a tall iced tea. She also brought two forks, which made Hope smile in a way she didn't imagine she could. They sat with the plate on top of a pile of resumes they'd received from the culinary school and ate together, chatting about nothing important, reminiscing on how they'd tested and tasted what seemed like one hundred different sauces before settling on the lime to elevate the guava cake from fantastic to fabulous.

Hope drew her finger through the last of the sauce and licked it off with a groan of pleasure.

"Delicious," she said.

"A little sour offsets the sweet," Lu offered. "It's a lesson in life."

Hope frowned. They'd circled back to Tyler without even mentioning his name. And with that, Lu left the office, blowing her a kiss as she closed the door behind her.

Now, Hope had no company, no cake and no reason not to spend the rest of the night thinking about Tyler and what the hell she was going to do next.

Stalking had never been Tyler's style, so hard as it was, he stayed as far away from Sunsets as he could while he figured out his next move. He considered texting Hope, but she'd either changed her number or blocked him. He didn't have social media and if he downloaded an app just to reach out to her, even *he'd* consider himself a creep.

By Sunday afternoon, he'd jotted out a note to have delivered to her apartment, maybe with flowers or chocolate, but he wasn't sure where she lived. He could have asked Ben or Lu, but he didn't want to put them in the uncomfortable position of turning him down. Mel would go to the grave before she told him so much as Hope's shoe size. Her tirade about Hope's lasting sadness over their broken engagement had prompted him to seek her out in the first place and judging by her rage when he'd showed up at the restaurant unannounced on Friday night, he'd poked that bear enough.

But he couldn't take the easy route anymore. He didn't want to. He'd earned her anger and he had to face her before either of them could move on. At the very least, he had to apologize to her for hurting her. In person. He had to explain how his mind had worked at the time, if she cared to listen.

He had to ask for forgiveness without expecting she'd give it.

Then he could figure out how to deal with the rejection when she flat-out refused.

Why would she forgive him? She could move on without it. She hadn't, but she could.

So why hadn't she?

Despite their traumatic childhoods, Tyler and Hope's romance had been sweet, like in a TV sitcom with a laugh track and a dog or toddler who'd steal scenes. When they were together, they could forget how their parents had abandoned them, how he'd lived on the streets for months and how she'd changed foster homes so often that sometimes the families who had taken her in didn't even know her name. All of it changed for both of them when they'd ended up at the Kapono home. They'd started off as foster siblings, then became friends, and amid the swell of puberty and hormones, boyfriend and girlfriend.

By the time she'd moved into the dorm at college, he'd started working sixty hour weeks at the restaurant. They'd barely scratched the surface of a physical relationship.

He'd longed for her. She wanted to be with him, too. But life and obligations always seemed to get in the way of them truly exploring what it meant to be intimate, close or committed. He'd thought an inexpensive ring and a sincere proposal would change the course of their relationship. And yeah, a part of him had prayed that a ring and a promise would be enough to hold onto her while she moved up in the world and he was trapped in a sweltering kitchen learning how to properly prepare taro root or butcher a pig for the pit.

He'd never experienced such intense happiness as he had the night she'd said yes to becoming his wife—that was, until Greek investor, Paolo Paredes, had sampled his food at the restaurant and then offered him a chance to travel and cook for him.

Hope had encouraged him to go. She had practically threatened to break up with him if he didn't. She was still in school. He could take this amazing opportunity to travel and learn and in a year or two, he'd come back and they'd get married. She'd graduate to running the business end of Sunsets and Tyler would run the kitchen.

But after only a year with Paolo, he'd realized that running the kitchen at Sunsets would not be enough for him. Not when there was so much more of the world to see—so much more to explore and learn and experience.

And to get more, he'd have to leave all his past dreams behind.

He'd honestly believed the rewards would be worth the price, but now he knew that he'd give back everything he'd gained if he could find a place to call home again.

He'd returned to LA a few times due to his job with Paolo, but he'd never had the guts to face the people he'd left behind. Running into Mel had been the catalyst for facing his truths, but now that he was here, he wasn't sure he could leave again. Not unless he knew that the next time he returned, he'd be welcome. Maybe that was too much to ask, but he had to at least try.

Once he'd come to terms with that, he decided to go see the Kaponos. He'd kept in touch with Ben by text and the occasional phone call, but Lu had been harder to connect with since she hated using the phone. But that was no excuse. Not any more. He owed his found family an apology, as well as an explanation about why he'd stayed away so long and why he'd finally come home.

Fact was, he missed them. He'd traveled the globe, but in no corner of the world had he felt as loved as he had in the Kaponos' kitchen. Without them, he never would have known how to peel an onion much less how to transform it into a meal. He would never have known what it felt like to trust that the adults in charge weren't going to pass out on the floor or forget to feed you.

He also would never have known what it felt like to fall in love.

Monday morning, he got up early, hit the market to purchase fresh passionfruit, sugar, butter and eggs, then returned to Paolo's borrowed apartment to whip up a batch of lilikoi bars before heading out to Santa Monica, north of Ventura, where the Kaponos still lived. As expected, Ben welcomed him with open arms. Lu was standoffish at first, but after three lilikoi bars, Hawaiian-grown coffee and three hour's worth of deep conversation, she returned to her warm and welcoming self. He answered every question they had about his life as a chef, his travels around the world and his immediate plans while in LA.

He answered honestly about the first two topics, but on the third, he had no answers to give. He purposefully kept Hope out of the conversation, which was hard to do since she was the reason he'd stayed behind after Paolo took off for France. He forced himself not to look at the photos of her that hung on the walls, some he'd seen a hundred times when he'd lived there, a few that were new and showed her smiling and enjoying events in her life he knew nothing about.

He bit back every question he had about her. He could not put the family in the middle. Mel had already made it clear that she was done with him. She was the self-appointed captain of Team Hope and he trusted that while Lu and Ben would try to stay neutral, they'd be torn. When he finally said the words, "I'm sorry," they wrapped him in their arms and forbade him from ever staying away so long again.

Just like that.

No recriminations. No criticism.

Just love.

He didn't deserve it, but he'd take it all the same.

After promising to cook dinner for them later in the week, he left, though instead of heading back to Paolo's LA condo, he decided to wander the old neighborhood and try to remember all the reasons why he loved the places he'd left behind.

When he'd first arrived in Los Angeles, he'd been alone, broke and scared. He'd had no family to run to—no friends to have his back except for the punks like him that he'd met on the streets. Truth was, he'd been just as displaced in Arizona, the geeky son of alcoholic parents who never showed up to parent-teacher conferences or signed him up for Little League, but who thought shoving a Ziploc of stale pizza in his backpack for lunch made them parents of the year.

When he'd landed in the Kapono home, he'd been wary. But their spirit, their dedication to the practice of *hānai*, won him over before he could resist. In their home kitchen and then the restaurant, he'd found his calling. He'd bussed tables and washed dishes for a year before Lu had given him a knife or taught him how to chop vegetables and filet a fish, but every sweaty, backbreaking moment had been magical, simply because they trusted him to do it.

As he strolled through the residential area west of downtown and blocks from the famous Santa Monica pier, he grinned, recalling how different this ordinary oasis was from the streets of west Hollywood, where he'd first tumbled out of a hitchhiker-friendly van.

He hadn't lasted long on those streets. A month? Maybe two? After getting pinched for shoplifting, he'd been placed in a group home where he'd further honed his criminal skills. That had led to a second juvie arrest, a short-term stint and then placement with a foster family whose name he couldn't recall and who had had too many kids to pay him any attention. Just after his sixteenth birthday, he'd been moved to the Kaponos and after that, the trajectory of his life had forever changed. With them, he'd learned a trade. He'd learned about family. He'd learned about love.

Before he knew it, he looked up and saw he had arrived at the park on Ozone Ave in Santa Monica, just a couple of blocks from the house. On a Monday afternoon, the place had a small spattering of young kids, their parents or babysitters, and a noisy half-dozen dogs rambling around the area fenced off just for them.

And there, under the large red arch that tethered the swings, he saw Hope.

His heart screeched to a stop. So did his feet. Unable to process seeing her here unexpectedly, he ducked behind a tree.

God, he was such an asshole. Why had he hidden? He should turn. Walk away.

No, he'd tried that already and it had been a massive mistake.

Still, she did not want to see him. She'd made that perfectly clear. But he hadn't come back to Los Angeles to leave old wounds untended to.

He had to talk to her.

He was stepping out toward the sandy area beneath the arches when he saw that Hope hadn't shown up alone. Mel had been chasing a couple of toddlers with a bright orange bubble gun, squealing with glee along with her pint-sized prey. Hope looked up from pushing another child on the swing when she caught sight of her sister's antics and burst into laughter.

The sight punched him in the gut. It was one thing to see her when she was filled with rage and pain, but it was entirely something else to see her standing in the sunlight, her skin dappled with sunlight and her smile bright with uninhibited happiness.

How could he take this moment away?

The choice was taken out of his hands when she looked out and their eyes locked.

As predicted, her smile dropped into a frown.

Part of him wanted to retreat, but his stronger urge was to march forward and prove he wasn't afraid to finally face what he'd done to her. But he also didn't want to be a bully. She'd asked him to leave her alone, which was why he couldn't believe it when she gestured for Mel, who'd also noticed him, to stay put and started walking toward him on her own.

As she came around the swinging children, her expression hardened.

"Are you following me?" she asked.

"No," he replied, his hands up in a sign of surrender. "I went to visit the Kaponos and took a walk around the neighborhood. They didn't say a word about you being here."

She pressed her lips together as if to contain the first words she'd wanted to say. He probably shouldn't have noticed how soft and luscious her lips looked or give himself permission to remember the taste of those lips on his, but he couldn't help himself.

This was why he hadn't come home. This is why he'd broken up with her over Facetime. His attraction to her muddled his brain, causing the blood to rush around his veins like white water rapids.

That, and because he was a jerk.

"They don't know we're here," she said. "Mel has to drop off some ukulele strings she ordered online for Ben and when we passed by the park and saw the swings, we decided to stop. It wasn't planned."

"Maybe it was kismet," he said.

"Maybe it was bad luck," she countered.

Her tone was clipped, but she didn't move. Did this mean she wanted to talk to him? Hope had never been shy with her opinions, criticisms or praise, as she'd proved Friday night. She could leave, but something was making her stay.

Maybe it was just curiosity, but at this point, he'd take what he could get.

He'd blindsided her at the restaurant and she'd reacted with justifiable anger. But though he'd surprised her by showing up here, this time, at least she'd known he was in town. And she wasn't trapped by customers or obligations. They were out in the sunshine at a familiar place.

Their place.

How many times had they snuck out of the Kapono's home after midnight to stroll to this park and jump on the swings? How many nights had they kissed under the trees, out of the sight of the streetlights so the neighbors who might call the police, or worse, call the Kaponos, wouldn't see? They'd come here after dates to finish off their In-and-Out chocolate shakes. They'd often come here to toss frisbees or footballs with Mel and the other fosters.

When he'd finally decided to ask her to marry him, this is where he'd done it. God, he'd forgotten. How could he have forgotten? He'd placed a cheap ring he'd bought off of a vendor at Ventura Beach on her finger, promising to get her something better as soon as he could afford it.

She'd said she didn't care about fancy jewelry. He still wanted something better. Not just a big diamond, but he wanted to offer her a better life than either of them had ever expected when they'd been just lost, overlooked, unwanted kids.

His life had been laid out like a roadmap to delinquency and poverty. Even when his parents were alive, they'd spent what little money they had at the local bar or liquor store rather than save a penny for his future.

When they'd died in a wreck, he hadn't been surprised. He'd been sad– devastated even–but not surprised. Losing his parents, neglectful as they were, to alcohol had been his darkest nightmare come true. Having to go live with his equally neglectful uncle hadn't changed his view that the only future he could look forward to included jail or an early grave. That's when he'd run. He figured his future couldn't be any worse in the California sunshine that it had been in the choking desert heat.

It had ended up being magical, especially when he'd reached sixteen and suddenly, the girl who shared a bedroom across the hall changed from being someone to play videogames with into the woman he'd wanted to kiss. Wanted to love.

Did love.

Then and now.

The flair of her dark blond hair in the breeze taunted him. The hint of her perfume teased his nostrils. But it was her eyes that tore him in two. She was struggling to make her expression passive and unreadable, but everything he needed to see was reflected in the mossy green centers of her irises.

He'd hurt her. Deeply.

"I'm sorry," he blurted.

The hazel gaze narrowed. "Sorry for what, Tyler?"

"For leaving. For not taking you with me."

"I couldn't go," Hope replied dismissively. "You knew I'd never leave LA. Not for long. Not when my future was here. The restaurant. The family. I couldn't leave that behind."

Yes, he'd known, just as they'd accepted that Tyler was not college material and he'd never had the means to even consider expensive culinary schools. The Kaponos had known that Hope had the smarts to get a degree. To him, they'd given all the kitchen experience and hands-on learning they could offer. They'd given her the higher education she'd always aspired to, as well as the responsibility to run Sunsets once she finished school. If he'd stayed, he would have run their kitchen, but he would never have known how to grow their legacy or see the endless possibilities outside their dream.

He'd used what he'd learned at Lu's side to snag himself an opportunity he never could have imagined as a thirteen-year-old sleeping behind a Dumpster at a church on Wilshire. His flair with traditional Hawaiian cuisine had brought him to Paolo's attention, but his hunger to be as adventurous in the kitchen as Paolo was in the world of finance was what had made him a success.

But now that he had the success he'd craved, what was left?

He'd fully intended to only do a year jetting around the globe and studying world cuisines before he returned home to Los Angeles to use his expanded knowledge to elevate the food at Sunsets and eventually open a restaurant he could call his own. But working for the high profile investor had been too seductive to limit to one year. Over the past six, he'd cooked for titans of finance, heads of state, Oscar winners and supermodels. He'd picked wild yams from a mountainside in Peru and prepared them over an open fire in a village square under the shadow of Machu Picchu. He'd shopped roadside farmers markets with former line cooks who now had their own shows on the Food Network or Netflix. He'd fished in the Great Barrier Reef and served his catch to a prime minister and her entourage.

He'd done all of those things…at the cost of his once-in-a-lifetime love.

"I'm sorry," he repeated.

This time, she waved the words away. "Don't, Tyler. You had a chance to do something amazing. I get why you went. I even understand why you broke things off." Her eyes narrowed. "Though, you might have considered doing it face to face rather than in a video call."

He winced at that direct hit. "I was stupid. Young, selfish, cowardly."

"Yes, you were." She shrugged, as if that wasn't the shittiest thing he could have done, though he knew it was. "What I do not understand is why you stayed away so long. Was it just because of me?"

Hope's eyes remained stoic even while her lips quivered. His fingers itched to cup her chin and smooth away her pain, but he did not have the right.

"No," he said.

"You're sure?" she pressed.

He could not lie to her. He'd already broken promises and caused her more anguish than he'd ever intended. He couldn't compound that with a blatant untruth.

"I couldn't face you," he confessed. "I couldn't face what I'd done to you. What I'd done to us."

She scowled. "You didn't do anything to me and there is no us anymore. You went off to live your best life. I would have been happy for you. I would have cheered you on. I did, if you remember."

"I know," he said. "And then I fucked it up by breaking up with you over the phone from across the world. I should have found a way to get back here to see you in person. I didn't want to hold you to the promises I knew I couldn't keep. But it was wrong. I messed up and I will be sorry for that for the rest of my life."

She mulled his confession. Her mouth moved as she considered his apology. Was she biting back what she really wanted to say or just biding her time until she could form all the sharpest barbs?

"Yeah, you messed up, Ty," she said, using the nickname she hadn't spoken for years. "But not by breaking up with me. Your biggest mistake was asking me to marry you when we were nineteen-year-old idiots who had no idea what the world had in store for us. And I made it worse by saying yes."

Her words were classic Hope–honest, self-deprecating and straight to the point.

"We were in love," he insisted.

"We were *kids* in love," she admitted. "I'm not minimizing how I felt about you then. Or even what I still feel now after all this time. But I've spent years blaming you for most of it and that's not fair. In a different time and in a different set of circumstances, we might have worked. But we didn't. I'm tired of wallowing in that. Aren't you?"

Tyler took a step back. He thought he'd been prepared for anything and everything she might say to him when he finally apologized, but he hadn't been ready for this.

The honest, heartfelt words that had come out of her mouth shocked even Hope. She hadn't planned to voice them; honestly, before this morning, she hadn't even considered them. They were true, though–she was tired of blaming him and definitely tired of wallowing.

She and Mel had spent the morning catching up, talking about nothing and feasting on burgers and beer from a food truck by the beach before heading over to the house. But they'd also managed to deconstruct more than a little about her feelings for Ty.

Ty. The first and only boy she'd ever kissed under the tree that had shaded the park and still did now.

The only man she'd ever loved.

Even now, after all the time and distance and pain, she was still blindsided by the power of her elemental response to his nearness. His boyish good looks had morphed into manly handsomeness. He was broader, older, devastatingly better.

His blue eyes blazed with surprise and then she spied a hint of the grin she'd always found so disarming, as if he couldn't believe there was a path to forgiveness for them, even though he'd offered an apology or two. Or three? Or a thousand unspoken ones, judging by his soulful eyes.

She was ready to accept them all.

The truth was, Hope had no more anger or resentment to hold onto. Somehow between Friday and today, it had evaporated into nothing. Perhaps it had dissipated a long time ago and she'd been holding onto the remnants in order to keep herself in an endless holding pattern. That part had not been his fault. She'd made choices, too, and it was time for her to own each and every one.

"Honestly, Hope," he said, taking a tentative step closer, "I haven't wallowed in my guilt half as much as I should have. I've been avoiding the past by living 100% in the present."

"That doesn't sound like a bad thing," she said.

He shook his head. "It wasn't necessarily bad, but it was the easy way out. Too easy. I appreciate you cutting me slack, but I don't want to leave here feeling good about bad decisions. I want to make it up to you."

"You don't owe me anything, Ty."

"Don't I?"

As much as she wanted to deny him and send him on his way, she couldn't. Her feelings for him were different now, but they weren't gone. If they had been, his absence wouldn't have thrown her into a void of loneliness she hadn't wanted to pull herself out of and his sudden reappearance wouldn't have thrown her into an emotional tailspin. Although she hadn't even realized it until this very moment, the truth was, she'd been waiting for him, just like she would have promised to if he'd given her the chance.

"Can I come by the restaurant tomorrow?" he asked. "Ben and Lu couldn't stop talking about all you have done at Sunsets and how you saved the restaurant when the pandemic and lockdowns hit. How you and Mel have built a community of locals that fills the place every night."

Her mouth quirked in a half-grin. She had never been comfortable with over-effusive praise. "We get new business, too. Mel is a master of TikTok."

He chuckled. "I bet she is."

"How about Wednesday?" she offered. She needed a beat. Time to process. Room to adjust. "We have our huli-huli chicken special on the menu," she added with a smile, "and a group that does *hula kahiko* that can't be seen anywhere else except the islands."

"That would be great." He glazed down for an instant and her brain immediately pictured the boy he'd been–the one who'd won her heart.

And that was her cue to leave.

When she turned to walk back to Mel, who'd likely been watching the entire time with a narrowed gaze, she thought she felt the warmth of his hand rising as if to touch her arm. She glanced over her shoulder in time to see him shove his hand into his pocket.

If he had made contact, what would she have done? Bolted or melted into his touch?

She didn't know and she wasn't prepared to find out.

The dance troupe that performed at Sunsets did so on Tuesdays, too. She'd pushed him off until Wednesday to buy herself more time. Everything she felt about him had shifted. All her emotions had changed. She needed to sort some of it out without putting him off forever. She had no idea how long he intended to stay. If she asked, she felt as if she would be telling him she wanted him to leave.

She didn't.

Damn it all, but she didn't.

"So?" Mel asked the minute they were close enough to talk over the squeals and shouts of the playing children.

She inhaled deeply. "We're good. He's coming to the restaurant Wednesday night to see all the updates and watch the show."

"You're *good*?" Mel asked, clearly shocked. "That's it? Six years of heartbreak and sadness and you're 'good' in one conversation?"

Mel even added the air quotes. Hope knew the proclamation sounded ridiculous, but the fact remained that she no longer wanted to tie herself up in knots over actions and decisions that happened before she and Ty had been old enough to drink.

She shrugged. "You said it yourself this morning. I can't move on if I hold onto my pain. What happened in the past is the past. It's time to move forward."

"With him?" Mel asked, not as incredulous in her tone as Hope expected.

"Don't be absurd," Hope said. "He hasn't seen the whole world yet. He still has his job. He won't be here long."

"He told you that?" Mel questioned.

"No," Hope said. "We didn't talk that much, but his dreams can't have changed. He's always wanted to travel and let the world be his classroom."

Mel's expression was doubtful. "You don't know what his dreams are anymore, Hope, but if you're wise, you'll take the time to find out."

Hope shook her head. "It's his life. His dreams are his business."

Mel hooked her arm in hers and led them toward where they'd parked their car. "And your dreams are your business. I just have a feeling you both have aspirations that overlap."

Hope forced herself to laugh. "You're crazy."

"Yes," Mel instantly agreed. "But that doesn't make me wrong."

———

Hope changed her clothes three times. First, she'd donned the uniform she usually wore, dark pants with a blouse made with the proprietary Sunsets pattern, but in soft greens and browns she'd had made for management. She looked good, she decided after a long perusal in the mirror, but too ordinary. She swapped her top out for one with the pinks and purples Mel preferred, but it washed out her makeup and made her look pale. If she added more blush or brightened her eyeshadow to make it work, she'd look like she was trying too hard.

It was bad enough that she was trying at all.

She wanted to look attractive for Ty. She could spend unnecessary energy trying to convince herself otherwise, but what was the point? Even if he planned to leave Los Angeles again–and she had no reason to believe he wouldn't–she'd rather him return to his new life remembering her at her best.

At last, she pulled out the dress that the designer from LaHaina had put together as a gift, one she'd been saving for a special occasion. It had hints of the Sunsets design with its wide hibiscus pattern, but it was otherwise unique. No one else at the restaurant had a dress that was short enough to skim her thighs, long, slightly belled sleeves impractical for serving food and a neckline that swooped from shoulder to shoulder, leaving her skin bare. Even the colors were special, a blend of her preferred earth tones with pops of gold and pink. Paired with sandals that would keep her from dropping into the kitchen without risking a code violation, she looked as if she was going on a first date rather than to work.

And frankly, she did not care.

The minute Ty came through the doors, she knew her choices had been the right ones.

Jenny, their hostess, immediately put on her best smile as Ty approached, but Hope dropped her hand on the young woman's shoulder to indicate that she'd be taking care of this customer on her own.

"Wow," he said. "You look amazing."

"Thanks," she said, overwhelmed by an uncharacteristic bashfulness. She'd never felt that before, not even with Ty. How could she have when they'd seen each other in their pajamas for years before they'd discovered that they no longer felt like childhood friends. "Do you want to try one of Mel's famous new signature drinks?"

He glanced into the mildly busy space. Mel hesitated a moment, then gifted him with a half-grin and a shrug. That was about as much of a welcome as her sister would give him, and it was more than Hope had expected.

"Doesn't look like I have a choice. She's not going to poison me, is she?" he asked, sotto voiced.

"And ruin the restaurant's perfect A grade? Never."

Hope joined him at the bar and Mel did an admirable job of acting as if she was happy to see him. She served him her signature Mai-Tai, not the overly fruity concoction her parents used to offer on their original menu, but the classic aged rum cocktail with orgeat almond and rich demerara syrups she blended herself and which had won her an award from a local food guide.

"This is fantastic," he declared, and then spent the next ten minutes talking shop about mixology.

Hope sipped a flavored sparkling water, marveling at how the vibe between the three of them had shifted like tectonic plates after a quake. The comfortable, familial tone set her off-kilter as much as sitting close enough to Tyler to breathe in the scent of his woodsy cologne. He wore soft jeans, a snug gray T-shirt and a breezy linen jacket rolled up at the cuffs, making him look casual and cosmopolitan at the same time. She remembered the days when she was lucky that the T-shirt he wore on a date wasn't torn or dotted with splashes of grease.

Only this wasn't a date.

It was …

What was it?

When the business in the bar picked up, she suggested they go visit Lu in the kitchen. Her foster mother took great pride introducing Tyler to the staff and inviting him to taste myriad dishes until she finally shooed them out to the table they kept open by the stage. They shared a plate of huli huli chicken and a wide assortment of sides including Lu's infamous macaroni salad. The unexpectedly comfortable conversation scratched the surface of "catching up," but impressed Hope with its depth. They'd both changed so much. Had learned so much. Had experienced so much.

And yet, nothing about him seemed foreign. He was the Tyler she'd known. The Tyler she'd loved. Just better.

The show provided a much-needed intermission to their conversation. She was overwhelmed with his nearness, his honesty, his love of cooking and travel and life. When Ben came on stage to sing the final set, ending with his heartfelt rendition of *Aloha-oe*, Ty reached across the two-top and enveloped her hand in his.

They both knew the history of the lyrics. Written by the last queen of the islands, Lili'uokalani, it was a love song to her land, her people and her culture. To most *haole*, it was a song they'd heard on television shows and movies. To Ben and Lu, it was a piece of their past, rife with longing. Ben always sang the verses first in his native Hawaiian and then in an English translation. When he reached the words, "Dearest one, yes, you are mine own, from you, true love shall never depart," Ty squeezed her hand tight.

Hope wasn't sure what happened next. The set ended. The customers applauded, milled about, ordered more drinks. Ben came by their table and chatted a few minutes with Ty. When their foster dad noticed their clasped hands, he raised his eyebrows and made an excuse to leave. After declining another round of cocktails from their server, Ty stood and gently tugged her up, guiding her to the lobby.

"I'd like to see the new patio," he said.

The suggestion shook her back to full consciousness. "We don't open it up during the week."

He pulled her a half-step closer. "I know."

This was insane. And it was also perfect. Hope took her turn leading him, unlocking the entrance to the patio and sliding the "no access," sign back into place before shutting the doors behind them.

She let go of him long enough to reach behind a cascade of hanging plants, flicking on the colorful fairy lights and activating the water feature. A rocky waterfall dotted with gas flames and flowers native to the area of Maui where Ben and Lu had first fallen in love splashed gently. Her foster parents had been around the same age as Hope and Ty when they'd decided to get married, sell everything they owned and emigrate to California to open the food shack that grew into Sunsets. Their leap of faith had brought their family so much prosperity, they'd immediately wanted to share it with children like Hope and Ty who'd never had anyone to show them the strength of 'ohana.

Hope moved closer to the fountain, sat on the smooth ledge and after a deep breath, gestured for Ty to join her.

"Beautiful," Ty said.

She knew he wasn't talking about the patio. He proved her right by reaching down and smoothing a single finger down her cheek. The sensation sent a vibration through her that reached every part of her. As he cupped her chin and tilted her face up, he lowered himself beside her and brushed a whisper of a kiss across her lips.

An explosion of need wracked her body. She shook. He pressed his hands on her bare shoulders and rhythmically rubbed.

"Cold?" he asked, leaning in to swipe another kiss across her cheek.

"No," she said. "This shouldn't feel this way. Not after all this time."

"What way? Familiar? Welcome?"

She nodded. "Safe," she had to admit. "But it's not safe, Ty. I could fall again so easily, risk my heart again, putting it right in your hands."

"Would that be such a bad thing?" he murmured.

"It could be. There's nothing to stop you from leaving again. I don't know if I can survive it a second time."

He sat back, disengaging from where he'd tangled his hand into her hair, but keeping his knees pressed against hers as if he could not bear to completely break contact.

"I don't want to leave again," he answered and the certainty in his voice snapped her gaze to his. "You were right that I needed to go and experience the world. I needed to see things I never would have if I'd stayed. But if I ever go exploring again, I want to do it with you, Hope."

Her heart thudded and her pulse raced as a long-forgotten hope tried to claw into her mind. "How can you possibly know that? We have to get to know each other all over again. I've changed. You've changed."

"We have grown, but no matter how much time has passed or how much distance has been between us, you've always been in my heart."

She couldn't reply, still unsure, torn between caution and hope.

"Hasn't it been the same for you?" he pressed.

She could not deny it. Of *course* it was the same for her. She and Ty were as linked as the water and the wind. They had been from the start.

Taking a deep breath, she thought for a moment…before letting her heart decide. She had no idea where this new path would lead them, but just as he'd had to fly from the nest to find his way home, she couldn't resist taking a chance at love with Ty.

"Yes, Ty," she finally whispered. "You have been in my heart since the day we met."

This time, the kiss was anything but tentative or sweet. Lips locked. Tongues danced. Hands touched and caressed. When they broke apart, they were so breathless, they couldn't help but laugh.

Ty dropped to the ground, his back against the ridge of the fountain where she still sat and leaned his head against her knee. She tangled a hand into his hair, brushing through the soft strands. He closed his eyes and tilted his head up as if lost in the intimacy before he gently coaxed her down beside him. She tugged her skirt down and crossed her feet at the ankles. He slid his hand down her thigh, captured her hand and slid it between them. The moment was sweet and ripe with endless possibilities.

"I never could have dreamed this, Hope. I guess I didn't think I deserved all this. A family. A home. A chance at true love."

She leaned her head on his shoulder. "I don't think I did, either."

"But we do. I know we do."

Hope shimmied closer to him, loving how his body heat melded with hers even as the artificial grass beneath her legs itched against her bare skin. She'd be lying to herself if she didn't confess that she'd fantasized about a moment like this when she'd dreamed up the design for the patio. Tyler had embedded himself in the foundation of her soul from the start. And now she knew she'd built a similar place in him.

"I don't know what's going to happen next," she admitted.

He tilted his head so she could see the naughty glimmer in his eye. "Don't you?"

She gave him a soft punch in the bicep. "You know what I mean."

He chuckled, the sound warm and homey, yet also exciting and sexy. "The only thing that matters is whatever next thing that happens, it will include both of us. Together."

Forever.

Thanks for reading. Check out the rest of my books at www.julieleto.com.

DARK PARADISE

KARINA HALLE

This short story was previously published as "Esteban." It features characters from the Dirty Angels Trilogy. Please note that it contains the following potential triggers: suicidal ideation, depression, and infidelity.

CHAPTER 1

I knew that the wave was too dangerous. I knew it and that was why I went for it. It came rolling into Hanalei Bay like a brilliant blue shock wave, diamond-studded from the sun, catching the attention of the bored surfers on this otherwise average day. It called to me like a slippery siren, just as it called to them. But instead of watching it pass underneath my dangling legs, like I had done with every surfable wave in the last hour, I decided to answer the call.

I decided it would be a good way to die.

Determined, I lay down on my stomach and began paddling like a madwoman, knowing the liquid beast was barreling up behind me. I could hear some of the territorial surfers out there were yelling, perhaps to get out of their way, perhaps to warn me, but I didn't care. The golden beach spread out in front of me as kids grabbed their bodyboards and fled from the surf, their parents yelling at them to be careful. They knew the dangers, just as I did.

I wasn't a great surfer. But then again, that was the point.

I sucked in my breath, salt dancing on my tongue, and got to my knees as I felt the massive pull of the wave take me and the board back.

My feet found the rough, beaten surface, my legs bracing for balance. The ocean roared beneath me. This wave was what every surfer could ever dream of, their holy grail, their Moby Dick, and I captured it like fireflies in a jar. I could feel the power, the surge, the sea spray, the sun on my skin. I could feel everything, as if I were finally alive and breathing and part of the world.

And yet living was the last thing on my mind.

I rode that wave for a few seconds that stretched out into eternity. Maybe my life flashed before my eyes, or maybe it flashed behind them. One moment I was up, feeling the immense girth of the wave curling up behind me, and the next I was down, a flower crushed in a closing hand. The board was yanked away from me so hard and fast that the cord was ripped off my ankle, and I was pulled in a million directions before the way down was the only way to go. The wave pummeled me until I took in water and gave up nothing in return.

No fight.

My eyes closed, burned by the salt, and my hair whipped around my head like seaweed. With heavy limbs and a heavy heart, I sank.

The ocean took me under, intent on holding me hostage with no ransom.

No one would have bartered for me anyway.

And then a hand reached out for me in the depths, wrapping around my wrist. I didn't know if it was the hand of life or death. But it had me.

Then another hand grabbed my arm and I felt the water around me surge, my body being pulled upward. I opened my eyes into the stinging blue glow, and past the rising bubbles and foam, I caught a glimpse of a man's face. His expression was twisted in turmoil; I suppose from the act of trying to save me. He obviously didn't know how little I'd appreciate it, how little I was worth it.

Suddenly, I was brought up to the surface, the sun and air hitting me just as the water began to rush out of my lungs. I could only cough until my chest ached, the rest of me completely useless as the man towed me toward the shore. My brain switched on and off, processing everything in splices of film:

The man's longish hair sticking to the back of his bare neck.

The gray clouds that hunkered down above the cliffs of the Na Pali coast.

The people on the beach watching my rescue, hands to their mouths, murmurs in the crowd.

The painfully vivid sky as the man laid me down on the beach, cradling the back of my head in his hands.

The man as he stared down at me—his disturbingly scarred face contrasting with his beautiful hazel eyes framed by wet lashes.

The face of a man I knew would be more dangerous than any wave.

And so, with consciousness slipping out of my hands again, I smiled at him, at the danger I recognized within.

And then the new world went black.

"Are you sure you don't want us to take you to the hospital?" the EMT asked me for the millionth time.

"I'm fine," I said deliberately. "Though I'm getting a headache from all your questions."

"It's really better if—"

I narrowed my eyes at the clean-cut man, even though it hurt my brain to do so. "I didn't call the ambulance, and I have no intention of riding in one to the hospital all the way in Lihue." I paused, inwardly wincing at what I was about to say. "I'm an artist and I'm uninsured."

He gave me a dry look. "Well, if you're going to continue surfing, perhaps looking into insurance is a good idea." But before I could say anything to that, he snapped up his kit and headed back to the ambulance that was purring behind the public restrooms.

I sighed from my perch on top of the picnic table and ignored the curious looks of the drifters who were hanging around underneath the shelter, drinking cheap beer. Water from the rains that had passed by a few hours ago was still dripping off the roof, smacking the concrete and sand below with a desolate sound. The looky-loos who had been twittering about me earlier had gone on their sunburned ways back to the sand and surf, and Hanalei Bay looked as it did before I nearly died.

I was back to being alone. Back to being caught in my thoughts. Back to everything I had tried to escape from.

Except now that I'd actually willed myself to give it all up, there was something that pushed at my mind.

Someone.

The man who had saved me.

Just where had he come from and where did he go? When I came to on the beach a few minutes later after I had blacked out yet again, he was gone, and I was stuck looking at the faces of the panicked tourists, one who must have called the ambulance for me. The man, with his scars that crisscrossed the side of his face, and his vibrant eyes that hinted at the depths within, had completely disappeared.

The least he could have done was stick around so I could thank him.

But *would* I have thanked him? Perhaps if I saw the darkness in him, he saw the same darkness in me.

I got off the table and stood on the stiff grass, careful not hurt my ankle. It was especially tender after my board was ripped away from me, but not bad enough to warrant spending the money to get it checked out. I wondered if my board had washed up on the beach somewhere or if it was lost to the waves, then decided to forget about it. I didn't want to spend an extra minute here, knowing that I'd made a fool of myself by almost dying and all that.

I fished my keys out of my board shorts and headed to the Jeep I'd rented during the last two weeks. I had one week left on it before I was supposed to return to the mainland, back to Doug and the life that was drowning me. I swallowed my bitterness at still having to find a way out of all of this.

On the way back to Kilauea, I drove fast—too fast—nearly smashing into a waiting car as I sped over the one-lane Hanalei bridge, stars in my eyes and the war raging on in my mind. It was a miracle I even pulled into the driveway of my rental house in one piece.

The fact is, I wanted to keep driving. I didn't want to come back even to here, the place that should have been the escape from my marriage, from my job that didn't even insure me, and everything. But that was the irony of trying to escape to an island. There was nowhere to go; you just kept going in circles, coming back to where you started.

I went inside to the kitchen and poured myself an extra-large glass of red wine, wishing I hadn't finished the bottle of Scotch the night before. Leaning against the counter, I stared at the backyard, which disappeared into a thicket of hibiscus and gardenia, the azure sea stretching beyond it. I'd stared at the same scene ever since I arrived, willing myself to paint it. There was a papaya tree in the corner, a small fish pond, a hole in the distressed wood fence where brightly colored feral chickens would come through. This should have been paradise—this should have brought me and my art back to life. But it hadn't.

My phone buzzed and vibrated on the counter. I didn't even look at it. I knew I probably had a million missed calls since I headed out surfing, and I knew they were all either from work or from Doug. Work, because I was sure the temp couldn't handle another day under my boss's direction, and Doug because he just had to know where I was. Not because he cared—he stopped caring two years after our wedding—but because the fact that I took off to Kauai by myself was the biggest fuck-you to his renegade ego that I could have done.

I wondered what he would have thought if he knew I'd almost drowned without his permission, what he could have said if I'd come home with a death certificate. Would he genuinely be upset, distraught at losing his wife because he loved me oh so much—or would he just write me off to be with Justine?

I gulped back the rest of the wine and thought about what the gravestone of Lani Morrison would say on it. Here lies a wife? Here lies an artist? Here lies one lost woman who never quite found her way?

I hoped it would be blank and that people could draw their own stories about my life. They'd all be better than the truth, that Lani Morrison died at the age of thirty-three, childless by choice, locked in an unhappy seven-year marriage with a man who'd been in love with someone else for most of it. She lost her parents to a car crash when she was seventeen, found mediocre fame in her twenties for her watercolor paintings, then when her muse, her "spirit" for the art, left her, she had to find work as a part-time assistant in an office selling dishwashers.

May she rest in peace.

Fuck peace.

I slammed down the glass and it shattered on the marble countertop, sending shards everywhere. As I looked down at the mess, I felt acutely overwhelmed for a second, before I decided to let it all go. I plucked the bottle of wine off the counter and headed out into the backyard, where I sat down on the back stoop and proceeded to drink until all the cab sav was gone and I was even more numb than before.

Though not numb enough to prevent my thoughts from going back to the mystery man, my savior. What was it about him that kept stealing my attention? Every time I tried to picture him, I either saw his face under the water, partially obscured by the bubbles rushing past my eyes, or the sun-kissed look of his neck, his wet hair clinging to it as he pulled me to the shore.

I closed my eyes and leaned my head against the back door, the images replaying over and over in my mind until a noise brought me to attention. It sounded like someone was outside the front of my house.

Carefully easing myself up, feeling more than a bit drunk, I made my way through the cool house to the front door. I opened it and had to blink a few times at what I was seeing.

It was my surfboard, leaning against a potted Phoenix palm. I walked over to it and ran my hands down the smooth sides, then looked around. The street was empty except for a lazy cat waddling through the neighbor's grass. Who dropped it off, and more importantly, how the hell did they know where I was staying?

For the first time that day I felt uneasy, my skin prickling with gooseflesh. As empty as I had been, the fact that someone must have followed me to my house to return it to me was a bit unsettling, yet considerate. I took in a steadying breath and picked up the board, about to take it inside, when a piece of paper fluttered to the pavement.

I placed the board back against the palm and scooped up the paper in my hands. In neat cursive handwriting, the note read: "The next time I save you, you'll want me to."

A strange thrill ran through me as I remembered the man with the face of danger.

I wondered if he *really* knew how hard it was to save me.

CHAPTER 2

I spent the next morning pacing up and down the hallway, trying to figure out what I was going to do with my day. Every now and then I'd wince as my bare feet found yet another slice of glass that I'd missed when I cleaned up the mess from the day before. From time to time I'd stride over to the windows and nervously peer out past the palm fronds, looking for a sign of that man who wanted to save me again.

It was kind of ridiculous, actually, but I was enjoying the suspense, the way my nerves rattled every time a car drove down my street. It gave me a strange sense of focus that had been missing the last few weeks . . . or months. Or years.

Finally around noon, after I managed to get down a bowl of cereal, I decided I'd had enough. I packed a beach bag, grabbed my board, and got in the Jeep. Though Hanalei was my favorite part of the island, I didn't want to head back there. I knew that the November surf was notoriously wicked on the North Shore, part of the reason why I had wanted to go there in the first place.

But this time, it wasn't really about being saved.

It wasn't about dying either.

I steered the Jeep onto the highway and decided to head southeast to Larsen's Beach. It wasn't the easiest beach to get to—I'd have to travel down a road that would coat the car in the island's infamous red dirt before heading down a dangerously steep path to the beach itself. But if this man really wanted to find me, if he wanted to chase me, to save me, all the way there . . . he would.

I parked the Jeep at the end of the red road, finding space along a fence of buffalo grass. I wasn't the only person that day with the idea of surfing at Larsen's; about seven other cars were crammed into the same area. Apparently everyone wanted to take advantage of the sunshine and light winds. Maybe some surfers would have been mad that other people would mean they'd be sharing the breaks, but it made me feel safe, as if I were going on a blind date with someone.

Except that I'd seen him before.

I took my time unloading my board and putting on my sneakers for the hike down, constantly looking over my shoulder in hopes of seeing a plume of red dust rising up through the air. Nothing yet. Maybe the man had just been nice in that note. Maybe he had no intention of saving me again.

I pulled my long black hair into a ponytail and headed past the open gate and down the steep, uneven path that went from the very top of the cliff to the golden beach below. I wasn't far along, still near the top, when I decided to take a moment and observe the waves. Steadying myself with my board still under my arm, I climbed onto a few volcanic boulders that were wedged into the cliffside, rising above the tall grass that obscured my view.

Below, the ocean glistened with patches of turquoise where the bottom was sand, and royal blue where it was rocky. The waves crashed on the reef just offshore, and the tiny figures of surfers were already catching the steady swells. You'd think that just looking at the water, imagining myself back out there, would have brought some fear into my chest, but my fear was different now.

The hair rose on the back of my neck.

"Don't jump," a low, accented voice growled.

I gasped and quickly spun around to see a man—my man—standing on the path and watching me. His eyes widened just as mine did. I had turned so fast with the board that I was toppling to the left, my foot trying to find stability and finding none.

I was going over.

Falling.

I cried out, whipping my head back around to see where I was going to end up, what my doom would be. I wasn't fearing death, but the amount of pain before death.

Or endless pain *without* death.

Then, with reflexes like a cat, he was at me, grabbing on to my arm as the ground beneath me turned to air. The surfboard crashed down the cliff but I was hanging on to him, staring up at his face as he pulled me to safety. Again.

"I wasn't going to jump," I said, breathless. Of course I'd be defensive.

"A simple thank-you would have sufficed," the man said. His accent was Mexican and now that he was standing right beside me, still gripping my arm, I finally had a clear look at him.

He was about six feet tall, with a nicely toned body he wasn't hiding very well under his board shorts and white wifebeater. His skin was this smooth, golden tone that you just wanted to run your fingers over and over again, and played off the strands of bronze in his wavy hair. Those hazel eyes of his were watching closely, and though his dark brows were furrowed with concern, maybe even anger, there was a startling brightness to them.

The scars that lacerated his left cheekbone were ugly as sin, yet there was something almost beautiful about them. They added depth and secrets to a man who was probably in his late twenties. He had a story to tell.

I wondered if I'd be around to hear it.

When I became aware that I was not only staring at him but that he still had a grasp on my arm, I pulled myself away. "You scared me," I explained. "I was watching the waves."

He cocked a brow. "Planning to surf so soon after yesterday?"

I crossed my arms. "It's none of your business what I do. I don't know you."

He smiled prettily. "I'm the man who saved you from a watery grave. I also delivered your board to you. And I believe I might have just saved your life again."

"As I said, you scared me."

He shrugged. "I couldn't be sure, not after yesterday. Hey," he peered over my shoulder, "want me to get your board again?"

I didn't want to look down in case I experienced a bout of vertigo. "It's fine. Maybe it's a sign I should give it up."

He gave me a curious look and then opened his mouth to say something. But he shut it with a smile and then turned around, heading to the path. "If you gave up surfing, how would I keep meeting you like this?"

He trotted down toward the beach. I watched him for a moment before I shook my head and went after him.

"Why are you doing this?" I asked him, carefully following him. Damn, he was quick. "I still don't know you."

"My name's Esteban," he shot over his shoulder. "Now you know me."

"You don't know my name," I called out after him, my knees starting to hurt from the quick descent. Oh God, I hoped he didn't know my name. That would be terrifying.

"I don't," he said without pausing. "But I figure you'll tell me eventually."

"Oh, really?" I called after him. Cocky little bastard. Well, tall bastard. And a savior instead of a bastard. Still . . . cocky.

When the path almost started to level out, he vaulted off into the wild greenery that clung to the cliffs, his athletic form disappearing. For a moment I couldn't hear anything but the sharp wind that rushed up to me, the cry of mynah birds and the waves crashing on the reef.

Time seemed to slow as I took stock of the situation. I had no idea who this guy was other than he was a pretty hot Latino and his name was Esteban. Yes, he was retrieving my surfboard for me—at least I think he was—and yes, he had saved my life. But he'd also followed me to my rental house and to the beach today. That took some sleuthing and was stretching the boundaries of being a Good Samaritan.

"Got it!"

I whirled around, surprised to see him appearing a few feet down the path, my board under his arm, while he wiped away the loose foliage that was clinging to his hair. He strode over to me proudly and lifted the board out in my direction.

When I reached for it, though, he pulled it back to his chest. "Not until you tell me your name."

I tried not to roll my eyes. "It's Lani."

"Lani? Interesting . . . short for something?"

Was this really the time and place for small talk? "It's short for Lelani."

"Lelani, hey? Are you Hawaiian? I thought you'd have better surfing skills than that."

"Actually," I said as I wrestled my board out of his grasp, "I have Hawaiian ancestry. My grandparents were from here. But I just like to come here to . . ."

"Escape life?"

I pursed my lips as I eyed him. Despite the sparkle in his eyes, there was still something odd about him. Though I didn't feel I was in danger, there was still a sense of unpredictability and circumstance that seemed to swirl around us.

"Yes," I said slowly. "To escape life."

He nodded, then asked. "Are you part Japanese?"

"My grandmother was, why?"

He smiled. "No reason other than you're strikingly beautiful."

"Well, thank you," I said, moving to walk past him, trying not to blush.

"That's it?" He reached out and grabbed the back of my board, pushing it to the side so I had to face him. "You smile and then you leave?"

I had no idea what to say. It wasn't that I wanted to leave, but I had a hard time processing anything new. I had been so happy to just plod along on this island, keeping quiet and looking for the easy way out.

Esteban cocked his head toward the beach. "Why not try surfing, like you'd planned? The waves look nice." He took a step toward me, and I imagined his eyes were darkening. "Or is that the problem? It's not dangerous enough for you."

My pulse raced as I bit my lip. I noticed beads of sweat on the crest of his forehead, and wondered if they would taste salty on my tongue.

I really needed to go.

"I was watching you, you know," he said. "I was out on the waves, too, though I know you didn't notice. You were just sitting there, watching every wave pass by. For the longest time, I thought maybe you were a total beginner. But even from far away, I could see it in your eyes."

Shocked, I swallowed hard. Though the sun was bright as sin, I felt a chill creeping up my limbs. "What could you see?" I whispered.

"The shadows," he said simply, as if he were making sense. "I have them, too. You have to in my line of work. But you wanted yours to pull you under."

"Look," I said, trying to appear cool and calm, as if he hadn't seen who I was out there. "It was really nice that you saved me and got my board, but I think we have to part ways here. I'm just here on vacation. I like to surf. I like to paint. I'm here to relax and have a good time, like everyone else." I stuck out my hand so I wouldn't look scared. "Good-bye, Esteban."

When I expected him to be put out, he just smiled at me, so pure against the scars. "Esteban Mendoza. I'm staying at the Princeville Saint Regis. If you ever feel like discussing those shadows of yours."

I was about to tell him I wouldn't be doing that, but he just turned around and headed down the path to the beach. From there I watched him trot toward the water's edge and dive into the clear blue water, swimming powerfully out to the reef. He made it past the breakers, disappearing into the foam before appearing out on the horizon, a tiny dot against the navy swells.

I could have sworn he waved good-bye to me. It must have been my imagination.

After the beach, I stopped by Foodland to pick up another bottle of Scotch and headed straight back to the house. I poured myself a drink, neat, and took it into the shower with me. I stood in there, washing and washing and washing until I felt raw and real and my skin had turned pruney. I could have stayed in there forever, just living in the warmth.

Oddly enough, it felt like I'd taken a shower for the first time in my life. God, how much of my day was always on autopilot.

When I finally dragged myself out, slipped on my robe, and wound my coarse hair into a braid, I decided to call Doug.

He picked up on the fourth ring. Just like always, he made himself seem too busy for me, yet would get mad if I didn't pick up right away.

"Hello?" His voice was distracted, and I heard the distinctive crinkle of a potato chip bag in the background.

"Hi, sweetie," I said, trying to sound cheery and sober.

A pause. "Nice of you to call me back, *finally*. I was trying to reach you yesterday. Where were you?"

"Surfing."

"Not painting?"

"Not painting," I said with a sigh. "So, how are things?"

Now it was his turn to exhale. He launched into tirade against some of the new clients at his work, the tightness of our purse strings, the lack of opportunities. With each sentence I could feel the stress and frustration pour out from him. He often used me as a venting board, though I assumed it was only on the days that Justine wasn't around.

I let him talk, not putting in a word edgewise, not even when he reminded me that the time I was spending in paradise was costing us money we didn't have, and if I wanted to truly make it worthwhile, I'd need to start painting. I'd need to create. I'd need to make something, and something of myself.

Instead I eventually hung up the phone with a stiff "I love you," and poured myself another glass. I let the drink burn on my tongue as I stared at the easels and blank canvases that were hidden in the shadows of the room.

Those damn shadows. They really were here with me, filtering out through my soul, permeating every inch of my life. Just how long had they been living my life for me?

I finished my drink, then placed it down on the counter with a desolate clink.

I googled the number for the Saint Regis and was put through to one Esteban Mendoza.

CHAPTER 3

The next morning I woke up to the sound of a motorcycle outside the house. I barely had time to register that I had slept through my alarm when there was a knock at the door.

Fantastic.

I quickly got out of bed and slipped on my pajama pants, all the while thinking it couldn't be Esteban. We had made plans to do something in the morning, but I'd assumed he would have called me first.

On the way to the door, I paused by the mirror and winced at my reflection. My eyes were sleepy and puffy with smudges of mascara underneath, my hair was a mess, and my nipples were poking out of my camisole. Another knock prevented me from trying to fix myself up.

I opened up the door and lo and behold, Esteban was on the other side, a motorcycle parked behind the Jeep.

He looked surprised at my disheveled appearance and couldn't hide the cheekiness in his grin. "I'm sorry," he said. "I thought we said noon."

I wiped underneath my eyes and crossed my arms over my chest the minute his eyes rested on my breasts.

"You said you'd call me first."

He shrugged, taking my body in, his gaze trailing from my tired face all the way to my bare toes. I felt like I was being dissected. Couldn't say a tiny part of me didn't enjoy it. I couldn't remember the last time Doug looked at me like that. I couldn't remember the last time I wanted him—or anyone—to mentally undress me.

"I'm sorry," he said more sincerely this time. "I should have called." He looked at his watch. "It's eleven thirty . . . want me to come back?"

I sighed. He was already here, and I didn't feel right about turning him away. Luckily I never took too long in getting dressed, so I invited him inside. He said he'd put on a pot of coffee while I got ready. I picked up my clothes for the day, hoping I wouldn't have to ride his motorcycle, and went into the bathroom to do my face.

The only problem with the vacation rental—and it wasn't a problem when you were alone—was that it was extremely *un*soundproof. While I washed my face and put on the barest touches of makeup, I could hear him puttering around in the kitchen. It was an odd feeling having a stranger in the house, doing domestic things while I was in another room. Of course he could have been casing the joint, stealing my camera and the few pieces of jewelry I had brought with me, but I didn't feel that was the case with him.

Then again, other than his name, I didn't know Esteban Mendoza at all.

When I came out of the bathroom I found him standing on the back steps, two cups of coffee in hand, admiring a pair of chickens that were strutting around the backyard. He shot me a winning smile and handed me my cup of coffee like we were old friends.

He nodded at it. "It's black. There was no milk and sugar in the house, so I figured you liked it dark."

I couldn't tell if that was sexual innuendo about his brown skin, but I tried not to dwell on it.

I took the hot mug from him, our fingertips brushing against each other. The brief contact caused my face to grow hot, something I didn't quite understand. I was never shy—introverted, but not shy—but this man made me feel like an awkward teenager again.

"Thank you," I said, tucking a strand of hair behind my ear.

He watched my movements like a hawk and just before his attention became too intense, he smiled. His dimples were such a contradiction to his scars. I had this terrible urge to reach out and touch them, to stroke his face and find out what shadows followed him.

Instead I cleared my throat and said, "Thanks for taking my call last night. I was . . ."

"I know," he said, taking such a large gulp of coffee that I winced, imagining it must have burned going down. "You don't have to explain why. I told you why. I'm just glad you called." He gestured to the yard with his free hand. "This is a beautiful spot."

I nodded. "It is."

"You're a painter."

I gave him a sharp look, feeling intruded.

He tilted his head. "I saw your easels. I saw no art, though, so I could only assume. You have the hands of a painter."

I sipped my drink, gathering my thoughts before I said anything. "I do paint. I came here to . . . but . . . I just haven't."

"You haven't been inspired."

I snorted and shot him a sideways glance. "If you can't be inspired on the most beautiful island on the planet, there's something wrong with you." My smile quickly faded at my last words. There *was* something wrong with me. Fatally.

"Maybe you're not looking in the right place. Inspiration isn't in your backyard or at the bottom of the ocean. It's somewhere else."

I glanced at him curiously. His face was grave but his eyes bright, shining like the sun.

"Come on," he said, tugging lightly at my arm. "I'll show you."

Minutes later I had finished my coffee and was climbing on the back of his bike. Legally you didn't have to wear helmets here, but he still gave me his to wear. Truth be told, I hated motorcycles—I hated the speed and uncertainty, finding them to be more constrictive than freeing. They also forced intimacy with the person you were riding with. Not only did I have Esteban's helmet on my head, which was damp from sweat, though it was a musky, pleasant smell, but I had to put my arms around his waist. This Harley was definitely not a cushy cruiser.

"Where are we going?" I shouted into his ear as he revved the engine.

"Around," he shouted back at me.

"That's not very helpful!"

"Don't worry, it will help you in the end!"

"How do I know that you're not taking me somewhere to kill me?"

He shot me a lopsided smile. "Because you'd already be dead. Besides . . . they call me the nice one."

"Who are *they?*"

He didn't answer. He accelerated and we were flying down the road toward the highway. Esteban was a safe driver, though, and didn't go much faster than the speed limit, which on Kauai was stupidly low, yet I still found myself holding on to him for dear life. My God, he had fucking abs of steel, and somehow I felt guilty just touching them.

It took about ten minutes of us heading south before I began to loosen up a bit and reduced my Kung-Fu grip on his T-shirt. I began to appreciate the speed as we picked it up and the road rushed past us. The scenery was breathtaking; to our right were deep-cut green mountains, straight from the scenes of *Jurassic Park*. To the left were the fields of tall grass and small farm stands, red dirt coating the signs while the Pacific sparkled in the distance.

But despite how much I relaxed, the ride—everything—felt dangerous. It wasn't the same type of danger that I'd been courting, though. This danger was more subtle, more menacing. This danger spelled trouble for the life I'd have to go on living.

Eventually we passed through the towns of Kapa'a, Lihue, and Poipu before I realized we were going quite far off the beaten track.

"Where are we going?" I yelled at him.

"You'll see," he said. "You're not afraid of heights, are you?"

I wasn't. But being afraid of a stranger pushing you off from a great height was a different story.

Soon we passed the ramshackle town of Hanapepe and started zooming up toward the mountains, heading inland. There was only one place for us to go, and I knew where we were going: Waimea Canyon.

It was one of the places I hadn't been before, thanks to its location at the south end of the island. Also, when you're traveling alone, you don't really feel like being a sightseeing tourist.

Eucalyptus trees flew past us as we ascended the mountain road, the foliage becoming greener, the earth redder, the air filling with ethereal mist.

When we zoomed past the most popular lookout over the canyon, I started to get a little nervous.

"Where are we going?" I asked again.

"That view is, how you say, overrated."

We accelerated as we rounded a corner, the colder air snapping against me. I went back to holding on to him for dear life as we passed more and more viewpoints filled with tourists. I started to wonder if this was such a good idea after all. It seemed he was taking me to the end of the road, the end of the line.

That idea hadn't scared me before; it was curious that it was scaring me now.

But eventually when the road did end, it did so at a parking lot with a couple of cars parked and some sightseers milling about. I breathed out a sigh of relief as the bike came to a stop and I was able to get off.

I slipped off the helmet, knowing my hair was probably sticking flat to my head, and Esteban stared at me curiously.

"You seemed a bit scared at the end," he noted.

I swallowed hard and looked away. "Well, I've never been good on bikes."

"It's a good sign to be scared, hey," he said. "When you stop feeling fear, that's when it becomes dangerous. That's when you die."

I resisted the urge to say something, to tell him he didn't know shit. He acted like he knew all this stuff about me, just because he rescued me and saw my "shadows," something we hadn't even touched on yet.

"This is the Puu o Kila Lookout," he said as he lightly touched my elbow and guided me toward an unpaved trail that sloped away from the parking lot. "Not many people know about it. They stop at the one before and never venture on. But this is better."

"And how do you know so much about this island?" I asked him.

"I like to do my research," he said in a low voice, and I followed him as we went down the smooth red banks until suddenly . . . I was breathless.

There, sprawled out in front of us, was a view like nothing I'd see before. The red dirt sloped off sharply with no guardrail to keep us back, and when the drop ended thousands of yards below, the valley begun. It ran green and wide toward the ocean, the cliffs rising up from it on either side, gouged out by millions of years of rainfall and weather. Though the sun was out, clouds passed through the valley, quickly scooting over our heads, so close at times that I wanted to reach out and touch them.

"Careful." His voice whispered at my neck as he gently put his hand around my waist and pulled me back a step. I looked down at my feet and recoiled with horror when I realized how close I had gotten to the edge. It was almost like I had really been going for the clouds.

"It's okay," he said, leading me away from the edge.

I was shaking; I couldn't help it. Jesus, I had been so close to going over.

"Come on, we can get the same view from up here." He took me to where the path sloped up. We were farther back, but the surreal view was the same. Too bad my heart was still beating so fast, my blood pumping loudly in my ears.

Esteban took his hand off me and I felt a strange chill in its absence. "Are you okay?" he asked, his eyes searching mine.

I nodded. "Yes," I said, licking my lips that were suddenly dry. "I'm fine."

"When women say they're fine, they're usually seconds from throwing their shoe at you."

I cracked a smile, my gaze flitting over to him. "Is this from personal experience?"

He shrugged and tucked his wavy hair behind his ear, the highlights catching the gleam of the sun. "I've pissed off my fair share of women. But it's not my fault they all fall so madly in love."

I laughed. "I think you're full of shit."

"Oh, I am," he said, facing me. "Perhaps that's why they throw the shoes."

We lapsed into silence, our attention turned back to the view. Now that I was calming down and we were farther away from the edge, I was able to take in the view as much as I could. It was like watching a moving painting. There was something so . . . unbelievable, unnatural about finding such beauty in real life. I felt like I had stepped into my own art.

And that was when it hit me like a kick to the shin.

I was inspired.

The feeling, the itch to paint, to capture the crazy, otherworldly beauty of this place, the rich, thriving greens and the opulent blues and the vista that seemed carved out of time.

"I told you so," Esteban said.

"Told me what?"

"That you were looking in the wrong place."

Thoughtfully, I rubbed the back of my hand across my lips, not sure what to say to that. But he was right. We stood there for a little while longer, not saying anything, and pretty soon the silence was as comfortable as warm flannel.

I thought about the man standing beside me, the relaxed yet intuitive way about him, the way my feelings about him swung from easygoing to vaguely fearful in the blink of an eye. He was handsome as hell, the scars only adding to his rugged appeal.

I needed to know more.

"So you said *they* call you the nice one," I said. "You never said who they were. How do I know I can trust their opinion?"

He scratched at his sideburn and squinted at the sun. "They're my colleagues. Out of all of them, I am the . . . most civilized. Though I guess that's not saying much, hey."

"What kind of work do you do?"

He shoved his hands in the pockets of his board shorts. "Oh, you know. This and that. I'm usually a tech guy. Sometimes I help out in other areas of the business."

"What business is it?" I asked, and immediately felt stupid for doing so. From his evasive nature, to the darkness, to his very scars, I knew whatever he did, it wasn't working at Target.

"I'll tell you the truth if you tell me the truth," he said without looking at me.

"Okay . . ." I started, feeling a little bit uneasy. "What do you want to know?"

When he picked up my left hand in his and raised it to eye level, my skin immediately began tingling.

"You're married. Why aren't you wearing your wedding ring?"

My chin jerked down. "How do you know I'm married?"

"Tan line," he said. "You live somewhere where you get a lot of sun, and normally you wear your ring. But here you don't. Why?"

I looked at my hand, at the sun spots and faint lines and a tiny splice of lightened skin where my ring usually was. "I don't know. I was in the water so much, I took the ring off. I guess I haven't put it back on. It's on my dresser."

"I see," he said.

I frowned. "It's true."

"I believe you. I was just curious."

I eyed his bare left hand. "Are you married?"

"Nope," he said with a smile. "I don't think I'm cut out for it."

"I'm glad you know that," I said solemnly as clouds momentarily blocked the sun. "Men aren't cut out for it. But so many think they are."

I knew he could tell I was talking from personal experience, but luckily he let it go. He cleared his throat. "Is that what you wanted to know? If I was available?"

The silky way he said "available" sent a rush of blood through me. "No.

What business are you in? I mean, unless you're a CIA agent and you'd have to kill me first."

"I'm Mexican," he said. "The closest thing we have to the CIA *is* the CIA."

I stared at him with impatience until he continued.

"I'm in the import and export business."

I raised a brow. "Of?"

"Drugs."

I froze. He couldn't be serious. Of course he wasn't. If you were involved in importing and exporting drugs, you didn't just tell a stranger that.

And that was when the hairs at the back of my neck danced. He wasn't joking, was he? I stared at him, afraid to see the truth in his eyes, but his scars and that glimmer of burning darkness within told me otherwise.

He was a drug dealer. He was part of a cartel. An actual fucking Mexican drug cartel.

I tried to swallow, feeling like there was a lump in my throat. "Oh," I said stupidly.

"Are you afraid of me now?" he asked with intensity.

I squared my shoulders and looked him in the eye. "No more than I was before."

"I saved your life, you know," he said. "You shouldn't fear someone who won't let you die."

"Why not?" I countered. "They might love granting something and then taking it away."

"Lani," he said, and my name never sounded so sweet. "You don't trust me because you don't trust yourself."

"You know nothing about me."

"I know you're in an unhappy marriage. That you're struggling to find your art again. That you feel this life holds nothing for you anymore, and you think that you're doing your husband and the world a favor if you just . . . disappeared."

I hated the way he—this stranger, this fucking drug dealer—thought he knew me.

"You're wrong," I lied.

"Then why are you here, with me, now, looking to find those shadows?"

I opened my mouth to speak, but nothing came out. I didn't even know what to say.

Esteban reached out and touched my arm gently. My skin buzzed under his fingers, feeling alive, as if it had been nothing but dead cells before.

"Some fear will kill you," he said. "Some fear will open your eyes. I know all about the difference."

I let out a shaky breath. He was getting under my skin and his occupation didn't help the situation. Still, I found myself asking, "So, what are you doing on Kauai?"

He smiled and removed his hand. "Ah, the million-dollar question. How about I tell you about it over dinner?"

I smiled warily. "Is that code for 'dump my body somewhere afterward'?"

"I told you," he said breezily, clapping his hands together, "that isn't my intention. You took a chance on coming here today, didn't you?"

I looked away, letting the scenery fill my sight. "I did."

"And it was worth it, wasn't it?"

I nodded, still not used to the competing feelings of fear and exhilaration running through me. "It was."

"Come on then," he said, stepping away from me and jerking his head toward the parking lot. The golden strands in his surfer hair caught the sunlight that was piercing through fast-moving clouds. "Let's get you home, get you rested. Maybe when I pick you up tonight, you'll be splattered with paint. That would make me very happy."

That would have made *me* very happy. I followed him to the bike and shot one last glance at the kaleidoscope of greens that tinted the lush cliffs. I couldn't imagine recreating such beauty, but I knew in my heart I was about to try.

CHAPTER 4

It wasn't that I didn't think there was something wrong with the scenario. It was more like what *wasn't* wrong with the scenario. Everything that had happened since the day I almost drowned had been nothing but wrong. Never mind my mental state, the thoughts of hopelessness, desperation, and despair. Never mind those shadows that trailed inky fingers over my skin and tried to pull me back under, to let everything go and forget.

There was Esteban, a total stranger, who had admitted to me that he was part of a drug cartel. He had rescued me in ways that were not just lucky but calculated. Nothing was accidental when it came to him. Then there was the fact that I willingly let him whisk me away to a perilous place, all while on the back of a motorcycle. And of course the fact that I had agreed to go to dinner with him.

Perhaps that was the most troubling part of all. I was a married woman —an unhappily married woman, as he so astutely pointed out—but a married one, nonetheless. My marriage vows at this point were no more sacred than my own life, but they still meant something, which in turn meant there was something so very wrong about agreeing to go to dinner with another man.

And yet, despite all these things, all the things that were red flags waving as obnoxiously as a matador's cape, I wasn't worried.

Why?

Because when Esteban came to pick me up later that night, I was in the backyard painting the last rays of the sunset. Streaks of pink, gold, and purple were in the sky and on my canvas and dotted on my white T-shirt. I was touched by color.

"That's beautiful," he commented, surprising me with his presence.

I only briefly looked over my shoulder at him, too afraid to take my eyes off the scene. A few doves cooed in the nearby bushes, and I wished I could add audio to my painting.

"I suppose you just waltzed into my house?" I asked mildly.

"Yes, sorry about that. I knocked a few times, but there was no response. I did tell you seven, didn't I?"

"You did," I said. I dabbed a bit of ochre on the horizon. "But I lost track of time."

"And I'm glad to see it." I heard him walk down the back steps and toward me. The chickens that had been pecking at the ground clucked and ran back through the hole in the fence in a flurry of feathers. I felt him stop right behind my back. "Should I come back later, Lani? Or perhaps, not at all?"

There was an edge, a coldness to his last words, as if he was hurt. It was absurd to think that a member of a drug cartel could feel slighted.

I sighed and carefully rested my paintbrush on the easel's ledge. Then I turned around and brushed my hair out of my eyes with the back of my hand, careful not to get any paint on my face. "I'm sorry," I said and offered him a shy smile. "This light is disappearing anyway. I was about to wrap it up. Give me a few minutes and I'll be ready to go."

He smiled in return, his greenish eyes softening. It was only then that I realized he cleaned up really well. Gone were the board shorts; instead he was wearing gray slacks and a short-sleeved white dress shirt with the first two buttons undone, his skin glowing gold. His hair was tamed by what looked like gel, and he'd shaven. His look was elegant and casual all at the same time, and had it not been for the scarring on his face, that constant reminder of his job, I would have thought he was like any well-dressed man out there.

But he wasn't like everyone else. Wasn't that why I picked up the paintbrush?

True to my word, I washed up quickly until the only traces of paint were lines of lavender caught in my cuticles. Then I touched up my makeup and slipped on a plain yellow shift dress. I debated on bringing a cardigan, but today was a few degrees warmer than normal, and I knew the evening would be just as balmy. I had no idea if we were going to a fancy restaurant, but this was Kauai and I had to assume that my flip-flops would be tolerated.

I walked out into the kitchen where Esteban was drinking a glass of white wine. I'd told him to help himself; I just didn't think he'd be so literal about it.

"You look beautiful," he said, his gaze raking over me.

I plucked the wineglass from his hands and took a sip. "Thank you." His eyes never left my lips. It should have made me feel uncomfortable, but it didn't. Though I knew if this kept up, the way he was looking at me, it eventually would. "Shall we get going?"

"With those shoes?" he asked, pointing at my Reefs. "You might lose them on the bike."

I smiled wryly and put down the glass, then picked up my purse from the counter. "I'm pretty good at keeping articles of clothing on." He opened his mouth to say something but I went on. "We'll take my Jeep. You just give me directions."

He appraised me for a moment, running his fingers along his dimpled chin. "All right. Nothing wrong with the woman calling the shots."

I rolled my eyes and we headed out to the car.

Though the restaurant ended up being close by, in the Princeville Resort where he was staying, being in a car with Esteban was more challenging than the motorcycle ride. I felt the need to keep the conversation going, but I wasn't sure how. The things I really wanted to talk about seemed inappropriate, and the way he stared at me didn't help either.

"You seem nervous," he said with an elbow propped up, leaning casually against the door.

I raised my brows. "I'm not nervous."

"You keep biting your lip."

"Maybe I'm just hungry."

"You've gotten funnier, you know that?"

I eyed him quickly. "Since when?"

"Since this morning."

"You don't know me very well. I'm often funny."

"Maybe in a past life. In this life, you've been nothing but sad."

When I shot him a look, he smiled. "It's all right, hey? You started painting. That made you happy. That's a start."

I tightened my grip on the wheel. The generic rock from the radio station hummed in the background. I was about to bite my lip but stopped, suddenly conscious.

Then I looked back to the road and cleared my throat. "You make it sound like you had something to do with it."

I could tell he was smiling when he said, "I just wanted you to be inspired. It worked."

"And tonight, is this the same thing?"

"You're awfully suspicious," he said. "I've saved your life, twice, brought back your inspiration for your art, and now I'm about to buy you an extraordinary meal."

"And that's it?"

He laughed. "Sure. That's it. I'll tell you this, though, the meal doesn't have to be the only . . . ," he paused, "*extraordinary* thing to happen tonight."

The silken quality to his words conjured up an image in my mind of me facedown in some swanky hotel room, with him removing my thong, dragging it down my legs with the tip of a 9mm handgun. I don't know why I conjured up that scene, but I found myself blanking on it, heat flushing on my chest and cheeks. I squirmed slightly in my seat.

"Does that interest you?" he said, his voice lower now.

I had to pretend that it didn't, even though my body was currently screaming the opposite.

"Dinner sounds wonderful," I said.

He smiled. "Good, good."

Soon we pulled up to the restaurant, and the valet took the jeep. Esteban held out his arm for me, and I hesitated for a moment before I took it.

The restaurant was beautiful, swanky in this beachy way with low lighting, sand-colored tablecloths, and dark teak furniture. A centerpiece of frangipani floated in a small dish lit by candles.

We were given an amazing seat, right by the edge, where the restaurant was open to the ocean. You could hear the steady roar of waves as they crashed against the cliffs in the darkness below. It was a dramatic and appropriately primal setting for someone like Esteban.

"Are you impressed?" he asked, a wicked curve to his mouth.

I nodded, knowing he must have requested the table especially for me, for *us*. I couldn't fathom why, though. He did know I was married, though he probably figured if it was that important to me, I wouldn't have come. There was nothing innocent or accidental about us being together anymore, not with the way my thoughts were turning toward him anyway, and he knew it.

He knew it and he was using it to his advantage. I wondered if I was there with him because I still felt I owed him. That was what the moral part of me wanted to think. But I was beginning to think that the moral part of me drowned in the ocean all those days ago. My morality was floating with the sharks.

Esteban quickly ordered us two mai tais, telling me that the bar at the restaurant had the best ones (as did every other place on the islands, apparently), and then folded his hands in front of him, a gold ring with a jade stone in it gleaming in the candlelight.

I was thankful for the conversation starter. "That's a lovely ring," I told him, gesturing to it.

He smiled. "Thank you."

Not as forthcoming as I had hoped. "Is that from a significant other?"

He raised a brow to that and then smiled politely at the waiter as our mai tais were delivered. He nodded at the drink. "Try it. Tell me I'm wrong."

He was skirting the question, but okay. I had a sip. Not too sweet, with just enough fruit and rum. It was pretty perfect as far as mai tais went. I started playing with the purple orchid it was served with.

"You are not wrong," I admitted.

"I rarely am."

"Who gave you the ring?"

He admired it on his hand. "Perhaps I bought it."

I shook my head. "No. It's not really your style. You're wearing it out of respect or obligation."

His mouth ticked up as he eyed me steadily. "You're good. You're very good. You should come work with me, hey?"

I kept watching him, waiting for an answer, something about him to hold on to.

He sighed. "It's from my brother."

"Your brother?"

"Yes," he said carefully. "He . . . has funny ways of showing his affection.

I almost died once, you know." His eyes flicked up to me, their green depths glittering. "But I wasn't trying to die."

I ignored that remark. "What happened?"

He shrugged. "Nothing out of the ordinary. A car bomb."

I choked on my drink and started coughing. He leaned over in his seat, concerned, but I waved him away, my hand flapping rapidly.

"I'm fine, I'm fine," I squeaked out when I could. When I finally got myself under control, I was still blinking at him in disbelief. The words couldn't quite settle into my brain. "A car bomb?" I whispered.

He stroked the scars on his face. "Where do you think I got these pretty little souvenirs?"

"Not from a car bomb," I said honestly as I glanced around to make sure no one was listening. The man had said he was part of a drug cartel, but I suppose I never really understood the reality of it. This wasn't some movie, some story. This was real life, a drug lord's life, and somehow I had gotten licked by it, like a hand darting in and out of a candle flame.

"Well, I did. Wrong place, right time. Or maybe not, maybe it's the other way around. It was, in some ways, the best thing that could have happened to me. Becoming so—tainted, physically—hurt my way around some of the women I was used to having, but on the other hand, I was able to stay low and play dead. I let my brother think I was gone. I let Javier think I was gone."

"Who is Javier?"

A darkness came over his eyes. "He is not important right at this minute, not here, with you." He took a sip of his drink. "By pretending I was dead, that I died in that bomb, I was able to get a second chance at life. I had a chance to go . . . straight, as you would call it. Unfortunately, there are certain types of people cut out for certain types of jobs. I am one of those people. Leaving is impossible. It wasn't long until I came back from the dead." He sighed and twisted the ring around his finger. "When my brother, Alex, found out, he gave me this ring. He said the jade would bless me and protect me, and in some ways, remind me that I was valuable."

He cleared his throat and splayed his long fingers out on the table. "The ring was the nicest thing he'd ever done for me. Soon after that, he went back to pretending I didn't exist. I guess giving me this eased his conscience. Perhaps he was too afraid I would disappear again. In this business, you push your loved ones away. You don't dare invite in the pain. Love is weakness."

"That's sad," I said.

He pursed his lips. "I would have assumed you, of all people, would have agreed."

I stiffened. There he was hitting me deep with things he shouldn't glean from me. He didn't know me. He didn't. He couldn't.

Esteban went on, stirring his drink. "Loving people *is* weak. We've all been taught that. It's the only way to survive in my business. But I am guessing it's the same for everyone. You may lose love to death. You may lose love to another man. Or you may lose love because you lost it somewhere along the way, and you were just too proud to stop and pick it up." He smiled coyly. "So, which way did you lose it?"

I lost it when my husband cheated on me with my best friend. When he continued his affair. And I continue to lose it, every single day. I'll lose it until I'm just an empty sieve.

I didn't say that to Esteban, of course. He already *thought* he knew me—it would be dangerous if he really did.

He wasn't waiting for a response, either. The green in his eyes shone knowingly. He let me keep my cards hidden.

The rest of dinner went well enough. The dinner was phenomenal, and the food—soft, flakey ono over red curry and rice—was a sharp reminder that my taste buds had been sleepwalking until then. The mai tais kept coming, and I felt warmth fill me up from the inside, especially when the conversation lulled and Esteban had taken to staring at me in this absolutely carnal way that just screamed sex.

I was tempted to slip off my flip-flops and slide my bare foot up his pants leg. It would be completely unlike me, completely objectionable and completely wrong. And yet, the sexual tension between us had been mounting, becoming unbearable. The high I got from painting was starting to wear off, and even though I could see the lilac around my fingernails, I wanted something more. Another chance to prove that I was alive, and that I had some spark left in me.

Just before I was about to suggest we take a walk on the beach, his phone rang, playing Darth Vader's theme from *Star Wars*. Okay, that had to be his boss.

He glanced at the screen in annoyance, and his finger hovered above it as he debated whether to answer it. Finally, he shot me an apologetic look. "Sorry, I have to take this," he said, and held it up to his ear.

"Yes?" he said into the phone, polite but brimming with thinly veiled annoyance. He listened, closing his eyes. "I am busy right now. Yes. Having dinner. Why? Fish. Of course I am not alone." A long pause and Esteban's gaze moved to me. "I'm sitting with a very stunning woman. You would like her. No, I will not tell you her name." Another pause. He looked at his watch. "I have fifteen minutes, there is plenty of time."

Time for what?

He sighed. "Must you? Fine." He cleared his throat and reached across the table to give me his phone. "He would like to speak with you."

I raised my brows. "Who? Your boss?"

He nodded, his lips twisting into a grimace.

"Why does he want to talk to me?" I asked, feeling utterly confused and frightened. I stared at the phone, not wanting to take it.

"Please," Esteban said. I could have sworn there was a hint of desperation on his face.

Jesus. Fine, I'd talk to him, the fucking boss of a drug cartel.

I gingerly took the phone from him and stared at the screen. It just said Darth Vader on it. Helpful.

"Hello?"

There was silence.

"Hello?" I said again.

Someone on the other end of the line took a breath. "You have a very pretty voice," a man said. His voice was smooth, glacial, and calm with only the slightest hint of a Mexican accent.

"Thank you?"

"What is your name?" the man asked.

I didn't want to say, now that Esteban wouldn't tell him. "What is *your* name?" I asked. "The phone says you're Darth Vader."

The man on the other end—Darth Vader—laughed. Esteban was staring at me, wide-eyed. Well, if didn't want me to tell his boss that, then he shouldn't have handed me the phone.

"Well," he said when he eventually recovered. "I can be Darth Vader for you, if you want." His voice was as seductive as satin sheets, but I wasn't fooled.

"So, why did you want to speak to me?" I asked, wanting nothing more than to hang up the phone and go back to the tiny slice of paradise that Esteban and I had created.

"I was just curious as to who had captured Este's eye, that is all. I also wanted to verify that he was indeed occupied. Though, from the sounds of it, you don't sound occupied enough."

"We were finishing up dinner when you called. We haven't had a chance," I told him. I didn't elaborate on what. I could tell that was going unsaid.

"What a pity," the man said. "Just so you know, if he gets his job done properly, he'll be leaving the day after tomorrow. So, perhaps you might want to plan around that."

"What is the job?" I couldn't help but ask.

The man chuckled, the sound creamy and rich. "He'd tell you, but he'd probably have to kill you. And I would definitely need to know your name." His voice became serious over that last word, serious enough to send a chill up my spine. This guy was not joking. I heard him inhale, a slow, wicked sound. "May I please speak to Este?"

Yeah, no problem. I didn't say anything, I just quickly handed the phone back to Esteban and told him I was going to the restroom. I felt extremely uneasy after that phone call, and needed to try to get my wits about me.

Inside the swanky bathroom with its polished chrome and gleaming glass sinks, I eyed myself in the mirror. I looked different somehow, like I was a foreigner in my own world. I looked scared but I also looked . . . pretty. My eyes were clear and bright, my skin flushed and glowing. My hair was glossed back into a smooth ponytail. I didn't think I had done anything different to myself, but maybe it was all in my head. Maybe the art had started to seep into my body.

Maybe I needed another way to get my fill.

I stared at myself for a few moments, running through all the scenarios in my head. There were only two. I would say good-bye to Esteban here. He would do whatever job he had to do—a job I had no business knowing. I would remain in Hawaii, trying to recapture the fire I'd felt earlier in the day. I'd try to find that finicky will to go on, alone. And if I couldn't . . . well, the ocean was always right there.

Or I could go back to the table. Take Esteban down to the beach. Try to find myself in his touch. And if I went out, I went out with a bang. A fleeting glimpse of the stars and possibility before the shadows came for me.

I'd lost love with my husband. I'd lost love with myself. I wanted to find something, anything, before I lost everything.

I went back to the table and saw Esteban standing, waiting for me with his chair pushed in. His phone was nowhere in sight. I quickly grabbed my purse and said, "Where shall we go next?"

His brows quirked up, as if unsure what to do with the question. "The beach?" he suggested. "There's a path by the cliff here."

I smiled. "You know everything, don't you?"

"That's why they call me the smart one."

"I thought they called you the nice one."

"Oh. That, too."

"Who was that on the phone?"

His eyes sought the ceiling. "My boss is Javier. He controls the operation. In fact, he controls pretty much all of Mexico. Well, almost. We're working on a few things."

"Are any of those things the reason you are here?"

He smiled, white teeth against tanned skin. His scars rippled with the movement, so darkly beautiful. He held his arm out for me. "Shall we go to the beach?"

I nodded, my nerves buzzing with possibilities.

We left the restaurant and he led me down the tiki-torch-lit paths past fancy condominiums. The night was beautiful; the stars were out along with a fingernail moon. It was impossibly romantic, impossibly dangerous. The path down the cliff was unlit, and thanks to the dark and the instability of my flip-flops, I was relying on Esteban to keep me safe. I put my trust in someone who probably couldn't be trusted.

And yet, eventually I felt sand beneath my feet. The wild ocean crashed against the beach in waves of ink dotted with silver sparkles, reflections from the moon. A balmy breeze caressed my face like a gentle lover. My whole body rippled with excitement I hadn't felt in years and years and years.

I felt like I was waking up.

We walked along the sand in silence, heading toward the surf. The foam churned steps away from our feet. Esteban was now holding his shoes in his hand and behind his back. He stared out at the dark horizon, breathing in deeply through his nose. The wind pushed his wavy hair off his face.

"What are you thinking?" I asked him softly, though I supposed I had no business to.

He didn't seem to mind. "I am thinking that I am lucky."

"How so?"

He turned to look at me, the moonlight in his gaze. "That I met you. I was not planning on meeting anyone. But here you are."

"But you leave soon."

He nodded once. "I am leaving. And I will go back to Mexico and all I'll have of you will be memories. We won't call each other. We won't write. We won't e-mail. What we have will remain in the Pacific. Where it belongs."

I didn't understand. How was that lucky?

"You're a beautiful woman, Lani. You're talented, smart. You have a lot going for you, which you refuse to see. Maybe you're too stubborn. Or maybe you still don't think you deserve a second chance. But I will leave here having known you and having made you smile. The memories will be good enough for me. I'll find someone else, someone available, someone who is cut out for my lifestyle. And I'll thank you for that."

Where the hell did his confidence come from, the idea that everything would be okay, even in the line of work he was in? I didn't understand it.

He turned his body so he was facing me and put his hand behind my neck, holding me there. His voice lowered. "Sometimes people come into our lives for just a second, just long enough to let us know that hope exists. Will you let me be your hope, if not for just this night?"

I didn't have time to react before he kissed me.

It went deep, deep inside, stoking a fire I never knew had been building.

I heard his shoes drop to the sand as he sank his hands into my hair. They tugged a little bit at the strands, and I cried out into his warm mouth. His tongue was silky and smooth, making me wet. He slid one hand down to my ass, cupping it firmly. I had never felt a need so powerful, and from the way he pressed his hard erection against me, I could tell he felt the same.

Until Darth Vader's theme song filled our ears.

"Shit!" Esteban groaned and pulled away, pulling the phone out of his pocket.

I felt like I should be annoyed, but knew I had no right to. "It's been more than fifteen minutes, hasn't it?"

He nodded and adjusted his pants before turning his back to me, the phone to his ear.

"*Sí*," he said quickly. There was a pause, then he hung up. He slowly turned to face me and a sober smile graced his lips. "I have to go. Now. I am so sorry."

I shook my head. My heart was still beating so fast, and my clit was throbbing like I was going to die without release. But I understood. I took in a deep breath. "It's fine. Go. Go do your job."

"You can get back up the hill?" he said. "I can carry you on my back, but I have to run."

"It's easier to go up than down," I told him reassuringly. "I'll be fine. I'll . . . talk to you tomorrow?"

"Yes," he said. Then he grabbed my face in his warm hands and kissed me hard. He took off sprinting across the sand. I had no idea where he was going, but whatever he was about to do, it would be something bad, part of a world I would never have to know about.

Once he disappeared up the path and my hormones had calmed down, I turned to look at the ocean. There was a strange hollowness in my chest. Was this it? Was this all there was to my life? Just the waves again, beckoning me to join them, to sink into depths where love couldn't touch me?

I stood there on the private beach, bathed in moonlight, and watched. And waited. Waited for my legs to start moving, to walk into the water and drown.

But I didn't. Because tomorrow was another day. And someone wanted to see me smile.

Though it was dark, it was still paradise.

———

Thanks for reading. Check out the rest of Karina Halle's books on her website at www.authorkarinahalle.com.

THE END OF US

KASEY METZGER

In the beginning we lied.

We lied about being friends. That it was all we were. We lied to each other and to anyone who asked.

It was the kind of relationship that didn't just end. It wasn't quick. No, the end of us was a slow, painful death that took almost two years.

I remember the last night of our true *relationship*. Before that night, we'd spent almost every day and night for six months together. Then he went away for the weekend and didn't come back the same. I barely saw him after that. I don't know what happened that weekend. Why it was over for him and why he couldn't tell me.

We lied in the end too. He lied about it being over, but he didn't let me go. I lied about moving on, but I couldn't. Not with him pulling me back in every time I thought I was over him. And then eventually, those lies took root and became true.

"Drinking tonight, Court?" Ryder nudges me.

"Sipping tonight," I tell her. "I'm drinking exactly one drink tonight and it's this one." I swirl around the beer bottle.

"How are you holding up?" She asks in that knowing way only a best friend can. I know her eyes are stuck on me the way mine are stuck on Brooks. He's engaged in one of Jimmy's insane stories about his latest outrageous injury, like tonight isn't goodbye and it's just another summer night. We're standing on the driveway of his childhood home on the last night before he leaves this place. He signed his life to the military the day he turned eighteen. A ticket out of this nowhere town in the Midwest.

"I'm good." A lie. "Great, actually." Another lie.

"Right." She squeezes my hand. "Well, I'm going to take shots and hit on your brother." She winks and walks away, leaving me to my own devices. I guess Ryder thinks it's funny to set her sights on Jack, for my brother to have a fling with my best friend seeing how I did the same thing to him.

It makes more sense for Jack to be here than me. Brooks and Jack grew up doing everything together. They're best friends while I was the annoying little sister, until I wasn't. Little sister isn't fair to say - we're Irish twins and have always been in the same grade level.

"Glad you could make it." Brooks stalks up to me.

I don't remember the last time I was this close to him. "You know I wouldn't miss this." I look up at him. He holds my gaze and the butterflies erupt inside me.

Even after these past few months of being done with whatever it was we had, I have to fight the urge to lean into him. He's not mine. Maybe he never was.

"Stay by me tonight?" He asks with a sincerity that makes me melt.

I can only nod in response. I'd stay with him every night.

The usual crowd shows. Any excuse to drink without being harassed by our parents, who are also present, just in the backyard. Over the years, our parents have all gotten close too. This is as much a goodbye party for them as it is for us. I think they've given up on the thought of us not drinking until twenty-one, and know we'd find a way to do it anyway with or without their consent.

Unfortunately, the usual crowd includes Rachel, Brooks' ex-girlfriend. They had been together since pretty much elementary school. Almost inseparable until a year ago when she ended things. They had been a package deal and she was around as much as Brooks was.

"I should go say hi," Brooks mumbles before leaving me for her.

I have no claim to him, and I was the one who came after her, but it stings all the same. When they broke up, he came around just as much as before, only he didn't have her around. Our house had been home base for everything. Jack's friends spent more time under our roof than their own. And when Jack and I got in trouble with our parents, his friends were invited over for the punishment as well. So, it wasn't unusual for any of them to be in our house without Jack around. It happened often enough that I was used to sharing the space with them. They could have been my friends in a different life, if Jack wasn't my brother. But he is, and that has always made me *Jack's sister*.

I guess that's how it started with Brooks and me. He stayed at our house the following weeks after their break up, with or without Jack. I've always been a home-body and was around. He didn't talk about Rachel and I didn't ask questions. We spent our time in the moment. Like the walls were a barrier and time stood still. It started with sharing blankets on the couch during shows. Then cooking together and sharing meals.

Soon we ventured outside the walls of the house for dinner or movies. The only difference from before when this happened was that we weren't in a group. This was just us since everyone else is busy.

One night, Rachel saw us out together and confronted Brooks. They ended up arguing outside the restaurant, and I made the decision I'd rather walk home than deal with whatever it was they had going on. But then Brooks came in and paid, even though I'd been paying for myself each time before, and asked me to take a drive with him. I didn't know what they fought about, only that something had changed. He didn't joke or laugh; it was like his shine was gone. What would have been sing-yelling our favorite songs in the car became talks about the future and who we want in it. We drove for hours, just winding through county roads, in different circles until we ended at his house. Not mine. It was the first time I stayed the night.

We slept in the living room, on separate couches with some dumb comedy movie on in the background. Rachel texted me the next day, asking what was going on between us, and I told her the truth. Nothing. Nothing had happened with us.

Brooks kissed me the next night. And every night after for the next six months. We spent each one together, either at his house or mine. Jack didn't have anything to say about it; not that we saw him much anyway. We stayed at Brooks' most of the time. It didn't matter if school was the next day or not. We were together.

In the halls though, we kept our distance. The looks Rachel shot me were enough to keep me away. I didn't mean to hurt her, and not that she believed me, but there truly was nothing going on when she had asked.

That was how it went, until it stopped. One weekend, Brooks went on a guy's trip with Jack and their other friends. When he returned, I surprised him in his bed. It didn't go well. Still, I didn't let one bad night ruin things, and since Valentine's day was right around the corner I planned a date for us. He showed. That was about the only good thing for the night. Something happened and when he came back, we were done, even if it took me time to realize that.

I didn't try after that, and neither did he. Slowly, we faded away into nothingness. He didn't come over as much, and when he did, I hid in my room. I couldn't see him, not when I didn't have any answers. Jack wasn't much help either. When I asked him about their trip, he told me the only time Brooks and I were mentioned was when everyone gave Brooks their approval. When I realized we were actually done, I didn't ask Jack if he knew what went wrong. He's my brother and Brooks is his friend. I didn't want to place him in the middle now, when he hadn't considered him when we started.

Jimmy rubs his hand on the small of my back pulling me away from whispers of the past. "Hey Courtney, you good over here?"

He's been as close to Jack and Brooks as anyone else; always a constant in their group. He's as handsome as Brooks and has never had issues finding someone to spend his time with. I can't say I've been immune to his good looks or charming personality either. But we've always been playful and neither one has dared to approach the line drawn in the sand. Not like Brooks and I did.

"Yeah." I smile but it feels hollow.

"How are you doing with everything?" He digs deeper.

"I'm okay, I guess. I'm going to miss him." I take a drink of the beer I've been rationing.

"Hey!" Brooks wanders over as soon as he sees Jimmy and me talking. "You talking to my girl?" He throws an arm around me and pulls me in. I'd forgotten what being his feels like, and the way he is now has me spinning.

Jimmy pushes Brooks' shoulder back light heartedly. "Only about how finally you might get some abs when they whip you into shape." They both laugh, and Brooks lifts his shirt revealing his already chiseled abdomen.

"If you're jealous just say so." He drops his shirt and ushers me away. "I thought you were going to stay by me," he whispers in my ear.

"I will," I answer back.

I don't remind him how he was the one to walk away from me to talk to Rachel when she showed up. I don't care anymore. Not when he left her to come back to me. I guess that's the game Rachel and I are stuck playing.

The end of the night finds us calling back to past days, and I end up in Brooks' bed once more. It's nothing more than sleep, but sleep where he holds me again. Another night when I think there will be no more.

But he's leaving. And he's leaving soon.

Breakfast is not much more than hungover grumblings between the usual crowd. I'm fine, having stuck true to my one beer for the night. Ryder looks rough, though. She took full advantage of parental-punishment-free drinking.

It's unceremonious, with the dry eggs and flimsy bacon and terrible service at our last gathering before everyone goes their separate ways. While Jack is staying in town for community college, Ryder and I were accepted at the state school a couple of hours away and plan to room together. Brooks is going to training camp and everyone else is starting their own plans as well. This really is the last time we'll all gather before life claims us.

Last night- last night with Brooks didn't feel like goodbye it felt like hello all over again. And I'd wait for him if he asked me to. I'd be his once more, no matter the distance.

But he didn't.

All I have is a couple more hours with him, reminding me that my heart has never really let him go.

The bill for food comes and I buy Jack's meal. He's my ride home and it feels like paying for him is the nice sister thing to do.

I'm not ready for the moment that's coming.

We all walk out of the diner and the world shifted in the time we were in the restaurant. For me, it's not the same. Not now, when everything I want is getting on a plane. The pit in my stomach opens up and might swallow me whole.

Brooks says goodbye to me first. He holds me tight and kisses the top of my head. He doesn't say anything and I can't either. I don't ask him what we are. I can't. Not when he's leaving and all we had was the ghost of a relationship. He releases me and that's it.

Small pebbles of hope I'd collected from lingering gazes and every "*my girl*" he said last night vanish into this abyss inside of me. As my stomach bottoms out, the muscles in my shoulders tighten.

I take a step back and Ryder gives him a hug while I say goodbye to the other guys. Jimmy picks me up and spins me around, causing me to laugh. It releases the tension built inside. While Brooks' leaving hurts the most, I'm going to miss them all. Life won't be the same without them as a constant. After Jimmy puts me down Jack approaches me and brings me off to his side before I can tell Ryder to call me later.

"Hey, I can't give you a ride home," he says and it looks like shame flashes over his face.

"Why not?" The pit inside opens again.

He sighs. "We're taking Brooks to the airport." He looks at the ground.

"Oh," I say when all I actually want to do is scream. I wasn't invited for this part. I don't blame Jack for it. I'd assumed I was his ride since that was how it has always played out. I still would have bought him breakfast either way. And up until last night Brooks hadn't shown interest in me being around him again.

"Ryder? Give me a ride home?" I ask, but don't wait for an answer as I head straight to her car. Brooks leaving hurts, but I don't expect the sting from not being included again. I guess I'd hoped after everything, after all this time, that I'd be more than *Jack's sister*. That for an occasion like this, I'd be included in the group. I know that in the past I have been taken with the group when they started the evening at my house. The invites haven't been extended otherwise.

She unlocks it just as I get there. I hold in the sobs until we're out of the parking lot. I can't let them hear me before we drive away. I don't look at them, at Brooks. I can't. I'm afraid that while I'm being torn apart from him leaving, I'll see that he's fine.

It's funny how much sober realities rip apart intoxicated confessions. Maybe it's not funny at all. Not when you believed them.

"He called me his girl," I say through tears.

"I know." Ryder sets her hand on my leg.

I think I could have gotten over him if I'd been able to forget what being his felt like.

Even in the bathroom, the speakers in our suite are entirely too loud. We would have normally gotten caught pre-gaming in our room solely because of how loud the music was. But Ryder assured me our RA was at a meeting halfway across campus and we were in the clear.

We're weeks into freshman year and living for every second of it. Ryder has become our floor's party concierge. Somehow she has ins with all the parties happening everywhere and can get us invited to whatever ones we want.

"A sip for you, a sip for me, but we're here to party. So, let's take shots while we're young and hot." We down the cheap tequila and bite the lime wedge. "Cheers to football boys." Ryder laughs.

"You're a menace." I turn back to the mirror to finish curling my hair.

"We've paid a lot of money to be here. I want to make the most of it."

"You're not going to remember your years here," I joke.

She takes another shot and grimaces after.

"Is it that kind of night?" I ask.

She shakes her head as she bites another lime wedge.

"That one was for courage," she says, avoiding my eyes. "Something came in the mail for you and I shouldn't have kept it from you, but I did."

I put the curling iron down and follow her out of the bathroom into our room. She digs through her purse and pulls out an envelope.

"I-" she pauses and holds the envelope back to her chest. "I don't like seeing you hurt." She extends her hand to give it to me.

I grab the envelope from her and see my name in the center, then look to the upper corner. It's from Brooks. He's in training right now so he hasn't been able to communicate with anyone. I've asked Jack and no one has heard from him at all.

"When did it come?" I ask.

"Today," she answers. "I saw it when I picked up your mail with mine."

I beeline for my bed and rip it open. I can't hide my smile even though I know Ryder is scowling, watching me. It's seven pages long.

"How's my girl?" It's the opening line.

My girl.

I try to read past that but I can't. It's there, inked forever onto me.

"Do you think you're going to come out tonight?" Ryder sits on the bed beside me.

I shake my head and show her the opening line. She releases a deep sigh and pats my leg before she stands without another word. I know she isn't thrilled about this, but I can't dismiss this. Not if there's another chance.

I don't write him back, but only because he asks me not to. He tells me how training is going, and about how much he misses home. How much he misses me. He has a graduation ceremony coming up, but I'm a college student and don't have the time to fly out, not that he gave me any details on it. Then he goes immediately into more training. There's no talk of when he'll be back. He ends the letter telling me he is holding onto hearing about my life when he sees me next. And that's what he's looking forward to. To hold onto that too, that he's coming back to me.

I read the letter before bed every night until the next one arrives a week later. It starts the same. *"How's my girl?"*

I squeal seeing it again.

After the weekly letters start, I go out less. I can see that Ryder disapproves but she doesn't voice it.

On Halloween night I relent and agree to go out since we had already planned out our sexy vampire costumes and, I have to admit, I was excited to have fun.

"We're going to a house party off campus tonight. It's going to be insane." Ryder dances in between curling her lashes. "There are going to be lots of cute guys, too." She glances quickly at me, I think to gauge my reaction.

"Well then, I will be the best wing-woman ever," I redirect.

"I could set you up with someone, too." She fumbles around in her make up bag.

"Ryder," I say.

"He's not even here! He sends you letters. That's it! He hasn't even asked you to wait for him or to write him back. He's a ghost." She meets my eyes, not shying away from the stinging words she spoke.

"That's not fair." My voice quivers. It's a truth I refuse to see.

"No. He's not fair. He's stringing you along because it makes him feel less lonely while he's gone. He could have actually officially asked you to be his girlfriend and take this on, but he didn't. He's a coward." She snaps her mouth shut. "I'm sorry."

My face reddens and I hold back tears. "It's always going to be him," I say. "I don't want it to be him, but I can't walk away if there's any chance."

She pulls me in for a hug. "Okay, okay" She shushes me, holding me tight.

Fuck. I drank too much. I peel myself out of bed and stumble to the bathroom, trying to keep my eyes as closed as possible. I splash some water on my face and brush my teeth. The person looking back in the mirror has definitely seen better days. I hear Ryder groan from her bed.

"What happened last night?" I call out with the toothbrush still in my mouth.

"I made you drink every time you talked about Brooks." She shuffles into the bathroom, tying her bed head into a bun on the top of her head.

"Really?" I spit the toothpaste out and set my brush back.

"For a bit. After a while though, I made a rule where if it looked like you were thinking about him you had to drink." She groans as she sits down to pee. She grabs make up wipes off the counter and starts to clean the residue of make up off her face.

"You're the worst," I say as I turn the shower on. I need to clean the night off of me. I have left over vampire makeup that I'm positive has stained my sheets. "You look like shit," I comment because I know I'm in the same state.

"You've never looked better." She remarks back sarcastically while I test the temperature of the water.

"Ouch." I climb into the shower. "Will you go get us coffee, please? I'll buy it. And maybe some cinnamon rolls?"

"Yes. Only because you drank like a champ last night," she calls over the water. "Be right back!" She flushes the toilet and I scream as the water runs ice cold. I hear her cackle as she closes the door to our room.

I let the hot water come back before I scrub the previous night away. I remember bits and pieces with the information Ryder gave me. At least I didn't throw up. I'd take a little bit of a foggy memory over being sick any day.

After my shower, I throw on sweats. I actually audibly moan with how comfortable they feel. I strip the sheets from my bed and stuff them into my hamper. Laundry is a future issue. I grab my extra set and as soon as my bed is made, I jump into it. I pull out my laptop- today is for streaming movies and nothing else. As soon as I find exactly what I want to watch and cozy up into the absolute perfect spot, there's a knock at the door.

"Use your key!" I call back to it. I found my comfort and I want to live in it. Ryder can figure out opening the door herself.

Another knock.

I groan loudly before closing my computer and throwing my blankets off.

"I just got comfortable," I whine as I open the door.

"Brooks." I say in whispered shock. The world stills for a moment. There is nothing else but him standing in front of me.

He's here. He's here and he's standing in front of me. "Brooks!" I throw my arms around him. He picks me up and I wrap my legs around him. He brings me back into the room before closing the door.

"I've missed you so much," he says against my ear.

"What are you doing here?" I don't let go. I don't quite believe he's here yet, and I'm afraid he'll disappear if I do.

"I had a day and I wanted to see you." He brings me to my bed. I'm not sure how he guessed the right one, but he did.

"But your family," I counter.

"I saw them at graduation," he says. "Plus, they grabbed me from the airport so I got to see them then."

"I can't believe you're really here." I bury my head in the crook of his neck.

The door swings open behind him. "Holy fucking shit. You bastard." Ryder says in disbelief mixed with annoyance.

"Hey Ryder." He chuckles.

"When do you leave?" she asks, walking into our room.

"Tomorrow morning," he answers and my heart sinks.

"Typical," she says as she sets my coffee on my desk.

I climb off of him.

"He can't help it." I grab my drink.

She stares him down. "I'm going to stay somewhere else." She packs a bag quickly. I watch her, but she doesn't look at me. Even knowing she hates seeing me hurt, I yearn for her approval. "I'd say it was nice to see you, but-" She leaves.

"So, she's not exactly my biggest fan," Brooks says.

"She doesn't like seeing me miss you," I admit.

"Aw, you miss me?" He grins.

"You know I do." I playfully push him.

"Yeah? How come you never write then?" He winks and I gasp.

"That's not fair! You told me not to!"

"I know. I'm teasing you. I wanted this. I wanted to hear about everything from you like this." He grabs my hand and interlocks his in mine.

I lean into him again. "This doesn't feel real, Brooks. You're actually in my dorm room."

"Are you going to show me around?" he asks. "I want to see where you go to class and eat and party."

"The party tour would have to be led by Ryder," I say. "But I can show you everything else."

I change and finish my coffee before giving him a very unofficial tour of the main places on campus. We end up near one of the campus stores.

"Do you promise to wear it?" I tease.

"As often as I'm allowed." He adjusts the hoodie in the store mirror.

"Jack doesn't even have one yet," I say.

"No? Well, he's slacking then."

After I pay, he grabs my hand as I show him the rest of campus. My favorite spot to read and the best place to get coffee. I tell him about everything that's happened since I last saw him- except the heartbreak and ache. I leave that out. I know my time with him is limited and I don't want my longing to put a damper on this moment, now that he's actually here with me.

"Can I take you to dinner tonight?" he asks as we walk over fallen leaves.

"I would love that."

"Where's the fanciest place in town, then?"

"Brooks. You're barely any money. I'm not taking the little you do have."

"Oh no. I didn't drive all this way not to take my girl out. Plus, what little I have made, I have multiplied in poker. Totally swept everyone last week." He brings my hand up and kisses it. "So please, tell me which restaurant I can get the best steak made in and we are going."

I relent. Not that I could ever truly say no to him.

We walk back to my room where I can change into something suitable for tonight. He does as well- as if he'd known he'd need nicer clothes. The butterflies in my stomach are in a fury.

He's mine again.

I quickly curl my hair and apply makeup before giving him the grand reveal. He stands and walks to me immediately, bringing me in for a hug. "You are stunning, Court."

"You smell amazing," I say. "Is that a new scent?"

He blushes, like actually blushes. "I stopped at a mall on the way here to find something nice. I got the clothes too."

My jaw drops slightly. "I can't believe you're doing all of this for me."

"You're my girl," he says in response and it's the answer for everything. I am his and he is mine.

He drives to dinner and holds every door open on the way. We don't order wine because I don't have a fake ID yet and he doesn't either. But we do get the most delicious steak and potatoes. My eyes well up at the first bite. It's honestly the best food I've ever had in my life. We sit in a secluded section of the restaurant, per Brooks' request, with only dim lights and candles to illuminate the room. He sits next to me, instead of across. Finding a way in each interaction to touch me. His gaze lingers as we exchange more stories about our time apart. If he's not holding my hand, then his arm is around me.

It's been the most romantic date I've been on. When we get back to my dorm, Brooks pulls a bottle of Riesling out of his bag.

"I got my mom to buy us a bottle," he says sheepishly. "I'm realizing now I should have put it in the fridge."

I laugh. "No. This is perfect. We can drink it with ice."

He climbs onto my bed as I find two clean glasses and grab a few ice cubes.

"I think this is the best day of my life, Brooks."

He fills our glasses.

"Mine too."

We clink our glasses together, in a silent toast to us.

I settle into him like we're molded to fit one another. It's so easy to get here. To fall back into us.

"I wrote you back, too." I confess. "I just never sent them."

"Can I see them?" he asks.

I sit up. "I don't want you to read them in front of me," I say.

"Can I bring them with me?"

I melt. I have melted and I am a puddle.

I get up and grab my polaroid camera. "Want some pictures too?" I hold it up.

"More than you can know."

We take a few of us together on my bed. One with me kissing his cheek. Then he insists he takes a couple of me to keep as well.

I run to the bathroom to make sure my hair and makeup still look good before letting him.

"There is never a moment where you are not the most beautiful woman in the world, Coutney," he says as I come out. "This morning. Right now. Always."

Heat floods my cheeks.

"Do they teach you how to smooth talk in the military?" I deflect the compliment.

"'I've learned a lot, but no. Not that." He holds the camera up and I smile.

After he snaps the first picture, he pulls the photo out and then brings the camera back up for another. I blow a kiss for this one.

After a few more photos, I take the camera. "My turn." I give him a devilish grin.

He smiles and I snap a picture before he can change his mind about posing.

"These would be a lot better if you were in them," he says.

"They would be a lot better if you were shirtless," I joke.

"I can make that happen." He moves up to his knees on my bed. I want to protest but he starts unbuttoning his shirt and there's no way in hell I'm passing this up.

I snap a picture of him unbuttoning, then another when he's taking it off, and finally one with him shirtless on my bed.

"How about you put the camera away and come here?" he asks and I immediately oblige.

I fall into him, like I've done it a million times before. My mind races but one thought stands out among all the rest. I'm his girl. He's here and I'm his girl.

I spend the night tangled up in him. I'd spend forever if I could.

The morning comes too quickly. Bastard always ruins my nights.

"I wish you didn't have to leave." Tears threaten a grand entrance.

"The only thing I want is to spend forever in that bed with you, Courtney." He pulls me in for a hug and kisses the top of my head.

"Can I write to you this time?" I ask as we finally untangle.

"I'll let you know." He winks and backs away. When he's halfway down the hall, he turns around and yells. "You're the only girl for me, Courntey!"

It dulls the pain of him leaving. When I can't see him any longer, I finally close my door. I crawl back into bed and decide that responsibilities can wait until tomorrow. Afterall, it's Sunday and there's nothing that's absolutely pressing.

My bed still smells like him. I close my eyes and hold my pillow and I can almost pretend he's still here with me.

"Do you two still need the room?" Ryder asks and I jolt up.

"It smells like him." I say as the only explanation.

She looks at me like I'm a wounded puppy, and maybe I am.

"Oh shit, Court." She climbs into bed with me. "You gotta stop doing this to yourself."

"It's different this time," I plea.

Famous last words.

It's been a week since I last saw Brooks. The night he left, I discovered his cologne with a note for me.

For my girl.

He left the entire bottle. I sprayed my pillow with it and the scent helped the ache at night. I still read his letters, and as I do, I imagine him reading mine. The pictures from the polaroid surround my bed, and I make one the background to my phone. The one of me kissing his cheek. I snapped a photo before he took it along with others.

I'm in the library studying when Ryder finds me. She looks annoyed. No, exasperated maybe.

"I've been looking for you." She sits next to me.

"Big test tomorrow. Everything is on Do Not Disturb. What's up?" I take the ear buds out.

"Jack texted me. Check your social media," she says with wary eyes.

"Weird my brother texted you. You still trying to hook up?" I tease.

"He couldn't reach you. Go check." She bites back.

I open and it's the first thing on my feed.

Rachel.

And not just Rachel... Rachel at Brooks' training graduation. She's in pictures with his family. There's some of them only. She flew down to watch him graduate. He never even let me know the time or place.

"Did you know?" Ryder asks.

I shake my head slowly.

He didn't tell me when he was here- that he saw her. That she flew hundreds of miles for something I didn't even know happened.

My heart had hoped once more when he showed up at my door.

And now.

Now, it's breaking all over again.

"Slut-ception," Ryder adds and I veto it.

"Sleep-a-thon?" I ask but she crinkles her nose at it.

"Hmm," she says, looking around our room like it will give her answers.

We decided I was going to actually get over Brooks. Even if it meant going through every guy at this school to do so.

"Whore-dom?" Her voice raises as she says it, like she's unsure even saying it.

"No," I say.

It still doesn't feel right. We've been trying to name the crusade I'm about to unleash on campus. Ryder is positive it needs a name, as if I am breaking a dam onto the student body.

"Whore-tism?" I ask.

"Feels common," she counters. "And sounds weird."

"Whore-icane?"

"That's it!" Ryder yells. "Yes, we finally have a name for this beautiful season of life into which you are entering." She claps her hands, and then dances to the bathroom.

I laugh but stop when she's out of sight. The pain floods the spaces I reserve for faking my way throughout the day. He didn't tell me Rachel flew out to see him. I have no idea what transpired between them. All I know is he didn't tell me.

I believe him in the regard that he didn't have much time allowed to go home and that he spent it with me. I know his schedule has been incredibly tight, and Jack has attested to that as well. No one else got letters, even still. No one mentioned if Rachel got any either, although I'm not sure if they would tell me.

"To get over him, get under someone else." It's what Ryder has been trying to drill into me the last couple days.

I can't forget him if I don't try. I look to my nightstand that has his cologne and pictures tucked away. I can't get rid of them. I believe in what we have with each other, even if it's breaking me. And it is breaking me.

Hope opened my heart once more, and now I'm reeling from the consequences of it.

"It's just heartless sex," I tell myself as a pep talk for the night. "I need to get over him."

I need to get over him. I need to get over him. I need to get over him.

I say it like it's a mantra. Maybe it is. I don't know if it will ever be true, though.

I lied to Ryder. It was the only way.

I told her I got over Brooks, that he was in my past and there would be no future with him. There couldn't be when he was impossible to reach and I was allegedly active on the dating apps.

I had been, for about two weeks into my whore-icane, then stopped when I got the next letter from Brooks. It was as if everything fell back into place. And this time, he asked me to write back. He admitted in his letters how before he knew he'd be able to surprise me, but he was now unsure of when he'd be able to come back home.

And I wrote back. I sent more pictures too. Some were a little bit racier than others. I didn't care if they had been screened by someone else as long as they got to Brooks.

His letters were proof they'd made it to him.

Semester break comes quickly, and the first half of my freshman year is over. I go back home while Ryder goes on vacation with her parents, along with a guy she's been seeing.

I don't expect any surprises from Brooks. I don't let myself hope to see him, not when his schedule is not his own. When his life is someone else's to dictate.

And I don't. No one hears from him in weeks, including me. I assume training has been too much and he has no time. Jack knows he came to see me, but doesn't know the details. I can't bring Brooks up to him, without presumably being told it wasn't a good idea. That's what everyone else on the outside has been telling me.

But they didn't see us. I could, though. I could see us.

I don't hear from him after Christmas either.

I still send letters. I write them in the library during study breaks so Ryder won't catch me. And when I know she'll be gone all night, I bring out the cologne and letters he once sent me.

My heart won't give up on him or us, even when everyone else does.

I finish my first year without ceremony. Ryder ended it in a relationship. He's nice; good to her, and most importantly he's present. But he's different from Brooks. The situation is different and that's what I tell myself to keep the jealousy at bay. But it's hard to watch Ryder get all the things I wanted with Brooks.

Halfway through the summer while sitting at my temp job, he calls. His name flashes on the screen of my phone, and I almost convince myself it can't be him before I answer.

"Brooks?" I ask hesitantly.

"Courtney," he answers and it nearly breaks me.

"Where have you been?" I cry.

"I'm home. I'm back for right now. Where are you?"

I tell him I'll come to him and before he can protest, I let my manager know I need the rest of the day off and run to my car. I actually had found a job closer to his house than my own. It's just a couple minute drive, but it still feels too long when I know our time is short.

I race through the streets, and on the way to his house I pass Rachel leaving the neighborhood.

My stomach drops.

I try giving myself reasonable explanations for why she was there before me, but none come to mind.

Still, I go. Still, I drive to his house.

He's standing on his driveway when I pull in and I don't know if it's to welcome me or to say goodbye to Rachel.

I get out, but stay next to my car.

"I saw Rachel leaving," I say. It isn't a question, but it might as well have been.

"She just left," he says shamefully.

"She was your first call?" I brace myself for the answer.

"No." He walks to me. "I didn't know I was coming home until the last minute. Her mom and my mom still see each other all the time. Her mom told her to come. I swear I didn't tell her I was coming home." He's at my side now.

"What about your graduation?" I ask, tears streaming down my face. There's no surprise on his face at this, like he knew that I'd found out.

"My mom invited her mom to make a mini vacation out of it, and she brought Rachel. That's it. I had no idea until she was there." He wipes my tears away.

"You could have told me." I stand tall.

"I should have. I'm sorry." He kisses the top of my head.

"I thought your mom liked me," I say with realization.

"She does. I think it's harder on Rachel's mom and she's been super pushy about things." He grabs my hands. "Please, come inside. I've missed you and I don't want to spend my time with you talking about her."

I nod my head and agree.

"Let's go."

I spend the weekend in his bed. We visit other places as well, but the highlights are his bed. It takes me back to when it had been just us, at our best. When we found ourselves through all the other shit going on.

When he leaves, he promises he'll have the opportunity to be better at communication. And he is. For the months following, he's been able to call me once a day and he spends his entire phone time with me. I schedule it out too. Ryder doesn't notice when we get back to school because she's been too busy with her boyfriend. But Brooks and I have found each other once again, even with all the miles between us.

"What do you want out of life, Court?" he asks me one night.

"I want to see the world. And I want to do it with you," I admit.

"I'm gonna give that to you someday." He mirrors my hopes and dreams. "Where to first?"

"Some place I've never been, that looks nothing like here. I've only ever been home and school. You've seen more of the world than me."

"Well, the extra I have seen hasn't been fun. Not yet anyway. What about Alaska?"

"Definitely on the list," I answer.

"What's number one on the list?" he asks.

"Well, what are the eligible locations where you'd end up?"

"Well, there's Alaska - already mentioned. Let's see... Colorado is a possibility. The mountains are nice. Oh, there's also Hawaii."

"Hawaii." I cut off the list there. "That would be my number one. I'd only ever go if you were stationed there."

"It's my top spot too. I'd have to be insanely lucky to get it, though. But you'd come out there for me?"

"Yeah... I would."

Each conversation leaves me more sure of where we stand. I'd finish my degree and then we'd see where he was at in his career. I'd follow him anywhere if he let me.

We end every conversation with a promise to talk again. The first night he doesn't call, I don't call him, but only wait for him. Then the next night is the same. And the nights that follow. I think that's what breaks me the most. I fell for it again.

I become a shell of my former self. Brooks made the parts of me I thought were shadows feel seen. Without that, without him, I'm hollow all over again.

Letters come sporadically, and with no real explanation for why the phone calls stop. They just do. And just when I think I might be able to move on, a new letter comes. I can't tell Ryder or Jack what's happening. I don't want to hear about how stupid I'm being with Brooks, again.

For weeks, I go through the motions until it happens again.

Rachel posts another photo of them together with the caption: *Somehow we always find our way back here*.

It breaks me.

I don't know when it was taken. I have no context. But I know I haven't heard from Brooks in a few weeks, and Rachel's picture shows the new ashy blonde look she recently changed to. He's also wearing the hoodie I bought him. So, I know it's not an old picture.

I recognize the place they were in too. He was home and he was with her and I hadn't heard anything.

I delete my accounts that night. And I also restart my dating apps. Not being with Brooks hurts, but knowing I wasn't with him and he was with her nearly kills me.

I block his number and stop writing letters.

I have to be done with him. I don't care if it ends up being some innocent occasion between them. We've never reached the level of relationship Brooks and Rachel had. And now it's apparent I never would.

Ryder goes home for semester break our sophomore year. Her boyfriend ended up not living too far away from where we had grown up, so she's able to see him during break as well.

On New Year's Eve, he throws a party at his brother's house. It isn't super far to drive and Ryder promised me a bed to sleep in when we eventually crash for the night.

The theme is black and white, and a couple of days prior I decided I'd make my hair match the theme. I had been able to get an appointment with a stylist who gave me my black and white hair, with the middle part splitting the black and white. It's perfect.

I find a dress in Ryder's closet that fits the theme as well. It's the time of year for resolutions - promises of new starts, and I'm in desperate need of one.

New Year's Eve day is spent with Ryder and I getting ready at her house, just as we do so many times at school. We dance and curl our hair and take shots. By the time we leave her house, I've loosened up and resolved myself to have a night filled with fun.

And fun turns out to be dominating the beer pong table.

I don't know what it is, but I'm on absolute fire. I team up with Ryder's boyfriend's friend, Nick. He and I absolutely sweep the competition. We have a twenty two game winning streak before we take a break to go play other games and see what's happening elsewhere. And for whatever reason, we stick by each other for the night. We aren't as good at tippy cup, but pump our egos back up again at the beer pong table.

And for the first time in a long time, I realize I haven't thought about Brooks. It isn't in a way that makes me miss him more, but in a way that makes me realize the ache is missing. I think that's what hits me the most as the clock counts down to midnight with this handsome stranger next to me. That for once, my day hasn't been affected by Brooks. So when the clock strikes midnight, I kiss him.

I barely know his name, but I know there's something happening in me.

A couple weeks go by and I've been texting with Nick, the guy from the party. He isn't spectacular, but he's new and most importantly, available. And he wants to see me when I come home to spend the weekend doing laundry.

He's nice enough, so I agree. I don't tell Jack or my mom I'm coming home. I just show up while mom's cooking dinner. Since Nick told me he was bringing us food, I don't eat but I sit with my mom while she does. She doesn't tell Jack I'm back but told him he should spend the night at home. I didn't get to see him that much during my break because he was working and I stayed away from home as much as I could to avoid questions.

But I have to admit, I've missed him, and it'll be nice to see him. And also to berate him with how he ended up with a giant TV in his room while I was gone. The family room still has a decent sized one, but he must have bought himself a nice set up.

Nick texts me when he arrives and I bring him downstairs right away because I don't want him to meet my mom yet. Not when we haven't been able to spend enough time to find out if it's worth it. My mom doesn't think Jack will be home tonight anyway, but at least I'll get to see him in the morning before I go back to school.

"Do you like scary movies?" Nick asks on the way downstairs.

"Only if I can follow them up with the cheesiest girly movie ever so that I'm able to fall asleep," I say in all seriousness.

"Deal. If I make you suffer through something, then I guess it's only fair you make me suffer through something as well." He smirks, but it doesn't ignite sparks in me like Brooks does.

We eat first before settling into a movie surrounding hauntings. They genuinely scare me, so it doesn't take long for me to bury myself against Nick. We eventually find that him lying on his back and me lying down on my side next to him offers the most comfortable position for us. I'm able to hide in him when I need to and he's able to still watch all the parts he wants. It's an added bonus that it means he's holding me the whole night.

Almost three quarters through the movie, the door to the basement bursts open and Jack waltzes in.

"Courtney!" he yells, clearly intoxicated. "You're home and I missed you. And I guess that's why mom told me to come home. But since I wanted to stay out celebrating with my friends, I brought my friends back. You and whoever this guy is, go take my room and we'll take the TV down here," he says as he falls onto the other end of the sectional.

I lean over to grab the remote as Jimmy walks in with Brooks behind him.

Brooks is home. Brooks is here.

Brooks is in my basement and I'm lying down cuddling on the couch with someone else. My face heats and my heart races. I'm not cheating but this feels the same. He's the one I want to bring me dinner and watch movies with on the couch.

He stops walking in as soon as he clocks the situation.

"What are you celebrating?" I ask, staring at Brooks.

"I got stationed," he answers. "I'm going to Hawaii. First stop in seeing the world."

The words gut punch me. I'm supposed to have that with him. To be with him through it. It's our dream and it's happening, but without me. And I have no idea if it's still something he wants with me. I've never known what he truly wants from me and for us because he's never let us become anything. And now that we've found ourselves here in this moment, I know that it never will. Because he could have included me in this- could have told Jack to tell me, but he didn't and I guess that's clear enough.

"Come on, Nick." I get up and walk straight past them to the stairs.

Jimmy stops Nick, though. "What are your intentions with Courney?" he asks through drunken slurs.

I stop going up the stairs.

"Right now, to get through our movies." It's a smart answer, and probably the correct answer but the tone sets Jimmy off.

"Hey!" he barks. "I'll kick your ass if you hurt her." He points as he sways.

"Leave him alone, Jimmy," I say defeated. Jimmy has always been my protector, and that's why no one outside of Ryder knew about Brooks and I this last year and a half. I could barely handle Ryder's hard truths. I wasn't going to be able to withstand it from everyone else, too.

I can't look at Brooks anymore. Because I know what I'll see. I'll see that I'm putting him through everything I went through.

I think that's what does it. Walking into the house and seeing me with someone else.

He stops pursuing me after that. No more letters, not that there had been any in a long time. I unblock him just to see what would happen, and there's nothing. I can't bring myself to reach out first, either.

I think I broke him the way he broke me.

Nick wasn't worth the fallout, worth hurting someone else over. We fizzled out quicker than we started. But he'd been a catalyst in the end.

I wanted someone to love me back.

Neither of them did.

But I broke free of Brooks.

I don't know if I lost him or if he lost me.

I do know it hurt a lot. Every part of being with him hurt. And every part of losing him did, too.

He made me believe in something that was never really there, and then didn't allow me to find it somewhere else. Not when he'd been able to reel me in with stolen glances and secret letters.

I guess in the end we'd lied too. He lied about it being over, but he didn't let me go. I lied about moving on, but I couldn't. And in the end, those lies had become the truth. I thought distance would be what made us move on. Turns out, it was proximity. I needed to be up close to see it all and he needed to see the fallout. And finally, years after the end, we found our finale.

He got over me and I moved on.

Or at least we tried.

BAECATION
A NAUGHTY NERDS SHORT STORY
KIMBERLY REESE

/'bā-'kā-shən/
    noun
    : a period of travel or recreational time spent away from home with a romantic partner

CHAPTER 1 - THEO

"Demi," I hiss. "I don't kn-know if I c-can do this."

A beat of silence passes before the familiar sound of an incoming call fills my ear. I pull my phone away and glance down to see a FaceTime request from my best friend filling the screen. I quickly accept it, and her serious, serene face replaces my slightly frantic one.

"Theo, it's going to be okay."

"How d-do you know?"

"Trust me, I have a—" She stops, leans closer to her phone, and squints. "Are you on the toilet?"

Of all the times to get distracted. "Yes, but I'm not using it." I lower my voice even further since I am, in fact, hiding out in Addy's bathroom.

I showed up at her apartment a few minutes ago and immediately excused myself to the restroom in an attempt to calm my nerves. When splashing cool water on my face didn't work, I panic texted Demi before giving in to the urge to call her. She's at her dad's house or else I would've initiated an in-person pep talk back at our place.

I don't want to risk Addy overhearing this conversation, so I get up to turn on the exhaust fan before moving away from the door and whispering, "In case you can't tell, I'm k-kinda freaking out."

"No, I had no idea," she whispers back dryly. My actions aside, she knows better than anyone how the resurgence of my stutter is a dead giveaway about my state of mind. "Do me a favor and take some deep breaths, please."

I breathe in through my nose and steadily release the air through my mouth a few times, and working through the familiar exercise helps to somewhat settle my nerves.

"Thanks."

A small smile lifts the corners of her lips. "Anytime, bestie. Now, I know why you're nervous, but you have no reason to be. Everything is going to work out beautifully."

I repeat my question from earlier. "How do you know?"

"I don't know for sure, but what I meant to say earlier is that I have a feeling. I know deep down, under all those nerves, you feel it too."

"What if . . .? What if she says . . .?" I stop myself. God, I can't even finish this train of thought.

"She won't." Demi pushes her glasses up her nose and leans in further. "You say you're not sure if you *can* do this anymore, but I think you should ask yourself if you still *want* to do this. Have your reasons for wanting to do this changed?"

There's no hesitation or doubt. I've never been more sure of anything in my life. "Of course, I still want to. I love her, and that will never change."

"And she loves you. So much." I know this too, but it still doesn't alleviate the mild panic.

"What if she thinks it's too soon?"

"Then you guys wait. You won't know for sure, though, until you throw it out into the universe. Take the risk."

Her advice brings to mind Cohen's words from when we first met. *No risk, no reward.*

Addy is the greatest reward I could possibly hope to earn, and I'm willing to risk putting myself out there if it means I can spend a lifetime trying to be worthy of her.

"Okay," I whisper.

Oh, God, this is happening.

"Okay," she echoes. Her smile is gentle and supportive.

Before either of us can say anything else, Addy's muffled voice sounds from the other side of the door.

"Hey, hot stuff. When you're done, could you grab the toiletry kit I left on the counter, please?"

The air leaves my lungs, and I choke out, "S-sure thing."

"Thanks!" Her footsteps grow fainter as she walks away, and I look down at Demi.

"I've gotta go."

She nods in understanding. "Have fun, stay safe, and have some faith, Theo."

"You're not gonna wish me luck?"

"Nope, because you won't need it. Now, go get your girl, tiger." Genuine encouragement radiates through the phone and practically smacks me in the face. "Keep me posted!"

With a promise to do just that, I hang up and exit my temporary panic room.

I find Addy in her bedroom packing, and like every time I see her, a warm feeling suffuses my chest. Wordlessly, I walk up to her, wrap my arms around her from behind, and drop the kit she asked for on the bed next to her suitcase.

My lips brush against her neck before I move them up to whisper in her ear. "Hi, beautiful."

A shiver moves through her body, and my effect on her causes the warmth I feel to settle lower and heat. She makes me just as dizzy as the day she bumped into me over a year and a half ago.

"Hey, you. Everything okay? You disappeared on me almost as soon as you arrived."

She doesn't sound upset, just curious, and the squeeze I give echoes the one around my heart.

"Yeah, I just wanted to refresh myself." She hums and tilts her head to the side as she considers what she has left to pack. "Are you almost ready to go? Is there any way I can help?"

"Yes, actually, there is a way you can help. Mind telling me where we're going? My curiosity is killing me."

I scoff lightly and give a playful nip to her shoulder. "Nice try. You'll find out soon. I can't really hide where we're off to once we hit the road."

"Please?"

For a split second, I almost cave; I want to give her everything, so she's hard to deny. Ever since I dropped the news we'd be traveling for spring break, she's been trying to get it out of me.

"Soon, baby. I promise."

A dramatic sigh leaves her before she playfully wiggles her butt against me, and my blood starts to rush south.

"You sure I can't convince you?" Her voice is husky, sly, and slightly smug. She knows exactly what she's doing to me.

I bite back a groan. Correction: she's *really* hard to deny. Speaking of hard
. . .

"Are you trying to scramble my brain so I tell you?"

She slowly reaches for something that's farthest from us on the bed and bumps her butt against me again, and I swear I feel a subtle grind.

"Is it working?"

I respond by shifting my hands down to grasp her hips, and instead of pulling away, I tug her closer and rub the evidence of my desire against her. She braces both hands against the bed to keep herself upright, and I smile at her gasp of pleasure.

Another twitch of her hips. "Are you trying to distract me so I stop asking?"

I mirror what she asked a moment ago. "Is it working?"

"Nope, not at all." Her words and the way she presses back against me say otherwise.

I chuckle as I easily lift her slight weight, spin her around, and deposit her onto the bed so she's on her back. I lean over her, an arm on either side of her head. Her flushed cheeks and glassy eyes tell me all I need to know.

"Mmhmm," I hum. "You'll find out soon enough, baby. We've gotta get going."

She nibbles on her lower lip as she gazes up at me, and I give in to the temptation to kiss her full, supple mouth. When I pull away, her words are breathy.

"Could I get a clue, please?" I debate with myself for a moment, but she makes up my mind for me when she adds, "Tell me what you're hiding."

I know she doesn't mean it in a negative way, just that she's dying to know what I have planned, but my nerves from earlier start to buzz back to life when I think of what I'm actually hiding. She deserves the best, so I want everything to go perfectly. Besides, as much as my girl begs for details, her love of surprises means she really doesn't want to know. She lives for the moment when a surprise is unveiled in all its glory and enjoys the push and pull leading up to the big reveal.

I shove my anxiety to the wayside and decide to give her a different truth. I back up until I'm kneeling on the floor and drag her yoga pants and underwear down with me. Her eyes widen in shock and excitement, and she moans when I press a kiss right above her clit. I smile against her skin and take a deep breath against her pussy.

Groaning, I say, "God, you smell so g-good." I swipe my tongue over her slit, the light pressure more teasing than fulfilling, and close my eyes in pleasure. "You taste even better."

"Oh, God," she cries. "I thought we had to go?" It comes out as a question, and the last word drags out when I nuzzle against her.

I peer at the face of my watch before glancing back down at the shining feast before me. Thankfully, we're only about ten minutes from the airport, so we'll both benefit from the close proximity.

"We do. We need to be somewhere in less than thirty. Think you can come *and* finish packing in twenty minutes or less?"

I don't wait for her response before I start pressing open-mouthed kisses against her pussy. I avoid her clit until she's squirming, which only takes a few minutes, and a sense of satisfaction washes over me when her hips buck up to meet my mouth. I may still struggle sometimes with words, but the way my body speaks to hers makes up for it; my tongue has definitely found other ways to compensate. When I finally bestow her clit with my attention, Addy makes a keening sound and arches her back off the bed.

"Yes," she finally pants. "Keep that up, and it'll be less than five."

I smile into her pussy and nibble, lick, and suck at her with dedicated fervor until she comes, and I don't let up until she's a shuddering, incoherent mess. Needless to say, she's sufficiently distracted. Hopefully, this pleasure-filled start to our carefully planned trip is a positive sign of things to come.

We make it to the airport with five minutes to spare.

CHAPTER 2 - ADDY

"We're going to *Maui*?"

If my sweet, thoughtful boyfriend is tired of me asking this question for the umpteenth time, he doesn't show it. Instead, he lets out a low laugh and gives my hand an affirmative squeeze.

The squeal I let out when I found out at baggage check reached a frequency range I'm sure only dogs could hear, but from Theo's look of joyful relief, my reaction was what he was hoping for. I probably sound like a broken record at this point, much to the annoyance of our fellow passengers, but I'm beyond thrilled that I'm going to Hawai'i with my favorite person.

My enthusiasm isn't dampened at the prospect of an almost twenty-hour flight with two stops. If anything, the anticipation over what he planned will continue to build.

I squeeze his hand in return. "You're a sneaky one. I love surprises."

"I know you do."

The smug confidence curving his lips is almost as sexy as his bashful smiles. Whatever look he's sporting, I want to kiss him right on his handsome face, so I do.

"Thank you," I say sincerely. "You know you didn't have to do something so extravagant. I would've been happy holed up with you in my apartment."

For someone as extroverted as I am, that's yet another sign of how much I love this man.

"It's my pleasure. And I know, but I thought we could use a little escape."

He doesn't have to elaborate. Life has been busy in the best way, but busy is still busy.

My recent promotion at the boutique PR firm I've been working for since graduation has kept me busy and fulfilled, but even at my busiest, I'm in awe of how Theo handles his schedule.

Between his classes—he took on additional coursework so he can try and graduate early—TA work, and the lessons he occasionally plans and teaches under Professor Wilder's guidance, I'm surprised he still balances his personal life so well. He spends quality time with loved ones, helps his mom around the house, swims regularly, finds time to get his nerd on, and dedicates every other ounce of free time to our relationship and spending time with me. If I didn't know better, I'd think he really was a superhero with how he juggles everything. At this point, I wouldn't be shocked to learn he has a clone or five.

Granted, he's better than any fictional superhero, but his dedication to everyone and everything he cares about is impressive. If anyone deserves a relaxing getaway, it's him.

I twist in my seat so I can face him head-on. "Thank you, Theo. I love you."

My soft words are met with an even softer blush that stains his cheeks.

"I love you too, Addy."

Our gazes hold, and I soak in the love his stare radiates. I've had plenty of guys spout some surface-level bull about how they feel about me, but Theo backs up his words with actions. Outside of family, he's the first and only person whose love I *feel* on a cellular level, and it's the ultimate game changer.

I'm a lucky, lucky girl, and I want him to know I know it.

"I can't get over how lucky I am to have you in my life."

His blush deepens, and it's so endearing and earnest that I want to straddle him and do naughty things that'll make it stick around longer. In the interest of not getting kicked off this flight at our first layover, I restrain myself and promise to blow his mind later. After all, I still owe him for the orgasm from earlier that left me barely able to walk. He's proven he's the best student on all fronts, and I feel the need to reciprocate.

His response shakes me of my dirty thoughts. "That's how I feel about you."

He lifts our entwined hands so he can place a kiss where our fingers meet, and the butterflies that never leave me in his presence flutter. I need to distract myself before I drag him into the bathroom to join the Mile High Club.

Don't end this baecation before it really starts, you perv, I think to myself.

"So, hot stuff, what's on our itinerary for Maui?"

Theo regards me quietly, a thick brow lifted in consideration. "Do you really want to know?"

My mouth opens but shuts just as quickly as I think carefully about how I want to respond. I love surprises more than anyone, but I don't think anything can really top finding out about this trip. Besides, the travel duration that didn't seem like an issue before now sounds interminably long to not know anything.

I settle for getting a tidbit. "What's one thing you have planned?"

He smirks as he reaches into his backpack, grabs the Venom folder I got him recently, and pulls out a piece of paper. He hands it to me, and once I register what it says, it takes effort to not crinkle it in my enthusiasm.

"We're going to Kahului Con?" Only our favorite word can convey how ecstatic I feel. "I think I just had a nerdgasm."

It's a struggle to keep my voice low. Since our epic first date, going to comic conventions has been our thing. Sometimes we go as a pair, sometimes with Demi, and we always have a blast. I'm proud that I manage to swallow my squeal, but it must be louder than I thought when a dog under a nearby seat whines in response, confirming my suspicion about the decibels my excitement can reach.

Theo busts out laughing, and he quickly presses his face into his hand to try and smother the sound. His wide shoulders shake, and I can't help but laugh along with him as quietly as I can.

"Y-yes," he gasps, and I know instantly his stutter is born from his laughter rather than nerves.

"Oh, my God. We're going to have so much fun. Thank you!" I swivel in my seat so I'm facing forward again, and I pull his arm into me so I can hug it. "I can't wait to pull up the schedule of events so we can plan around the panels we want to see. Are there any you know you want to add?"

Once his laughter eventually subsides, he leans over, presses a kiss to the top of my head, and lets out a contented sigh.

"I haven't looked yet, but I'm down for anything as long as it's with you."

My heart skips a beat because I feel the same, and considering the beautiful destination we're headed to, it's only fitting that I borrow my response from one of my favorite Jack Johnson songs.

"Same. It's always better when we're together."

CHAPTER 3 - THEO

"Oh, my God, my feet."

Concern and amusement battle each other for supremacy as I watch Addy duck walk around the college where Kahului Con is taking place. It's the second and last day of the convention, and we haven't had a moment of respite as we've bounced around between panels, photo ops, vendors, and food. We've seen all we want to see, spent an obscene amount on souvenirs for ourselves and loved ones, and have just been casually strolling the last hour, so it may be time to call it quits.

"Addy, hold on," I call out from behind her.

She halts and rotates her weight from hip to hip to try and alleviate the pressure on her feet. I move to stand in front of her and kneel down, arms outstretched behind me in a signal to hop on.

She doesn't hesitate to press herself against my back and wrap her arms around my neck, and when I grasp her thighs and straighten, her groan of relief is borderline indecent.

"You're my hero."

You'd think I have a small Arc Reactor in my chest from the surge of power I feel at her words of gratitude. I have no delusions of grandeur at all and know I'm not a comic-book character, but being there for Addy, even in this small way, is beyond fulfilling.

I enjoy satisfying her needs, and right now, fatigue isn't the only thing plaguing her.

"Let's go grab some food and head back to the hotel."

She lets out another groan of thanks as I maneuver us through the still-packed crowd and outside to the food trucks. It takes a few minutes to find a place to sit, but once I do, I deposit her into her seat and mentally tally the trucks I need to visit.

"I'll be right back," I say as I turn to leave.

"I can go with you."

Her half-hearted attempt to move out of the seat is beyond cute, and I turn back to drop a kiss to her forehead.

"No, you stay. You can save our seats. Besides, your Lambor-feeties need to rest."

Her wide-brown eyes blink up at me. "My . . . Lambor-feeties?"

I pointedly look down at her feet and waggle my brows, and she starts to giggle.

"You're adorkable, and I love it." A few seconds pass before she adds, "Thanks for being so thoughtful. I'll give my Shoe-barus a break."

It's my turn to stare at her. It's been almost two years, and I'm still floored that she's just as nerdy as I am. In some respects, she's an even bigger nerd, and it's sexy as hell.

"You do that." I start to leave but pause one last time. "And by the way, you're adorkable too."

She winks, and as I wait in line at different trucks, my eyes can't help but track back to our table to make sure she's safe and comfortable. She's a magnetic social butterfly, and even though she's talking animatedly with the couple next to her, she blows me a kiss or makes a funny face whenever our gazes collide.

Her attention helps the twenty-five minutes it takes to wait in line and order at four different trucks and stands worth it, and once our food is ready, our table is almost overflowing with bento boxes.

"I've been dreaming about you," Addy coos to her ahi poke bowl, and her eyes close in bliss as she takes her first bite. "Oh, God, it's almost too good. There's something about überfresh seafood in a tropical paradise that just hits different."

I might be jealous over the sounds she just made if I didn't agree, and I nod as I stuff my own face full of alternating bites of spam musubi, garlic shrimp scampi, and Portuguese sausage.

"We'll need to come back," I throw out casually, and I'm rewarded when her posture straightens, and her eyes brighten.

"Please! If not every year, maybe every other year. If we didn't have loved ones and lives we'd miss way too much in New York, I'd be begging to move here. Maybe one day when we're retired and have the luxury to explore more."

My heart thuds heavily when I hear her talk about our future together. Tomorrow is, after all, when I have the biggest surprise planned, and her words give me a boost of hope.

"I know what you mean, so we'll have to see what we can do to make that happen."

"Yes! Hawai'i baecations for the win. We can't go wrong." She holds up a finger and starts ticking off items, adding a digit for each pro she names. "The people? Amazing and friendly. The scenery? Stunning. The weather? Excuse me, New York winters, we don't know you. The food and drinks? I need more stomachs, that's how good it all is."

She takes a long swig of lilikoi-orange-guava juice, and I follow suit with my own drink. The flavors of the refreshing liquid dance on my tongue, but Addy's next words cause me to choke a little while in the middle of my next gulp.

"I know you and Wilder are obsessed with oranges, but I think guava takes the prize as my favorite juicy fruit."

"Cohen's the obsessed one. I think I'm partial to the lilikoi myself," I admit. I can feel the tips of my ears heating to what must be a bright red.

Cohen and I have grown closer as friends and colleagues, and I've kept my promise to keep the sex advice he gave using an orange as a teaching prop strictly between us. Addy may not know the details, but Cohen's seemingly endless supply of the citrus means I end up eating the tangy fruit in his office more often than not.

I thought he stocked them for me because I was the first to bring one to his office that fateful day, but with how often he eats and replenishes them, I've idly wondered if he has an oral fixation. Perhaps he's trying to replace one habit with another and needs the distraction so as to not give in to another itch he'd like to scratch. Maybe he eats the fruit simply because it's a healthy snack, or maybe the man just loves oranges. Regardless of the reason, I'm orange-guilty by association.

My thoughts are pulled back to Addy when she leans back in her seat to pat at her midsection. Her *Lucifer* crop top rides up further, exposing the small swell of her normally flat stomach. The roundness from all our eating looks good on her, and my brain can't help but imagine a day, far from now and only if and when we're both ready, when she has our baby in her belly.

God, she'd look more gorgeous than ever pregnant, swollen and glowing and waddling around as she nests in our home and rubs her baby bump.

I feel my dick start to thicken in my briefs and try to discreetly adjust myself. Thankfully, no one notices me perving out over a future I may or may not have, and the rest of our lunch passes by without incident.

Tomorrow is the day I put myself out there more than I ever have, and with the amount of planning I've done and the hope Addy's words from earlier have given me, I'm feeling confident.

Things are going to be perfect.

THE NEXT DAY

I spoke too soon.

Everything that could go wrong has.

I had it all planned. We'd pick up malasadas for breakfast, drive out to Lahaina for a ziplining tour, go whale watching, grab a romantic dinner, and then end the day by catching the sunset at Haleakalā. It's at this last stop that I planned to get down on one knee and ask Addison Mitchell to be my wife.

So far, the bakery we visited ran out of malasadas, and the company where I booked our ziplining tour accidentally overbooked us. Everyone has been really kind and has worked to make things right, but it's been one disappointment after another. I want to kick myself as well because I mistakenly booked the whale-watching tour for tomorrow, and they were fully booked for today. There's plenty of time until sunset, but I hope the universe isn't conspiring against me or giving me some sign that I'm not supposed to propose today.

As each carefully planned activity begins to unravel, so does my composure.

Thankfully, Addy has taken everything in stride and doesn't seem the least bit disappointed. I've never been more grateful that she's as chill as she is and that we're in an island paradise where every view is worthy of a postcard.

I'm yanked from my thoughts of how to salvage today when Addy, who had been talking to a young woman nearby while I tried to clear things up with the tour office, taps on my arm to get my attention.

"Hey, babe. Guess what?" She's practically buzzing.

"What?"

"I made a new friend! She's super nice, and now we *have* to come back so we can see her again." Her rapid-fire words are brimming with excitement, and I can't help but smile. "Anyway, I told Keala what happened with our tour mix-ups, and she said her brother gives surfing lessons at Kamehameha Iki Park Beach." She says the name slowly and carefully, as if she practiced. "It isn't far at all. What do you say to a beach day? She invited us out for a free surf lesson, and after, she said we're welcome to join their lūʻau for an early dinner. We can always go hiking tomorrow."

Message from the universe received.

I think back to the ring hiding snugly in my pocket and resign myself to the fact that maybe today isn't meant to be. After all, I can't bring myself to disappoint Addy when this sounds like something she'd love to do. And, if I'm being honest, it sounds good to me too.

Once I accept that my carefully laid plans are in the dust, a feeling of calmness settles over me. An unplanned beach day is exactly what we both need, and with the pressure I was feeling finally put away for the time being, I can finally let go, relax, and just be.

"That sounds amazing."

CHAPTER 4 - ADDY

"Damn, girl, you've got it bad," Keala teases from her spot next to me.

"Don't I know it," I murmur.

There's no point in denying that I'm so far gone for my insanely sexy boyfriend.

We're sunbathing at the beach in Lahaina while Koa, her brother, hangs out with Theo for his surf lesson. The lifeguards instructed us that only very experienced swimmers and surfers should be out on the water since the waves are strong today, and since I'm not the strongest swimmer, Keala was kind enough to keep me company.

Not that I'm complaining, though, because the views are spectacular. My attention shifts between looking out over Lana'i and my boyfriend. His hair is dark from the water, and whenever he's close enough for our eyes to meet, his chocolatey eyes heat until they're molten.

It's easier to admire his strong, lean form as he paddles out on his board or surfs, and the wetsuit only serves to highlight the beautiful shifting of his muscles. I'll probably never surf, but I'm fine with being a spectator because *damn. I knew his shoulders were broad, but that wetsuit makes him extra yummy,* I think.

"For someone who hasn't surfed before, he's actually pretty good," she observes.

I can't help but agree. My swimming machine took to surfing like he was born to it—he really is the best student—and it wouldn't faze me if the world-class surfing and the new friends we made became additional reasons to come back to beautiful Hawai'i.

"His favorite pastime is swimming, so I feel like this is a natural extension of that. Your brother may have created a monster."

"Then he can join the club. Every brah on the island is a surf nut," she says fondly. "By the way, you two look so cute together."

"Thank you. I'm totally biased, but I agree. Ugh, all this thirsting is making me hungry."

Keala chuckles and rolls over so she's on her stomach and facing me, her left cheek pressed against her forearm. "Good, because my family always goes overboard at lū'aus. My mom and aunties made poke, taro bread, guava pies, and loco moco with potatoes." She groans and smacks her lips. "My dad roasted kalua pork and made shoyu chicken, and my sister ordered from Zippy's. If you haven't tried their famous chili with rice, you haven't lived. My mouth is watering just thinking about everything."

Even though we've been snacking intermittently on roasted macadamia nuts, my stomach chooses that moment to let out an unholy grumble, which causes us both to cackle.

"Clearly, I'm hungry as well. I think I've done more eating than anything else on this trip, and I have no regrets whatsoever."

"I love to hear it. You're gonna need that appetite, girlie."

"Then I can't wait to start living." I smile as I flop down on my stomach to join her. "What should Theo and I bring?"

"Just bring yourselves. In the spirit of aloha, we just want you guys to have a good time and are honored to have you join us."

My cheeks heat from more than the sun. As beautiful as Hawai'i is, the warmth and welcoming nature of the locals are most beautiful of all.

CHAPTER 5 - THEO

The beach day and lū'au turned out better than I thought, and if I'm keeping it real, we probably had more fun being spontaneous than we would've had if we had stuck to my meticulous plans. We were both out of our element yet somehow wholly in it at the same time as we played, conversed, and enjoyed the sunshine.

Good food. Good people. Good vibes.

Talk about a winning recipe for success.

We stroll hand in hand down Lahaina's Front Street in an attempt to walk off our dinner, and I'm savoring our alone time. Keala and Koa's family treated us like their own, not tourists, and my stomach hurts from both the food and laughter. They were an entertaining bunch, and I hope we stay in touch with them. However, it's still nice to have Addy to myself after such a long day of interacting with others.

I look across the street and see Banyan Court Park, which one of Koa's aunties told me about. Wordlessly, I steer us in that direction and don't stop until we reach an empty bench under the famous, mammoth banyan tree.

"Wow," Addy whispers reverently as we each sit. "This is beautiful."

It is. We're surrounded by trees in Ithaca, but none of them look like this. The wide canopy feels like we're being sheltered and embraced in a hug, and the aerial roots creep down and sway gently in the island breeze. Shafts of fading sunlight peek through and light up small sections around the base of the tree, and it feels like we've been transported to another world. The lack of people in this moment is surprising but welcome, and I take advantage of our solitude.

I mirror her hushed voice as I relay what I learned today.

"Some say this tree is the heart of Lahaina," I start. "It was brought from India in the late 1800s and is Hawai'i's oldest non-native tree. It's home to hundreds of mynah birds that are also native to India, and I can see why they choose this as their home. It feels safe."

Addy cranes her neck to look up and around us, and the short hair she wasn't sure she loved a month ago brushes the tops of her shoulders at the movement. I love how it draws attention to her throat, and even in the fading sunlight, I can see how our beach day and the sun have brought out the platinum highlights in her honey-blonde strands.

She tilts her head toward me, and my gaze dips to her sunburnt cheeks and nose. She's never looked more beautiful, lobster cheeks and all. Her smile unfurls slowly like the petals of a flower, and my breath catches at the look of adoration in her expression.

"It does. It reminds me of how I feel when I'm with you."

Her words are stronger than the mythical weapons used to slay the biggest, baddest villains. I'm just an ordinary guy, but the way I feel for her is anything but. She slays me.

She looks like a painting, and I wish I had a shred of artistic talent so I could capture how lovely she looks. Instead, I'll have to rely on my big brain to preserve this memory and the way she makes me feel.

It's at this moment that I make a choice. Plans be damned. I'm gonna do it.

"Banyan trees symbolize wish fulfillment, and Addy, there's a w-wish I want to sh-share with you."

My stutter recaptures her attention, and she turns to look at me fully.

"I had today all p-planned out, and while I was disappointed at first, it turned out to be the b-best day."

"It did," she agrees.

I use the moment to catch my breath and gather my thoughts.

"I learned that it d-doesn't matter if plans go wr-wrong because the only thing that matters is who I'm w-with. Things don't have to p-perfect as long as they're real. *We're* real, Addy. The w-world can throw whatever it wants at me, and I'll be happy because I'm with y-you."

Her eyes start to mist, and her lips part to say something in return. Before she can do so, I continue.

"Last month, I made a p-promise to you in my Valentine's Day love note. I promised to sh-show you all the ways putting you and what we have first will always r-ring t-true."

Sucking in a deep breath, I shift off of the seat and drop down so I'm on one knee. I pull the ring I've been carrying around for months out of my pocket and present it to her as if it were my heart on a platter.

"Oh, my God. Theo," she whispers, emotion clogging her throat.

My own throat thickens with feeling, and I bump my glasses back up my nose with one hand before I continue.

"Addison Mitchell, I l-love you. Every n-nerdy part of me is yours. I w-want to grow o-old with you. You were my f-first," I say, and a blush starts to heat my face. "And I want you to be my o-only. We can w-wait as long as you need, but my h-heart, mind, and body know you're the one. If you'll let me, I'll f-fill your life with love, happiness, and all the n-nerdgasms you could ever desire. A life with you is my greatest w-wish. P-please, will you m-marry me?"

The last word is barely out of my mouth before I'm tackled to the ground and laid flat on my back. I look up at Addy's overjoyed, tear-filled face and the dappled canopy serving as her backdrop. This is yet another moment I wish I could paint.

"Yes, Theo, I'd love to marry you." She leans down and presses a kiss to my smiling lips. "I don't want to do life with anyone else." Another kiss. "We're both perfectly imperfect on our own, but what we have? That's my idea of perfect. I love you, I love you, I love you."

She peppers kisses all over my face until I'm laughing and kissing her back, but I reluctantly pull away so I can slide the vintage ring I thought suited her perfectly onto her finger.

Her voice sounds watery as she takes it in. "I love it, but I love you most of all. Now, Theodore Cadwell, please take me back to our hotel. We should start our celebration with some nerdgasms."

I thought I knew bliss before, but it doesn't compare to the unfettered joy pulsing through me now. Without a word, I sweep her into my arms and away from the charmed, ethereal courtyard. I may not be an artist, and I may very well lose my memory one day, but I'm content knowing that this moment we shared will forever be sheltered in the safe arms of the banyan tree.

CHAPTER 6 - ADDY

The comforting weight of my engagement ring gives me a thrill because it means what just happened isn't a figment of my imagination.

Theo proposed. He wants to marry me. We're going to get married.

I don't even remember the drive back to the hotel, that's how euphoric I feel.

My happiness bubbles over into my kiss, and I twist so that Theo is pressed against the elevator wall, my front plastered to his. I lift up onto my toes and try to rub against the hard ridge taunting me. His responding growl sends a shiver down my spine, and my panties flood when he grasps my hips, spins me around, and switches our positions so he's dominating me, not the other way around. He grinds into me, and it feels like a fever is burning me up from the inside out. The only way I'll feel better in my own skin is if I shatter and am put back together again.

He pulls away from me, and I'm about to cry out for more when he surprises me by dipping down and lifting me by my thighs so my pelvis presses against his.

Well, hello.

I get one firm grind that's pleasurable enough to make my eyelids flutter when the elevator dings, signaling that we've reached our floor. Theo turns, and if seeing an older couple waiting to go down to the lobby flusters him, he doesn't let on. I smile and wave at them as we pass, but I miss their reaction because every step he takes bumps his dick against my aching pussy. We're in the room farthest down the hall, and every step is pleasure-induced torture.

I start to wriggle in his arms, but he keeps me in place with a firm grip and a light chuckle.

"Almost there, baby. Nerdgasm number one, coming up shortly."

The seconds tick by, and once we reach our door, he reaches into his pocket for his phone so he can access our digital-room key. Moments later, we're inside, and I'm pressed against the back of the door as if no time passed from the elevator to now.

"Theo," I whine. In another life, I might be embarrassed about the needy sounds coming out of my mouth, but all I can think of is the relief I know is waiting for me.

"I know, baby."

He drops down to his knees so my feet can find purchase on the floor, and before I have the chance to protest, his head is underneath my sundress. The rough pads of his fingers trail up my thighs, and wetness saturates my swimsuit bottoms further when he grabs my ass and presses a kiss against my clit through the slick fabric. His moan is like an adrenaline shot to my system.

"Coconuts and sunshine," he groans roughly.

As much as I want to come, I want him to feel good too.

"Let me go down on you."

Cool air kisses my core when his fingers peel the fabric to the side.

"After." It comes out more like a grunt before he pops his head back out.

"Hold the fabric up, baby. I need to do this. The last time I went down on you was to distract my girlfriend. This time, it's to worship my f-future w-wife."

Emotion grips me at his words, and I barely follow his instruction before his mouth is eating at me like he's been starved for my taste. Oh, God. The long strokes of his tongue tighten into tight circles around my clit, and the trembling of my legs when he sucks it between his lips makes it difficult to stay upright. I'm not going to last, and that is proven with stunning clarity when Theo inserts two long fingers inside me and presses against the spot only he has ever been able to find.

I detonate and scream as my orgasm rips through me, and he continues to lap gently and hold me up until my limbs are as soft as Jello.

It's almost criminal how good he's become at playing my body. I've never been with anyone more eager to please or willing to learn what makes me tick. Thank God I'm marrying him; I'm going to be the happiest wife ever on all fronts, emotional and physical.

"Okay, my turn, hot stuff," I pant.

My brain can't believe that the same man who beams up at me with the sweetest smile is the same one who short-circuited my brain. I don't know how he does it, but for how naughty he's learned to be, he still manages to look innocent.

As if he can read my thoughts, he smirks. "That's one."

A gentle hand presses against my lower back and presses me over his shoulder. Once he ensures I'm secure, he stands and carries me to the bed so he can plop me down. I quickly swat my hair out of the way so I can watch him unveil the body that reaps the benefits of all his swimming.

My mouth dries, and any moisture left in my body moves south when he slowly removes his shirt and shucks his swim trunks.

Stretches of sun-bronzed skin and lean, trim muscle greet me, and I track each cut edge and delicious divot down to his cock. I scoot closer to him so I can grasp his long, thick length, and his little inhale of breath makes me smile. When I lick up and around his head and twist my fist just the way he likes, his full-body shudder makes me moan.

He may be accustomed to my touch and all the ways we make each other feel good, but he never takes it for granted. Each touch is treated like his first introduction to pleasure, and he always meets me with wonder, gratitude, and boundless enthusiasm. The main difference, however, is his stamina.

I lose count of the nerdgasms we give each other, and it isn't until pale-pink light crests the horizon and disrupts the darkness that we give in to the fatigue.

In moments like this, when I'm wrapped in his arms, I'm extra grateful to have a partner who checks every box, even the ones I didn't know I had. Our baecation turned into the beginning of our forever, and I look forward to every first, last, and everything in between with my naughty nerd by side.

EPILOGUE

Professor Cohen Wilder

"Theo, I have a question for you when you have a spare moment."

I remove my glasses, place them on my desk next to the stack of abysmal papers I've been reading for the past hour, and rub my temples. I swear, most of my students can't string together a coherent sentence let alone an original thought.

"I have a moment now. What do you need?"

What I need are more students like him: sincere, intelligent, hardworking, and studious. I'm not ignorant; I know why many undergraduate students sign up for my courses, but it doesn't mean I can't die a little inside. However, that's not what I want to talk to him about.

"I've been asked to lead a short-term study abroad program this summer. It was very last minute, but the professor they had lined up had a family emergency come up, so they needed a flexible replacement."

His eyebrows lift in surprise. "That could be fun or an absolute disaster. When and where will you be going?"

I smile. These details are the silver lining to the dean's request.

"The first summer session, so almost three weeks . . . in Greece."

His jaw drops. He's almost as passionate about mythology as I am, which is one reason we get along so well. Needless to say, this destination is a dream.

"There's no way that could be an absolute disaster. It's Greece! It'll be amazing."

My smile widens as I go in for the kill. "I know. The location alone silenced my initial reservations. Would you like to go with me? I'm allowed to bring a TA. I could use your help, especially since the program will be brief but rigorous."

"I would l-love to," he says. I feel triumphant for two seconds before he adds, "But I can't. I'm so s-sorry."

"There's no need to apologize. Is there a reason why you can't? The university will, of course, cover your expenses and will continue to provide your stipend. We can make sure they adjust it appropriately to account for costs there."

"Th-that's not it." He gulps, and when I raise an eyebrow as a signal for him to continue, he explains. "I already committed to spending that time with Addy's f-family at their s-summer house. We've both been so b-busy that it seemed like the perfect time for us to bond, especially now that we're en-engaged."

Ah, of course. I'm disappointed on my own behalf, but I get it.

"No worries. I hope you have fun with her family. I wish you could go, but I understand why you can't. Mutual appreciation for the destination aside, I'll be hard-pressed to find a trustworthy, competent TA in such a short turnaround. If you know anyone who may suit my needs, please send them my way."

I wasn't expecting him to recommend someone right this moment, so his swift reply surprises me.

"Actually, I think I do. I happen to know they're available, and they're smart, organized, and reliable. I just need to see if they'd be interested."

"I'm listening."

Theo leans forward in his seat. "You know Demi, my best friend?" His brow furrows, and he looks contemplative. "Now that I think about it, I don't think you've met, but I know you've at least seen her with me. If she's willing and able to go, she fits what you're looking for. Of course, her dad would need to sign off on it, but he works here too, so I don't see why he'd have a problem since it's for school."

I keep my face impassive, but there's a sinking feeling deep in my gut.

Yes, I've seen his best friend. There's no way I *can't* see the curvy little temptress whenever she's in my line of sight, can't feel her presence like a siren's call.

My reaction to her is baffling. Until she showed up in my class one day to pick up Theo, students never interested me sexually or romantically. She's been a long-term thorn in my side without even knowing it, and of-fucking-course her father would also be a colleague of some sort.

If she TAs for me, it's a tangled, disastrous wreck waiting to happen. I should say no, absolutely not. I'll take anyone else, or I'll go alone.

Instead, I seal my fate.

"Send her my way."

I've been told that my hubris would be my downfall one day, but I have a feeling it'll be her.

Read *Nerdgasm* today for Theo and Addy's love story. Connect with Kimberly to get updates on upcoming books and exclusive sneak peeks.

REUNITED

AN AFTER CARE REUNION

L.B. DUNBAR

FIVE YEARS

For five years we've been coming to this beautiful Hawaiian island to regroup and celebrate.

The good news about my remission from breast cancer.

The reminder of our first meeting.

The anniversary of our wedding.

As I sit on the edge of the pool, I smile at the three children playing in the water. Their father isn't far away, watching his brood who are now ten, eight, and four. Gage Everly is a lucky man. One of his greatest fortunes, though, is the woman sitting beside me.

"Granger! Don't splash your sister," Ivy calls out, scowling at her four-year-old son. The blonde happens to be my niece through marriage, but she's also become one of my best friends despite an age difference that numbers in decades, not years. She's like a second daughter to me and I know I've been a second mother to her. She lost hers to an awful disease.

Fortunately, for me, I'd been able to beat cancer. Five years free.

When I first met Ivy, I was sitting on this very pool's edge, self-consciously fiddling with a scarf on my head, covering the fuzz growing in but not fully restored. My hair never was the same after chemotherapy. I keep it short now, and the blonde streaks blend with the sudden onset of white. My hair is also curlier than it was before.

Before Tommy.

Glancing up from my position, where I dangle my feet in the pool and softly kick my legs back and forth in the cool water, I find him across the pool deck.

Tommy. Not Tom. Not Thomas. Not even his stage name of Lawson Colt. Just Tommy.

My Tommy.

A man now in his fifties but as fit as any young stud. His barrel chest is still solid. Said chest is covered in a blend of black and white curls. A jaw bristling with the same combination of ink and silver. A tempting trail leads down his abs to his waistband. Firm legs hold up his tall form. And dark aviator glasses cover deep brown eyes.

He's more casually dressed in a brightly-colored bathing suit than when I first met him poolside five years ago, but he's no less intense.

Because despite those reflective lenses covering his eyes, I know he's focused on me, and a shiver ripples up my spine.

The good kind of quiver that makes you warm in private places and sets your heart fluttering. When you know your man is watching you, wanting you. And Tommy Carrigan loves me.

I fight a smile, chew the corner of my lip, and tear my glance away to take in the kids splashing in the pool.

"Think he'll ever relax, Edie?" Ivy asks me about her uncle.

I gaze back at Tommy and softly chuckle. "Someday. Maybe."

Although we return to this resort every winter-holiday season—because a tradition had been set before I'd met any of them—Tommy is always on high alert around the pool.

When you manage a famous rock band, who want to spend family time with their wives and kids, being in such a public place like the resort pool puts Tommy on edge.

When I met him, one of the first things he said to me was to move away from his niece when I had no idea who she was or who she was married to.

I didn't know Gage Everly was someone I *should* know. Or that Collision was one of the hottest bands.

Now, *the boys*—despite being men in their late thirties—are family. And everyone has gathered for the next two weeks.

Gage and Ivy with Ava, Emmaline, and Granger. Jared and Lexi. West. Petty.

"Hello, beautiful." Thinking of the devil, Petty collapses beside me and bumps my shoulder with his. The curly haired blond is still a giant child, and he knows it pisses off Tommy when he flirts with me.

Being that Tommy's on the other side of the pool, we're safe from scrutiny for the moment.

"Hey yourself, troublemaker," I tease. Petty is the last man standing in the band when it comes to love. "I'm surprised to see you so early."

"It's almost noon," he says, holding up his wrist as if he wears a watch. He doesn't. He's dressed in orange board shorts and nothing else, and looks freshly rolled-out-of-bed.

"That's early for you," Ivy jokes from the other side of me.

Petty squints at the chaos in the pool. "Well, we don't all have little munchkins to wake us at the crack of dawn."

Ivy playfully huffs, agreeing with him. Her kids are early risers. We've been at the pool for hours already.

"Uh-oh. Here comes the big bad wolf," Petty mutters, before slipping into the pool and swimming to the center, joining Gage with his children.

"He did that on purpose," Ivy says.

"Uh-huh," I agree.

Petty's trying to dodge Tommy who is now stalking around the pool toward us. The band manager can be a grumpy bear when it comes to his crew, especially when they overindulge and miss band practice. Petty can be the worst culprit.

"Darlin'," he addresses me as he nears.

"Tommy," I reply mimicking his Southern drawl *and* the edge in his tone.

"Come have a seat, Uncle Tommy," Ivy suggests, patting the space beside her but knowing he'll pass her and sit beside me.

He does. Extra close. Like his thigh is touching mine. We're shoulder to shoulder, and he hooks one of his feet underneath my leg dangling in the water.

"He's avoiding me, isn't he?" Tommy states, eyeing Collision's drummer spinning skinny Granger around in the water. "He hit on you?"

"He's always a flirt," I remind him.

"He's such a punk," Tommy mutters, but he doesn't mean it. Each of the boys has had their issues over the years. Tommy's been there for every one of their sticky situations, because he loves each of these men like they are his sons. Especially Petty. His restless nature reminds Tommy of himself.

Then again, each of the band members has a spark that mirrors their manager.

Gage and his silent, broody personae, but also a deep love for his wife and children.

Jared and his book smart, all business sense about the band.

West, who was newish to the band when I met them, and eager to just play music.

And Petty, who has had his share of hardships and heartbreak but disguises it all with a joke and flirtation.

"He's innocent," I state.

Tommy snorts in disagreement. I bump his shoulder with mine and he turns his head, giving me a soft smile.

"You're too sweet on him, darlin'."

"Only have eyes for you, honey." The endearment does the trick. Tommy visibly relaxes beside me. Shoulders lowering a little. Arms going back to support him. Foot curling tighter around my leg and rubbing downward. He leans sideways to kiss my shoulder before settling back into his easier position.

"You've got to let them have a little fun. This is a vacation." Tommy doesn't really need the reminder. He's just tense for the first few days we are here, until he finds his relaxation groove.

"Speaking of vacation . . ." Tommy nods toward something and I follow his gaze, noticing Masie, West and Caleb finally arriving at the pool.

My smile grows and I lift an arm to exaggerate a wave for their attention. Caleb and Masie are also family. As in, my adult children.

Caleb is practically announcing his arrival. "Is that Ava Bear and Emmaline Jelly Belly in the pool?" He doesn't wait for answers but does a little skip before tucking his legs, and dropping into the refreshing water, exploding a giant splash at Gage and his kids.

My twenty-seven-year-old son loves to rile up the girls, especially Ava who is on the cusp of adolescence and sometimes agitated by the nickname Caleb has given her. As a minor league baseball player, he's finally been called up to the pros and he's thrilled to be starting with the Chicago Anchors next spring.

My daughter Masie graduated college last spring and has decided to go to medical school to be a midwife. She originally went to college to be an oncology nurse after all she'd lived through during my three years with the disease while she was still in high school. After a rotation with infants, though, she fell in love with the idea of helping bring babies into the world. A happier profession than oncology, in my opinion.

My smile falters a bit as I watch the awkwardness between West and Masie. They've been on-again, off-again. In private. In public. For four years. As a college student, it was difficult to date a rock star. Their five-year age difference had me concerned at first, especially since Masie was still *in* high school when they met. But she's twenty-three and has become the level-headed woman I knew she'd be. She has goals of her own, and while her heart might want to chase the rock star, her head pulls her toward a career for herself.

"How are they doing?" Tommy asks, as if he doesn't know. As if he doesn't see the tension nearly visible between Masie and West. Regardless of whatever strain is between them right now, West is still a gentleman. He carried Masie's bag, and he spreads out her towel on a lounge chair in the VIP section Tommy demands the band reserves for some semblance of privacy. Masie is polite as she thanks West, but their movements are too stilted, too reserved for a young couple.

Tommy slips his hand against mine and entwines our fingers, giving mine a squeeze. "They'll figure it out," he states when I don't answer him immediately. The comment is a reminder to *let* them figure it out. Tommy knows it's been a struggle for me. I don't want to see my girl's heart broken. I don't want West's to break either.

"Okay, swimming time," Tommy says, slipping into the pool while still holding my hand and distracting me from my children.

"Tommy," I warn as he tugs me forward, not releasing my fingers, until I'm almost falling into the water face first.

"Pool, darlin'," he murmurs, dipping his broad body lower and blowing bubbles against the surface.

Gingerly, I slide into the pool. "It's cold." I suck in a breath at the sudden shock creeping up my body, especially over my waistline.

Tommy reaches out and tugs me flush to him. "I'll warm you up."

"Thomas," I warn. His tone is recognizable. Sight unseen, I'm certain there's a gleam in his eyes. He wants to do *things* in this pool that need to be saved for the privacy of our room.

His hands coast over my hips and around to my backside, drawing me tighter against him. I wrap my arms around his neck and lower my body beneath the surface, lining us up in all the ways we shouldn't be, considering this is a crowded resort pool in broad daylight.

Tommy hums, squeezing my ass cheeks underneath the water. "I remember the first time I saw you here."

"Really?" My brows lift as I pull back and stare at my reflection in his sunglasses.

"Prettiest woman at the pool."

I laugh, deep and loud. He's so full of shit. "Really?" Sarcasm drips from the question.

Tommy tugs me harder, forcing my legs to spread wider and wrap around his hips. "Knew you were going to wreck me in the best of ways."

"You knew no such thing." I chuckle.

"Saw you staring at me. Drinking me in."

"So, it was all about you. *Your* ego," I tease. Tommy might be the most level-headed man I know. He's had his time in the limelight, and he's happy to be on the sidelines now, managing Collision and helping this newer, younger band be all they can be. He's the first to say fame is fleeting. Enjoy it while you can. Let it go when you can't enjoy it anymore.

Tommy chuckles. "More like all about my dick, darlin'." His bluntness does not surprise me. "But my heart was already singing a tune as well."

"Really?" I ask again. "And what song was it singing?"

I'm awful at music trivia and Tommy's going to tell me some obscure song I've never heard of by some band he thinks I should know but won't. It's our own inside joke. Then again, he's a closet Bee-Gees fan, and it's one of my favorite things about him. When we watched a documentary about the Gibb brothers, I understood Tommy's attraction to them even more. They were musical geniuses.

"Reunited." Tommy hums a few bars of the 1970s song.

"Wasn't that a breakup song?"

Tommy continues to hum, his gravelly sound growing stronger and louder. "Was. But I mean the title is perfect for us. You're the other half of my heart. Now I'm whole."

"Tommy," I whisper. He can be too charming when he wants to be. Lifting his glasses so I can see his dark eyes, I'm not surprised the brown is nearly eclipsed with black. "You're the other half of me, too, honey."

I should have expected it, but I didn't. The rush of his mouth. The firm hand on the back of my head. The thrust of his tongue. When he's sweet toward me and I'm sweet right back, it's like a switch flips. He's on fire for me.

"We need out of this pool," he mutters against my lips. "Because you in this suit . . . it needs to come off."

He tugs at the bottom of my tankini beneath the water, letting it snap back against my skin before abruptly standing with me still wrapped around him.

I lower my legs to stand on my own and Tommy slips a hand between us to adjust himself. He's about to give everyone a show, because beneath that form fitting suit of his is a steel rod of desire that can't be disguised. Tommy spins me so my back is to his front, and he walks us to the stairs, using me as his shield.

"Gonna get a room, old man?" Petty teases from where he sits on a lounger in the VIP section.

"Be respectful," Tommy snaps at his band member.

Petty's gaze snaps to me, and he mouths, *Sorry.* I shake my head, dismissing him. Sometimes the over-fifty band *manager* is as bad as the younger set in the horny department.

Tommy wraps a towel around his waist and leans forward to snag my beach bag while I wrap a skirt around my lower half.

"Where you going, Uncle Tommy?" Emmaline calls from the pool, all innocent and sweet. Her blond curls are slicked back from the water.

"Naptime, baby girl," he calls back, taking my hand in his.

"You're too old for naps." She giggles with love for her great-uncle.

"Never too old for afternoon delight," he mumbles, squeezing my hand.

"What's afternoon delight?" Ava asks next, louder than her little sister. The wise brunette sees and hears everything lately.

"Jesus," Gage mutters from his spot in the pool. "Really, old man?" He arches a brow at his uncle by marriage, band manager, and truest friend. As if Gage is any less affectionate toward his wife in front of his children. Sometimes when he kisses her, it's almost obscene.

"Watch who you're calling old. When you're my age, you'll still be wishing you could nap like me."

The sexual euphemisms are flying like weakly aimed arrows and it's time to end this charade of napping.

"Tommy," I whisper, and his attention comes back to me. "Take me to bed."

"Working on it, darlin'." My arm is almost pulled from the socket as he leads me through the pool area and into the lobby of the hotel.

I expect us to head directly to our suite. The penthouse is still rented by the Everly's, especially as their family has grown. Tommy got us a luxury suite, and for the first time, purchased a separate room for Masie. Caleb doesn't mind bunking with West and Petty.

Instead of our room, though, Tommy detours us down a hallway that leads toward the bar. I'm a little disappointed as I wasn't anticipating a drink first.

Then he veers us again and we're walking down a hallway that brings back all the memories.

Me leaving the bar early. Him chasing me. Then Tommy dragging me into an empty conference room like he's doing right now.

"Tommy." I giggle like a schoolgirl. "It's the middle of the day."

"Perfect time for afternoon delight." He spins me once we are inside the vacant space and locks the door behind me.

He drops my pool bag and I'm instantly pressed up against the door. His mouth captures mine, making me almost dizzy with his urgency. Five years later, and he still kisses me like he might lose me. Like I might disappear, which I'd never do to him.

His large hand skims down the front of my still wet bathing suit and slips underneath my beach skirt.

"Drop the bottoms, darlin'."

I should scold him. Remind him we're in a public space. Someone could walk in at any moment. But this is our routine. Once a year, upon our return, we reunite with this room where he first kissed me and touched me after years of sexual drought. And we'd only met about six hours earlier.

I wasn't like that. I didn't attract men like a magnet or let them touch me within a blink of meeting them.

But Tommy had been different.

And I do as he asks, knowing I'm not getting out of this room without him touching me.

It takes some effort to roll down my tankini bottoms, also still wet and clinging to my skin. Once I do, I step out of them and Tommy swipes them up like dainty panties, not water-drenched spandex. He drops the wet mess into my bag before sliding his hand between my thighs again. His fingers disappear beneath the skirt and easily find what he seeks.

"You're soaked."

I don't have a chance to respond as his mouth covers mine at the same time two fingers glide into me. My breath hitches with the suddenness, but I quickly settle into the rhythm he sets, working me over with the strength of his fingers and the intensity of his touch.

I moan against his mouth, warning him with the sound how close I am. His kisses deepen. His tongue swirls. His fingers thrust until I crash like the ocean waves outside.

"That's it, darlin'," he hums, knowing what he's done to my body. "God, I love you."

"I love you." The declaration is a breathless whisper as I'm still spiraling from his touch.

"Return the favor." It's another private joke and more of a question than a command, like that first time. He's asking permission, acknowledging this room isn't the dark, late-night escape from a bar but filtered with late afternoon sunlight streaming through the limited windows covered by lowered blinds.

Spinning, I give him my back, giving him my answer. I hear the rip of the

Velcro securing his swim shorts and feel the breeze of air conditioning as my bare backside is exposed when Tommy lifts my skirt.

"Gonna be quick," he warns. Tommy is a ferocious lover for his age. Gentle and sweet sometimes. Hot and rushed at others.

This is what I do to him. And what he does to me.

I lower my forehead to the closed door and brace for the swiftness of his thrust. Once planted inside me, he stills, and I melt over him. He pauses a second, nibbling along my neck before biting me in that spot that will turn me into a puddle.

"Darlin'," he growls before pulling back and surging forward again, setting a new pace that expresses his urgent desire. He reaches around me, plucking at my clit, but this round is all for him and I brush his hand away. He typically doesn't like that—me denying him—but I'll let him make it up to me once we are in our room. For now, I want him to break.

My breath hitches. My back arches. I groan deep and throaty, carving his name into two syllables. "Tom-my."

He releases a strained grunt to accompany his finish as he pours into me. His fingertips dig into my hips. His body slowing but still thrusting, dipping, filling me.

"Edie," he groans, lowering his forehead to my shoulder as we both pant from the exertion. We aren't as young as we used to be, but our desire for one another remains on the rise.

"You undo me. Every damn time," he murmurs against my cool skin. Next, he moves to my ear, his bristly cheek brushing mine. His voice drops, serious but tender. "I'm so grateful you married me."

"I'm thankful, too," I whisper, caught off guard by a sudden swell of emotion.

"No regrets," he says, leaning so he can better see my face.

I twist to view him over my shoulder. "Never."

He smiles slowly, crooking up one side of his mouth before the other joins. Then, he's kissing me, slow and sweet, assuring me with his kiss he's never regretted a day together either.

From the moment *I* saw this man, I had no idea he'd undo me in all the ways he has. He made me feel desired and loved, despite all my body and heart had been through in the past. He'd been good to me. And he'd wanted me in his life, constantly by his side.

It's why he asked me to be his wife. And why I accepted.

And during this holiday vacation we'll be celebrating how we'd married on New Year's Day, wanting to start another year with love in our hearts and holding each other's hand.

In the exact place where it all started—beautiful Hawaii.

Want the full story of Tommy and Edie? Read *After Care*. Stay up to date on all things L.B. Dunbar at www.lbdunbar.com.

HORNY AND HEALING IN HAWAII

LAUREN ROWE

CHAPTER 1

Bye, Bye, Brayden

I'm trembling as Brayden looks into my eyes and delivers his wedding vows. My heart is pounding like a drum against my chest. The soft sounds of audience members sniffling through happy tears are drowned out by the rush of emotions coursing through me. Rage at how effectively Brayden fooled and betrayed me. Shame that I didn't suspect the truth before finding those texts. Not once. How could I have been so blind and stupid?

"And that's when I knew you'd become my wife one day," Brayden says, his blue eyes locked with mine, and my stomach somersaults. Now that I know his words are all lies, watching him say them so smoothly and convincingly is actually terrifying. Have I been in love with a monster this whole time? He smiles and says, "I knew in that moment I'd never find a better wife or mother to my children. Julia, I knew right then I wanted to grow old with you. To protect you and love you and be your best friend and teammate through life, forever. Julia, I promise to always . . ."

I can't take it anymore. I tune him out, even as I maintain eye contact. When I overheard Brayden's phone conversation two days ago, I couldn't believe my ears. *I had to have misheard him,* I thought. *Misunderstood somehow.* But then, after clever, loyal Delilah easily figured out the passcode to her big brother's phone, and I was able to get into my fiancé's closely guarded device while he slept, the truth couldn't be denied any longer. In less than twenty hours, I was scheduled to marry a serial cheater. A liar. A man who clearly never really loved me. *A gold digger.*

I would have cancelled the wedding right then and there, if I could have gotten even half the money back for my father. But since the wedding was too close to recoup a single dime, I decided not to let the money go to waste. What better reason to party and celebrate with the people I love the most than me escaping from a monster, mere hours before pledging my eternal love to him? Hatching my plan gave me a reason to stop sobbing on the bathroom floor. It made me put down the bottle of sleeping pills, get up, and start furiously writing the speech I'm mere seconds away from delivering to Brayden in front of all his family and friends.

"Julia?" the wedding officiant says, right on cue. Brayden has finished his personalized vows. It's my turn now.

With shaking hands, I pull the folded paper from my bra, making everyone in the congregation chuckle. I've always been a planner. Nothing left to chance. That's Julia for you. Do you have a headache? Ask Julia. Surely, she's got some Tylenol in her purse. A button popped off your dress? Ask Julia. She's probably got a needle and thread in her purse. But what could I have stuffed into my purse to prepare for this moment—when the man I thought I loved would turn out to be a fucking sociopath?

I take a deep breath as I survey the typewritten words in my trembling hand, and when I've mustered my courage, I look into Brayden's smiling face. "Brayden, I thought about it, and couldn't figure out the perfect words for this one-of-a-kind, special moment, so I decided to quote you, since you always know exactly what to say, no matter the situation or occasion. I'll never forget the first time you said to me, 'Julia, I'll love you forever and a day, come what may.' It brought tears to my eyes. You saw how much that touched me, so you made it your mantra. Your catchphrase, if you will. And I loved it.'" I look at the audience. "I genuinely believed him. Loved him, heart and soul." I return to Brayden. "But, as it turns out, on one of the days you said those words to me—on Thursday of last week, to be exact—you also told a gorgeous blonde named Beth, an exotic dancer with extremely large breasts, 'I can't wait to taste your sweet pussy again, baby. I can't wait to—'"

As gasps and shocked exclamations rumble through the chapel, Brayden snatches the paper out of my hands. But I don't need the paper now. Brayden's betrayals are burned into my gray matter.

"And to a woman named Willow," I say, raising my voice to be heard above the rising chaos in the chapel, "you texted: 'My work meeting finished early, baby. I'm heading over now. Get ready to get railed.'"

Even louder gasps and exclamations erupt in the chapel. People are standing. Moving. Brayden holds up his palms to the audience. "My phone was hacked. If you'll give us a minute, we'll—"

"There's no more 'we,' Brayden," I grit out. "There's me and the liar who can go fuck himself." I turn to the audience. "The date and time of his text to Willow was three minutes after we'd finished tasting cakes for our wedding reception. We unexpectedly fell in love with the first cake and cut the tasting short. Brayden supposedly rushed back to work to close an important deal after that. Little did I know, he was actually rushing off to *rail* Willow."

Brayden grabs my arm. He says he can explain everything. He begs me to listen to him. But when the best man thankfully pulls him away from me, I'm able to continue my planned speech.

"I would have cancelled the wedding, but I only found out the truth yesterday—too late to get any of my father's money back." I look at him. "I'm sorry, Dad. Thank you for giving me my dream wedding. Too bad the groom is a cunt, huh?" As the gathered audience titters and murmurs, I continue, "So, anyway, since the reception is already paid for, and everything I've planned is going to be amazing and perfect, let's not waste any of it. Let's have ourselves a 'Fuck you, Brayden!' party—a celebration that I've narrowly dodged the worst bullet of my life."

I turn to look at Delilah in the line of bridesmaids—my guardian angel—and send her a secret wink of thanks, and my honorary sister returns the gesture. If it weren't for Brayden's little sister helping me find out the full truth yesterday, this officiant would be pronouncing me Brayden's wife right this very minute.

"Anyone who wants to celebrate this happy day, other than Brayden and his parents, of course, please head to the reception hall now. I'm going to eat, drink, and dance the night away with you, before hopping onto my scheduled flight to Hawaii tomorrow morning." I look at Brayden. "Oh, yes. I'm still going to Hawaii to enjoy what should have been our honeymoon. And to be clear, by *enjoy*, I mean I'm going to drink rum punch like water and get myself *railed*, every single night, the same way you railed Willow after tasting wedding cakes with me.'"

CHAPTER 2

Hello, Handsome Stranger

I talked a good game yesterday in the church about getting myself railed here in Hawaii, but as I trudge up the walkway toward my rented bungalow for the week, the last thing I want to do is hit the bars or the beach or dating apps in search of an appropriate candidate to perform the deed. I feel hung over and exhausted and not the least bit interested in human interaction. I don't even want to talk to another person, let alone let someone fuck me. All I want to do is spend the next week in solitude. Reading. Sleeping. Looking at the ocean and trying to piece together what went wrong. How I missed the signs.

After double checking the entry code on my phone, I enter the digits on the keypad on the bungalow door, but it doesn't open. I try again. And again. But, still, nothing. What the heck? I find the phone number connected to my confirmation email. But when I call it, no dice. My call goes straight to voicemail.

As I'm leaving a voicemail, I notice a rock nestled in a cluster of flowers. It looks suspiciously like the fake rock that holds my spare house key back home. I pick it up, and sure enough, it's as fake as the tits on that exotic dancer on Brayden's phone. I open the small, plastic door on the bottom of the rock, and, voila, I've found a key. Will it fit in the lock on the bungalow door? That's the question.

I head to the door. Slide in the key. Turn the lock. And just like that, my problem is solved. When I step inside the bungalow, I'm overjoyed and relieved. It's stunning. Every bit as gorgeous as the photos led me to believe. The perfect place for me to lick my wounds and process the worst betrayal and shame of my life.

First things first, I need to pee. I ditch my rolling suitcase in the middle of the living area and head toward a closed door. Nope. It's a closet. I try the next door and shriek when I come face to face with a naked, dripping-wet man.

"What the fuck?" he shouts, jerking back, as I scream, "Oh my god!"

I bolt out of the bathroom and straight out the front door. But since I've left my suitcase and purse and phone inside the bungalow, I can't go any farther than that. *Jesus Christ*. What the hell is he doing here? He's probably not a burglar, given that he just took a shower. Also, now that I think about it, I saw a suitcase on the bed as I raced past the bedroom on my way out.

I pace in front of the front door, trying to figure out what to do. He was definitely hot, I'll give him that. In fact, I've never seen a naked man who's *that* hot, in person. When my friends took me to a male strip show for my bachelorette party in Vegas, some of the dancers were that hot. But I certainly didn't see them *naked*. I haven't seen that many dicks in my twenty-eight years, since I've always been a serial monogamist; so I can't be positive that guy's dick was as massively thick and long, compared to the general population of dicks, as it seemed to me in the moment. It was definitely bigger than any dick I've had inside me, though. That's for fucking sure. After yesterday's fiasco, did my bridesmaids quickly chip in to buy me a paid boy toy for my solo week in Hawaii? Did they call the strip club we went to in Vegas and ask if anyone knew anyone in Kauai who might want the job of cheering up a runaway bride?

The front door opens and the fit man from the bathroom comes out in nothing but board shorts. His bare chest is delectable. Tan and muscular. His dark hair is still wet from his shower and slightly curled. His eyes are dark brown and his teeth straight and white.

"Why are you here?" I say.

"I was about to you ask you the same thing."

"I've rented this bungalow for the week."

"I've got this place for the whole week. You must have the wrong address. Or the wrong dates."

"I can show you," I say. "My phone is inside." We head back inside and compare our respective booking confirmations, and quickly realize the unfortunate situation: the rental company has doubled-booked this place. I call the number from before and leave another voicemail. And when that's done, I sit on the couch with my face in my hands.

"I'll find another place," the guy mutters on an exhale. "Is it okay with you if I sit on the couch while searching for somewhere else to go?"

I didn't expect such chivalry. I thought I'd have a fight on my hands. "Of course, you can sit. I feel bad, though. This isn't your fault."

"It's okay. These things happen. I'll figure something out. Do you mind if I make myself a drink to enjoy while searching for a new place? I stopped on my way here from the airport to get ingredients for cocktails for the week."

"You literally just got here?" I say.

"Twenty minutes before you. That's good, though. At least, I'm not all settled in and drunk off my ass yet. If this was going to happen to me, I'd prefer it happen now."

He's handling this cluster fuck remarkably well. If I'd walked into this bungalow with Brayden at my side, as originally planned, and we found this man here, I'm positive Brayden would have turned the situation into something confrontational and combative, without even giving this handsome, laid-back man a chance to react kindly, as he's doing now.

"Of course, you can make yourself a drink," I say. "But only if you make one for me, too."

He smiles. "Deal."

He heads to the kitchen and gets to work. As he makes the drinks, I ask, "What brings you here for the week?"

"My brother's cancelled wedding. He was supposed to get married here yesterday, but he found out a week ago his fiancée had cheated on him with one of his friends."

"Oh no."

"He couldn't get his money back for the honeymoon, but he didn't have the heart to come here alone. So, he gave the place to me." He chuckles. "Or so he thought. Apparently, not so much."

During the flight here, I told myself I wouldn't tell the story of my cancelled wedding to anyone I met in Hawaii. Maybe not to anyone, ever, for the rest of my life. But certainly, not here. In Kauai, I told myself, I'd pretend to be a mysterious, sultry woman on the prowl. A woman who came to Hawaii for nothing but fun. A woman at the top of her game who's never been rejected in her life.

But suddenly, after hearing this handsome stranger's tale, I can't help blurting, "A broken engagement and cancelled honeymoon brought me here, too. Except, in this case, I'm the one who was supposed to get married."

He looks deeply sympathetic. "I'm sorry to hear that." He hands me a concoction that looks like paradise in a glass, and we head to the couch with our drinks. Once settled, I tell him the rest of my embarrassing tale. Every single detail of it, including the fact that I told the entire congregation in that church that I planned to go to Hawaii to get myself "railed" every single night of my vacation, the same way Brayden had "railed" the woman on his phone named Willow.

By the time I'm done talking, we've both finished our delicious drinks and the handsome stranger sitting next to me has a noticeable bulge in his board shorts. Clearly, his dick is now at full mast, thanks to the last part of my story—the part where I vowed to get myself railed in Hawaii.

When I notice the evidence of his arousal, excitement courses through me. Tingles skate across my skin and awaken the nerve endings between my legs. I put down my empty glass on the coffee table with a smirk and ask, "Are you single, by any chance?"

He matches my smirk. Doesn't break eye contact. "I am, yes."

"Please, don't lie to me about this. I need you to be honest with me."

"I'm single." He gnaws on the inside of his cheek for a moment. "Actually, it wasn't my brother who got cheated on by his fiancée. It was me. I was too embarrassed to admit that to a stranger when you first walked in. But in light of what you've told me, I feel like you deserve to know the truth. We're in the same boat."

"I'm sorry to hear that." I am. Truly. But also, I'm *not*.

He sighs. "Honestly, I came here to lick my wounds for a week. Get shitfaced and feel sorry for myself."

I wouldn't normally be this forward, but the man's visibly hard as a rock behind his shorts. Plus, he handled the double-booking so damned well. And it certainly doesn't hurt that he's hot as fuck and makes an incredible tropical cocktail.

"Listen, I don't know if this is a crazy thing to suggest," I say. "I don't know if you're at all attracted to me, but I'm wondering if you'd like to be the guy who rails me tonight. I'm thinking maybe we could lick each other tonight, rather than licking our wounds."

One side of his handsome mouth tilts up. "You're a mind-reader."

I motion to the bugle in his shorts. "Well, a dick reader, anyway."

He chuckles. "In this particular moment, they're one and the same. Yes, I'm attracted to you. Extremely attracted to you. And yes that sounds like a fantastic idea to me."

"If all goes well tonight, and we're both feeling it in the morning, maybe you wouldn't need to look for another place to stay this week. Maybe you could stay here with me and we could have ourselves a weeklong vacation fling—something to help us both get our groove back, so to speak, before we need to go back home and figure out how to return all the wedding presents."

"What happens in Hawaii stays in Hawaii?"

"Exactly. A fun distraction to make us forget . . ." I stop speaking, as emotion unexpectedly rises up inside me. I take a deep breath and finish my sentence. "All the lies and deceit. Even if it's only for one night."

His chest heaves. He rises from the couch and extends his hand. "Come with me. Let me make you feel good."

I can barely breathe. "I'll meet you in the bedroom. I want to take a shower first."

"Take your time. I'll be waiting for you, naked in bed.

A shock of arousal courses through me. "Sounds good."

"I'm Mateo, by the way."

I laugh. "Julia. Nice to meet you."

"Nice to meet you, Julia. Meet me in the bedroom, whenever you're ready."

CHAPTER 3

Mateo's Got A Big Dick and He Knows How To Use It

I walk into the bedroom, my hair wet from my shower, my naked body wrapped in a skimpy towel. I've never had sex on a first date before, let alone within minutes of meeting someone. I don't even know Mateo's last name! But in this moment, not knowing anything about him, knowing I'll never see him again after tonight, or this week, if all goes well, is thrilling. I feel reckless. Sexy. Untethered and uninhibited.

Mateo is on the bed with the bedding pulled back. His tan, naked body looks delectable against the stark white sheet. As I approach, he gets out of bed and takes my face in his palms. The tip of his hard-on nudges my belly as his soft lips meet mine, and we both jolt at the dual connection of our flesh. He smells good. Looks good. I don't know what he's like in real life. Why his ex-fiancée wasn't faithful to him. And I don't want to know any of it. For me, Mateo is a fantasy. A form of therapy from whom I intend to squeeze every amount of pleasure as possible before returning to reality. The last thing I need this week is for Mateo to know my last name and google me — and then figure out that my father has done exceedingly well for himself and assume, incorrectly, that I'm living a life that's fancier than my own kindergarten teacher salary affords.

I open my lips slightly, and Mateo slides his tongue inside my mouth. As our tongues tangle and dance, rockets of pleasure shoot through me, all of them zapping me between the legs. With each passing second, I'm getting more and more turned on. More and more certain this was a brilliant idea.

There's no sense of urgency in our kiss. He's taking my temperature, I think. Getting a read on me. Luring me in, slowly. And the tactic, if that's what it is, is impeccably effective. Soon, I'm aching for more. Pulsing, and then pounding, between my legs, as arousal floods me. By the time Mateo guides me to the bed, my most sensitive flesh is swollen. My tip is hard and beating like a steel drum.

From my mouth, Mateo's lips travel to my cheek, my jawline and neck, as his fingers begin gently stroking between my legs. I can feel myself getting wetter and wetter with his touch, my clit harder and harder and more swollen and aching.

"You're beautiful," he whispers. "He's an idiot."

Before I walked into this bedroom, I would have assumed any mention of Brayden would be a mistake. A turn off. But as it's turned out, his comment is sheer perfection. The precise words I needed to hear in this moment; and I let him know it with a loud and husky moan.

His mouth returns to mine, as his fingers begin dipping in and out of me. By the way his fingers are moving with ease, I must be insanely wet down there. Wetter than Brayden ever got me, that's for sure. If Mateo plunged himself inside me now, he'd burrow into me like a knife in warm butter.

I gyrate into his fingers and deepen our kiss, aching for penetration. But he doesn't go in. No, he leaves my mouth again and starts kissing his way down my torso, all the way to the bullseye between my legs. He repositions himself between my thighs and gets to work on me in earnest. And in less than a minute, I'm gripping the sheet beneath me and coming with a loud roar that's surely traveling through the open window to the nearby beach. But I don't care if random strangers hear me having the best sexual experience of my life. This moment is too delicious to hold back. Fuck anyone who's clutching their pearls. *I'm reborn.*

When the waves of pleasure subside, I open my eyes to find Mateo's glorious hard-on wrapped up and ready to go. He climbs over my body like a panther, grabs my hands and lifts them above my head, and then plunges himself inside me. As his body stretches mine and fills me up, I feel like I'm being injected with a narcotic. Like I'm being transported to a state of bliss on a rocket.

I wrap my thighs around his hips as he gyrates on top of me and match the movement of my pelvis with his, until we're both moving as one. Maximizing the depth of each and every thrust. It's sublime. And not only for me, based on the way Mateo is groaning with pleasure.

"Julia," he whispers into my ear. "You feel so fucking good. Jesus Christ. You're incredible."

I've never had a lover who talked during sex before. Every partner I've ever had goes about his business silently, so I've always followed suit. And now I know what I've been missing out on, because the groaning dirty talk thing Mateo is doing is taking my pleasure to another level.

We kiss passionately as our bodies move, more and more enthusiastically. With each thrust, and each swirl of my tongue with Mateo's, I suddenly feel hope that the gashes and wounds in my heart could heal. In fact, I suddenly know, for a fact, I'll one day soon be as good as new. Better than ever, as a matter of fact. I didn't even know my body could feel this good. What else have I been missing out on?

Mateo touches my face with urgency and looks at me with blazing eyes, right before he snaps his pelvis forward and releases with a loud growl. When he's done climaxing, he slides out of me, as expected. But then, he does something I'm not expecting. He kisses me deeply while massaging my clit with his fingers. I'm thinking it's wishful thinking on his part. I've never had two orgasms during sex in my life. But in short order, it's clear I'm hurtling toward another release. One that's going to be a good one.

When it comes, it curls my toes and makes me groan, even more loudly than the last time. But when the waves of pleasure subside this time, I realize I've got tears streaming down my cheeks.

"Aw, hey," Mateo coos. He wipes my tears with his thumb. "Did I hurt you?"

"No, not at all. You made me feel better than I've ever felt in my life," I admit. "I'm crying because it felt so *good*."

He sighs with relief and kisses me, and we make out for a while . . . until Mateo is suddenly hard and ready to go again. This time, I suck his big cock for a while before mounting him and riding him like a bucking bronco.

And to my shock, I wind up having an orgasm with his hard dick still inside me. It's a first for me — having an orgasm during actual intercourse. A delicious one. One that only makes me want to do it again and again and again.

When we're both sweaty and spent and in desperate need of water, we head to the kitchen, naked, to fuel up and recharge. I take a seat on a stool with a glass of water, while Mateo cuts up fresh fruit he picked up earlier on his way to the bungalow.

"You don't need to find another place this week, as far as I'm concerned," I say. "In fact, I'd really, really, *really* like it if you'd stay."

"Are you sure?"

"Can you promise to keep fucking me this week with the same kind of enthusiasm you just had in there?"

He chuckles. "Yeah, I can definitely promise you that."

"Then, yes. I'm sure."

He holds up his glass of water. "Cheers to that."

I clink his glass. "Cheers to us — to a week of fun in paradise. Absolutely no strings attached. And cheers to both of us dodging the biggest bullets of our lives."

CHAPTER 4

Fun, Fun, Fun

I open my eyes and smile when I see Mateo's stunning face on the pillow next to mine. He's already awake and reading a book.

"Whatcha reading?" I ask, resting my cheek in my palm.

He tilts the book cover toward me and smiles. It's a self-help book with a subtitle about unlocking your best self.

"Is it any good?"

"So far, yeah. I'm not fully unlocked yet, I don't think. But I'm working on it."

"You're giving me a lady boner. I love to read so much. Do you read a lot?"

"A book a week, usually."

"All of it self-help?"

"No, I read all kinds of things." He lists off some of the genres he reads, and I'm so turned on, I sling my leg over him and press myself against him, letting him know I'm feeling horny again. Other than going out for food and taking walks along the shore, Mateo and I have spent the past three days exactly like this, naked and physically entangled in this bed. Or on the couch. And as a result, we've become insanely comfortable around each other in record speed. We'll never know each other's last names, and we'll never see each other again after this crazy week, but while we're here, my body is his to enjoy and vice versa, as much as possible. The sex has been so amazing with Mateo, in fact, I'm kicking myself for settling for so much less heat in all my past relationships. Granted, I didn't know what I was missing at the time; but now that I do, I feel stupid for putting up with lukewarm, mediocre sex for so damned long.

"What do you do for a living, Mateo?" I ask. We haven't shared any personal details. That's been part of the fun. But suddenly, I'm craving information about him—the tiniest peek into his real life beyond the bubble of paradise.

"I'm in marketing. You?"

"I'm a kindergarten teacher."

His features soften. "That's amazing. I can totally see you doing that."

"How dare you, sir. I'm a sex pot."

He laughs. "Yes, you are. Damn straight." He touches a lock of hair and grins. "And you're *also* a very sweet, gentle person who seems like she'd be fantastic with kids."

I blush. "Thank you."

"Your ex is an idiot, Julia. You didn't deserve what he did, okay? What he did has nothing to do with you. If it wasn't you, he'd have done it to whoever else."

"Back at you. What your ex did has nothing to do with you . . . Right?"

He chuckles. "You're not sure?"

"Well, I mean, you're the man here. And men can be dogs. I'm not saying you deserved to be cheated on. Absolutely not. That's despicable. But I'm just wondering . . ."

"What I did to her first?"

I grimace. "Kind of. Yeah."

To my relief, he smiles. "I got injured on the job and had to do some rehab and take some time off, and that was pretty hard on the relationship. But even harder was the fact that, when my employer renewed my contract, the bump in my salary wasn't as much as she was hoping for. Not nearly as much as the bump my co-worker got. So, she decided to get with him, instead. Imagine that."

"Oh my gosh. I'm so sorry, Mateo."

He shrugs. "I'm just glad I found out before having a kid with her. That would have been a true catastrophe."

My heart is thrumming. "You want to have a kid?"

"I'd love to have a kid. You?"

"Two or three."

"Same."

"Are you still injured now?"

"No, I'm fine now. It was my knee. I had surgery and I'm all better now. Good as new."

I crinkle my forehead. Mateo got injured doing his job in marketing?

"So, listen," Mateo says, before I've mustered the courage to ask for further details about his injury. He slides his palm to rest on the curve of my bare ass. It's become the default resting spot for his palm. The place it belongs. "I've got a bunch of reservations-for-two this week, stuff that can't be refunded. If any of it interests you, we could do some of it together." He lists off the activities he's got booked: parasailing, snorkeling, jet skiing, a sunset dinner cruise. And I laugh and tell him I'm in the exact same situation —holding multiple reservations-for-two that can't be refunded at this point.

We open our calendars and cross-reference all the reservations and come up with an exciting itinerary—one that will keep us plenty busy throughout the entire week, when we're not fucking each other's brains out. I can't believe it. When I made the various reservations for daily activities for Brayden and me, I knew he'd probably poop out for some of it. But I figured we'd go with the flow, once we got here, and pick and choose the things we wanted to do and let the other stuff go to waste. But now, out of nowhere, I've got a willing, excited companion for *everything* I'd planned for this week— and even more than that, since Mateo's also got a bunch of fun stuff to share with me, too.

"So, which activity should we pick for today?" I ask excitedly, looking between our two calendars.

"How about my private boat cruise?" he suggests. "You had snorkeling booked today and sightseeing tomorrow, but we can combine both activities if we take the private boat I've got booked all day."

"Awesome."

"My excursion also includes a private chef making us a gourmet dinner on the yacht at sunset."

Yacht? He called it a boat before. And now it's a yacht? Is he being literal or silly by using that fancy word? If we're truly going on a yacht today, and not a simple boat, then Mateo's excursion will definitely be fancier than any of the reservations I've made for the week. "Yeah, that sounds perfect," I say, trying to play it cool. "How much time before we need to leave? I definitely want to take a shower before we go."

Mateo squeezes my ass, pulling me into him, and I feel the unmistakable sensation of his hard-on nudging against my thigh. "We have plenty of time to shower *after* I fuck you senseless again," he coos. "It wouldn't be a good day in Hawaii, if it didn't start with me making Pretty Julia scream before getting out of bed."

CHAPTER 5

Catching Feelings

It's a yacht.

A fancy one, too.

Holy fuck.

"Hello, Mr. Ribaldi," the captain says, shaking his hand vigorously. "Welcome. I'm a fan." He takes my hand. "Mrs. Ribaldi. Congratulations."

Mateo doesn't correct the man, and I don't blame him. He booked today's excursion as part of a honeymoon package, and explaining the truth would be highly embarrassing. Who wants to explain the cancellation of their wedding to a complete stranger? Not me, that's for sure. Also, this guy's a *fan*? Of *what*?

"We've got welcome champagne and food set up for you here, sir," another crew member says. A waiter of some sort. "And, of course, a full bar. Anything you'd like, you just let me know. I'm Leo, and I'll be taking care of you today."

"Thanks, Leo," Mateo says. "We appreciate that."

We get a tour of the yacht and Mateo is polite and kind to everyone. My father always says, "Watch how someone treats waiters and service staff. It'll tell you everything you need to know about them." Judging by Mateo's easy charm with everyone, he certainly *seems* like a good guy. But then again, I'm a gullible idiot, so . . .

At the end of the tour, we're shown where the equipment is for snorkeling, paddle boarding, and kayaking, and asked what we'd prefer to tackle first. When Mateo and I easily decide on snorkeling, off the yacht goes toward some nearby cove that's supposedly the perfect spot.

As we make our way to our destination, Mateo and I sit and drink champagne and graze on the charcuterie board set out for us. But the second Mateo gets up to use the bathroom—the very nanosecond he's gone!—I pull out my phone and search "Mateo Ribaldi." And when his name comes up, along with a smiling photo that confirms I've found the right man, I gasp audibly. *Mateo is a famous soccer player.* A professional one who plays for a popular team in Spain—and, holy shit, his most recent contract, signed earlier this year after he battled back from a knee injury, was for ten million dollars per year! *That wasn't enough for his ex? What the fuck?*

I peek toward the bathroom to make sure Mateo's not coming out, and quickly return to my research. Mateo's not the star of his team. The star is another guy who just signed a contract for forty million per year. But still, Mateo is widely respected and considered a huge reason for the team's success. On chat boards, plenty of posts say something along the lines of "Mr. Big wouldn't have half as many goals if it weren't for Ribaldi."

"Got you a rum punch," Mateo says.

I jerk my head up and smile. "Thanks so much." I put down my phone, face down, and raise my glass. "Cheers."

"Cheers. Thanks for being game to do this with me. It would have been a shame to waste the reservation."

"No, this is amazing. Fabulous. I'm thrilled."

He leans back. "You googled me."

"Hmm?"

"You heard that guy say my last name and the minute I left, you googled me. It's written all over your beautiful face, Julia."

I blush and nod and hold up my phone, which is currently displaying the Reddit board I was reading about Mateo's team. "I'm sorry," I say. "I couldn't resist."

He grins. "I did the same thing, basically. Right off the bat. While you were in the shower that first time, I looked at your driver's license and called the information into my assistant, who then ran a background check on you."

I gasp. "*A backgrouind check?* Why?"

"To make sure you weren't a crazy stalker fan who'd tracked me down on my honeymoon, intending to kill my new wife and take her place. For all I knew, you'd photoshopped that booking confirmation for the bungalow."

I giggle. "Well, what'd you find out about me? Anything exciting?"

"Very exciting. I found out you're a sweet kindergarten teacher who's deeply adored by your students and their parents and everyone else who's ever crossed paths with you, basically. You won a big science fair in seventh grade and got to go to Washington DC to present it. And your father invented some computer-chip something twenty years ago that he licensed and it's now made him a whole lot of money."

"He's not leaving it to me. My mother died of cancer, so he's leaving half his money to cancer research and the other half to some children's charities. I'll get an inheritance one day, but I'm not going to be obscenely loaded, by any stretch."

Mateo chuckles. "You're worried I've been fucking you this week to get a piece of a possible future inheritance?"

When he says it like that, it sounds pretty silly. "No. I'm not worried about that. I've always had my guard up about that particular topic. But, no, I don't think that at all."

"Good. Because I fucked you that first time on a whim. I needed to escape my feelings, as much as you did." His dark eyes sparkle. "And I kept on fucking you because you're the most fun I've ever had."

My heart leaps. "Really? Because you're like a magic portal to me, Mateo."

He laughs. "*What?*"

"You take me places I've never been. Make me feel things I've never felt. It's like you're a magic portal into another dimension—another version of me."

He raises his glass. "Well, cheers to that. To new versions of ourselves. The best ones."

I clink. "Cheers to that." I take a sip. "I promise I didn't recognize you when I walked into the bungalow. I don't follow soccer. I honestly don't know a single player's name. Well, other than yours now and that other guy on your team." I say the name, and Mateo's face falls. And suddenly, I realize my mistake. I look around to make sure none of the crew is nearby and whisper, "Is *he* the one who slept with your fiancée?"

Mateo nods.

"I'm so sorry, Mateo."

"It's fine."

"No, it's terrible. How are you going to play with him now, game after game, knowing—"

"I'm not. I told my agent to get me released or traded as soon as possible. I'm waiting to find out where I'm going next."

"When will you find out?"

He shrugs. "A week, probably. Two, at most."

"Where will you go before then? Where do you live?"

"Nowhere at the moment. I don't want to go back to Barcelona any time soon. Paparazzi follows me whenever I'm there. That's why I planned my honeymoon on the other side of the world. So we wouldn't be bothered. I'm sure the scandal will get out soon. These things never stay private. And once that story hits the tabloids, I won't want to step foot back in Barcelona."

"Scandal?"

"My ex is a popular model and actress in Spain. From what I've been told, he's still with her. So, if they get caught together, anywhere, I'm sure the full story will break, including the part where she dumped me for him."

Oh, my heart. "I'm really sorry." I reach across the small table to touch his hand. "Let's book another week and stay here until you know where you're going. Why not? We're having so much fun. Let's keep having fun."

"You don't need to get back sooner than that?"

"I'm off from work for the whole summer. That's the best perk of being a teacher."

A wide grin spreads across his gorgeous face. "Okay, yeah, let's do it. I'll figure out the arrangements when we get back tonight."

"Awesome. We'll have fun in paradise and forget the real world even exists."

CHAPTER 6

Feelings Officially Caught

I rest my cheek on Mateo's broad shoulder and sigh as I watch the sun dipping below the horizon. The sky before us is painted in vibrant hues of pink, orange, and red—beautiful colors that would make my soul soar, if my heart weren't aching so badly. After two weeks with Mateo in paradise, he's heading to his new hometown tomorrow. LA. To his shock, the team that signed him is the LA Galaxy. Which means he's going to be living about two hours from my hometown of San Diego. Not gonna lie, when he told me about his new contract, I immediately wondered if he'd be interested in seeing me again in the real world, given how geographically close we'll be to one another. But I banished the thought, as quickly as I had it. From the get-go, we both agreed to a no-strings fling. That was the deal.

"I wish we could press some kind of cosmic pause button," he murmurs. "I wish we could stay in paradise like this forever."

"Mm hmm," I say. I don't want to let myself hope he's thinking about a future with me. I don't want to think that way and set myself up for disappointment. Two weeks ago, I was ready to say "I do" to Brayden, after all. Clearly, it's way too soon for me to even think about getting seriously involved with anyone else. Even someone as amazing as Mateo.

"When I decided to go on my cancelled honeymoon by myself," Mateo says, "I never in a million years thought I'd meet someone like you here. Never."

"Same here."

"Not true. You told the whole church you intended to get yourself 'railed.'"

We both crack up.

"Turns out, you did a whole lot more than rail me," I admit. "You've brought me back to life. Joined me on a fantastic adventure. I'll never forget this time with you. Ever."

It's all true. But there's more to it than that. *I'm in love with him.* That's not part of our deal, though. Also, it's a batshit crazy thing to feel, given the white dress and veil I was wearing a mere two weeks ago. Indeed, if I went home and told my family about Mateo, and admitted my feelings for him, they'd rightly get me involuntarily committed. But the fact remains, even if I'm smart enough not to say it out loud, that I really do have love in my heart for Mateo. I know we're not going to wind up together, obviously. I know what I feel is partly situational. He's a Band-Aid. An extremely hot, kind, gentle, laid-back, handsome, hot, hot, hot Band-Aid. But a girl can love a Band-Aid, can't she? As long as she's not stupid enough to tell the Band-Aid what she's feeling? If you ask me, the answer to that question is a resounding *yes*.

"So, listen," Mateo says. "This might sound crazy, but—"

"Yes."

Mateo laughs. "You don't know what I'm going to ask you."

"Whatever it is, my answer is yes. I'm open to anything, especially if you have to preface it with 'This might sound crazy.'"

"God, you're fun. I love that about you."

My heart races. That's a big word, even if it's only a figure of speech.

He kisses my cheek. "I was going to ask if you'd let me share you, sexually, with all my new teammates. That's a thing all players do in the league, when they join a new team. They share their girlfriend with—"

I punch his shoulder playfully. "Say what you were really going to say, you dork."

He's laughing too hard to continue for a long moment. As he laughs, it suddenly occurs to me: he just now used the word *girlfriend*. He said it in the midst of a joke, of course. But was the girlfriend part as much of a joke as the sharing thing, or was that part sincere?

Mateo collects himself. "To be clear, I'd never want to share you with anyone. The very idea makes me feel physically sick. I want you all to myself. What I was actually going to say when you jumped to yes so fast is that I'm not ready to say goodbye to you yet. I'd like you to come to LA."

My heart leaps. "Of course, I'll come visit you! LA is only two hours from San Diego, so we can easily—"

"No, no. I mean come *with* me." He takes my hand and kisses the top of it. "They're putting me up in a furnished house on the beach for the rest of the summer, until I can figure out where to live permanently. Come stay with me there, Julia. You've still got eight weeks till you have to get back to work, right? Spend it with me."

My breathing is erratic. My heart lodged in my throat. Is there any reason why I need to go back to San Diego? My friends live there. My father, too. But no, I can't think of a single reason why I can't say yes to this crazy idea. "Yes!" I blurt excitedly. "I'd love to come with you."

Mateo cups my face in his hands and kisses me, but soon, we're both smiling too much to continue smooching.

"It really is a crazy thing for me to do," I tease.

"Absolutely bonkers," he agrees.

"Seriously, my family is going to worry about me. They'll think I've rebounded way too fast. They'll tell me I'm jumping in too deep, too fast. And they'll probably be right."

"My family will think the same thing. And maybe they'll be right, too. But what if they're all wrong? What if this is meant to be, Julia? We owe it to ourselves to find out, don't you think?"

"I do. We'll continue having fun, just like this, till the end of summer. And if it's not working out by then, we'll call it quits and thank each other for the memories."

"Exactly. And if it's still going this well, we'll figure out what to do about it then."

"Right? We don't have to have all the answers right now. It's not like we're making any promises to each other."

"Of course, we're not. Why would we do that after two weeks?"

"Two weeks in paradise."

"After two broken engagements."

"Exactly. It's a perfect storm for making bad romantic decisions."

"And we know that. Which is why we're not making any long-term commitments here. We're simply having fun."

"Yep."

Mateo gnaws on his lower lip. "Except I'd like to introduce you to my new teammates and coaches as my girlfriend, if that's okay with you. I don't want them thinking you're just some chick I'm dating. I don't want anyone thinking you're fair game to hit on. Because you're *not*."

My heart is hammering. "I'd love to be introduced as your girlfriend, Mateo."

Mateo pauses. "Well, to be clear, you actually would *be* my girlfriend. For real. I wouldn't simply be introducing you that way."

I chuckle. "Even better."

"Starting right now," he whispers, right before leaning in and pressing his soft lips to mine. This time, neither of us laughs or giggles. This time, our kiss is passionate. Full of heat. This time, we're sealing something real with a kiss. I'm moving to LA to be with my hot boyfriend, and anyone who thinks I'm making a huge mistake because I'm brokenhearted and not thinking clearly can kiss my ass cheek. You know, the one that's got bite marks on it from where Mateo's been nibbling on me for the past two weeks.

CHAPTER 7

"Fated Mates"

I'm trembling as Mateo looks into my eyes, preparing to deliver his wedding vows to me. My heart is pounding like a drum against my chest. The soft sounds of the nearby ocean waves are drowned out by the rush of joy coursing through me. I've found my soul mate and I don't have a single doubt about that. We're meant to be, Mateo and me. And I can't wait to become his wife.

"Julia," Mateo says. "I feel like I've waited a lifetime to call you my wife. Mere days after meeting you, someone on a yacht mistakenly called you Mrs. Ribaldi, and in that moment, I knew it was only a matter of time before we'd be standing here, just like this, pledging forever to each other on a beach in Hawaii. Call me crazy, but I swear I knew it, right then."

Mateo's never told me that before, and the revelation brings tears to my eyes.

Mateo gently squeezes my hands and smiles. "Julia, I promise to be the best husband, friend, protector, lover, and father to our baby I can possibly be. I'll love you forever, and you'll never have to wonder about my loyalty or faithfulness. You'll wake up knowing you're the center of my universe, and fall asleep knowing it, too. My love, you're my fate. My destiny. I'd take every sling and arrow and heartbreak that brought us together, all over again, in a thousand lifetimes, if it meant I'd get to wind up here with you, again and again and again." To cap off his beautiful speech, Mateo leans in to kiss me, and I burst into tears of joy as his lips meet mine. Chuckling, Mateo pulls out a hanky and wipes my tears and kisses my cheeks. And of course, everyone sitting in the audience laughs and swoons along with me.

I turn to look at my bridesmaids to see their reactions, and my eyes meet Delilah's—the young woman who would have been my sister-in-law right now, if she hadn't helped me uncover the truth a year and a half ago. My guardian angel. It was a pity when Brayden was shot and killed by the enraged husband who'd caught Brayden fucking his wife. Well, a pity for Delilah, anyway. She's always loved her big brother, despite his flaws. Personally, I didn't care about Brayden's demise. It seemed a fitting end for him, to be honest. But I did and still do care very much about Delilah, so I felt sorry about *her* heartache. The good news, however, is that Brayden's untimely death only brought Delilah and me, even closer. She's now, one hundred percent, the little sister I never had.

"Julia?" the wedding officiant says.

I wink at Delilah and return to Mateo, my soon-to-be-husband. The father of the baby boy growing inside me. I considered typing out my vows and reading them to Mateo today. But upon reflection, I realized my words don't need to be perfect. They only need to be honest and true. I realized that whatever I felt when looking into Mateo's gorgeous brown eyes would be perfect in that moment. That's how it always is with Mateo. Natural. Easy. *Right*. The old Julia never would never have winged it like this; but the new

Julia knows, as long as she's got Mateo by her side, every moment will be perfect.

"Mateo," I begin, holding his hands in mine. "You're the fantasy who became a reality. And the reality is better than any fantasy. I promise to always love, respect, support, and adore you, as long as I'm lucky enough to walk this earth alongside you, as your devoted wife. Thank you for being my destiny. My Fated Mate-e-o." As everyone laughs at my silly play on words, I lean in and seal my words with a tender kiss. Rings are exchanged. A prayer said. And a mere minutes later, I'm officially Mrs. Ribaldi.

"By the power vested in me by the State of Hawaii, it is my pleasure and honor to introduce to you, for the very first time, Mr. and Mrs. Mateo and Julia Ribaldi!"

Mateo takes my hand and holds it up and whoops, and we bound excitedly down the aisle toward our happily ever after.

Thanks for reading. Check out the rest of Lauren's books on her website at www.laurenrowebooks.com.

MAUI DREAM GIRL
LEX MARTIN

CHAPTER 1 - CAM

Leaning forward to shoot the intruder on my flatscreen, I yell into my headset, "Head around the back and cut off his partner!"

"Already on it," a husky female voice murmurs in my ear.

NerdyNinjaGrl's handle flashes on the corner of the screen as she confirms the kill.

"So bloodthirsty," I tease.

Her sexy laugh in my ear has me debating this situation for the hundredth time.

If you meet up, you'll ruin a good thing, I remind myself.

There's no denying this any longer. I want to meet her. We've been playing together for the last year, and somehow, she's become more interesting than all of the party girls downstairs.

Look, I'm not an asshole. I don't buy my own hype. I know full well that the women who want to climb in my bed are all here for the same thing. They want to fuck a football player. It's practically a full-contact sport around here, if the headboard thumping against my wall is any indication.

Feminine laughter echoes down the hall before Jinxy opens my door so hard, it slams against the wall. "Bro, that chick Denise is asking for you. She said she wants to tag team you this time instead of the other way around."

Jesus Christ.

I wince, hoping NerdyNinjaGrl didn't hear. Because I'm not sure she would believe that's all in my past.

The truth? Yeah, I might've shared my dates with my best friend Billy a few times, but after one of our sexcapades landed in a gossip blog last year, complete with photos the blogger herself took, he and I decided we were playing with fire and called our hedonistic days over.

I point at my headset, but my housemate doesn't seem to understand.

NerdyNinjaGrl clears her throat. "Sounds like you're busy. We can play another time."

I scowl at Jinxy, who holds up a hand as he leaves, while I try to explain. "The guys are celebrating the win." When she doesn't respond, I clarify. "You know, the national championship."

Silence.

I chuckle. "Are you sure you're a student here?"

"I warned you that I don't watch football, Mr. Super Fan." She thinks I'm a fan. That's adorable. "You do know it's a Tuesday, right?"

"The celebration of football has no boundaries."

I toss the bag of ice I had wrapped to my shoulder into a giant bowl at my feet. It's tempting to tell her I scored the final touchdown of yesterday's game, but then she could easily identify me. It's also possible she'd think I'm full of shit.

Of course, if she really wanted to figure it out, my screen name, BackfieldBlzr23, isn't exactly creative. Backfield because I'm a running back. Blazer because I'm fast, and 23 is my jersey number.

But Ninja has never asked me the significance of my handle, so I figure she doesn't get it or doesn't care.

I'm not crazy about either of those options. I've been talking to this woman for a while, and the fact that she's never inquired about it bugs me a little. While I don't want a football fangirl, it would be nice to share an appreciation for the sport I've been obsessed with since I was four.

It's been the one thing that's kept me from taking this further.

Sighing, I stare up at Miss Maui, who decorates my wall. Kelani Kekoa smiles back at me. Her thick mermaid hair blows in the wind as she stands on a golden, tropical beach. My older brother sent that poster to me to be a dick because he went to Maui on vacation last year while I was stuck here for football practice. He gave me some bullshit line about Kelani attending college here, but that makes no sense. Why would she attend school in the Texas Hill Country?

Now, I love women of all shapes and sizes, but if I had to pick an ideal woman, it's Kelani. There's something mysterious about her smile that I love.

Plus, she's hot as fuck.

Too bad she probably lives thirty-five hundred miles away.

It's a sad state of affairs that I have hardcore crushes on two women I've never met. I guess it's easier this way since real-life entanglements are messy. My parents' divorce was so volatile, so full of hatred, that I swore I'd never subject myself to a serious relationship.

Maybe that's why I fucked around for the first few years of college. I'd probably still be that guy were it not for that gossip blog calling me out, which made me realize how hollow I felt in the aftermath of those nights. It didn't help that several of my teammates have serious girlfriends. They make relationships look *almost* appealing.

So yeah, I'm over wild sexcapades and casual hookups.

I'm thinking it's time I move on to a friends with benefits situation. That way no one catches feelings. I already know I won't. I'm not wired that way. Wouldn't I have experienced it before now, my junior year of college? But it would be nice to get to know a woman better. To know exactly what to do to make her fall apart and not have to guess.

Then again, if she's into my sport, would that make a situationship messier?

Maybe it's better if Nerdy doesn't give a shit about football.

"We should meet." My heart pounds like I'm sprinting toward the end zone as I wait for her response. I rub my chest, a little freaked by my body's response. I'm usually cool under pressure because women don't send me into a tailspin.

Her laugh is light. "Are you sure, Blazer? What if I'm a troll?"

I snort. "Impossible." There's no way this girl is unattractive. It's impossible for someone with such a beautiful soul.

Christ, that's cheesy.

Except NerdyNinjaGrl is a sweetheart. Funny. Sarcastic. Smart. Between juggling her own classes, she also babysits her little niece so her older sister can finish her degree. And she volunteers at some old folks' home. My grandmother would say she has a good heart.

My Nerdy Ninja won't tell me her major, though. Or where she volunteers.

"You babysitting tonight?" I ask when I realize she hasn't agreed to meet up, and my pulse finally slows down. I'm disappointed but also relieved. Some part of me doesn't want to ruin the good thing we have. If we meet and fuck, then that claustrophobic feeling will wrap around me until I can't breathe, and I'll need space.

Hm. Maybe I'm not ready for friends with benefits.

It's better if we don't meet. I'll never disappoint her or break her heart or any of that screwed up crap I try to avoid at all costs. We'll just be buddies.

"No. Her classes haven't started yet."

"Does your sister attend Lone Star State too?"

"No. She goes to a local high school that offers night school to get her GED." She's quiet a moment. "Do you need to get back to your party?"

She can probably hear the bass through my headset since I can feel it through the floor. "Nah. I had a couple beers with the guys this afternoon. Shit's starting to get crazy downstairs, and I'm not in the mood."

Her voice gets quiet. "So... what are you in the mood for?"

Everything in me stills.

Except for one part of my body that gets hard.

I adjust myself and lean back in my chair and pray I'm not reading her wrong. "Tsk. Tsk, Sexy Ninja. I'm not sure you wanna hear what's going through my head right now."

We've never done this before. We've talked about life and politics and our families while gaming. I know her parents passed away a couple years ago, and she knows mine fight like rabid animals. Sometimes, we just hang out in this virtual waiting room and chat. We've even talked late into the night about how she loves stargazing and learning the names of the constellations and how that will send her on a wild frenzy to read all of those Greek myths.

Sure, we've flirted a little, but things have never gotten sexual.

She hums. "Maybe I'm curious."

My heart kicks hard in my chest. "Do you really want to know?"

I close my eyes and listen to her throaty purr as she hums again. "Yeah, I think I do."

Here goes nothing. "I'm wishing you were here."

"In your room?"

"Yeah. In my room. The lights are low. Except for the TV." Our game is long over, and neither of us bothered to jump on another session. I stretch out on my comforter and groan. "Fuck, I'm sore."

"Did you just crawl into bed?"

I chuckle. "Yeah. My ass was falling asleep in my gaming chair."

"Want to know what I'm really good at?" she asks almost hesitantly.

There's no helping my erection at this point because her voice is so damn sexy, but it feels wrong to rub one out when I'm not a hundred percent sure that's where this is headed.

"Tell me."

"Massages. I give great massages."

I groan, unable to help it. Reaching down, I give myself a firm tug. "Stop. You're turning me on."

"Um... really?"

Did I imagine her breathlessness? "Yes, I'm hard as steel right now." I close my eyes on a wince. "Sorry if that's TMI."

Her voice goes to a whisper. "Have you ever had phone sex?"

Fuck, yes. We're doing this. "Nope. Never." I clear my throat. "Full confession, I've sexted before, but I'm not a fan. I can't coordinate texting and jerking off at the same time." Thank god for hands-free headsets.

She laughs, and it's full bodied and beautiful. "I can see how that would be difficult."

I'm dying to cut to the chase. "Are we gonna have phone sex, little Ninja?"

Silence.

As it stretches awkwardly, I debate how to backtrack out of this, but what she says next changes everything. "I'm down if you are."

I glance at my crotch. "There's nothing *down* about what's happening in my shorts." Her giggle makes me smile. "I don't think I've mentioned this before, but your voice is sexy as fuck."

"Well, if we're going for honesty, then I have to admit your voice is hot too. It's deep and kinda gritty. Like you're a nice guy in the streets but a freak in the sheets."

It's my turn to laugh. "I'm definitely a freak in the sheets." I leap out of bed to lock my door so none of those fuckers downstairs can barge in, and then I'm back in bed. "If we're going to get off, don't you think we should share our first names? I'm gonna feel weird later when I'm replaying this in my head and having to call you Ninja or Nerdy."

"Call me Kelly."

Kelly. I smile so wide, my face hurts. Fucking finally. "I'm Cam."

"Hi, Cam."

"Hi, gorgeous."

"You don't know what I look like."

"True, but I have a great imagination, and you're a total fox in my head. Hold on." I strip off my t-shirt, readjust my headset, and sprawl out on my bed again.

"What did you just do?"

"Took off my shirt."

"Mm. Tell me more about this. What do you look like?" She laughs. "Is it weird that we've been gaming together for a year and I haven't a clue what you look like?"

"Not weird, no. You and I have been on a low setting the way my housemate Jinxy makes dinner in a crockpot. And to be honest, I've enjoyed getting to know you like this." I don't want to tell her I'm tired of never having a personal connection with the girls I sleep with. "Let's see, I'm six feet two, two hundred and ten pounds. I'll spare you my football stats." What else do women usually want to know? It's been a while since I've had to talk myself up. "Um, blond hair that probably needs a trim and blue eyes. Have you ever seen that show *Vikings*? With that guy Travis Fimmel?"

"Ragnar."

"Yeah, that dude. My friends call me the Viking because they say I look like him."

"So you're stupidly hot."

I snort. "Before I started weightlifting, I was a beanpole nerd with braces, so that keeps me humble."

"Aww, I have a thing for nerds. But you're basically the opposite of me. I'm tiny, petite. Dark hair, dark eyes."

My attention drifts to the Hawaiian mermaid on my wall, and my heart goes a little erratic. Could this be Kelani?

No, dumbass. Ninja said her name is Kelly. Don't fuck this up by confusing what this is. And for the love of God, don't call her by the wrong name.

Turning my head, I stare up at the ceiling. "So I'm going to tower over you?"

"Yes. You could crush me if you wanted."

"I definitely want to do some crushing, but only the good kind. The kind you'll like."

Something rustles in the background. "There. I locked my door and took off my shirt too."

Christ. "Tell me about this layout. Small tits? Big? Bouncy? Bite sized? I love them all, so spare no detail."

She chuckles. "Are you a boob man?"

"I have a deep and abiding appreciation for breasts."

"Well, my boobs are decent. High. Round. A full C-cup."

"Are they sensitive?"

"Not too much. Sometimes you have to give them a good squeeze or bite."

I let out a breath. "I'm available for those activities."

She laughs again. "What about you?"

"I do not have boobs." In between her chuckles, I add, "But if I did, I'd be fondling them all day." I know what she's asking me, though. "Not gonna lie. My chest is probably my best feature." I work my ass off in training and the benefit is a sculpted body.

"Not your face?"

"I have a scar across my eyebrow, so lower your expectations."

"From football?"

"From my brother. He threw a trophy across the room when we were kids, and it landed on my skull."

"Ouch. Poor baby."

"Yes, poor me. I think you should kiss it."

"Perhaps I should."

I could listen to her sultry purr all night. "Are you in bed? I need you to set the stage."

"I'm in bed, the lights are off except for a small lamp. I'm still wearing running shorts."

I already know Kelly runs every day. I close my eyes and consider the legs on this woman. They've got to be sleek. "You said you're petite. Think you could wrap your legs around me?"

"I'd like to try."

God, this woman turns me on. "Tug down your shorts. Leave on your underwear. But I need descriptions of everything."

I hear the smile in her voice as she responds. "I'm leaving on my boy shorts. They're a pale pink with lace on the edges."

Why is everything about her so attractive? "Are they wet, baby?"

She takes a breath. "Yeah."

"Look down your body. What do you see?"

"My tan is fading, but it's chilly in here, so my nipples are hard."

"If I were there, I'd take one little bud between my teeth and nibble on it. Lick it. Suck. Take your nipple between your fingers and pinch it. Pretend it's my mouth." Her responding moan has me reaching into my shorts where I give my cock a tug. "Then run your hand down to your panties and rub yourself, but over the fabric."

"Wh-what are you doing?"

"I'm stroking my dick. I've been hard for you for the last three months, so I need relief."

She laughs. "Want to know a secret? Sometimes, in the shower, I think about you."

Thank god she can't see me because I'm smiling like a lunatic. "How do you get yourself off in there? Fingers?"

"Showerhead."

I squeeze my cock hard because the visual she's giving me is too hot. I don't want to come yet. "So you run it against your clit?"

"Yeah. And..."

"And what?" I'm literally holding my breath, wondering what naughty little things she does to herself when she's all alone.

"I run it all over myself. My opening. My..."

"Your asshole."

"Yes. Everywhere. Until I can't stand it any longer, and then I jam two fingers inside myself and hold the showerhead to my clit and come."

"Jesus." I stare down at my swollen cock. "That description alone makes me want to jizz myself."

She pants. "I'm pretty close. I'm gonna slide my hand into my panties now."

Yes. "Stick your fingers in yourself. Start with two, and then add a third."

"I usually just do two."

I debate how to say this, but fuck it. We either mesh sexually or we don't. "Baby, you should use three..."

CHAPTER 2 - KELLY

Cam's voice is a sexy grumble.

I shiver. "Why three?"

He pauses. "I'm, uh, girthy, so..."

My core throbs as he grunts that in my ear. I swallow, my mouth dry. "Let me try."

Everything about Cam turns me on. The sound of his voice. His sense of humor. His laidback personality. How hard he trains for football.

But I also know he's one of the biggest players on campus, something he's admitted to in a roundabout way. Which I only confirmed when his roommate basically shouted that he's done threesomes.

I've wanted to meet Cam a hundred times over the last several months, but frankly, I don't want to get hurt.

Except he's here, talking to me after his big win instead of at the party raging in his own house.

In fact, the last few weeks, he's played with me on Friday *and* Saturday nights. He has to be interested, right?

I kick off my panties and reach between my legs. "I'm dripping." I'd usually be mortified to admit that out loud, but isn't description key to good phone sex? Everything about this thing with Cam requires a leap of faith, and I'm tired of pretending to be unaffected.

He affects me. A lot.

"Kelly, baby, put those fingers in your sweet little pussy."

I can barely breathe, but I do as he says. "I'll start with two. I like to close my legs and slide my fingers down my front. Kinda feels like..." Do I just say it?

"Like a cock."

"Yeah." I groan on the first pass, shiver with the second. "I'm spreading my legs to try three. I need a second to get past my knuckles." But I can't do it at this angle. "I have to lift my knees, but I'm pushing in now. God, it's tight."

I can hear him breathing in my ear.

"Bet you feel fucking amazing. I've got a death grip on my dick right now." He laughs, and it turns into a groan.

"Do you like getting head?" Jesus, Kel. That's a stupid question. Doesn't every man?

"Are you offering?"

"Depends. Will you gag me on it?"

"God, no. I'm not one of those guys who will jam you down on my crotch."

I probably shouldn't have taken those hits off my sister's joint earlier because now I have no filter. "Hmm. Too bad. I'm kinda into that."

He makes a choking sound, and I laugh. "Christ, Kelly. I mean, I'm more than happy to accommodate you."

"I want to come. If you were here, how would we do it?" I spread my legs and look down as he huffs in my ear.

"You mean after I lick you to oblivion?"

"Yes, after that."

"I'd probably kneel between your legs. Slowly work myself in. At that angle, I can watch myself impale you. Watch you stretch around me. Then I'd lift your gorgeous ass so my cock could rub along your g-spot as I rubbed soft circles on your clit."

"Oh god." My whole body tightens as my core pulses around my fingers.

He makes this sexy grunt, and I know he's coming too.

Afterward, I flop on my bed, panting. "I don't think you can top what just happened."

His sexy laugh makes me smile, ear to ear. "I'd like to try."

CHAPTER 3 - KELLY

The next morning, I groan when I think about all the things I said to Cam last night.

"Why are you over there making weird noises," my sister Lana asks as she pours her coffee.

"Trust me when I say you don't want to know."

She smirks. "Does this have anything to do with your sexy football player slash gamer boy?"

If Cam was being honest, there's nothing boyish about him. "Possibly."

Lana's eyebrows lift as she waits for me to spill my guts. "And?"

I peer over my shoulder where my five-year-old niece Gia is watching cartoons in the living room and whisper. "We had phone sex. Except it was online."

"While you were playing your little shoot 'em up game?"

"Warriors of the Vanguard is not some 'shoot 'em up game.' It requires skill. Teamwork. Strategy."

She rolls her eyes. "My bad, gamer girl." After taking a sip from her steaming mug of coffee, she asks, "Well? How was it?"

"We won."

"Not that, goofball. How was the sex?" she hisses. "Spare no detail. I need to live vicariously through you."

"So, so hot." I fan myself, remembering. "We're supposed to meet today, but I'm scared."

"That he's a psycho?"

"No, Lana. That we'll mess this up. That meeting will destroy our vibe online. I finally have a great game partner, and this could ruin everything."

Reaching for the bread box, she shrugs. "I still can't believe you haven't cyberstalked this dude yet."

"I know, it's crazy." I press a hand to my stomach. "Let's do it now. Let's look him up."

"You said you wouldn't do that. You said you didn't want to know anything personal about him."

"That's before I agreed to meet him." I grab her hand and drag her back to my room while she yells about spilling her coffee. "This will only take a minute. He said his name was Cam, and he's on the football team. How many Cams do you think there are?"

I don't wait for her response before I pop open my laptop and search for the Lone Star State Bronco roster.

"Cam is short for Cameron, right?" I ask as I type it in. "Damn it."

She peers over my shoulder and laughs. "It's just your luck that there are three dudes named that."

"But only two are blond." I squint at the screen. "And one is a freshman, which leaves this guy, Cameron Fletcher." And there's that scar over his eyebrow.

Silence fills the room as Lana stares at the Adonis with shaggy blond hair and a roguish smile. "Holy hell, he's hot." But then she goes into mom-mode. "You said you were done dating athletes."

I sigh. "I know. It's just... I think he might be different."

"Kel, that's exactly what I said to myself nine months before I spawned Gia."

"But I'm approaching this differently. I'm going to straight-out tell him I'm only interested if he wants to date and be monogamous. None of this dine and dash bullshit. He can either take me on dates and spend real time with me, or he can bang the girls who go to his parties."

"That's gonna scare him away."

"It might." I nibble my bottom lip. "But that's a risk I'm willing to take. I want what Mom and Dad had, and I'm never going to get that if I don't raise my expectations."

My sister hugs me, and I lean my head on her shoulder. It's been tough since our parents died in that car crash. Sometimes my heart hurts with how much I miss them. My mom would know what to do right now.

She always said when she was confused about life and big decisions, she'd ask the universe for a sign.

So I close my eyes and put that wish out there.

Mom, I need a sign. I want to know whether or not I should take a chance on Cam.

By the time I get to the coffee house, I'm a nervous wreck. I check my reflection in the rearview mirror one more time. I'm just wearing a little mascara and some tinted lip balm. I don't usually wear much makeup, and I don't want to bait and switch the man.

My ex gave me so much shit for not dressing up more. There's probably some truth to starting the way you intend to go. I intend to wear jeans and t-shirts for the foreseeable future unless we're spending a nice night out and I *feel* like dressing up. But because I *want* to and not because some man thinks I *need* to.

Out of the corner of my eye, I spot a tall guy in a letterman jacket head up the sidewalk to Rise 'N Grind. He's wearing a black beanie, though, so I can't tell if he's blond or not.

Then I notice the bouquet of flowers in his hands.

My insides go sideways. *Please let that be Cam.*

Because I want a man who brings me flowers on a first date. I know I'm supposed to be all about girl power and doing shit for myself, but it's nice to be treated like a princess once in a while, and I'm not too proud to admit that.

I slowly get out of my car and wrap my coat tighter around myself. Texas seems like it would always be hot, but it's cloudy and cold in the hill country. There's even talk of snow flurries this weekend.

When I reach the door, I take a deep breath and pull it open. Between the warm air from the coffee house and the cold air whipping behind me, my hair whirls around my face and I bat it away with a laugh. I should've tucked my hair under my hat, but I wasn't expecting to get caught up in a mini-tornado.

After I step inside, I instantly connect with a brilliant pair of blue eyes.

"Kelly?"

God, he's even more gorgeous in person. "Cam?"

I pull off my hat and brush my hair out of my face again, and he does the same.

We stare at each other a long minute before we both start laughing. He pulls me into a hug and lifts me off my feet.

When I'm back down on the ground, he hands me a bouquet. "These are for you."

I sniff the beautiful white flowers. "Gardenias are my favorite flower."

He smiles. "I remember. You told me last summer when we did that round robin challenge online."

My heart pounds like I'm in some kind of fairy tale.

Slow your roll, girl. Don't get carried away. Have some coffee before you plan your honeymoon.

But in my head, I'm wondering if that's the sign I'm looking for? How will I know?

I'm fidgety as we order our drinks. When I glance up at him, he's already looking down at me.

"Cameron!" The barista yells, leaning over the counter to give him a fist jab. "Holy shit, man. That play in the fourth quarter was cray-cray!"

He chuckles. "Thanks."

A few guys come up to talk to him and slap him on the back, and I'm immediately reminded that his team just won a national championship. More people notice him and circle around us.

After a minute, though, he grabs my hand and starts to lead me away. "Sorry, y'all. I don't want to leave my date hanging."

He views this as a date too. Solid point in his favor.

Everyone's respectful, but one guy screams, "Go Broncos!" and rips his shirt down the middle.

"Your fans are hard core," I say with a chuckle as he leads me to a booth in the corner.

We sit across from each other, and I blow on my coffee to cool it down.

At first, we just look at each other.

Then he clears his throat. "This is gonna sound creepy," he says slowly, "but for the sake of full disclosure, there's something you should know."

"Don't scare me," I say with a laugh.

His face flushes, and he smiles like he's embarrassed. "Last winter, my brother went somewhere for vacation while I was stuck here for football. And the asshole brought me a touristy poster of this gorgeous girl to rub the whole thing in my face."

I nod, not knowing where he's going with this.

He rubs the back of his neck. "For the last year, I've had a poster of a stunning Miss Maui in a tiny bikini on my wall."

My eyes widen. "Oh."

"Now, I'm not one to really believe in fate or kismet or anything like that, but, *Kelani,* don't you think it's a little weird I've had a poster of you on my wall since about the time we met online?"

My eyes sting as I think about the wish I made this morning, but I'm too choked up to say anything.

"I'm sorry," he says quickly. "I didn't mean to upset you. I swear I'm not a creep."

I wipe my eyes as I smile. "This just reminds me of something my mother used to say. Maybe I'll tell you about it someday."

He nods, and the sweet look he gives me makes me want to crawl into his lap, except we're not there yet.

But this all feels too heavy, and I want us to relax and really get to know each other. "So, Cam, if we're going to be hanging out, maybe you should explain this football stuff to me."

He gives me a huge smile and reaches for the sugar packets at the far edge of the table and spreads them out. "Let's start with offense."

CHAPTER 4 - KELLY

After coffee and pizza at a restaurant down the street and some hot chocolate where we basically closed down the joint, we head back to my car arm in arm. I have my gardenias in my messenger bag, which is slung around my shoulder, and every time the wind blows, I can smell their heavenly scent.

"I had a great time."

He squeezes my arm. "I did too."

We talked about a million things today. How I ended up moving to Texas to be with my sister after our parents died. How I did that pageant because it was something my mom had done at my age, and I wanted to honor her. And how my dad got me into gaming when I was a kid.

He shared how stressed he's been this season, and how he games to relax and stop worrying about his future. He's not sure whether or not he should go for the NFL Draft this spring. His dad thinks he should do it on the heels of the championship, but his mom wants him to finish his degree.

The thought of him leaving in a few months makes a pit form in my stomach because I feel like I just found him.

Again, that's jumping ahead of myself.

When we get to my car, I lean back against the door as he hugs me. I barely come to his shoulders. And, oh my god, he smells good. Like spicy cologne and leather.

He nuzzles against my neck, and I shiver.

This has literally been the best date I've ever been on. Cam's been sweet and considerate. He brought me flowers and treated me to dinner. Our conversations were great, and we never had any awkward stretches. It's almost too good to be true.

"When can I see you again?" he asks in my ear.

Do it, Kelani. Don't chicken out.

It's dark outside now, and maybe that helps me be brave and say things I'd have a tough time admitting in the full light of day. "Can I ask you something? This is totally awkward, and I know it's way too early to say this, but we've basically been talking for a year, and I want to put my cards on the table."

He leans back and stares down at me, his brows furrowed. "You can ask me anything."

I clench my hands to stop them from trembling. "What is this between us? Because I'm looking for something serious. I don't want casual, and I get the feeling that's what you're into. As much as I've enjoyed today, I really don't want to be just a notch on your bedpost. But if you're not looking for a relationship, we can just go back to gaming, stay friends, and forget about last night."

He lets go of me, and I immediately want to retract what I said. *Stay strong, Kelani. Those were some tough words, but they needed to be said.*

With a sigh, he runs his hand through his hair and looks away.

His silence feels foreboding.

Disappointment washes over me. I knew he was too good to be true.

"It's fine, Cam. Maybe I'll see you online next weekend."

I turn around to unlock my door when he puts his hand on my elbow. "Wait."

Staring down at my shoes, I gather the remnants of my tattered pride and turn around. "It's too much for you. I get it."

He swallows. "I'm sure you've heard about the team's reputation. Maybe even mine personally, but I'm over partying like that. And honestly, I'm over hooking up. Lately, I've been thinking I'd like a friends with benefits situation."

I give him a tight smile. "Good luck with that." I go to turn around, but he stops me.

"I'm not done," he says gruffly.

Folding my arms over my chest, I brace myself for whatever else he's going to level at me. "Sorry. Please continue."

He rubs the back of his neck. "Before I met you, I was pretty sure I needed something casual but with one person."

Frustration bubbles up in me. "I'm not looking to convince you of anything. You don't need to change what you want for me."

Cam gives me a soft smile and pulls me against him and whispers in my ear, "But that's the thing. You make me want more."

It takes a second for his words to sink in. "Oh."

He rubs his cold nose against my jaw. "What do you say, Kelani? Would you like to be my girlfriend? But fair warning, I'll probably be terrible at this. I haven't had a girlfriend since high school, and I'm pretty rusty at this stuff."

"You did good with the flowers and dinner." I wrap my arms around him and lean my head against his broad chest. "I don't need perfection. I just need you to try."

He hugs me tight. "I'm gonna nerd out for a second and quote the great Jedi master Yoda. 'Do or do not do. There is no try.'"

I smile up at him. "I thought I was the nerd."

He shakes his head. "Don't you know? You're my Maui dream girl."

Inside, I melt into a puddle.

Running his thumb over my bottom lip, he leans down. "Can I kiss you, Kelani?"

Something about the way he says my name makes me feel like we've known each other forever.

"I thought you'd never ask."

The touch of his lips on mine shoots little bolts of electricity through my limbs.

Reaching up, I wrap my arms around his neck as his fingers spear into my hair. Pulling me closer, he brings me flush to his hard body. I can feel his heart racing, a tandem beat to mine.

When he licks my bottom lip, I open to him.

And then I'm lost.

To his kiss. To his scent. To the way the whole world seems to revolve around this solitary spot where we stand.

After a moment, we part and stare at each other for a long-drawn-out minute as our breaths swirl between us. The dazed expression on his face feels like a reflection of my own.

I touch my lips with a laugh. "What was that?"

His voice is low and rich with promise as he smiles. "The world's best first kiss."

CHAPTER 5 - CAM

Three months later

"Watch that corner! Go, go, go!" I lean over to the side as though that will help me keep up with Kelani's niece Gia, who's kicking my ass in this game.

When her car crosses the finish line first, she leaps in the air. "I did it!"

I high five her, and then she leaps in my arms with a laugh.

Behind us, Lana razzes me. "She beat you again?"

"Yup." I raise Gia's arms in victory, and we dance around the living room.

"I'm ready!" Kelly walks down the hall from her bedroom, and I freeze. She's all decked out in this tiny little black dress and heels. Damn, she's gorgeous.

"Babe." I go over to her and kiss her before I whisper in her ear. "You should give a guy some warning. I almost sported wood around the kid over there."

She adjusts my tie. "You're pretty handsome yourself."

There's a new restaurant I wanted to take her to, and since she said she was in the mood to dress up, I thought I'd go the extra mile to make my girl feel special. Plus, I have some news I need to share with her.

Kelani and I have been going strong since we started dating, but I think tonight's finally the night. We decided we needed some time hanging out in person before we had sex. Given my issues and her concerns, I was fully on board taking things slow. And we're not monks. We've messed around a little. Had some hot makeout sessions. We just haven't gone all the way yet.

When we reach the restaurant, I slide into her side of the booth. I kiss the top of her head and wrap my arm around her slender shoulders. "You smell so good. I might need to lick you from head to toe when we get out of here."

She gives me a sultry smile and runs her palm up my thigh. "I'm game if you are."

I adjust myself, and she laughs.

After our delicious dinner, I take her hand in mine. "Kelly, I wanted to let you know I made a decision about the draft."

Her shoulders go stiff, and she waves her other hand. "Tell me. I can't take the suspense anymore."

Because if I get drafted this spring, we'd have to do long distance for a year while she finishes her degree. It's not ideal.

"You know I don't want to leave you…"

She bites her lip and nods. Her head tilts down, and her hair falls like a curtain between us. "But."

I tuck her long tresses behind her ear. "But nothing. I'm not going for the draft this year."

Her eyes shoot up at me. "But you kicked ass at the Combine. And what if the Broncos don't do as well next season?"

"You trying to get rid of me?"

She grabs my face and kisses me. "No. In fact, this has been eating away at me. I don't want you to go. At the same time, you've worked so hard to get to this point, and I don't want you to regret not going for the NFL when you have this great opportunity."

"The truth is I want to finish my degree. And, bonus, that would mean spending my senior year with you." I take a deep breath. "However, if I *do* get drafted next year, are you open to coming with me?" Laughing awkwardly, I shrug. "I know this is really fucking early to ask you this, but like you said on our first date, I want to get my cards on the table."

Her eyes get soft, and she crawls into my lap and burrows her nose in my neck. "Yes. I'll go with you. Can my sister and niece tag along too? I don't mean they have to live with us, but they're my only family, and it would suck not to be near them."

I tangle my fingers in her long, thick hair and kiss her. "Of course."

It feels like a huge boulder just got lifted off my shoulders. But on the walk back to my car, I'm nervous for another reason.

"Um. So tonight… Do you want me to drop you off at home?"

She lifts an eyebrow. "Really? You want to take me home when I wore this dress for you? You'd better take me back to your house and strip me out of it before I spontaneously combust."

"Thank god." I laugh and start jogging down the street, pulling her along.

Her giggle has me smiling.

At the crosswalk, I scoop her into my arms and really start to run. "Don't want you to twist an ankle in those heels. Plus, you're going too slow."

She pats my chest and wraps her arms around me. "Okay, big guy."

When we get to my place, I'm dragging her through the living room, which is filled with people. She waves to some of my teammates, but I don't bother stopping.

"Viking!" one of the guys yells. "You in a hurry or something?"

I hold up my middle finger and drag my girlfriend up the stairs as they laugh.

When we get to my room, I kick the door closed and lift her in my arms. She immediately wraps her legs around my waist as we frantically kiss.

"I thought we'd never get home," I grouse as I take her ass in both hands.

"What was with that traffic?" she asks as she pulls off my tie and starts unbuttoning my shirt.

We tumble into bed. I settle between her thighs and lean down to kiss down her tight little body. "It's like the citizens of Charming were deliberately trying to cock block me."

She laughs so hard, she snorts and slaps a hand over her mouth.

I lift my head to look at her. "Did my little beauty queen just snort?"

"No, sir." She shakes her head, and I chuckle.

"It's okay. I plan to get you to make all sorts of sounds tonight." I slip the spaghetti straps off her shoulders and nibble on her collarbone and then down between her pert breasts where I nuzzle her soft skin. "You smell fucking delicious."

Her hands tighten in my hair when I take her nipple in my mouth and give it a tug.

"Yes! Harder."

I love that she never hesitates to tell me exactly what she needs. It's fucking hot to be with a woman who has this kind of confidence.

She arches as I suck and squeeze her gorgeous tits. Eager to make my girl come apart, I reach down and slide my hand into her panties where I drag my finger through her damp folds the way she likes a few times to tease her. When she starts making those needy sounds, I push into her with one finger, then two.

She feels like heaven. A tight. Wet. Heaven.

The anticipation makes my dick pulse against my zipper. I kneel to drag my shirt off while she reaches for my belt. It takes a few minutes to kick off the rest of our clothes.

I stare at the stunning woman beneath me as I stroke myself. "Fuck, Kelani. You're gorgeous."

She watches me jerk off a second before she scrambles to her knees and takes me in hand. Before she puts me in her gorgeous mouth, she looks up at me. "Choke me on it and pull my hair." And then my little siren winks. "I like it rough."

Holy hell.

My cock throbs when she licks the crown like I'm her favorite lollypop.

I gather her hair and brush it off her face so I can watch her run her mouth up and down my length. "If, uh, if I push too hard, or it's too much, tap my thigh."

She nods with a smile, only she's stuffed full of me. It's a wickedly beautiful sight.

I let her play on my cock for a while. She deep throats me so good, my balls tighten.

When she comes up for air, I tighten my hand in her hair to keep her from going down again. "Not yet." Instead, I rub the tip of my erection against her perfect lips. Her tongue darts out to wiggle against my slit. Little by little, I let her take more.

After I'm sure I'm not gonna blow, I shove her back down. For a second,

I'm afraid I'm too rough, but she groans around me and pushes deeper until I bottom out against her throat.

It's like I've died and gone to heaven. To the paradise of Kelani.

As she shuttles back and forth with that sinful mouth, I clench my eyes shut and drop my head back while I try to keep from coming.

Having this beautiful woman on her knees and worshiping my cock is a heady experience. I'm not sure what I've done to deserve her, but I aim to prove myself worthy.

"That's enough." I pull her off me with a pop. "Now it's your turn."

She wipes her mouth, confused. "But you haven't come yet."

"And I won't be coming until you do the honors first. Get your cute ass on the bed and spread your legs."

Her eyes glaze over and she nods.

I watch, enraptured as she tosses her hair over my pillows and stretches out before me. When her thighs part, I grab myself and squeeze my dick to calm the fuck down.

"Reach down and spread yourself for me."

She swallows and then does what I've asked, spreading her pretty pink pussy with her hand. I settle between her thighs and run my finger through her wetness.

"You're soaked, baby. Is this all for me?"

She nods. "Yes. Hurry up before I die."

I chuckle and lean close to blow on her swollen clit. Her thighs tighten around me, and I wedge my body deeper to keep her open. "Be a good girl and keep your legs open."

CHAPTER 6 - KELLY

When he tells me to be a good girl, my clit pulses.

"Hurry, Cam," I moan.

Reaching down with both hands, I spread myself for him. He looks ravenous, like a man who hasn't eaten for months and I just sat him before a buffet.

He's a big man. Tall, broad, with muscles everywhere. So it stands to reason that his touch might not be gentle.

Only the first swipe of his tongue is featherlight. So light, my toes curl.

With all of the sexual tension that's built up between us, I expect him to rush to the main event, but he takes his time working me over. He circles my clit so long, his hot breath warming my nub, I'm pretty sure I'm going to melt into his mattress before he finally reaches the destination.

Then he sinks two fingers into my body.

"Oh god." His fingers are much thicker than mine, and considering his dick is enormous, maybe that's a good thing. It'll acclimate me to his size.

He gets a rhythm going with his hand that has me arching my back. That's when he starts laving my clit.

I jam my hand into his hair to hold him to me as I quake with an orgasm. I make sounds I've never made before as I shiver and shake and come apart beneath him.

I finally open my eyes and look down at him. "Again?" he asks.

Laughing, I shake my head. "Get up here. The next time I come had better be on your dick."

Like a big jungle cat, he prowls up my body and settles between my thighs where his cock nudges at my opening.

We've already had the birth control talk. Last month, we also went to the clinic together to get tested for everything under the sun. Since I'm religious about taking my pill every morning, and condoms make me itch, we've decided the pill is enough.

He kisses me, and I suck his tongue into my mouth while he grinds against me. Everything feels so good, I claw his back to get closer. "More."

Bracing on one arm, he uses the other hand to rub himself along my opening. I pull my knees to my chest because it's going to be a tight squeeze down there. I can't wait.

"I'll go slow, baby," he assures me.

"I can take it." I think.

He starts to sink into me, and I groan in delight. He's so thick, and the stretch is incredible. "Oh my god, Cam, don't stop."

When he finally bottoms out, I rest my knees against his chest. I'm too overwhelmed to say anything.

"You okay?" he asks, almost out of breath.

"It's so good," I pant as I try to get him to move. "Fuck me, Cam." With a groan, he pulls back, all the way to his tip before he sinks back down again. "Faster. Faster!"

Something in him snaps, and he starts to move. Our bodies slap together as his big body starts nudging me higher up the bed.

I reach between us and circle his dick with my thumb and finger as it descends into me, and he pulses.

"Kelani," he grits out. "I'm gonna come if you're not careful."

"That sounds like a challenge." I hike my legs over his shoulders. "Get there, babe."

He nods, that feral look in his eyes gobbling me up as he starts to fuck me hard. His attention zeroes in on my tits that bounce with every thrust.

I take my nipples between my fingers and twist and pinch as he watches. When his thighs spread more, he hits the perfect angle, and I cry out as I come again.

"Fuck, baby. Fuck." He drops onto me, and after a few more hard thrusts, he comes, swelling thick between my thighs and setting off another round of pulses through my body.

We lie tangled together and out of breath. He finally lifts his head and looks at me, an expression of wonder on his handsome face. "What was that?"

I smile, tired and sleepy but so well sated. "An out of body experience?"

Still lodged deep in my body, he kisses me, slow and soft. I drag my fingers through his damp hair. "Let's clean up. Did you want me to stay over? Or do you want to drop me off at home?"

We've had long conversations about how he feels after sex, and the last thing I want him to feel is claustrophobic.

He frowns. "Kelly, there's no way in hell I'm letting you out of my bed tonight."

"It's okay if you want to sleep alone. I'm not going to judge you or be hurt. Tell me what you need."

Twisting, he pulls me on top of him. "Smother me. I can take it."

I laugh and rest my chin on my palm as I stare down at this beautiful man. "I like you, Cam. A lot." I more than like him, but I don't want to overwhelm him.

His smile widens. "Good, because I'm pretty sure I'm in love with you, and it would be a damn shame if you didn't like me."

My heart goes into a frenzy at his sweet words. I lean down to kiss him. "I love you too, my sexy Viking. Now get your ass up unless you want to sleep on the wet spot."

That night, we sleep in spurts, waking up every few hours to reach for each other. It's magical.

The next morning, we sit side by side on his bed and stare at our competition on his flatscreen.

"What's our strategy? Do you want a direct hit or should I stalk them from behind?" I ask in between bites of my bagel. I'm wearing one of his big t-shirts, and he's wearing a pair of gym shorts.

"Stalk from behind," he says, pausing to give me a look. "Speaking of which, you look damn good from behind. Especially with your ass in the air."

I laugh and playfully smack him. "Focus on the game. And if you're a good boy, I'll let you do that thing again."

He winks. "You're on."

Leaning over, I grab his face to kiss him. "I love you."

"Love you too, baby."

That kiss goes from a sweet peck to something hotter in a flash.

"Fuck it." He flings his controller onto his desk and reaches for me. "We'll play later. I need my Nerdy Ninja."

Laughing, we both fall onto his bed. "Bring it, Blazer."

Thanks for reading Maui Dream Girl! Cam is a supporting character in the Varsity Dads, a series by Lex Martin that features single dads or soon-to-be fathers. You can start the series with The Varsity Dad Dilemma or find more info at lexmartinwrites.com.

FIRST CLASS SCOUNDREL

LIV MORRIS

CHAPTER 1

"Excuse me, Miss." I look up from the pages of my book and see the friendly flight attendant smiling at me. "Would you like a glass of wine?"

She's holding a bottle of something red and inviting that could help me unwind. I nod my head and reach for my wallet.

"It's included with your first-class ticket." Her whisper saves me my dignity. "Is red okay?"

"Yes, thank you." I pull out the tray from the sidearm of the chair and she sits the nearly full glass with a cocktail napkin in front of me. The motion of the plane causes the wine to ripple. I glance down at my lily-white sundress and wonder if red was a good choice after all.

"I'll be back with some warm nuts. Enjoy." She turns to the couple sitting across from me and goes through the same spiel.

I pick up the glass and take my first sip. I wasn't expecting it to taste so good and I pray refills are free, because I need something to help me forget why I'm escaping Kansas City.

The reason starts with a man and ends with a woman. The man was mine for a while, but the woman wasn't me. I wish he would've made his choice before he left me standing at the altar.

I keep telling myself I'm better off without him and it's true, but the truth doesn't help ease the pain. I keep thinking this sick feeling in my stomach will get better soon. I'm putting my faith in the healing powers of the turquoise sea. Several months on a tropical island should help I hope.

The flight attendant begins talking to the man one row up and diagonal from me. My scattered state must be to blame for the fact that I missed him before since he's stunningly handsome. The panty-melting kind of hot. Even with the short distance between us, he exudes an almost animal-like sexuality. Like a wolf in Savile Row's finest, he's dressed in a bespoke black suit. The tailored kind that likely costs more than my month's salary. A crisp white shirt peeks out around his collar.

He begins to speak and his deep voice is smoother than the wine I'm holding. His jawline is severe with a broad appearance. The wisp of scruff etched across it makes me bite my lip. I've always loved a little five o'clock shadow. His thick black hair is slicked back in a controlled professional type style. He probably uses more hair product than me, but the result is well worth it.

He stretches out his arm and long fingers curl around the offered wine glass. I watch the sleeve of his suit coat inch back enough to reveal an onyx cufflink. He oozes money, class, sex, and.... marriage.

I spot the thick gold band adorning his wedding finger and take a deep breath. All the good ones make it down the aisle it appears.

Returning to my romance novel, I continue the story of that one incredible man who would do anything for his love. To make the fairytale seem possible, I indulge in the bottomless wine pours, not to mention the delicious food served in the "special" section of the plane.

I'm only sitting here by pure luck, since the airline receptionist solved the problem of me having to pay for three suitcases at check in. It would've been two hundred and fifty dollars. An outrageous fee for someone living on a teacher's salary. But those three suitcases contain all the essentials for my three-month stay in Maui over the summer.

The receptionist upgraded me to first class on my Los Angeles to Maui flight for one hundred-fifty dollars. The simple act let me have all my bags checked for free. Plus I am now a first-class snob with enough legroom for a giant.

I glance over at the married man and frown as I see his legs barely contained in the generous area. He isn't just hot he's tall. Handsome and hitched. I sigh at my always-present bad luck.

He must have felt me looking at him, because he swivels in his seat and his eyes meet mine. For the first time I'm able to see his face fully. No partial side view, but his entire glorious face.

He's devastating with dark eyes that draw me in as if I have no will. A nose and cheekbones so precise, a master may have sculpted them.

I've never called a man beautiful, but he is simply breathtaking. Face to face as we are now, he possesses an untamed sexuality that is overwhelming. I shake my head a couple of times and melt back into my seat hoping I can escape his pull.

A slow smile slides across his face as he observes my discomfort. He knows exactly how he's unnerving me, but I'm helpless. I offer a weak smile in surrender and silently chant, "He's married," over and over.

The flight attendant breaks my pathetic trance as she walks by. I bury my head in my book and don't glance his way until we are preparing to land.

I believe I read the same two pages in my novel for about forty-five minutes. The book might as well have been upside-down, because my concentration stopped the second his eyes met mine. *Damn him.*

I dutifully readjust my seat and secure my tray table. The flight attendant makes one more round to make sure her chosen subjects are buckled in.

Against my better judgment, I stop fighting this crazy pull he has over me, and glance over at the subject of my naughty thoughts. He's fiddling with his wedding ring, and to my shock I watch him brazenly remove the band and stuff it into his suit pocket. I blink a couple of times in hopes I will see the ring reappear on his finger. But instead all that lingers is a prominent tan line and a blatant disregard of his wedding vows.

This man reeks of mendacity. He's nothing more than a first-class scoundrel. If we weren't two seconds from landing, I'd get out of my seat and slap him on behalf of his poor wife who's probably home counting the days till his return. What a complete jerk.

CHAPTER 2

Most of the other passengers have walked away from the airport's open-air baggage claim with their bags in tow. The buzz of conversation has turned to silence, and I find myself waiting for my three suitcases with the one person I didn't want to see again, Mr. Married with No Ring.

He stands tall across from me with his legs slightly a part and arms crossed over his chest. Even in the empty space his presence crowds me. I take a deep breath with the intention of turning my eyes down toward the baggage claim, but I can't force them away from his hypnotic gaze.

He's looking at me with an impassive expression, and I can't help but wonder what he's thinking as he appears to assess me.

I watch his eyes travel from my face to my chest and he stops in a fixed stare to gaze at my boobs. This act solidifies him as a typical player and shouldn't have an effect on me, but I squirm and stand a little straighter. Something about him makes any willpower I have disappear.

Then a devilish grin crosses his disgustingly handsome face. *Bastard.* He throws his head backwards in a small laugh which makes me a little unnerved and curious. So I glance down where his stare was targeted and see a perfectly round drop of wine staining my white sundress. The large drop has landed exactly where my nipple is located with the help of my push-up bra.

Deep red marks the spot and the color of my face. *Damn him.*

I glance back up and I swear he winks at me. The gall of this horrible creature makes my blood boil. I turn my body, so he no longer has a view of my chest. His show and my humiliation are now over.

I toss my purse over my shoulder and pray my suitcases appear. I need to escape this sexual magnet of a man. He's on the prowl and God help the woman, or more likely women, who succumb to his evil ways on this island.

Even as I think this, there's a part of me that wonders what it would be like to succumb to a man like him. Have his long fingers lingering over my body. Touching me in private places, and having his full lips kiss me with passion. I bet he's a powerhouse in bed.

What in the hell is wrong with me?

I should pinch myself for even entertaining what this Adonis is like in bed. Even if it has been nearly six months since a man touched me.

My three suitcases finally appear and I start to lift them off the belt. I grit my teeth as I pull each one of them to a standing position. Now I need to find a cab to get me to my best friend Sarah's villa.

"Mal." I turn to see Sarah walking toward me or more like walk running. She was supposed to be working tonight, but I sure am happy to see her. It's been way too long.

"You made it!"

She's embracing me before I can even respond. "Of course I made it. I've been counting the seconds. I thought you had to work late?"

"The powers that be let me leave early." Sarah works as an emergency room nurse at the island's only hospital. They sponsor a program to help new graduates pay off student loans in exchange for a few years service in paradise. She accepted their offer and has been down here for a year.

"Thank God. I worried about taking a cab to your place. I've only been here once, and it was just for a few days."

"It's all good. And you look great, but way too pale." She scans my exposed arms. As a true redhead only my freckles tan. "We need to dip you daily in a vat of sunscreen."

"Funny," I laugh, but she's right. I had a horrible sunburn when I visited her over Christmas, and I was sitting in the shade. She said the sun's reflection off the sand cooked me.

I frown at the thought of Christmas. I used my supposed honeymoon ticket for the island to visit her instead. I drank half the island's rum, which is a feat, but it didn't do much to numb the hurt.

"I know that face." She scolds me, because it's impossible to hide anything from my closest friend. "I promised to never bring up his name, but I did enjoy hearing the slut left him for a Chiefs' running back."

"I might have celebrated with friends the day I saw the news," I added.

It didn't make me feel better in the end, but I wasn't upset that he knew the pain and embarrassment I endured when he cheated on me and didn't show up for our wedding. At least his betrayal of me didn't make the front page of the newspaper's gossip column. That had to sting. "I know I'm better off without him."

"Yes you are." Sarah glances at the three suitcases parked next to me. "Are you planning on moving here?" Her goodhearted laugh makes me laugh too.

"It's possible." I tease as she starts to walk away with two of my suitcases. There's a part of me that would love a new beginning in a faraway place, but I'm not a risk taker like Sarah.

"I've heard from many mainland transplants that it's best to purchase a one-way ticket here. Just in case."

We make our way to the outside parking lot, and I run into the back of Sarah as she stops dead in her tracks. I peek over her shoulder to see the first-class scoundrel crossing our path.

He's dragging two extra-large rolling bags toward a taxi, which seems odd for a weekend getaway to cheat on his wife. Surely, he will only need a couple changes of clothes and a Costco size box of condoms. *Jerk.*

"Whoa," Sarah practically purrs. "What a man." I roll my eyes so hard I think I pull a muscle.

"He's a pretty package, but he's also on a mission to cheat on his wife." Sarah turns her head toward me as I move to her side. She knits her brows and silently asks me to continue. "He sat near me on the plane. I watched him pocket his wedding band."

Sarah crinkles up her face and mouths the word "no," but I nod in return. "It's true. Swear."

"I've never seen him before. But there's a constant flow of men who fly here from Los Angeles to *explore* the island." She winks at me and I understand what she means by explore. "I always look for a tan line on the ring finger."

"Oh he's definitely got one of those. Promise." I want to say I'm thankful I saw him remove his ring, because I might have succumbed to his charming ways if he showed any interest in me.

I watch him take off his suit jacket, throw it into the taxi, and roll up his sleeves to expose bare arms built like a weight lifter's. He proceeds to help the cabbie lift his bags into the vehicle, and his broad shoulders pull the seams of his shirt. If that wasn't bad enough, he bends over to pick up something the cabbie dropped, and I'm greeted by a perfectly tight butt.

"Mal?" I notice Sarah shaking my arm as I hear her voice. "Mallory? Are you okay?"

"Sure." I blink the sight of him away and fix on a smile. "He's a jerk, right?"

"The worst kind. So hot you might forget why he's a scoundrel." I crack a grin. If the shoe fits...

We walk away from the culprit of my wet panties toward Sarah's car in the parking lot. After maneuvering through a lot of vehicles packed in like sardines, we load my gear, and we pull up to the airport's parking pay station. There are two lanes and I glance to my right and see the scoundrel staring back at me from the back seat of his taxi.

I turn my head toward the windshield and lower myself in my seat. Since I'm apparently a sex-deprived mess, I have no self-control and peek over at him again.

This time he's grinning at me with pearly-whites so bright I almost need to squint. However it's his eyes that draw me closer to the car's window. They're gleaming with mischief and dare I say, *sex.* I cross my legs to control the odd sensation his look causes.

Determination hits me, and I grab my sunglasses out of my purse and nearly slam them on. I face forward, but I feel his stare like the noonday sun on my cheek.

Thankfully, Sarah's car pulls ahead breaking his spell over me. She hands the attendant her lot ticket and the gate bar rises up.

"Yes! Free for the first thirty minutes." She turns my way and starts to smile until she sees me. "What's with the glasses? It's almost dark."

"Nothing." I pull the glasses off and tuck them back into my purse. Hoping that I can tuck away the thoughts of Mr. Hottie too. "What are the plans for tonight? You mentioned something about watching the sunset from that bar on the beach."

"I think we need to make a stop at my place before we head there. You have a big red stain on your boob. And believe me you have a big enough rack that you don't need to give the men another reason to gawk." She giggles and I try to smile, but I remember that *man* laughing at me instead.

CHAPTER 3

"I'm picking out your clothes." Sarah leaves no room for arguments as she digs through a closet containing all the colors of the rainbow. "I have an awesome dress that would look great on you."

I start to protest as I'm hit in the face with a small piece of bright green material. It falls to the floor, and after picking it up I realize it's Sarah chosen garment for me to wear.

"There's not enough here to cover me below the waist." I stretch the dress and gasp when the size almost doubles.

"See." Sarah points to the now larger dress. "Trust me. It will look just right and tight."

"Oh my God. You're out to get me laid my first night here aren't you?" I'm tempted to fling the dress back at her; instead I decide to give it a try.

"Okay, turn around." I demand, and Sarah huffs while spinning around to walk back into her closet.

"Whatever. I was your roommate for four years. I've seen it all." Her voice echoes out to me from the depths of her floral abyss.

I remove my stained clothing and step into the sinful dress as best I can. I shimmy it up my legs and realize it's nothing more than a tube of green fabric contouring over my curves.

I remove my bra and adjust the girls. They stay in place because there's barely enough room for me to breath.

"See, it fits." I don't miss the smug look on Sarah's face when she walks out of the closet wearing a bikini top and a matching sarong. "And so what if I'm trying to get you dolled up for some action. You need something besides that battery operated friend."

"God, don't remind me." I lean over her dresser to get closer to her mirror so I can freshen up my makeup. I decide to leave my hair down in waves around my shoulders since I'm showing so much skin.

"Some of the island guys around here are pretty good at helping a lady burn off a little steam. And that guy at the airport, though he's scum, seemed to have you worked up."

"He was a charming snake!" I won't admit it out loud but I get tingles just thinking about those eyes of his staring at me. I don't remember a man giving me *that* look before. It was pretty damn incredible even if he's a seasoned cheater. I swear I have the crappiest luck when it comes to men.

"Yeah, he's the kind that would charm the clothes off you."

Truthfully, I would love to meet a decent guy tonight and do a little fooling around. Maybe even help each other out mutually without having full-blown sex.

Sarah stands next to me and looks at me in the mirror. "That dress leaves little to the imagination. Your red hair goes perfectly with the green color too. If you put on some lipstick, I'm pretty sure I'll have to beat them away tonight."

"I could use a few guys giving me some attention." I sound desperate, and I am.

"Okay, grab your purse and let's go."

Sarah heads to the door and we're off to her favorite bar, Over the Cliff. Tourists are seldom found there, so it's guaranteed we'll see the locals gathered around the place. Since Sarah makes friends when someone comes within two feet of her, I'm sure she'll know everyone there.

As soon as we walk into the open-sided bar, people start saying hello to Sarah. I recognize a few of them from when I was here a few months ago, and hope my former state doesn't scare them away from me. I was the total definition of a hot mess after the wedding fiasco. I should have worn a sign that said, *jilted bride.*

"Hey Patty." Sarah addresses a woman a little older than us sitting at a pub table by herself. I'd guess she's around thirty-years-old. "I want you to meet my best friend, Mallory. She's here for the summer."

"Hi," Patty moves her tote off the chair next to her and we sit down around the table. "Welcome. The summer is the best time to come here. Less touristy. You'll get a better feel for the island."

"It was crawling with people when I was here last Christmas."

"That's the highest of the high season. It's much more chill here now." Patty gives me a lazy smile that matches her words.

"It felt different today. Even the airport was practically empty."

I really like how easy Sarah's friend is to talk to. I'm not the most social person, especially at bars when I've not had a drink yet.

Damn, the word airport reminds me of that handsome jerk. I shake my head and look to the side and see what I hope is a lust-inspired mirage. However I'm pretty sure it's Mr. Cheater himself.

"What's wrong Mallory?" I ignore Sarah's question, mostly because I am too shocked to move. "You look as if you've seen a ghost."

I break through my paralysis and grab Sarah's arm. "He's here." I move my head a couple times in his direction. "Over there."

"No way." I hear Sarah's shock though it mixes with what sounds like the beginning of a laugh.

"Yes, and he's even hotter now." I said that last part out loud, dammit. I loosen my death grip on Sarah's arm, and pull my hair over my face to hide. "Do you think he saw me?"

Half of me wants Sarah to say yes. The other side, which is clothed in a too tight dress, hopes he didn't.

"I'm not sure." I glance over at Sarah and she's narrowing her eyes. "Patty do you know that tall, handsome guy over there? The one with the dark hair and baby blue t-shirt plastered to his pecs.

I peek through the strands of my hair to see what his pecs look like. Yep, they're outstanding, the bastard.

"I've never seen him before, but the guy he's standing next to is some hotshot investor here to build a resort," Patty sounds none to pleased with the cheater's companion. They're both likely here to plan, party, and quickly depart. I've been here for five years and their type isn't new."

"Mallory saw the tall one take off his wedding ring and stash it in his pocket. He definitely plans on partying. I bet he flew here for the weekend just to get a quick fuck."

"He's looking over at our table now," Patty shares the play-by-play with me and I'm itching to see what he's doing. "He's got his friend turned our way too."

Just as I'm about to tell Sarah I needed a drink like five minutes ago, a rum punch suddenly appears in front of me on the table.

"Your drink. Courtesy of David Lawson." I flick my eyes to the just-following-orders server. He takes a step back when he sees the snarl on my face, because I have a hunch *who* this David character might be.

"Care to point him out?" I ask with a raised brow.

"He's the gentleman in blue at the end of the bar," says the server. Poor guy is just doing his job and didn't realize he was entering a blasting zone.

I straighten up in my chair and turn toward the so-called gentleman. What a gigantic mistake it was to look over at him, because now I'm having trouble breathing.

He's sporting a different smile than the one earlier at the airport. This one's more a sexy smirk. The kind you might see on the devil himself. Maybe the two of them are brothers? It would make perfect sense if they were.

I pick up my drink and put it back on the server's tray. "I can't accept it from *him*." I hiss the last word and the poor server appears confused.

"What do you want me to do with it?" His question baffles me. Surely someone has turned down a free drink here before.

"Dump it down the sink for all I care."

"Or dump it over the a-hole's head," Patty pipes in.

The server moves after Patty's suggestion, and scurries away to the bar. I put on my best smug face and direct it toward David. He definitely witnessed me rejecting his "free" cocktail. I would bet he thought it would get him to at least third base with me. Instead he struck out and appears crestfallen. Odd since every other woman in the bar is likely panting over him.

"Wow," Sarah says. "He looks as if you kicked his puppy."

"He's just looking for a chase. Once he has someone caught and bedded, he'll move on to the next conquest," Patty sums him up perfectly. "I've seen his type for years down here. They think it's an adult spring break."

"He's still staring at you, Mallory." I glance over to see him looking peeved. I have hurt his delicate ego. I smile to myself and sit up proudly, even though there's a part of me that wants to go comfort him.

I am totally sick to even think those thoughts.

"Would you mind if we went to a different place?" I pout and put on my best puppy-dog eyes, because I don't know if I can stand being in the same small space with him any longer. I am here to escape stress not feel so wound up.

"I think it's a good idea. He's really into you and he's the last man on earth you need to get involved with." Sarah reaches across the table and gives my hand a soft squeeze as she turns to Patty. "Her last boyfriend was just as bad."

"I'm sorry," Patty says. "I've had some bad luck with love myself."

"*Men,*" Sarah's tone says it all. "They're almost not worth the trouble."

"True." I push off the pub stool and grab my purse. "Let me visit the Ladies before we go."

"Wanna join us Patty? The night is young." Sarah gives Patty a wink. "I'm still hoping my friend gets lucky tonight. Look at her damn dress."

"Both sound good," Patty turns to me and winks. "Mercy's Child is playing at Cane Bay down the road."

"You all can figure out our next move. I'll be right back." I pull the dress down at the hem and up at the top's edge. I want the fullest coverage before I walk across the bar to the restroom, because I can still feel his burning gaze on me.

After walking to the back of the bar without turning his direction, I do my business and start to exit through the bathroom door. What I don't expect to see is David standing like a giant directly in front of me.

I bring my hand to my chest and simultaneously gasp. "What are you doing here?"

"I want to talk to you." He's moving his gorgeous full lips to speak and I can't help imagining what he tastes like. I'm guessing whiskey because he smells like a mix of Jameson and spice.

He's placed one hand on the top of the door's frame, which makes his body lean forward even closer to me. I hear the door's handle click behind me and I press against the wood for strength.

At this point there is barely a foot separating me from this man and his half-quirked smile that makes my knees almost give way. I should pray for help from on high with him so close, but he's likely scared all the angels away.

Staring up into his lust-filled eyes, I'm pulled into his sexual thrall. And since I'm a weak, sex-deprived woman standing in front of a godlike demon of a man, my body doesn't want to retreat. Nope. It wants to attack, pounce, and ride.

Yes, I went there, or would like to go there with him. It makes me feel sick to admit this truth, and I need to remember the *truth* about David.

He's *married*.

I chant these words over and over in my head, and picture a sweet young woman about my age dusting off a wedding picture. She gazes at it longingly while wishing David was at home with her. Add a small child or two and I'm back to where I should be. *Disgusted!*

"Well, I want to tell you *this* first." He leans even closer to me as he waits for me to speak. He bites his lip and gives me a sly smile. It's going to be so fun to cut him down to size. "You. Are. *Repulsive*."

David appears stunned by my verbal attack and removes his hand from the door as he stands up giving me some needed personal space. I exhale a deep breath and prepare for a little show and tell. I want him to know why I've come to this conclusion about his character. I grab his left hand and bring it up between us.

"See this tan line on your ring finger." He drops his eyes down to look with me and brings them back up to mine. "It's missing something very important. A gold band."

I drop his hand like he's carrying a plague and, knowing his behavior, he might have a sexual one.

"I saw you take off your wedding ring on the plane. So let me introduce myself. My name is Mallory O'Connor, and on behalf of all the women on this planet, this is for you."

I reach my right hand up high and slap him across his jawline. He steps back and with eyes wide, rubs his jaw. A hand-printed, razor sharp jaw on a beautiful cheating face. *Damn him.*

He starts to speak but looks at my chest and smiles his trademark scoundrel grin. My eyes continue down and I see the reason he's smirking. I've had a major wardrobe malfunction thanks to my barely there dress. My right nipple is exposed and ready to cut glass. Forget a drink, I need a damn bottle.

CHAPTER 4

"*Sarah.*" I hear a knock at the front door, or maybe it's the pounding in my head. I indulged in way too many Pain Killers last night. I quit counting at four.

Boom, boom, boom. The noise continues from somewhere, so I yell out to Sarah again. "I think someone's at the door."

I see a wild-haired Sarah walk by the guest room I'm sleeping in. I push back the covers and look down to discover I'm still in the green dress from last night. However, it's more like a belt leaving everything exposed.

Exposed. That word is the reason I drank a gallon of rum. David saw my nipple. A turned on, needing his immediate attention one too.

Kill me.

I swing my legs over the bed and wobble on my two feet. I think I'm still under the influence. I manage to find a pair of shorts and a t-shirt in my suitcase and quickly change. I'm tempted to burn the dress on Sarah's barbeque outside.

"Mallory. Look at this." I finish adjusting my shirt and see Sarah at the door holding a large vase of roses.

"What the heck are those?" I walk toward her and she holds up an envelope with my name on it.

"I bet I know who these flowers are from." I shake my head at Sarah and assess the flowers. They're gorgeous bright yellow roses with a sherbet orange on their tips. I look up at Sarah in shock. "Over the top right?"

"I don't get it. I told David fuck off and followed it with a slap to the face. Why would he send them after that? And how the hell did he find me?"

"I know the answer to the last question. It's a small island. Everyone knew you were with me. Some probably remember you from Christmas. I want to know the why. Open it."

I take the envelope from her and consider burning it along with the dress, but I'm too curious. The seal breaks easily and I expect to find a card but instead it's a couple sheets of paper. Strange.

"What does it say?" Sarah buzzes around me like a bee. I'm more worried at how I'll feel if it's truly from David.

I straighten out the sheets of paper and see that they're written in long hand not typed. His handwriting reflects him, strong and polished. He's written a ton of words, so I dive in.

Dear Mallory,

(He's used a term of endearment. I guess that's okay.)

Please hear me out. There has been a big misunderstanding and I want to clear up one major thing. I'm no longer married. I was married for four years to a woman who left me six months ago for her best friend, Margot. If you Google my name and my ex-wife, Anna, along with the word divorce, I'm sure you can verify what I'm saying. Our breakup made the headlines in the Los Angeles Times.

My divorce was final yesterday afternoon. My attorney called me with the news as I traveled to catch the flight to Maui.

Yes, you saw me remove my wedding band. Due to legal issues, I was told by my attorney to leave it on until the last paper was signed. I thought about my freedom from my ex during the entire flight and decided I

*needed a fresh start. I saw the ring on my finger right before we touched
ground, and knew it was the first change I wanted to make. So off it went.*

(Wow. I stop to catch my breath. If what he wrote is true, I'm in a bad
Hawaiian version of Pride and Prejudice. *Help me, Jane!*)

*Now to you. I've always had a thing for red heads and beautiful
women. When I saw you standing in your white dress across from me, you
looked like an angel.*

(How sweet his words, and here I called *him* the devil's brother. What a
judgy bitch I turned out to be, and he's so damn hot.)

*We started off on the wrong foot, but there's something about you I
can't seem to shake. You're the first woman since Anna left me that has
made me want to know more. Who you are? Why you're here on the
island? What movies do you like to see? How your lips taste when I
kiss you?*

(I might need to read this in private. I'm sure Sarah is watching me
squirm and turn red.)

*Even this misunderstanding has left me intrigued because I loved
seeing the fire in your eyes when you confronted me. It makes me wonder
what other passions live within you.*

(Holy hell. This man has written me into a sexual hot flash.)

*If you can look past our beginning, I would like to take you out to
dinner this evening. Text me at 202-555-0131, if you're interested in
joining me. I have dinner reservations tonight for seven o'clock at Mama's
Fish House.*

I hope you give me a chance. I want to see more of you…

(Oh, he does have a bad side, because I'm sure he's referring to the nipple
sneak peek.)

*Yours truly,
David*

I sit back in the over-stuffed chair that I somehow ended up in while I was
reading David's letter. The steamy tone has me now using the sheets of paper
as a fan. What an idiot I was for jumping to the wrong conclusion about him.
Now I need to verify what he outlined about his marriage, I didn't want to
answer with a text until I was certain he was telling the truth.

I ponder that I might be a rebound for him. It's not even a question really since he's only been officially divorced for twenty-four hours. I *am* a rebound.

It's not like I'm looking for a relationship, so I am not going to worry about it. I prefer to think of him as a tropical diversion below my equator, and a hot as hell one too.

I hand over the letter to Sarah. There's no need to keep it from her, she'll ask me a million exhausting question if I don't.

"Here." I dangle the papers in front of Sarah. "I need to search the Internet. Can I use your computer?"

She grabs the letter from my hands and points to the dining room table. I have a few seconds before she starts in so I hurry to the chair in front of the computer and fire it up.

I type these words into the browser. David Lawson, Anna Lawson, divorce, and Margot. I press enter and wait for the results. Within seconds I see link after link tagging David and his ex-wife. I click on the first LA Times' article in the search results and begin to read.

"Hotel heir and former playboy, David Lawson and his wife, Anna, are calling it quits after four years. The cause of their breakup seems to be his wife's best friend Margot. It appears they will be sharing a closet. Good thing they both wear a size 2."

"Ouch! David doesn't appear to be heartbroken, but I can't imagine seeing my breakup in the headlines. I'd still be in bed if it was me. It makes me want to comfort him and give him a hug. One that includes my legs wrapped around his waist tightly, which reminds me that I should do some grooming prep for tonight.

"You better text his hot ass." Sarah sounds like she's finished the letter, and I answer her with a quick nod.

Now I'm off to find my phone. I need to confirm a dinner reservation with a walking, talking sex god.

CHAPTER 5

I am trying to relax and forget the nagging remnants of my hangover as Sarah fusses with my hair and makeup. She keeps telling me that less is more with the island humidity, but she hasn't finished working on me yet. I've tried on every outfit in her closet at least twice. I may need a nap before David arrives because I'm exhausted.

We finally decide on a turquoise blue dress. The skirt of the dress is just about mid-thigh with a flirty flair. My favorite part of the outfit is the halter-top. I'm able to position my boobs with an enticing cleavage and still not wear a bra. And if there's some romance later tonight, one quick release of a button and I'm showing him the girls.

"I think you're ready." Sarah stands back and assesses me from head to toe. "Here are the nude wedge heels that will go perfectly."

"Thanks." I take the shoes and slip them on my feet. We lucked out because we both wear the same size in clothes and shoes. Just like David's ex and her girlfriend. Poor beautiful man. "Is it normal to be this nervous on a first date? I feel like I'm sixteen again."

"Well he's GQ hot and you've been basically living like a nun for six months. You just need to get back on the horse and ride it."

"You are disgusting, but right. I need to get laid." I watch Sarah pump her fists into the air. She may be doing an island-mating dance as she circles around me.

"Damn right!" She stops and eyes me. "My advice. Take it one orgasm at a time."

"I've never had a double one, but if there's a man who might give me one…"

With the windows open, we hear the sounds of wheels hitting the gravel of Sarah's driveway.

"Shit," I curse as my stomach starts to flutter. "Do I look all right?" I ask the usual silly girl question.

"You are beautiful. He's going to have a boner all night."

A light knock comes from the front door, and I know he's here. Sarah gives me a side hug and a kiss on the cheek. "Don't come home until you can tell me whether it's boxers or briefs."

I hug her back and head to the door. Once I open it up, my breath hitches at the sight of David standing before me looking like he walked out of a resort magazine. He has on a crisp white linen shirt with the sleeves rolled to the elbows. Two of the buttons are open at the top and I can see a light smattering of chest hair. I try not to lick my lips, but there's no stopping them. It's been way too long.

"Hello, Mallory." David's voice sings to me and I swear the melody caresses my skin. Six month without sex can do that to a girl.

"Hello." My response is weak, but at least I uttered something intelligible back to him.

"You look lovely." He reaches for my hand and raises it to his mouth. The slight brushing touch of lips circulates through my body and my nerves melt away with a sigh. "That color was made for you."

"Thanks." I need to compose myself, or I'll be climaxing in the driveway.

He doesn't release my hand. Instead he gently pulls me from the porch to his car and opens the passenger door for me. So far he's been a perfect gentleman, but I'd be okay with a dash of scoundrel too. There's something about a hot guy mixed with some bad boy tendencies that unravels me.

"I'm glad you gave me a chance." His remarks make me nearly laugh at loud. I wouldn't deny this man a date after finding out the truth. Actually there's very little I would deny him right now. I may be sliding down the sleep-on-the-first-date slope tonight.

He places his hand on the small of my back to help me into the car. I'm amazed how right his simple touch and guidance feels to me.

Closing my door, he hurries around the front end of the car. I shiver watching his body move with such grace. Daydreaming, I picture him moving over the top of me in bed. Slow and steady.

Once he's buckled up, I turn to him. "I think you're the one taking a chance on me. I did slap you. Hard. Not a very good first impression."

"Oh, you left an impression. I had a handprint on my face hours later. And the memory of something else to drive me wild."

I let my eyes fall to the floor when I think about my nipple slip. Now I'm aching for his touch.

The road to the restaurant hugs the island's coastline giving us scenic views. He explained the reason he is visiting. His hotel chain is building a class-A resort in Maui. A group of his employees has been working with the government to secure the necessary permits, but issues have arisen that demand his presence. I'm trying not to appear too excited at the news he's staying on island for the foreseeable future.

He pulls up to the front of the restaurant. I can see the beach below us and the ocean stretches out for as far as the eye can see. It's a perfect lookout point. The sunset appears to be seconds away as the last of the round orange glow hits the ocean's edge on the horizon.

The view takes my breath away along with the person sitting to my left. I look his way just to make sure I'm not dreaming. Nope. He's real and gazing at me... intensely.

"I'm sorry you've run into trouble with your hotel, but I'm not sorry you need to be down here for a while." I bite my lip in remorse and he stares at me. *Hard.* I watch his eyes darken and I become lost in them.

"I want to kiss you, but I think it's too soon. I confess I've been thinking about you nonstop since yesterday."

"It's not too soon," I respond in a raspy voice that surprises me with how needy it sounds. Desperate describes the sound better.

He brushes his long fingers over my cheek and cups the side of my face. I lean into his gentle touch as a chill runs through me, though I'm anything but cold. I close my eyes as I feel his warm breath against me. When his lips touch mine, I surrender.

He parts my lips with his tongue and deepens our kiss. I feel his hands at my waist pulling me toward him. We are breathlessly driving each other wild. I run my hands up over his hard biceps and thread my fingers in his hair. He presses harder against my lips and then suddenly pulls away.

"I need to stop, or you might slap me again." He's breathing hard and so am I.

"No more slapping, unless you like that kind of thing." I whisper the last words. I know he hears them, because his fingers stop lingering up my arm.

"I hope you find out." Goose bumps break out over my flesh at his words of promise. "But I'll settle for a nice long dinner here with you." He gently touches my forehead with his lips, and for now, a dinner will have to do.

David forks the last bite of cheesecake left on the dessert plate. I watch him lick his lips after he swallows. His full lips are wet and so am I. I never thought eating could be a sensual act until now. Everything thing this man does personifies sex.

Usually at this point on a first date, when the last plate is cleared away, I wonder what my date expects from me. A goodnight kiss at the door when he brings me home? Or will he push for more or ask to come inside? That last question could be taken many ways.

Tonight is different because I'm the one with expectations. I want him. All of him. He appears to be as attracted to me as I am to him. During dinner, he kept touching me in subtle ways. Reminding me, and everyone watching, that I was here with him.

David encloses my hand in his and circles his thumb over my skin. "I have to confess something to you."

His words and actions have my undivided attention, and I brace myself for what he's about to say. The rejection from being a jilted bride still hovers over me, so I prepare for the worst.

"It's been over a year since I've been with a woman."

"What do you mean?" I can't believe a man as virile as David could abstain from sex. He *is* sex.

"My wife left me a year ago."

"But the paper, I mean, I thought she left you six months ago." I hate to admit I searched him online, but I did it on his suggestion.

"True, but she stopped sleeping with me before she moved out. I tried to work things out with her, and I am not the cheating type. I took my vows seriously. She did not." He gazes down at the table and spins an unused spoon. He has looked away to hide the pain.

"Then after she left..." I can't finish my question, as it seems too personal for a first date. "I'm sorry. It's none of my business."

"I don't want to drag my past into this night with you, but I want you to know where I'm coming from. I kept myself away from women while the divorce proceedings were pending. I focused on work, weight-training, and long showers."

"Weights and long showers," I say in a dreamy voice. I imagine this muscled man pleasuring himself while hot water runs down his body. It's almost too much for me in my sex-starved state.

"I don't want to presume, but would you like to go back to my villa for a drink? You can decide where the night goes from there."

I nod my head at David and glance around for our server. When I spot him a couple tables away, I call him over with a look.

"I'm ready." I squeeze David's hand and his lips roll into a sly smile. One that's meant for only me.

CHAPTER 6

When he asked me to come back to his villa, he should've said his mansion. The place we are pulling up to spreads out over the top of a large hill. It could easily pass as a small resort.

"Is this where you are living?" I whisper.

"It belongs to a family friend. They're off island for the summer and opened their home to me." His answer makes me realize our worlds are miles apart. I exist on a fourth grade teacher's salary and was raised by middle class parents.

A black wrought-iron gate stands in the way of us entering the property. David clicks a remote attached to his sun visor and the gate slides to the right so we can enter.

"It's beautiful." Palm trees line the driveway and lights illuminate our path. David parks under a tall stucco portico and comes around to open my door.

He helps me out of the car and guides me inside the house. I'm greeted by floor to ceiling window in an expansive room. My entire apartment in Kansas City could fit inside the area.

"It's amazing." I walk forward and notice a glimmering swimming pool beyond the patio doors. "Do you swim?"

"I was on the swim team in high school. Typical Los Angeles kid."

"There's nothing typical about you. I bet you drove the girls wild in your Speedo." We continue onto the patio and stop a few feet from the pool's edge. The sides and bottom are painted an ethereal blue. "It looks so inviting."

I haven't even felt the sand under my feet since I arrived. We hurried to the bar last night, then today was hangover recovery and date prep, so I slip off my sandals and dip a toe in the water.

"The pool's guest house has spare swimsuits if you're interested." David comes up behind me and wraps his hands around my waist. He brings his lips to my neck and trails kisses over my sensitive skin. I close my eyes and let my head fall to the side. He stops at my ear and whispers, "Let's go change."

"Yes." I hope I'm able to repeat this word to him many times tonight.

David stands near the shallow end of the pool when I make my way outside after changing. The dressing room had several colorful options. I chose a turquoise string bikini since he loved that color on me tonight. From the ear-to-ear grin on David's face he appears to approve.

"Stunning," He takes my towel and tosses it onto a lounger.

"Thanks." His attention and admiration overwhelms me. It's been ages since a man has showered me with praise.

"Join me." He places his hand on the small of my back and leads me down the water- covered steps. He stops when I'm in waist deep and brings me into an embrace. "May I kiss you again?"

"Please." I beg.

In one swift move, he picks me up. I circle my legs around his hips and my arms around his neck. I press against his erection hoping to relieve my aching need. Damn he is large and hard. I forgot how good it feels to be held by a man. When his lips find mine, we moan together.

Since we both have pent up desires, things begin to escalate quickly. He needs to know I want him, now, and I'll be his for the night.

"Take me." I remove my lips from his for a brief second then return for more.

"Here?" I nod in reply. "I don't have a condom."

"I'm on the pill and clean. Tested after my cheating fiancé." I grind shameless against him and I'm already close to screaming his name.

"Same with me." His kisses begin on my neck and he lifts me higher so he can reach the top of my breasts. "I need you naked."

"You too." He walks us over to the side of the pool with me still clinging to him. He sits me down on the edge.

He moves my hair to the side and reaches behind my neck. He tugs on the tied strings holding my top together, and the garment falls to my waist. My nipples pebble to peaks under his stare and the night's breeze.

"Beautiful," he mutters while covering my nipple with his mouth. I arch my back and wrap my legs around him again. Desperate for more friction between my legs.

He switches from one breast to the other. Tongues, lips, and teeth bring me sensations I'd never known before as he devours me like he can't get enough.

He eases my bottom to the pool's edge. I'm spread out before him with only a little scrap of fabric covering me. He fingers the strings of my bikini bottoms and yanks them. Now nothing keeps my most private parts from his view.

He pushes a finger inside me and I close my eyes as a climax begins. "So close."

"Hold on, baby." David says as his mouth trails down my stomach to my sex. He keeps his finger moving in and out of me while flicking my clitoris with his tongue.

I climax under his skilled mouth and scream in sheer ecstasy. His skills are tonguetasitc.

"That was unreal." I let my head fall from side-to-side since I've lost the strength to sit up on my own.

"I need to be inside you." I come out of my blissed state to see David's hooded eyes staring at me.

His intense gaze is scary sexy and I have only one answer to give him. "Yes."

The next second, I'm hoisted up and placed back in the water. He removes my top completely and sheds his trunks. Nothing stands between us now.

"Wrap your legs around me." His voice is raspy with need. I do as he bids and the feel of him bare against me sets off more moans from us both.

"Are you ready?" I nod my head as he looks me in the eye to confirm my words. He takes his erection in one hand and places it at my entrance. His other arm is wrapped around me tightly and he pulls me down on him. I scream as he fills me in one quick movement. He pushes deep and I'm lost in the feeling.

I throw my head back, and he brings his mouth to my breast. Up and down he controls my body as he pushes into me. I hold on tight as the sensations of another orgasm build.

"David," I whimper. "Harder."

He answers my plea by cupping my bottom and pulling me hard to him with each stroke. Maybe it's the way the water makes me weightless, but sex has never felt like this before.

I tighten my legs around him and match his relentless rhythm. Screams fall from my lips as I climax around him. With three hard pushes from his hips, he joins me too.

I fall into his chest as nothing more than a boneless body. All my strength has been thoroughly screwed out of me.

"Thank you, Mallory." He leans into me and whispers sweet words as I smile against his chest.

"I've never had sex like this before, so I should be thanking you." He chuckles at me and I look him in the eye. "I'm serious. I never knew sex could be like that."

"I'm just getting started with you. Please stay the night." He tilts his head to the side and searches my face for the answer.

"I'll stay." He smiles the same blinding grin he gave me yesterday at the airport. So much has happened in one day. He went from a cheating scoundrel to the best lover I've had.

CHAPTER 7 - DAVID

Mallory has stayed with me every night over the last three months. She even resigned from her teaching position when I hired her on as my personal assistant.

She's attended meetings with me, handled calls, and took care of any special needs that might've arisen. I have to say she handled that last part with skill and I've returned the favor. She calls *me* tonguetastic.

She's in the bedroom getting ready to go out for dinner as I savor a glass of my favorite scotch. We've only been together for a short time, but I know she's the one. During my divorce, I reflected on the mistakes I made in my marriage. No one shares all the blame in our failure, because I didn't open myself up fully to my ex. I lived in a guarded way, waiting to feel safe enough to reveal my real self. That day never came.

Mallory's sweetness soothes the vulnerability I had in all my previous relationships. The after-divorce-me bears no resemblance the person in the mirror now.

"Are you ready?" I turn to see her walking toward me in a colorful dress.

Her boobs look fucking spectacular in the low-cut top, and I wonder if I have time to pull her onto the table for a quickie.

"Always ready when you're around." I waggle my brows suggestively at her. "You look beautiful tonight."

"You bought me this dress in Puerto Rico last week. Thanks." She reaches up on her tiptoes and kisses my lips.

I grab her around the waist and press into her for more. She lets out a squeal in surprise. I love catching her off guard. I push her dress up and cup her sweet ass only to find her bare beneath my hands.

"Commando? You're asking for it aren't you?" I pick her up and sit her down on the dining room table. I think we've only used it to fuck on so far, but then again I love feasting on her. "Spread your legs."

I'm greeted by her perfectly pink pussy, and I'm on her in a split-second. She tastes so damn good, and I lick her until she's squirming under my tongue. I do some finger magic and she's over the edge.

Once she's ridden the wave, I stand up and unzip my pants. I pull out my dick and pump it a couple of times. Since she's glistening and ready from her orgasm, I dive in balls deep.

"Harder," she cries out after a few pushes. My baby likes it on the edge of rough, so I pick up my pace and thrust with more force. I notice her legs beginning to quiver, so I bring my finger to her clit. I press against her in small circles, and she's coming undone. A few seconds later, I follow behind her as my orgasm builds from down deep and releases.

I lean my forearms onto the table and stare into her satisfied eyes. A stray piece of hair covers part of her face and I brush it away. Then she gazes at me like I'm her world and something snaps within me.

"I love you Mallory."

My profession comes spilling out before I realize what I've said. It's the first time she's heard me say these words to her. I wait for her reaction and see her soulful eyes fill with tears. When one falls down her cheek, I kiss it away.

"Oh David, my sweet scoundrel. I love you too."

The End

Thanks for reading. Check out the rest of Liv's books at www.livmorris.com.

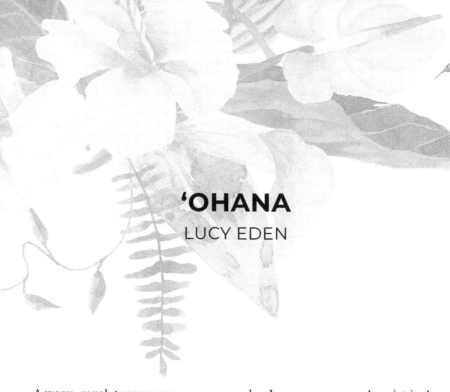

'OHANA
LUCY EDEN

A warm, rough tongue passes over my palm. I open my eyes and squint in the moonlight that passes through our bedroom window. A huge lion stares back at me from the side of the bed.

I can tell it's Pete because his mane is shorter and darker and he doesn't have a scar over his eye like Jake. I also know it's Pete because he always greets me when he comes in for the night. I don't know if it's because he misses me while he does whatever he and Jake do as lions in the cover of darkness. Maybe, it's because he senses that I worry about them and he can't wait to let me know that they're safe. Whatever the reason, it's my favorite part of the day.

When I first met my lions, our connection was strong and instant but Jake was the only one who accepted it right away. Pete and I took some time to come around to the idea. He didn't like the idea of having a human for a mate and I didn't think I could handle living in Hawaii. Aside from the salty air and humidity wreaking havoc on my 3C hair, I was leaving my friends, family and my entire life behind in New York. But once we finally came together—pun intended—life with my two boys has been perfect. It's true when they say you can't escape fate and with fated mates like Jacob Palakiko and Peter Kahananui, I'll never want to. After years of running from love and almost giving up on my soulmates when they found me, I'm finally in the place where I belong, between my lions.

"Hey, handsome," I whisper and scoot closer to the edge of the mattress so I can run my hand over his muzzle and scratch behind his ear. "Did you have a good night? I can't wait to hear about it." He rubs his warm wet nose into my palm and licks me again which I take as a yes before he turns and moves toward our bath- room, swishing his tail contentedly. The shower is already running which means Jake is in there, fully returned to manhood, possibly washing off blood from a fresh kill. I wonder if it was a feral hog or a deer, but I suppose he'll tell me later.

Their deep voices carry out of the bathroom door, which they've left open as an invitation because I'm sure Pete has told Jake that I'm awake. Usually, I wouldn't pass up this opportunity

but today my boys took me to The Big Island and we spent the day hiking mountain trails. The sights were so beautiful that I could weep but despite being a New York City girl who usually spent most of her day walking, I was completely unprepared for how sore hours of trekking up and down dormant volcanoes would make me. They took turns massaging my aching muscles on the plane ride back to Oahu. Once we were home, they took turns massaging me in other places until I drifted off to sleep. I hug my pillow and listen to their muffled voices and laughter wearing a lazy smile. I imagine Jake using a giant sponge to massage Pete's back, pressing his brand of rough kisses on his shoulder. I imagine Pete threading his fingers through Jake's long dark hair, rubbing shampoo into his scalp while lovingly gazing into his dark brown eyes. The temptation to creep into the shower is becoming unbearable when I hear the water stop. My boys fill the doorway, with dark, golden brown glistening skin, all bulk and sinewy muscle covered with a light sheen from the water.

Pete has a towel wrapped around his waist, showing off the tattoo that covers his entire left arm and half of his chest. Jake is completely nude except for the towel wrapped around his head in a makeshift turban. He knows it makes me laugh and I giggle as they stalk towards me, Pete's muscles flexing and rippling; Jake's long hard cock bobbing with every step that brought them closer to home, closer to me.

They crawl on either side of me, smelling like soap and mint. Four strong arms cage me in, locking me into an embrace you would think is reserved for lovers reuniting after a long journey, but this is the way they hold me every night after they come home from prowling the night as lions, my lions. My lovers, protectors, best friends, and fated mates.

"Hey, beautiful," Jake whispers and plants a kiss on my neck. "How are you feeling?"

"Tired." I punctuate the word with a small yawn. "And still sore from hiking."

"So, we'll let you get your rest." Pete presses a kiss to my shoulder. "Right, Jake?" He shoots a stern, pointed look at our mate, which Jake ignores.

"Is that what you want, Dawn?" Jake's brown eyes bore into mine with a mischievous glint. The muscles between my thighs tighten and my belly flutters.

Sleep is the last thing I want.

I shake my head. He kisses me and says, "I think Pete needs a little convincing." It doesn't take much, because when I reach under the towel around Pete's waist I find a rod of velvety steel. I squeeze and stroke him as he finds my mouth with his and slides his tongue over mine in a soft hungry kiss.

"You're such a greedy girl, aren't you?" Pete whispers when our lips separate and I nod. "You're lucky there are two of us. I don't think one of us would be enough for you." He shoots a look at Jake, who has pulled off his towel turban before pressing kisses and licks on my spine making me shiver.

"Definitely not," Jake whispers, "but there isn't anyone else I would want to share her with." He pushes me onto my back and slides a hand over my belly to lock hands with Pete as they move

in unison down my naked body, teasing, tasting, and kissing. Two heads jockey for position between my legs as my thighs are spread and hoisted onto muscular shoulders. The hands inter- locked on my belly hold me in place as I squirm, squeal and dig my heels into the backs of my lovers. I'm overwhelmed with sensation and ecstasy as I'm being licked, kissed, and nibbled past the point of sanity. My hands shoot between my legs to palm Pete's bald head and tangle my fingers in Jake's damp and messy brown locks with highlighted golden strands kissed by a lifetime of living in the sun.

Two fingers find their way into my pulsing, clenching pussy and a probing digit replaces the tongue lavishing the tight pucker of my ass. Pete and Jake take breaks from kissing me to kiss each other in a sexy chorus of ravenous slurps, growls, and groans. I want to prop myself up on my elbows to watch but I can't coordinate my limbs to make the necessary movements.

Every single one of my senses is on high alert and inflamed, pushed past the point of reason. I can smell the scent of my arousal, mingled with sweat and the lingering floral smell of the shower. Every nerve ending in my body is ringing with sensation. The messy wet sloshing sound of Jake and Pete working between my legs is ringing in my ears, mingled with my own desperate whimpers and grunts. I can taste their lingering kisses, but I can't see them.

I need to see them.

After somehow summoning the focus and strength to pull my elbows underneath my body, I peek between my thighs. The sight reminds me of a National Geographic documentary. Two lions working on devouring a freshly caught prey, and that's exactly what it is, but instead of an antelope, it's me. It's the sexiest fucking thing I've ever seen and I'll never get tired of it. I suck my bottom lip and bite down trying to stifle a loud moan. It doesn't work.

Jake notices me first. He pauses for a second, which is how I know it's his thick finger twisting and probing the tight bud of my asshole. He grins with his mustache and beard covered in the glistening evidence of my desire for them. Pete picks up his head next and they're both gazing at me, smiling.

"She's watching us," Pete whispers to Jake, loud enough for me to hear while never taking his eyes from mine.

"Do you think she likes what she sees?" He grins, also watching me like I was prey. I love it when they do this. They talk about me like I'm not a sentient being, I'm just a vessel for pleasure and my pleasure belongs only to them.

"Should we show her more?" Pete raises and eyebrow and glances at Jake.

"Yes," I breathe out in a desperate whisper. "Yes, you should." The fingers filling my cunt curl in response. A moan tears itself from my chest.

"So greedy." Jake shakes his head and clucks his tongue before lowering his mouth to my core, covering the sensitive fleshy pearl between my thighs with his lips and gently sucking. My hips buck against the strong hands holding me into place on the bed. My elbows fly out from under me and I flop backward onto the mattress, drowning in waves of ecstasy and endorphins as a giant orgasm hits me like a truck. Their fingers and hands vacate my body, making me feel empty and weightless. I feel like I can float but I don't. Instead I giggle as a heady rush of euphoria washes over me.

Jake and Pete rejoin me in the bed and are holding me again.

"Has our little flower had enough?" Pete asks, adjusting the knot in my headscarf so he can kiss my sweaty forehead.

"No," I shake my head. "Not even close." I roll over onto my stomach and crawl between my gentle giant's legs. I pull my knees underneath my body and raise my ass in the air as an invitation to Jake.

"Fuck, Dawn," Pete hisses as I grip his length and stroke up and down before running the tip of my tongue along the thick crown of his cock.

"Yes, little flower." Jake is smoothing a palm over one round globe of my ass as he watches Pete's dick disappear and reappear into my mouth. "I'm gonna fuck you while I watch you make our mate feel good. Would you like that?"

"Yes," I moan. "Please, fuck me. Please." The dripping slit of my cunt is hoisted in the air, pulsating, achingly empty and desperate to be filled.

Jake doesn't make me wait long before wrapping his huge hands around my waist and filling me with one smooth motion. I grunt in shock and pleasure, humming as my head bobs between Pete's legs.

"Yes, little flower," he moans. "Shit. Your mouth feels so good. So fucking good."

"You should feel her pussy, Pete." Jake's voice is husky with need as he fucks me slowly, feeling me stretch and tighten around his cock. "How does that feel, little flower."

"Mmmm," I moan around Pete and I feel his muscles clench. It's too soon and I'm nowhere near to being done with him.

"No, not yet, baby," I pant when I pull away. "I need to feel you. I need to feel both of you."

I look over my shoulder at Jake who gives himself one more deep stroke in my pussy before he withdraws and leaves the bed. I'm sleepy, sore, and sensitive but so far from sated. I crawl into Pete's lap and straddle him, wrapping my arms around his neck. I lean down and plant a kiss on the large black paw print tattooed over his heart and run my tongue along the four raised claw marks etched into his skin, Jake's mark.

"Hi," I whisper when I pick up my head and brush my lips over his.

"Hi," he answers before sucking my bottom lip between his teeth and biting down. I make a mewling noise like a cat and roll my hips back and forth, sliding his erection between the swollen lips of my pussy, desperate for the pressure and friction against my clit as we wait for our third to complete us. "I love you, Dawn," he whispers.

"I love you too, Dawn." The mattress dips as Jake walks over to us on his knees and settles behind me on the bed.

"And I love you. Both of you. More than I ever thought was possible." I feel tears stinging my eyes before Pete leans forward to kiss them away.

"Finding you was the best thing that ever happened to us." He sighs and traces his long healed bite mark on my shoulder with his tongue and lips.

"I'm glad you're finally admitting it," Jake chuckles. Pete narrows his eyes at our mate and Jake responds with a wink and a soft chuckle.

"Are you ready for us, sweetheart?" Jake whispers to me before planting a kiss on bite mark he gave me on the opposite shoulder.

"Always." I smile at him over my shoulder and he rewards me with a sloppy, desperate kiss.

"You're up, Pete." Jake squeezes lube onto my lower back, making me flinch from the chill. "Sorry, babe." He drags a slick finger down the seam of my backside and begins to massage the puckered opening again. I scoot forward on my knees and rise, preparing to impale myself on Pete.

"Ugngh," he hisses as I raise and lower myself onto his hips.

"So good, little flower. So good."

Jake is now working two fingers in and out of my ass as I whimper and moan.

"Jake, hurry, she feels too good," Pete groans.

"I know." He leans forward and plants a kiss on my back.

"Relax, beautiful. It's going to feel like heaven when we're both inside you."

"It always does." I lean forward and press my weight onto Pete's chest, letting him support me. I'm even more exhausted than before.

I don't want to move.

I don't want to think.

I only want to feel.

I want to be dragged screaming and moaning into the mind-blowing orgasms only my lions can give me.

I suck in a deep breath and release it slowly as I feel Jake press into the part of me his fingers just vacated with a burst of sweet pain followed by a sweet release of hormonal pleasure that makes me shudder.

"Oh my god," I murmur into Pete's chest. "Oh my god."

"How do you feel, baby? Talk to us."

"P . . . p . . . perfect," is all I can say. I relax and feel boneless as Jake pumps into me from above and Pete from below. I don't know if minutes or hours pass before I feel the first climax roll over me. It's quickly followed by another and another. I'm squealing and shuddering while being crushed between them. The clamping and rippling of my muscles sets off a chain reaction. Jake grips my hips and pushes himself into me until he clenches and spends his release into my channel, his loud growls filling our bedroom.

He pulls out and flops onto the bed, his chest heaving. Pete rolls me onto my back and pushes into my swollen cunt again. His pupils are wide and dark, limned with golden brown irises, remnants of his lion bubbling beneath the surface. His pace quickens and the power of his thrusts increase. It hurts so much but it feels so good and though I didn't think it was possible, I'm coming again and again. My eyes are squeezed shut and I feel tears rolling down the sides of face.

"You're so beautiful like this, little flower," Jake whispers. I open my eyes to find my face inches from his. He begins to stroke my cheek as Pete climaxes above me.

"Jesus fucking Christ," he pants on the other side of me.

"You're going to be the death of me, Dawn."

"I could think of worse ways to go." Jake yawns and kisses my shoulder before he climbs out of bed.

"Stay put, gorgeous. Do you want something for the pain?" Pete asks. I nod before he kisses my nose and follows Jake into the bathroom, giving him a sharp slap on his sculpted ass. The bathroom door is left open again but there is no way I'm leaving this bed. I'm not really sure if I can.

They return after a few minutes, again smelling of soap and mint. Pete is carrying a washcloth and Jake is holding a glass of water and a bottle of Tylenol. I usually take Advil but I assume it

will have the same effect on my sore limbs and aching sex. I drink the water and swallow the pain relievers while Pete kneels between my legs, cleaning me and inspecting me for damage. When he's satisfied, he climbs into bed where Jake has already folded me in his arms and I'm drifting off to sleep.

"Hey," I say sleepily. "Why did you give me Tylenol instead of Advil?"

"Because you can't have Advil anymore." Jake is wearing his trademarked sexy, silly grin and it confuses me.

"What? Why not?" I furrow my brow and blink, trying very hard to stay awake and focus. I would remember if I'd suddenly developed some weird allergy to ibuprofen.

"We've known for a couple of weeks, pretty girl. You smell different." Pete says.

"You definitely taste different," Jake adds with a yawn. "We were waiting for you tell us."

"Tell you what?" I glance between their sleepy smiling faces.

"You're pregnant, Miss Washington." This is what Pete calls me when he wants to tease me about my sluggish wedding planning. We haven't even set a date.

"What?" I sit up. Strong arms settle me back down on to the mattress and cradle me. "Are you sure?"

"Yes. We definitely know what a pregnant female smells like.Now, go to sleep, gorgeous. We'll talk about it in the morning."

I'm pregnant.

It seems too incredible to be true, but it has to be. My lions have what my best friend Chellie jokingly calls "super shifter senses." She is married to a bear shifter, after all.

Jake and Pete can smell my every emotion. They're so accurate at predicting my period—there's always a pint of Mama Palakiko's homemade mango or lilikoi ice cream in the freezer two days before it starts—that I stopped keeping track.

I am really pregnant . . . with a lion shifter cub.

Pete and Jake and I will have a bond stronger than fate or love or lust.

"Jake?" I whisper.

"Yeah, babe?"

"What's the Hawaiian word for family again?"

"'Ohana," they whisper in unison and tighten their arms around my body.

"But you already knew that, gorgeous," Jake says with his lips pressed onto my shoulder.

"I did," I say in a sleepy giggle, "but I love hearing you say it."

"Not as much as we love hearing you say it," Pete grins at me and I can't help kissing him one last time before exhaustion takes me.

"'Ohana," I repeat before closing my eyes and drifting off, dreaming about lion cubs.

Thanks for reading. Check out the rest of my books at www.lucyeden.com.

EL DIABLO

M. ROBINSON

SECOND CHANCE CONTRACT

AUTUMN

"Your husband is such a barbarian," Camila, Dr. Aiden Pierce's wife, who became a part of the family, teased over the phone.

"Yeah… he's always been that way. It's actually one of the things I love the most about him. Julian doesn't care who you are or what you think about him, he's going to be an asshole to you regardless."

She laughed on the other end as I finished up cooking dinner. Mixing in the enchilada sauce the way she'd advised.

"Capri never stood a chance," I added, shaking my head. Thinking about all the times my husband guarded our fifteen-year-old daughter, like it was his sole purpose to ruin her life.

Just last week they were going back and forth about her wanting to wear a purple bikini.

"But, Daddy… every girl is wearing two-piece bathing suits."
He took one look at the bikini in her hands before he snatched it away.
"That's just string!"
"You're ruining my life!"
"Julian, come on she's—"
With one look, he rendered me speechless, but that didn't stop Capri.
"It's called a string bikini for a reason!"

"Which is why you aren't wearing it!"

To think, how I thought my father and brother were bad when I was growing up. They weren't anywhere near the level of overprotective Julian was with our only daughter.

"Does he know Capri has a boy over?"

"Umm... not exactly."

"So, you lied?"

"Of course not."

"So, Julian knows?"

"Hell no!"

She busted out laughing.

Julian had left me no choice. Capri would be turning sixteen soon, and as soon as she started socializing with other kids, he turned into a rabid dog. Especially now that we were in Maui for vacation, she was meeting new friends everywhere while he worked on some business he was starting.

No one was good enough for his baby girl.

Not one single boy.

We had to hide her boyfriends, her guy friends, her study partners, exactly how we were doing right now. Anything or anyone that pertained to the opposite sex was hidden from her father, or else he'd threaten to "break his legs." His words not mine.

The sad thing was...

I wasn't exaggerating.

"Where are they now?"

"In the living room, on the couch watching a movie."

"That's probably safe when Julian comes back."

"He never comes home before the sun goes down." I half-joked.

He was the best daddy.

My husband was like having a fourth child. However, I loved him with every last part of my soul. He was mine.

Past.

Present.

Forever.

Before she could reply, Capri hollered, "Mom!"

"Give me a second, honey!"

"But, Mom I need you now!"

"Alright, Camila, I gotta go."

"Me too. The boys just got home. Talk soon."

"Bye." I hung up.

"MOM!"

"Oh my God, Capri!" I shouted in response, walking down the hall toward the living room. "Why all the screaming?"

"Because you said daddy wasn't coming home till later tonight! We'd be safe from him, so we could hang out!"

I rounded the corner, coming into the living room, "He isn't, honey. You're safe from your dad," I expressed, stopping dead in my tracks when I saw him sitting there.

Cocky.

Pissed.

Looking all Julian Locke like with his suit on and a snide grin and intoxicating eyes...

Glaring directly at me.

Our intense stares locked. He didn't hesitate, speaking with conviction, calling me by his nickname for me since I was a kid.

"You're not, kid."

JULIAN

Autumn Locke.

Autumn fucking Locke.

Even after all these years, she was still a pain in my ass.

Except now, I had two fucking hurricanes destroying everything in their path in the form of my wife and my baby girl.

Autumn's eyes went wide, looking beautiful. "Oh, shit," she muttered.

"My thoughts exactly," I snarled, shifting my glare over to the teenage motherfucker sitting next to my baby.

"Dad..." Capri coaxed in an uneasy tone. "Be nice..."

"I'm always nice."

"Daddy, we're just hanging out. Look." She held up the remote. "Just watching a movie."

I didn't waver, eyeing only the guy. "No one will protect you from me, boy."

"Julian!" Autumn reprimanded.

"Sir, we're just friends," he agreed.

"Her momma was my best friend too, but that didn't stop me from making her mine. Now did it?"

"It's not like that between us."

"Better stay that way, boy. Your dick goes near her, I'll fuck you up."

"Dad!"

Autumn grabbed ahold of Capri's arm. "Why don't you guys head to the beach on your bikes? Here's some money."

"But, Mom—"

"Do you see your father's face? Go, now."

She grumbled, "Michael, let's go before my daddy chops your balls off."

"Capri!"

"What?" She shrugged, pointing to me. "That's what he says. I'm just repeating Daddy's words."

Damn straight she was.

Autumn shook her head, but I didn't pay her any mind. I was too busy plotting this boy's death.

As soon as Autumn walked back into the room, after shoving them out the door, I stated, "My cock isn't going suck itself, sweetheart."

Her mouth dropped open.

"Now get on your knees and show me how sorry you are."

"You arrogant asshole!"

"Not gonna say it again, kid. You're up to no good, right?"

"No," she sternly stated, looking me straight in the eyes.

"Think you can lie to me? Think I wouldn't have fucking found out? Walk me through your thought process, baby. Please, enlighten me."

"I'm not talking to you when you're like this," she replied, shaking her head. Crossing her arms over her chest, she caused her tits to pop out at the seams of her yellow summer dress.

My cock twitched at the sight of her.

"I didn't lie to you."

"You didn't exactly tell me the truth either. I'm not going to ask again, Autumn. Did you think I wouldn't have found out?"

She sighed, knowing I wasn't going to let up until I got a straight answer.

"What am I supposed to do? You remember how I was raised, right? Of course, you do. You're the guy my parents tried to keep me away from, remember?"

"You of all people can understand my protection over Capri. I don't want her falling in love with an asshole like me. Do you understand me?"

"Julian, the more you shelter her, the more she's going to want to rebel. *Do you understand me?*"

"No, but I will."

"What's that supposed to mean?"

Before the last word even left her mouth, I was in her face. Gripping onto her ass, hard.

"Ow! Julian!"

In two seconds flat, I was lifting her up my body, wrapping her legs around my waist.

"Now, do you understand me?" I patronized, rocking her hips against my bulge. "Not sassing me, are you? Not when your pussy is dry fucking my cock."

She swallowed hard, waiting for my next move.

"Yeah… that's what I thought," I added, backing her into the wall.

I was over this bullshit. These little punk ass kids trying to piss on my territory. I needed to shut that shit down really fucking quick. It wasn't going to happen.

Not now.

Not ever.

"I protect Capri's guy friends from you."

"Is that right?"

"Yeah, that's right."

"Then who's gonna protect you from me?"

"I don't need protection from you, Julian Locke."

"Is that right?" I repeated, mirroring her loving stare.

"Yeah, I'm your girl. Been your girl for as long as I can remember."

"No, sweetheart, you're my wife. Who's being a pain in my ass. Let me handle my business, Autumn."

"Stop bossing me around."

"Stop fussing like you don't want me to. We both know how wet this is making your silk panties," I mocked, smacking her ass for good measure.

"You're such an asshole!" She tried to push me away, but I didn't move an inch.

"Babe, we both know... if I want in, I'm getting in."

I smiled, cocking my head to the side. Getting closer to her face, I started kissing my way from the corner of her lips, down to her chin and neck. Working my way toward her tits that were just as eager for my touch.

She unconsciously moaned, unable to help it. It's what I always did to her.

Made her wet.

Come.

Love me.

"I should spank your ass raw for this stunt you just pulled," I growled. Never once letting up on my sweet torture of rocking my hard cock against her pussy. "Who do you think you're fucking with, kid? I know everything, especially when it comes to my property."

"Your property, huh?"

Hiking her a little higher, I unzipped my jeans and stroked my cock.

I always loved her this way...

At my mercy.

Since the first time I claimed her in my bed.

"Tonight, you're mine, and you're going to give me what I want. Fuck my face, Autumn."

She purred.

"You like that, do you? The wetter you are, the harder I'm going to tongue fuck you."

And the little minx replied, "Prove it, Julian."

I didn't have to be told twice. I sucked her clit into my mouth, and she loudly moaned, melting against my lips. There was no stopping there—I was just getting started.

Savoring the taste of her.

The feel of her.

Her hips rocked against my face as I pushed my tongue into her cunt before sucking her clit into my mouth. Up and down, side to side, I took what I wanted. What she was giving. Knowing I was the first man to have her this way did something primitive to me. I turned into a fucking caveman.

She was so wet.

Tasted so good.

Her pussy throbbed.

Her body shook.

It didn't take long to have her come undone.

"Julian," she panted, climaxing in my mouth. "Julian, please..." she begged for mercy, but still—I didn't stop. I couldn't.

She consumed me.

From my mind to my soul, to my goddamn cock.

A heady growl vibrated from deep within my chest, conscious of the fact that she was trying to save me from myself while I was destroying her in the process. Ruining her for every other man. The mere thought pissed me off, and I took my frustration out on her cunt.

"Julian!" she exclaimed, coming down my neck. Her body fell forward, and she held herself up on the headboard.

"Are you a squirter, baby? We're about to find out. Give me what I want, Autumn."

She did, proving that she was indeed a dirty little girl. Squirting down my face and chest, but it wasn't enough for me. I was a man possessed, licking her fucking clean, from her opening to her clit. I wanted every last drop of her come. Not allowing her any time to recover, I flipped us over and crawled my way up to her mouth, kissing her and making her taste herself.

She moaned, sucking on my tongue.

"So fucking good." I sat up on my knees, never once breaking our heated stares as I unbuckled my jeans to kick them off with my boxer briefs.

Through dark, dilated, hooded eyes, she took in the size of my hard cock for the first time. I fisted my shaft, jerking myself off in front of her. She watched with an expression full of desire and nothing else. I smiled, appreciating the look in her eyes.

I was a fucking goner. There wasn't a chance in hell I wouldn't have stolen her virginity.

It was mine.

It belonged to me.

I'd stolen everything else, and this would be mine as well.

Still fucking my hand, I made my way back up her body. "I can go as slow as you need."

It was her turn to smile as she sat up, kissing me. Silently demanding I keep going. When I didn't move fast enough, she reached for my dick and wrapped her hand around my shaft, causing my breath to hitch against her lips and my dick to jerk in her grasp.

"Yeah, baby, just like that," I scoffed out, biting her bottom lip. "Stroke my cock. Harder. Faster."

She was a very good listener. Driving me to the brink of insanity. I'd never been with a virgin before. It was too personal, and I was the fuck 'em and leave 'em kind of man.

With Autumn, it was different, and there was no denying that.

"After I'm done with you, I'm going to fuck you again. Just so you remember, only I belong inside of you."

She slid her tongue into my mouth, and I let her take the lead.

"Julian, I want you." She positioned my dick at her entrance.

I groaned, "I want you more than I've ever wanted anything. Are you ready for me?"

"Yes, I've always been ready for you."

"Once I thrust my cock inside of you, there's no going back, kid. You know that, right?"

She beamed. "Promise?"

"I don't deserve you. Not your heart or your pussy, but I'm a selfish bastard, and I want both regardless."

"I'm yours forever."

"You remember the first time I made you mine?"

"I've always been yours."

And she was.

She always had been.

"I know," I stated, grinning like a fool. "Nothing's changed since then... always doing what you want, never listening to a word I say. No matter how many damn times I tell you, it's always done in Autumn's way."

She giggled. "At least I'm consistent."

She pushed me too far over the edge this time. I was going to have my way with her, exactly how I wanted to.

Gliding her panties to the side, I slid the tip of my cock into her warm, welcoming heat.

"Julian, I love you."

"I bet you do, sweetheart."

"Please..."

"Please, what?"

"Forgive me for being a bad girl."

In one hard thrust, I slammed my cock into her pussy. "Fuck..." I groaned in a low, rumbling tone. "How you always feel this fucking good?"

Seconds later, I was thrusting in and out of her in a slow, tortuous rhythm that had her coming undone. Making it much easier to fuck her the way I wanted. The slapping sound of my balls against her ass cheeks with each hard thrust echoed off the walls.

I leaned forward, brushing her hair to the side of her neck. Giving me access to kiss and lick her overly heated, sensitive skin.

I knew what she liked.

What she loved.

What she craved.

I fuckin' taught her.

"Please..." she shamelessly begged, pleading with me to give her what she wanted.

"Please, yeah? What do you want? Want me to touch you, here?" I taunted, my fingers rubbing her clit. Leaving nothing but desire in my wake. Purposely trying to drive her insane.

"Oh God," she panted, her legs trembling while her cunt gripped onto my dick like a goddamn vice.

"Please... please... don't stop... please..."

And right when she was about to explode like a fucking volcano, I pulled out.

Dropping her ass down to the ground.

My balls throbbed and my cock ached to be back inside her, but that wasn't the point in this sudden lesson.

I grinned, gazing down at her while she peered up at me through dark, hooded eyes.

"This is bullshit!"

"No, what's bullshit is you lying to me about my baby girl."

"*Our* baby girl."

"If you ever want come again, don't fucking try me. You understand me?"

Meaning every last word.

Thanks for reading. Check out the rest of Monica's books on her website at www.authormrobinson.com.

CALL ME SWEETHEART

MARIA LUIS

Because sometimes we need a story full of sunshine. Also, in case you ever wondered about the love child of Cinderella, Star Wars, *and* Pride & Prejudice *. . . I imagine this is the level of chaos that would commence. Happy Reading!*

CHAPTER 1 - JORDAN

New Orleans, Louisiana

Here's the thing about working at a tattoo shop on Bourbon Street:

You see crazy shit on the daily.

Like this one time when I was trying to beat the clock on my way in and accidentally stepped on a dude playing dead in the middle of the street. He'd been decked out in a clown onesie and all I can say is—trauma. Or this other time when I was scarfing down a po'boy during my break, only to have my lunch be sideswiped by an ass.

This is not a metaphor.

My sandwich was quite literally taken out by one of the mules that cart tourists around the French Quarter for a very lofty sum of money. The carriage rattled along, its passengers none the wiser, while I stared forlornly down at my scattered fried shrimp, stomach grumbling pitifully.

So, my very long-winded point is this: I'm a veteran around these here parts. More jaded than hopeful. I'd say that New Orleans ages you like fine wine but these days, I feel more like the forgotten spritzer in the back of your fridge—desperate to be drunk but ever fearful that the minute you pop me open, I'll have forgotten how to fizz.

Which is probably why I'm staring out the front window of Inked on

Bourbon, jaw flapping, at what *has* to be the singular most ridiculous thing I've seen in at least six months.

"The absolute fuck is that?" my boss, Owen Harvey, grunts as he comes up beside me.

I tilt my head to the side, hoping that might offer a little perspective. "Do you think there's a real human beneath all that hair?"

It's shades of neon pink, for starters, and thick enough to double as a winter coat. I'd feel an ounce of sympathy for the sucker stuck wearing the damn thing except, of course, for the fact that they probably thought it was a good idea. In the middle of a *heat wave*. I have serious concerns for all of humanity.

Owen lifts his water bottle for a drink.

Idly, I comment, "I wonder if they're thirsty."

His tatted arm lowers as his head swings my way. "Is that you telling me to water them?"

I roll my eyes. "They aren't a *plant*, Harvey. Clearly, they're a . . ." Settling my hands on my hips, I stare a little harder at the figure now careening into a tourist holding a Hand Grenade. The acholic beverage goes everywhere, including all over that pink fur. "Well, fuck. I really have no clue."

"Big Foot?" Owen suggests after a moment of shared silence.

"Don't think so."

"A bear on acid?"

I spare him a glance. "I worry for your children."

"Child," he corrects, as if I don't already know this. "I have one child."

"I was talking about your harem of cats. Don't give them acid. It's bad for their digestion."

"Bad for their digestion—"

Mr. Grumpy-Pants is promptly cut off because whatever *That Thing Is* has now somehow become acquainted with Inked's storefront window. I don't think they intended to make love to the pane of hundred-year-old glass but it's as good a visual that I can come up with right now. This close, I can see that there are little holes cut out of the furry face for the poor sucker's eyes—and those eyes are a bright, brilliant green framed by thick, black lashes. Then those green eyes blink, crinkling at the corners, and I have the distinct impression that I've just met someone with a sense of humor to rival my own.

And listen, I'm not proud of the way my dick hardens at the prolonged length of eye contact, but here we are. I have very little in the way of boundaries and, apparently, this Big Foot-Bear-on-Acid costume is doing it for me.

I move around Owen to head for the front door.

From behind me, I hear him let out a groan. "You've got to be fuckin' kidding me."

"I make no apologies."

"Do you ever?"

"Rarely." I peer back at him over my shoulder and offer a shit-eating grin. "Don't wait up, Grandpa."

"*Grandpa?*" His brows furrow. "You little shit—"

I let the door slam shut behind me before he can add any more flavoring, and then I walk right out into a puddle of sunshine.

CHAPTER 2 - KINSLEY

New Orleans is hot as hell.

I mean, that would be the case even if I wasn't in costume—a suit that cost me way too much money, by the way—but I'm also talking about . . . the scenery.

Wide-eyed, I watch the good-looking guy from inside the tattoo parlor step out onto the sidewalk. He's all loose limbs and big, flirty grins. The kind of guy who would seem equally at home on the back of a Harley as he would driving a rusted-out truck. Soft-looking jeans ride low on his hips, and those hips must have some sort of mesmerizing allure because I find myself in a trance, watching that swagger like it's the last thing I'll ever do, before realizing that he's stopped less than an arm's length away.

I drag my gaze north, past a lean chest decked out in a plain, white T, to a handsomely rugged face.

His lips are still smiling.

A quick peek upward reveals that his brown eyes are smiling, too.

Something warm fizzles in my chest, and I feel myself smile back, even though he definitely can't tell while I'm still decked out as—

"Big Foot."

"What?"

He crosses his arms over his chest and peers down at me, his head angled like he's giving all of this—all of *me*—a good deal of thought. "My boss guessed that you might be dolled up as Big Foot."

"Do *you* think I'm Big Foot?"

"Nah, doesn't seem to fit the bill."

"What's that supposed to mean?"

"It means that I've never seen anything quite like you."

I blink up at him, feeling an absurd urge to laugh because I have a feeling that he's playing with me. Not in a mean, judgmental way, but because a guy like him tries to find whatever bits of joy he can in life. Since I tend to operate the same way, I ask, "Is that the best pick-up line you've got?"

His dark eyes flash in challenge. "I have a feeling you're actually wanting the *worst* pick-up lines in my repertoire."

"I'm surprised you know the meaning of the word repertoire."

"Just learned it the other day," he quips without missing a beat. Then he adds, "I may not be Fred Flintstone, but I bet I can make your Bed Rock."

Lifting one of my furry paws to my mouth, I pretend to yawn. "Pass."

"Is your name Ariel? Cause we were Mermaid for each other."

"It's Kinsley, actually, and I don't Mer-mate on the first date."

"Is this a first date?"

"I don't know, how do you feel about *Star Wars*?"

"Yoda only one for me."

"You didn't," I say, cringing even as I burst out laughing.

"I did," he replies, and then he starts laughing, too.

"Yoda only—" I shake my head. "Oh, my God, that's *awful*."

His brown eyes twinkle in delight. "It really, really is."

"Has it worked for you before?"

"Never."

"Good. I wouldn't want to question humanity."

"Is this the point in our first date when I confess that *you* have me questioning humanity? Put me out of my misery, please. What the hell are you?"

"Chewbacca, obviously."

"There is no *obviously* about it." He stares me up and down, lips firming like he's trying hard not to laugh. "You're neon, Kinsley. Tell me you have a mirror at home."

"Of course, I do."

"Tell me that you *used* it."

"Now that would be a lie."

"And you never lie?"

His voice goes a little husky at the end, and maybe it's the sun beating down on me or the fact that I'm wearing a costume that I bought for this past Mardi Gras season—to walk in the infamous *Star Wars*-themed, Krewe of Chewbacchus, naturally—but I suddenly want to strip out everything that's made of faux fur because I feel hot and sticky and kind of nervous.

And silly. Very, very silly.

It's one thing to play dress up when everyone else is, too, and another thing entirely to do it on your own accord because your kid-sister had a crap week at school, and you know it's the right move to cheer her up. Speaking of kid-sisters—*shit*, I am most definitely late to pick her up.

I hastily step back. "I have to go."

He steps forward. "Now?"

"No, I mean, *yes*. Now."

"Can I have your number?"

"No."

His jaw drops a little at that. "No?"

"I'm a horrible girlfriend," I say, edging backward into the crowd. "And I don't like people."

"Who *does* like people?" he counters easily.

"Matthew MacFayden in *Pride & Prejudice* is my one true love. It's the hand clench that does it for me. No one's ever hand-clenched for me before and I admit, I have very high standards."

"I have no idea what any of that means but I lift weights on occasion and can promise you at least a mediocre hand-clench. Except on days when I've spent too much time playing tennis, in which case you'll have to accept a limp hand-clench, but we all can't be perfect. It's unhealthy to set unrealistic expectations."

I narrow my eyes. "You're a smooth talker."

"I tattoo people for a living. All I do is talk."

"I thought you don't like people?"

"I think that I could like *you*."

Choking out a laugh, I retreat yet again. "Another terrible pick-up line?"

"Terrible, sure, but surprisingly heartfelt." He reaches for the back pocket of his jeans for his cell phone. "Give me your number, Kinsley."

"I really—what I mean to say is—" Floundering, I meet his gaze. "I've got to go."

And then I run away like a furry coward.

CHAPTER 3 - JORDAN

It's not every day that I fall for someone in a neon-pink Chewbacca costume.

Honestly, the thought alone haunts me, but then I remember the peel of happy laughter from the woman *wearing* the neon-pink Chewbacca costume and my heart starts beating triple-time all over again.

I have ninety-nine problems but clearly self-awareness ain't one of them.

Humming, I tap POST on my phone and sit back, waiting for the internet to do what the internet does best. The image sets the stage—a hastily captured picture of Kinsley running off into the crowd, confused expressions rampant as a life-sized Chewbacca stormed the streets of New Orleans—but the caption really seals the deal, I think. It reads:

Tattoo Artist Seeks Lost Chewbacca. Return To Sender if Found.

Below, I tagged Inked on Bourbon's Instagram handle, which I know will drive Harvey up a wall, which means I've successfully killed two birds with one stone. Okay, maybe just one bird with one stone since there's a very good chance that I won't ever see Kinsley again.

And I would very, very much like to see her again.

I don't even know what she looks like but that doesn't seem to matter when her wit turns me on. Most people tend to think that I talk too much—they aren't wrong—and if it's not me talking too much that's a problem, the general consensus is that I don't have anything of real substance to say. Which isn't the case at all. I have opinions on a lot of things, but what I love most is making people *laugh*.

It's just not as often that people make me laugh in return.

A little too eagerly, I tap my phone to bring the screen back to life and then heave a huge sigh of disappointment when the only notification is from Savannah, Owen's wife, who's commented with: *Nothing about this surprises me.*

I let my head fall forward onto my desk with a heavy *thud*.

Fuck, this is going to be a lot harder than I thought.

. . .

A few weeks later, I still haven't found Kinsley.

I'm halfway convinced that she was either a figment of my imagination or, at the very least, a tourist who popped into town for the weekend from Maui, or Norway, or who-the-fuck-knows-where. Somewhere not even remotely close to New Orleans, which means that I'll never, ever see her again.

And then I get a DM on a stormy Saturday afternoon.

It reads, and I quote, "Your Lost Chewbacca loves afternoon strolls in the rain with her trusty sidekick Kassie."

I reply: Where do these afternoon strolls usually take place?

I'm pleased to report that when the anonymous DMer sends another message a few minutes later, it's of a view that I've seen often enough. All said, I'm out the door in five minutes flat. Sure, the messenger with the little Yoda avatar as its profile picture could be a murderer trying to lure me to my death, but I choose to shoot my shot because I haven't come this far in life without standing at the edge of a cliff every now and then, practically daring the world to take me out.

By the time I conquer rush-hour traffic on my way across the Crescent City Connection, the sun is already setting over the Mississippi River. I park my car illegally, slide out from the driver's side, and sprint up the levee's steep grassy incline. I'm not out of my breath when I make it to the top, but you wouldn't know it from the way I'm practically chomping at the bit to go another round with Kinsley.

Except, now that I'm up here, I don't see anyone at all.

An old steamboat is winding down the river and then there's a group of kids playing near the water while a few adults hover nearby, just in case. I turn in a semi-circle, letting my gaze roam the area before taking out my phone again.

Me: You're awful with saying goodbye.

It takes a few moments for the DM to go from SENT to SEEN, but when it does, I immediately get the feeling that Kinsley is on the other end of this thread, no matter what she might want me to believe.

Finally, there's a reply: *You're awfully certain that you're speaking to the right girl.*

Me: Should I prove it?

Anonymous: You can try.

Me: Did you know that Matthew MacFayden improvised the infamous Hand Clench?

Anonymous: First, I love that you capitalized Hand Clench. As it should forever be referenced. Amen.

She attaches a GIF of a set of praying hands, along with a second GIF from the *Pride & Prejudice* scene in question, which makes me smile.

Anonymous: Second . . . did you look up facts about the movie?

Me: I also WATCHED the movie.

Anonymous: Smooth move, Jordan.

I stare at her latest message, letting a hum of awareness settle low in my gut. Yeah, I might have no idea what this girl looks like, besides the memory of those pretty green eyes of hers, but I'm intrigued. More than intrigued, if I'm being honest about it. I want her, and from nothing more than a quick rapport that has me eager for more conversation.

Me: So, you know my name.

Anonymous: You're ridiculously easy to stalk online.

Me: Can't say the same about you, Lost Chewbacca. I resorted to drastic measures.

Anonymous: I told myself I should feel flattered.

Me: But you're not?

Anonymous: Could be a red flag.

Me: Speaking of red flags, did you know that your boy MacFayden has terrible eyesight? When Mr. Darcy is walking through the mist toward Lizzie, the director had to hold up actual red flags to help guide MacFayden on where to go.

Anonymous: That's . . .

Me: Wildly endearing? Yes, yes, I am. How forward of you for mentioning it.

Anonymous: I shouldn't be laughing.

Me: That feels like a green flag. Making you laugh, I mean.

Anonymous: Yellow, maybe.

Me: Proceed with caution? I can work with that.

The second my message is marked as SEEN, but there's no immediate reply, I want to give myself a swift kick in the ass. The way we talk, it feels seamless. Feels *right*. Leave it up to me and my fast mouth to take it one step too far, though, even after trying to keep things breezy and fun.

Me: I'm sorry. That was too much.

I'm often *too much*. Everyone tells me so—friends, family, exes.

Swallowing tightly, I close my eyes for a beat before forcing myself to return to our conversation. Being vulnerable isn't always my strong suit but it feels necessary.

Me: I don't want you to feel uncomfortable, Kinsley. I didn't the day we met, and I don't want that now, either. Something about you . . . Something about you makes me want to stay, but I'm not oblivious to the fact that something about me makes you wanna run.

Anonymous: I didn't run.

Me: Didn't you?

Anonymous: I'm close by. Like, really, really close by. I didn't lie about wanting to meet you, but I did lose my nerve.

Me: Because I make you nervous?

Anonymous: Because I shouldn't feel so comfortable with you when I barely even know you.

Me: So, let me get to know you.

Anonymous: I don't think it's supposed to be that easy.

Me: Can't it?

Me: Hold on, gonna find a spot to sit.

I park myself on an elevated strip of land protruding out into the river, letting my long legs hang down over the side of the levee. The rain's cleared out, leaving the air thick with humidity. Across the way, the sun is just starting to set over the Quarter, the sky an artist's fever dream of pink and orange hues. Without giving it a second thought, I hold up my phone and take a picture, making sure to capture the length of my legs in the same frame with the river glistening under the falling sun. I send it off with a smile, thinking that maybe Kinsley will appreciate the fact that I'm willing to go at whatever pace she needs to make this feel right for her, too.

Not even sure when I started to feel the need to go at *any* pace, but here I am.

Me: Tell me something no one else knows. Something that makes you lie in bed at night and think, *what if*.

CHAPTER 4 - KINSLEY

The *what-if*'s are starting to torment me.

I mean, every night when I go to bed, I do so with Jordan's husky voice whispering "good night, Kinsley," in my ear, and every morning when I wake up, it's to another DM where he's either sent me a groggy voice message on his way into work or a picture of his morning drink of choice.

Some days it's honest-to-God tea, like he's a real-life Mr. Darcy.

Other days it's coffee in a travel mug the size of my head.

And none of that's even taking into account the constant stream of messages that fill my days to overflowing. In the span of two months, I've learned more about Jordan Knight than I have anyone else since college.

I know that he got into tattooing after he couldn't land a job at any of the fancy art galleries in town.

I know that he's the youngest of five brothers, and while he loves them all, sometimes he feels guilty for enjoying the fact that they all live out of state. Growing up, he told me, was a weird contradiction of expectations — being babied because as the youngest, no one expected anything more from him, while simultaneously being told to grow up and stop acting like a kid.

I also know that he's never had a long-term girlfriend.

He's the guy with the loose limbs and big, flirty grins, and I'm falling so hard for him, I can barely catch my breath.

"Kins?" he says now in my ear. "You still there?"

"Yeah. Yeah, I'm still here."

He goes quiet for a moment, but I've talked to him so many times on the phone at this point that I know his sudden bout of silence has nothing to do with my awkwardness and everything to do with him fiddling with his station at Inked.

Jordan Knight is also the guy everyone thinks of as a good time. Always down for a party but never thought of once the music turns off and the lights go on. It hurt me when he let that slip, both because I often feel the same way and also because I hate the thought of him not feeling seen. And from what I've gathered, no one's really bothered to stick around long enough to realize that when Jordan loves something, he throws his whole soul into it. That's how he feels about tattooing, and that's why I booked myself an appointment with him today — even though he has no idea that it'll be me he's inking.

I can't live with the *what-if*'s anymore.

"You have an appointment soon, don't you?"

If he can hear the slight quiver in my voice, he doesn't mention it. "Yeah, an hour from now. Hey, do you want to watch a movie this weekend, me, you, and Kassie? Was thinkin' that we could set everything up, so we start it at the same time? Maybe get on the phone so we can be total animals and run commentary together while we watch?"

Goddamn this man.

My heart is practically in my throat when I say, "My sister hates it when I yell at the TV."

"And yet, here I had this gut feelin' that you're just like me. Guess I was right."

"Is this a weird way of complimenting yourself?"

"I don't know, Kins, do you feel complimented?"

I press a hand to my warm cheek, because, yes, I am a goner for this guy, and, yes, I'm totally blushing. "I'm hanging up," I tell him. "I have better things to do than listen to you stroke your own ego."

"Like, what?"

"Like . . ."

"I'm waiting," he hums pleasantly. "Please, go on."

Looking away from the blinking cursor on my Word doc, I bite my bottom lip.

"You've got nothing, do you, sweetheart?"

My cheeks flame even hotter. "What did I say about endearments?"

"You vetoed me calling you my Lost Chewbacca, that's it."

He lets out an aggrieved sigh like I've done him a great disservice, and because I can't stand the thought of *actually* hanging up the phone just yet, I say, "Mr. Darcy would never subject Lizzie to this level of harassment."

"Pretty sure Lizzie overheard Mr. Darcy call her ugly."

"He did *not* say that she's ugly."

"Fair point, he said something very British-sounding about her being tolerable but not handsome enough to—"

"I'm hanging up the phone."

"You do that, sweetheart."

"And just for the record, an attack on Mr. Darcy is an attack on all mankind."

"You're right," Jordan says agreeably. "As soon as we hang up, I'll go repent."

"You're laughing at me right now, aren't you."

"I'd never dare."

"I hate you, Jordan Knight."

"So, we're still on for the movie this weekend?"

Every day, he runs me in circles, and still I come back for more. "Yes," I say begrudgingly, even as my heart flutters fast.

"Perfect," he chirps, and then he ends the call before I can have the honor of doing it myself.

CHAPTER 5 - JORDAN

"Your noon appointment is here."

Glancing up at Owen from my sketchbook, I tilt my chin in acknowledgement and slide out from behind the desk. It's been a busy morning so we don't bother with shooting the shit, the way we normally would. Owen takes my place at the desk, probably to make some phone calls while he's got a minute, and I head for the front of the parlor.

Working at Inked on Bourbon feels like a dream. I dropped out of college early on and spent a few years selling my artwork down in Jackson Square. Barely eked out a living while I was at it. When I tried to get a job at an art gallery, just to earn a consistent paycheck, I was met with a lot of rejections.

It all worked out in the end, though, because Owen Harvey came into my life and swept me off my feet like my very own fairy godmother.

Sunshine filters in through the front bay window. Outside, New Orleans rages on, but inside Inked, it's just the low hum of music playing and the jittery nerves of a foot tap-tapping against the floor. My gaze lands on the woman seated in one of the oversized chairs, taking in the long black hair that hangs halfway down her back. Her shoulders are set a little stiffly, and I'm thinking that maybe this might be her very first tattoo when she suddenly seems to realize that she's no longer alone.

Her head snaps up and then bright, beautiful green eyes meet mine.

Kinsley.

Fuck, I—

I—

Shit. Where the hell are my goddamn *words*?

I open my mouth and nothing—seriously, nothing—comes out.

Kinsley hops up onto her feet, her purse hitting her in the hip as she levers the strap onto one shoulder. "Hi. I'm here for my appointment? For the yellow hibiscus?"

I momentarily falter.

Are we really doing this? Really pretending that I didn't immediately recognize her—if not from her gorgeous green eyes than from the sweet tenor of her voice? I have *dreamt* of her voice. I've made myself come, just thinking of how prettily she might sigh my name if we ever had the opportunity to be more than our friends-who-flirt-daily situation.

This isn't at all when I envisioned.

But even if it isn't, that doesn't stop me from soaking her in. The expressive, dark brows. The long, black lashes. Her bottom lip is a little fuller than the top, and she must be feeling nervous because she sinks her teeth into the soft flesh, and I nearly groan out loud. What I wouldn't fucking give to lean in close and—

"Is this okay?"

Her soft voice interrupts my thoughts, and I immediately shake off the lingering grip of desire to really focus on Kinsley—*my* Kinsley, standing right there in front of me.

I can't believe she's actually here.

Over the last few months, I've grown to learn her through the various inflections of her voice. I've heard her happy and I've heard her giddy, and one time, when her sister was having another bad day at school, I listened with my hands balled into fists as Kinsley broke down on the other end of the line. Thirteen-year-old Kassie lives with her big sister full-time, and while Kinsley hasn't gotten into all the gritty details of why her parents decided they'd rather go see the world than take care of their youngest daughter, I respect the hell out of her for giving everything she has to raise Kassie in a loving home.

Right now, I force myself to ignore what I already know in my heart so that I can learn Kinsley in an entirely different way. I take in the tight grip she has on her purse, same as I notice the shimmer of worry in her green eyes. Everything about her stance says she's on the brink of running, not because she doesn't want me—want *this*—but because she's spent years putting up walls to protect herself and her sister, and she's finding it difficult to tear them all back down, brick by brick.

If I had a set of parents take off on me, too, I'd probably react the same way.

I don't move any closer, letting her have whatever space she needs to feel safe, and in control, but lower my voice, so she knows that this isn't a joke to me. *She* isn't a joke to me. Whatever she needs, I'll give it to her.

"This is okay," I murmur gently. "I promise."

"I-I want this." Her knuckles are white with tension. "I want this so bad, but I'm scared."

"Because I make you nervous?"

It's a throwback question to our very conversation on Instagram, and she seems to remember it, too, because she quickly shakes her head. "Because you already feel like home."

"Fuck, sweetheart." I let out a heavy breath that seems to leave a crater-sized hole in my chest. I'm desperate to pull her closer to me; desperate to press my lips to her skin and inhale her scent. Desperate, really, for anything that she'll give me.

I've never felt this way before.

It leaves me disoriented, like even the earth beneath my feet is shifting.

After briefly squeezing my eyes shut, in search of restraint, I stare down at this slip of a woman who's thrown my entire world off its axis. "What do you want?"

"To kiss you," she whispers.

"What do you *need*?" I ask hoarsely.

"To let you ink my skin. To talk and listen and understand you."

"Then that's what we'll do."

Her tremulous smile could brighten even the darkest of days.

I lead her to my station, and within minutes, we find our groove. She tells me about the cluster of yellow hibiscuses that I'm tattooing on her forearm, about how the trip she took with Kassie to Maui was the first vacation she ever paid for on her own, with money she made from the romance novels she published. She listens when I tell her about how most days, I feel like my real family is the group of people that I work with at Inked on Bourbon. Owen and his twin, Gage. Their wives, Savannah and Lizzie. How I'd do anything for them, or their kids, even when I barely see my own brothers for the holidays.

She waits until I've lifted the tattoo machine away from her skin to reach out with her free hand to squeeze my bicep, and I'm suddenly struck with the realization that we understand each other on a level I've never felt with anyone else.

I ask her about Kassie, and she tells me that her little sister has a massive heart, with a streak of empathy a mile-long, but how the kids at school sometimes take advantage of how *good* she is. Then she peppers me in return with a million questions about my life—how I got into playing tennis, what style of ink really gets my blood pumping, and whether or not I prefer Matthew MacFayden or Colin Firth as Mr. Darcy.

"This feels like a trick question," I tell her.

"It'll only impact the rest of our relationship," she says blithely.

"Oh, that's all?"

Her smile is quick and breath-taking. "That's all, Mr. Knight."

I top off her tattoo with some ointment, then carefully wrap it up. "I'm a smart man, Kinsley."

"Never said you weren't."

"So, I know what you *want* me to say."

Her brows flash upward. "Why do I hear a *but* coming?"

"There isn't one."

"*But?*"

"May I request your hand, please?"

Those gorgeous green widen with surprise and a dash of uncertainty. "I . . . I mean—" And then I watch as she seems to force out every disquieting thought from her head. She squares her shoulders and curves her lips in a wicked grin and thrusts her hand in my direction. "You may, good sir. Proceed as you will."

Laughter creeps up my throat.

Clutching her fingers in mine, I hold her gaze as I slowly lower my head and press my lips to the inside of her wrist. I hover there, for just a moment, letting the first sensation of her skin against mine settle into a memory that I can revisit for the rest of my life. Her soft gasp quickens my pulse. Without saying a word, I press a kiss to the base of her hand and then another to the center of her palm. I kiss each one of her fingertips and try to ignore the way she wriggles in her chair, breathing out my name.

Then, and only then, do I slide my hand alongside hers, palm to palm, and gently squeeze.

"A hand-clench?" Kinsley whimpers like I've killed her. "*Really?*"

"My take on it, anyway." I squeeze her hand again. Half a heartbeat later, she squeezes mine back.

"Jordan?"

I lift my gaze. "Yeah, sweetheart?"

"Can you kiss me now? *Please?*"

So, I do.

I cup her jaw with both my hands, let my lips hover over hers, until she's begging for me to do it already, and then I kiss her.

A first kiss in the same breath that it's my last.

Because even as she parts her lips to let me inside, I already know that there's no one else for me but her.

EPILOGUE - KINSLEY

'Tis the Season for Mardi Gras

"I can't believe you made me wear this."

I tear my gaze away from the massive crowd ahead of us to look at my little sister. All I can see is a pair of flashing green eyes staring back at me; the rest of her face is covered by neon-green fur. Undaunted, I throw my hands up in excitement. "Family bonding time!"

Kassie looks from me to Jordan. Deadpan, she says, "You should dump her."

"What?" I exclaim. "Why?"

But Kassie won't be deterred. With her entire attention fixated on my boyfriend, she starts ticking off bullet points with her furry paws. "She makes you watch *Pride & Prejudice* at least twice a month. She forced you into wearing a *neon-yellow Chewbacca* suit. Should I continue?"

A little smile plays at the corner of Jordan's mouth. "Feel free."

"Hey!"

Kassie summarily ignores me. "She locks herself away in her office for days at a time. Sometimes we have to force-feed her because she forgets to eat."

"It was one time, y'all. That's it!"

"She hates interacting with people but loves dressing up for Mardi Gras, and she doesn't even care if drunk people fall all over her because it's part of the *experience*."

"I prefer to call it research. For my books."

"She thinks *The Phantom Menace* is actually a good movie and that, right there, should say everything. It's awful, Jord. *Awful*."

Jordan's smile deepens. "Anything else to add?"

Kassie blows out a big breath. "Probably. Yeah." She spares me a glance that reeks of teenage sass. "But I won't."

I poke her in the arm. "Because you love me?"

"Because I don't want to crush your self-esteem," she sniffs, but then she's laughing so hard that her shoulders are shaking and she's diving into my wide-open arms the way she has since she was small enough that I could pick her up. "I love you, Kins," she says into my neck. "You're too easy to mess with."

Before I can say anything else, she scampers off to meet her group of friends, and I'm left alone with Jordan, who throws a furry arm over my shoulder and drags me close to press a kiss to the top of my costumed head.

I wrap an arm around his waist. "Regretting dating me yet?"

He hums a little under his breath. "Hmm. You are a pretty bad girlfriend."

Snorting, I elbow him in the side. "Watch yourself, Knight."

He pulls me to his front, so that we're facing each other. He looks ridiculous decked out as Chewbacca but that's the fun of New Orleans, and that's the fun of *us*. Jordan is always down for a good time, yes, but he's also the same man who holds me when I'm sad and listens while I rant and chases me whenever I toss him a look that says, *come and get me.*

"My feelings will not be repressed," he says, swaying us side to side. "You must allow me to tell you how ardently—"

"Oh, my God. Not again." I try to scamper away, but he holds on tight, deep laughter barreling up from his chest.

"—I admire and love you," he continues.

"Jordan," I squeal, giggling despite my best intentions to seem disapproving, "you can't just steal Mr. Darcy's words whenever you want to be romantic. It's plagiarism. Theft!"

"In vein I have struggled—"

"*Jordan.*"

"To tell you all the ways I love you."

I blink up at him because he's gone off script and feel my heart lurch. It's not the first time he's said the words—*his* words, mind you, not a rip off Mr. Darcy's—but they never fail to make me swoon. "Say it again," I tell him.

His brown eyes warm. "I love you, Kins."

"Again."

"I love you."

"One more time."

He laughs, and if he weren't in that stupid costume, I know that joy would be dimpling his cheeks right about now. "I *love* you. Now say it—"

I skip out of his reach.

"Chase me first," I say, "and then I'll tell you all the ways I love you."

So, I run.

But this time, he catches me, and he doesn't ever let me go.

Thank you so much for reading! If you're curious about the other couples of Inked on Bourbon, start with Tempt Me With Forever and Love Me Tomorrow. And don't worry, those ones have spice. ::slow clap::

ICE SURFING
MJ FIELDS

CHAPTER 1 - NALANI

Looking up into the sky at the kaleidoscope of autumn colors blanketing the landscape surrounding me, it's more beautiful than I ever imagined it would be. The crisp New England air carries the faint smell of autumn leaves and pumpkin spice. Okay, maybe the last part is exaggerated, but that's all I see around here—pumpkin spice this, and pumpkin spice that. I do have to admit that pumpkin spice lattes are amazing.

It's not quite dark. The sun is still peeking through the leaves and kissing my skin. Skin that I just now noticed is losing its golden bronze color. How is it that I only left the island a couple months ago and I'm already losing my tan?

Home. I miss it. I miss wearing flip flops or sandals instead of tennis shoes and boots. I miss my family. I miss shorts and tank tops. Most of all, I miss the sand beneath my toes and the sound of the water crashing into the shore. I miss it just like I thought I would, but much sooner than I expected.

Don't get me wrong; I love it here. It's exactly what I wanted—a smaller school with diversity, and seasons that changed in vivid and living color.

Maui has been my home my entire life. My family's ancestry chart reaches back hundreds of years on both sides. You can't get more native than that. I plan to return when I'm finished with my degrees, running the law department of my family's hotel business. Until then, I want to experience other parts of the world. Vermont was my first choice. My parents were apprehensive, but my ex begged me to stay. He is attending university in Maui, and so is my ex-best friend.

I'm not sure who I feel most betrayed by—him or her. My best friend and my boyfriend got caught in the act … by me, one week before graduation. On my family's restricted beach, of all places.

They are attending the same university he talked me into going to because he "couldn't imagine not seeing me every day." He emotionally manipulated me by saying, "If you love me—if you're serious about us—you won't leave."

It's been nearly six months, and I'm finally at the point where I no longer question what I may have done wrong or why I wasn't enough. I now realize he's simply a vile human being, and she's an opportunistic bitch.

I reach into my bag and pull out my cream-colored cable knit sweater, pulling it over my head and covering the flimsy tee-shirt sporting my letters, all while trying to not ruin my perfectly plaited hair.

"Are you insane?" Sofia's eyes widen in astonishment. "Lani, it's seventy degrees and sunny."

Laughing, I pull my hair out from the collar. "I'll survive. It's just going to take some time to get used to it."

"Babe, here in Vermont, seventy is not something you get used to; it's something you celebrate."

"I'll celebrate the hell out of it when I'm wearing, hats, gloves, boots, and a parka," I agree. "I just didn't expect tonight to be so chilly."

"Any excuse to accessorize," Sofia chides as she pulls two tumblers from the bag we brought from our dorm.

"Damn right," I agree.

She hands me mine. "The alcohol will warm you up; the dancing will keep you that way."

"If the band ever starts."

She holds up her drink. "Cheers."

I tap it. "Hipa hipa."

After taking a drink, she declares, "You're hooking up with someone tonight."

"I'm open to the possibility."

Sofia makes that face, the one I'm sure I make when I see a perfect wave coming in from behind me, her body almost shaking with excitement. I know the only reason she hasn't dived on me is because I'm still holding my drink to my lips.

"You're going to live your Hallmark dream," she all but squeals as I set the tumbler down. And just as I knew she would, she dives on me.

I correct her, "We're too young for Hallmark moments. We watch the movies to prepare ourselves for being miserably single at thirty during the holidays and snowed in at a quaint B&B."

"I'm gonna be like that *Mean Girls* actress who's starred in a million of them."

"Lacey Chabert? She's an icon."

"Of course you know her name." She pushes off me.

"I've lived in a snowless region my entire life—I've been deprived."

"Don't even. You've lived a lifetime of spring breaks."

"Hey, ladies."

We look up and see both of our sorority big sisters, Lauren and Noelle.

Sofia springs up. "Hey, how are you? What are you doing here?" She's about ready to drown herself in questions that I've learned she asks when she gets anxious.

"About time. Let's dance." I hop up just as the band starts.

When I first arrived here, fresh from betrayal, I was leery of making friends or letting anyone in. But Hayward, as small as it is, is bigger than my private high school. People are less up in your business and more focused on education and sisterhood. KET was my first choice for a sorority—they're the most diverse. Thankfully, they chose me.

I know it's new, but so far, the overall environment seems to foster positive, supportive, and mature relationships. Bonus: they know how to have a good time.

I'm totally here for that, too.

We sway and twirl beneath the setting Vermont sun, surrounded by the "pretty decent music" from a "semi-famous local band" that they all seem to know. Those terms left little hope that the music wasn't going to suck; the fact that they're good is a happy coincidence. More and more people begin to dance as they start playing covers.

Amongst the warm hues, in the fading sun, my eye catches a group of big guys standing a few yards away. There's one who catches my eye. He's tall; at least a foot taller than me and a few inches taller than his friends. Even in this light, I can see he's athletically built; his broad shoulders taper down to a trim waist. His body looks ... powerful. I can tell his skin is darker than most of the others—he's tan—which leads me to believe he must love the outdoors. *Same.* His hair is thick, jet black, with a nice wave to it. When he turns, I see a strong, square jawline and full lips. Well, at least his left side. It would be a shame if the right didn't match.

He's looking in this direction, so I can't shield my eyes to check him out without being obvious, which sucks. As he moves, more light shines from behind him, and I can no longer see his face at all. But I do see the way he moves through the crowd.

His dark Henley stretches across his chest, accentuating his extraordinarily defined muscles. Paired with his light-colored jeans, he looks more casual than his stature should allow. While moving closer, people stop him. He pauses, leans down, and gives them his attention. I'm enchanted by the way people seem to be drawn to this mountain of a man who could easily be intimidating yet exudes a casual charm.

"Who is that?" I ask who I thought was Sofia, but it's Lauren.

She grins. "That's The Cock."

"The Cock?" I laugh.

"The Cock." She nods as if some understanding has just passed.

It hasn't. I'm clueless.

I step back right into a hard body as the music stops. "Sorry."

"Don't be." The deep voice sends a shiver up my spine. "Dance?"

"Sure?" I ask, looking at Sofia, whose jaw is dusting the ground.

"You positive?" He chuckles.

"She's positive." Sofia gives two thumbs-up, and I can't help but laugh.

Two hands grip my hips, and heat begins to emanate where they flex then relax. The female guitar player takes the mic and begins to sing.

I close my eyes, trying to stay lost in the music, in this moment—the present, not in my past—as we begin to sway to Miley Cyrus's "Flowers."

His hands grip a little firmer, but the feeling is gentle as he moves us in sync with the melody. Nothing about the way he holds me makes me think of my ex, and although his touch is foreign, it feels so familiar. Maybe it's because I want it to be. Maybe it's because I miss physical contact so much that, at this point, I'll take what I can get.

I flinch at my self-deprecating thought, causing his hands to immediately loosen, and then ... then I feel his thumbs begin to make a soothing circular motion against my exposed skin. Yep, I ditched the sweater when we started to dance, and I'm so glad I did because ... fuck him—the ex, not The Cock— for the epic mind-fuck which included but was not limited to blowing up my social media when I downloaded Tinder a month after the breakup. The messages, things like, "Where is your self-respect?" or "Are you that desperate?" and "Are you trying to embarrass me by fucking around with *insert every damn guy I chilled with, even friends who happen to have a penis* because it's you who should be embarrassed."

It got to the point he was calling me a whore and ... worse. I never once responded to his messages, but I did finally have enough self-respect to block him.

It's not any of those things, though. It's that I'm nervous to turn around and face this man, knowing that as much as I want to let myself get to a place that allows me to be vulnerable again, a part of me knows I'm not ready. A bigger part of me knows that relationships of every kind are precious to me, and falling in love is unwise as a first-year student in college. All that added to the fact I know I'm going on to law school then back home to work with those I cherish the most—my family.

Holy shit, get ahold of yourself, I scold myself. *He asked you to dance, not to get married.*

I turn to face the man who has, in the most ridiculous way, already been judged and sent into exile for breaking my heart. Facing his broad chest, I lift my chin to meet his eyes.

"Holy shit," I mumble as I finally see the entirety of his stunning face.

His lips turn up slightly and his eyes—he has gorgeous eyes—are twinkling cognac pools of sexiness. "Aloha."

I bite my lower lip to stop the spread of what I know will be a smile so huge and disturbing he'll run for the hills if I don't take a moment to tone it down.

I swear to God, I'm going to kill Sofia, I think after I ask the world's most poorly-timed and wildly inappropriate question. "So, they call you The Cock —why?"

He sucks in his lips, suppressing a grin, but it doesn't hide the insanely deep dimples on both sides of his stunning face.

"Jesus, really?" I turn away, fully intent on walking all the way back to the dorms and forcing myself not to look back.

CHAPTER 2 - KOA

"Hold up." I laugh as I attempt to catch up to her.

My steps are quick, fueled by a mix of determination and curiosity. It's been years since that summer we all hung out at the beach, years in which I have transformed a bit, but I didn't think I was unrecognizable. She isn't to me—she never has been. As soon as I saw her on that dance floor, my heart recognized her before my eyes did.

Nalani, the girl who left me angry and with a hurt that never really faded. Memories of sunsets and laughter, of a connection that once felt unbreakable, until she ended up with Joey Buchannan.

She's walking ahead, her pace steady, but I close the gap between us, feeling both anticipation and a hint of trepidation.

When I reach her, my voice breaks through the music that seems to have disappeared into our silence. "Nalani."

She looks back at me, surprise flashing in her eyes. She's beautiful, just like I remember. Her eyes carry a certain kind of light, like moonlight dancing on water. I couldn't ever mistake her for anyone else. The curve of her smile, the one that used to make my heart race—*it still does*—hasn't changed either.

For a moment, her gaze searches mine, as if she's trying to place me. And then I see it—the confusion dawning in her eyes. She still doesn't recognize me. The years have changed me, but that much? Okay, maybe. The gym will do that to you, and so will a growth spurt sophomore year, one so radical my mother took me to the doctors, concerned with growth plates and shit. My youngest sister—a *Twilight* movie fan and "Team Jacob"—was convinced I was turning. My oldest sister told her she was stupid, and not because of the whole turning thing, but because she hadn't read the books or she'd be "Team Edward." I'll never admit it, but I read them then watched the movies. I'm "Team Seth." That kid had the type of unbreakable loyalty that I admire.

Nalani may not recognize me, but I recognize her. I see her younger version in every curve of her face, in the way she tilts her head when she's trying to figure something out. I see her in the way she worries her bottom lip, a nervous habit she's obviously carried from back then.

There's a mix of emotions swirling inside me—old memories, the thrill of seeing her here at Hayward, and the uncertainty of what comes next.

"Nalani," I repeat, my voice softer this time, a thread of vulnerability weaving through her name. "It's Koa."

Her eyes widen, and I see shock flicker across her face before she manages to school her features.

Koa. My name hangs in the air between us as her gaze searches my eyes.

And then, slowly, the corner of her mouth begins to move, but instead of smiling, her lips turn down.

"Koa," she repeats, and in that one mention, I hear recognition. It's not just my name; it's an acknowledgment of shared history.

She steps forward and pushes against my chest. "Did he tell you to watch me?" She pushes me again. "Did he tell you to—"

"Fuck no." Annoyance boils inside of me that she thinks I'm here for him. That mixed with the alcohol I rarely put into my system has me in my damn feels. "Your boyfriend is a first-class asshole. He may think he runs the island, but he doesn't. Wailea is a small part of a much bigger picture, one he'll never be able to see."

She lifts her nose in the air, giving me a reminder of why I lost the girl before I even had her. I didn't know it when I met her, but Nalani's family has more money than I'll ever see. I would never have known that because her grandmother lives in my town—Kihei—which is the reason I met Nalani. She came for surfing lessons from my father and bought a board, one I helped build and finish with a sweet lavender-colored paint job.

"How about you call and ask the king of Wailea why he left Baldwin," I huff. "Spoiler alert: it's because he lost captain of the football team to me, and it bruised his massive ego."

"Ex-boyfriend." She crosses her arms and narrows her eyes.

I cross mine and try my best to mirror her facial expression. "Ex-teammate."

She looks me over skeptically and shakes her head, releasing some of the tension. "Your dad taught me to surf, which I appreciate, but *you* introduced me to Joey."

"Unintentionally," I state.

"He told me—" She stops herself.

"Let me guess, he told you I wanted you to meet him."

She unties her sweater from her waist and nods as she pulls it over her head.

"I wanted him to meet you because *I* was interested."

She stands frozen with her arms in the air, sweater blanketing her face.

"You stuck? Need some help?" I begin pulling it down. My cock jumps a bit when I see her nipples poking against her shirt, but I force myself to do the right thing—stop staring and keep pulling the sweater down. When her face appears, I see she's blushing.

"Was," she whispers as she looks down at her feet.

I lift her chin with my finger, getting her eyes back to mine. "That connection out there, before I even knew it was you, tells me it's still there. And this time, it's not one-sided."

"I didn't know," she defends.

I pop my pecks. "Or maybe you just didn't notice."

Stepping back, amusement dancing in her eyes, she waves her hand up and down. "You think it's because you look like ... that?" Then she rolls her eyes. "As if."

"I own a mirror—I know what I look like. I know what women see and what they want. And I know you were looking at me the same way they do."

"I was looking for a rebound before I knew it was you."

And I'm looking for a do-over, I think.

"Look around." I tip my head backward, toward the crowd. "Do you think any one of those guys believes they have a chance with you now?"

She shoves me again jokingly. I don't move.

"You're so full of yourself."

"Just a heads-up: eventually, you're going to be so full of me you'll realize immediately that, even before the growth spurt, I've always been the bigger man."

She laughs out loud. "You're going to realize even quicker that a man they call 'The Cock' hasn't got a chance in—"

"Hell no." I laugh. "You can't take what you already gave me. Do you know how much restraint I used to make sure I did not get hard when your sexy ass was grinding against me?"

She fires back, "I can take away consent anytime I want." She again playfully tries to shove me. This time, I take her hand, and she doesn't try to pull it away. "That wasn't a call to action; that was dancing."

"Dancing?" I shake my head.

"And an attempt to stay warm. It's freezing here, and you're like a furnace."

"There's a lot of cold nights in Vermont; you may want to rethink this."

"I promised myself this wouldn't be another one-bed situation for me." She rocks back on her heels, still holding my hand. "I have to keep my options open. I'm a single college girl. I'm not planning on being *wifed up*. I wasted years of my life doing that."

"Okay." I nod, even though it's not, but hey, I'm not about to force her hand this early in the game.

I let go of her hand and shove mine in my pockets. "When you get sick of the dating game and want something *regular*, let me know. But Nalani, once you and I've gone there, there's no one else."

She crosses her arms over the sweater that swallows her up. "The campus Cock isn't what I'm looking for."

"Cock is a nickname that—"

She barks out a laugh. "I'm sure it is."

"That," I speak over her, "my teammate gave me."

"That doesn't make it any better." She continues to laugh.

"Replace the Cs with Ks and drop the last one," I explain.

"What?" She shakes her head.

"Get your mind out of the gutter, Nalani Kāne. K.O.K are my initials. Koa Olu Kelekolio—Cock."

"That may be so, but when I asked my friend who you were, she said *The*

Cock. It wasn't in a K.O.K tone." I start to object, but she holds up her hand. "No judgment. But I've sworn off football players."

A smile creeps up my face. "Good to know." I nod to the crowd. "Let me walk you back over."

She looks me over again, and I notice the slight shake of her head. She's clearly shocked.

Good.

After making sure Nalani's back with her friends, I decide it's time to relocate the party.

I head over to our team's co-captain, Dash. "You ready to take this back to the house?"

"Yeah, man, of course." He rubs his hands together. "Let's roll."

I lift my chin toward Nalani and her friends. "Those four need an invite. My name needs to be left out of it."

"Little brunette?" he asks.

"She's off limits."

CHAPTER 3 - NALANI

"I can't believe we're being invited to our first house party," Sofia whispers as we walk out of the sorority house, following Lauren and Noelle.

"We've been to house parties," I remind her.

"Not ones on Athlete Row." I frown, and she relays, "It's the hockey team, not football. You specifically said no football."

"I'm losing on a technicality?" I ask.

"Good lesson to learn here and not in the court of law." She giggles.

When Lauren and Noelle turn on flashlights, I stop.

"Pledge week's over, right?" I ask because, although they didn't haze hard, there were some shenanigans involving a scavenger hunt I don't particularly want to relive.

Noelle laughs. "The hockey house is behind ours."

"So convenient." Lauren giggles.

Noelle looks back at us. "Which is code for Lauren's sneaky link lives there."

Lauren smacks her arm. "Really?"

Noelle giggles. "What? They're our littles, our ride or dies; they'll take it to the grave."

Lauren turns, shining her flashlight right under her chin and making a deranged face. Sofia screams and jumps at me, causing me to spill my drink.

"Girl, relax." I laugh as I help steady her.

Noelle throws her arm around Sofia and tries to keep a straight face. "You're safe with us, babe. Mama's got you."

"I'm reliving past trauma here. This is no laughing matter." Sofia pouts.

"Were you ...?" Lauren asks with concern in her voice.

"No, no, no," she replies. "I was eight when my cousins took me snipe hunting, and I'll never be the same."

"What's a snipe?" Noelle asks.

Sofia begins, "It's—"

"It's a flightless bird," Lauren quickly cuts her off, "nearly extinct, that's worth a lot of money to, um … bird watchers who want to save the snipes."

"Why do they want them hunted?" Noelle asks.

When I see Lauren and Sofia faltering, I decide to chime in with my *knowledge* of the very elusive snipe. "They're trying to get them off the endangered species list by putting them in natural-ish environments that enhances the likelihood of them breeding."

"We should do a fundraiser," Noelle states.

"We most definitely should." Lauren laughs as she lifts the latch to the gate and pushes it open.

Stepping in, I look up and see strings of lights hanging diagonally across the yard. Music plays softer than it does at the frat parties we've attended. I also notice there's no beer pong table set up. Instead, there's a massive Jenga puzzle, shuffleboard, and a giant chess game. There's also an outdoor Tiki bar. On top of it is a giant rooster, with a sign around its neck that says, "*KOK's BAR.*"

"What the hell?" I ask then hear a low chuckle from behind me. My spine straightens, the fine hairs on the back of my neck stand up, and … my nipples stiffen.

"Aloha."

I whirl around and place my hands on my hips. "What is going on here?"

He nods toward the bar, takes my hand, and pulls me behind him. "Let's get you a drink."

"Hey, Nalani," one of the guys says as we pass by.

"Joel. He's right wing," Koa explains.

I swear I'm at a loss for words for the second time tonight.

"Welcome, Nalani," the guy I saw Koa talking to after he deposited me back with the girls says.

"That's Dash—team's center and co-captain."

"What the hell?" I mumble.

"What's up, girl?" a guy with a girl on each leg asks.

"Hey, Nalani," they say in unison.

"Tiny—he's goalie. The girls? I haven't got a clue." Koa chuckles.

Gaping at them, I feel a tug at my hand.

"Watch your step."

I glance down and step up onto the wooden platform.

"Have a seat. Let me make you a drink." He pulls out a tall, wooden slatted chair with a cushion on it. As I sit, he walks around the bar.

"Why are you at the ice hockey house?" I ask, watching him set a paper plate on the bar, tear open a packet of instant hot cocoa, and pour it onto the plate.

"Got taken out my last game at Baldwin, lost my football scholarship to

Texas." He pulls a paper towel off the roll, dips it in a cup of something, and then rims a plastic martini glass.

"I'm sorry. That's horrible but still doesn't explain"—I wave my hand about—"this."

"Academic scholarship that I turned down was offered back. I took it." He pours vanilla vodka into a cup of ice, looks up, and winks at me. "And she's thinking, *all this and he's smart, too.*"

I was totally thinking that but shake my head. "Still not sold."

He grabs a bottle of coffee liquor in one hand and chocolate liquor in another, tipping them both into the cup with ice and vanilla vodka. "Got into a pissing match with Dash over hogging the squat rack; ended up being friends. He dared me to try out for the team during walk-on tryouts." He places an empty cup on top of the one filled with alcohol and shakes it before pouring it into the martini glass. "I made the team."

He pushes the drink over to me as I stare at those deep dimples. Water pools in my mouth, because since he left me at the concert, all I've done is try not to think about him, like fully tried, and here he is again, all gorgeous and dimpled.

"What's this?"

"Your favorite drink." His lips quip.

"And what's that?"

"Tall, dark, and handsome." He leans forward, resting his elbows on the bar, fingers steepled. "Blond was never your color."

Joey was blond.

"No?"

He's so close and looking at me with obvious intent, but that's not what's causing my reservations to crumble.

Even before the summer his dad taught me how to surf, I knew who Koa was. The town he lives in—and my grandmother lives in—Kihei, embodies everything I love about my island. The sense of community, the strength of family, the way people help one another without expecting anything in return, but knowing they'll receive it when needed. They don't want to be paid for kindness because they don't hold money above community. It's vastly different than the way people who live in the bigger cities and tourist traps behave. I can honestly say I don't think one friend I've ever had wanted to be my friend because of who I am as a person. It was all about who I *was.*

Koa's different.

My grandmother was sick the summer before I learned to surf. When I visited and asked what I could do to help, Koa had already done things for her, like taking care of the landscaping and trimming the grass. But that wasn't all. He brought her fresh flowers every few days when it was too difficult for her to go get them herself. I distinctly remember her mentioning he'd slept on her couch when there'd been a terrible storm and my mother couldn't get to her.

He pushes off the bar and stands tall, so freaking tall. "Tell me I'm wrong."

I shake my head and take a sip.

He lifts his chin. "Go find your first date."

I nearly choke on my drink. Seconds ago, he was giving me not just hookup vibes, but something more along the lines of what he'd offered before. Something steady. "Someone to keep me warm on cold nights."

"At least make the effort to act out your bad girl bit." He smirks.

I slide off my chair and hold up my glass. "When this is gone, you gonna make me another when I come back?"

"Of course I will."

I slam the whole damn drink then set the glass on the bar and climb back in the chair.

Eyes dancing, he asks, "What can I get for you?"

"Something tall, dark, and handsome."

Making me another, he asks, "You know what you're getting into?"

"You've given me a pretty good idea."

"Nalani, I gave you the entire blueprint." He rims the glass. "You're mine and no one else's." He glances up at me. "Don't break my heart again."

"I didn't!" I protest.

He lifts a shoulder. "Not knowingly." He pours the drink then slides a full glass back to me. "I'll never break yours. I'll protect it."

I could tell him I've heard that before, but if I'm honest with myself, I haven't. I just assumed that's the way it went.

"You better." I lean forward. "That's the expectation when you get naked and share your body with someone."

He shakes his head. "Not gonna lie to you. I've been naked and sweaty with a few women. None asked for that, and I never offered it to them. I'm offering it to you because it's not just your body I want you to share with me. I want more." He steps back. "Doesn't work for you, at any time, you can tag out."

"Same goes for you, but could you do so before you get naked and sweaty with someone else?"

"I'm not that guy."

I look up at the sign and giggle. "You think they know that?"

"In my defense, I didn't put that damn thing up."

"Let me guess, one of your hookups did."

He scrubs a hand over his insanely handsome face. "Actually, it was Tiny."

CHAPTER 4 - KOA

Sitting under the stars with a drunk Nalani on my lap, she's giving me kiss-me eyes ... again.

"Ku'uipo, I'm not kissing you for the first time and end up being the only one who remembers it."

"You don't know what you're missing."

"I've got an idea." I brush her hair away from her eyes.

"Yeah?"

I whisper in her ear, "Been dreaming about your lips for years."

"Anyone ever tell you you're a tease?" she asks.

"Nope," I answer her honestly, giving her what I expect back.

She eyes me suspiciously.

"Ask me anything; you'll get the truth. You need to do that, and I understand. I can tell you over and over I'm not him, and I will if that's what you need. But I'm gonna do more than that. I'm gonna show you."

"I'm not putting that on you. It's not your responsibility to fix what he broke in me."

"You say that like it's a burden." I shake my head. "It's not. It's a fucking privilege."

She licks her lips and looks at mine. "You keep saying these things and expect me not to want to kiss you?" She curls up to a seated position. "I should head back, because the longer I sit on you"—she wiggles her ass against my semi—"the more I'm going to want more than a kiss."

"You're staying here tonight."

"Really?" She acts like I'm kidding.

"Gonna wake up with you in my bed, in my arms, kiss you, and—"

"You won't kiss me when I'm drunk for the first time"—she holds up her hand when I start to explain why again—"don't you even try kissing me before I brush my teeth."

Holding back a laugh, I watch as she stands up and holds out her hand. "You're staying with me tonight because my toothbrush is not here."

I stand and take both her hands, walking backward toward the French doors of the house. "I have extras and no roommates in my room."

"Extras, huh?" she asks.

"Mom sends them in bulk." I step back across the threshold. "She's a dental hygienist. The answer to the question you're not asking but want to"—I swoop her up—"no hook-up has ever stayed the night with me."

"Them's the rules," Dash says as we walk past him and Lauren in the kitchen. "They're not yours, they don't stay."

I watch Lauren cross her arms and stick her nose in the air.

"Lauren, you think you can get Sofia back to her and Nalani's dorm?" I ask as we hit the bottom of the stairs.

"Sure thing," she answers.

"Why isn't Dash committing?" Nalani asks.

"It's not Dash." I climb the stairs.

"Oh, wow."

I can't help but laugh. "You were hell-bent on playing the field, too."

She yawns. "Her prerogative."

"It is." I walk us into my room, kicking the door shut behind us, then move and set her on my bed. "You are so beautiful, ku'uipo."

"You, too." She smiles and begins looking around. "Your room's so big and clean."

"The dorms suck." I head over to the closet and grab her a shirt to sleep in. "Move into KET next semester."

"That's the plan." She stands up and pulls off the sweater I helped her put on.

Then your sophomore year, move in with me, is what I'd like to say, but she'd think it's a bit premature.

When she lifts her shirt over her head, I freeze. She looks at me as she unbuttons her jeans and shimmies them down.

Fuck.

Bending, she picks up her clothes and walks over to drape them over the chair. "My swimsuits are skimpier than this."

"That may be true, but you in red lace, in my bedroom ..." I make a hand gesture. "Mind blown."

"Mind blown, huh?" She mimics my movement.

"The realization that my imagination is shit has me second-guessing myself. Beautiful doesn't even come close to describing you."

She takes the tee-shirt and pulls it over her head. It swallows her up. Only then do I step forward and help her pull her long, thick, jet-black braids from the collar.

She swallows hard and asks, "Do you have a hair tie?"

I take her hand. "Right this way."

We walk out of my room, just as Tiny and the two chicks he's been playing with for the past week crest the stairs.

"You two have a great night." He winks as they walk by and down the hall.

"Back at you," Nalani calls to them as we cross the hall and into the bathroom.

Looking around, she states, "This is clean, too."

"Secret?" I squat down and open the cupboard, pulling out my bathroom tote.

"Tell me all of them." She smiles as I hand her an unopened toothbrush.

"The four of us chip in and have someone clean the bathrooms and kitchen once a week." I stand and open the medicine cabinet, grab the paste, my brush, and two hair ties. "Another secret: I can't sleep with my hair down, so ..." I pull my hair up into a bun then move to gather her braids and place them into a ponytail.

"You're insanely sexy." She turns on the water and wets her toothbrush. "Always were. Even when your father was teaching me how to surf, it was hard paying attention when you were out there." She closes her eyes. "I can't believe he tricked me into thinking you wanted him and I together."

I pull my shirt over my head and toss it in the hamper. Then I grab two washcloths from my shelf and set them on the counter. "Always hated that saying—everything happens for a reason. When I realized it was actually you and not some doppelganger, I didn't hate it as much."

A smile creeps up her flawless face, and she opens her eyes. When she slaps her hand over them, I bark out a laugh.

She elbows me. "You could have given me a heads-up."

I turn on the water. "Just giving you the same as you gave me."

"You have tattoos?"

"No," I answer.

She pulls her hand away from her face. "You totally do."

I squirt toothpaste on her brush then mine. "Where *I* come from, this is called kākau uhi."

She looks over my left arm from my shoulder to my wrist.

"When I told my father I wanted a tattoo, he told me if I was going to mark my body, it needed to be done traditionally." I chuckle. "When he took me, it wasn't to a shop, and there were no guns or needles. It was to the mountains and done by a priest who only uses the traditional method called tapping."

She lifts my arm with one hand and skates her fingertips down my side, where I had more work done this past summer.

"I plan on getting my leg done next."

"It's stunning."

"Each pattern represents something about our culture." A yawn escapes me.

"Tired?"

"I have practice at seven and a game at four." I hold up my toothbrush, and she taps hers against mine.

When we're finished brushing our teeth and washing our faces, we head back across the hall.

I wave my hand toward the bed. "My lady first."

She climbs in. It's sexy. "I want a tour."

I slide in beside her. "Not much to the place. Four bedrooms and—"

"Of your body, your art, *our* cultural meaning behind it."

Pulling her against me, I tell her, "If I wake up tomorrow and this hasn't been a dream, I'll give you whatever you want."

She yawns and whispers, "Same."

A few minutes later, she looks up at me. "I'm not that drunk."

I press my lips to the top of her forehead. "None of our firsts are going to be distorted by anything, not drink or exhaustion. After that, I promise wild, drunken make-outs and dirty, sloppy sex anytime you want it."

I feel her smile against my chest, and then ... "What the ...? Is your nipple pierced?"

I chuckle when I think about how shocked she's going to be when she sees what else I've pierced.

"Let's sleep. Tomorrow, I'll give you the grand tour."

"You're sleeping in jeans?" she asks.

"Tonight, I am."

I wake to Nalani scampering off the bed and am blinded by the light when she throws the door open.

"Nalani, you okay?" I hop out of bed just as she throws up.

Fuck.

CHAPTER 5 - NALANI

When Koa tried to wake me up, I faked sleep … due to mortification. Then he whispered, "See you when I get back."

As soon as I hear him leave, I drag my ass out of bed, find my phone, which he sweetly put on a charger on his side of the bed, and immediately message Sofia to find out where she is. I then sneak out of the house and freeze my ass off in yesterday's clothes as I run through the small patch of woods to KET, because hell no I'm not going to see him until I've pulled myself together, washed off my embarrassment, and thrown on some dignity … and lip gloss.

I cannot believe I threw up. I can, but I hate it. I drank more than I should've, which is not me. In my defense, I was drinking for courage.

"Come on." Sofia opens the door, letting me in.

I follow her up the stairs, into Lauren and Noelle's room, and sink down into the queen-sized air mattress. Sofia lies next to me.

"Please let me sleep until graduation."

The three of them giggle, but I don't tell them I'm dead ass serious.

Ten minutes later—or at least, it feels that way—Sofia is shaking me. "Wake up."

"Did they call my name?"

"What?"

"To get my diploma?" I rub my eyes.

"No one called your name, but there is a very hot hockey player downstairs, surrounded by some thirsty sisters, cooking breakfast. He's requested your presence."

"What?" I say in unison with Lauren as I spring up.

Sofia grins. "Oh, and there's also a *Dash* of a little something else downstairs. My advice, you two shower and get downstairs before your boyfriend—"

"My what?" I ask.

"That's what he told Hilda"—the house mom—"when she asked him who he was trying to impress."

"What'd Dash say?" Noelle asks.

"He said he wasn't at liberty to discuss his motives." She claps her hands loudly. "Now move it!"

Walking down the stairs, freshly showered and dressed in silky red and clean pajama shorts and a matching button-down shirt that Lauren insisted I wear, I hear his laugh, and everything inside me clenches, except my heart, which begins beating to a rhythm I have never felt before.

Walking into the massive kitchen, I can't help but notice how tiny it looks with him standing at the stove, flipping pancakes. He's in track pants and a tank top, his damp hair pulled up. His back is ripped, just like his chest and abs, and his shoulders and arms … pornographic.

"First round's up." Dash lifts a platter full over his head and walks to the table in the adjacent dining room. Pausing when he sees us, he winks at Lauren, who's in black. "Morning, ladies. You'll have to wait your turn. No perks for sleeping half the day away."

"The cook disagrees." Koa turns and looks me over. "My lady gets whatever she wants, whenever she wants it."

"Remind me to call my grandmother and ream her out for not living next to a hot guy my age with a lawnmower," one of the girls mutters.

"I'm calling my father and shunning him for not owning a surfing school," another sputters.

"Your father owns a chain of hardware stores," Noelle reminds her.

"Not the kind of hardware I like," the other sputters back, walking toward me.

I'm not sure if I should trip her or …

The stabby thoughts stop when she pops a kiss to my cheek. "Can we schedule this every Saturday morning?"

"You'll have to ask the chef. I'm not his boss."

She gives him a pleading look.

He chuckles. "My lady doesn't reside on Athens Lane."

She smiles. "We have an extra bedroom."

"She's not wrong—Sheena dropped," another girl pipes in. "You can move in with—"

"So did Hannah," yet another adds. "I have a bed free."

I catch Sofia out of my peripheral, wilting like a flower.

"Not sure that's how it works with housing, but even if it did, I'm never leaving Sofia."

"The house could use the funds," Hilda pipes in from where she's sitting in the corner, reading the paper. "I'd be open to talking to the advisors; see if they'd talk to housing. You girls would have to speak to your parents, and you two"—she points to the two sisters with spare beds—"would have to move in together." She looks at Koa. "Before any of that happens, you'd have to commit to cooking breakfast Saturday mornings for my girls."

He chuckles. "I'd love to, but we have away games—"

"The Saturdays you don't."

He lifts his chin at me, as if looking for my input.

I hold up my hands. "This has nothing to do with me."

"Ku'uipo," he says in a smoldering tone. "It has everything to do with you."

"Oh my God, that's so sweet." Sofia sighs. "Wait—what does ku'uipo mean?"

"Sweetheart," Koa and I answer in unison.

"I thought I was completely ruined by romance novels, and now I know it's real." Sofia pouts out her lip. "I'm gonna end up having five cats and living in my childhood home, in a room that's Barbie pink and looks like a library exploded in it."

"You say that like it's a bad thing." Hilda pulls her e-reader out from under the newspaper she's pretending to read and winks.

Everyone, including Koa, cracks up.

Sitting on the bleachers at Hayward arena, wearing Koa's jersey from last year, I'm a mix of exhausted and excited.

Sofia sneakily tries to hand me a tumbler.

"Hell no."

"It's hot cocoa," she assures me. "I didn't want you to freeze."

"You don't have to take care of me." I lean into her. "Thanks."

"You're like my fairy godmother. First, a hockey party, and now we're moving into KET early? I'd rub your feet." She shakes her head. "If I liked feet and you asked me to … even though I seriously hate feet."

"I can't believe we may be moving again so soon."

"Maybe?" She laughs. "We totally are!"

"It's not approved by housing yet. Even though my parents and yours said they didn't care about losing money, I do."

"And I love that about you. I'll make sure to tell everyone how you valiantly fought against this because people are starving and stuff, but—"

"Stop!" I laugh.

"I swear, I'll be the villain in order to save us from those dreadful dorms."

"I kind of like them. I met you there."

"These seats taken?"

I look up at an older couple. They're wearing Lincoln Lions scarves.

"This is the student section," Sofia informs them, "for Hayward students."

They look around at the empty section, and then the woman asks, "Where is your university's team spirit?"

"Right?" I ask.

She points to my key lanyard. "KET?"

I nod. "We both are."

"I was a KET." She beams proudly.

I move my bag. "Please, have a seat."

Smiling, she sits beside me. "I promise not to 'dis' your team. But when our Dean does something amazing, we have to applaud him."

"Your Dean?" I ask, keeping the conversation rolling. This woman is seriously adorable.

"Our grandson is the goalie for the Lincoln Lions." She looks around. "We just had a new arena constructed. It's state of the art." She reaches into her Birkin bag, pulls out her wallet, and removes a card. "You should have your people contact me when they decide to give your team a much-needed remodel."

I take it, even though I don't have "people" to remodel an arena.

"My information is on it, too. It's always nice to have KET contacts. Shoot me a text message so I have yours."

"Will do." I smile.

Sofia looks around me. "This is Nalani's first game, not mine. Yet, I admittedly never paid attention, so she and I are pretty clueless."

She leans in and whispers, "I don't know much more."

The Lions skate onto the rink, and this sweet woman jumps to her feet, pulls a massive foam finger from inside her coat, and holds it up. "That's our Dean!"

I choke back a laugh.

"We're so fucked," Sofia whispers.

"Totally are. But she's adorable."

A tap and a gasp from beside me causes me to look from Sofia toward the rink.

Koa winks at me as he places his giant gloved hand against the glass. I hold mine against it. He then skates off.

"Oh my, that must be the young man our Dean spoke about. The Cock, right?" she asks.

I nearly lose it. However, I manage to gather myself quickly and turn to her. "That's what they call him. His name is Koa."

"Interesting." She watches the ice. "But the name Coc—"

"His full name is Koa Olu Kelekolio. His initials K.O.K, so …" I shrug.

"He's Nalani's boyfriend," Sofia informs her.

"*Ooo* … very, *very* interesting." She grins.

"Very," Sofia whispers.

With minutes left before the start, the stadium begins to fill.

"Notice it's mostly women," Mrs. Costello states. "How smart are we women to let them think they rule the world."

"So true." I laugh.

"Very." She gives me a long wink.

The game begins, and Koa is on the ice. The rest of the world fades away.

It's obvious that he and Dash are the stars of the team, but Koa rules the ice … on Hayward's side. I wondered how someone who played football could make such a switch. I quickly realize it has nothing to do with football.

Koa's on the water; it's just frozen. He's surfing but doing it on blades. He's in his element, and he's absolutely amazing.

Even though the Lions are killing them.

CHAPTER 6 - KOA

Walking out of the locker room, I can't help but smile at the message from Nalani.

You're amazing! I'm in the parking lot, chatting with the couple that sat with us .

I hit her back.

I'll meet you out there

When I see her, she's standing in the middle of a whole group of people, including my coach, the Lions coach, and a few of their players.

"There's The Cock." An older woman claps her hands. "Bravo!"

Coach Tallman pulls his hat down as he shakes his head.

I tip my head to the woman. "Thank you. We tried."

"And a valiant effort at that." She takes my hand. "This is Coach Kosta."

I reach out and shake his hand. "Nice to meet you."

"Son, you don't belong here," he states.

"Jesus, Brad, right in front of me?" Coach Tallman snaps.

Kosta looks at him. "Damn right. When this kid goes pro, he's gonna say Tallman was the man who took a chance on a kid who ..." He pauses and looks at Nalani. "What was that again?"

She blushes, giving me an apologetic look. "I just said you were surfing on ice."

Kosta clamps his hand on my shoulder. "You're a beast and a natural. With a couple years, I can skate you off college ice and right into the NHL."

"You're losing your team at the end of this season," Tallman sneers.

"I'm losing four seniors and my first line, all of them being courted by the NHL. I'm not losing my team. I have a center who can carry it just like this one does yours." He pauses and looks at Tallman. "I'm giving you the opportunity to do the right thing. Tell him why he should play with us."

"It's not done yet. We have this season," Tallman snaps.

Not one for confrontation outside of a healthy competitive sport, I walk over and pull Nalani under my arm, kissing the top of her head.

She looks up. "You should listen to them."

"We have plans."

She places her hand over my heart. "We'll still have the same plans. Give them a minute."

I look at Coach Tallman, who shrugs. "There's a possibility that we won't have a team next year. They're cutting costs. Since Hayward is more of an academic school, sports will be the first to go."

"I'm here on an academic scholarship." I look down at Nalani. "I'm not going anywhere."

"Son," Costello begins, "you'd be given a full ride—housing and the possibility of endorsements—"

"With a name like The Cock, you'll make millions," the older woman states.

I have no fucking clue how to reply to her. None. She's older than my grandmother. She's ...

"You'll have cock everywhere. Cock jerseys, cock tennis shoes, cock boxers and tank tops. Cock stadium seat cushions will be under the derrieres of millions. People will be eating cock cookies and drinking cock energy drinks out of official cock cups, through official cock straws."

Nalani shakes in silent laughter, her face buried against my side.

"No disrespect, but the only person I want drinking my—"

"Don't you dare!" Nalani yells at me, and I can't help but laugh.

The goalie steps forward, holding out his phone, "Your parents own a business? A snack bar and surf and bait shop?"

I nod.

He lifts a shoulder. "Cock Bait will be everywhere."

The older woman takes his face in her hands. "You're genius."

Holy shit, I think. "Not sure that's something—"

"Cock Bait," she interrupts me, sweeping a hand across the air. "A little pop-up style snack stand, selling phallic-shaped snacks. It will bring more ladies to the arena, and the gays from the theatre to the ice."

"Grandma." The goalie holds back a laugh while shaking his head. It's obvious he adores his grandmother.

"Oh please, Dean, hockey needs the gays. Imagine how fabulous it would be."

"I'm not sure 'the gays' is the term—"

She waves him off. "I have my pronouns in my Instagram biography, Dean—I know a thing or two."

"How the hell did I lose this conversation?" Kosta mumbles, and Nalani giggles. "You wanna help me out here?"

"I think it's a great opportunity, but it's his decision."

"Mrs. Costello says you're KET. We have a chapter at Lincoln." He's now dangling *cock bait* in front of her.

"That's a lot to think about," I say over the crowd. "But my lady and I have plans tonight."

Coach Kosta hands me his card. "We'd love to have you next season."

I take his card to be polite.

"Let's get the hell out of here."

Three players—Leo Stone, Evan Smith, and Bass Guilietti—walk over.

Leo shakes his head. "Seriously, man, Kosta is the best and has great connections. We're all heading pro. Theo Rivera and you would be unstoppable."

"Something to think about." I shake all their hands as Nalani says goodbye to her new friend, Mrs. Costello. Then, finally, we're heading to the parking lot.

As I unlock the door to the old Jeep I bought when I arrived, with money I saved over the last three summers, I can't help but think about what endorsements would mean to my family, to me, to my community, and to the ability to take care of Nalani the way I want to.

I open the door, and she gets in. Before I close it, however, she turns toward me. "Talk to me."

"That woman was a trip."

"You have no idea." Her eyes widen, and so does her smile. Then she reaches out and takes my hand. "We can unpack that bag later. Koa, this could be life-changing."

I motion between us. "This is life-changing. I'm not willing to walk away from you."

"We have plenty of time to figure out what's best for *you*. Right now, you should kiss me—"

"Not here. I won't be able to stop."

Smiling, she turns in her seat. "Then let's go."

"Who's home?" she asks as I walk briskly toward the house.

"No one. We have the place to ourselves for three hours."

She tugs on my hand, and I stop and look back. "Then, why the race?" She points down at her feet. "These boots have killer heels."

I grab her hips. "I like you in flip flops." I then lift her up. "Wrap those legs arou—yeah, just like that."

She grabs my hair and pulls me toward her.

I'm not sure whose lips touch whose first, but there's no slow build-up to this. A fucking bomb goes off, one that changes me forever.

Her mouth is hot, and sweet—*so fucking sweet*—and again, I'm faced with the fact my imagination is shit. I look forward to being continually proven wrong by her.

I'm not sure how we make it in the house, let alone up the stairs and into my room, but we do. I even manage to get her boots off of her.

I set her on the bed, pull her shirt over her head, and toss it to the ground. "I can't wait to taste your tits."

She pushes down my track pants and gasps.

"Yeah, the tour." I chuckle. "Forgot to mention it."

She grips my cock.

"Fuuuck."

"It's pierced!"

I can't see her face—her hair is curtaining it—but I don't miss her tongue swirling around the tip of my dick, or her sucking on the barbell.

"Fuck yes," I groan. "But hold up." I lift her up from under her arms and stand her on the bed. She glares down at me. Then I unbutton her jeans and laugh. "I've been dreaming about devouring your pussy for years. I get to go first." After I remove her jeans and hot pink thong, I try to grab her.

Stepping back, she says, "Get naked."

I do so quickly.

"Now lay on the bed."

I arch a brow. "This how it's going to be?"

She rolls her eyes, and I do what I'm told.

When she stands over me, pretty pink pussy staring down at me, I groan, "Fuck yes."

She turns and faces the end of the bed, lowering herself.

I breathe out, "Goddess."

Our mouths are on each other, feasting, pleasuring, taking and giving, and when she comes, I bury my face against her, lapping up her wetness and bathing in her essence.

I try to stop her when my balls draw up.

"Clean?"

"Fuck yes," I groan.

She doesn't relent; she swallows everything I give her and doesn't stop until I'm bone dry. Then she moves off of me, pushing her hair over her shoulder and swiping the back of her hand over her lips. My heart briefly stops.

"I could lie here and look at you forever." I curl up to a seated position.

"I'd give my left nut to do that." Gripping the back of her head, I pull her into another kiss, expecting it to be less heated than the first. It's not.

I move over her, and she shoves her hand between us, dragging my still hard cock through her scorching wet folds.

I hold the sides of her face. "I'm not ever leaving you."

She nods. "I know."

Seven words between us mean more than the three words some people wait their entire lives to hear.

"I need to get a condom."

"I'm on the pill."

"Never gone raw." I push in slowly. She's so tight, so hot, so wet. "I'm never fucking leaving you. I wanna die inside your pussy."

She gasps as I push in further, eyes rolling back.

"You feel exquisite."

"You're huge."

"Am I hurting—"

"Doesn't matter," she pants out. "I was meant for you."

"Fucking hell," I groan as I bury my face in her neck and thrust in fully.

She whimpers, moving her hips slowly, getting accustomed to my size.

Quickly, we hit a rhythm, our bodies moving together in a way that I've never moved with anyone.

"Not ever going to be able to hold back with you," I groan out, seated deep inside her, before pulling back out and slamming in again, because I need to be in her. I need it more than I need air or water.

"Better not."

We go thrust for thrust until we both come again. This time, we do it looking into one another's eyes.

As we lie sated, still touching each other's bodies, she whispers, "I think you should consider Kosta's offer."

"You'd be willing to take that shot with me? Because I was serious when I told you I was never leaving you."

"Wouldn't have suggested it otherwise," she says, lips to my chest. "Next season?"

"Next season."

This hot little novella is part of the Taking The Shot series of stand-alone novels. It was written as a complete stand alone, short story for the Aloha Anthology.

THE MERCER CURSE

PREQUEL TO THE JEWELRY BOX SERIES

PEPPER WINTERS

To those who love a little pain with their pleasure.

CHAPTER 1 - Q

"*MAÎTRE?*"

I groaned and squeezed the back of my neck.

Whenever she called me that, bad things happened.

Hot, dark, deliciously bad things.

"*Esclave...*I told you. Give me thirty minutes and then I'll fuck you within an inch of your life. *Distrayez-moi et vous saignerez pour l'erreur.*" (Distract me and you'll be bleeding for the mistake).

The soft whispers of her bare feet on carpet sounded behind me. "I haven't come for you to pleasure me or punish me, master."

"Oh?" I ran my fingers over the figures of the latest building development in Amsterdam. "Why are you here then? Corrupting me like you always do..."

She didn't reply, creeping up behind me like a girl who wanted to provoke every despicable monster that lived within me.

I shuddered.

I felt the darkness unfurl and get ready to play.

The short leash I kept myself on had ensured I'd lived a lonely, miserable existence before Tess tripped over my doorstep, spat with such intoxicating fury, and ensured I tumbled right into the darkness with her.

She was the only slave I'd ever touched.

The only woman I'd ever loved.

The only mate I wanted, now and forever.

Doing my best to ignore her games, I kept my gaze on the spreadsheet. I'd been offered the deal by a middle-ranking Dutch Mafia member—a bastard who thought he could go behind his bosses and make some coin on the side by enticing me and my overly inflated bank account.

Pity for him, I knew exactly what he was and cast out my line, fishing with bait I knew he wouldn't be able to refuse.

I'd said I needed a special sort of incentive to work with him.

He'd laughed and told me to meet him in the red-light district.

I'd gone, purely because I'd heard rumours. And rumours always started in truth. He dabbled in slavery. Sold living, breathing girls and boys as if they were coins to buy him power.

It was up to me to see if that was true.

And do something about it if it was.

Despite my wife's fury, I'd flown to Amsterdam three days ago, allowed the bastard to seduce and flatter me, but the moment he'd closed the hotel suite's door and paraded a whimpering sixteen-year-old girl shot to hell with heroin toward me, he'd signed his death warrant.

The girl was a gift.

For me.

Like always.

My reputation preceded me in almost every country on this godforsaken planet.

Police knew who I was.

Criminals knew who I was.

Both of them had a different story, truth mixed with lies online, and neither of them were the wiser.

I'd swallowed down my rage as the broken, skinny girl stumbled toward me. I'd allowed her to crumple at my feet and pretended to listen to the bastard's demands.

I would've killed him right then but...he wasn't the only one trying to forge this alliance. Instead of giving into my bloodlust, I kept my smile in place, accepted the girl, and flew her back to my estate in France on my private plane.

His death would come...once I knew how many other girls he had and where I could find them.

Tess didn't blink an eye as I carried yet another slave into our marital home. She merely summoned Suzette, told Mrs Sucre to get cooking, and Franco pushed open the door to one of the many rooms for this purpose as I strode through opulence and tucked the drugged-up girl into safety.

The doctor had come.

Two days into the girl's detox and she'd finally stopped screaming. She'd now turned catatonic instead.

"You haven't touched me since you returned from Amsterdam," Tess murmured as she pushed me back in my chair and deliberately sat her pretty ass on my desk, squashing my paperwork. "You went without my permission.

You put yourself in danger. You made me mad, Q Mercer, and you know what happens when you do that."

I smirked and reclined. "Remind me, wife…what happens when I make you mad?"

"I make you lose your mind."

My blood heated. "And what is your plan tonight, *esclave*? How are you planning on making me come undone?" My hand dropped between my legs, fisting the hard-on she caused every time I caught her scent. "Because I will be coming…whether you will too is a matter of discussion."

"Oh, you'll make me come, husband. You won't have a choice."

I chuckled and stroked myself. "Bold, Tess. Very bold."

"You left me." Her hands went to the belt holding her satiny, sexy dressing gown closed. The faint lilac gown had looked stunning on its hanger in the lingerie shop in Amsterdam, but on her?

She made it fucking sinful.

"You brought home another woman." She unthreaded the bow, letting the material slip like water from her delectable skin. Skin I'd marked, bit, branded, and whipped. Skin that bloomed a perfect shade of red. Skin that always healed so I could do it all over again.

A tremor ran through me as my cock hit full mast, growing painful in my slacks. With steady hands, I reached for my belt.

Her eyes shot to where I unhooked the leather, no doubt remembering the many times I'd had her spread over my desk, her hips in the air, and the crack of my belt landing against her ass.

"Go on…" I whispered, my French accent thickening like it always did when she tempted me. "Tell me why I should tolerate you being mad at me for saving yet another slave or doing what I must to repent for what I am."

"What you are?" With a shudder, she spread her legs, planting her heels on my rock-hard thighs. "What you are is *mine*. My monster. And I want to get mauled." The gown fell away, leaving swathes of skin from collarbone to pussy. The swell of her breasts teased me, the Q branded over her heart enraged me, and the wetness glimmering on her thighs fucking broke me.

I groaned. "*Je vais me régaler de toi, femme.*" (I'm going to feast on you, wife).

"Promise?" Her hand trailed down her belly, heading south.

Unzipping my slacks, I pulled my cock out, digging my thumb painfully into the tip. I couldn't look away as she swirled her clit. Her long, wavy blonde hair cascaded over her shoulders, the soft light from my desk lamp caping her in shadows and secrets.

Tess had always been beautiful. Even when she'd broken my black fucking heart, she'd been the most stunning creature I'd ever seen.

But now that she was my wife?

Now that she mine in every way—blooded, bonded, and betrothed…I couldn't look at another woman without comparing them. Comparing their strength to hers. Their light to hers. Her ability to make me feel when everyone else in the world made me shut down.

"Don't you want a taste, *maître*?"

"*Merde*." My heart pounded. My ears rushed with white noise. I wanted her moaning in pleasure and screaming in pain. I wanted to hug her and hurt her at the same time. I wanted her blood on my tongue and her cum on my fingers. I both loved and hated her. Her power. Her fight. Her undeniable claim over me.

The one girl who'd come to me unbroken.

The one girl to break me in return.

She moaned as her finger dipped inside. The nightgown darkened beneath her ass with her need.

Swallowing hard, I growled, "If you get that paperwork wet, you're in trouble."

Moaning, she tipped her head back. "You know what your threats do to me."

"Fuck yes, I do." I shot up from my chair, fisting my cock with one hand and snatching at her hip with the other. Yanking her to the edge of the desk, paper fluttered to the floor, but I didn't give a fuck.

Tess deserved to pay for making me this senseless. She needed another endless night in chains while I did whatever I damn well wanted to her.

I wanted to taste.

But not the part of her she was expecting.

Grabbing the sharp letter opener glinting by my lamp, I dropped my head between her thighs. The scent of her arousal made a ripple of need work up my cock. She always did this to me. Made me too eager. Too willing to blur the lines between husband and beast.

Her breath turned thin and quick as I blew a stream of air on her clit.

"Q. Yes. God, please…"

Keeping my eyes locked on the most vulnerable part of her—the part no one else would ever see or touch unless they wanted to have their heart ripped out by my bare hands—I dragged the letter opener along the inside of her trembling thigh.

She stiffened at the sharpness.

She stopped breathing as I dug the point into the crease where her pussy met her leg. Such a delicate place. Paper thin skin, easily damaged, and beautifully bruised with spiderwebs of arteries and veins.

"You couldn't give me an hour to finish, wife? You had to come and interrupt me."

"I missed you."

"I wouldn't admit that if I were you." I dipped my head and ran my tongue from her wet entrance to her tight little clit. "I'll get a god complex."

"Don't care." She shuddered as I nipped her, dragging my tongue back to her entrance, my hand tightening around the letter opener as a flush of her desire coated my lips.

"You don't care that I hold your life in my hands?" I bit her again, making her cry out. "You don't care that I get off knowing I could so easily hurt you?"

She squirmed on my desk, locking onto the two words that'd become an awful aphrodisiac between us. Between a sadist and his masochist. Between two monsters who'd found each other in the dark.

"Hurt me," she breathed.

"I thought you'd never ask." I fell on her pussy, lapping up her every drop of need, biting, laving, driving my tongue as deep as it would go. Her moans came quick with intoxicating gasps.

I let her think I would take her to the edge. That I would let her come on my tongue. Her thighs clenched, her toes dug into my thighs where she still had her feet planted. Her moans turned to whimpers. The first squeeze of her pussy around my tongue—

Ripping my face from her, I soared upright and pressed the letter opener right over her jugular.

My cock speared up, sticking out from my suit. I was fully dressed, and my Tess was naked on an altar to be eaten. So pretty. So pure. So perfect.

My teeth ached to bite. My tongue burned to taste.

Her eyes met mine with a flash of condemning black fire that also burned inside me. Fire that only grew hotter the longer we played.

Ever so slowly, she turned her neck, surrendering to me, giving me every shred of trust and submission. "Do it."

My lips pulled back as I traced her vein with the small stationery dagger.

My black heart pounded. My lips, still coated in her desire, stung for a different sort of flavour. One far more intimate than sexual pleasure. One of sickness and depravity. One that I needed to sate because her blood was my temporary cure. A shot of medicine to restrain myself for another day.

I didn't look away from her as I pressed the dagger just a little harder.

She flinched and moaned.

Everything inside me froze into predatory stillness as the first bead of ruby welled on her throat. The colour. The glisten. Her lifeforce and very essence.

Fuck.

Crushing her into my desk, I rocked my cock through her drenched folds as my mouth latched onto the droplet.

The moment her sweet, metallic, hot, hot, hot blood soaked into my tongue, I snapped.

She wanted to be fucked?

She just got her wish.

"Spread," I snarled, pushing her knees as wide as they'd go.

Lying back on my desk, her hair strewn over my laptop and other junk, she presented herself to me.

Tossing the letter opener away, my eyes locked on another droplet of crimson as it welled down her skin, down and down, coming to a stop in the hollow of her collarbone.

Fuck.

Me.

Dragging her hips the final inch off the desk, I sucked in a haggard breath. "Who are you, *esclave?*"

Her smile glinted with sharp canines. "*Le vôtre. Je suis à vous.*" (Yours. I'm yours).

My vision shot black.

I thrust.

The sensation of her body closing hot and wet around mine made all the blackness, all the wickedness, all the perversion inside me snarl.

I wanted to break her apart as I withdrew and plunged back in.

I wanted her screaming my name in both pleasure and terror.

My mouth locked over that little droplet of blood. Cooler, less viscous, already beginning to congeal.

I lost myself to her.

Fucking her against my desk, I snatched her jaw and planted my lips over hers.

I groaned as her tongue instantly stroked mine. Fierce and snake-fast, she met me with war and violence.

The desk creaked as I turned manic.

The sounds of our flesh slapping together was a perfect melody.

Something crashed to the floor, I didn't care.

Tess's moans turned to animalistic grunts, I rejoiced.

My own roar built louder and louder in my belly the longer I drove myself deeper and deeper into my wife, punishing her, remembering her, eradicating any distance of the past few days.

Her breakable hands landed on my cheeks as I fucked her like I despised her. Her nails dug into my five o'clock shadow, threatening to draw my blood just like I'd drawn hers.

We were sick.

We were contagious.

We were free in this cage of our own making.

"Fuck, Tess. I can't—"

"Come. Come, *maître.*"

It was her job to obey me. Her purpose to submit. But in that moment, she was my master and I let go.

The stinging, shooting waves of release jettisoned out of me and into her. Splashing deep, wake after wake, full of bone-snapping pleasure.

Her hand shot between her legs, rubbing herself as I watched my cock spear in and out of her.

With a scream, she shattered, milking me in thick, erotic waves, dragging out my own release until we both collapsed onto the desk. Her bare chest panted beneath my suit-covered one. I pressed a worshipping kiss to the small wound I'd caused. "*Je t'aime*, Tess. With all my heart."

She stretched beneath me, making my cock hit different parts of her. "I love you too. With every part of me."

I kissed her sweetly, reverently.

What did I do to deserve this minx?

How had I been lucky enough to marry this wonderful woman?

Whatever it was, I was grateful. So fucking grateful she was mine.

My evening of work faded beneath images of taking her to our bedroom and pulling out the toy chest. I'd cuff her to the foot of the bed and—

"Eh, *maître*?"

Ah, fucking hell.

Having Tess call me her master made me ready to rut like a beast. Having my staff call me their master sent cold water of reality dousing over me.

Freezing, I glowered over my shoulder.

Suzette stood with her back to the open door, her maid uniform pressed and neat like always. Clearly, she'd seen Tess spread half-naked with my cock impaled inside her, but I didn't try to cover up or explain.

She'd seen far worse.

All of our staff had.

Because...our household was unique.

Tess and I's relationship wasn't explainable to outsiders yet those who lived with us accepted us. They were trustworthy. They were our friends...family.

No one blinked an eye if Tess appeared at breakfast with teeth marks on her throat or crawled beneath the table at the snap of my fingers for her to suck me.

It'd taken a while to accept that they wouldn't judge who I was. And even longer to indulge in my deviant appetites.

But now, nothing could stop me because...I was happy.

I was fucking *happy* even with scum running around in the world. Buying and trading, kidnapping and trafficking. Scum that would one day die by my hand or someone else's. Scum that I used to believe lived inside me until Tess showed me I only wanted to kill her because she was my mirroring piece. My reflection of depravity. My monster just like I was hers.

"Not now, Suzette," Tess moaned and flopped her wrist like some frustrated damsel. "Can't you see we're a little busy."

Suzette's soft laughter came from the hallway. "I did see and I can't unsee, *mon ami*. But...Q is needed downstairs. There's someone here to see him."

"What?" Sighing hard, I withdrew and stuffed my wet cock into my dark grey slacks and zipped up. "Who the hell is making house calls at seven p.m. on a Sunday?" I rolled my eyes as I helped Tess up and wrapped her in her dressing gown. "It's not my asshat of a friend Frederick is it? If it is, tell him I'm about to play with my wife and whatever nonsense he has to say, it can wait until tomorrow at the office."

"It's not Frederick," Suzette said quietly. "It's eh...I don't really know how to say this, Q, but...it's your brother."

CHAPTER 2 - Q

BROTHER?

I didn't have a fucking brother.

I was an only child.

Well, only *legitimate* child.

My raping cunt of a father sired many others, with many other women who weren't my alcoholic mother. Other kids who I'd found hidden in a room attached to the stable block tucked in the estate's sprawling gardens. Kids ranging from infants to almost teens. All of them scared into silence and beaten into obedience. Their short lives used as a leash to control the unwilling harem my father kept in his bed.

Tess chased me down the stairs, her hands tying her belt, hiding away her nakedness. Rounding on her at the bottom, I snarled, "No way is another man seeing you in that scrap of a gown. I can see your nipples, *esclave*."

"It's your cum trickling down my leg, no one else's."

My heart kicked. "And let's keep it that way. Go." I pointed back up the stairs. "Go and change. Give me ten minutes. I want to speak to him alone."

Her eyes flashed with familiar grey-blue fire.

Catching her around the nape, I breathed into her ear, "And don't rinse my cum away. I want you sticky and used. I want you to stay in that state until I have you again tonight."

Her lips twitched as she bowed her head, then flew back the way she'd come.

I had to readjust my cock again.

Damn woman.

Suzette skirted past me, heading to Franco's awaiting arm. He hugged her and shrugged at me. "What's going on?" he asked quietly.

I raised an eyebrow. "Who the fuck knows. Extortion? A threat? If he thinks he can milk me for money, he's going to find out it's a very bad idea to mess with me."

"He's in the library," Suzette said, keeping her voice down. "When I first opened the door, I swear I was looking at a younger version of you, Q, but...different too. I knew he had your blood even before he told me who he was."

"And who is he?" I raked a hand through my short dark hair, doing my best to stop thinking about Tess and my cum leaking down her leg.

"His name is Henri Ward."

"Nationality?"

Where did this little bastard end up when I'd shot my father and freed all his slaves? I'd done my best to give each woman a substantial fortune to live off after a lifetime of horror. And for those women with rape-begot children, I'd forged any document they asked for, then flew them to whatever country they wanted to build a new life in.

Over the years, I'd kept tabs on them. I'd ensured they'd found some semblance of a happy existence. A few had died. A few lived on. And a few had obviously told their offspring about their true origins, even though that'd been my one condition.

I would protect them financially. I would atone for what my father had done to them but...under no circumstances were they to tell them about me or my father.

I had enough shit to deal with without impromptu family reunions.

"He has an English accent but he spoke French to me," Suzette replied.

"Age?" I shot a look at the closed doors to the library. The glass wasn't opaqued and I could see a shadow of someone standing by the limited edition leather bound classics by the fireplace.

"I'm guessing late twenties? Maybe a bit younger?"

Fuck.

He would've been one of the older ones in my father's stable then.

Did he remember living here?

Did he remember me marching into the midst of them, covered in patriarchal blood, gun in hand, and leading a trail of broken women to claim their bastards?

My hand shook a little as I shoved it into my pocket and spun on my heel. Tess appeared at the top of the stairs. The same stairs I'd stood on when Franco pushed her over my doorstep and commanded her to kneel before me.

She'd refused then and she'd refused me ever since.

Pity for both of us, her refusals got me hard and her wet and we'd become a match made in fucked up heaven.

"You." I pointed a finger in her face. "Stay there. I need to do this on my own." My eyes narrowed and I added a tad more gently, like a doting lover should, "We'll finish our conversation after."

Her lips quirked. "Conversation, huh? Very well, I very much look forward to *conversing* with you, husband."

My palm itched to remind her of her place all while I fought the lust and darkly tangled love she always drowned me in. "Behave and obey, Tess. Don't interrupt."

Stalking to the library, I wrenched open the double doors, and came face to face with my half-brother.

One of many.

Hopefully, the only one who would ever know of my existence.

He was tall.

Maybe a shade taller than me.

Broad shouldered and lean waisted, with the type of physique that said he'd been in a few fights in his time and won.

He spun around as I closed the doors behind me and flicked the switch for privacy. The glass instantly went dark, blocking my nosy wife's eyes, giving me time to assess this new threat.

Because he was a threat.

A big one.

Motherfucking huge.

I'd chosen my family.

I didn't want any more springing from the shadows.

Especially ones with my father's blood running in their veins.

I had firsthand knowledge of that curse.

The Mercer Curse that'd been passed down by a man who raped, mutilated, and abused. I wouldn't will it on anyone. And I had every intention of avoiding all those who shared it because chances were very fucking high that I'd have to kill them for the very reasons I strived to deserve to live.

I hunted monsters.

I killed paedophiles and tore out the hearts of traffickers.

I made others hurt, all while the one person who should hurt the most was me.

The moment our gazes locked, he froze.

Grey eyes.

Stern mouth.

Stare of a beast.

He shared my unfortunate sharp widow's peak, same short dark hair, same five o'clock shadow that refused to be tamed by a razor, no matter how many times I shaved.

His jaw he'd inherited from our sadistic father, his cheekbones from an unfamiliar slave. His brows furrowed, casting his eyes in deeper shadows. His fists curled, matching mine, sensing my unwelcome without saying a word.

Neither of us spoke for the longest moment. Both assessing. Both forming conclusions on faces alone.

Finally, he said, "*Elle disait la verité.*" (She was telling the truth).

I stiffened. Who was telling the truth? His mother? Some woman I'd done my best to protect, even at a personal cost?

"*Je suis désolé.*" (I'm sorry). He tipped his chin, fighting for social etiquette. "*Je suis désolé de faire irruption comme ça mais…je n'avais pas le choix.*" (I'm sorry to barge in like this but…I didn't have a choice).

Suzette was right. His French was impeccable but the faintest English accent lurked beneath. Which slave was he welped to? Which one broke her promise and told him about me?

A headache bloomed in my temples as I tried to recall the numerous women my father kept. Some from Asia, others from far off continents. There'd been a few from the United Kingdom but not many.

Prowling forward, I did my best to keep my voice civil. "You may speak in English."

"Okay…" He never took his eyes off me as I chose one of the matching wingbacks and sat stiffly. Copying me, he took the other one, our bodies facing one another, the empty fireplace full of shadows. "I, eh…there's no easy way to say this so—"

"You're the son of a slave. She told you about your origins and that my father was the cunt that created you. Am I correct?"

He stiffened. Clearing his throat, he nodded once. "That's about the gist of it."

"And why did you think you'd be welcome here?"

His eyes narrowed. "Because we're blood. Because I wanted to meet my—"

"We are not brothers. We merely share the unfortunate disease of similar DNA."

"It's because of that DNA that I'm here."

"In a place where you're not wanted."

Temper flared over his face. "Look, all I'm after is—"

"Money?"

His shoulders swooped back with offense. "No. Fuck. Is that what you think? That I've come here with my hand out?"

"Didn't you? You must've researched me. You must know who I am if you've been clever enough to find my personal address."

The faintest tinge of embarrassment covered his cheeks. "I'll admit, I did spend a fair deal of time learning what I could about you."

I went deathly still. "And...what did you find out?"

He studied my coiled muscles. He read my body language correctly: understanding I was moments away from snapping and throwing him out of my home.

Would he run or would he fight?

Leaning back in the chair, doing his best to project calm, he said, "You're successful. Beyond successful. Your company is worth billions. You own real estate globally. On paper, you are nothing more than a bigshot corporate bastard who's probably done his fair share of dodgy dealings to get where he is but..."

"But?" I snarled.

"I also found a few articles on your wife. The interview you both gave of how she came into your life. A slave you fell in love with. A girl who returned to you even when you freed her."

Fuck.

That article had been Tess's idea and one I'd spent a fuck-ton of money suppressing ever since. My role in slaughtering traffickers relied on them being confused on who I truly was. Sure, it didn't hurt for them to see things online stating me as a wholesome family man. Someone trying to do the right thing. If anything, it helped form the persona that I was a straying son of a bitch who liked to keep broken women and cheat on his meek little wife, but I would prefer not to have criminals think the way to ruin me was to take Tess.

That'd already happened.

It'd almost killed me finding her.

The heart of the man who took her still rotted beneath a rose bush outside.

And despite all my efforts to find her, fix her, and love her the way she needed me to love her, she'd shut down, shut me out, and put me through absolute fucking hell.

I traced one of the faint silver scars on my face from when she'd whipped me. A whipping that'd taken all my strength to endure but it had brought her back to me.

I'd chosen love over loneliness and some dark part of my heart nudged me to listen to this man.

I knew what it was like to hit rock bottom.

To feel so alone that death lured like a welcome utopia.

Forcing myself to relax a little, I softened my snarl. "Seeing as you know so much about me...let's talk about you." Steepling my fingers and resting my elbows on the wingback arms, I looked him up and down. "Henri Ward. Is that your real name? Where are you from? Why are you here? Tell me in as few words as possible why I should tolerate you in my home and why I should trust a thing out of your mouth."

Silence fell as he shifted uncomfortably. His lips twisted as if he chewed on words and discarded them before selecting a few and saying, "Can I have your vow that you'll listen with no judgement? The whole journey here I promised myself I wouldn't do this. That I'd follow the usual expectations of conversation between strangers, even if those strangers share blood. I wasn't going to blurt out my life story or every sordid mistake I've ever made. I mean...who does that? Who barges into someone else's house and vomits up their worst confessions. But..." He shrugged. "If I can't be honest with my brother, then who can I be? Chances are you won't want a thing to do with me anyway, so what have I lost by speaking the truth for the first time in my godforsaken life? I can't tell a therapist. I can't tell a friend. I definitely can't tell a lover. I've got no one else and...well, that makes you uniquely qualified for me to—"

"Get on with it," I snapped. "Speak."

He hung his head. "I need to be fucking honest for the first time in my life. I need...fuck, I need." He sighed and looked at the floor. "I-I was going to kill myself last month."

I sucked in a breath, shooting a glance at the library doors to make sure Tess stayed away like a good *esclave*.

"Go on," I said quietly.

He didn't look up, preferring to keep his eyes on the swirling, rich patterns of the carpet. "I...I'm sick." He growled under his breath. "No, that's wrong. I'm diseased. Not physically but spiritually. There's something broken inside me. I've felt it ever since I hit puberty...fuck." He laughed coldly. "That's a lie. I've felt it for far longer than that. Even when I was a boy, I felt different whenever I'd see violence in a movie or watch lovers have a quarrel in public. I'd get hot and tight and I didn't understand what the crawling, gnawing sensation was until I had my first wet dream."

I waited for him to gather his thoughts, not making it any easier on him. I might not care what he had to say, but I gave him the quietness he needed to spill his confessions.

"I dreamed of blood."

It was my turn to stiffen.

His story so far sounded eerily close to mine.

"I dreamed of fucking a girl and hurting her." He winced. "I woke and found my sheets a mess. And ever since that day, I can't get those fantasies out of my head. I hid from them for as long as I could. I had a girlfriend in high school—for a couple of weeks at least. But she dumped my ass when she got sick of my lack of interest. I'd burn in shame whenever she'd reach for me because her innocent, gentle hand only made me soft." He wiped his mouth. "There I was, a fifteen-year-old guy, and I couldn't get it up. But whenever I'd break my self-control and watch porn late at night, I'd get hard as a fucking rock."

"What sort of porn?" I asked.

He didn't raise his eyes. "Bad stuff. Choking. Breath play. BDSM but... not the role play kind. The real kind where the tears are real, the pain is real, the blood is...real."

I dropped my hands and gripped my knees. "Why are you telling me this? You're a complete stranger. No one in their right mind would come to a stranger's house and confess all the shit inside them."

His grey eyes met mine, swimming in troubles and begging for salvation. "I-I have no where else to go. My mother....she, eh—" He cleared his throat. "She's been ill for most of my life. Recurring breast cancer with periods of remission. It finally claimed her last month. One of the last things she told me was who my father was."

Ah, so it was a deathbed confession.

Something that'd eaten her alive and now she'd passed that demon onto her only son.

Stupid woman.

Why couldn't she have let that filth die with her?

She'd only condemned her son to a worser fate.

"Is that why you wanted to kill yourself?" I asked clinically, feeling no emotion to the thought of him alive or in a grave.

"No. I mean...it was the slippery slope that led to it but no. I loved her deeply. She was my only family. She told me that my father ran off when she was pregnant with me. That she had no other kin to turn to. How she ended up in Devon when we aren't originally English is a question she didn't have time to answer."

"You're not English?"

"I have a feeling she might have been French Canadian. She raised me bilingual but her accent never sounded Parisian. She also taught me Spanish but never told me why, or how she knew it."

I frowned, drawn in despite myself. "So you're raised in a village where no one really knew you and then a month after your mother dies, you decide to commit suicide?"

He flashed me a tight smile. "Sounds pathetic when you say it like that. It makes me sound like some poor little boy who can't survive without his mother." Sighing hard, he said, "The thing is...with her gone, I allowed the parts of myself that I've always suppressed out to play."

Ah, fuck.

That wasn't good news.

I could almost see where he was going with this.

Where I'd gone.

Why I'd forbidden myself from touching a woman unless it was a paid professional, until Tess came along. Why I'd murdered my father in cold blood and spent my entire life repenting for what he'd done.

I couldn't cure myself.

I couldn't turn off the blackness inside me.

I could merely live within the cage Tess kept me content in, ever so fucking grateful that she could withstand my violence, my sickness, my curse.

"You killed a girl?" I kept my voice deliberately calm.

His answer would determine on him walking out of here alive or dying right there in the wingback.

He caught my gaze, flinching at whatever he saw in me. "No, I didn't go that far. But...I did hurt her. Badly. I was the idiot who took a one-night stand back to my family home, where I'd nursed my sick mother for the last seven months, and spilled her blood all over my childhood bedroom."

My hands balled. My gut churned. My mouth watered to end him.

"And you're here for me to bail you out? To get you off a criminal charge?"

"No." He slouched into the chair as if he wanted all his sins to devour him. "I know what I did. I know how badly I fucked up. I compensated her, and she didn't press charges. Thank God." Licking his bottom lip, he took his time forming his next sentence. "I came because...the moment I held that knife to my wrists—ready to draw my own blood for drawing hers—I remembered what my mother had said. That she'd been taken and raped for over a decade. That she'd birthed me in some chateau in France. That she'd done her best to raise me when she was granted the permission to spend time with me."

I studied him.

Did he remember that time?

Did he remember me?

His eyes locked on mine; he answered my unspoken question. "I thought I'd recall something from my childhood driving up here. I thought for sure I'd recognise you if what she said is true. How could I have spent the first eight years of my life in a place I can't remember? How could I have a half-brother that I've never met? How could I have this disease inside me and have no way to get rid of it?"

The doors cracked open as Tess stuck her head in. "Q...everything okay?"

My heart skipped then hardened. "Not now, Tess."

"But—"

"I said...not now."

Her eyes fought mine. I had no doubt I'd get a fucking tongue lashing later, but I didn't want her hearing this. Not because she couldn't tolerate the darkness Henri spoke about but because she'd cajole me into letting him stay.

She'd force me to welcome him into the family.

She'd command me to give him somewhere safe.

She'd do that because...he was me.

This fucking stranger was *me*.

And it twisted me up in ways I didn't want to acknowledge.

I want him gone.

Now.

Shifting in my chair, I went to stand as Tess obediently drew the doors closed, leaving us alone. "Look, I'm sorry for your loss and for everything you're dealing with, but you have to leave—"

"Wait." Henri shot to his feet, towering over me while I still sat.

Ever so slowly, calculatingly, I stood until our eyes were in line, our hearts at the same height. "Don't *ever* think you can command me in my own home, boy."

"Boy? I'm only eight years younger than you."

"Just because you saw my date of birth online doesn't mean—"

"I know because my mother told me you were sixteen when you shot your father. That you freed them. That you did everything you could to get them home to their own families."

I froze.

Fuck, how much had this woman told him and how the hell did he not remember a thing from before?

Not that I had many memories of that time.

I'd deliberately forced them away. Preferring to forget what went on in this house before it was mine.

Henri stepped into me, our chests almost touching. "That's why I'm here, brother. Not for your money or your help with whatever sickness stalks inside me. At least I know now where that sickness comes from. I didn't come to blame you. I didn't come to thank you. I came because...all my life I've always felt alone. My mother loved me but I always got the feeling she hated me too. Which makes sense now I know who created me. I've always done my best to be good. To obey the rules. To be like the others. But...I've never fit in. I never wanted what others wanted. I barely sleep because I don't have the strength to dream such sickening things. I barely exist because I'm fucking petrified I'm going to slip and hurt someone. I hate myself. I hate what I am and I hate that I'm so fucking alone."

Breathing hard, he went to the fireplace and ran a finger over one of the very few pictures of Tess and me. It'd been taken outside in full summer with the sun shining and Tess sprawled over my belly and me on my back. We'd both fallen asleep because the night before I'd proposed to her, put my ring on her finger, and then seared my brand into her chest.

She'd branded me in return.

We'd fucked like absolute deviants.

And then, we'd passed out like teenagers on the lawn.

I smothered my snarl as he ran his finger over Tess's perfect face. Hanging his head, he murmured, "I want what you have. I came here to ask if you suffer the way I do. If you fight every damn day not to hurt those you desire but...I don't need to ask. I know." Turning to face me, he shrugged. "I saw it in the way you spoke to her. The way you looked at her. The way she looked at you. You walk a fine line of disrespect and devotion and I...I want that."

I bared my teeth. "You think I can snap my fingers and conjure you a wife?" I laughed. "You'd be better off asking me for money."

Crossing his arms, all his grief and loneliness vanished beneath a mask of ferocity. It was like looking in a fucking mirror and I hated it. "I don't want money and I don't expect you to find me a wife. I've long come to terms with the fact that I'll exist alone and I'll die alone but...in the small window of time I have left, I would very much like to know what it feels like to belong."

"Belong?" I crossed my arms, matching him. "What's that supposed to mean?"

"It means I want my brother. I want at least one person to know who I truly am with no fear of being arrested or—"

"I'd do worst than just arrest you," I said. "If you'd killed that girl, you wouldn't be breathing right now."

He froze. He studied me to see if I lied. When he found no such evidence, he braced his shoulders. "So...you didn't just stop murdering with our father? You kill other men like him? Other men like...us?"

Jesus Christ, how did he jump to that conclusion so quickly and why did I like it?

Why did my interest in him creep from intolerance to mild curiosity?

"I'd be careful if I were you." I stalked around the library, moving toward the window. The very window where Tess had made me swear a blood oath to try loving her. She'd returned to me after I'd set her free. She'd become my air, my reason, my gravity and—

"Q, I'm sorry, but I really must interrupt." The object of my affection and annoyance came bounding through the doors again, heading straight toward Henri.

I pinched the bridge of my nose. "Fucking hell, Tess. You try my patience."

She flipped me the bird as she stopped in front of my unknown brother. She gasped as she studied his face. I growled as she cupped his cheek and traced his cheekbones that weren't mine on a face that clearly shared my genes.

"*Esclave, enlève tes mains de lui.*" (Get your hands off him).

Spinning to face me, she didn't flinch as I crossed the room and grabbed her wrist, tugging her away from Henri.

Her eyes widened, brimming with joy. "Oh my God, it's real. He's really related to you." She looked back at Henri. "I-I have no idea how this is possible—"

"It's possible because my father was a raping bastard who sowed seeds that shouldn't be sowed. You've met him and now he's leaving. Say goodbye—"

"Goodbye?" Her nose wrinkled. "But he just got here."

"And now he's leaving.

"But—"

"Say *au revoir*, Tess."

"Please..." Henri was wise enough not to come near us but the smile he shot my wife almost made me strangle him. "It's an honour to meet my sister-in-law."

"Nothing about her is yours," I snarled. "It's time you left—"

"Will you think on my request at least?" Henri asked. "It would mean—"

"What request?" Tess asked, pulling her wrist from my pinching hold. "I deserve to know. You're family." She elbowed me in the side. "He's family, Q. Your brother."

"Half-brother." I scowled, rubbing where her sharp little appendage caught me.

"He's still blood."

"Yes, and he likes to *spill* blood," I hissed.

Her eyebrows raised. "As do you if I'm not mistaken."

Henri sucked in a breath.

I groaned. "*Esclave*, you're really not—"

"*Esclave*?" Henri scowled. "You call your wife *slave*? What the fuck?"

Tess grinned. "Think of it as sweetheart or darling. I always knew, even from the very first moment he called me that, that he was madly in love with me."

"Madly obsessed with you more like," I muttered. "Dangerously obsessed. There's a difference."

"Not for us there isn't." She winked. "And we all lived happily ever after, even with your fetishes."

Goddammit, this woman.

Pressing a kiss to my cheek, she waved between me and Henri. "So... what's the story? You've been in here ages and are still glowering daggers at each other. Let's go get a drink. Have some dinner. Mrs Sucre is getting mighty tetchy that her souffle is ruined because we didn't eat it in time."

"Tess, my love." I gritted my teeth. "Please leave. I'll escort Henri out and—"

"Dinner would be great," Henri interrupted, throwing a hesitant smile at Tess. "If it wouldn't be too much trouble?"

"Trouble? Oh, no, Mrs Sucre always cooks far too much. You can meet Suzette and Franco and—"

"He's not staying, Tess." I did my best to hold on to my temper, failing by the second.

"Why not?"

"Because he's not welcome."

"So that's what this is about?" Tess asked, flicking both of us a look. "Henri came looking for family and you're refusing to give him one? How can you not welcome your own flesh and blood, Q?"

Fucking woman.

She'd always read me too easily.

Always put her nose in where it didn't belong.

Before I could form an answer, Henri murmured, "I don't know a thing about either of you, and you don't know a thing about me but…I feel more myself in the twenty minutes I've been here than I have in my entire life. I feel like I can breathe. Like I'm…free. Not fully. I doubt I'll ever know what true freedom feels like, but I do feel as if I can relax a little. Like I won't fuck everything up by saying the wrong thing or admitting who I truly am." His grey eyes landed on mine. "If I can have that freedom for a few more hours before I'm evicted from your lives, then—"

"Nonsense." Tess smiled kindly. "You're my brother-in-law—"

"He's nothing to you, Tess. Just like you are nothing to him," I snapped.

"Jeez, stop being such a monster, *maître*."

Everything inside me went still, dark, dangerous. "Careful, Tess."

She drew herself up but didn't back down. "He came for you, Q. Don't you see? He needs you."

Henri wisely stayed silent.

I tripped into Tess's beguiling blue-grey eyes.

I could never refuse her anything when she got stroppy like this. Fiery and fierce and tempting my palm to bring her back into line all while she made me fucking beg.

"What do you need from him to prove he's looking for nothing more than company?" Tess crossed her arms.

At least she'd changed into a faint blue jumper and jeans. She looked young and innocent, belying the temptress beneath. The temptress that'd turned me inside out and back to front all because she could handle the filth inside me.

An idea sparked.

An idea I tried to crush but couldn't.

She called me a monster?

I didn't like that label but it fit.

It had always fit.

I *was* a monster.

To my enemies and my loved ones.

The curse never lifted.

The needs never faded.

I'd learned to exist despite them.

I was happy in *spite* of them.

But I remembered all too well the haunting, harrowing existence I'd lived before Tess came along. The agony of wanting what I couldn't have. The despicable need burning me up. The lust that came with so much disgust and shame.

If Henri fought such battles, I wasn't surprised he'd turned to suicide.

I'd contemplated it a few times.

But each time I sank into such self-pity, I threw myself deeper into my work. I saved more slaves. I rescued those that'd been hurt by men like me. I did my best to erase my shame by giving back those lives that were ruined because of bastards that deserved to be dead.

Wiping my mouth, I shook my head a little.

The idea kept evolving, spreading, unfolding like a map before me.

He could be useful.

He could be my secret weapon to infiltrate the clubs that knew who I truly was.

The traffickers I'd dealt with in the past and managed to slaughter, only for new ones to spring up like weeds, fully aware of what I did and always one step ahead of my usual methods to hunt them down.

Lowering my hand, I studied Henri with new eyes.

Would he have the strength?

Would he lose his rotten soul if I threw him into the darkness where we both belonged?

"What are you thinking, Q?" Tess asked quietly. "I know that look and it's not good."

Ignoring my meddling little wife, I locked gazes with my half-brother and said the words that would ultimately break him or save him. "You want to belong? You want a ready-made family that sees you and accepts you? Fine."

Henri sucked in a harsh breath. "Really? Fuck, I can't thank—"

"There's a club. It's called The Jewelry Box and is run by a sadist called Victor Grand. I've been trying to bring him down for years. I don't know where his club is, but I do know he's trafficked hundreds, possibly thousands, of girls and boys through his doors. Not one has ever been found. All of them lost without a trace. I can't touch him because I have no one to infiltrate his operation. His intelligence is clever and always seems to find a link between the mercenaries I send in and me. He's ruthless, calculating, and a dangerous son of a bitch."

"Q...don't say what I think you're about to say," Tess murmured.

"I will welcome you with open arms, brother." I smiled coldly. "All you have to do is prove yourself."

"Prove myself?" Henri asked, equally as coldly. "Prove myself how?"

"Go to Paris. Befriend whoever you need to befriend to get an invitation into The Jewelry Box. I'll put a tracker on you and, if and when you're welcomed into this sordid, sickening world, you will lead me right to his estate and will help me exterminate him, once and for all."

"You want me to infiltrate a sex ring?" Henri's face went white. "I've just told you why I can't be around that sort of thing. Why I'm here instead of in a ditch somewhere. I-I wouldn't be able to survive the temptation."

I shrugged. "That's your problem, not mine. You asked to be accepted. I'm saying I'll accept you, but only if you prove that you're like me. That you suffer the same desires. Drown beneath the same darkness, yet you're strong enough to stay in the light. It takes strength to survive the curse we've been given. And if you're too weak, then...I want nothing to do with you."

Wrapping my arm around Tess, I led her toward the door. Before heading into the foyer and the dining room beyond, I turned to look back at Henri. "You can think it over tonight. I'll give you a bed. I'll tolerate your presence. But until you prove that you aren't like our father. That you won't give in and become him. That you're better than all the evil swimming in our veins...you won't be permitted to stay."

Henri raked a hand through his hair. "And if I don't?"

"If you don't?" I gave my half-brother my final promise. "If you fail at helping me destroy Victor and his Jewelry Box. If you fail to resist the temptation of broken slaves, bound and ready to serve your darkest whim. If you fail at keeping your dick in your pants and your hands free from blood, then...so help you, I will find you, I will hurt you, and you will wish you never set foot in my house, kin or no kin."

"You'd kill me?" Henri winced. "You'd kill me just because I'm sired by the same bastard who sired you?"

"I'd kill you because I know what you suffer. I know how close I've come to hurting others. Therefore, I know what you're capable of. I'd kill you to protect those innocents, but I'd also kill you to free you from the same pain that's driven me mad all my life."

"And if I succeed?"

"Then you are worthy of the Mercer name and you will never be alone again."

Henri looked at Tess snuggled against my side and a look of such visceral longing, such heart-wrenching hope twisted his strangely familiar face.

He'd managed to survive this long but it wasn't a life he'd been living.

It'd been a prison.

A carefully fortified jail to keep himself in check.

If he could prove he was better than our father, that he had the power to control himself, then I would teach him how to find joy even while being the worst kind of beast.

I would help him find a woman capable of taming him.

I would help him be free.

But so help me God, if he failed, his guts would be ribbons, his blood would be spilled, and his heart would join the other one rotting under my rose bush...

Thank you for reading this short, steamy prequel! Henri Ward's Dark Romance will release in 2023 with Ruby Tears. Or start at the beginning with Tears of Tess.

EBB & FLOW

REN ALEXANDER

CHAPTER 1

"I hope a rabid squirrel gnaws off his lopsided nuts!" I ugly cry the rest of my makeup off my face as Simone watches me in horror. "I fucking hate him!" I squeal, not caring who the hell sees me.

Simone leaves her front door to pull me into a hug on the stoop. "Sharla, I'm so sorry he did that to you."

"Two weeks before our wedding!"

She nods against my head. "I know, girl. He's an asshole."

"A whole ass!" I yell over her shoulder, noticing her mother, Julie, standing in the foyer. I pull away from Simone and wipe my face with the sides of my thumbs. Right now, I'm positive I look horrid next to Simone, whose skin and hair exude a golden glow and contrast my brown hair and ivory coloring.

Simone picks up my suitcase. "Come on. My mom made her famous brownies." It's funny that her mother is a dentist but always serves sugary sweets when I'm here. I won't argue with that.

Still, double chocolate brownies can't fix my broken world. I sigh and sulk after Simone. She shuts the door as Julie holds out her arms. "Sharla, come here." Her mother also gives the best hugs ever.

Simone takes my suitcase to the bottom of the staircase. Julie sighs and shakes her head as she lets go of my shoulders and twirls strands of my chin-length hair. "I just don't understand how he could do this to you."

"How did you find out?"

"I mistakenly grabbed his phone when I left for my final gown fitting. We both have black cases. Anyway, when I got to the boutique, I checked my phone for messages but realized I had Teddy's phone. I entered his PIN so I could call my phone. That's when I saw the texts from one of his coworkers, Dane."

Simone makes a face. "I'm afraid to ask."

"I should've been afraid to look because a dick blew up in my face!" Simone hides her smile, and I scowl. She never misses an opportunity to laugh or to crack a joke at my expense. Sometimes, I think Simone's in eighth grade all over again. We became friends when I moved to Dover, Delaware, in seventh grade, bonding over our love of boys, retro 80s movies, and makeup. But I've always been responsible and subdued compared to her spontaneity and charisma. Not much has changed with me at twenty-four and her at twenty-three, even as adults, except that now those boys are men. Sometimes.

"And then sexts. Teddy had described what he wanted to do to Dane! Sucking, thrusting, rimming—"

Simone says, "Stop right there. We get the picture. I mean, not that one, but..."

Julie nods and clasps her hands. "Good Lord, sweetheart. I don't know what rimming is, but it doesn't sound good."

Julie says, "Simone, why don't you take Sharla to your room? The brownies are still baking. I'll call you when they're ready."

Simone picks up my suitcase and heads upstairs. I've been at this house so much during my school years for homework, parties, and sleepovers. I loved staying here for Simone, but also for another reason.

We walk past a door, but I stop and push it open, inhaling. Simone sighs and whips around. "Finn isn't here. Move on, girl. He's married and has a kid. That ship has sailed and sunk."

I pout. "It still smells like him."

"That's disgusting," Simone grumbles, storming into her bedroom across from her older brother's. Finn Wilder was my schoolgirl crush. Back then, he was handsome and has only become hotter. His wife is one lucky girl. Nearly a decade older than Simone, he didn't live with her for long but was here often enough during college and then to visit afterward. Finn is now Richmond, Virginia's favorite sportscaster, whose viewers dare him to do sport-related stunts. His favorite is to jump off a bridge in West Virginia every year in October.

I shut his bedroom door and follow Simone into hers. Her old yellow and pink room brightens my gloom for a minute before I remember my life crashing down on me only hours ago.

Simone sits on her bed, and I sit at her desk. Picking up her pink stapler, I turn it over in my hand. "I'm sorry about you being stuck with a dress you'll never wear."

She waves her hand with a shrug. "Forget it. I'll *Pretty in Pink* it."

I smile and return the stapler. "You can't sew."

"You can help me. If not, I'll figure it out. Who cares about the dress?"

"I can't believe Teddy cheated on me. Why didn't he break up with me instead of entering a marriage he didn't want?"

Simone frowns as she twists one of her earrings. "Men do shit like that. But remember that you're a goddamn catch, Sharla. I hate standing next to you." She laughs, but it's not a typical giggle for Simone. It's more like she's going through the motions.

"Where's your man? Greg?"

She tosses herself back onto pillows and throws another one over her face with a muffled, "I don't want to talk about him or my problems."

"I don't want to talk about mine, either."

We're quiet until Simone sits up. "Let's not, then. We should go out."

I make a face. "You know I don't enjoy clubbing."

"Why not? I just graduated from college two years past due. Celebrate with me."

Nodding, I tease, "Oh, yeah. You majored in drug rehab, right?"

"Kind of. I wanted to work in outreach for drug addicts in recovery. Now, I'm not so sure."

I scoff, "You're changing your mind *again*? You changed your mind from a model to a teacher to a real estate agent and then a news anchor to work with your brother. What happened to our shared dream of fashion design? We strived to be partners in a big fashion house before starting our own. Now, it's only me aspiring to be a fashion designer. You dumped me."

"Jesus, Sharla. I'm sorry I can't make up my damn mind and complicate your plans."

"I sacrificed for you, Simone. After we graduated high school, you convinced me to put off college for a year to make time for road trips, parties, and doing nothing. Now, I'm behind on my career path. And alone."

"For fuck's sake! Why didn't you tell me you didn't want to take a break? You sure liked seeing new places while the wind blew through your hair! Teddy hurt you, so I'm your punching bag now? Fine! But don't blame me for holding you back! I didn't hold a gun to your head!"

We glare at each other until there's a knock at the door, and it opens. "What's going on, ladies? Brownies are ready."

Simone covers her face again, muffling her voice. "Just talking."

Julie walks into the room, pushing her hands into her jeans pockets. Her short, dirty-blonde hair is the same style I've always known her to wear while her familiar smile dazzles, possessing the power to lift a dark mood. "Now is not the time to turn on each other. Both of you have suffered recent losses in love."

I brush a tear from my cheek. "I wouldn't know about Simone's since she tells me nothing."

She shoves the pillow from her face and sits up. "You've had your head up your ass, planning your wedding!"

Julie says, "Simone, that's not fair."

"Wait until you're planning your wedding someday," I mumble.

"Shove it, Sharla. Stop being a snot," Simone argues. Her eyes shine, but

Simone isn't prone to tearful outbursts like me. I've seen her cry twice in all the years I've known her.

"Me?"

Julie sits on the corner of Simone's mattress. "Ding, ding. Back to your corners. You need each other right now. I heard you talking about road trips. What are you doing about your honeymoon, sweetheart?"

"Oh, jeez. I didn't think about that."

"Hawaii, isn't it?"

"Yes—Maui, to be exact. A week. I always wanted to go there."

Julie laughs. "Why can't you still?"

"Well, because I... It's a honeymoon."

"Only if you label it as one. Didn't your parents give you the trip as a wedding present?" I nod. "Since it's already booked, they'd want you to use it for everything you've been through. Take someone with you."

I glance at Simone, who stares at her lap. "Simone, we could call it a divamoon."

"Pussymoon," she says, smiling as her blue eyes meet mine.

"We're not calling it that."

"BBmoon."

"Babymoon?"

"What the hell, Mom? BBmoon." Julie and I stare at her, and she rolls her eyes. "Bad bitches."

I frown. "We'll work on that." I then turn to Julie. "How do we do this?"

"I'm so on board."

"Whoa, whoa. First, brownies, and then we'll make calls."

CHAPTER 2

"This is the shit," Simone whispers as we raise our sunglasses and observe the hotel lobby in a 360-degree circle.

"This looks so much better than the brochure."

The floor is a random pattern of earth-tone tiles with wide columns jutting from the floor to the ceiling, dotted with large, dome-like light fixtures. Love seats and chairs pepper the massive room that appears endless. Green, gold, and cream carpeting covers the floor, and on the other side of the lobby, small tables and chairs and a long counter with stools pervade the area.

We check-in, the desk clerk explains the amenities, fastens green plastic bracelets around our wrists to keep a running tab on our food and drinks, and offers us a bellhop to help with our luggage. However, Simone grabs the surfboard room keys and advises him we'll handle it ourselves. I don't want us to do everything on this trip. I'm here to relax and... I don't know what else. I'm afraid to make it that far.

We roll our suitcases along the tiles, echoing a hollow, sandy sound. It's late afternoon and the bright blue ocean shimmers with sunshine beyond the expansive windows on our way to the bank of elevators. The salty sea air drifts into the lobby, peeling away some of my sadness.

The doors close with only Simone and me, and she says, "Thanks for bringing me along."

"Of course. There's no one else I'd bring other than my mom."

Simone waves her hands like she's swatting flies. "This trip must be epic and life-changing for you, Sharla."

"It already is since it's *not* my honeymoon."

"Yes. That's what I need you to remember. You're single. No attachment."

"Thanks? God, Simone. Kick me while I'm down."

"I'm trying to elevate you. You will do the unthinkable. Something you've never considered doing. I dare you to have a one-night stand."

I laugh. "You're hilarious and sound like your brother."

"Sharla, this is Maui. You will live. A lot. All your life, you've played it safe."

"I want whatever you're huffing."

The elevator opens on the eighth floor to a blue-and-cream carpeted hallway. People roll suitcases past us while laughing and talking. There's a thrill in the air from being in paradise.

We look at a room key and the directory sign on the wall and swing left as I mull Simone's suggestion. I've never imagined having a one-night stand. They seem impersonal and a little transactional.

Finding our suite, Simone enters a card, and the door opens with a green light and a click. She steps aside and allows me to enter first. I lug my two stacked suitcases and makeup case into the room with a balcony and an ocean view. "Sweet aloha!"

Simone rushes into the room after me. "Fuck me to Maui," she utters with the same amount of awe.

"I second that." Luckily, the hotel allowed me to switch our room from a one-king-bed suite to a double queen. The cream-and-gray carpet resembles rippled sand. There is an ocean canvas picture spanning the distance of the bright white beds.

"I can't believe we're here!" I marvel, walking over to the window.

Simone laughs. "I know it's not a honeymoon, but I believe with all my heart that this trip will change your life."

I'm dubious and ask, "What do we do first?" I claim the bed closest to the balcony because I deserve it. I separate my suitcases and set the smaller cases on the bed.

Simone bounces onto her bed. "I already gave you an assignment."

I shake my head as I dig into my makeup bag. "I'm not having sex with a random stranger."

"Why? Your ex-fiancé was fucking a specific coworker."

I spin around. "Simone, come on!"

She crosses her legs and studies her manicure. "You need to do it. I brought condoms. You'll be fine."

"God, I can't believe you're trying to talk me into being someone I'm not."

"No, just less uptight. Have you seen yourself lately? You need a redo. And I will pick out a man for you."

"Wait! What? There's no way!"

"Yes way, because your outrageous standards suck."

"You'll pick out some beach bum with bad breath and body odor."

"Give me some goddamn credit, Sharla. I've done this before."

Curious, I sit across from her on my bed. "Oh, yeah. The night you lost your virginity."

"Donovan Abernathy. So cute, but so dumb. And he lasted five minutes. Disappointing. I almost swore off sex and joined a convent."

"Why did you do it? I was at the party but was downstairs."

She shrugs. "I dared him to pop my cherry. We went into Mason's bedroom, and Donovan didn't know how to put on a condom correctly. I wonder how many girls he impregnated, but it would not be me." Simone makes a face and runs her hands over her thighs like she wants to forget it now.

"Then what?"

"Not much else, except Mason watched us. It was creepy as fuck. Donovan didn't give me time to get in the mood and thrusted maybe ten times, and it was over. I cried, but it wasn't from ecstasy. For a little pecker, that shit hurt. Zero stars."

I laugh. "What did Mason do?"

"Nothing. Apparently, Donovan and I were not jerking material." Simone sighs. "Anyway, we'll find you a man. You'll fuck his brains out and give him a fake phone number."

"I can't do this."

Simone claps her hands and bounces on the bed. "Ooh. Maybe there's a cute bartender who'll notice you. Maybe you should act sick to get his attention."

"My life isn't *Cocktail,* and I'm sure the bartender is no Tom Cruise."

"Well, then get changed, and we'll head down to the pool for some drinks and to search for your lay. Not the floral kind of lei."

"It doesn't have to be today."

"Right. Then, tomorrow we'll scour the beach for an available cock."

I groan as she pulls her hair into a ponytail. "This sounds dirty and unsafe."

Simone rolls her eyes. "Loosen up. You're not walking the plank. And the sooner we find you a man, the better. Fuck that Teddy out of you. You can't let his dick define your pussy." Simone stands to dig through her suitcase.

"What about you? Are you grabbing a one-nighter too?"

She pauses before shaking her head. "Maybe when we go to Jamaica."

"That is not a good enough reason why you're not doing this too. I'll pick out a guy for you."

Simone snorts. "Hysterical. You've had four boyfriends in your whole life and only slept with two."

"Well, you're hiding something. Will you tell me what happened to you in these past months?"

She peers into her suitcase. "Not much."

Exasperated and dubious, I argue, "That's a lie."

Simone pauses her digging and glances at me. "It's not worth talking about."

I cross my arms with a sigh and move closer to her bed. "Here's the deal. If I have a one-night stand with someone you throw at me, you must tell me what went down with Greg." I haven't met Greg yet, but from what pictures I've seen of him on her phone, he's yummy. She told me they were sleeping together, but their complicated relationship ebbs and flows with the tide. She won't admit it, but I know she's in love with him.

"That's not part of the deal, Sharla."

"It is now." I pick up my black bikini and toiletry bag and head into the bathroom.

CHAPTER 3

"Where do you want to sit?"

I observe the tall, umbrellaed stone tables beside a grass-roof bar. On the other side of the large patio is a stage adorned with the same grass and a band playing upbeat cover songs on it. "I guess near the bar?"

Simone grins, and since there aren't many available tables, we hurry to one in the corner. I already notice Simone surveying people at nearby tables and the bar, but when she frowns, I relax a little.

I adjust my swimsuit cover-up, and Simone says, "Take that off. How are men supposed to see the goods you're selling?"

"Excuse me?" I ask with a worried laugh. "You're not my pimp."

"I prefer madam."

"I don't want to sit in my bikini since I'm not wearing shorts like you."

"It's not like you're the only one in a bikini. At a beach. In paradise. Jesus. You're not making this easy, Sharla."

"If I remove it, you talk." I pull it off, and Simone bites her lip and gazes at the ocean.

I hang the cover-up on my chair as Simone gasps, watching people at another table.

"What?" She'd better not be stalling.

"That waiter. I swear to God he was checking you out."

Seeing a man with his back to us, wearing a blue-and-green polo shirt and khaki shorts, I shoot her a look. "You mean the one with his back to us?"

Simone rolls her eyes. "Well, duh. He wasn't two seconds ago. He's cute and has a nice ass and legs."

We watch the guy laughing with the guests and gesturing as he tells some lively story. "Because they're all that matter."

Simone sighs as she shakes her head at me. "It's a one-night stand, not picking out the father of your children. Teddy wasn't all that great looking."

"For real?" I shriek. "Teddy is cute." Not so much after the things he said and did to someone else.

"If you like spaghetti arms, pancake ass, and mismatching facial hair to the hair on his head. Weird."

I cross my arms and argue, "I can't believe you, Simone. Why didn't you say anything to me?"

"Sure. You would've loved that. Why are you pissed off? The dickhead topped a guy on your couch. You showed me the sexts."

My face crinkles, but I shake my head and sit up like it'll reset my emotions. "But—"

"No. Name three things about him you didn't like."

"He cheated on me. His lips were thin and dry. The sex was mediocre."

She claps and giggles at my frown. "There you go! Don't you feel better?" No. It reminds me of how gullible I'd been.

"Hello, ladies. I hope I can make your day better. My name is Kaz. What can I get you to drink?"

The man at our table smiles, and it's mesmerizing. Even with the umbrella's shade, his gray eyes sparkle with his megawatt smile. He has nice lips, definitely not thin and dry. His loose medium-brown curls catch the sun and light up streaks of golden brown.

Simone's jaw drops, and she's speechless for the first time in our friendship. But she rebounds with a smile that men find irresistible. "I'd like any kind of drink in a coconut."

"Coco-Loco. It's one of my favorites."

He doesn't take his eyes off Simone, which isn't surprising. Simone attracts men without trying with her smile alone.

Sulking and feeling sorry for myself, I study the menu again, unsure what I want or if I care anymore. Simone says, "As long as there's plenty of coco for my loco. I'm Simone. *Kaz*. That's a unique name I haven't heard before."

I look up from the menu as he props his hands on the table and leans closer to Simone. "You know? Me neither. Let's keep it our little secret, or everyone will want it, and there's not enough to go around."

Simone says, "I'm horrible at keeping secrets." She sure knows how to hide her own.

He straightens with a laugh. "It's short for *Kasra*, but only my mother and grandparents call me that. It's Persian, originating from a king."

"Are you from Hawaii?"

"No. I grew up in Pennsylvania, but my mother is Iranian."

"That's cool. I'm from Delaware, and so is my mother. Boring. Do you like living here?"

Kaz shrugs as a breeze tosses his lazy curls. "It has its moments, but it's great here if you don't mind living on an island in the middle of the ocean."

Simone sighs. "Yeah. That probably would get old. What brought you to Maui?" I roll my eyes at the menu. When Simone wants a man, she reels him without delay. She can stay at his place, then. I'm not listening to banging the waitstaff.

The table vibrates as he leans on it again, and I look up. I try to stay out of their conversation since he's auditioning to be her flavor of the night. "A Boeing 767."

"Stop!" Simone smacks the table with a giggle.

Kaz sighs, and it sounds sad. "Love. I thought it was, at least. She moved here for a job. I quit my job to help her and to try out living here. Three months later, she ditched me for a bartender from another resort."

"How awful. Do you have a girlfriend now?"

His responding smirk oozes sexiness, and my face reddens. Even though I'm not involved in this discussion, he's magnetic, and I can't stop staring at him. Kaz tilts his head. "Why should I tell you? You can't keep a secret."

Their tedious flirting makes me grateful for the music. If this guy says he has a girlfriend, all this is for naught, and I won't be in the awkward position of lusting after her newest conquest.

Simone grabs his hand, and I envy her boldness. "Because we're friends now."

Kaz takes back his hand and almost appears embarrassed. "What about you? Do you have a girlfriend or a boyfriend?"

Simone says, "No girlfriend."

Before Kaz responds, I grab the chance to find answers and ask, "What about a boyfriend, Simone?"

Kaz side-eyes me and purses his lips like he forgot I'm here. Simone sighs with a pout. "Not technically." What kind of answer is that?

Kaz taps his notepad against his palm. "To answer your question, I don't have a girlfriend, but I'm accepting applications." Okay, then. Now, I think I'm pouting.

They laugh, and I interrupt their merriment. "I think I want a Mai Tai."

Kaz's bright smile radiates until he turns to me and douses it. His pretty eyes travel over me, and he mumbles, "Sure."

Simone motions to me. "This is my friend, Sharla. Please tell her to chillax. We're here on vacation. Her fiancé cheated on her two weeks before their wedding."

"Simone!" I squeal, annoyed. Simone bites her lip and widens her eyes at me. I'm not helping her score her thousandth boyfriend at my expense.

Kaz's gray gaze still pierces me, and he probably surmises I'm cuckoo. "I'm sorry to hear that. His loss for sure." He then seems weirded out and trips over his words. "You... I... I'll be back with your drinks."

As Kaz walks away, two women stop him, and his smile returns. When he heads to the bar, Simone twists to watch him while I sigh and check my phone. "The ocean has nothing on you drooling after our waiter." Or me, but I hide it better. Damn, though.

Simone wheels around to grab my wrist. "Holy fucking shit, Sharla. Did you even see him?"

I jerk my arm out of her grip. "Yes. If you want to ask him out, you'd better do it before another woman snatches him." Like me. I wish.

She bobs her head. "Yes! You!"

Dubious, I laugh. "Hysterical."

"His whole demeanor changed when he looked at you."

"Yes. He remembered he was doing a job. Besides, he's supposed to flirt." It's probably in the employee handbook.

Simone crinkles her nose. "Who in the hell says? He's not a stripper."

"I can't believe you don't know if that's a side hustle. You know everything else about him now."

"For *you*."

I smile but remember what she wants me to do with Kaz. "Why wouldn't you want him for yourself?" Though I won't use him, I don't want her to, either.

She sits back and drags her fingertips across the polished granite. "Because."

"We have a deal. No technical boyfriend? What *is* that? Tell me about you and Greg."

"There's nothing to tell. He's doing his thing. I'm doing mine." Simone peers around us. "Maybe we'll see dolphins or a whale. I need to pet a whale."

"Sure. A humpback whale will pop out of the water, begging you to scratch his blowhole."

She wrinkles her freckled nose. "You make it sound gross."

"You pretended to be married to Greg after being legally married to him to con your father. Why did you end it?"

Simone taps her fingernails on the table while observing the stage. "He helped me and then moved on. Now, I'm here with you."

"You're leaving out such a huge chunk."

She swings her around and cranes her neck to see the bar better. "I wonder how we pay for our drinks."

"He'll scan our bracelets. Stop changing the subject."

She slumps over the table. "It's such a dead subject."

"Do you love Greg?"

She arches a blonde eyebrow but swallows hard and drops her gaze to the table. "I don't know. We can't stop hurting each other just so we don't lose touch. When we're together, all we do is argue and/or screw. How damn sick is that?"

"I'm sorry I haven't been there for you. With the wedding, I..."

Simone shakes her head and sits up. "I understand. I don't want to think about Greg because I'll lose my mind." She clutches my arm again. "Please don't waste this chance here. Have fun and purge stupid Teddy for good. At least you discovered what he's doing before you married the fucker."

I nod. "True. This could be a whole lot messier."

"Here we are, Simone." Kaz delivers a coconut to Simone with a grin. "I made sure it's extra coconutty for you."

She takes an eager sip through the fuchsia straw, and her blue eyes light up brighter than the early evening sky. "Holy shit. This is heaven!"

His eyes meet mine but then slide to my drink. "And here you are, Sharla. I hope it's enough mai to the tai."

Simone hums and asks, "Did you put extra cream in Sharla's too?"

My eyebrows tighten as I gasp. "Simone!"

Kaz laughs with a blush, which is charming. He crosses his arms and shakes his head. "Um, yeah. I can't go there. Just wow. I'll need to scan your bracelets."

Simone giggles as she offers him her wrist. "Sharla thinks you have beautiful eyes." She glances at me with a puckered smile, trying to contain her amusement.

Kaz bites his smiling lip as he rubs his chin. I offer him my wrist and blurt, "I'm sure women tell you that all the time."

He holds my hand and scans my wrist. His skin is soft. Kaz shrugs as his eyes meet mine. His dark eyebrows match his hair, unlike Teddy's mismatched situation. I like how Kaz's sideburns blend into his faint stubble. I've never seen a man who can pull off sideburns like him. "But your blue eyes beat mine. Nobody wants gray."

"I wouldn't say that," I murmur, realizing I said it aloud. He releases my hand, and we stare at each other until I laugh, feeling so out of my depth.

His voice shakes when he asks, "Are you from Delaware too, Sharla?" He sounded different with Simone. Do I turn off everyone?

"Detroit, originally. No, I didn't run into Eminem."

His crooked smile is fiery sex on a summer night. "Well, there goes my next question."

"But my grandmother knew Aretha Franklin."

"That's fantastic." Simone scrutinizes us with delight, and I'm unsure what's happening.

I comb my fingers through my chin-length bob. "For now, I live in Dover, Delaware." I notice I'm nervous, so I pick up my drink and take a tentative sip while Kaz and Simone watch me. I set the glass down and smile. "That's the best Mai Tai I've ever had."

When I look up at Kaz, his attention is glued to me until he blinks and glances at people walking past him. His gray eyes bounce back to me, but his jaw clenches this time. "Good. I don't like to disappoint."

"I doubt you could."

Simone looks back and forth between us. "One of you needs to pull the damn trigger."

Another waiter says Kaz's name, and he turns to answer him. I check out his arms, which are muscular but not bulky. His greenish-blue polo complements his olive skin.

Simone giggles, and I frown at her. "What?"

"He's hot, right? Ask him out."

"I don't know how," I say, hating how stupid I sound.

She rolls her eyes. "Seriously?" When Kaz turns back to us, she says, "Sharla wants to ask you something."

I freeze for five seconds before Simone nudges my leg with her foot, and I grasp at straws. "What time do you get off?" Simone coughs on her drink, stuck between hacking and laughing. I rush to say, "From *work*. Simone's mind is a trash fire."

Kaz laughs, and his teeth are so perfect. "I assumed that's what you meant."

"But she *so* wants the other," Simone wheezes, and I kick her back.

He checks his black watch. "I get off…whichever way you take it…in ten minutes."

I clear my throat, fidget, and cross and uncross my legs. "Would you want to…?"

Simone perches her chin on her hand. "She's asking you to rock her world for tonight only." She swings her head to me, where I glare at her, but I couldn't have said it better.

Kaz grins but dips his head to hide it, almost like he's overjoyed. His smile is more subdued when he looks up at me before he laughs. "Rock your world. Do you mean to…?"

Simone covers her face with her hands and muffles, "Jesus Christ, yes! *Fuck* her!"

I swat Simone's arm. "Drama queen."

Simone's phone dings, and she drops her hands. A text flashes from Greg, and she picks it up with a scowl. "Well, your shit is painful to watch. I thought *my* life was fucked up." She shakes her head, and her blonde ponytail swishes against her neck.

Kaz hides his mouth behind the side of his fist, but it doesn't hide his smile. When he drops his hand, he says, "I'm up for whatever."

The phone dings with more messages, and Simone inhales before rising from her chair. "I'll hang out here or at the beach for a couple of hours. Text me later." She digs into her phone wallet, pulls out two yellow foil squares, and hands them to Kaz. "Have fun, but stay safe, kids."

His wide-eyed expression matches mine as he fists the condoms and stuffs them into his pocket. Simone is unreal sometimes, but she has the experience and guts I lack. I cringe at Kaz, "I'm sorry. This is weird. We don't have to do anything involving…those. I'm okay with walking on the beach or anywhere, really."

Kaz drags a deep breath as his eyes linger on me. "Whatever you want. Give me a few minutes, and I'll meet you back here."

I nod, but I grab my things when he leaves and bolt.

Such a chicken.

CHAPTER 4

Orange-tinted white sand fills my sandals as I shuffle past sunbathers. I stop on the hot sand to remove my shoes and head toward the cooler, wet sand. Waves crashing into the shore and the smell of salt and coconuts coax me to stop and absorb the sight. All my problems melt in the sun and wash away with the foamy tide.

Simone wants to help me, but it's hard after being with Teddy for five years. But as the shock dissolves, I realize we existed together. I cared about him, but he was a safe choice. I don't want to be afraid of living. I've missed out on so much, staying with a man I didn't love with all my heart. I want a love that will rock my world permanently.

I turn to look at the hotel, regretting I ditched Kaz like his girlfriend had. Maybe he gave her a reason to leave. Or perhaps he's like me, trying to start over but not knowing how.

My cover-up flutters, and my hair whips around my face. I sigh and turn back to the ocean.

"You left."

I see a man wearing khaki shorts and a gray shirt walking toward me, carrying shoes. I squint in the sun, unsure if he's talking to me. When his body blocks the sunlight, blinding me, I blink to see Kaz. "Oh!" I'm shocked but then smile.

Kaz stops next to me. "I saw Simone, and she said you probably went to the beach. She also told me not to blow you off. Like I ever could."

I scrape the hair from my face. Kaz is more than a good-looking man. His straight nose, sharp cheekbones, and rugged jaw make him beautiful. "You don't have to stick around for me. Simone should focus on her own guy problems."

With his hair waving in the sea breeze, Kaz smirks out at the water, but his wrinkled forehead reveals his confusion when he looks back at me. "I'm a guy problem for you?"

I cover my laugh with my fingertips. "No. I just... I'm not some horny tourist looking for a good time."

He nods and appears maybe disappointed as he glances at the surf and then up to my face. "Well, I'm not some horny local looking for a good time with a tourist. Believe me. I get enough propositions I don't want." He shrugs, and his smile is almost shy. "But I'm willing to make an exception."

I lick my salty lips and stare at his. "Why?"

"At the risk of sounding cheddar, you do something to me. Being around you feels different."

Before I stop myself, I say, "I feel the same way about you. But we don't know each other, and I don't know how to do any of this."

Kaz drops his tennis shoes and raises his hands. "I have no expectations, regardless of what Simone said. Honestly, I don't know what I'm doing, either." I nod with a smile, and his crooked grin makes my heart stutter. "You don't know me? Let's fix that. I'm Kaz Cervenka—my dad is Czech. I'm twenty-five. Your turn."

"I'm Sharla Hertzler. My parents are primarily German and English. I'm twenty-four."

He grins. "There. Now we know each other." Kaz holds out his hand. "Let's walk." When he sees me hesitate, he shakes his head. "I swear I'm not a serial killer."

"That's good. Because I am."

Kaz bends to pick up his shoes with a laugh. "I'll take my chances."

I take his hand, and a thrill zips through me. "Do you live far from here?" He looks at me with a smirk, and I nudge his arm with mine. "Not that I'm interested in going there."

"About three miles from here. I left my car with my parents, so I bus it. Do you live with Simone?"

"No. She's in Richmond, Virginia now. I'm not sure what she plans to do. She was planning to go to graduate school in Dover, but after she dropped a bomb at her college graduation, I don't know."

"What did she do? Please tell me it wasn't an actual bomb."

My feet sink into the wet sand, and I love the feel of it and holding Kaz's hand. "No. You'll need to ask her. She tells the story so much better."

"Okay. I will. How long will you be here?"

"Seven days. Six now. This trip was supposed to be my honeymoon."

"Damn. I'm sorry. He wasn't the one for you."

"Oh, yeah?" I squeeze his hand, and my heart hammers against my ribs. But when he squeezes mine back, my heart squeals to a stop before soaring high. "I want to find the one who is."

Kaz shrugs. "I don't think you'll have to look very hard."

"I'm a romantic dreamer. I need my person."

"I'm the same way. I wish Melody hadn't waited until I was here to dump me, but I'm glad she let me go. I wasn't hers to keep."

"No, you weren't."

He slows us to a stop and points to the water. "Dolphins."

"Sweet!" I watch their fins dipping through the water near the colorful horizon. "I'll never tire of seeing dolphins."

We watch them until they're harder to see. Kaz puts his arm around my shoulders and tugs me as he resumes walking. At first, I don't know where to put my arm until I roll my eyes at myself and slide it around his waist. "So, how long have you lived here?"

"Six months, but I'm ready to go back. I have a graphic design degree and miss seeing my family."

"I want to be a fashion designer and move to New York."

"That'd be a great place to go."

I nod, thinking of more things to ask to keep him talking. "Do you have any siblings? I'm an only child."

"I have two younger sisters. My mother moved to the US with her parents as a teen. When she met my dad, she spoke little English, but they still fell in love."

I smile at the thought of finding love in a new place. "Do you speak any Persian?"

"Yes, but I don't use it often. Mostly around my grandmother."

"And she still calls you *Kasra*."

He smirks, and his lips are fascinating. "Yes. But I don't hold it against her."

"I like your name."

"Thanks. I don't hear that often." His stormy eyes hold mine, and it's like they cast a spell on me, and I can't look anywhere else.

"What's your middle name?"

Kaz swipes his hair, and the damp air slicks it back. If I thought he couldn't get hotter, I was so wrong. "Delancy. It's my other grandmother's maiden name. Yours?"

"Penelope. Like you, my parents also named me after a grandmother."

He smiles. "Nice."

We walk until the hotel disappears, and then we turn around. We chat about everything and watch the sunset in all its red, purple, yellow, and pink glory. I feel like we've known each other forever by the time the hotel springs into view. I ask, "Would you like to have room service with me? And possibly Simone? I don't want to banish her from the room all night."

"I'm up for anything." His smile wavers, and he licks his lips. I don't have a witty response like Simone would and smile back at Kaz.

The dry sand is cooler, and the twinkle lights around the hotel's courtyard sparkle. We put our shoes on and go to the main entrance. Inside, I stop to text Simone. She responds that she's talking to new friends on the patio. And then asks if we did *it* yet. I roll my eyes with a sour frown and put my phone back into my beach bag.

Kaz looks at his phone and then arches an eyebrow at me. "Would you like my number?"

At first, I'm dumbfounded. Men have flirted with me and asked for my phone number, but I ignored them since I didn't give anyone a chance. I've never had a man offer *his* number. I nod with a doubtful grin as if he'll change his mind. "Absolutely."

After trading numbers, I feel bold and grab his hand, which he readily takes. We reach the elevators, but before getting into one, I let go of his hand and spin around to face him. "You're not really going to rob me blind, are you? Or are you scamming me?" I laugh, but it could happen.

Kaz sucks in his top lip like he's considering it. I wonder what his lips would feel like on mine. "Now that you mention it…" He laughs, and I gasp with a smile. His eyes drift to my lips, but mine aren't as pillowy as his. "Sharla, I don't need your money or care. I made good money working with my father's friend, but just because I'm waiting tables doesn't mean I'm broke."

"I didn't mean that. I've never invited a man I've known for mere hours to my hotel room."

"I've never been that guy, either." People bustle around us in the lobby while Kaz and I stare at each other, unsure if we should go further. He sighs and drops his gaze. "I get it. If you don't want me around tonight, I'll go."

I grab his hand and pull Kaz toward an open elevator. We stand on opposite sides of the crowded car, and it's ridiculous how I miss him. It's not a feeling I've ever felt with Teddy. I didn't want to be close to him and resented it most of the time. Kaz is not him.

When we stop at the eighth floor, I follow two other people and look behind me for Kaz, but I don't see him. Maybe I missed him getting off on another floor. Maybe he didn't want my baggage. Maybe I truly offended him. I'm such a bitch, as Simone calls me.

I turn toward the elevator and see Kaz squeezing between a stroller and an enormous suitcase. Our small smiles feel forced, and I hate that I may have ruined any possibility with him. If so, why is he still here?

We proceed down the hall, and I stop at our door to unlock it with my card. I set my beach bag next to my purse and Simone's on the dresser. "Have a seat. I'll be back." I slip into the bathroom and throw my hands over my face, nervous and horrified I hurt his feelings. I take a deep breath and remember that I'm far from home and have only known Kaz for one day. Still, I need to chillax, like Simone ranted.

I use the bathroom, and when I return, Kaz is sitting on a chair, scrolling through his phone. I say, "It's yours if you want it."

He lifts his gaze from the phone and cocks his head. "Uh, okay."

When he can't hide his smirk, I say, "The *bathroom*, Kasra. Simone is already a bad influence on you."

He shrugs as he stands. "She's entertaining."

"Everyone loves Simone. She's gorgeous and bubbly." I wish Greg felt the same way because, despite her laughter, she's dying inside.

Kaz starts to say something but walks past me to the bathroom. I sit on the bed, but it may be too forward, so I stand. But then I look too eager, so I sit on the chair. Then I stand because Kaz was sitting there. I grab the desk chair and pull that out, but I don't want to seem distant.

Heat overwhelms me, and I remove my cover-up and go to my suitcase, but the bathroom door opens. I sigh and turn toward Kaz. "I'm sorry for hurting your feelings in the lobby. I don't think you're... Well, I'm sorry."

His eyes swirl around me before they settle on my face. "You didn't." He shakes his head. "A little, but there are people out there who rip off unsuspecting tourists." Kaz's gaze again falls to my body, but then he runs a hand over his mouth and looks out the window. "Maybe I should go."

I'm self-sabotaging and will lose this opportunity if I can call it that anymore. I won't be leaving here feeling the same. Because of Kaz.

"Don't leave. Not yet," I murmur.

He nods with a laugh as he rubs the back of his neck. "Right. Simone ordered me to rock your world."

I go to him and slide my trembling hands onto his chest. Kaz looks away from the window, and his gray eyes darken. I whisper, "Then rock my world, Kasra."

Kaz puts his hands on my hips and pulls me closer. "I don't know how to not fuck this up, Sharla. I've never felt like this."

"Like what?"

"Anxious. Eager. Conflicted. Turned on. All at the same time."

"You described me." I move my hands to his jaw and pull him to my lips. His quiet gasp melts me, and our lips are slow and tentative.

Kaz pulls away, looks into my eyes, and then dives back to my lips. His fingers stroke my cheeks, causing my body to tighten and ache everywhere. On an impulse, I drop a hand from his jaw, feel for his crotch between us, and grab a handful of his hard-on.

Our moans fill each other's mouths, and our kiss intensifies as I stroke his dick through his shorts. We end our kiss to breathe against each other's lips, but our magnetic attraction is undeniable. I return to his soft lips, and when his tongue enters my mouth, I suck on it. His hands slide over my ribs until he's cupping my breasts. When he sweeps his thumbs over my nipples, I'm close to begging him to fuck me.

Needing more of him, I move my hands to the button of his fly and pop it open. I grab his shorts and underwear waistbands and shove them until they fall to the floor. I end our breathless kiss to work on his shirt. He yanks it over his head, making his brown curls bounce and stick up.

Kaz stands naked before me. His body is perfect. He tosses his shirt onto the chair and wraps his arms around my waist. His dick rubs against my stomach, and on another whim, I leave his mouth and drop to my knees. I lick the wet tip, and his groan floods the room. I hold on to his shaft as I lap around the tip before taking more into my mouth. My lips and tongue caress him, and he digs his fingers into my hair. "Sharla, your tongue is…" He moans, and I smile around him and suck as I stroke. He thrusts his hips but then slows. "I can't, or I'll come. You're that damn good."

With a pop, I let him fall out of my mouth, and he offers me his hand. When I'm standing, Kaz kisses me again, and he slides his hands to the back of my bikini top and unhooks the back. He pulls away from my lips to slip the top down my arms. The top falls, and Kaz yanks down the bottom. I step out of them, and he cups my pussy. He kisses my jaw to my ear and whispers, "I want you. I've never said that to anyone." He pushes a finger into me and kisses below my ear. He slips in and out of me. "Your wet pussy is driving me crazy."

"I need your hard cock inside it." Kaz kisses me breathless, and I pull him to the bed. I break the kiss to pull down the duvet and get into the bed while he picks up his shorts and removes a condom from his pocket. Kaz then climbs into bed next to me. He hovers over me and kisses my neck. His hot breath blowing against my skin makes me squirm beneath him. He fingers my nipple before moving down to suck it into his mouth.

I moan, "Kaz," and lift my hips.

He releases my nipple and says, "You're sexy, Sharla. I was so damn nervous around you. But I couldn't stop thinking about making love to you with my tongue." Kaz shifts and spreads my legs but bends to lick my thigh before his burning tongue slides over my clit and darts inside me. I hold on to his head as I pant his name over and over. He then glides a finger into me, and I bounce my hips against his mouth.

He groans into my pussy, and I wheeze, "Kaz, I'm coming." Kaz licks and thrusts faster until an orgasm erupts over his soft lips and into his mouth. His wet licks draw out my orgasm, and he pants against my clit, making me fall apart again.

When my orgasm ends, he crawls up to me while I catch my breath. I grab his face and kiss him, and his hard-on jumps against my stomach. I push him onto his back, and his dick slides close to my soaked entrance. The tip of his dick breeches my pussy, and he groans before pulling back. He slides his hand across the mattress and tears open the condom package. "Are you on birth control?"

I nod. "It's been months since… But he was kind enough to use a condom when he cheated on me. I've been clean, otherwise."

He moves to put the condom on but then hands it to me. "I never have sex without one, so…"

"Okay." I frown somewhat, not because of that but because even if it feels like we've known each other forever, we haven't. And he doesn't trust me, which is fair since I accused him of wanting to mug me.

Kaz shakes his head. "I didn't mean that I have a problem with you. I don't want you to get pregnant because I wasn't careful, Sharla. I want to rock your world, not wreck your life." His concern for me is sweet and nothing Teddy ever considered.

I straddle him and align the condom over him before rolling it down. "I know."

I lean down, and my pussy grinds along his shaft. Kaz moans, and I kiss his jaw. He whispers, "I'm close already."

"That's okay." He holds onto my hips as I kiss his neck.

I grind more against him, and he pants, "I can't take it anymore. Fuck me."

I swoop my hips up, and he thrusts into me. I moan, "Fuck," and ride him hard until he stops my hips.

"Not yet. Goddamn, though."

Smiling, I kiss his lips, and we move slower. I sit up, and his hands move from my hips to my breasts. He looks me in the eye and whispers something in Persian. I don't know what he said, but the expression on his face shoots shivers up my spine.

"Oh, Kaz." I move faster while Kaz's solid thrusts into me spark another orgasm. I yell and moan as this one rolls through, and my body grips his shaft.

"Sharla," he pants. "I'm going to come." Kaz bucks into me and freezes as I feel his dick jerking. He sits up some, and his ab muscles crunch.

After Kaz relaxes and lies back down, I move off him, and he rolls to his side and kisses me. I put my hand on his cheek and sit back. "That was… Never in my life… Sex with you is different."

He swallows with a frown as his eyebrows tighten. "I didn't know sex could be like that."

I whisper, "Is that good or bad?" I clench my teeth and purse my lips, ready for the worst.

Kaz grins and rubs his nose over mine. "Very good. That was the fastest I've ever finished. Wow."

"That doesn't sound very good."

He laughs but sobers when he sees my anxious expression. "Before, it was something to do. This time, it was something more. I wanted you so much."

Kaz dips his head to kiss me, but before he does, I ask, "What did you say to me in Persian?"

His crooked smile makes me smile. "That's a secret."

"I can keep a secret."

He kisses my cheek and whispers, "So can I."

I sigh as Kaz gets out of bed and goes to the bathroom. My phone dings, and I reach over to the nightstand and see Simone's name, asking if I got laid yet.

I text back no. I'm not discussing that over a text. I then tell her to give me half an hour. She sends a picture of another Coco-Loco and four people I don't know sitting with her.

"Is Simone asking if I kidnapped you?"

"No. Are you?"

"For now." Instead of getting dressed, Kaz gets back into bed with me, but I get up and use the bathroom.

When I return, he watches me as I return to bed. I ask, "What?"

"Damn, you're hot."

I laugh. "Um, thank you. You're hot, too. I've never seen steel-gray eyes before."

"I got them from my mother. I'm partial to blue."

Kaz looks into my eyes, and I giggle. "You already got me into bed. You don't have to feed me lines."

"I haven't fed you any."

My grin falls, and I say, "I think we made a mistake with having each other's phone numbers."

His eyes widen, and I hear him swallowing. "Why?"

"One-night stands are…one night. Not even a full night, right? I'm asking because I don't know. But I guess neither do you."

Kaz's eyebrows pull together, causing lines on his forehead. He bows his head toward the mattress and mutters, "Shit."

"What's wrong?"

He sighs and raises his head but doesn't look at me. "I need to go." The smile on his face no longer shines, and a glower storms into its place.

"You don't want to stay for dinner? Room service. Remember?"

Kaz tosses the sheet back and gets out of bed. "Uh, no. I forgot I have somewhere to be."

My chest tightens as I watch him get dressed. I didn't think this would be weird. Simone made it sound like one-night stands are a fuck-and-duck event. I'm not a fan.

Keeping his back to me, Kaz picks up his shirt from the chair. I'm desperate to end this on good terms without having to end this at all. "Do you work tomorrow?"

He sits on the bed to put on his shoes. "I'm not sure. I haven't looked at my schedule."

"Oh. I'll probably see you before Simone and I go home. If I don't…"

"I don't know if you will. Maybe." He stands but looks everywhere but at me.

I need to be an adult about this. No sprouting feelings for a guy I just met. And fucked. Teddy flipped my life upside down. I need to get a grip and not fall for the first guy who looks my way or lures me into bed. Though, I did the luring. Or Simone did.

I don't even know what to say to Kaz. "You don't have to rush off. I'm not chasing you away. We can watch TV, rejoin Simone, or…" I glance at the bed, and when I turn back to him, he drags his gaze from me and shakes his head. His curls are now messy but in such a sexy way.

"I wish I could, but…" Kaz doesn't move, but I feel his buzz to leave.

What do I say to a temporary sexual partner? Tell him it was fun? Ask him for a sequel? Confess that I might have a crush on him? Being with him felt like more, but that's how messed up I am. I'm vulnerable after the breakup. Someone needs to remind my heart to slow the hell down.

"I'll text you?" I ask, hoping he'll smile.

"Um, sure." He growls a little like he's annoyed with me. But then Kaz steps over to me and kisses my cheek.

I grab his jaw. "Why is this weird now?"

He purses his lips, and his eyes don't stay there when he looks at my face. "I'm late. That's all."

I nod, but unable to resist his lips, I kiss him. Kaz doesn't hesitate and kisses me back. He growls again but pulls away from me, and without another word, he leaves the room.

CHAPTER 5

"Ho, you'd better tell me what happened with you and Kaz right now."

Stirring my straw, I mope and look around our table every five seconds. "We kissed a little, Simone. It wasn't a big deal." And every second that passes, I miss him more. Sex with Teddy never came close to what Kaz and I had days ago. How could that happen? I've known Teddy for years and Kaz for mere days. Or hours since I haven't seen him since our one night. "Where are all your new friends?"

"They left. We leave tomorrow morning, Sharla, and he's not been at work. Something's not right."

I grip the table's edge and glare at my phone. "He won't answer my texts. Or yours since you stole his number from me."

"Damn right, I did. I even threatened to kick his ass, but he won't answer. I thought he was my friend, but it looks like he's another asshole."

I shake my head. "He was so nice, but we wouldn't have spent time together if you hadn't pushed us. Do my standards suck that much?"

"Like a black hole. Did Kaz fuck you as instructed? Yes or no?"

I sigh. "Only if you tell me if you're still sleeping with Greg."

She sighs back at me and shoves her empty coconut. "God, yes. We're obsessed with fucking each other. After everything we've been through together, it doesn't matter that he's seeing another woman or that I'm his ex-wife who ended our sham marriage."

"Besides marrying him because of your father, what all have you been through with Greg?"

Simone shakes her head and glares at the table. "I don't want to go there right now. I'm not drunk enough. Maybe later."

I nod. "I'm sorry. Okay. Yes. Kaz and I had sex."

Brightening, Simone dances in her seat and twists, searching the crowded patio. "We need more drinks, damn it!"

"No. This is my limit. And why would I celebrate a one-night stand?"

She frowns and pulls the coconut back to her. "I thought it wouldn't be one."

I gasp and lean over the table. "What the hell?"

"Yeah. I thought you two would fall madly in love, and you'd hatch his babies." I thought I'd have that with Teddy.

"He lives in Maui, Simone. I'm not doing a long-distance thing *that* far. And Kaz didn't seem into me once he was out of me. Now, he's not even responding or showing up here."

"Maybe he gave you a fake number."

"No. It was real." But who am I to say since everything else that night wasn't?

A bearded waiter in a greenish-blue polo shirt walks past our table, and Simone leans in her chair to stop him. "Excuse me…Miguel. Where is Kaz tonight?"

Miguel glances at me and then back to Simone. "I thought I saw him earlier. Maybe check the bar. He might be there again."

I ask, "Again? He can do that?"

Miguel laughs. Stupid tourists. "Yeah. He's been there most of the week. Can I refill your drinks?"

I shake my head, and Simone whines when he walks away. "Why did you tell him no? Mama needs another drink."

"That dick," I mutter and turn toward the bar with the brown grass roof, but I don't see him.

"Yep. By the way, how *was* his dick?"

"Come on. It was fine." More than fine.

She clicks her tongue. "I bet he's hung like the goddamn moon. Greg is. I'll tell anyone that." Teddy was bigger than Kaz, but he didn't know how to use it. That's for damn sure. Simone frowns as if she's remembering something. "Just get me another Coco-Loco. Tell Kaz extra coconutty, and I might not curse his existence."

I get off my bar-height chair and walk over to the crowded bar. I dodge around people, trying to see who's working the bar. When I peer over the shoulder of the woman in front of me, I see brown curls bouncing as he slides a drink over the counter. Kaz smiles somewhat, but his hooded eyes don't twinkle like they did at the beach or in the hotel room.

I shuffle to the crowd's edge and see three bartenders and many waiters gathering their orders on the other side of the bar. Between customers, Kaz cranes his neck to look past them but frowns.

Taking a deep breath, I approach the building and say, "Excuse me. I'm feeling a little faint. Can I have some water?"

Kaz does a double take, first with a smile and then dropping it as guilt colors his face. "Sharla... Hey."

"Hey," I drone, crossing my arms. "Can we talk when you have a chance?"

The woman bartender next to him checks me out and asks, "Is that her?"

Kaz throws her a look. "Don't worry about it. I'm taking a break."

He nods toward the rear of the small building. "Meet me at the back door."

Anxious, I adjust the spaghetti strap of my mint-green tankini and smooth my black sarong. Regardless, I'm not here for a fashion show, but I feel like an exhibition.

I turn the corner as Kaz exits the shack. We stare at each other silently until I ask, "Why are you avoiding me?"

The guilt remains on his face and voice while he watches people walking past us. "I'm not. I've been working."

"Working? I've been here every day, about every hour, and haven't seen you."

He shrugs, but his shifty eyes don't match that nonchalance. "Why does it matter if you see me? It was one night."

I nod. "I know, but..." I cross my arms and look at the shack and the hotel behind us. The warm air soothes my skin, being near Kaz's chilliness. "What did I do? You got into my pants, so you're done with me? Am I another gullible tourist? Another flower in your lei?"

Kaz chuckles darkly, still unable to face me. "Sharla, that's the way these things go. Right?" Kaz sighs, and I hate staring at his strong profile. Around us, vacationers enjoy themselves in a tropical paradise while I grasp the harsh reality of a night I fought to avoid. But I didn't and used Kaz for a one-time fuck to forget my heartbreak. Only, I didn't know he would fuck me over and add to it.

I mutter, "Okay. I'm glad we had this illuminating chat." Before I crumble in front of him, I search for a break in the crowd, but Kaz grabs my hand. He hauls me to a side entrance, scans his employee card, and holds the door open. I don't know where Kaz wants me to go, but I enter and wait for him. Bright light fills the hallway, but he opens another door, nodding for me to go first.

The light in this room isn't as bright and appears to be an employee lounge with tables, chairs, a microwave, and an old, green couch, probably from the 70s.

I wipe my eye but don't worry about smearing my mascara since I didn't wear makeup today. Kaz moves around, still avoiding being close to me. He pushes in a chair, tosses a paper cup into the trash, and then stands in the middle of the room with his hands on his hips, staring at a wall.

"Did you bring me in here for a reason?"

Kaz doesn't acknowledge me. Knowing I'm wasting my time, I turn to leave, but he says, "Don't go. Because I won't follow you."

I fold my arms over my chest and spin around. "What?"

He sighs, bows, and mutters things to the floor in Persian. He then switches to English. "I don't know what you want from me, Sharla. You wanted me to rock your world for one night. Done. Why are you here now?"

At first, I'm speechless. I thought he knew. "Because you rocked my world, Kasra. I thought maybe I had rocked yours."

Kaz looks up at me. His gray eyes darken like an impending storm despite the light. "Do you know how many women have propositioned me since I moved here?" I shake my head as my throat strangles me. "Over two hundred."

I clear my throat. "Thanks for using a condom with me. Jesus."

He shakes his head. "See? You think I lied to you when I said I've never had a one-night stand. I didn't accept any of them. Until you. But you'll only see me as a casual fuck."

"No, I don't, but you don't care. When I didn't serve a purpose anymore, you ditched me. Like Teddy did."

Kaz pivots toward me and raises his voice, bouncing it off the walls. "He had pledged his commitment to you but *cheated*, and you're comparing me to *him*? That fucking sucks."

I close my eyes to shove that thought away. When I open them, Kaz's gray eyes slice into me. "Look, I'm sorry that I keep hurting your feelings. That's never my intention. We both regret our night together for different reasons."

"You think I regret our night together?" Kaz shakes his head and throws out his hands. "Our night was goddamn amazing, Sharla. The best of my life. You rocked my universe. But whatever we thought we had between us? Our baggage is way too fucking much. There's nowhere for this to go if that's what you're searching for. I'm here because I followed a woman I thought was my future. Now, my life is a question mark. Even if it weren't, you live thousands of miles away and leave tomorrow morning."

"And you weren't going to say goodbye?"

He laughs but covers it with the side of his fist. He drops his hand, and his bitter laughter chills me. "Like I didn't care? Jesus Christ. I've been watching you all week at the bar. I didn't want to say goodbye because it guts me that I was only a fling for you."

"You were more than that to me. You said I was different. I felt something for you, Kaz."

His eyes widen, and he mumbles, "We've run out of steam."

Dazed, I collapse onto the couch. "Why did I listen to Simone? I'm not cut out for a one-night stand. And now I'm here, whining because you did your part but didn't bid me farewell."

"Sharla, no," Kaz argues, his voice hoarse. He sits down next to me as I wipe my cheek. "I'm not good at this, either." Kaz's voice cracks, and he clears his throat. "I don't know what else to say."

I look at his face and scrounge a smile, but I can't fake anything. "Since my flight is at 9:00 tomorrow morning, this is the last time I'll see you. Bye, Kasra. Thank you for..." I laugh as I shrug. "I seriously don't know what I'm doing."

Kaz whispers, "Me neither." When I look up, he kisses me. His lips are soft but commanding, and his tongue is forceful as it plunders my mouth. I slide my arms around his neck, savoring our last kiss. He moves closer to me, and his right hand falls to my knee while his left rests on my back.

Kaz leans into me more as our kiss heats up until he tips us over. He shifts to hover above me and returns to my lips. I slide my hands into his hair and lift my hips. His rigid erection pushes between my legs and against my clit. We groan together, and I leave his hair to work on his shorts while he reaches underneath my skirt and pulls down the bottom of my bikini. Kaz sits up and hurries to remove his wallet from his back pocket. The second condom Simone gave him flashes in front of me as I drop my swimsuit bottom to the floor. This couch smells like burnt popcorn and has years of dirt on it, but I don't give a fuck. With Teddy, I wouldn't have done such a thing.

Kaz rolls the condom down his shaft, and I moan, watching him. His dusky stare pierces me, and when he crawls back, he says, "You're the most beautiful woman I've ever seen. God. I want you," and then kisses me with a passion I've never felt. While our kiss intensifies, he enters me slowly, but when I slant my hips to meet him, he drives into me the rest of the way. His arm goes above my head, and his powerful lunges shake the couch.

Kaz steals his lips from mine, breathless. He pauses, and I clasp his jaw. His piña colada scent marks my soul. Though he doesn't want to give up his life, following another woman across the country and then some, I kiss his lips and whisper, "I've fallen for you." But I say it in Spanish as a loophole, having confessed my feelings under lock and key. And maybe tit for tat since he said something in Persian but won't translate.

In response, he closes his eyes and dips his head. His hot breath bathing my skin with the guttural sounds he makes near my ear shoots me into oblivion. Kaz grabs the couch's arm and resumes ramming into me until less than a minute later. I pant, "I'm coming. Oh, my God." A tsunami slams me with little warning when an orgasm shreds me. I arch my back. "Fuck! Kaz!" I cry as he fucks me fast. The room disappears. I hear nothing beyond our panting and fall further into an inescapable hell.

Vaguely, I hear Kaz gasping, "Sharla, holy shit," as his orgasm counters mine. Despite him wearing a condom, I feel his hot cum exploding into me as his shouts and grunts echo off the tile floor.

Though we've reached the end, we still move together. I don't want this to end, but it is. I can't be casual friends with Kaz, sending occasional and painful texts to check in with him.

I hear knocking on the door, and Kaz yells, "Okay, I heard you! Give me a minute!" Pushing himself up and out of me, he mutters, "Sorry. We need to go."

When he stands to remove the condom, I can't help but watch him as I try to get dressed in a rush. Kaz wraps it in a paper towel and throws it away before going to his fly.

I hear people talking outside in the hallway. How damn humiliating, doing the walk of shame in front of an immediate audience. But I'm another vacay cock hopper to them. At least, I think that's the phrase Simone used.

I inhale a deep breath and glance at Kaz, buttoning his shorts. His deflating hard-on persists, and he frowns with a sigh, appearing to be at a loss for words. "I'll leave the room first and do crowd control. There are only a few of my coworkers out there, though. They won't bother you."

I nod as sorrow squeezes my chest and throat. There's nothing to say that'll make this better. "Bye, Kasra. I won't forget...this. Or you."

Kaz says, "I'm no longer a one-night stand. If that matters..." He bites his frowning lip and hurdles his gaze to the floor.

Folding my arms so I don't hug him or make this worse, I walk to the door and wait for him to go first. But when he reaches for the handle, his shaky breath makes me look at him. His gray eyes are thick smoke swirling behind glass, but I don't see them long because he leans over to kiss me. I keep my arms locked against me and pull away from him. He whispers, "Let me know when you get home."

Quiet tears stream my face, and I nod without looking at him. He sniffs before opening the door. Kaz talks to them, and I hear them mumbling as I leave.

Before I open the exit door, I hear Kaz say, "No. Leave her alone. Damn it to hell. I can't fucking do this."

Outside, the harmonious steel drums and guitars accompany my numb sadness. I head to the side entrance but remember Simone is at the table. I backtrack and stop beside her, and she looks annoyed at me. "Where's my Coco-Loco, bitch?"

I shake my head and swallow before answering, "You'll have to get it. I can't."

"Sharla?" she asks, angling her head to see my face, partially hiding behind my hair. "What happened? Did you talk to Kaz?"

"Uh, yeah. We said goodbye. I'm heading upstairs."

Simone looks over her shoulder and then back up at my face. "What did he say?"

"Exactly what I told you."

Fury ignites her blue eyes, and she mutters, "I'll kill him."

I grab her shoulder. "No, you won't. He did nothing wrong, Simone." I inhale and brace my hands on the table. "What the fuck did Gregory Rodwell do to you?"

Simone's anger disintegrates, and she scrunches her face into swift sobs. Stunned, I pull her to me. Since I'm standing next to her high stool and we're about the same height, she lays her head on my shoulder and cries into my neck. I've never been in this reverse situation with Simone. The two times she's cried, I was crying with her.

I rub her back and whisper, "Let's go upstairs and talk."

She nods against me before sitting up. "Go ahead. I want to finish your drink before leaving. I'm not buzzing yet."

I smile but don't feel it. "Okay." She pulls my glass closer and hands me my beach bag, and I leave. Peering over at the bar, I don't see Kaz, and it's better I don't.

It's going to be a rough night. One of many.

CHAPTER 6

"Did you double-check the bathroom, under the bed, the drawers, and the nightstands?"

"I didn't know that was my job," I mutter with a yawn and drag fingers through my bedhead that I don't care to fix this morning.

"It was. You're the responsible bitch. I'm the fun bitch. BBmoon. Remember?"

"Yep. We packed everything, including the free toiletries and coffee. Can we just leave?" The memories in paradise aren't all pure joy.

She pulls her phone from her purse. "Our ride is still twelve minutes away. We'll check out and wait." Simone opens the door, and I look out the window one last time, needing the ocean again to cleanse my wounded soul.

I roll my suitcase behind me, but when I step into the hall, a man leaning against the wall with his deep golden legs crossed at the ankles stops me. His gray eyes wake me, and my heart hammers, unable to handle more pain. I swallow hard. "Kaz?"

His crooked smirk appears. "The one."

I clear my throat, but it's still tight. "We said our goodbyes."

He nods, and I notice he's wearing cargo jean shorts and a white Panama Jack T-shirt. "Yeah. We did."

My gaze falls from his face, and I notice the large suitcase parked next to him. Confused, I move out of the way of people passing us in the hallway. Simone closes our suite door, seeing Kaz. "Oh, you're here. It's about damn time, fool."

"I had a few things to do," he mutters, not looking away.

I walk, wheeling my suitcase closer to him. "Where are you going?"

"Home." When I say nothing, he uncrosses his ankles and shoves himself off the wall. "I'm going back to Camp Hill, Pennsylvania. That's where I'm from."

I don't respond, and Simone says, "Hertzler, look alive."

I shake my head, but nothing still makes sense. "Okay. Um, have a safe flight. Good luck with whatever you do." I smile at Kaz to stop myself from screaming. I walk past him and push the down arrow for the elevator.

Simone sighs. "This is not going as planned, Kaz." She wheels her suitcase to the elevator area and says, "Get back here, Sharla."

"What?"

Kaz rolls his suitcase and stops in front of me. "I won't be thousands of miles away from Dover. A little over a hundred miles."

"Okay. Still, what does that mean? You said you won't follow another woman. Message received."

Simone slumps against the wall and growls, "For fuck's sake."

Kaz laughs at her but then sobers when he looks at me. "I'm not following you. We're not even on the same flight, Sharla."

I sigh. "Why does it feel like you're teasing me? Like, you'll be closer, but tough luck. Have a nice life."

He licks his lips. "That's not what I'm doing."

"Then what? Last night hurt me. You have no idea how much."

"I do. I'm trying to fix it."

"It was more painful than being cheated on and losing my fiancé."

Kaz inhales and releases a slow breath like he didn't expect to hear me admit that. "Last night was excruciating for me, and I've only known you for a goddamn week. Melody leaving me didn't come close to how shitty I felt. So, after you left, I quit my job and stuffed everything I brought back into my suitcase. When I get home, I have calls to make and a few favors to collect for a job in New York."

"New York? That's where I want to go."

He nods. "Yeah. I was thinking maybe we could eventually work together. Kind of like a package deal. Maybe even start a company together. Graphic design and fashion design…"

A smile tugs at my lips, but I'm not there yet. "This package deal. Does it include you being mine?"

Kaz's smirk melts me. "Sharla, from the moment I saw you on the patio, I wanted you to notice me. Your table wasn't even in my section. All my coworkers knew who you were because it was obvious how much I was attracted to you."

I giggle. "I knew what drink I wanted. I just didn't want you to leave."

"And I won't." Kaz's hands go to the sides of my head, and he kisses me.

Simone claps. "Thank you, Baby Jesus! That was more painful than a period. And our ride is here."

She reaches around me to hit the button. Kaz releases me, and Simone throws her arms around his neck and hugs him but then lets go of him to smack his chest. "You're such a dipshit, but you know. I kicked ass and saved the day."

I clutch her arm. "What did you do?"

Kaz says, "Simone grabbed me by the shirt and said some choice things. But that was after I quit the hotel and was heading out."

Simone rolls her eyes. "He wouldn't be here this morning if I hadn't hurried him along."

I frown. "Oh, really?"

Kaz shakes his head. "I would've moved back, but probably not for a few days. But all I've thought about was something you said last night."

Simone's glee is nice after everything she told me last night. "Kaz, I don't know if your girlfriend told you, but I'm ordained to marry in the Commonwealth of Virginia."

Kaz and I freeze. Simone rolls her eyes. "Calm the hell down. It's okay if you have the babies first."

Kaz buries his hand into his hair, lifting it, and I fidget with my tank top as fear creeps into both of us. She mutters, "Christ. You two need a lot of work."

The elevator dings, and the doors open. People exit, and then we step into it. I stand next to Kaz, and he leans against the wall and puts his hands behind him on the rail. I ask, "What did I say last night?"

Simone giggles and faces us. "You snagged a good one, Sharla. Your boyfriend has so many talents that aren't sexual. And for the love of tacos on a Wednesday, don't tell me. But he makes a mean Coco-Loco, is an accomplished stalker, and the fucker knows how to speak two damn languages."

Kaz's sexy smirk returns as he looks at me. *"Tres. Yo hablo español."*

I gasp, "Oh, hell, Kasra."

He slides closer to me and whispers, "You know, you're one of the few who gets away with calling me that."

I whisper, "So… You know what I told you last night?"

He laughs, but his eyes reveal more. "Maybe."

"Then, what did you say to me in Persian?"

He shrugs with a full-blown grin. "I guess that's for you to figure out. Just know, I said it first."

My grin could break my face. "You're not following a woman, right?"

Before he reaches my lips, he says, "Nope. This time, I'm following my heart, Sharla."

If you haven't read Hadley's story, check out the Wild Sparks Series, Chasing the Wild Sparks.

MY DARK TRIBUTE

AN EAGLE ELITE SHORT

RACHEL VAN DYKEN

SERGIO AND VAL

Aloha. Hello. Welcome.

People never really want to hear the truth. It's one of those things that stings and bites at you no matter how many times they ask you or lie that they want to know, no matter the consequences, no matter the cost…

I stare down at my hands.

So much blood has been spilled.

So. Fucking. Much.

I stare down at the ocean, I'm fascinated at how ocean life works, everything almost floats carelessly through the water as the tide comes in. We came to Hawaii for one purpose—to relax. I was told by my wife, Val, that if I didn't stop and take a minute that she'd force me to and quite honestly, since we've been married she's gotten scarier and scarier and I feel like I've turned into this soft man because of it. The more intense she gets in all ways of the Cosa Nostra the more I feel I need to give in and take a deep breath—even if that means that I'm not adding any more tattoos of my kills to my body.

She even asked me to see a therapist.

I laughed.

She didn't.

So I try.

I try every day to get closer to normalcy, but that's basically impossible when you're literally one of the assassins of the Five Families.

And now I'm staring at a damn turtle floating around in front of me, smelling coconut and watching a yellow fish just swim around by my feet.

Life is weird.

Truly strange if you ask me.

I have blood staining my hands constantly and yet I'm watching a sea turtle and smiling, a blessing to be able to afford an expensive vacation in Hawaii, a curse knowing that everything always has an end, and I'll be back in Chicago soon, back to work, back to doing what I do best.

Silencing everyone and everything next to the Families and making sure that they stay silenced. Maybe I should back up a bit, you see, years ago I was in love—rare for any of us because love isn't something any of us rich bastards can really afford, but I was—and she changed me, she ruined me actually. I loved her so hard; I loved her the way you love how the wind presses against your cheek and tells you you're alive.

But she died.

She literally died in my arms.

It wasn't my fault though, it wasn't something I could control, it wasn't something that any of us could prevent. No, this was nature, just like the turtle swimming in front of me, just like the yellow fish casually floating by, it was just...life.

But when Andi died, when she twirled twice in my arms in front of the sunrise then collapsed at my feet and told me she loved me, it nearly killed my soul, in fact I initially thought about just following her into that place.

Instead, I met Val, and my life changed.

I didn't want it to change though; you know how you almost want to just sink into your grief? Into your darkness? I wanted that. I wanted to punish myself for not being able to save the love of my life and I hated Val, my current wife, for making it better, for making me smile.

Damn, the first time I did smile after meeting her, I literally grabbed one of my knives and thought. It would be so easy to draw some blood, to feel again, to make myself feel better, because at the end of the day? The Five Families would come after me anyway and maybe it was better that way, maybe it was better if I just didn't exist.

Grief does that to you. It makes you dive deep, so deep into yourself that you're afraid of your own thoughts. Sickness does the same thing... you have those weak moments of like, okay do I deserve this? Maybe?

Does this world really need me?

You become unrecognizable even to yourself until all you think about is diving deeper into that darkness, just like the stupid turtle diving down into the beautiful blue ocean waves I'm currently watching hit the rocks in front of my feet over and over again.

Life is like this ocean.

Life is like this sunrise.

I stare out and take a deep breath.

I run my hands through my thick dark hair, it's touching my shoulders, I came outside without a shirt wearing only a pair of black board shorts. Everyone else is still sleeping, the sun is rising. We're in Kona, Hawaii.

Waikoloa Resort, a place that Val said she'd always wanted to visit, it's far away from downtown Kona on the big Island which is full of volcanic rock.

Beautiful if you ask me, because it's almost like seeing scars from the island itself only to bloom into the best soil for new growth to continue to build the islands more and more.

My mom used to come here often.

Technically, it always felt like a second home, but we never stayed in this general area. We always stayed at the huge resorts near downtown.

But now, I'm a bit further away and I realize the draw.

It's quiet.

I'm not used to quiet.

Maybe I should try harder.

People are starting to wake up, the whole dolphin area is buzzing with the trainers getting ready for the day, and I can see older couples start to walk by me near the swimming pond inside the actual resort.

They make it so easy to relax here, but I can't relax, and I have my reasons, I almost laugh maybe that's not my journey, relaxation, though Val is convinced that if I just breathed in and out for five seconds, my life would change.

I lean back on my elbows in the sand and stare out at the ocean, sinking my body into the sand. Hawaii is truly beautiful.

I try to breathe deep.

I inhale, exhale.

I close my eyes.

And then.

A shadow or something crosses over me.

A cloud?

I blink up and she's there.

My wife.

Val.

Her hands are on her hips, oh shit, why is she so pretty? Her dark hair's braided across her shoulder, her blue eyes are staring down at me, she has no makeup on, is wearing a white bikini that barely covers her body and I'm pretty sure if she turned around I would see nothing but ass... not complaining.

We're on a kid free vacation and my body is suddenly fully aware that I can take her back to the room.

"Hi." It's all I have.

She doesn't respond, just sits next to me and then reaches for my hand.

I've killed.

I've taken so many lives that it just feels like going to work and clocking in and yet the way that she grabs my hand has me nervous. Me, of all people.

"Come on." She grips it and stands.

I stand with her. I would walk with her anywhere, even to my own death.

"Are we going to breakfast?"

She shakes her head, is she crying? "No, we have more important things to do."

"Like, save the turtles?"

She laughs. "No, I think they're okay, they're bonding with the fish and now you and I get to bond."

I'm confused, but honestly, maybe it's the fact that I've been so lost in my thoughts watching a freaking turtle float around. I'm feeling sorry for myself, and I know why.

Because ten years ago today—I lost Andi to cancer. My first love.

Ten years ago today I watched the sun rise with her in my arms.

And I watched the sun set and buried her.

My throat hurts from trying not to cry because no matter how much happiness I've found with my wife—it still hurts, it will always hurt and I feel even more guilty because I have the best and most understanding wife in the world and it hurts me to even talk about it to her.

I take a deep breath, force a smile, and hold Val's hand as we both walk away from the shore. I have no clue where she's taking me, but she seems almost... vividly happy.

Maybe she forgot the date.

Maybe I'm just needing a strong drink and a nap.

I hold her hand and just keep thinking, I want to feel again and yet I don't. I don't want to cry, maybe it's better to be numb, maybe it's better to just... exist and go through the motions. Honestly, it's probably better for everyone to just move on like I have been.

Her memory will always be with me.

Her love.

And despite what I do for a living, I was given someone else, someone who loves me for me despite the crazy life we live.

We have so much, but that's the shit part about survivor's guilt, you always think about it, especially on days like today, why her, why not me? I'm the killer here and while she was part of the Russian Mob, and a badass in her own right, why did she get taken?

Why?

And why am I sitting in Hawaii with my wife, living my best life?

It's just a rough day and I don't often allow myself to dig deep into my emotions, but every year, on this day, I truly allow myself to struggle, to breathe, to feel it, the guilt, the sadness, the horror of losing someone close to me and knowing that I had no way to stop it.

I don't know if that makes me a better husband, dad, killer... who knows?

All I have are moments like this, holding my wife's hand and I've learned to just take them in and treasure them.

Because you never know.

"So..." Val squeezes my hand. "I have a surprise for you."

I smile. "Okay. Sounds good."

"You hate surprises."

"I literally want to run away screaming right now, but if you're surprising me, it means you planned which makes me want to know what it is."

She shoves me.

I laugh and it feels good, so damn good. She's always been able to pull me out of the darkness. It's always been just seamless with us despite the grief and past between us. Our relationship started in grief, but she was the light in the darkness.

She saved me.

God, I don't deserve her.

We walk up a small hill on the resort. I can hear the ocean waves, people are starting to wake up and the sun is finally rising, weird how she even knew where I was, then again, mafia. We know things.

I smile at my own joke.

Val elbows me, then stops walking and grips my hands. "Kiss me."

I don't need to be asked again.

Our mouths meet and I never want to let go. I cling to her hands and tug her against my chest, pressing my lips against hers, tasting her, needing her more than ever. Her hands wrap around my neck, fingers dig into my hair while she holds me close. Her tongue slides past my bottom lip, and I just rest in the feeling of the way she deepens the kiss, the way she clings to me and devours me with each touch of her lips, with each breath.

My heart rips to pieces, a tear slides down my cheek and I hate the weakness there, I hate that she's done nothing wrong and everything right and all I can think of is I don't deserve her, I love her.

I love her so damn much.

I pull away. "You know how much I love you?"

"A lot." She smiles, tears in her eyes, one escapes down her cheek. "But do you truly know how much I love you?"

"Yes," I say without hesitation. "You've been through a lot, dealt with a lot, and you're just... present, always present, by my side. What more could a person ask for, then having the love of their life standing next to them? You don't even need to speak and I feel you, I know you, I see you."

Her eyes fill with more tears. "Good answer."

"Truth always is the best answer."

"When I met you..." She sniffles. "...you were broken, a shell of a man, and with each day I saw you heal more and more, but the thing about scars, Sergio, they always exist and if we don't acknowledge their presence they still don't fade, they haunt, so today, I wanted to do something for yours."

"What?" I almost stumble backward. I wasn't expecting any of this and I already feel too vulnerable to even talk, let alone follow one word after another.

Her hands trace the tally marks on my arm, the kills I've made, they trace across my chest, and finally they fall on the tattoo on my lower stomach.

Two. Twirls.

I don't back away, but it feels almost invasive even though it's my wife touching me, I slowly lower my head. Her hands fall away and then she grips mine and keeps walking.

I follow her.

I would follow her anywhere. She knows this. I no longer ask questions. I've always been a leader, but with her? Nah, with her I keep walking, following her footsteps as pain sears in my soul as I hear the waves crash as I realize that I could have so easily fallen.

But I had an angel that saved me.

I had her.

Her hand grips mine tighter.

We stop.

I finally look up at the small chapel and frown. It overlooks one of the cliffs on the resort, could maybe hold fifty people tops. The brown shutters are open and in front as we walk in and see the small rows of pews—he stands there.

Phoenix.

The worst of us.

The one that rose above the ashes in the Cosa Nostra.

The one that once was unredeemable in all of our eyes, and he's standing in a chapel.

His dark hair falls by his ears, his tattoos line down his skin, but stand out against it, the family crests almost glisten on his forearms.

His smile is wide, happy... rare for someone who everyone's afraid of. "Hi." He's against a backdrop of the blue ocean.

Nobody else is present.

Or so I think.

And then I feel them.

I feel people, I don't know how I know, I just do.

Suddenly the room fills, it's slow, purposeful.

My entire family.

Abandonato, Campisi, Nicolasi, De Lange, Alfero, and finally Sinacore, and Petrov.

They all stand with their kids at their sides.

They all stare straight ahead, not even looking at me.

And Val holds my hand tighter.

"We are all here"—Phoenix starts—"to honor those who have fallen, not just by our own hands, but because of tragedy. We're here to do one more thing that we are now adding to our own family tradition." His smile is sad, he looks down while his wife, Bee, comes up to him and grips his hand. He lets out a sigh I feel deep in my soul. It's filled with all my regrets, maybe even his. "Today is the anniversary of Andi Petrov..." His voice catches.

I almost can't look at him.

His eyes meet mine. "Death can be the beginning of something beautiful, it can be a new start, and I'd like to think—no believe—that her death brought our Families together. Enemies to friends and lovers. We have so much to be thankful for, but what we really want to honor here is Sergio and Val, happy anniversary. We're a lot of things, we have a very..." He pauses and smiles. "Interesting career."

Laughter and small chuckles erupt around the small chapel, hopefully we don't get lightning hitting us anytime soon since technically our jobs are a bit dark but instead, it's almost like more light breaks through the clouds and into that chapel.

I want to believe it's Andi laughing with us.

I want to believe that she's looking down and smiling.

"Two twirls, Sergio. Life should include more than one, otherwise, why else are you living, if you can't indulge in more? We deserve at least one more. You." She pressed her hand against my chest. *"Deserve joy. Do you even know what that is?"*

I frowned. "Joy? It's being happy."

"No." She shook her head. *"Joy isn't being happy just like sleep isn't actual rest, resting is when your mind shuts off, sleep is what you do at night or attempt to accomplish. But rest? Rest is when you wake up like you've been sleeping a really long time without any intruding thoughts knowing that you're better. Rest is healing. When you die, you rest, but you know the really wonderful part? The morning always comes. Whether it's in your dreams or after you pass. Rest is what humanity needs, it's where I'm going but before I go rest for a little bit and allow my soul to heal, remember this..."* She turned in her white dress, the pearls she refused to take off spun along with it dancing on her chest. *"You need at least two."*

"Two twirls." I repeated.

She was barefoot in the field. "You try."

"I'm not dancing barefoot in a field, you do remember I tried to kill you the minute I met you?"

She threw her head back and laughed, her blonde hair moved across her shoulders touching her skin like a kiss and I remembered thinking, wow, how pretty. "I was already dead."

I froze in that moment, hating her truth.

She shrugged though. "Life isn't worth living if you don't take every moment, so now, husband who was forced to marry me at gunpoint—two twirls, otherwise I'm grabbing my dagger."

"The one strapped to your thigh or the one by your ankle?"

"Both?"

"Is that a question?"

"Thought it was more of an answer, but sure, both."

I laughed. "I kind of hate you right now, if the guys see me twirling in a field, I'll never hear the end of it."

Her eyes filled with tears. "Good."

I twirled so hard and fast you'd think I'd studied ballet. I twirled, and I twirled.

I twirled for her.

For my dying wife.

Sometimes, I think I'm still twirling now.

Sometimes I think my life is nothing but chaotic circles and the only ones that center me are my family.

My kids.
My wife.

Phoenix looks toward the door, I wasn't even paying attention, lost in my own thoughts, but there are at least a hundred people lined up down to the shore and each of them are wearing leis of different colors.

I've always thought I was a strong man, but when I see them standing, and when they start singing, I nearly lose it.

It's Lei Hali'a by Keali'i Reichel I lose it.

I completely lose my ability to function.

All I have is my wife's hand and my family around me.

"The earth gives and takes," Phoenix whispers. "Today we give back. Every family member will be donating to Hawaii, and every single one of us will be releasing a lei into the ocean in honor of Andi and to those that have fallen, and in the end... we'll dance, the way that she did every day until she died."

I don't know how I manage to leave the chapel and walk, maybe it's because Val is holding my hand, but we make it down to the beach. The sun is high, bright, pure.

I want to smile, I want to honor her as someone hands me a lei of pink and purple flowers, slowly my family does the same and comes up beside me. The tide hits my feet as they sink into the white sand. She's not coming home.

She's already there.

She's free.

A tear slides down my cheek as my wife walks past me, I expect her to put the lei in the water, instead she puts it around her neck and slowly while the sun shines down, she walks further into the water, it's like watching a baptism, and then with all of us watching she turns once, twice, and slowly lays back into the water.

It is a baptism.

Of new life.

Of what was, what is now, all I see is her dark hair, the sun, and her lei floating around her.

And then she smiles and looks up at the sky. "Two twirls, Andi, always two twirls. I love you, you'll never be forgotten."

Slowly, one by one, my entire family, some of the most terrifying mafia bosses in the world, walk into the water and do the same.

Our mourning ends with us in the water, looking up at the sky.

And then, in the perfect ending, Phoenix says, "Amen."

I've been Catholic my entire life.

I have never until that moment understood the fullness of the closure.

The ending.

Only to have our Capo add on. "Selah."

In Hebrew it can mean forgiveness and some even say forever.

So I whisper to the sky, "Forever."

And I grab my wife's hand.

I have no clue how long we stay that way, all of us in the water probably looking like psychopaths, but I smile.

And in the end, sadness turns into laughter.

And forever?

Well, forever is forever, isn't it?

When I walk back up the beach, I swear I can hear her laughter and when I feel the sun on my back and watch all the kids play, I nod.

It's good.

It's so good.

Life isn't perfect, but moments are. And they are etched in our souls forever, always, and nothing can take that away.

Thank you for reading. Enjoy more Eagle Elite books by Rachel Van Dyken starting with book one, Elite.

GOODBYE AND HELLO

SKYE WARREN

JANE

"Aloha."

The guide puts a lei of fresh pink flowers around Paige's neck, who squeals in delight. Unable to contain her excitement, she dashes across the beach. White sand kicks up behind her, leaving a spray in her wake before she hits the foamy water.

Emily laughs, chasing after her daughter.

The ocean is the color of jade, sand the color of ivory. Impossibly tall palm trees line the beach. The sun is so bright, it makes the entire world look like it's made of glass. Waves crash in relentless rushes, a steady roar beneath the shouts of playful children.

Gardenias, jasmine, and other flowers waft through the air. Heavy with floral notes and cool drops of morning dew, they coat the beach like an invisible blanket.

Beau and I accept our leis with grace, having learned that it's rude to refuse them. I force my nose not to twitch because I also learned that I'm allergic to whatever these flowers are. We give our thanks. Only when the guide is out of sight does Beau pull the flowers from around my neck.

Finally, I allow myself a big sneeze.

It startles a seagull into flight.

Beau grins. "There's my girl."

"It's like I'm allergic to luxury."

"You're allergic to pollen. Simple as that."

I scrunch my toes into the warm sand, trying to remind myself that this is real. Not a dream. Not a fantasy. I'm really standing on a beach in Hawaii, my skin sun-warmed, my blood leavened with pina coladas. It's paradise. It's my life now.

Hard to believe.

Hard to accept, really.

I guess part of me, the young, childish part, started to believe I couldn't have nice things. That I lost my parents and lived in a shitty foster home because that's what I deserved.

Beau's blue eyes match the expansive sky behind him. "Sweetheart," he says, his voice gentle.

I force a smile, but he sees right through me. "It's too nice," I say, my voice coming out shaky.

A strong hand behind my neck pulls me in. A soft kiss on my forehead promises me a lifetime of *too nice*. "You'll get used to it. Being spoiled. You'll be so pampered it will feel normal to you. I swear it."

I glance up at Beau, feeling safe in his arms, but something else lingers in my chest. Fear. I'm terrified that this is all a dream - that I'll wake up in the cold, stale air of a foster home or worse, alone in my grief. Maybe it's because I've never had anything this good happen to me before. Maybe I'm too damaged to accept happiness.

His lips brush against my temple, his hand rubbing soothing circles on my back. "You don't have to pretend with me, you know," he murmurs. "I know it's overwhelming, but it's okay to enjoy it. To let yourself be happy."

I nod, but the anxiety doesn't dissipate. It's a constant hum in my veins, a reminder of all the times I've been hurt. One day my father was with me. The next day he was gone. How do I know this paradise won't disappear just as fast?"

Beau tilts my chin up, his thumb stroking my cheek. "I won't let anything hurt you again."

"Let's go back to the room," I say because that's how he can distract me. It's how he can convince me, for a few moments of bliss, that this is forever.

His eyes darken to sapphire. "I'll tell Mateo we're leaving."

"Leaving?" Mateo asks, appearing with drinks in both hands. "Where could you possibly be going, two people on their honeymoon?"

"I would punch you if you weren't holding pina coladas."

"One virgin," he says, holding up a drink in a plastic cup. "For Paige. And one not-so-virgin for Em."

Perhaps it would seem unconventional to have a double honeymoon but after everything we've been through together, the four of us, along with Paige, it feels right.

"We'll meet you for the tour?" I ask.

"Seven thirty at the marina," Mateo confirms. "Now all we have to do is make sure Beau doesn't spear any dolphins."

"Hilarious," Beau says drily.

"Hey," his best friend says, unrepentant. "Once a fisherman, always a fisherman."

"Lobsters, man. We caught lobsters. And I was a kid."

Paige pinwheels her arms back over to us, excitedly showing Mateo her new pink lei. He has settled into the life of a father rather well, considering he was a Hollywood heartthrob not that long ago. He still is, but he's taking a break from acting while he settles into his new role as stepfather. He's patient and playful with her, something she needs after so little levity in her life.

We say our goodbyes, laughing at how quickly Paige waves goodbye. She's flush with grownups these days, and I'm glad. When I first met her, her mother was in hiding, her father dead. She was orphaned with only a somewhat clueless uncle to care for her.

Beau hired me as her live-in nanny.

That was only the start of our adventure.

And this? This isn't the end. It's the next chapter.

Beau leads me down the gorgeous, lush pathways through the private resort toward our tower. We pass someone with a table who draws names with tropical leaves and seashells decorating them.

I pause, looking over the names they have displayed as samples. William. Alana. Jeremy. These children are loved. Everyone at this resort, everyone who commissions these paintings. My heart feels overfull with it.

"Do you want one for Paige?" Beau murmurs, running a hand up my back, massaging the tension from my neck.

"Yes. No. Maybe." I imagine the big letters P A I G E with coconuts and flamingos around them. That would be cute for her room at home. "I have a better idea."

There are scraps of paper for us to write the names. Instead of writing that, I sketch out a rectangle with a box at the top. TURTLE TOWN, I write in block letters. Then I sketch out a turtle covering part of the box.

Then I show it to Beau. He smiles, recognizing the shape of a Monopoly property square. Not one from the board game. This one's based on the place we went snorkeling yesterday. The reef contained clear, calm waters, perfect for viewing the marine life. Especially the endangered sea turtles.

"Perfect," he says, taking out his wallet to pay the artist. "Do you think she'll end up designing board games when she grows up?"

"Maybe," I say. "More likely she'll end up being a real estate tycoon with actual property."

The corners of his eyes crinkle. He had been completely unprepared for the stubborn grief-stricken child, but he'd done his best. He'd cared for her when the rest of the world had thrown her away. I could love him for that alone.

Of course, I love him for a million other reasons, too.

The villa we booked has broad floor-to-ceiling sliding doors that open onto a private infinity pool. There are three bedrooms—one for me and Beau. One for Mateo and Emily. And one for Paige.

The perfect honeymoon for our unconventional group.

Beau's eyes are dark as he leads me into our bedroom. Even here we have expansive views of the ocean. Hesitant, nervous, I reach for the button that closes the blackout blinds. After all, if we're going to have sex...

His hand stops me. "I want to see you," he murmurs.

I shiver underneath the air conditioner. The deep V-neck swimsuit and sheer sarong felt appropriate on the warm beach. Here in the hotel room, it feels scandalous.

My nipples turn hard beneath his hot regard.

He takes a step closer, his hand trailing along my bare arm. I shiver at his touch, my body responding immediately to his proximity. I can feel his hard length pressing against me, and I know he wants me just as badly as I want him.

"God, you're beautiful," he whispers, his breath warm against my temple.

I tilt my head back, offering him better access. He takes it, trailing kisses along my collarbone, down to the top of my swimsuit. He unties the knot of the sarong and the fabric falls away. He pulls down the straps of my swimsuit, letting it drop to the floor at my feet, leaving me bare to him.

He groans at the sight, his hand cupping my breast, thumb teasing my nipple. I moan, pleasure shooting through me.

Awareness rushes through me. Vulnerability.

He kisses me, his tongue exploring my mouth with a hunger that matches my own. I wrap my arms around his neck, pulling him closer, wanting to feel him against me.

He breaks the kiss, trailing hot kisses down my neck.

I'm not the only one vulnerable. He's wearing only board shorts, revealing a broad muscular chest. I run my hands over the hard musculature.

Perhaps it was formed when he was young, hauling lobster traps. He never got soft, not even building his financial empire in California. Not even returning home.

His strength is more than attraction. It's part of who he is.

Someone who fights for his family.

Someone who fights for what's right.

The thin fabric of the sarong swishes around me, and my eyes widen. "What are you doing?"

He doesn't answer. Not with words. Instead, he reaches behind me, tying my wrists together.

My breath catches.

"Relax," he murmurs, pulling me down to the bed. "Let me show you how much you deserve."

My heart pounds as he fastens the other end of the sarong to the headboard. Excitement swirls through me as I realize I'm trapped, completely at his mercy.

He kisses down my belly and I pull against the restraints. I can't fight him, can't escape.

"Beau," I breathe.

A hand moves between my legs, stroking me in that place where I'm already wet and hypersensitized.

"Beau," I say, pleading. I need him inside me.

He presses a finger between my sensitive folds. "I'm taking my time," he murmurs, kissing up my body. Every kiss, every touch of his hands erotic and possessive.

I whimper as he teases me, not giving me what I need. "Let me touch you," I gasp.

"No."

"I need you."

"Don't you know that you already have me? I'm yours, sweetheart. Yours irrevocably." His voice is hard with determination. Molten with lust. Like a volcano, both solid rock and incandescent lava. "Which means I have to give it to you right."

I arch my hips to him, trying to get off the bed. He holds me in place with a hand on my stomach, but his mouth moves over my breasts, light scruff teasing my nipples. The sensation is subtle, but I can feel it everywhere.

I'm still whimpering. He trails kisses down my cleavage, further, until he reaches my stomach. He looks up at me and grins. I can feel his erection against me, throbbing.

"I deserve this," he murmurs against my stomach. "Say it."

"I-I-oh God, Beau. Please."

"Say it. It's the only way to get what you want."

He's merciless, pushing apart my legs, pressing his mouth to my sex. I gasp my pleasure, my pain, my absolute refusal to say the words. No, no, no. I don't deserve it. Not any of it. Not these thousand thread count sheets or the infinity pool. Not Beau and Emily and Paige. Not happiness.

It's not for me.

I'm an imposter here. Years of living alone and afraid, a childhood spent facing abuse or the streets, hammered that home every day until it became an undeniable truth.

Falling in love didn't fix me.

It just made me yearn for what I should never have.

He circles my clit with his tongue, wide and cruel, avoiding the pressure I need to come. "I deserve this. Say the words. I deserve that tongue on my clit. I deserve that cock in my pussy. I deserve to come so hard, again and again, until I'm limp, until I'm exhausted, until I sleep long and dreamless."

"That's—" I gasp a laugh, trying for playfulness. "That's a long thing to repeat. I'm not sure I can remember all the words."

He nips the tender inside of my thigh. "Try."

His teeth press harder. I cry out, begging for him to stop.

And my voice cracks.

I've lost.

"You deserve this," he says again. I feel the words deep in my bones. "You deserve everything good. And though that doesn't include me, and I belong to you. Every inch of me, every breath. My cock. My heart. My soul. I belong to you."

He moves between my legs, his erection hot against my folds. I whimper, still wet, still swollen from his torment. "Now let me fuck you." His voice breaks, revealing the lust he's been holding back. "Please."

The hoarse agony in his voice makes me shudder. "I deserve this. I deserve you and pleasure and your c-"

"Finish it," he says between gritted teeth, lining up his cock against my slick, swollen entrance.

"I deserve your cock."

The words unlock his passion. They unlock his ferocity. He's so big and hard. I gasp as he enters me. He fucks me slow and deep, but I'm so tight, it's enough to send me over the edge. I'm already so close.

I'm coming, my body spasming as pleasure sweeps over me. He fucks me harder, those blue eyes burning, and I can feel him getting closer.

His body tenses, his arms trembling with effort.

I wish I could touch him. I wish I could ask him to untie me so I can feel him go over.

But I'm trapped.

I squirm against the sarong, desperate to touch him. He groans, lifting his hips, creating a delicious friction against my clit.

"Now," I say. "I want to feel you come when I do."

He grunts, his cock pulsing inside of me, his orgasm even harder than mine.

I'm spent, exhausted. I close my eyes, sinking into a trance-like state of complete satisfaction.

And then I hear it. Tap.

Tap.

My eyes fly open, and I stare at the ceiling, which isn't the source of the unfamiliar sound. It's coming from the windows, which reveal a beautiful view.

A private view.

And a seagull.

It taps the glass with its long beak, tilting its head inquisitively as if to say, *Do you have any fish?*

Laughter breaks over me like a cresting wave, releasing some of the tension. Sometimes this life feels too fancy for me, but something like this? Well, that's what makes it accessible. And fun. And mine.

"I'll shoo it away," Beau says, starting to get up.

I hold onto the warm blanket of his body. "No, let him watch, the little voyeur. I don't want to let go of you."

Crystal eyes soften. "Never."

That evening on the dolphin cruise we meet up with Mateo and Emily.

Paige chatters about the sandcastle she built.

It's not a large boat, but a catamaran with just enough room for all of us. There might be some truth to Mateo's words because Beau looks completely at home on the deck, wind in his brown hair. Once a lobsterman, always a lobsterman. Even though he built his fortune, which he currently manages from our home in Maine, there's a part of him that's always rugged. A part of him that belongs near the water.

I'm coming to terms with that as I come to terms with everything else.

The dolphins come alongside the catamaran, making good-natured sounds as they leap out of the ocean. I didn't grow up around nature. Houston is mostly concrete and sod grass. A rare field trip to Galveston had only revealed muddy water and washed-up seaweed. I must sound childish as I exclaim over their grace.

Paige is disappointed that she can't convince a dolphin to come closer to the boat, even when she shouts promises of endless amounts of fish as a reward.

"We don't want them to get too comfortable with people," Emily explains to her daughter. "They're still wild animals. And not all people are kind to them."

A shadow crosses Paige's eyes because even though she has boundless joy and safety now, she's also seen the dark side of humanity.

Emily, too. Her fragile beauty covers a core of steel. She survived her abuse and danger, walking through the figurative fire so she could protect her child.

I'm watching her when the realization hits me.

Paige is sitting in between us. Her hand is in both of ours as she looks out towards the dolphins. She's not my daughter, but she is part of my flesh and blood. My family. Mine. Along with Emily and even Mateo. We're more than two couples on a honeymoon.

We're a family.

We love each other, all of us.

Beau settles in beside me, his shoulder brushing mine.

It takes me a moment to realize that he's watching me.

He smiles, a slight upturning of his lips.

"What?" I whisper, smiling back.

"Nothing," he says. "I'm just glad you're here."

His words sink in, just like they should.

Beau Rochester is the most amazing man I've ever met. I'm lucky to have him in my life.

"I love you, Beau."

He smiles. "I love you, too."

"I love you both," Paige says.

I laugh, though it's a watery laugh, and squeeze her tight. I never dreamed that I'd have a family again. Never dreamed that I would be worthy of one.

When I made plans in foster care, I wanted to graduate college. To become a social worker so I could help other children. Children like Paige. And like me.

I dreamed about helping other people because I knew deep in my bones that it was too late for me.

I was wrong. That's the realization I have as the pink sunset washes over us, casting long, beautiful shadows. It's not too late. It's only just beginning.

Paige throws her arms around us, and I squeeze back.
And then, as the lei tickles my nose, I sneeze.

Thank you for reading Goodbye and Hello, which features the honeymoon of Beau and Jane from PRIVATE PROPERTY. I loved exploring Hawaii with them…and with you.

THE WEDDING DATE

TARA BROWN

CHAPTER 1

The mirror in the airport restroom held an honesty I didn't appreciate.

Not today.

Of all days.

I washed my hands and dried them, trying to shake the level of disbelief or surrealness I feared I wouldn't be able to.

Hopefully, I could hide it from him. He deserved every bit of joy the weekend might offer.

Clenching my trembling fingers around the damp paper towel, I took a deep breath and remembered Linnie's words from earlier. A sinister smile crept across my lips as her offer to murder them both and ensure no one found out was still on the table.

A vibration in my pocket brought me back from the terrible journey my mind took. I pulled out my phone and winced at the text from the stranger.

He was here. Waiting. His flight had just landed too.

Every ounce of my being wanted to back out.

Go home.

Bile bit at the back of my throat.

My hands quivered as I contemplated texting back, getting sick, passing out, or taking a fight home.

The phone buzzed, catching me off guard and I nearly threw it, but a face I needed and yet wanted to avoid flashed across the screen simultaneously. "Hi," I answered but was cut off by my best friend's shouting.

"Get your ass out of that bathroom, now! You think I'm not mapping you?" The words held all the rage gingers were known for and a little something else. A little something more. That was who she was. A spicy ginger who loved and hated with equal amounts of passion and venom. Normally, I was on the side of passion. "He's waiting at the Maple Leaf Lounge. Go!"

"I-I can't do—"

"Yes, you fucking can." My phone vibrated again as she changed the call to Facetime. I accepted and stared at her concerned gaze.

"I can't. They'll know," I pleaded.

"This is going to play out one of two ways. Either you are going to go with this fucking genius plan and make your sister and that douchebag suffer this weekend. Or run home and miss your brother's wedding and let them win. That's all there is. Win or you lose. There's no middle ground here. We both know you're not going without a date."

My lip trembled but I nodded, quite aware of the situation. Both options sucked. But attending the wedding with someone, even a stranger, was the only option I could take.

"You're gorgeous. You're funny. You're strong. There's no one I'd rather take to battle." Linnie smiled softly, her gray eyes shining with emotion. "They rattled you, Nicole. But that's all it was. Shake it off and go meet your date. He's perfect. You're going to hit it off."

"Did you hire him?" I finally asked the one question that was driving me obsessively insane.

"What?" She gasped. "Of course not. He's one of Skin Suit's besties." Her boyfriend's nickname made me smile.

"Is he a professional athlete too?" I needed details.

"I'm not telling you anything. You have to trust me." She winked. "Have I ever steered you wrong?"

I parted my lips to answer.

"Don't you dare bring up eleventh grade. I love you, have a great weekend, and remember who the fuck you are." She ended the call, leaving me smiling. As always.

Except in eleventh grade, but I was over that. Mostly. There was no way she could have known the party we were sneaking into was an adult fetish party. It wasn't something they advertised.

Before I could stop myself or think for a moment longer, I grabbed my carry-on and rolled it out of the restroom. My feet glided over the shiny floor of the nearly empty airport. That was the one perk of taking a late-night flight. Though I nearly missed the plane from Vancouver.

Before I had a chance to back out, I was flashing my Amex and walking into the Maple Leaf Lounge. The front desk ladies whispered with cheeks flushed in excitement over something.

The lounge was empty, as expected, except for one person sitting across the room. I could only see his back. Short dark hair. Broad shoulders.

I was silent, but as if he knew I was there, he turned and stood.

Sunglasses?

At night?

"Linnie," I grumbled as I got closer, scared this was eleventh grade all over again.

"Nicole?" Was that a British accent?

He wore a suit for a flight to Hawaii.

Was he a spy?

He could easily have been cast as a young James Bond.

Perfect amount of dark stubble over his stunning jaw and juicy lips. Thick dark eyebrows. Fit, as far as I could tell. But was he soccer fit?

"I'm James," he said, making me laugh.

"Bond?" I asked before I could stop myself.

"Smythe." He grinned—a good one. For a whole second, I was positive Linnie had paid him, but he was worth every penny. Or pound. Would he pound me?

Oh God, did I actually think that?

My cheeks were aflame.

He walked with ease and confidence. Two traits I was currently missing. Perhaps they'd been missing for a while. Maybe considered dead.

James pulled off the sunglasses and my whole body covered with pins and needles.

"Oh no," I muttered. "You're James Belvedere," the words fell flat as I panicked quietly on the inside.

Nervous spasms shot up and down me.

He stopped straight in front of me and offered a large hand, but I didn't take it. I couldn't move. "I'm James Smythe, my professional name is James Belvedere. It's a long story." He brushed his hand through his hair instead of shaking mine, when he realized I wasn't moving.

A cold sweat beaded across my entire body. My fingers buzzed. My feet were numb. "James Belvedere," I whispered.

"You can just call me James." He scowled. "You don't have to keep saying Belvedere. Really."

I laughed but it wasn't a laugh. It was a noise but not a fun one.

"Or you can call me Smithy, a lot of my friends call me Smithy." He scowled at that and turned to point in the direction of the seats where he had been. "Shall we get acquainted before we leave? We should have the entire backstory created before we leave." He winked and I died a little. He was smooth.

I wasn't sure if I would kill Linnie for hiring the most famous European soccer player to fake date me, or if I'd die of shock before I had the chance.

Either way, the "Sexiest Man Alive" for this year, according to magazines, led me to my seat.

We chatted, which consisted of him asking questions and me answering while trying not to stutter or stare at him in disbelief. I didn't want to be rude, but my head was spinning on a revolving rotation of what, where, why, and how.

"So, we met through Linnie and Jack last month. I knew right away I liked you. You're funny, caring, and kind. You mentioned the wedding and I of course wanted to come. We've been dating for a month, secretly, so the press doesn't find out. You hate the idea of the spotlight." He leaned forward in his seat facing me and took my sweaty fingers in his, eating them up. "We're still early days, but I've got a good feeling about this." He flashed that smile. I nodded along, not really hearing any of it. I couldn't believe he was touching my fingertips. We were touching. Me and James Belvedere.

Could he tell my fingers were sweaty?

Sexiest Man Alive.

What the fuck was I doing?

CHAPTER 2

The sun shone in the window with a sparkle we never experienced back home in Canada. Hawaiian sun held a little more magic, from what I'd seen from my balcony.

My phone vibrated, flashing a beautiful face. I answered the Facetime call as I finished applying makeup at the vanity. "Hey!"

"How was the drive to the hotel? James says you're delightful," she added an English accent, flawlessly.

"He did?" I paused and stared down at her.

"He said it was a smooth introduction—it's very easy to talk to you and he's excited to spend the weekend hanging out." She beamed.

"Well, he's right about one thing. It was easier than I expected. He's super nice. Though I don't understand why he's doing this."

"He's a nice guy." Linnie bit her lip. She was lying about something.

A knock at the door interrupted us. "I think that's him. I'll Facetime you later. I want fucking answers, Linnie. Did you pay him? Is this blackmail? What's going on?"

"Okay, love you, bye." She ended the call.

I stood up straight, mustering strength before getting the door.

He was less intense this morning, wearing a white short-sleeved linen button-up and taupe shorts. The sunglasses were on top of his head but the smile was the same. How was he so easygoing? "Good morning," he said politely. His manners were flawless.

My lips parted to ask what the hell was going on. Something I'd been too starstruck to do the night before. But the door down the hall opened and my father stepped into the hallway.

"Nicky!" he shouted, hurrying toward us. "We were wondering if you made it."

James stepped back from the threshold so my father could offer me a massive hug.

"Hi, Dad," I said, but my gaze stuck, locked on the deep gray eyes staring down on me from behind my father. "This is James." I offered, pulling back. "James, this is my dad, Stephen."

"Lovely to meet you, sir." James presented a hand.

Dad squinted as he greeted him, they shook for a moment too long. "You too, son. Do I—do I know you?"

"I doubt it," I said with a laugh, quite aware he recognized him. And not only because my mother bought every magazine and loved the "Sexiest Man Alive" edition.

Mom joined us in the hallway. "Nicky." She smiled at me, but it was gone the moment she saw him. I knew precisely how she felt. Starstruck. "James Belvedere? My God! Are you staying here too?" she gushed, standing straighter and brushing her hands lightly over the pale floral dress she wore. "What a coincidence. Is the whole team here?" She rushed over to us, taking his hands in hers as if that wasn't an insane thing to do.

"Mom, this is James. He's—my date." I didn't know how else to say it, but the word "date" felt wrong.

Her eyes widened as my father added up the name "James Belvedere" in his head.

They spoke in unison as they both touched his hands like weirdos.

"Of course, James Belvedere! My God—how on earth do you know each other—what a treat! A real star at the wedding! Your brother is going to lose his mind— soccer is his favorite sport!"

"Okay, uhh let's let James settle in. And get some breakfast, perhaps." I gave him a contrite glance. "We should all have breakfast. Break the fast and such. Breaking."

As if he noticed my distress, James took over. "Yes, let's get something to eat." He swooped an arm around both my parents and led them to the stairs. Leaving me to catch my breath and stop saying the word "break."

When we arrived downstairs the fanfare around him was a whirlwind of chaos.

Only my brother, Jacob, noticed I was at the bottom of the stairs. He hurried over and swept me into his arms. "Banana! I'm so glad you actually came. I thought I'd have to fly home and force you on the plane."

"I couldn't miss it," I mumbled, trying to ignore the nickname in hopes he wouldn't use it in front of anyone else.

"I should be angry that you've upstaged my entire wedding, but I suspect Linnie is to blame," he whispered, quite aware of Linnie's antics and her boyfriend who also played professional European soccer.

"I'm so sorry," I muttered and gripped him a little too tightly.

"Don't be. Are you ready for the money shot?" He turned me to face the family surrounding James.

"Money shot?" I questioned his wording before seeing what he already had. Our sister Rachelle and my ex-fiancé Thomas had joined the fanfare.

Thomas slid an arm around Rachelle who was suddenly in the middle of the groupies, presenting her delicate hand to James. She batted her eyelashes and offered that sexy grin. The one I imagined she used to steal Thomas from me.

The world slowed.

My heart ached.

In my blurred vision I noticed James didn't take her hand. Smoothly, he turned and pointed at me. His lips moved as my brother whispered in my ear, "Three, two, one."

Rachelle's eyes widened. Thomas's face flushed. And somehow, James managed to offer me the most loving look any human had ever given me.

Sweat formed on my face.

I offered a weak wave, at the behest of my brother moving my hand like a puppeteer.

James winked.

He was worth every penny, whatever it had cost Linnie. He walked from the crowd, leaving them gaping. Jacob inched me forward slightly, into James's embrace. I was akin to a prop in a play. Jacob and James were directing. A script Linnie had written.

James spun so his arm was around me and kissed the top of my head. Words continued to leave his lips, I felt them on my steaming head. My family gushed at this display.

He peered down at me, seemingly miles away and yet right there. I stared up into those gray eyes and lost myself. I offered something back I hoped was a smile at least. But my body was no longer under my control. Had it ever been? He grinned wide and placed another kiss on the top of my head.

Had I washed my hair? Did it smell nice or like hair? I recalled nothing of my life before this moment. I was in a haze as I turned back to the family.

Jacob was right.

Money shot.

There, in the middle of the crowd of people who knew my sister had taken my fiancé as if she were borrowing a shirt, were Rachelle and Thomas. Pinched expressions. Red faces. Annoyance and disgust. Rachelle stared at James as if I'd offered her a new challenge and Thomas knew it.

But that was not in Linnie's script. And James knew his part well.

My future sister-in-law, Simone, rushed forward from the crowd. She hugged me quickly. "I'm so glad you guys made it," she said quite practiced as if this were how she greeted every person who arrived at the small affair.

"Thank you for having us," James said and offered her his hand. "You must be Simone and Jacob. It's lovely to meet you both. I'm James. Congratulations on your engagement. I suppose I'm a little late with that." He was too good at this. Too easy and natural.

Jacob grinned wide, his smile far too knowing. "You must be friends with Jack and Linnie."

"Jack and I have been mates since we were playing footy as babies. But I've only met Linnie twice."

"Scary, isn't she?" Simone asked, making Jacob burst into laughter. I tried to laugh but my nerves were on edge. Something resembling a chuckle or maybe a goat bleating left my lips as my gaze darted between us and my sister who was trying not to look at me but failing miserably.

"I'll never admit this to anyone who plays, but I've always found rugby players to be some of the more terrifying people in the world," James said teasingly. "Especially the Irish and Scottish ones. They're mad, the lot of them."

"You didn't tell him?" Jacob arched an eyebrow at me.

My cheeks grew hotter, but I knew they couldn't get redder. My entire body felt flushed. The humidity didn't help that.

"Tell me what?" James asked.

"Nicole played for years. She and Linnie were Team Canada together." Simone smirked at him.

"Team Canada?" James asked quite sarcastically, also arching a dark eyebrow. His tone changed as if I'd betrayed him somehow.

"That was a long time ago." I changed the subject, "What's the plan for today, again? I know you have the rehearsal and dinner but what was the other thing?" I hadn't really read the invite. My dread of coming to the wedding at all had bested me for the three months since it was announced.

"We booked a six-hour day at the Kulaniapia Falls. We're all going to paddleboard and swim and eat a delicious picnic. It'll be great. Then, when we get back, we'll do the rehearsal quick and have a massive dinner on the beach," Simone gushed with excitement. Her gaze drew to my brother's and they looked at each other the way people were supposed to when they were madly in love. I felt like a voyeur seeing it until James rescued me.

"Well, we should eat quickly so we can change." He slid an arm behind my back and led me to one of the small tables where only two could sit and pulled out a chair for me.

"Thanks," I sat, managing to take a huge inhale.

"Coffee?" A server appeared out of nowhere and spoke directly to James. I might as well have been *Bella Swan* to his *Edward*.

"She would love coffee and I would like some tea please. Black tea. None of that Earl Grey."

"Of course," she said with a breathy glow.

"Thanks," I said but she didn't hear or see me.

She stared at him. Mouth breathing.

He nodded at her, again saying, "Thank you."

But she didn't move.

She stared for a heartbeat longer before finally turning and rushing away. I saw the heart emojis lifting off her like steam.

"That has to be weird," I said before I thought.

"Very weird. It was fine before the ridiculous Sexiest Man thing. No one in the US knew who I was. But now . . ." he sighed as if lamenting being fanned over or being so sexy. He was the sexiest.

"Okay, I need you to be real with me." I leaned across the table, drawing myself as close as it would allow and lowered my voice, "Why did you agree to this?"

He sat back, putting distance between us. His gray eyes narrowed as he contemplated.

"Linnie wouldn't give me anything. I didn't even know you were famous or athletic."

"Team Canada?"

"Are—are you changing the subject?" I laughed and it might have been the first real one in what felt like a lifetime.

He pressed his lips together.

"Please, just tell me. How much did Linnie pay you?"

His grin fell from his lips as confusion crept across his brow. "Pay?" He seemed to ponder the word before speaking again, "Oh, like a prostie?"

"Setting me up with the 'Sexiest Man Alive' seems a little suspect, doesn't it?" I whispered, hoping I hadn't offended him.

"Being sexiest could be profitable, I suppose." A twinkle of humor returned to his eyes as his lips toyed with a smile. "I wish I'd thought of that myself. Probably could have made a few quid off it." He winked. "But Linnie wouldn't have been able to afford me."

I laughed again, relieved he wasn't taking the question to heart, though I'd meant it.

"Coming here was my idea," he said flatly. "Jack told me about the wedding and I offered. This was never Linnie's idea."

"Your idea?" That felt worse somehow. Like he had learned of my tragic story and taken pity on me. "Sexiest Man Alive" level of pity.

"Your coffee and tea," the server interrupted. She was followed by my family pushing tables up to ours so we might all eat together. So they could eat with him. He was a star on the field and a star at the breakfast table. He smiled and laughed and acted as the perfect fit with my family. And every second of it made steam whistle out my sister's ears.

I struggled to eat at all, threatened entirely by IBS and nerves, but at least the coffee was almost as stunning as James's performance. Even I started to fall for it.

CHAPTER 3

"He's carrying my nana's bag and a chair for her to sit in at the shore since her hip likely won't cope with the beach blankets or picnic tables," I whispered into the phone.

"Yeah, he's a sweet boy. He's literally Jack's favorite friend," Linnie said as if the fact James Belvedere was at my brother's wedding was nothing. A simple fact. The sky was also blue.

"You promise you didn't pay him?" I asked flatly.

"He makes sixteen million pounds a year, Banana. I can't afford to pay him," she said with a laugh. "Hell, Skin Suit can hardly afford him."

"Well, as pathetic as it is, the pity date is working out perfectly. Everyone in the family adores him. Rachelle looks like she might shit herself if she can't win him over, and he acts like she isn't even here. But better yet, she's acting like Thomas isn't here." I chuckled at the sight of James carrying a beach chair, Nana's massive bag, and letting her cling to his free arm along the dirt trail.

"I told you this would work."

"Okay, I should go. I love you. Even if you're evil."

"Mmhmm. Love you too." She ended the call, and I focused on catching up to the crowd that was getting further from me.

Rachelle managed out of her sarong and handed it to Thomas, dumping it onto his armful of her crap he already carried, before she hurried to catch up to James and Nana. She took Nana's other arm and laughed loudly, obviously at something James had said.

I might have been jealous had this been real, but it wasn't.

Instead, I caught up to my father who walked a bit slower with his new hip and linked my arm in his.

"I'm really glad you came," Dad said. "I hoped that bad business with Rachelle and Thomas wouldn't keep you away." He peered down at me. "We can't help who we fall in love with. Can we?" he asked but I let it be rhetorical. I wasn't positive about what he knew, as far as the whole affair went. I had only told Jacob and Linnie what happened that fateful night six months ago.

I had borrowed Rachelle's car and was returning it, listening to the radio, absentmindedly. Only to have the Bluetooth link up to her phone as I pulled into her driveway. And there was my fiancé telling her he needed to be careful breaking things off with me as I was madly in love with him. And it killed him having to touch me or sleep next to me. He missed her, his cock of course missed her the most. The one-sided conversation went on for two minutes before he asked if she was still there.

Of course, words wouldn't leave my lips. They couldn't. Nothing could have shocked me more.

Not even her face popping out the front door, seeing mine, though it would haunt me forever.

I climbed out of the car, leaving it running with him saying hello over and over. I walked home, a fifteen-kilometer walk. It was one in the morning when I got there. I was home but I was lost.

He was gone.

His stuff was gone.

A letter remained, like we were in the 1900s.

An envelope sitting on the counter staring at me with my name across the front.

I didn't know where he'd gotten the envelope until I opened it.

He'd bought me an *Our Condolences* greeting card.

It had lilies on the front and pretty font swirling the words *"We're Sorry"* over top.

I never read what was inside.

What did it matter?

Clearly, he had bought it a while ago.

I didn't even care how long ago.

Seeing him trying to catch up to James and Rachelle, struggling with all her things, seemed funny now. It wasn't the karma he merited but it was a start.

My dad's eyes narrowed as he scrutinized Rachelle flirting with James over top of Nana's little gray head. "We're all so starstruck by him," he said with an awkward laugh but there was no denying the view or Rachelle's intentions. "How did you two meet, again?"

"Linnie. He's besties with Jack, her boyfriend."

Dad blanked.

"Skin Suit."

"Oh right, that's nice." He remembered the story. "How is Linnie? I thought she might end up as your plus one."

"She's busy," I lied. Linnie had been my intended plus one, but there was no way she wanted to risk ruining Jacob's wedding by murdering Thomas and beating Rachelle within an inch of her life. She loved Jacob. All my friends did. It had been an issue when we were younger.

"Well, I'm glad you brought James. He seems nice. Polite."

"He is, Dad," I said with a forced smile as Rachelle giggled away and Thomas tripped over a root he didn't see with the massive load in his arms.

Six months we'd been separated but the love I'd felt for him hadn't died off. It had changed its shape, becoming vile hatred, but I knew how close it remained to love. I hated that too.

The sound of the waterfall began to spill over from the shores of the river into the jungle trail.

My family's gasps joined in as they reached the destination and the stunning view. The waterfall was massive and the huge pool it fell into was the perfect swimming hole.

Paddleboards lined the shores and the picnic tables were already set up with drinks and cutlery awaiting the food.

Jacob made his way to us. "You doing okay, Dad?"

"Oh yeah, still breaking in the new hip." Dad stopped walking. "This is stunning, Son. What a beautiful location."

"It's gorgeous, Jacob," I agreed.

James settled Nana into her chair. Jacob followed my gaze to where Rachelle was readjusting her tiny bikini and turning her perfect bum to James, visibly asking him to tie the strings across her back. As if it weren't already a well tied double knot that Thomas had done.

James gave her a troubled look before turning to Thomas. He held his hands out for Thomas to give him the armload of stuff Rachelle required to exist on a beach for a day, so he might tie his own girlfriend's bathing suit.

Thomas gladly offloaded the haul and hurried to Rachelle who swatted him and huffed off with him on her heels.

It was a pathetic display.

Jacob sighed and Dad parted his lips as though he might try to explain the whole thing, but Mom walked over with a cool drink for him. "Darling, your favorite." She lifted the blood orange San Pellegrino. Condensation dripped from the sides of the ice-cold can.

"Oh good. I'm hot," Dad said, but his eyes stayed on Thomas and Rachelle as they squabbled. He followed Mom to sit at the picnic table.

"Did you tell them what actually happened?" Jacob asked as we watched the show.

"It's your wedding." I turned to him. "She's not ruining that. Let's swim and try not to drown in the waterfall."

He took a deep breath and switched back to the fun version of himself this weekend would require. "Okay, everyone! Let's get this party started." He clapped his hands and ran to his bride-to-be.

James made his way over to me with a mango-infused sparkling water in both hands. He handed me one. "Thirsty?"

"How did you know this is my favorite?" I asked as I took it and cracked it open.

"I'm a man of mystery, Nicky." He took a large drink from his own. There was something bizarrely sexy about the way he drank and licked his lips and breathed and wore clothes and existed. Adding swimsuits to the list of things he did sexily was making it harder not to stare.

I gulped. No drink, just gulping. Even worse, I gulped on nothing but air.

He offered an intense stare. "You ready to swim?"

"Swim?" I asked, saying the word as if I'd never heard of it. I was lost at sea in a gray ocean.

He blinked and brought me back to shore. "I'd love to," I lied. I didn't look the same way Rachelle did in a bikini. I didn't even own a bikini. I was a one-piece girl. I was a shorts and tee shirt girl. I was a wet suit girl.

"Let's do this then." He finished his sparkling water as if fizz didn't faze him and started unbuttoning his shirt. Each open button exposed a little bit more of him. I licked my lips. It was the least cool thing I'd done. But he didn't seem bothered by it. In fact, his sexy, fun smile turned to something else. Our eyes locked as he unbuttoned the rest of it and slid it off, revealing his ridiculous body. Perfectly chiselled muscles. Flawless skin that seemed kissed by the sun in a way that never damaged it. He glowed with vitality and sinewy strength. A dark-haired Adonis. A raven-haired Achilles.

I gulped again.

My can buckled a little in my hand under my grip, spilling sparkling water down my arm and startling me with the crushing can sound.

His eyes widened with mine, though he seemed oblivious to the icy water on my skin.

He adjusted the black swimming shorts he wore and nodded at me. "It's your turn."

I took a sip of the water and handed him my slightly crinkled can.

It was as if no one else was there as I slid my tee shirt from my body, revealing a black athletic one piece. No cleavage visible. No sexy lines. Nana and I had the same suit. At least something similar.

Why didn't I let Linnie pack my suitcase?

James didn't seem to notice. He drank my water and offered his hand to hold my shirt. I gave it to him and struggled out of my shorts, catching a flip-flop I'd failed to remove and nearly falling over.

"Do you want to paddleboard first or swim?" he asked, genuinely.

"Paddleboard. That water is going to be freezing." My answer was a confident one. I'd boarded a lot in Canada.

"You should be accustomed to freezing cold water," he teased and carried our clothes to the spot where everyone was putting theirs.

I grabbed a tandem board and paddle and set us up. He jogged over, earning a stare from every member of ours and Simone's families. His muscles flexed and moved in slow motion, I swear. He smiled wide, making me return the look.

It was impossible to feel sorry for myself in his presence. He was enjoyable. Completely. And weirdly wholesome in a sexy way. I wasn't sure what was happening, but I was one hundred percent certain Linnie understood the assignment. He was perfect.

"You can swim, right?" I asked when he got closer.

"Like an Olympian," he answered. "It's how I like to do everything." He beamed and I gulped again. Like an idiot, fighting the urge to chant "Hercules" at him. "Do you like being in the front or the back?"

I blinked, wanting so badly to say on top. I'm a top. That was my answer. *Top. Top, please.*

He narrowed his gaze. "You seem like the kind of girl who wants to steer. Why don't you go up front, then?"

I nodded, unable to say anything that wasn't top. My brain had overheated and glitched.

He smiled pointed at the board. "Get on the board."

"What?" I bit my lip and clung to the paddle, confused until I realized I was waiting for the sex dream in my head to play out to the end. "Right," I said. "Okay." It took a whole other second for my body to be able to move. "Being in the front is probably a better idea," I muttered, suddenly aware of how distracting he was. I'd steer us right into the waterfall at this rate. Hopefully, it would put out the fire inside me at least.

We giggled and paddled about, escaping several near misses as everyone else fell into the water one by one. All except for Rachelle who sat on the end of her paddleboard as Thomas paddled her around the pool, as if she were on vacation in Venice. Every time I glanced in their direction she was focused on James. It was creepy.

But James was an incredible distraction from my woes. "You have amazing core," he said as I steered us as near to the waterfall as you could get without falling in.

"You have amazing core," I replied. "I have okay core. I haven't done much in the last six months." The confession stung and was inappropriate here in this sexy daydream.

"Fifteen years of intense rugby suggests otherwise." He scoffed.

"I guess," I said and realized what he'd said. "Wait, how do you know that? It's almost seventeen, but how did you know how long I played?"

"Linnie said she played that long," he said casually. "I assumed it was the same amount of time."

"Yeah, I quit a little before her. Got my second concussion and that was it." It wasn't entirely the truth. Thomas had demanded I quit; the concussion was simply the breaking point. I turned around and faced James. "Guess I could have started playing the fairer sport. You lot never seem to have concussions. Not real ones anyway," I teased, letting my guard down a bit more.

"You would love football. I could teach you."

"You mean when we get back to the real world?" I joked but he didn't smile.

"Absolutely." His intense stare sucked me in again.

I lost time until my mother shouted something about lunch.

I handed him the paddle. "Want a turn?"

He stared at it for a second and shook his head. "Nope, I think it's time you get wet," he said.

"What?" Was it crude to tell there was a good chance I was already quite wet?

I didn't have a chance as he rushed me, tipping the board, and sending us sinking into the icy water below.

The current from the river pulled a little, but he found me in the dark and swam us both to the surface. We broke the waves together, gasping for air. He was sexier wet, with water dripping down his face and coating his lips. I stared at them, noting every curve, and wondering how they felt.

He grabbed the paddleboard with a long arm and pulled it to us for me to grip, but I remained treading water and staring at him.

He smiled deliciously and took my hand in his, creating warmth in the cool water. "Ready for lunch now that you're not so hot and sweaty?"

Were his questions all sexy or was my brain switched to the sexy setting?

The better question was, *Would it be wrong to have sex with him?*

Did a pity date include sex?

CHAPTER 4

The rehearsal dinner was done but the party continued. The lights and torches all around us created a romantic glow.

Music played loudly, making talking an intimate affair.

James danced with Nana, leading her next to Jacob and Simone. I began to wonder if Nana knew who he was and was smitten. Rachelle and Thomas made their way closer to them. Her dress was stunning. An obvious attempt to upstage the bride but Simone didn't seem to notice. She and Jacob were focused only on each other. I'd never seen him this way. Not even when he and Linnie dated briefly in high school.

I sipped my glass of sangria, noting this one was slightly stronger.

When the song ended, James made his way over to me. He took my sangria and finished it in one large drink. He shuddered. "I think that bartender is trying to get you a little bollocksed," he said with a wince and glanced in her direction. "Oof, she's just your type. Allow me to get the drinks." He walked off, leaving me questioning how he knew she was exactly my type.

Was that something Linnie would have shared?

It seemed like a weird thing to bring up.

He came back a moment later. "She knew it was for you. It's twice as strong."

I laughed. "Maybe she's trying to help you out." I took the drink.

"Nicky, I don't need alcohol to seduce you," he said, as if it was a simple statement. A fact. His stare bored down into mine, again holding me hostage. "Let's have a dance." He offered a hand.

"Okay," I said, taking his hand.

He led me to the dance floor where the band played an interesting version of "Free Bird."

Our eyes locked and I was hostage.

Desperate for a distraction, I decided we needed to get to know each other better. "Tell me about you," I demanded a little heavily for the conversation starter. "Three things you don't like talking about."

"I'm an only child. I had a brother but he died when I was eleven. He was fifteen. He was born sick, but he fought. He was amazing. Nathanial." James spun me around the dance floor like he'd had lessons. He was right, he did everything like an Olympian. "My cat, Percy Jackson, is my best mate. He rescued me three years ago when he showed up on my doorstep in Kensington. I learned how to crochet so I could make him jumpers. He has one for every holiday."

I laughed at that one.

He smiled but I was lost in the dance steps as he whirled me around. His movements were sharp and direct, firm and controlling. He was bizarrely talented.

"And lastly, I've followed your career."

"What?" I tried to comprehend his sentence. "What do you mean?"

He danced us to the far side of the stunning platform overlooking the sea. He stopped dancing when we reached the corner. His eyes were iridescent with the light of the torches beside us. "You can't judge me on this, okay?"

"Okay," I lied.

He bit his lip, pausing as though he might not say it, but he took a deep breath. "Fuck it. When I was thirteen, I went to a girls' rugby tourney in Ireland. A cousin was playing for England. There was a girl there, she was fifteen. She was the most beautiful girl I'd ever seen. She played with such heart it put everyone I knew to shame. She scored a try in the last seconds of the game. It was the fiercest thing I'd ever seen. She broke her ankle but kept pushing. She played on a broken bone."

I gasped, remembering how painful that had been but was immediately distracted by what he was about to say.

"We hung out all weekend. I bought her a slushy drink and made her laugh. I kept the receipt."

"Smithy," I whispered slowly, recalling with perfect detail his face as a thirteen-year-old boy. I'd considered him too young, but he was so cute. *How was this possible?*

"I followed her from then on. When she was invited onto the Canadian Olympic team, I made my mates come celebrate with me. I went to every game I could from the moment I made money playing football." He closed his eyes as if humiliated. But it got worse, and I realized that was why he closed his eyes. "I ordered her posters and had a tee shirt of her card made. I wore it under my kit for good luck. It's still in my locker at Stamford Bridge."

"Oh my God." I lifted my hands to my mouth. I was judging. It was accidental.

"I know. It gets worse, believe it or not. Fucking hell." He nodded, not yet meeting my gaze. "When my mate started dating her friend, I begged them to set me up. I even showed her friend my childhood bedroom with the posters of her friend on my walls. Still."

I pressed my lips together and shook my head in tiny twitches. I wasn't upset that he was a stalker, I was humiliated for him. I imagined how this must feel to tell this story. It was awful. And yet, I'd never had a fan before. Not like this. Recognition of women's rugby in Canada was still a bit sad instead of celebrated as it should be. And Linnie would have tortured him.

"Her friend said she was engaged to a horrid bloke and there was no chance. I was crushed. But then he cheated on her a couple of months later with her little sister and broke her heart." His stare found mine again. My eyes watered and his glistened with the light around us. "So, for six months I waited for the chance to tell her. Until this wedding came along. It was the moment I'd waited for my whole life."

"Oh my God," I repeated.

"It's been fifteen years since I saw you play rugby. It's why I know that bartender looks astonishingly similar to the girl you dated year twelve or senior year. It's why I know mango sparkling water is your favorite. It's why I know the scar on your ankle is from the surgery you had to have when you returned to Canada."

It was unbelievable. I had no response. How was this possible?

"For every person in the world who has fanned over me, I have spent an entire life as your biggest fan."

I blinked, stunned.

"Don't look at me like that. You play with more heart than anyone I have met and that is saying a lot. And for fifteen years I wished I could do this." He stepped closer. "Can I kiss you?"

I didn't answer him with words. I lifted my face as he lowered his and lightly brushed his lips against mine. It wasn't a kiss in the making for fifteen years; it was soft and delicate and caged.

The subtle vibration behind it suggested it wasn't even the tip of the iceberg.

Carefully, I brushed my tongue against his lips, hoping to send the signal that he didn't need to hold back. His arms wrapped around me, his fingers digging in, lifting me off the ground and pressing me into him.

"Can I have everyone's attention?" my brother's voice drifted in like a bad dream. "Banana," he said loudly.

I pulled back, dying at the sound of my nickname over a microphone.

The music had ended and everyone was watching us.

James carefully placed my feet back on the earth, ending the ecstasy and dream I was stuck in.

"Would all the male-presenting people of the wedding come with me for a night of Polynesian ceremony? As you all know, we chose this spot because it's entirely Indigenous owned and operated to ensure Hawaiians benefit from our tourism. One of the perks of choosing this space was this night that's offered." Jacob directed us to a man who seemed to appear out of nowhere. He was bare chested and wearing stunning Polynesian garments. "This is Jare. He'll be escorting us to the other side of the resort. We have to paddle there."

Jare waved and everyone in the party waved back.

"And I'm asking the fairer side of our families to please join me in the spa. We will sleep in the lush rooms there and wake to an early regime of health and wellness the islands are known for," Simone spoke loudly, not needing the microphone.

I glanced up at James, regretting that we hadn't escaped before this moment.

"Fuck," James muttered. His eyes were wild with the conversation we'd been having and not having. There was still so much to be said.

"See you tomorrow?" I asked, hoping he didn't regret telling me his insane secret.

He leaned down and pressed his lips into mine once more.

He made a sound like a grumble as he pulled away and walked off with my brother, trying to seem excited to be there.

I couldn't feign the same feelings since all the people I liked were going that way.

"Come along, Nicky, don't hold everyone up," Mom called after me as she followed Simone and her mother and sisters down the stairs to the trail back to the spa.

Rachelle waited for me at the bottom of the stairs.

"Worst night ever," I muttered as I made my way over there.

"You could stay and hide here," the bartender said as I passed her.

"You have no idea how tempting that is," I said and winked at her. "Have a nice night."

"You too!"

"Big sister," Rachelle said as I started to descend. "You have to tell me the story of how you two met."

"Why do you care?" I had nothing for her. As far as I was concerned, she had the blood of my broken heart on her hands.

"It's crazy that you happen to show up to the wedding with this surprise guest. No warning you were bringing a celebrity to steal Simone's thunder."

"Ya know, Rachelle, I want to forgive you for doing something so horrid to me." I stopped at the bottom stair so I was her height. "Because I finally see you did me the biggest favor. You did that for me. You saved me from marrying a villain." I wrapped my arms around her stiff body and hugged tightly. "Thank you." I pulled back, smiling genuinely. "If you hadn't freed me, I never would have found my way back to James."

"Back?"

"Yes, back. We've known each other since we were thirteen and fifteen." I loved that. Even if he was a weird fanboy, I loved it. For the first time in my life, I felt seen.

"That doesn't even make sense. You're lying. Linnie's boyfriend probably made him do this."

"Night, Rachelle." I waved overhead and headed for the spa.

CHAPTER 5

He was waiting at the entrance to the tent, dressed in his suit, looking fresh faced and handsome. My heart skipped a beat seeing him. I'd thought about him all night long, reliving that summer of rugby and meeting him and his friends. It was crazy I hadn't recognized him but understandable since it had been fifteen years, and my ankle was broken at the time.

I hurried in my off-the-shoulder white and blue floral A-line as fast as I could without sweating in the heat and humidity. Hawaii was wet. The air was wet. The wind heavy. The ground damp. Not like the interior of Canada at all. More like Vancouver in the summer after a heavy rainfall. A situation I always tried to avoid.

His lips curled into a wide smile when he realized I was walking to him.

"You are stunning," he said as he walked over and pressed a gentle kiss into my cheek right where he wouldn't smudge any makeup.

"You also look stunning." I reached up and brushed a hand on his cheek. "You shaved."

"Of course. It's not proper for a bloke to show up to a wedding unshaven. How was the hen do?"

"What?"

"The—" he flourished his hands in the direction of the spa. "The night and spa and such."

"Ohhhhhh hens. Right." I chuckled. "It was great. I managed to get a massage and detox wrap and water therapy. How was the Polynesian night?"

"Top night. Your brother's great."

Something in his tone suggested otherwise. "Did he threaten to kill you?"

"Twice." He held his fingers up, smiling wide.

"He's been weird since the whole—" My eyes darted to the spot my sister sat with Thomas. "I think he saw some things he shouldn't have." My mind did a tour of the many days my brother showed up at my small apartment to force me out of bed.

"He loves you."

I turned back to him and sighed. "He does. You want to take a seat?"

"Let's," he said and wrapped an arm around my back. The heat from his fingers through the thin fabric of the dress made my skin shiver. We sat with my parents and sister and Thomas. I made sure Nana was between us and Thomas. I couldn't bear to sit near him.

I crossed my legs as James slid a hand on my knee. He was a furnace.

"Have you ever contemplated coaching rugby?" James asked casually as we waited for the wedding to start.

"I was coaching—the year before." I didn't have the heart to tell him I never went back because my heart hurt too much.

"I know someone looking for a coach. Good job. In London."

"I can't afford London, James." I scoffed. "The people in London can't afford London."

"I'll rent you something." He said it sincerely but the idea of him paying for me made me want to run away. I recoiled. "Whatever that did to you, I'm sorry."

Realizing he was simply being nice, and my horror show of a past was making me a psycho, I shook my head. "Nothing to be sorry for." I lowered my voice, deciding it was my turn. "Three things I don't like talking about. Everyone in my family, including Linnie, calls me Banana because I ate so many when I was little, I got sick in front of everyone. It was a ride." I closed my eyes, reliving my own horrors. "I got sick on everyone on the ride. Banana vomit."

"Oof."

"Yup." I wrinkled my nose but continued, "I didn't get my period until I was sixteen. I was a freak show to my mom. It was humiliating. She dragged me to doctors. Mortifying me. I finally stopped her by pretending I got my period by rubbing my nose during allergy season and forcing nose bleeds in my underwear." I covered my eyes for a second.

"That's ghastly. Child cruelty." He struggled not to laugh. "I'm sorry. The nose thing is brilliant."

"It came a couple of months later so it was fine." I lowered my voice more, leaning right in so I could feel the warmth of him. "When my sister and Thomas got together, he wouldn't allow me to stay in the condo we lived in. He wanted to rent it out and make money and live with Rachelle. Playing rugby, I never made much money. I was broke. So, I had to move into a studio in a bad part of town. It was scary. Domestic violence all around me all the time. Assaults. Robberies. Break-ins. I lived in total fear for four months until I could find another job and save up and move into a better place."

"Jesus."

"Yeah. I never told anyone where I was living except my brother. I was so ashamed. But it was my own fault for letting Thomas be the money maker while I played rugby. I should have been prepared for the worst instead of living blindly in the best."

"He kicked you out?" His tone was dangerous. Something you didn't expect with him being so sweet and fun.

"He did." I nodded. "It all caught me off guard. I wasn't prepared financially."

"Of course, you didn't expect to have the rug pulled out from under you." His free hand clenched into a fist.

"Right. And I vowed I wouldn't do that again. I would be smart with money and never let someone take care of me or set me up for failure. You know?"

He squeezed my knee but couldn't say anything as my brother walked to the arch facing the sea.

The music started and Simone's stunning sisters began their walk down the aisle. The flower girl was an adorable little thing who left a sporadic display of rose petals.

We all stood as Simone appeared with her father. Her dress was breathtaking. She beamed as she stared down the aisle at my brother.

James slid his hand into mine, enveloping it and squeezing as they walked down the aisle.

The ceremony was stunning and my brother cried more than she did.

Love was all around us.

Dinner and dancing were in the same place as the night before, but they had added to the white decor and lights to make it all brighter. The whole scene glistened in the twilight.

We ate and laughed and danced and I sensed the walls around my heart weakening.

It was a start.

A beginning.

It was hope.

Dizzy with champagne and lust, I collapsed into James's arms. Out of breath but in sync with him, I leaned in and whispered, "Let's go."

His eyes widened and he stared as if checking to be sure. I was sure. I smiled coyly and laced my fingers into his.

He led me off the dance floor and down the stairs toward the rooms.

Our steps were hurried and our grip tightening, but we didn't speak. Instead, we raced to his room. He was on the main floor. He fished for his key card, his hand slightly trembling as he tapped it. His stare found mine as he cracked the door open. I moved into his embrace, letting him consume me as he dragged me into the darkness of his room.

It smelled like him and cologne.

The door closed and my back hit it as he pressed himself into me, caressing too many places all at once. Lips, hips, stomach, breasts. Hands tugging at my dress, sliding it down me until I stood in front of him in nothing but ballet flats and Spanx.

Shit.

I forgot about the Spanx.

I was going to take it off before.

"Why do you gals all wear this fucking second skin?" he questioned as he slid his fingers into the waistband and rolled it down as one would a condom. It clearly wasn't his first Spanx rodeo. He removed it so fast I hardly felt the pinch of the removal.

I stepped out of it and my shoes all at once.

He stood pressing his fully dressed body against my naked form.

His lips devoured me.

Hands lifting me into him.

I fumbled with his buttons, removing his shirt and freeing his blazing skin.

He was firm and rigid against the softness of my body.

A moan escaped my lips as he slid his massive fingers down my stomach and between my legs, delicately pleasing all the right places.

His kisses grew more intense as his fingers moved expertly.

I was drowning in pleasure and unable to get a full breath.

He increased his pressure and speed, sending me over the edge. My body tensed as my knees threatened to buckle. He held me up, forcing me to remain as I was while I orgasmed violently. He knew how to drag it out, making me beg for mercy by the end.

Gasping for air, I found my way to his belt and the button then zipper of his pants. I felt him through the fabric of his underwear but didn't get a chance to touch him. He lifted me and carried me to the bed, forcing me under his weight. The sound of the condom wrapper and our heaving breaths created a strange moment before he continued to kiss my neck, pushing himself against me, easing into me.

"Ready?" he asked.

"Yeah," I answered breathily.

But I wasn't.

He pushed himself inside me, taking my breath away.

There was bliss in losing this control over my body. He moved rhythmically, sending me over the edge yet again as every nerve was stroked and lit on fire. He was perfection.

Nothing had felt like this before.

Two bodies meant to fit with one another.

The bed became a sea of madness and lust as we set sail, taking turns controlling the waves rocking the boat.

There was a holy moment as I rode him, his hands cupping my breasts, and my head tilted back. Through the window, fireworks went off from the wedding celebrations outside, coinciding with the fireworks inside me.

The light of them bounced off our bodies and the walls and ceiling.

As they ended, I collapsed in the darkness, sated and blown away by the best sex I'd ever had.

He was worth every pound.

"Is that what fifteen years in the making feels like?" I asked as I lay down next to him.

"No. I rushed it." His kiss whispered against the side of my face. "I'll show you fifteen years' worth of angst tomorrow."

I laughed and for the first time in a long time, I felt completely at ease with the person lying next to me.

CHAPTER 6

"Your shirt's inside out. And actually backwards, for fuck's sake," my brother murmured as I took pancakes and sausages from the breakfast buffet. "I think you had better wedding-night sex than I did."

"Gross." I glanced down at the tag sticking out. "Shit." I handed him my plate and slid my arms in and turned it so at least the tag was at the back.

I glimpsed back at the table where James sat, laughing with my parents, a picture of perfection. Even his dark hair suited the messy bed-head boy band look. I'd put mine in a messy bun to hide the disarray.

"You actually like him, don't you?" Jacob asked, handing back my plate.

"I do," I said, though it was scary to admit that.

"Linnie chose wisely, I guess."

"It wasn't her. He asked to be set up with me. We met fifteen years ago."

"Weird. How the hell did that happen?—ohhh rugby. Of course. Little Miss Team Canada." He put it together so much faster than I expected. "Those Brits do love rugby too. But are you really up for something?" Jacob's stare flooded with concern.

"Nothing is something yet. I'm up for a casual hookup for your wedding, and we'll see where that takes us." I leaned in and hugged him with one arm awkwardly. "Thanks for being a weirdo big brother."

His eyes darted to Rachelle and Thomas. "One snake in the family is more than enough."

"He won't last, Jacob. She never makes it past a year."

"We'll see." Jacob walked away with his plate of food.

I sauntered back to the table to find Dad regaling James with stories of being a young man in the military before he figured what he wanted to do, as if playing football was the same.

James took it better than I might have.

I didn't have the heart to tell Dad how much James made.

Realizing the time, I kissed my dad and promised my mom I would call when I arrived home safely.

I hugged my brother and Simone and bid them farewell on their Hawaiian island-tour honeymoon.

Ignoring my sister and Thomas, I linked my fingers into James's and hurried to get my bags for the flight home.

"Meet out front in ten?" I asked and kissed him at my door.

"Okay." He kissed me a second time and hurried for his own room.

Immediately, I Facetimed Linnie and started shoving my things into my carry-on.

"Aloha!" she said excitedly. "How was the trip? Are you back yet or is this the ceiling of your room I'm looking at?"

"You suck. You couldn't have warned me that we met him fifteen years ago and that he has posters of me on his walls?" I grabbed the phone and carried her into the bathroom.

"In my defense—absolutely not. There weren't words for it. How do you tell someone they have the 'Sexiest Man Alive' as their fanboy? Would you have even believed me?"

"I guess not." I laughed.

"When are you home?"

"Few hours. I fly out soon. We're on our way to the airport in five." I did a circle around the room checking for anything I'd missed.

"Call when you get home so I can hear the details."

"What details?" I scowled at her.

"He fucked you so hard your shirt is inside out and your hair has a cowlick in the front of that messy bun. I think one of your fake eyelashes is stuck to your lower lashes. Chat soon." She ended the call.

Groaning, I hurried to the door to find him already there. He grabbed my bag and hurried down the stairs to the lobby.

We raced out to the waiting car.

Where we sat in a strange silence to the airport.

I didn't know what to say.

The cold realization of our situation hit harder with every kilometer we drove.

He lived in London and had a short offseason.

I worked in BC and couldn't afford to visit him.

I peered down at my inside-out shirt and smiled.

At least we had this. We had Hawaii.

We arrived and walked to security together with just our boarding passes and carry-on luggage.

My fingers were linked in his right up to my gate.

I lifted my face to tell him I was so glad we met again, but he kissed me before I could speak.

"How long is the flight to Vancouver?" he whispered against my cheek.

"Five hours, -ish. And then a three-hour delay. And then a quick forty-five minutes to Kamloops where I live."

"Jesus. I'll be in London faster than that."

"But you'll have jet lag and I won't," I teased but my heart wasn't in it. I had a weird feeling, a fearful question. What if we didn't see each other again?

"How long until you can come to London to visit?"

"I don't get time off again until December and I googled your game schedule. December is the worst."

He led me to the far side of the gate by the window and pulled off his sunglasses. "Take the job in London. We can figure out the housing thing. You can stay with me." The desperation in his stare made my insides ache.

"I can't," I whispered. "Not yet. Not like this."

"Not yet?" He arched a dark eyebrow. "When?"

I gulped. I wasn't certain I'd ever gulped in my life before I met him. It was impossible to say no to those gray eyes. I caught myself lost in them again. Time passed and I drifted. No answers. Just wishes.

The flight attendant announced the boarding of the flight to Vancouver.

"When?" he repeated.

I wanted to joke about the fifteen years he'd pined already, but there was nothing left of my sense of humor. It had died in the car somewhere along the road.

The crushing heartbreak on his face destroyed me.

I lifted to my tiptoes and pressed my lips against his.

It felt like a goodbye.

One I didn't want to make.

There were no words to say, so I kissed him again and headed to the gate.

I turned back once more before walking through the door for the loading bridge. He placed a hand on his heart as a swarm of people realized who he was. I lost him in the crowd.

The ache worsened as I sat in my seat, staring out my tiny window up to the massive one where the horde of people forced him to be kind and jovial. I couldn't see him, he was surrounded.

Before thinking I texted.

If I show up next week, can I get a ride from Heathrow? I heard the taxis are pricy.

The text was sent but I still stared at it in disbelief.

What was I thinking?

Hope.

It was hope.

For the first time in a long time.

Thanks for reading. Check out the rest of Tara's books on her website at www.tarabrownauthor.com.

A LITTLE TEASE

TIA LOUISE

AIDEN

"Terra said he got her key out of her pocket without her even knowing he'd touched her, and you know how tight she wears those jeans." Deputy Doug scrubs his palm against the back of his gray head, his brown eyes worried.

My brow furrows. "Was he trying to steal her car?"

"Nope—he just gave it back to her. Said it was a demonstration of what he could've done if he'd wanted to. She was pretty spooked by it."

"Who is this guy?" Annoyance creeps into my tone.

As the sheriff of Eureka, South Carolina, population three thousand, I don't like creeps showing up at our one local hangout and scaring the customers.

"Dunno. She said he had dark hair and an accent. I was thinking if he's a magician, maybe we should pull the mayor in on this one, see if she has any ideas."

"A pickpocket is not a magician." I'm on my feet, headed for the door of my office. "And the mayor has retired from magic."

It was the only condition my dad had for staying on as sheriff after she was elected. Having a former magician as mayor was bad enough. The last thing he needed was everyone looking for her to give them signs and make predictions.

I remember him saying that's how you end up with all the townsfolk sitting on top of their houses in their bathrobes waiting for the world to end.

"She could be like a secret weapon." Doug looks down at his boots. "I watched this whole show the other night about psychic detectives, and you wouldn't believe the things they were able to uncover."

"Edna is *not* a psychic." And I'm done with this conversation.

I agree with my late father. Edna Brewer has done a better job as mayor of Eureka than any of us expected, and I'm not messing with success by adding a bunch of carnival-sideshow antics to the mix.

"Her daughter's a psychic." Doug follows me into the main room of the courthouse. "We could see if Gwen has any insights."

"Gwen is a tarot reader." And as fake as her mother the mayor, I mentally add. "So that's all you got? A mysterious stranger showed up, picked a pocket, and left?"

"Terra said he was looking for somebody."

That catches my interest. "Who?"

"She didn't recognize the name, so she didn't remember it. You know how Terra is. If it's not about pickles, it's not on her radar."

"Is he still hanging around?"

"He could be back again tonight. It's Friday, after all." He gives me a look as if to imply *somebody* should do a stake-out at the El Rio bar.

Doug is pushing sixty, whereas I'm almost thirty-five. Still, I've got a son at home, and all his kids have moved away.

"Why don't you have dinner and hang around a while to see if anything happens."

"Aw, Sheriff. You know I like to turn in early."

"And Mom has her bridge game on the first Friday of every month."

"You don't have a sitter?"

"Mom is my sitter."

I level my gaze on my sole deputy, and he holds up both hands as if I pulled my gun. "Okay, okay. I'll see if the wife is up for Mexican tonight."

"They say regular date nights keep your marriage healthy." As if I'd know anything about a healthy marriage.

My wife died three years ago, and then later, when I was packing up her things, I found a series of love letters between her and the town librarian. It put the final nail in the coffin of love for me, figuratively speaking.

Doug laughs, shaking his shoulders. "After forty years, we're about as healthy as we're going to get."

"Let me know if you learn anything." My voice is growly now.

Any time the subject of marriage comes up, it spoils my mood. Doug hustles out the door, and I glance at the clock. It's after five, and I need to pick up Own. He goes to my mom's house after school until I get off from work, and he's the only thing that makes me smile these days.

Edna's at her door when I pass it, and I give her a brief, non-engaging, courtesy nod. "Have a good weekend."

"You too." Her tone is distracted, and she's not smiling like she usually is.

I blame Doug for what happens next.

"Everything okay?" As the words leave my mouth, I regret speaking them.

I typically don't dig too deep into Edna's personal life, mostly because I have no idea what lunacy might come up—like pulling a rabbit from a hat or a series of scarves from her sleeve, I want no part of it.

"Oh, it's my granddaughter's last night in town." She exhales, shaking her head sadly. "I tried to get her to stay, but she's hell-bent on moving to Greenville and forging her own path."

My eyebrow arches. I hadn't paid too much attention to Britt Bailey—partly because she's seven years younger than me, but mostly because she's Edna's granddaughter, and kooky Gwen's daughter.

Britt's a cute little blonde with a round ass and cowboy boots she likes to wear with cutoff blue jeans, but I have no interest in romance—fool me once —and I especially have no interest in getting mixed up with their nutty family.

"There's not a lot of jobs here in Eureka." My voice is rough and final, not engaging in the conversation. "It's probably best that she goes somewhere else."

"That's just it. She's training to be a forensic photographer. I was hoping she'd join the force with you and Doug. Not that Doug lends much to the force."

She can say that again, but shit, the last thing I need is another Brewer-Bailey around here.

"Well, I've got to pick up Owen." I clear my throat, backing away. "Maybe she'll come back to visit."

"She will." Edan's voice trails off, and she lets out another deep sigh. "Goodnight, Sheriff."

I hustle out the door to my parked truck, feeling like I've been dodging landmines for the last hour—first with Doug trying to get me to go out on a Friday night, then with Edna trying to pull me into her family troubles.

I'm picking up my son, and we're going to have a quiet night at home. No strangers, who probably aren't as mysterious as Terra would like them to be, or family drama. All quiet, just how I like it.

It's a short drive to the old, oversized farmhouse where we grew up. It's white with a large, wrap-around porch, short palmettos, and towering, thick-trunked oak trees in the front yard, and too many memories to count.

Parking in the long drive, I hop out when I hear Owen calling my name.

"Dad! Dad!" He runs to where I'm standing, blue eyes bright and breathing hard. "Gran said I can spend the night with Ryan tonight! And we're going to swim and pop popcorn and eat hotdogs…"

"Hey, catch your breath, buddy." I lean down to give him a hug.

Warmth squeezes my chest when I see the excitement in his eyes. Owen is the one good thing in my life. The one thing that makes all that old pain feel worth it. At least it gave me him.

"It's okay, Dad? Isn't it?"

"You're spending the night with Ryan?" My brow furrows, and I look up to see my youngest brother Adam walking out onto the porch.

"Mom's keeping Owen and Ryan tonight. You're coming with me to a party."

Standing, I slide my thumbs along the waist of my pants, just above the gun belt on my hips. "Is that so?"

Ryan is the son of my brother's friend Piper, and Owen's best friend. Since her boyfriend died, my brother took over taking care of Piper and her son. None of us have been able to figure out their relationship, and they keep a lid on it tighter than Fort Knox.

"Yeah, and you need to get moving," Adam continues.

"What about the Bridge game?"

"Canceled—one of the old ladies got poison ivy working in her garden, and you have to have four people to play the game."

"I know how Bridge works."

"I'm sure you do, Grandpaw." He rolls his blue eyes, same color as mine. "You're old, but you're not old enough to spend every Friday night at home alone. Mom agrees with me."

Placing my hands on my hips, I scowl. "I'm not old, and I like spending the weekends with my son. It's our time together."

"That's very admirable, but tonight you're coming with me." He catches my arm, pulling me to the truck. "Let's go, so you can put on something more festive."

I hold up a hand, taking a minute to step inside and speak to our mom. I make sure she doesn't need anything, and that she's actually fine with keeping two seven-year-old boys this evening.

"I like you and Adam spending time together." Smiling, Mom slides her hand in the crook of my arm, walking down the porch steps with me and pausing at a bushy green shrub covered in giant red blooms. "Just look at my hibiscus! Here, take one. It's my souvenir of our honeymoon in Hawaii—the one time your father took me on a beach vacation."

She plucks a vibrant flower off the bush, and before I can stop her, she actually loops it behind my right ear.

"Mom." I reach up to swipe it away, but she catches my hand.

"Hibiscus flowers symbolize joy, and wearing one behind your right ear means you're on the market." She winks, clearly in cahoots with my brother.

It only makes me frown more, and I take the flower off my head. "I'm not on the market."

"Aiden..." Compassion fills her eyes and her tone. "I know it's hard to move on after the death of a spouse, but you can't be single forever."

Pity bristles my skin, and she has no idea the farce my marriage was. I never told anyone about Annemarie's infidelity, because Owen deserves to have good memories of his mother.

"I noticed you've never remarried."

"Well, I was an old lady when your father died. That part of my life had ended."

"That part of my life has ended, too."

Her lips press into a thin line, and I know she wants to argue. I don't give her a chance. "Thanks for keeping Owen. I'll be here early tomorrow to get him."

"Not too early." She smiles as the two boys run out to the pool yelling *cannonball* before jumping in. "They'll play all night and sleep late tomorrow."

"If it's too much—"

"It keeps me young." Her eyes dance, and she kisses my cheek. "I want you to stay open to what the future holds."

"Let's go." Adam walks up beside us, kissing my mother's cheek and hustling me to the truck.

I give up the fight. I figure we'll check out whatever party he has, then head over to El Rio for a bit, where I can relieve Doug. Maybe catch a glimpse of this mysterious stranger.

Shania Twain music is blasting when we pull up at the large house, and I see a group of Adam's old school friends spilling onto the front porch.

"Why are we at Gwen's?" I frown, as my brother parks the car and opens the door.

"It's where the party's at." He cuts his eyes at my expression, and laughs. "Don't worry, nobody's going to try and read your future. Gwen's not even here."

He slams the door, and I step out, surveying the crowd. "Hanging out with a bunch of kids is not my idea of a party."

"Last I checked, we were all over twenty-five."

I'm about to leave on foot—Eureka's small enough that almost every place is within walking distance, including my house—when I see pale blonde waves highlighted by the moon.

Her soft laugh and sunny smile hold me in place, and like a siren call on the ocean, I find myself walking towards her instead of away.

"I'll stay a few minutes, then I'm heading home."

"That's the spirit." My brother slaps me on the back. "I'll grab us a few drinks."

A mermaid fountain is in Gwen's front yard, and a bush that smells like gardenia. Soft-yellow twinkle lights are wrapped around the beams over her front porch, and hurricane candles line the steps.

As I slowly follow my brother towards the house, my eyes go to the pretty girl holding a glass of sparkling wine and smiling like sunshine.

The first time I remember seeing Britt Bailey, I was seventeen and she was ten. She was wearing a maroon velvet dress, and her long, blonde hair was in a thick braid over her shoulder. A black beret was on her head, and she stood by her mother on the deck of a large ship, watching the dark waves churning in the ocean.

We were all there, because her father, the famous escape artist Lars Bailey, was performing a much-publicized, death-defying stunt. All the ads said it was the same stunt that had brought down the great Houdini. He was strapped in a straight jacket, sealed in a waterproof box, and lowered into the ocean.

The claim was he'd triumphantly rise to the surface of the ocean in less than four minutes, and people came from miles around to watch him do it. They even set up huge screens, so the people on shore could see the moment he broke through the waves.

The Brewer-Bailey family drove my dad nuts, but I always thought Lars Bailey's act was fun to watch.

Nothing was fun that day. I'll never forget the sick feeling in the pit of my stomach as four minutes turned to six, as my dad tried to get them to send in the rescue team, as Lars's manager argued to give him more time. The sealed box had air for up to fifteen minutes, he'd said...

More time passed, and my dad finally pulled rank and forced them to haul the box out of the water. I'll never forget seeing it rise, seeing the saltwater rushing out of it as the truth broke over all of us. Lars Bailey was dead.

Gwen's scream is a sound I'll never forget as long as I live. I'll never forget Britt's young face, stricken and lost. She looked so alone, and I wondered if anyone would comfort her.

Three weeks later, I left for Annapolis, but that memory never left me.

"Everybody stay cool—nobody called in a noise complaint." My brother's joking voice pulls me from that dark past.

Now everyone's looking at me as he hands me a red solo cup of what I expect is Natural Light, the cheapest, most watered-down beer on the planet.

"You're really making me want to stay," I growl, studying the piss in my cup.

"Glad you're here, Sheriff." A petite, young woman with dark red hair and serious hazel eyes steps forward and shakes my hand firmly. "Piper Jackson, future publisher of the *Eureka Gazette*."

"We've met." I deadpan.

"Yes, but not in my official capacity."

"I thought newspapers had gone the way of the dinosaur."

Over the years, the once-thriving town paper had dwindled down to a four-page obituary and public-notice mullet wrapper.

"Citizens have no idea how much value they get from a local paper." Piper lifts her chin defiantly. "I plan to remind them."

"Good luck, I guess." Last thing I need is a nosey reporter stirring up trouble around the courthouse.

"Let me help you with this." She takes the solo cup from my hand and disappears into the crowd.

I'm left standing on the porch gazing through the open front door into the living room where Britt and another girl are swaying their hips and calling out, "Man, I feel like a woman!" to the music.

Piper reappears, placing a clear plastic cup of caramel-colored liquid in my hand. I take the cup and she taps hers against mine. "To being allies in support of the town."

"What's this?" My eyebrow quirks as I study the drink.

"It's your brother's single-barrel reserve. He gives me free booze. I give him free publicity."

"You might be all right, Jackson." I tip the cup at her and take a sip of the smooth whiskey my middle brother Alex distills.

It's good shit, and he makes a killing selling it to high-end distributors—when he's not giving it away to family and friends for free.

"Let me know when you need a refill." She disappears into the crowd, and I step carefully into the wood-paneled hallway.

Above the fireplace is a sign that reads *Farewell Britt*, and the room is crowded with Adam's friends. I walk over to the large, round table in the back corner, and I see it's laden with bar food—pigs in blankets, buffalo wings, sliders, and even giant pretzels.

A new Shania Twain song starts, and I glance over to see Britt and her friend are pouring more champagne into their glasses and dancing as they sing. She moves gracefully, and her long hair sways down her back.

Someone bumps my arm, and I look down to see Piper is refilling my cup. "You should try a slider." She shouts over the music. "They're meat free, but they're delicious."

"Adam made them?" I have to shout as well, and she nods, grabbing one and holding it up before returning to the party.

I'm not hungry, but I am curious about this house. I can't help wondering what a pseudo-psychic, tarot-card reader formerly married to an escape artist considers interior design.

Taking another sip of whiskey, I walk down the hallway, but it's disappointingly normal. The walls hold pictures of Britt as a little girl, Britt as a graduating senior, a photo of Edna, Gwen, and Britt at the beach...

The kitchen doesn't have any potions or magical blends on the shelves. It's all canned beans, tomatoes, bananas, and coffee. A glass vase holding dried lavender mixed with eucalyptus is the most exotic element, filling the air with its distinctive scent of woody flowers—fresh and almost minty.

"Are you lost?" A soft voice startles me, and I turn to see Britt standing in the small kitchen holding her clear cup of sparkling wine.

"Ah, no..." I glance down, exhaling a laugh that she caught me snooping. "I was just looking around."

She's quiet a moment, studying me in a shy way that stirs an unexpected heat in my lower stomach. It's a heat I haven't felt in a long time, and I'm not sure what to do with it.

"It's cooler on the back porch." She motions to the back door, and I follow her outside, where the fall air is turning crisp.

The noise of frogs and crickets beat rhythmically in the night, and I glance up to see the sky is full of stars. It's one of the perks of living in a small town, away from all the big developments and their light pollution.

"I'm surprised Adam convinced you to come." Her voice is light.

"He didn't say where we were going." Realizing that might seem rude, I quickly add, "I heard you're moving to Greenville."

"Yeah, I got a job working with one of the detectives there. I like taking pictures, and I've been told I'm really good with details. When I heard there was something called forensic photography, I thought, why not?"

"Why not?" The simple question makes me chuckle. "Maybe because you'll be seeing a lot of gruesome things you might not want to see."

"I don't mind. I've always liked working on puzzles and finding clues. And not every crime is a brutal murder. A lot of times it's just routine stuff— robberies, breaking and entering, vandalism."

Silence falls between us, and I consider she's right. We've never had a murder in Eureka as long as I've been here. Glancing over at her, I study her cute little nose, her full pink lips.

She's leaving home. I think of that old song my mom used to play. *Bye, bye...* "I remember when I moved to San Diego for service, I never thought I'd come back."

"Why did you?" Her bright green eyes are so earnest, I take a step closer.

"Ma asked me to. Alex was on active duty, and Adam was off flying planes. My dad was gone, and I felt like she needed me."

"Now you have Owen, and you're the sheriff." She's even closer to me somehow.

Close enough to slide my hands down her arms, to pull her to my chest, to seal my lips firmly over hers. I wonder how she'd taste. I wonder what sounds she'd make if I moved my lips down the column of her throat, pulled the skin of her collar bone between my teeth. I wonder how she'd sound if I sealed my lips over her pussy...

"It all worked out for you." The statement pulls me back.

"I wouldn't say that, but having my son makes it worthwhile."

"At least people take you seriously."

"You don't think people take you seriously?"

She exhales a laugh. "I'm one of the town clowns."

"I would never call you a clown." The words cause me to look closer, consider what I would call her. "You're a smart girl. I bet you do well."

Her chin lifts, putting her lips closer to mine. So close... "You do?"

Her words slip out on a breath, and for the first time in a very long time the thought of acting on my impulse heats my veins.

I'm ready to concede what my younger brother has been saying, what my mother has been saying, hell, what everybody has been saying—it's time for me to get back in the game. I'm too young to be put out to pasture. I still have life in me.

My arm lifts, and I slide my hand up to her elbow. "Yes."

Our eyes meet, and I lean down, driven by what I want to happen. I'm pretty sure she's stretching taller. My lips grow heavy. We're right there, when...

"Hey, bro! Here you are!" The noise of the screen door banging open followed by my brother's loud voice throws us to opposite sides of the porch.

She goes to the wall, hiding in the shadows, and I step quickly to the rail, into the bright light of the full moon.

"It's been longer than thirty minutes, and you're still here. Are you actually enjoying yourself?"

He's so casual, while my heart is galloping in my chest. It only takes me a moment to get my shit together and realize what I almost did. I almost kissed Edna's granddaughter... Gwen's daughter.

I shake my head, snapping out of the trance. "I gotta go."

Britt seems to disappear, and I don't question it. What almost happened here was a combination of too much whiskey, too much moonlight, and too little sleep. Hell, for all I know, it could've been a spell conjured by the witchy women in this family.

If I believed in shit like that.

No, I stopped believing in romance a long time ago, and one fall night on a moonlit porch with a pretty girl isn't going to change me. The sooner I get my head back in the game the better.

Adam drops me off at my house, but I'm too keyed up to sleep. The place feels too quiet, and I can't get the thought of Britt's soft lips out of my head. Grabbing my keys, I drive to town and park in my reserved space in front of the courthouse.

The noise of music and laughter is muted, but I know it's coming from El Rio, a few blocks away. It's early, and I decide to give Doug a break. I'll have one drink, and if no mysterious strangers appear, I'll walk home. I need to burn off some of this pent-up energy.

The music grows louder as I approach the festive, Mexican restaurant. It's only been open a few years, but the local kids love it. I appreciate the owner doing his part to uphold the small-town vibe by shutting everything down at midnight.

"Hey, Sheriff!" Doug is at my arm when I walk through the door. "Did you find a babysitter after all?"

Looking around, I see a few of the kids who were at Britt's party are here. No sign of my brother or Britt, though. It's a good thing. I need to get my head straight and remember I'm a dad, not a player. I'm the sheriff of Eureka, not some trust-fund frat boy out of Hilton Head.

"The Bridge game got canceled. Have you seen anything here?"

"Actually..." He turns, nodding in the direction of a dark corner. "The mysterious stranger is here."

The frustration burning in my stomach is all the motivation I need.

Stalking around the bar, I approach the man with my brow lowered. "Hey, there, pal. I heard you were hassling one of the customers here last night."

The man stands, his dark eyes narrowed, and he looks me up and down. "And you are?"

"Aiden Stone, sheriff of Eureka. What's your name?"

"A new Sheriff Stone? Interesting." I can't place his accent. It could be Italian or Russian for all I know. "Are you as competent as the former Sheriff Stone?"

My hand tightens into a fist, and I'm ready to teach this guy a lesson. "Are you insulting my dad?"

He holds up both hands. "Not at all. I'll simply pay my bill and leave. No harm done."

"I'll take care of your bill. You take care of the leaving. And don't come back."

An oily smile curls his lips, and he studies my face in a way that puts me on guard. "I'll be going then, but I have unfinished business here."

"Find another way to finish it. The next time I hear you're hassling the citizens of Eureka, I'll lock you up."

"You won't see me here again."

He nods, exiting the bar, but a sick feeling in my gut makes me suspect this isn't over. The man walks out of the bar, and Doug joins me in the corner.

"You really handled that guy." Doug smiles, slapping me on the back. "I never worried when your dad was in charge, and I'm just as confident now. Eureka is in good hands."

"Yeah." I nod, signaling to the bartender. "I'll cover that guy's bill."

He brings me the statement, and I pay for Doug and the weird stranger. The frustration has cooled in my chest, but I'm not convinced the storm has passed.

I'm starting to feel like things are just beginning in our small town, but don't be alarmed. Doug is right. I'm more than up to the task of keeping this small-town safe.

Whatever's coming better look out for me.

Thanks for reading this prequel story to A Little Taste. Find out what happens when a sudden crime wave brings Britt home to work with Aiden on solving a mystery. Learn more about my books at TiaLouise.com.

MELE KALIKI MAKE OUT WITH ME

TRILINA PUCCI

The smile hasn't left my face since we stepped off the private plane.

Because we're in Hawaii…for Christmas. Well, technically, the day after, but still. These boys will never stop being the very fucking best. It's crazy to think that it's been two years with Reed, Alec, Cole, and Jace—my guys.

The best two years. They even handle my father like champs. However, in all honesty, I think they needed this trip more than me. My father really put them through their paces last week. But fair's fair when four guys are trying to date your daughter.

Thank god for my sister, Eleanor, and her husband, Crew, *annnd* the sexual tension between Millie and Crew's friends because without them, I think I may have lost my mind.

"Welcome to the island of Kauai."

A lei is offered by a man in a colorful shirt as I bend forward. I feel like I'm in a movie until Reed gently bumps my shoulder and whispers, "Sunshine, did you just get laid by some rando before we fucked you?"

"Shuuttt up," I whisper back, trying not to laugh. "You're such a child."

He nuzzles my neck, growling and making me squeal before I reach for Jace and escape.

"Will you tell your friend to settle down? We're in public."

Jace sweeps me up into his arms and spins me around, eliciting a carefree laugh.

"Cutie, we're on our own private little piece of heaven. You'll be lucky to keep any of us off you."

Reed dips in, kissing my cheek before he adds, "I'm gonna do whatever the fuck I want, sunshine." He licks his lips before giving me a wink. "But that's never been a problem before... Are you telling me you want my lips off you?"

Damn. When he does this and looks at me with those sexy bedroom eyes, I lose all focus. But Jace is right. I'll take all the hands all the time. Still, it's more fun when I make them work for it.

"This is my dance space..." I tease, pushing against Jace, pointing to the millimeters of space between us, even though he keeps holding me off the ground. "And this is your dance space."

His forehead touches mine, a smirk on his face as he sets me to the ground. "All right, baby. But only because I can see Cole over your shoulder, and he's about to kill me for bogarting our girl."

My head swings over my shoulder, the smile on my face permanent as I land on Cole's grumpy face, mainly because his neck is garnished with a colorful lei. Everything about it is a contradiction. Grumpy meeting happy. Cole's jaw tenses, so I immediately turn and walk toward him.

"You look good in flowers," I say with a wink, looking up at his chiseled jaw. It has stubble, and it never has stubble. And that makes me really like vacation Cole.

"It's actually maile leaves and a berry called mokihana."

Details, details. He's very good at paying attention to those. *In every way.*

"Good to know. Maybe you guys can wear them like you did with the Santa hats last year."

His chest rises and slowly lowers as he lets out a long breath, staring down at me like he's contemplating what he's going to do.

"Princess, you keep teasing me, and I'll make everyone sleep outside the room while I fuck you raw."

"Promises, promises."

Cole grabs the back of my jean shorts, dipping his fingers just inside the waistband, and spins me around before cracking his hand directly across my ass.

I squeal as he growls, "Move it."

Alec holds out his hand for me to take, so I let him lead me toward the jeeps that are waiting to take us to our villa. He opens the door for me, bringing my hand to his lips.

"Your chariot awaits, gorgeous. But before you get in, I want to hear that we can do whatever we want...all fucking weekend."

Mele Kaliki-make out with me right fucking now, asking a question like that. Alec already knows what I'm going to say, but goddammit, it's so hot when he demands it.

I bite my bottom lip, staring into Alec's eyes, letting it drag out slowly. But before it pops out, Alec reaches up and tugs it out, immediately sealing his mouth over mine. His hand slides down my body until my gasp is eaten because he's grabbing my pussy. As he pulls back, his eyes lock on mine.

"Gimme."

Reed growls loudly, playfully shoving me inside the car. "That's my fucking line, dick."

I'm laughing as my guys pile in and the engine rumbles because I think this is about to be the most memorable XXX-mas of my life.

"What's that?"

I blink a couple of times as I stare, pointing at the bed...a bed that's on a lanai...overlooking the freaking ocean.

"Looks like a four-poster bed," Cole offers, walking past me with his hands clasped behind his back and a smirk before giving me a tiny poke to my side. I jerk sideways, letting out a quiet laugh.

Jace passes by my other side, making my head jerk in his direction to see him licking his lips before he says, "With an endless ocean view."

"Hmmm..." I smile. "So it seems."

I swallow, feeling their eyes on me. Reed's big hands attach themselves to my hips, tugging me backward into his warm body. His lips skim my earlobe, sending shivers down my spine.

"You asked for paradise, sunshine. So, win-win."

"Win-win?"

"Yeah, because all we want is you."

Reed lets me go before I can even finish a breath and joins the other two guys as Alec's fingers guide my chin to his gaze.

"Fellas," he says in a low rumble, "I think it's time for our present."

Another present? And I bet it's something dirty. Here I thought Hawaii was the gift. I smile to myself because what was I thinking? We're never making it out of this room.

Everything is the perfect decadent romantic setup for a fuckfest. They're going to put me in a coma, and all I'll get are dreams of Hawaii. My mouth opens, then closes, then pops open again with insults laced with humor.

"You're the absolute worst men. You're all the goddamn delicious worst. I see what you're doing. And I love you with my whole heart, but I have demands—"

Alec smirks and nods, running his thumb over my bottom lip before pressing it inside my mouth. And because I'm a damn tramp, I suck and instantly get wet listening to him groan.

"We love you too, gorgeous. Forever."

But the moment he pulls it out, I lick my lips and rush my words out, mainly because I'm now being surrounded, and I know I only have a few seconds before the best kind of debauchery ensues.

"For the record, fellas, I want snorkeling in those silly masks with the goofy spouts. And an underwater picture of all of us for the penthouse."

My purse is slipped off my shoulder.

"And I want a romantic dinner on the beach with drinks that have umbrellas in them and you guys in Hawaiian shirts."

The hem of my tee is untucked from my shorts.

"And I swear to god, if we don't go surfing or see a waterfall, I will riot."

Reed grins, dragging my shirt up and over my head, making me laugh. I'm spun around by someone... No, not just someone... Cole.

Our eyes connect, and everything slows, stills, and quiets. Damn, he has a way of making his presence known. Cole licks his lips as his eyes dart to the swells of my breasts, which are still hidden in my bra.

"That's a problem for me. Solve it."

I smirk as I reach up and pop the clasp nestled within my cleavage, setting my tits free.

"Solved. Sir. And about my demands?"

Cole leans in so only I can hear him.

"Baby, you can have anything and everything you want. I'll make the world kneel for you. Always."

My eyes close for the softest second. He cups my breast, pinching my nipple between his fingers, making me gasp before I melt back into the other hard body behind me. My chest rises and falls with instant need as fingers scrape over my scalp, making my head fall back too. I rasp a moan, feeling lips drag over my collarbone and a hand run down my stomach.

The whole gang's here.

My eyes open as I lift my head, engulfed by my men. But my eyes are on Cole. He yanks my button-fly shorts open with two tugs, making room for the wandering hand and grins.

Jace's voice tickles my ear because he's the body behind me, just as his fingers dip inside my underwear. *Fuck.*

"You're so wet, cutie, but let me make you wetter. I want to play with this sweet clit until you're begging. Would you like that? Use your words and tell us."

I'm already breathing heavily, completely lost to the feeling of hands, lips, and their warmth as I nod and rush out a "Yes...I'd like that."

God, they're always so all-consuming. The moment they touch me, I'm so overwhelmed that it feels like I can't take it, even though I can't get enough.

Cole's hands spread over my hips, jerking my jean shorts off my body, taking my panties with them, eliciting a gasp.

Jace's hand presses to my stomach, sealing my back to his front and his hard cock as he begins rubbing small, too-gentle circles around my clit. Fuck, it's sweet torture. My hair is gripped by Reed before he tilts my head so that my neck is exposed. His teeth graze my skin before he sucks.

"Fuck." I groan, pressing my hips forward, trying to rock into Jace's hand.

But it's Reed's voice that gives me shivers as Cole stares me down, rubbing himself through his slacks.

"I'm going to mark your entire body—" Reed whispers with that sexy gravel. "—so everyone knows what a dirty little slut you are. Because who do you belong to, sunshine?"

My hips rock, feeling Jace apply more pressure as I lick my lips. Cole raises a brow, waiting for my answer, but they all know it.

"You," I breathe out. "I belong to all of you."

"I can't fucking wait anymore," Alec booms from beside me.

Jace's hand leaves my pussy as I'm swept off my feet, my arm landing over Alec's shoulder as he carries me toward the bed. I can't help but look over his shoulder because the vision of Reed, Cole, and Jace following like predatory fucking animals is enough to make me come on the spot.

The moment we hit the patio, the cool ocean breeze pricks my skin and makes me shiver as the sun simultaneously warms me. I'm dropped onto the soft fabric of the bed as I situate myself and look around them. They're standing, each at an end of the bed with a hand holding the post, as thin, almost transparent silk that's draped along the posts blows around them.

I press my lips together, hiding my smile, because it's so sexy but also kind of like a cover off those romance novels you see in grocery stores.

Maybe Cole can be a pirate and Reed a cowboy, Alec can be a swashbuckler, and Jace...he can be the stable boy. The giggle I give narrows their eyes, making me smile harder before they shut me up—because they're taking their clothes off.

Hot. Damn.

This part never gets old. I mean, none of our fivesomes do, but watching them strip is a top three favorite part of my life. Because not every girl is lucky enough to have four men who exude sex appeal. And forget about the muscles, even though how could I?

Between Jace's taut pecs adorned with nipple piercings and the fact that he is covered in tattoos—including his new one, a red bow with five loops. It's just like the one I tied around myself at Christmas when I gifted *me* to *them*.

And don't get me started on the way that Cole's body is sheer lean muscle perfection. There's not a mistake, a regret, or an improvement to be had. He even has the most defined lines leading down to his giant cock. Sometimes, I spend hours daydreaming about what it would be like to lick his entire fucking body. But he'd never give me that much control, and I love him for it.

Then there's Reed, who honestly could afford to be uglier because it's not fair to be this charming and also that fucking hot. He's a god, and he knows it. But my favorite part about him is his mouth—it's full of the dirtiest talk and also makes me constantly think of kissing...*not just my mouth either*. I've never been with someone who eats pussy as if it's his Olympic sport and he's the world's record holder. The man defends his title like a true champion, and like, *here's your medal, sorry it's wet.*

God, thinking about it is making my body squirm. As if he's reading my mind, he winks, and I press my thighs together.

Alec reaches under the bed and tosses a white box onto the bed. It's long and has a red ribbon on it. Fucking red ribbons. I smile, giving him my attention, partially ignoring the box because he's nude, holding his rock-hard cock in his hand.

I'm happily reminded of how Alec has the most beautiful dick I've ever seen. It's perfectly proportional between length and girth. And the veins snake up the side, creating ridges along his tan flesh. His dick makes my mouth water, mainly because not only do I want it there, but I know he wants to watch me put it there.

I don't know what's hotter—sucking him off or knowing he's captivated by watching me do it.

His thumb spreads the precum over the bulging head, and I can't help myself. I start crawling over the bed toward him.

Alec releases himself, weaving his fingers into my hair as I slowly run my tongue over his tip before letting him push my head down over his dick all the way until it hits my throat.

"Oh, fuck. You're such a good girl for me." He pulls me back before lowering my head again, rasping his words toward the ceiling. "Such a good fucking girl for me."

I suck, bobbing my head, letting him move my hair aside so he can see me take his cock deep into my throat, making myself gag before I release him and do it again. As I open my throat, letting him go deeper to cut off my air, wetness runs over my asshole, making me jump. But my hips are held still, and the tip of a cock presses to the tight hole, rimming it before I feel the tip slide inside.

Oh, fuck. I didn't even feel anyone come up behind me. *Yessss.*

I moan, but all my air is cut off again, then given back. Alec takes over fucking my mouth as the large cock in my ass begins to glide in and out.

"Fuck, that feels good" is groaned from behind me—Jace saying the words, I'm thinking.

My back arches as I try and make my ass meet each time Jace thrusts inside me. But the hottest part is that every time I'm pushed forward, I'm forced to swallow Alec's dick in a dirty rhythm.

Jace and Alec fuck me, one in my mouth, one in my ass, as I hear Cole and Reed offer dirty praises.

"Let them use you, baby, like a good whore."

"Yeah, warm her up until she's begging like a good girl."

I'm fucked slow and steady— no rush, just pleasure.

I feel Reed's hands glide over my tits. "Look at those tits bounce. I'm going to fuck them and come all over your face, whore. And you're going to thank me."

"Oh, fuck," Jace growls. "Our girl liked that. Her ass just gripped my cock so tight."

Jace grips my ass cheeks, kneading, pulling the cheeks apart to watch himself glide in and out as Alec holds my hair tighter. But just as I begin to mewl, begging for more, I feel Reed's mouth against my clit.

Jesus Christ.

My body bucks, but neither Jace nor Alec give an inch as Reed eats my pussy from underneath me. Fuck, it's too much. His mouth is sealed over my clit, sucking and licking like he's starving as my body bounces in rhythm between the other two fucking me senseless.

I can't take it. My palm slaps the blanket, needing and wanting more. Fuck, make me come. I want to come.

Reed growls into my pussy, and my arms buckle, but Alec's hand closes around my throat, keeping me upright as Jace grips my hips from behind.

"Take it," Cole growls. "You will fucking take it all until we say otherwise. Do you hear me?"

Alec uses my hair to pull me off his cock.

"Yes, Daddy."

The minute I answer, Alec thrusts back inside my mouth as the others continue their assault. Fuck, Reed's tongue feels so good. I try to slide my knees open over the blanket to spread my legs and get closer to his face because he's teasing me, barely flicking my clit with his tongue before sucking it and then pulling away again.

Fuck. I want it.

His fingers part my wet lips, opening my pussy as he presses his tongue flat against me. I want to moan, but Alec's hand is forceful, bobbing my head as he fucks my face faster.

"Fuck yes, let me have that throat. Choke on my cock, gorgeous."

Oh god, Jace picks up speed too, bucking harder into my body, making me quiver. Oh, he fucks my ass so good, filling it with his giant cock, punishing the tender flesh around my hips as he digs his fingers in.

I'm gripping the fabric of the blanker for dear life, wanting and needing to come as I'm fucked over and over, again and again. Finally, Reed stops teasing and seals his mouth over my pussy and devours me. He's taking no prisoners, licking, sucking, moving his tongue in a figure eight as he groans, pawing at my tits.

I just need...I need..fuck...

"Enough," thunders through the heavens.

There it is...exactly what I need. Cole.

The gasp that pulls from my body feels like a small earthquake inside of me because suddenly, everyone pulls out and moves, leaving me feral. Seriously fucking feral.

My body drops on the bed as I press my pussy into it, trying to find any kind of friction I can.

"Fuck me," I beg, rolling over and spreading my legs for them to see.

"Oh, you dirty bitch. Let Daddy help you."

Reed hovers over me for too brief a moment and licks my cunt before he stands again, grinning.

I hate him. I love him. No, I definitely hate him.

Spit glistens over my lips, my mouth agape as I breathe hard, eyes fluttering, trying to connect to Cole's. He's standing like a god next to Alec, muscular arms crossed over his chest, hard cock bobbing against his lower stomach. My fingers dart to my center, but my wrist is caught by Jace as Cole slaps my clit.

"Behave."

My entire body shudders.

"Princess, that's not how you come today," Cole levels. "Because you haven't opened your present."

The slender box I crawled over is lifted from the bed, and I watch Cole opening it as he keeps his eyes on me.

The minute it's revealed, my entire body heats—no fucking way. Oh my god.

"Is that a—" I rasp, still breathing hard.

"Spreader bar?" Reed smirks, finishing my sentence. He's come close now, pressing his soft lips against my rib cage. "Yeah, sunshine. It is. See, Alec wants you wide open so he can watch that pretty pussy come so hard it spills down your ass. And they"—he lifts his chin toward Cole and Alec—"need leverage. They're gonna fill your cunt like the dirty little slut you are. Together. While Jace takes your ass again and I straddle that pretty little mouth."

Fuck. I asked for this. It was one of those nights where we'd fucked and then fucked some more, and while we were still all half-delirious and tangled up, I'd said I wanted to know what two of them felt like inside me while the other two took my ass and mouth.

I wanted all my guys inside me. Correction, I *want* all my guys inside me —filling me, fucking me, until I can't scream loud enough to god in appreciation.

The click of the bar makes my shoulders jump, but not a sound comes out of me because Cole's grabbed my ankle, and he's dragging me down the bed toward him and Alec.

"Let's get you ready," Alec growls, running his hands up between my legs, pressing them open.

Alec brings the soft cuff to my ankle, wrapping it around just as Cole does the same. Holy shit. I will not be able to close my legs. I'm completely at their mercy.

My eyes are glued to Alec's profile, watching the attention he gives. His deft fingers ghost my skin before he fastens the strap and tightens it just enough to make me smirk. I lick my lips as our eyes meet, and he gives me a wink.

"I like you like this."

I shiver before turning my attention to Cole, who's rougher on the other side. He tugs me forward, making me draw my leg back toward myself like the brat I like to be.

His jaw tenses before he tightens the fuck out of the strap, then grabs the middle of the bar and flips me the fuck over.

I scream, face-planted into the softness of the comforter just before my ass rings with heat.

"Do you need another?"

I shake my head, then suck in a breath, feeling his lips soothe the spot he just smacked.

This time, he gently rolls me over onto my back, and I prop up on my elbows, taking it all in—my legs strapped between the silver bar, only able to move in sync and completely incapable of closing, and the men who are about to fuck my pussy at the same time. I drop my head back, feeling flushed and turned on.

"God, you look beautiful," Alec croons as Reed takes my nipple into his mouth. "She does. But she'll look even better with our cum on her."

"Cutie—" Jace's voice calls my attention up to my left as he sits down on the bed, running his fingers through my hair, pulling an appreciative moan. "—are you ready for this? They're gonna stretch you, and if it hurts, all you gotta do is say stop. Okay? But we know you want this, and so do we."

I nod and suck in a breath as he runs his rough hand over my bare breast and continues.

"I'm gonna lift you up now and lay underneath you. But just relax because I'll do the work." He tucks a strand of my hair behind my ear. "I promise to be rough, so just breathe, baby." His lips press to my cheek, whispering his words into my skin. "Cuz I know you like it."

Yes. Yes. And fucking yes.

Suddenly, my head is shifted so that I'm face-to-face with Reed.

"That means I get to fill that pretty little throat with cum. But first—" He dives down, sealing his mouth over mine, and I can't help but tangle my hands in his hair.

My body shifts as we kiss because Jace is lifting me, positioning himself underneath me. I melt into everything, my body pliable and manipulated. Cole tugs at the bar, and I smile as Reed pulls away, diving back to bite my lip, then lick it before he cradles my jaw.

"The way I'm going to abuse this mouth will make us both go to hell." He looks past me. "J, keep your arms around her because I'm straddling her face."

"Heaven's overrated," I pant, smiling back as I feel Jace's arms circle around me.

Before he can say anything else, the fucking bar clicks, and my legs spread wider.

"Holy shit," I exhale.

I should have stretched for this. How will I explain this when I end up at the hospital with a sprained poosayy. *Sorry, Doc, I was being double stuffed like an Oreo and assumed that the one yoga class I took one hundred and fifty-four years ago was sufficient preparation.*

Jace and Reed work out their spaces as my mind becomes one singular thought—fill me.

The bar is raised, taking my legs with it as my hips are lifted, and Jace slides back inside my ass.

"Oh, fuck," I groan.

Cole leans in and brings his finger to my clit, running it slowly over the swelling bud, making my body buck as he rims my entrance. I know it's him, even though all I can see is Reed's cock, because he says, "Alec, look how fucking wet our girl is."

"Open," Reed commands, and I do, immediately tasting his precum at the back of my throat. He wasn't lying about abusing my throat because he's already fucking my face like a man possessed.

"I fucking love this mouth," he growls as Jace speaks words into my neck. "I want to see my cum drip from your ass and mix with what they fill you with."

Cole thrusts his finger inside me, and I suck in a breath. The filthy sound of my desire sings as he thrusts in and out before adding more fingers. The sound of waves crashes below us, but all I can hear is my own panting because Cole won't stop. He adds more fingers, and I'm pretty sure he has four inside me.

"Let that cunt stretch for us."

"Don't stop," I plead as Reed's cock leaves my lips, my body writhing against Jace's cock inside me.

I'm so wet that I'm dripping as he fucks me faster, and I feel a different set of fingers.

Oh my god. They're both finger-fucking me, Cole and Alec.

I'm moaning, begging the only way I can while sucking Reed's cock and staring up at the smirk on his face. He pulls his cock out of my mouth again, holding it before he slaps my mouth with it.

"Use your manners, slut."

"Fuck me...please."

Reed touches the head of his cock to my lips, so I open my mouth, but he raises his brows. God, the feeling of my pussy being stretched and Jace fucking my ass is making my head spin, and I can't form words anymore.

So I open my mouth wider, pleading for it with my eyes. Reed bites his bottom lip and winks, feeding it to me slowly, further, and further down my throat until tears prick at my eyes.

Thank you. That's the only look on my face, and it's received because he's pushing in and out, over and over.

The bar clicks again, and my legs are impossibly spread just as I feel the tip of a cock at my entrance. Oh, fuck. I feel drunk, completely out of control with want.

Jace slows, as does Reed, who looks over his shoulder.

"Oh fuck, sunshine. You should your cunt. It's never been wetter."

I'm lost to the sensations because my arms are pinned inside Jace's. So I claw at his legs, whimpering around Reed's cock just as the first hard cock presses inside. Jace moans, feeling the sensation as Reed cradles my jaw gently.

"Easy, baby."

I relax my jaw, realizing I sucked hard.

The cock in my pussy begins moving, finding a rhythm with Jace. Reed pulls his cock out of my mouth, jerking it in front of my face.

"Let them hear how much my little slut like it."

"Fuck. Yes…I want more. I want all of you."

Groans and growls erupt around me, and I feel another cock at my entrance. Oh god. I can barely breathe, panting as I'm fucked, staring at the wet sounds of Reed's cock chasing its release.

"You want me in your mouth. Or on your face."

"Oh…fuck." I'm quivering, completely overrun by desire.

Sex is thick in the air, debauchery our only guide.

I blink, speaking the only truth I know.

"I want your cum to drip down my throat and then to cover my face."

"Deep breath" is all that's said in response before my pussy is completely filled, stretched with the most delectable sting.

"Yes," I moan before lifting my head, chasing Reed's cock back into my mouth.

There is no restraint, no composure. I am fucked. Cocks punish and pound my cunt, fighting for space as Jace thrusts inside my ass, fucking me harder and harder, angling underneath me to go deeper.

My fingernails dig into his tatted thighs as my body builds. They fuck me harder and harder, wet sounds ringing out between my mouth and cunt. It feels like an out-of-body experience, only tethered by their dirty praises and degradations.

I'm climbing higher and higher, moaning and begging around Reed's cock for them to let me come.

"Your pussy was meant for this, gorgeous. Do you feel us inside you, rubbing your fucking soft walls."

Oh god.

"Suck that cock like a good whore. Take it all. Gimme that throat. Swallow it back."

All my wind is cut off as Reed closes his hand around my throat to feel how deep he is.

"Fuck." Jace groans, biting my shoulder like an animal, fucking me senseless. "I can't get enough of this tight ass. You feel how deep I am. We're all rubbing inside you."

The vision of their cocks rubbing heads, pressing against each other and inside me, makes my mind explode and my eyes flutter back.

His hand slides down over my clit, and that's all it takes. My body shakes and writhes as every muscle I have suddenly contracts harder and harder until I'm seized.

"She's coming," thunders out, but I'm barely aware of anything else other than the orgasm that is rocketing through my body.

Reed takes his cock from my mouth, and a strangled scream erupts in a "Yesssssssss," mixed with their secondhand "Cunt" … "Ass" … "Tits" … "Mouth."

I feel one of the cocks inside me pull out, and I know it's Alec because he wants to watch.

Jace and Cole return and hammer inside me just as Reed takes my mouth again. I'm a pile of mush being fucked beyond measure, still riding a high and suddenly climbing again.

"That's it, cutie. Give us one more. Soak our dicks."

"Oh, fuck. Oh, fuck." Cole groans, and Jace follows suit until they're fucking me with no care in the world other than to come.

"My turn," Reed grits out before thrusting his cock into my mouth.

They're fucking and fucking and fucking me until I feel my body coming all over again, and this time, they follow. Reed grips my hair so hard it stings as he hammers inside my mouth before pulling back to the tip and letting his warm cum spurt inside my mouth. But just like he promised, he doesn't stay there, pulling out and pressing the tip to my face, letting it drip over my mouth and cheeks as I feel Cole coming inside my pussy.

"Fuck, princess."

He pulls out too, letting some of his cum drip down my pussy and mix with what Jace has left to leak from my asshole.

"Oh god," I exhale as Reed moves off me, along with Jace and Cole.

Alec comes into view, jerking his hard length, tugging it faster and faster, eyes hooded as he stares at my used body until his stomach contracts, and he releases all over my tits, covering me.

I'm soaked in their cum. Perfectly used.

Reed smears his finger over my cheek as Alec does the same to my tits. I shiver, looking around them, still overcome by the moment. I feel Cole dip inside my pussy, making me gasp as Jace runs his finger over my ass.

And before I can process, one by one, they feed me their cum, letting me suck their fingers as they stare down with love and appreciation.

I'm worshipped. There is no other definition.

Reed's arms come underneath me, lifting and carrying me like a bride as he walks completely nude off the lanai and onto the sand, straight for the ocean.

I feel euphoric and free, and my men follow me into the water. I suck in a breath because the salt water stings my overused pussy, but the feeling goes away as soon as it came, and I'm left to focus on the hands swiping over my body, cleaning me, washing away all our sins.

Alec runs his wet hands over my hair, staring down at me before he presses a chaste kiss to my lips.

"I love you, gorgeous. Marry us. Today."

My lips part immediately, seized by his words. But Cole brushes his knuckles over my jaw tenderly, stealing my attention. "It wouldn't be legal, just ceremonial…but—"

"But," Jace cuts in, making me spin towards his voice, "it would mean something to us, and if you want, we can make it real. We talked about it. Worked out the details."

Jace kisses my cheeks and the tears that are streaming down my face.

Strong hands take my waist, guiding me around until I'm staring up at Reed, who looks like the sun. So beautiful and bright. Almost boyish.

"Say yes, sunshine. Because we want forever."

Two Christmases ago, I met the men of my dreams. And tonight, I'll be able to call them my husbands.

"Yes."

If you loved this naughty fivesome or just want more of this series, run don't walk to read Tangled in Tinsel, and Knot So Lucky.

A NIGHT WITH YOU

FALL IN LOVE AGAIN, BOOK 3
WILLOW WINTERS

PROLOGUE

I can't help but smile as those fluttering feelings go through me. The little butterflies that just won't quit whenever Bennet looks at me like that.

"Stop it," I mutter as I playfully bat his right arm. "Focus on driving," I tell him, grinning so hard my cheeks hurt and I'm certain they're bright red as well. His hand lands on my bare thigh and the rough pad of his thumb runs soothing circles against my heated skin.

His charming smile stays right where it is as he glances at me from the driver's seat of his truck and promises he's doing the best he can 'when you look like that'.

"If you wanted me to focus on anything other than you, maybe you should have thought twice about that dress."

"Oh yeah," I play along, leaning closer to him and letting my hand fall on top of his. His touch does something to me I've never felt before.

"Yeah," he tells me, glancing again at me with those puppy dog eyes. "I love that color on you."

Love.

That little word has a ball of emotion swelling in my throat but I'm quick to swallow it down and I don't think my expression changed in the least. Staring straight ahead I ignore the one word I've been hoping he'd say and instead I tell him, "well next time I'll wear a paper bag."

He chuckles deep and rough and I love it.

Just like I love the way he makes me feel, I love every minute we spend together… I love his flannel shirt that he never buttons. I love the white tee underneath that's stretched tight over his broad shoulders. I love his tanned skin and the little grooves of his corded muscles, I love his jeans and the sound they make while he's kicking them off and making my bed groan as we get lost in the sheets every night.

I don't say what I want though when I glance back at him at the red light before we get back to his place from a long night out.

He winces slightly and then rubs the back of his neck.

"You looking to get a massage?" I ask him playfully and then offer it up rather than tease and torment Bennet. "You could just ask," I tell him.

He chuckles again and then says it's just a little headache but he's more than happy to take me up on that offer.

Before the light turns green, I swear he's about to say something else... something that brings a shine to his eyes, but the damn thing interrupts us... just like everything else in the small town that was never prepared for a love like ours.

CHAPTER 1 - AUBREY

I can't shake the nerves from the day no matter what I do. For all intents and purposes, it was a wonderful meeting with the publishers, and the promotion to head editor is something I never expected. As I pull the high waisted floral skirt into place and adjust my white sleeve blouse so it's loosely tucked in, I know I love my job but I never expected this.

It's been a dream of mine for as long as I can remember. Today feels like so much more. Digging through my makeup bag, I settle on a deep rouge lipstick that will pair well with my heels.

My phone pings and I suppress my sigh and eye roll and opt for a grin instead. The girls are taking me out tonight to celebrate and I wonder if that's why I'm a bundle of nerves. It's been a long damn time since we've been out on the town and I know they're going to try to hook me up with someone.

And finding a guy, let alone hooking up with one, is not on my to do list.

The phone pings again on the sink countertop and I glance down at it.

The text reads: *You almost ready?*

Lauren is always ready early and she knows I'm almost always five minutes late.

I wouldn't be surprised if she walks across the street past her perfectly manicured rose bushes and knocks on my front door within the next two minutes.

Just as I pucker and smack my lips, there's a knock on the door and I nearly laugh out loud. I know it's not Lauren though when my front door opens.

"Bree!" I slip the lipstick into my clutch, snag my phone in my left hand, heels in the right. "Let's go!" Marlena and Gemma both call out.

"I'm coming!" My heart beats even faster on the trip through my house to the entryway, where my friends are checking themselves out in the mirror by the door.I laugh at Gemma blowing herself a kiss in the mirror. Her little red cotton sun dress is adorable. "We just need--"

The front door opens again, and Lauren steps in.

"You did it!" she shouts, and then I'm surrounded by a hug and squeals from my friends, all of them shrieking with happiness.

"Stop, stop, I'm going to get lipstick everywhere!"

My friends release me, laughing. Lauren rolls her eyes. "Please, Bree. You're perfect. I can't wait to get to the bar and show you off."

A shiver runs down my spine. "I don't need to be shown off, I just want to celebrate with you three."

Lauren cocks a brow and Gemma lets out a laugh before sharing a look with Marlena.

I hook my arm through Lauren's, my pulse coming quicker.

"Where are we going anyway?" I question and their answer is easy. The breeze moves through my hair on the way to Lauren's SUV. She's always DD. As the seatbelt clicks into place,I feel practically giddy. Maybe there's just something in the air. I'm excited about the promotion, of course, but I worked hard for it. As shocked as I was to get the title of Head Editor, it also seems to fit.

Who knows? Maybe it's *tonight* that's special. Maybe tonight is the night that I'm finally the person I've been working towards being, with nothing from the past holding me back. What is it that people say? It's the first day of the rest of my life.

The bar is lit up from the inside, practically beckoning us to the door. For a minute, as we get closer, it almost feels like high school again. The nights we went to football games and ate pizza at the little restaurant downtown were like magic. We felt like the world was just opening up for us, like anything could happen. Like anyone could walk through the door.

Though at the time, it wasn't just anyone I thought about.

It was someone very specific.

And tonight reminds me of him, even though it's a night out with the girls, and he moved across the country a long time ago.

I try to shake off the memories, and Lauren pulls me closer to her. "Cold?"

"Excited!"

She laughs. "Yeah, I bet! It's been way too long since we went out. Now that you're head editor, you'll have more time for us, right?"

"I'm pretty sure it's the other way around."

"No, no!" Gemma says. "You're the boss. You get to set your own schedule. That means you *have* to let us steal you away for wine down Wednesdays again."

"She's right," Marlena agrees. "You have to. Or else one day you'll turn around and realize you missed everything."

"Shh," scolds Lauren. "Bree's been here for everything. All the important stuff. Nothing else matters."

I make a silent promise to myself that I *will* spend more time with my friends. More responsibility at work doesn't mean I can let friendships fall by the wayside. I'm not willing to let any of them get away, not after–

Gemma pulls the front door of the bar open. Noise pours out onto the sidewalk. People talk over one another, music plays, and glasses clink.

"Drinks!" Lauren says over the noise, and pulls me with her toward the bar. A couple attached to each other at the lips veers into our path, and Lauren shoos them out of the way. The man's taller, and the woman has her hands in his shirt, and the way they're kissing is so intense that I don't see him at first.

But then my heart stops and my entire body freezes.

Bennet Thompson.

He stands behind the bar, tall and handsome just like he was in high school, his hands moving confidently on a glass and bottles while he mixes a drink. My heart does a loop in my chest and straight up to my throat. I've thought about Bennet Thompson at least a few times a week since I graduated.

That's what happens when you have a crush on somebody. A crush is different from other kinds of love. It hides in your heart and pops up when you least expect it. Refusing to just go away because it was never even given a chance.

My whole face heats as Lauren pulls us toward the bar. I had no business having a crush on Bennet in high school, because he was dating Pamela. I have no business feeling this giddy at the sight of him now, but what am I supposed to say? I can't tell Lauren to stop, and more importantly I don't want to. I can't believe he's back in town.

I want to see him up close.

Oh, God, he's even more attractive up close. How is he hotter than my memories of him that kept me up at night?

He slides the glass across the bar to the woman it's for, brushes off his hands, and looks up.

Our eyes meet.

It's the first time I've looked him in the eyes since he moved across the country and the shock is no less powerful than it was all those years ago. The pale blue of his eyes lights up, and a slow smile spreads across his face. That's the smile of a heartbreaker, right there.

And oh, my heart is going to break. Because just looking at him makes me feel like I'd do anything to be near him, anything to see that smile again.

I'm in trouble.

Huge trouble. The kind of trouble that'll shatter my heart. I just know it. I'll be left with nothing but memories.

A wiser person might turn away and forget Bennet Thompson.

I smile back at him instead.

CHAPTER 2 - BENNET

At first, I think I have to be imagining her.

Aubrey Peters, with her doe eyes staring straight at me and her beautiful red lips parted just slightly, proving she's just as shocked to see me as I am to see her. All I've got on is worn blue jeans and a white tee, and this gorgeous woman's little black dress and red heels put her way above my league.

There's no way Aubrey Peters is standing in my bar. Or--the one I work at since Steve let me bartend until I get settled back in town. There's no way she's standing there with her arm hooked through her friend's, looking at me with a beautiful blush spreading over her cheeks, exactly the way she used to look at me in school.

It takes great effort not to show every emotion on my face and keep my cool. Her friend--Lauren--says something to her, and the two of them come closer.

She's real. Aubrey is standing there, right in front of me, making my heart race all over again. The bar lights shine down on her hair and men on the other side of the bar turn to check her out, and I'm not surprised by the flare of jealousy straight through my chest. She and Lauren are at the bar in a matter of steps. I lean over to take their order, and I swear there's a magnetic pull between us.

"Hi," Aubrey says. I only half-hear the order Lauren places. My hands move automatically to make the drinks, and suddenly Lauren's gone. It's just Aubrey, leaning in too, her face lit up with surprise. "I didn't know you were back in town."

"I am." I open my arms and gesture at the bar. "This is what I do now."

"Flirt with women?"

I give her wide eyes. "Is that what it looks like I'm doing?"

"You're smiling a lot."

I can't help myself as she sways back and forth in front of me, "I'm smiling at you."

Even though half the ice completely misses the glass,I keep going on the drinks as if I'm not hot and bothered. Aubrey laughs, tossing her hair over her shoulder, and I want to run my fingers through it. I want it so much I could jump over the bar and capture her in my arms, but I don't. I have more self-control than that.

I've been back for nearly two weeks now, working at the bar all week, and I haven't heard anything about her other than she's settled down in Cedar Lane. Although a quick glance at her finger tells me my definition of 'settled down' might be different from what I thought before.

"What have you been up to lately? You come here a lot?"

She grins, her eyes twinkling. "Working. I got a promotion, actually. That's why we're out tonight."

"A promotion?"

"Head Editor." Bree looks so damn proud of herself, and hell if I'm not proud, too. "I didn't realize they'd give it to me, honestly, but I'm thrilled they have."

"Drinks," I say, wanting to ask her a hundred questions about her new job. About her life since I've been gone.

But she picks up the tray I've pushed across the bar at her with a quick, soft *thanks*.

"It's good to see you," she says over her shoulder as she turns toward her friends and walks away.

I can't keep my eyes off her.

No matter how hard I try, I keep looking back at her table for the rest of the evening. Just being in the same room with her gives me a high like I haven't felt since I moved.

A few times, I catch her glancing at me. And each time I let an asymmetric grin slip into place.

The bar is busy and loud. People drink and enjoy themselves without stopping, but no matter how many orders I fill, I can't stop watching her. Nobody in this entire bar is as captivating as this woman, and my heart beats fast just to be in the same room as her.

How did I manage to stay away all this time? The memories flash by, college, a start up company and then selling it before being convinced to come back home for family... life is a wild ride but I never expected it to bring me back to her.

It's toward the end of the night when she comes back to the bar, her eyes bright from a night of drinking. She's confident and beautiful and leans right in.

"I wanted to say goodbye before I left," she said.

"Just goodbye?"

She bites at her lip, giving me a little grin that drives me wild. "I don't know. They've redone the bar since I came last. You could..." Her voice goes low with suggestion. "Show me the back... I heard there's a game room now or something?" One of her friends calls her name. "Just a second," she says back, her eyes hot on mine.

"It's this way." I play it cool on my way out from behind the bar. I know Steve is working on an expansion, but honestly I just wanted a job to keep me busy and to get back into the swing of things. I tell her, leading the way, "It's different from how I remember it, but it's nice."

The narrow hall in the back pushes us close together, and Aubrey leans into it a little, her elbow brushing mine.

"Supply closet." I point at one of the doors. "And then back here is where the pool table will go I think, and a little more space for storage."

The space is barren, drywalled and the ceiling is all beams and HVAC systems. "It's not much to look at but it will be nice I think."

I flick the light switch but they don't turn on. "Not quite ready yet," I comment and then glance behind me, knowing full well the bar is waiting with the faded chatter just barely slipping through.

"Oh." Aubrey steps closer, her lips pursed, looking at the space. She makes a slow turn, her eyes traveling over everything, not moving away an inch. "You're right. It *is* nice."

"You're nice."

"You're not too bad yourself."

She tilts her face up, just a little, and I take that as a sign that I should kiss her. There's no holding back, now that we're alone in this shadowy back room, nobody watching.

My hands go to her face like we were never apart. Aubrey's eyes flutter closed, and then my mouth is on hers.

Bree's lips are just how I always thought they would be. Soft and sweet, tasting like the last cocktails I made. She dives right into the kiss, her hands going around my neck, and I back her carefully against the wall. Those soft curves. The feel of her. I can't think of anything else.

Somebody moans... not one of us and it's someone in the office.

My brow rises as the both of us look up and to the doorway.

The sound echoes out of a nearby background, and Aubrey puts her hand to her mouth and laughs. "Oh my god. We weren't the only ones with this idea."

A smile widens on my face as I look down at her. I brush her hair away from her face, unable to stop myself from laughing, too. "Well, it was a good idea I think. Come on. We'll go out this way."

Aubrey takes her phone out as soon as we step outside behind the bar, looking a little rumpled and sweet. "My friends are looking for me."

"You better go find them."

She sways slightly and I wonder what she's thinking.

"I'm glad you came out tonight Bree," I tell her and she grins like there's some secret only she knows. "Even more glad you wanted to see the backroom," I joke, running my hand through my hair.

Her teeth sink into her bottom lip and she nods before saying, "Same. I'm so glad I got to see you. Maybe I'll see you again?"

"Damn right you will," I tell her and then glance back to the bar, knowing it's waiting on me.

She smiles although her eyes hold so many questions, and I'll be damned if my heart doesn't skip a beat. "How about one more good night kiss?"

I lean down and kiss her, softer than before, and she laughs into it. The sound fills me with something like heat, something like joy, and I'm not going to get too far ahead of myself, no matter how right this feels.

Aubrey pulls back, the wind rustling her hair. "God, that was--that was nice. I have to go."

She whirls away, leaving me behind, and I lean against the back wall of the bar with a smirk spreading across my face.

This time, it doesn't seem so permanent to let her walk away.

Aubrey glances back at me just before she turns the corner and gives me a little wave. Then she's gone.

There goes my dream girl, giving me a memory and a view of her I'll hold onto forever.

CHAPTER 3 - AUBREY

With my eyes heavy and a slight hangover, I wake up slowly, images from my dreams hanging on until the last possible second. Bennet Thompson was the star of all of them. I can't remember exactly what we were supposed to be doing in the dream, but I can remember what we did instead.

I remember the heat of his hands on my body and his mouth capturing mine and how perfect it was to be so close to him, like we were always meant to kiss like that.

In the dream, the lighting was dim, the way it was in the back of the bar in that room under construction. I kept expecting for someone to walk in on us-- I think I could hear voices--but nobody did. And there was nobody else moaning in the dream. It was just the two of us, and Bennet seemed as absorbed with me as I was with him.

It felt so vivid, like it wasn't just a dream. Almost like we'd been dropped into another life and found each other there. Even in my dream-life, I guess my main priority is to make out with him in a darkened room.

In my dream life, he was an amazing kisser... just like he is in real life.

I flip my pillow to the cool side and stretch, but it doesn't do anything to get rid of the electric sensation of needing more.

Smiling into the pillow, it's almost embarrassing how much I want him. I still can't believe I kissed him. I almost did it out there in front of everyone. A quick peck and then run off. But I wanted to make sure I wasn't making it up in my head and that he really wanted me.

I squeal into my pillow, reliving that memory from last night.

It's been a long time since I felt this needy over a man. I might've felt this way back in school, but I don't think I had the words--or the courage to kiss him, to be honest.

Now I do.

Now I've done it, and it feels like my entire life is starting. A promotion. Bennet back in town. I know my life has technically been happening all along--I've worked hard for it--but something about this morning feels fresh and new and a little headachey.

I had a bit too much to drink last night.

How much *did* I have to drink last night?

My phone buzzes on the table next to my bed, and I pick it up lazily and hold it in front of my face.

There are *tons* of messages.

Another one comes in as I'm scrolling through them. It's from Gemma, sent to our group chat. My heart speeds up as the words sink in.

Did you two hook up last night?? Bree, answer us!

One from Marlena pops up just below that.

If they did hook up, he's a five-minute kind of guy.

There's no way, Gemma answers.

I hold shaking fingers over the screen and type out my own message. This isn't a dream, that's for sure. It's real sunlight streaming in through my bedroom window and real messages pouring onto my cell phone's screen. I glance at the clock reading nearly 9 am as my fingers fly across my phone and I type out a response.

Wait--did he tell people we hooked up?? I'm just now seeing all these, I slept in!!

Gemma sends five winking emojis, and then she's typing something else. I hold my breath and wait for the message to arrive.

He said you kissed but nothing else.

Good, I write back, adrenaline surging through my body. I *just* woke up. There hasn't been time for me to tell anybody anything, and now Bennet's put out a press release about the kiss we shared? I don't know whether to be embarrassed or excited or both.

There's nothing like living in a small town. The gossip has a way of bringing things to life that never should have existed. As if a small kiss between the two of us could ever be a scandal.

Good why? Marlena writes.

Because that's what happened

I leave it at that, fresh warmth spreading all over my face.

Gemma sends another text: *You made out with Bennet last night?!?!*

My front door opens downstairs, and this is it--this is when I talk about Bennet with my best friend in the entire world. If that doesn't make last night real and life-changing, I don't know what does.

"Aubrey Lynn Peters," yells Lauren.

It feels like the entire world has crowded into my bedroom. I know it's just my friends, but part of me thought that last night had been...subtle. That maybe nobody had noticed. That Bennet and I had been in our own little world.

That couldn't be farther from the truth. They *all* noticed. And then he went and told people, and I don't know what that means. Is he trying to play it off like it was no big deal, or is he telling people out of the same kind of excitement that I feel?

My face goes hot, and I burrow into my sheets and blankets as footsteps climb the stairs. A few seconds later, my bedroom door creaks as it opens wide.

"I know you're in here," Lauren scolds. "I can see you under the covers. Oh my God, Bree!"

I peek out from the blankets and find her smiling, her eyes wide and shocked at the same time. I've spent the last few years throwing myself into work and not spending nearly enough time with my friends, and now, on our first night out, I kissed a guy in the back room of the bar. No wonder she finds it surprising.

Lauren crosses her arms over her chest and shakes her head. "You don't waste any time, do you?"

"I guess not." I pull the blankets back up and hide in them for another few seconds until it gets too warm. "The town is saying we hooked up last night? As in--*hooked up* hooked up?"

"Well, *someone* did last night." Lauren raises her eyebrows. "The town is saying it's the two of you."

My heart stops dead in its tracks. "We didn't do *that* last night."

"If it wasn't you and Bennet, then who was it?"

CHAPTER 4 - BENNET

I pick up another glass out of the rack behind the bar and wipe it down, watching Steve drop his face into his hands across from me. He looks tired, the way he always does--the man owns a bar, and he doesn't get much sleep even when things are good.

Hell, *I* didn't get any sleep last night, for almost the same reasons he didn't, which he's just spilled to me over a pot of coffee.

"Steve." He looks at me from over his hands. "You've got to be kidding me."

"Look." Steve lets out a heavy sigh. "No one can know. I'm serious."

"Nobody can know you kissed your wife last night?"

He grimaces. "She's not my wife."

"You're separated, not divorced."

"I know that, but she said before--"

"I'm pretty sure she's changed her mind if she kissed you last night."

"She doesn't want anyone to know," he insists. "Everything is so damn complicated right now."

I put the glass in its place and pick up another one. "But?"

"But I felt it." He lets his hands fall onto the bar, palms up. "Sparks. Whatever you want to call them. I felt it when she came into the office last night. It's not over between us and I can't let some gossip and busy bodies get between us. I need to make this right with her."

"So you want me to take the fall for kissing *your* wife?"

"We're separated," he repeats back to me. "It wouldn't be the end of the world if--you know…" he trails off. The poor guy is stuck between a rock and a hard spot. "If the town thought it was you and Bree and they stayed out of our business…"

Steve looks desperate, and I feel for him.

I just…

I can't agree to this. The town talking about Bree and spreading gossip that I don't think she'd be comfortable with … it's not just me who would have to agree.

Steve's right about one thing. It *is* complicated. He's the one who offered me the job and helped move me back to town. I owe him for that at the very least. I don't want to let him down and I know he still loves his wife. And I know how this town can be. But what I feel for Bree is real and I can't risk hurting the only chance I might ever have with her.

If it were anything else within reason, I'd be the first in line to help him.

"I don't do hookups in the back of bars," I tell him.

"Bennet, it's not like your boss is going to fire you."

I shoot him a look. "Isn't that a safety hazard, anyway?"

"I was in the office, for fuck's sake." Steve's phone lights up on the bar, and he checks it with a nervous twitch in his hands. "I'm afraid it'll be too much for her if the town starts talking and puts two and two together. You know how people like to play detective and give their opinion on everything.

I've messed up Bennet. Putting this bar before her. Working our lives away and not being there for her when I should have been. She wants to give it another shot but without the judgment and all that shit."

It's harder to have trouble in your marriage when you know that everybody and their brother is going to be gossiping. I don't know everything about Steve's marriage, but I have to imagine the stress of the bar and a small business could weigh on anyone. I feel bad for Steve. I really do. If he has a chance with his wife, then I want that for him, but it's not Steve and his wife everybody will be talking about.

It's Aubrey.

And there is just no way I'm doing that to her.

I can't. I won't.

"I'm sorry, Steve." I look him dead in the eyes. "I can't lie; you know I'm a bad liar."

"No, no--you don't have to lie. Just don't say anything."

I huff and look away, not liking any of this. A lie of omission is as good as the real thing. I'm not going to lie about Aubrey, even through keeping my mouth shut. Protectiveness shoots across my chest like fire, which only makes me empathize harder with Steve. He's trying to protect his wife, too, but he's going to have to find another way.

"If it was just me, then fine. I don't care. But Aubrey was with me last night."

"Bree isn't even interested in dating. They'd never believe it and if they did, hell, they'd probably be happy she was getting some action."

A flare of disbelief and even a hint of anger run through me. People would run away with that rumor about Bree. They'd never shut up about it. He needs to be more careful with what he says, or–

Or what? One kiss doesn't mean *I'm* dating Aubrey. I inhale a deep breath and steady myself. It doesn't mean I have any claim on her. I can't shut Steve down right now, or he'll think I've lost my mind.

Blowing up at Steve over an off-handed comment, as much as I hate it, would probably get around town, too, and it would have the same result. People would talk about Aubrey. They'd make all kinds of assumptions about her private life, and nobody needs to be doing that.

Not when she's–

Mine.

It sounds clear in my head. Right. *She's mine.* I know she's not. I know that whatever was between us last night, it doesn't mean I can speak for her in the light of day.

The best move is to keep things focused on Steve and his wife, because that's what this is about. Not me and Aubrey.

I dry off another glass. "You need to come clean, Steve. That's the only thing there is to do. If you and your wife want privacy, you can ask for it. But I can't let people think Aubrey and I slept together when we didn't."

Steve runs his hand over his face and leans back in his barstool. It creaks behind him, and I wonder when the last time it was that he had a full night off. Maybe if he had more time to spend with his wife, they wouldn't be in any kind of situation right now.

"I know, I know. I'm sorry." He pauses with his hand still over his eyes. "Wait...Bree?"

"No, wait." Steve uncovers his eyes and looks me over. He leans closer, his eyes narrowed, and I know he's about a second from figuring out what happened between us. Shit, shit, shit. I never should have said anything. I should have kept her out of it. "Did something else--"

"Steve--"

"Did something else happen last night other than me falling back in love with my ex?"

Steve's eyes are bright, and he pushes his fingers into the bar like a detective on one of those cop shows who's just been handed a major clue. "You and Bree? You and her are a real thing?"

It's like he just now realized what half the town already knows. I can tell he's happy for me, even if he thinks his world is going to crumble because this town doesn't shut up and his marriage is at the mercy of rumors and late nights.

I don't know what to say. I open my mouth to answer him, because he's sitting right there and I can't ignore the question, but I have no idea how to explain what happened last night without making things harder for Aubrey.

Just then, there's a sound up front--the latch on the door clicking into place.

Then the door swings open, and I can't say a thing because she's standing right in front of us.

CHAPTER 5 - AUBREY

I don't know what I expected when I got in my car and drove over here, but it wasn't the awkward silence that falls when I push open the door of the bar and step inside.

Bennet looks at me, his eyes wide, like he's surprised to see me, which is justifiable. And Steve– the man who has owned this bar for as long as I can remember--looks at me with a strange expression I can't pinpoint. The music is off. It's so quiet I can hear my own heartbeat.

"Hi." My voice sounds too loud without all the chatter of other people and the constant music that played last night, along with the game on the TV behind the bar, and my face heats up all over again. This is the tenth time today. "I know you're not open, Steve, but if I could just..."

I motion to Bennet, who's wiping down the glasses behind the bar.

"Of course." Steve waves me over to the barstool next to him, rearranging his face. A little alarm goes off in the back of my mind, but I could be reading too much into it. Also, my heart is going a million miles an hour. "Good to see you, Aubrey."

"Good to see you, too."

This time, there's nobody else. I'm front and center. No distractions, no friends, nothing but the two of us. And no liquid courage. My heart flutters. At the center of that feeling is a warm spark that's pure excitement.

I'm not going to beat around the bush. "Did you hear the rumors?"

Steve frowns. "Did you want me to step out?"

"It doesn't matter." I look back at Bennet. He seems shocked, and his hands are in the air, the glass he was drying abandoned on the counter. "I wanted to ask you."

"I swear, Bree, I'm setting the record straight--" Bennet starts.

"No one believes it, Bree. Don't pay them any mind," Steve says. He glances over at Bennet, and they share a look. Okay--something's definitely off, like the way he frowned, but I can't put the pieces together when my heart is pounding.

Bennet lowers his hands, placing them flat on the bar. "I hope you're not thinking last night was a mistake."

I steel myself and pretend it's just the two of us.

"Last night was wonderful for me, Bennet, but I don't want anyone thinking anything else happened unless..."

"Unless what?" Steve interrupts.

Bennet sighs and then scowls at Steve, "Maybe you should head to the back and do some inventory or something."

Stew swallows hard, the color draining from his face. He looks *panicked*. Is that why everything feels so off?

"Are you okay, Steve?" I ask, because if he's having some kind of emergency...if something's going *on* here...

"It's just, you know...it's not--it's like this, I--" He grips his coffee cup like it's a lifeline. "Hey, Bree, could I ask you a favor?"

Bennet looks his friend over. "I'm telling you it's going to be fine. The truth is always the best way to go."

"I can't lose her again," Steve murmurs, softly and with so much concern, and my heart sinks.

"What's going on?" I ask, keeping my voice as quiet as his.

Steve looks me in the eye, a flush spreading across his face. "It was me and Sarah last night. In the back. We were--" He shakes his head. "She doesn't know what to think of it all, but she doesn't want the town prying into our marriage again."

I let out a breath.

"Oh my god."

I was as surprised as anyone to hear that Steve and Sarah, who were high school sweethearts, were on the rocks. But I also heard about how stressful it had become to run the bar. A remodel earlier this year had tons of delays, which meant the bar was closed for longer than they wanted. On top of that, Sarah had been through some tough times with her family. My heart aches for them.

"Please," Steve pleads with me and I don't understand.

"Please what?"

"Let them think it was you two," he asks and just as his request registers, he hurries out more words, "I know it's a shitty ask and I know town gossip can be awful, but I'm begging you. I just want my wife to love me again and to work on our marriage in private."

I look away from him and at Bennet, whose eyes move between me and Steve, his mouth pressed into a thin line.

Holy shit. That was not at all what I was expecting.

"Either way Bree, if you say no, I'll respect it," Steve tells me and I look back at him, knowing full well that I don't care about town gossip in the least, but I know it played a part in what happened with Steve and his wife.

"I'm not a good liar," I start and the hope in Steve's eyes dim until I add, "I guess if you took me out to dinner tonight..." Bennet raises his eyebrows at my suggestion. "We wouldn't have to confirm anything, but we also don't have to deny anything?"

Our gazes lock. It feels like last night, only hotter, only more energy between us, and that kiss plays again in my memory.

Bennet cocks a smile.

"The Bree I remember was a good girl with a good reputation," he points out, his voice at a low, sultry pitch.

"*This* Bree cares less about what the town is talking about and more about whether or not you want to go out with me."

Steve lets out a 'thank you Bree', and I give him my biggest, brightest smile.

"This town loves to talk," Bennet counters.

"Yeah, they do," I agree. "We could give them something to talk about."

His smile turns hotter, though no less charming than I remember from school, and last night, and my dreams.

"Would you like that?" he questions, and then it really is like we're the only two people in the room. The heat in his eyes says we *could* be in a private room in a matter of minutes, and it would be just like the dreams I had last night. That heat rushes down my body from my face to my toes, and my skin actually aches for him to touch me again. I'd like it if we had more time, hours and hours...

"I think I would," I tell him.

Steve exhales and immediately picks up his phone off the bar and starts tapping at it, his fingers flying. I imagine he's telling his wife she doesn't have to worry.

Steve says matter of factly, even with a hint of emotion still in his tone. "Well, that settles it. Bennet, you're taking Aubrey out to dinner." Poor guy doesn't seem like he slept last night.

Bennet gives him a look. "I have my shift tonight."

"No, you don't." Steve looks up from his phone, relief clear on his face, then gets up from the barstool and makes a beeline for the back. "You officially have the night off," he calls over his shoulder.

I watch him go, hoping with all my heart that he and Sarah will be able to work things out. I want both of them to be okay

"So," Bennet says, drawing my attention back to him. His eyes travel slowly over my face, and I could swear I feel heat wherever his gaze touches my skin. I'm already craving more of it. I want to be on the other side of the bar with him, in his arms, but for now I'll let him look at me just like this. "I'll pick you up tonight, then? At...five?"

I smile back at him, feeling my face settle into an expression that's more *want* than *grin*. "It's a date."

CHAPTER 6 - BENNET

Steve didn't just give me the night off from the bar. He let me borrow his truck, too, since I don't have a vehicle of my own quite yet. I didn't need one in the city, and I haven't had time to find one, and...

All this is a distraction from my nervousness.

I couldn't figure out what the hell to wear or where to go. I'm more nervous for this date than I've ever been for anything else in all my life. My heart has been practically jumping out of my chest since Aubrey walked out of the bar earlier today.

If I'm honest, it's been causing a ruckus in my chest since I saw her last night. I couldn't sleep, thinking of her. I thought of a hundred different scenarios for how we might meet again since I didn't ask for her number. What I'd say if she showed up at the bar with her friends. What I'd say if we ran into each other at the grocery store. What I'd say if I went to her house and knocked on the door and told her I wanted a repeat of what happened at the bar.

In the end, none of them happened, because she walked into the bar, sat down across from me, and stole my heart.

If I'm honest...

I think she stole it a long time ago. I'm not sure why it took so long for me to notice, but that's the only explanation for how I feel about this date. Almost like it's already happened, and we're just catching up to how things are supposed to be.

I blow out a breath and try my damndest not to get ahead of myself.

I just want tonight to be perfect. That's what this is.

I can't even bring myself to mind that Steve and Sarah are in over their heads, because in a way, they gave us a nudge. Steve looked so pathetic sitting across the bar from me that it's no wonder Aubrey agreed to a date.

Though...

She didn't look like she needed much encouragement. If Steve hadn't been there, we might have ended up having the same conversation.

And I'd have ended up here, behind the wheel of the truck in my own driveway, losing my shit over a first date.

My phone pings.

It's a text from my dad. I unhook my hands from the wheel and pick up the phone to read it.

Dad: *So, Aubrey Peters and you? You better be treating that girl right.*

Word really does travel fast in a small town. I roll my eyes. What I do with Aubrey is none of anybody's business. I drop the phone back into my cupholder and ignore the text. Damn, this town is something else. I loved growing up in a small town, but I had to leave after high school.

Partly because there was one girl I couldn't stop thinking about. Days. Nights. Weeks. Months. Years. I thought about her constantly. And back then Aubrey never looked twice at me. After all, I had dated one of her good friends and broke her heart. Aubrey never knew but it was because I couldn't stop thinking of her. It wasn't right to her friend, who's long gone and living her happily ever after on the other side of the country.

My phone pings again.

Dad: *P.S. I heard she likes peonies. Heard it from Dale at the flower shop.*

I pause, cocking my head and deciding small town gossip is good for something after all.

Okay. I have one stop to make before I pick up Aubrey. Good thing I got ready way too early, so there's plenty of extra time.

The flower shop isn't too far away from the bar. It's a little white storefront with three parking spots in front. I pull in less than five minutes later and jump out of the truck, my muscles aching like I've been sitting for days.

It's only been fifteen minutes, tops, but I'm so wound up about this date that I feel like I've been trapped in a chair for a day's worth of classes or meetings or *anything* that keeps me away from Aubrey.

The bells above the door chime as I go into the flower shop. It's crowded with plants in different arrangements. I make my way around them to the counter in the back, where Dale is waiting with his wife.

The guy looks way too casual. His glasses perch on his dark hair, and he peers down at the cash register with a careful look on his face, like he's trying to hide that my dad clearly talked to him about me. His wife stands at his side, beaming. She's not doing a damn thing to hide how excited she is. As I get closer, she nudges Dale with her elbow.

He does the fakest startle I've ever seen and clears his throat. "Bennet! What can I get for you?"

"Mind if I take a look at your bouquets?"

I'm already halfway around the counter, headed for the cold room where they keep the pre-made bouquets, expecting that Dale will wave me through.

"Bennet, wait."

I turn back, and his wife is standing there with a gorgeous bouquet in her hands. Peonies in pastel colors burst from the top. It's better than anything I could have picked out in the back, and it's clearly been made just for Aubrey.

"I just made this one," she says and before I can say anything the bell chimes again, taking my attention back to the front door.

A woman steps into the flower shop, pushing a lock of hair out of her face. She looks vaguely familiar, a bit older, but I'm not sure why I recognize her. Half of this town is like that. I can't place her so I look back at the flowers. Dale's wife has them all ready for me, tied with a ribbon.

"I think I'll go ahead and take those off your hands," I tell her.

I take a few steps forward and get my wallet out of my pocket, then hand over my card. Dale plucks it out of my hand and runs it, his wife still grinning about the flowers, and I can't wait to see Aubrey's face when I give them to her--even if my dad is a busybody, along with everybody else in this town.

I guess sometimes it pays off, though I'll never admit that to my dad.

Dale hands me my card back, and then his wife gives me the bouquet. It has a decent weight in my arm. The scent of peonies is perfect. Near the door, the woman has stopped doing whatever it was she was doing with her purse, and our eyes meet again when she's about halfway through the flower shop.

She stops dead, her eyes going wide, surprise transforming her face. "Bennet? Is that you?"

It takes me a moment to realize I do know her. "Mrs. Baker," I lament as it hits me. She's a teacher from my high school, looking just a bit older with slight wrinkles around her eyes.

"How are you doing?" she questions with a wide smile but before I can answer she says, "I heard you were back in town."

My eyebrow shoots up, likely to my forehead, "You did, did you?" I've only been back a week and I'm barely moved in. "I'm still waiting on a few boxes but mostly back."

"I heard you came back to town for a reason," she peers down at the flowers in my hands and makes a little face like she's in on the secret. "I'm so happy you're doing well," she tells me and then brightens, "you two have fun."

Words escape me as I turn and watch Mrs. Baker, in all her glory, smug as can be, gather up a bunch of carnations and shoo me on.

I swear, this town's memory is as long as the summer days

CHAPTER 7 - AUBREY

My street has never been more captivating than when I'm waiting for Bennet to park in front of my house. Although for a Saturday, it's uneventful apart from Miss Shaw gardening at the far end of the street.

I watch through the front window like the outdoors is a movie, watching the late-afternoon light come down on the street. It makes everything gold. The leaves rustling in the trees. A flag on the house across the street waving in the sun. Everything seems more beautiful, in deeper colors, and it's all because I can't wait for this date to start.

I shake out the nerves and check my reflection in the front room mirror when the minutes tick by.

Finally, a truck comes down the street and slows in front of my house. It's Steve's truck, which means Steve must have been really desperate...or else he *really* wanted Bennet to be able to take me out.

Maybe it was both. It probably doesn't matter, in the end. From what I've gathered, between last night chatter and this morning messages from town gossip, Bennet sold a startup company for a decent penny and flew home for a family event but decided to stay.

Whether or not that's true though is something I aim to ask tonight. A quick kiss in the back of the bar was one thing, a date another.

I open it to reveal Bennet, who's dressed up from his bartending clothes. He wears slacks and a white button-down with the sleeves pulled up to his elbow, and I can't take it. He did that on purpose... showing off his forearms. How am I supposed to look at him all evening when he's this hot? It's hardly fair.

Bennet bites his lip, looking at me like he's thinking the same thing.

"Hi," I say.

In response he pulls a bouquet out from behind his back. Peonies. "Oh my gosh," I let out with genuine surprise. The bouquet paper crinkles as I happily accept the flowers. I inhale deeply, loving the fragrance.

"I love them," I tell him and then catch myself. My heart races. I try to keep it casual as I invite him in so I can at least put the flowers in water. "They're beautiful, thank you," I tell him and keep it lighter. Lauren gave me one rule and it was not to use the "L" word. I've already blown it.

"I'm glad you like them," he says as I look up from the mason jar and find him staring down at me in my kitchen. My mind races and I can just imagine all the dirty things we could do on this very clean countertop.

As if reading my mind, he shakes his head, a grin lighting up his face. "Ready to go?"

"I am." I swallow thickly and let him lead the way.

Bennet waits while I lock up, then offers me his arm and escorts me to the truck. With my hand wrapped around his forearm, skin against skin, more of last night comes back to me. The stolen glances and blush that came to his cheeks when he saw me across the bar.

It's almost too good to be true. He reaches ahead of us to open the door for me. I hold his hand tight as I climb into the truck. Again there's this shock and pull and the idea that all of this must be a dream.

"What a gentleman," I say, holding his hand for a few seconds longer.

"I'm trying," he says, then squeezes my hand and lets go. The truck jostles slightly as he closes the door.

"You're doing a good job, in my book," I tell him through the open window and he grins before jogging around the truck and climbing behind the wheel.

"The flowers especially. Brownie points," I tell him with a grin although I can't look him in the eyes as I do.

Bennet flashes another smile at me, and my heart skips a beat. "I'll keep it up, then."

He drives us to a little restaurant downtown. There aren't many upscale places in a town this size, and this one's known as the 'date' restaurant.

"Oooh, you're going all out tonight," I remark and Bennet laughs.

"It's the least I can do to say thank you for what you're doing for Steve," he tells me and I wonder if that's really what he thinks this is.

"Don't forget," I tell him, "we're here to be seen." As if this date is only for Steve.

"You're right," he agrees, then hops out and comes around to my side of the truck to help me back out. "I will definitely be playing it up for the crowd," he says with an uncontained smile.

"I guess I'll play along too then," I tell him before biting down on my smile to keep it from being a bit too much. It feels almost like a dare. Almost like the rules don't matter.

Bennet threads his fingers through mine on the way to the front door, giving me a wink as we go. The hostess looks between us, her eyebrows going up for a fraction of a second. I smile at her like I have no idea what's going on.

"Reservation for Thompson," Bennet says.

"Right this way." The hostess smiles even wider, then leads us to a table in the front windows of the restaurant. We're surrounded by glass on three sides. Anybody walking past can see that we're here on a date.

Bennet pulls my chair out for me. "This okay?" he murmurs.

"More than okay. This is the whole point, right?"

"Mmm," he says. That's not a *yes*. My heart speeds up again as he takes his seat across from me and spreads his napkin over his lap. "Now. A lot's changed since high school... mind catching me up."

"That's a lot to cover in one date," I tell him with a simper as I smooth my own napkin over my lap.

Bennet shrugs, like he'd actually sit here in this restaurant until I'd told him absolutely everything about me. "Start at the beginning."

"I was born in town, went to school here..." I say jokingly.

"Oh, I remember that." His eyes light up. "But go on."

"I got into editing during college."

"You went to state right?" he asks and I nod, surprised he knew that.

"And when I saw the open job here, it just made sense to interview."

"Had enough of the city?"

"Yes." Memories resurface from my time away from town. "It wasn't bad. I had some really happy times in college. But I guess I just felt like I was meant to be here."

A waitress with a simple black shift dress leans in to fill our water glasses and take our orders, and we're off.

Over warm bread and butter, I tell Bennet about the first apartment I ever rented during senior year and how scary it felt to take out a mortgage to buy my house and how the first year of my job drained the hell out of me but at the same time was a dream come true.

"Did you always know you wanted to do that?" he asks, and for a few seconds I can't answer. I'm too taken with the shape of his lips and the carved lines of his face and the way his eyes linger on mine. There's that heat again, in every inch of me.

In that same moment, I feel other eyes on me and glance away from the table.

"I just don't remember you talking about editing or publishing back in high school."

It's not a big restaurant, and at least one person at all of the closest tables quickly looks away, pretending to be absorbed in their food.

"I..." I turn back to Bennet. "I always loved reading but I didn't realize I wanted a career in publishing until later."

He smirks as he catches me looking over my shoulder again.

He leans in, darting a glance out to the rest of the space. "They're all looking at us, aren't they?"

"Yeah. They're staring."

We share a barely heard laugh at the ridiculousness of this town before I get to ask him what happened when he left. Business school took up most of his time and it turns out the start up was wonderful, the payout was even better and helped his parents get out of debt, but he found himself alone afterwards not knowing what to do. The conversation moves easily enough and the dishes come and go leaving us with nothing but drinks and laughter and more and more questions. Several times we were interrupted by old neighbors and classmates who just wanted to say hi and tell Bennet they're glad he's back. Their eyes linger on me and I simply keep my lips sealed tight. *Let them talk. This old town needs its entertainment.*

"So what's your plan?"

"Well I guess I'm doing it."

"What do you mean?"

"I wanted to come back home, be with my friends again, have a moment to slow down while catching up with the life I left behind."

The way he says 'left behind' resonates and I find myself staring down at the small pool of red liquid left in my glass.

"You want to get out of here?"

I sip the last of my wine and make it a point to look at him, not at anybody else, even though we've felt eyes on us all night. "With everyone talking, it does have me wondering."

"Wondering what?"

I'm so excited that my breath comes short and shallow. Bennet's still just as hot as he was at the beginning of our date. Watching him eat has only made me want him more.

"What it'd be like." I pause and put the wine glass down. "You know. If you and I... They're already saying it and I figure we might as well... "

I let the sentence trail off suggestively, and Bennet's eyes darken. He shifts in his seat. He's *clearly* feeling the same as me, clearly wants me, and I'd like to be somewhere *without* a bunch of people staring at us so I can find out what Bennet Thompson is like when he lets himself go after something he wants.

When he lets himself go after *me*.

Bennet clears his throat and sits up straight. The energy coming off him is pure desire, even here in this little restaurant with half the town watching.

He doesn't seem to notice any of them. Doesn't seem to care at all that everybody's going to talk about us for the rest of the evening.

"You want to go back to my place?"

CHAPTER 8 - BENNET

I can't keep my hands off Aubrey, and this time, I don't have to.

There's no high school friend groups in the way.

No bar full of people watching and talking. There's no one but us and what we both want.

I drive her back to my place, a bachelor pad I'm renting from a friend until I get my own place. It's quiet as we drive although her hand is held tight in mine and I'm pushing the speed limit. The second we're through the front door, she's on me.

Or I'm on her.

She ends up with her legs wrapped around my waist, her back against the door, and her arms around my neck. I kiss her like I've been starved for her. She tastes sweet and moans softly, urging me on and kisses me back like she doesn't know the meaning of a *good, small-town girl*. It's the hottest kiss I've ever shared with anyone. I'm hard as a rock by the time she starts clawing at the buttons of my shirt.

I don't have time to second guess the barely furnished place. Or what she'll think of the boxes still sprawled out. Without the lights on, it's dark anyway. We bump into a few boxes and find ourselves up against the wall before I can open the bedroom door.

I've never had anybody go after my clothes like that. Aubrey bites her lip and focuses hard on getting those buttons undone. She wants my clothes *off*.

I let her work on it while I shove open the door and carry her in, then put her on her knees on the bed and let her shove my shirt off me. I've never done anything as hot as strip Bree's dress off over her head, revealing a lace bra and panty set that I want to take off with my teeth.

So I do, gently pushing her back and crawling between her legs to make my intentions known. She falls back onto my bed with a gasp. I hold the lace gently between my teeth so I don't rip it. Aubrey moans the whole time. I think she'd actually like it if I did rip a pair of panties off her, but it's our first night together. Everything's going to come out the other side in one piece, especially the lace.

We're naked inside of a minute, and she stretches herself out for me. All her curves are on display. I run my hands over every one of them. Her skin like fire under mine. Tease her nipples with the pad of my thumb. Taste them, too. I could spend hours kissing every inch of her body, but it's not long before I find my way to her hips, then between her legs.

Aubrey buries her hands in my hair and holds on while I suck and nibble and lick her with reckless abandon. Her nails dig into my shoulders as her back arches and I use her body to guide me. Her taste is sweet and with every clench and moan I know I'm close. It doesn't take her long. Her thighs tremble around my head and I fucking love it. God, it's hot. *She's hot.*

"I need you," she moans, tugging on my arms and I've never heard anything sexier. Her hair is laid out like a halo, her cheeks flushed and legs spread wide enough for me to be right where I'm wanted. And then I'm pushing in, and the words come out of my mouth without any thought or control.

"Oh, fuck, Bree, you're so tight. I just-I want--"

She kisses me in the middle of me pushing into her deeper and deeper and I can't say a damn thing.

Not that I need to say anything. She feels like fucking heaven. I pick up my pace and love how she throws her head back. I love how she grips onto me, and calls out my name as she gets closer and closer.

I fuck her like she's mine.

It's perfect. Every second of her in my bed is perfect. And just as I'm about to come, she pushes at my shoulders until I roll over. Bree rides it out on top of me, her hands planted on my chest, staring down into my eyes and my heart stutters. Just as she gets close, she slows and I can't have that. I reach up, kissing her and molding her lips to mine and roll her back over to help her find her release. I fuck her harder and faster, kissing her while she cries out my name as she finds her release with me.

As our breathing levels out, and our warm breath mingles, I slowly come back down to reality.

We didn't bother to turn any lights on, but there's a streetlight not far from my window, and her eyes sparkle in the dim light.

I rest my hands on her waist and she tucks herself into my side.

"I don't want to screw this up," I admit as I pull her close and drop a kiss to her temple.

I can feel her smiling. "I could cut to the chase for you?"

Fuck, she's stunning. Confident and beautiful and everything I've ever wanted.

I let out a huff of a laugh and reply, "I'd appreciate that."

"Okay." Aubrey pulls the sheets up to her chest "I want a relationship that's easy. I have a very small checklist. No pressure, just commitment that you aren't..." She takes a deep breath and looks at the ceiling, swallows and then looks back to me.

I push myself up on one elbow, staring down at her so she knows I'm serious. "I want a relationship...*relationship*. I want to settle down, I mean."

She smiles shyly at me and whispers, "I want that, too."

"I want to take my girl out on the town and when people stare, I want to wrap my arm around her waist and kiss her neck." I demonstrate, wrapping my arm around her waist and kissing her neck. "Right here."

"That feels good," she whispers.

"I want to be with my girl every night I can. Not just a fling but something real." There's no way in hell I'm letting her walk out of here now. Not when my skin still tingles from how good it felt to fuck her. But it's more than that, too. Kissing her gets me just as high. It all feels perfect with Aubrey. "And wake up with her in the morning."

"Are you talking about moving in?" she jokes.

"Well, not just yet. We can take it slow." No part of me actually wants to take it slow, but I want to do right by her. That's what matters most. "As long as we get where we want to go and it's the same place. But really I was just asking if you want to stay the night tonight."

She smiles this shy smile, "That sounds like a plan and yeah I think I would." Aubrey tips her face up and kisses me, and this time, there's no rush. It's as deep and hot as it was when we first got here, but we can take our time. Kissing her feels like sparks in my chest, like the embers of a fire.

"I want to fall in love and not have my heart broken," Aubrey whispers against my lips.

God. I think I've always been in love with her. I'm already there.

"I wouldn't," I promise her, though I want to tell her that for me, it's already over. She's the one.

"One step at a time?" Aubrey questions.

"That's what I'm thinking. One step at a time." I kiss her again, slow, but this time I tease her a little bit, licking at her bottom lip and giving it a gentle bite.

"Maybe we could repeat some steps?" Aubrey's breathing heavier now. "Like...the last step was nice."

"Was it? We should do it again to make sure."

I pull her under the covers with me, and she lets out a squeal. Then we go back over every step we took, again and again, just to make sure it's perfect.

CHAPTER 9 - AUBREY

I wake up in the morning in a bed that's not mine.

The sun's pretty high in the sky, and it comes back to me in a blink--the reason I slept so late is that we stayed up so late last night.

Me and Bennet.

Together. Tangled in the sheets. Me all over him, him all over me. The memories zing through my body with a palpable energy. I can *feel* how he was last night, even if he's not touching me right now.

He's *not* touching me, but the bed is warm, and I can hear him breathing. I close my eyes and savor the heat of him on the mattress next to me. This is how I wished it could be when I woke up yesterday, and now it is.

I almost want to go back to sleep for a few minutes so I can wake up next to him all over again.

Almost.

I roll over and find Bennet watching me from his pillow, his hair sticking up in all directions. It's the most handsome bedhead I've ever seen. Men have it so damn easy. Just at the thought I wonder what my hair looks like and I do what I can to tame it but then I'm caught red handed.

"Morning," Bennet smiles at me.

I smile back, not able to hide my blush and then snuggle back into the sheets.

"Now I guess when the town says we hooked up, they won't be lying." Bennet's voice is low and gravelly from sleep, and I like it a *lot*. He stretches out, yawning and manages to wrap an arm around me.

"What will you say when they do?"

The corner of his mouth turns up. "That I plan on hooking up with you again tonight, and if they have opinions on it, maybe they should tell someone who cares."

That makes me laugh although he's quick to add, "or whatever you want me to tell them."

I shrug, "I don't care much to be honest. I like the idea of maybe telling them we're a thing though," I suggest. My attempt at being casual falls flat though and a bit of nervousness comes over me as I twist my hair around my finger.

"I like the idea of saying that too."

A small smile slips into place as I think about dinner last night and how word may have gotten around. Not that it matters.

"What about Steve and Sarah?"

"It's none of my business." His face softens. "I just hope they come out of whatever they're going through alright. And knowing the two of them, they will."

"Yeah. Me too."

He reaches over and brushes a lock of hair out of my face. "They'll be alright."

"And we'll be alright," I agree.

"I think we're going to be better than alright, Bree baby."

My face goes completely hot. *Bree baby.*

"Ooh," Bennet says softly. "I love that color on you."

I laugh again, and he rolls me over onto my back and kisses me. Now it's not just my face that's hot. It's my whole body. Warmth, all down through my chest and my belly and my hips. Warmth everywhere.

He kisses me slow and deep, taking his time, letting his body rest above me in the bed. When he finally breaks the kiss, it's with a soft sound, like it's the worst thing in the world to stop.

"What time do you have to be in the office?" he asks.

"I work from home, and..." I reach down to the floor, where I dropped my phone last night. "Not for another two hours."

"Oh." His face lights up. I *love* watching his expression change that way. His eyes get brighter, and his cheeks lift, and he looks thrilled. "That's plenty of time."

Bennet starts by taking off the big T-shirt I slept in last night--one of his-- then finds the hollow of my collarbone and kisses it until I'm wriggling underneath him. His lips are so soft, and I've never met a man who likes to focus on such a small part of me.

"Bennet," I breathe a little while later. "You have to--you can't just--"

"Yes, I can," he says. "But I'll stop kissing this lovely little part of you and go lower." He kisses teasingly down between my ribs, then over my belly button. "How about here?" Bennet drops another kiss to that place and glances up at me with a wicked grin.

"Lower," I beg.

"Lower," he echoes, and then his face is between my thighs again. He holds me open with both hands this time. I thought he'd been thorough last night, but he's meticulous now. There's no part of me that Bennet leaves unkissed, licked or nibbled. My mind turns lust filled with the sensation of his tongue sliding over all the softest parts of me. He drags his tongue over my clit once, then twice, and once I've come hard on that tongue he makes me do it again.

I almost feel feverish when he stops, lifting himself to kiss my belly button again before he turns me over on the pillows and arranges himself behind me. Bennet folds his body over mine, covering me, and kisses the curve of my shoulder as he thrusts in. He fills me in a single moment and ecstasy drapes itself around me.

I'm glad for the pillows, because my legs are made of jelly and my arms are useless. Bennet curls his fingers through mine, and I grab the pillow with my other hand and hold on. He groans against the nape of my neck.

My eyes close and I revel in his embrace.

"You feel so good," I tell him, because he does, though it's hard to breathe. He's so strong, and he takes up every inch of space inside me. I meet him the best I can. Bennet curls the fingers of his other hand over my hip and holds me still, panting as he fucks me harder and harder.

I know I'm close and as my legs tremble he tells me to come and I'll be damned if I don't simply because of the rough timbre of his demand. I'm helpless beneath him as pleasure takes over and this might be the most intimate moment of my life. Bennet's just as warm above me, his weight on mine, and that heat is everywhere.

"Fuck," he says as we meet our release together, then he rolls us over onto the pillows both of our chests heaving. I move until my head is on his chest, and he wraps both arms around me. His heart beats fast but steady.

I did that to him. I did that *with* him. I made him feel that way.

I think again that this has to be a dream. It's just too good to be true.

"I don't want you to get out of bed," he says.

"I don't want to get out of bed."

"But you have to spend at least part of that two hours getting ready, don't you?"

"No," I decide instantly. "I can be late," I tell him and then kiss him again before I start thinking about the "L" word Lauren told me not to say.

CHAPTER 10 - BENNET

Waking up in bed with Aubrey Peters is the best thing ever to happen to me.

That stays the same the day after she comes to my place, and the day after that, and the day after that. Sometimes we stay at her house, sometimes at mine, but we're together pretty much every night.

A few weeks goes by, and there's no big drama about me and Aubrey getting together. Yeah, a few people talk about it. There are a few comments at the bar. But mostly, the town just accepts it for what it is--a romance that's nearly a decade in the making. It doesn't really have much to do with them.

I roll over onto my back and look up at the ceiling as the early morning light slips in and the bed groans. Aubrey's already up and she leans over and kisses my cheek. "What are you thinking about?"

I fold her under my arm and cuddle her close. She's warm all through the night. I never thought I was missing out, sleeping in my own bed with nobody else, but it turns out I was. It's a hell of a lot better with her.

"I was thinking it's lucky that this town talks."

She snorts, a cute little sound that makes me crazy about her every time I hear it. "What do you mean?"

"We got to skip a lot of little steps and get right to the good stuff."

Aubrey laughs louder. "Is that what you call sex? The good stuff?"

"Nah." I swallow down any worries and just say it, "But falling in love is the good stuff."

I knew from the minute she walked into the bar that night that I was falling for her. It took a little time to realize it for everything it was, but now that I have, I know--I've felt that all along. I've never fallen slowly for Aubrey Peters. It happened the second I saw her, and it'll never stop. Those years we spent apart were just a detour. It was time we needed to see that something was missing in our lives, and it was each other.

It was never going to be right without her.

It never *will* be right without her.

After a minute, Aubrey pushes herself up on one elbow and looks down at me, her hair falling in a wave down to my chest. She studies my face like it's one of her editing jobs. Aubrey always pays attention to the smallest details, and when she looks at me like this, I know she can see everything about me.

And she doesn't mind looking.

"Bennet Thompson," she says, a tremble in her voice. "Are you saying you love me?"

"I think I am, Aubrey Peters."

Aubrey bites down on her lip to keep herself from smiling even harder. Her cheeks flush pink. That blush on her is so gorgeous it makes my heart stop. I want a photo of this moment. Maybe a hundred of them, or a painting-- something that I could keep forever so I never forget this exact shade.

Then again, I don't think I'll be able to forget. There's a certain clarity about Aubrey. Everything she does locks into my brain, and it's just like it was back in school. I can't stop thinking about her.

"Well," she says, seeming almost shy about it. "I think I might love you, too."

I push her hair back from her face and tuck it behind her ear. "I know you love me."

I'm sure of it. Aubrey Peters loves me. From the way she kisses me and the way she talks to me and the way she sleeps next to me at night, she's loved me all this time, too.

I let my hand curl around the back of her neck and run my thumb over her cheekbone, my heart picking up. I don't have a ring, and I don't have a plan. Aubrey deserves both. She deserves the entire world.

But with the way she's smiling at me now...

"You want to maybe change your name one day?"

"Oooh." She wrinkles her nose, smiling bigger. "Big steps, not baby steps there."

"I'm just asking what your timeline might look like... I'm not booking the honeymoon to Maui just yet." Because I'd marry her tomorrow, if I could. Hell, I'd marry her right now. I'd go and bang on the door of the courthouse until they opened up and declared us husband and wife. I can picture that, too, just like it's playing out in a movie. Aubrey in a white dress, me in a suit, our signatures on a sheet of paper, a last-minute ring on her finger...

That would be good enough for me. It might even be good enough for her. I don't know, because I haven't asked her, but I'm going to, just as soon as–

"Change it to what?"

I blink back up at Aubrey, and...her face is different. She was grinning before, laughing, but now she looks serious.

"What do you mean?"

"What's your name?" Aubrey's voice is softer than before, almost like she's not right next to me, in my arms where she belongs.

"What? What's my name?" I ask her and a chill comes over me when she stares back at me with red rimmed eyes and a quivering lip.

"Bennet, tell them what your name is."

BENNET

Beep...beep...beep.

My head is more than groggy and my body more than sore as I'm slow to lift my heavy eyes. Everything swirls in my vision as I slowly move my head forward. I fall back and several hands steady me. A voice calls out telling me it's alright.

"Where am I?" I question and that's when I realize how dry my throat is. "What happened?"

Three faces I've never seen come into focus. All three in blue scrubs.

"Mister. Can you tell us your name?" the first one asks, a young brunette with wide, dark brown eyes and tan skin. She waits a moment, keeping my gaze and it's then I realize that I don't know.

I can't remember. Blinking rapidly, I look down and register that I'm in a hospital bed and wearing one of those cheap gowns. I clench my hand closed and open and reach for my leg but other nurse stops me.

She's taller than the first and looks a bit older with her blonde hair tucked back in a tight bun. "Sir please, could you tell us your name?"

Chills run down my arms and I don't know why. It's like a memory that won't come into focus.

I say the only thing I keep thinking, "Where's Bree?"

"Can you tell me who Bree is?" The first nurse asks me, calmness I'm not sure is real.

That chill comes back and my head pounds with a pain that refuses to be ignored.

But all I can focus on is her. *Bree.* "Where is she? Is she okay?"

"We can find her for you. Do you know her last name?" the third nurse asks but I don't know and fear takes a grip on me. I don't remember anything. Not my address, my own name. I don't know.

They keep asking me questions and telling me it's alright when I know it's not.

As emotions tighten my voice, I tell them the only thing I know, "I don't remember anything, but I know I need Bree."

This is not the end… The *Fall in Love Again* series will feature Bennet and Bree falling in love on the small fictional street of Cedar Lane over and over again while the real world has had other plans for them. Find out more at www.willowwinterswrites.com.

Made in the USA
Coppell, TX
16 September 2023

21625753R20446